Myths Among Us

When Timeless Tales Return to Life

Craig Chalquist

Book Two of the Living Myth Series

World Soul Books
an imprint of Worldrede Academy
5400 Hollister Avenue
Goleta, CA 93111

Printed in the United States of America
ISBN-13: 978-0-9826279-6-9

Cover art: "Muses" (1985) by Kurt Wenner - kurtwenner.com

Visit the author's website at Chalquist.com.

Contents

The Living Myth Series

It has been claimed that we live in a time without myth. But if C.G. Jung, Joseph Campbell, Hermann Hesse, Thomas Mann, Mary Shelley, Robert Graves, Jorge Luis Borges, F. Scott Momaday, and a host of other preeminent minds are correct, then myth is always with us and all around us as the basic psychic weave that holds our relations with ourselves, each other, and the living world. The real question is whether we resonate to the weave of myth consciously or unconsciously, knowingly or involuntarily, even tragically.

The Living Myth Series seeks to foster consciousness of the presence and power of myth in our lives. In the end myth is story, and story always says more about the heights and depths of human experience than facts or figures can by themselves.

The Series is being published at a time when the humanities have yet again been deprived of public funding for being insufficiently "practical." Yet if we knew our stories and traditions better, and valued the richness of our literary and artistic legacies, we might treat each other and the planet itself with greater understanding and compassion. At its best, the study of myth requires imaginative engagement, thinking in the round, intensive self-questioning, and growth of a capacity for grasping contrasting "pantheons" of choices, possibilities, and perspectives. It expands the heart as well as the mind. An education of the soul reaching into multiple levels of the naturally relational self is what this Series hopes to encourage.

ACKNOWLEDGMENTS

Hearty thanks to Sigmar Schwarz, who introduced me to the work of Jung and Hesse; to Marilyn Fowler and Vernice Solimar for giving me my first opportunity to teach Archetypal Mythology; to Devdutt Pattanaik for prompt and intelligent feedback on my various mythology activities; to Brian Swimme for our ongoing discussion about science and myth; to Christine Downing, whose classes deprived me of my mythological virginity; to Dennis Patrick Slattery for conversation and inspiration; to Maren Hansen for giving me new ways to imagine working with myth; and of course to my students, who have given me such meaningful feedback over the years.

My thanks as well to Lakshmi Mayya, May-Linn Hammer, and Tiana Ellauri for working so tirelessly to gather the necessary background material. Special thanks to Lola McCrary for critical comments and questions.

I also give a nod to the shade of Roger Zelazny, whose storytelling awakened me to the power of myth retold. May his spirit inhabit a celestial Castle Amber where, guarding the basement, a lantern at his feet, he has plenty of time to compose, conspire, and chuckle evilly.

"Let me tell you a story." When I hear those words, I relax and put aside whatever it was that I was thinking about or doing. I prepare to concentrate on that which I'm about to hear because those words are a special invitation to step into another reality, into another time or into another way of thinking... I may become more sensitized to the feelings of others as I find myself experiencing the world from another perspective. Hopefully, I will learn something new.

—Kay Olan

Myth is no fiction, but a reality; it is, however, one of a different order from that of so-called empirical fact.

—Nikolai Berdyaev

Myth is the truth of the fact, not fact the truth of the myth.

—Kathleen Raine

The god who has his oracle at Delphi neither conceals or reveals; he speaks in signs.

—Heraclitus

A myth is a tissue of symbolism clothing a mystery.

—Richmond Hathorn

Considering the condition of the world and how we're so caught up in the media and music and all this other stuff, we've forgotten as human beings how to talk to one another, and communicate instead of doing it through text messages and through email and instant messages. We've got to get back to this one-on-one face-to-face communication, and I think the best way to propagate that is through storytelling.

—Lopaka Kapanui

To stake your claim over culture, your cultural practice, you have to tell your stories. Ultimately, mythology is about place and belonging.

—Monica Mody

The more enlightened our houses are, the more their walls ooze ghosts.

—Italo Calvino

We are all part of the old stories; whether we know the stories or not, the old stories know about us.

—Leslie Marmon Silko

Mythology is historical, because it reflects upon the traditional values of the past in order to make sense of the moral challenge of the present. Mythology makes an unspoken but underlying assumption: *the future depends not on what people believe, but on their responsible actions in the here and now.*

—Duane Champagne

Every positive statement about ultimate things must be made in the suggestive form of myth, of poetry... Myth is a symbolic story which demonstrates the inner meaning of the universe and of human life.

—Alan Watts

Storytelling is part of the oral tradition of indigenous peoples. Stories impart values, language, memories, ethics and philosophy, passing them to the next generation. A lot of people think of storytelling as just entertainment for kids, but for the Diné [Navajo] it helps maintain tradition and language.

—Laura Tohe

Since the language of myth is close to the language of poetry and does not belong to the genre of rational and reasoned-out discourse, it takes a different disposition from the common, run-of-the-mill prosaic mind of 20th century man to understand it fully. But the power of the mythopoetic mind of ancient Vietnam was such that we can still feel its reverberations.

—Ngoc Binh Nguyen

Through migration and assimilation many of my Caribbean relatives forgot their history or chose to not remember. I see this to be detrimental to preserving our history and culture. I think this is why telling the stories of T&T's [Trinidad and Tobago's] folklore was so important to me. There was power in the story. The story is what got us through slavery, made sense out of chaos and allowed us to be free and creative in a constricted world.

—Marjuan Canady

Storytelling used to be very a popular art form in the Arab world. The Hakawati, the Arabic word for the storyteller, would sit in a cafe, sip tea and tell amazing stories to people belonging to any age or color. My aim in life is to bring that human contact back into the people's lives through storytelling.

—Abeer Soliman

When the Dong people in southern China offer sacrifices to their ancestors, they gather together to sing songs and dance to entertain the gods... As a traditional genre that was primarily created in the ancient past and has been transmitted for thousands of years, myth has deeply influenced people's ordinary lives throughout history. It often helps to shape people's attitudes toward the world, provides evidence and reasons for their behaviors, and supplies meanings and models for their current lives.

—Lihui Yang

The serious dogmatism in religion, the ideology in culture, and the literalism in historiography are smashed by myth, which, though dealing with powerful ideas and meanings, is after all merely myth. It is fiction, story, and hypothesis misread as biography, science and history.

—David Miller

There is hope in myths and rituals, balm to heal and dynamite with which to shatter the hardest prejudice.

—Marina Warner

In all the wild imaginings of mythology, a fanciful spirit is playing on the border-line between jest and earnest.

—Bronislaw Malinowski

Myths help us to enter the complexity of our situations more deeply, with more love of the perplexities themselves and of those caught up in them.
—Christine Downing

Myth speaks to the extraordinary in us and to the innate nobility of our souls. Hearing a mythic story awakens the myth living in each of us. As the story enters us, we enter the timeless territory of myth. We become mythic again, a knowing participant in our own story and a seeker near its source.

—Michael Meade

To create a myth, that is to say, to venture beyond the reality of the sense to find a superior reality, is the most manifest sign of the greatness of the human soul and the proof of its capacity for infinite growth and development.

—Louis-Auguste Sabatier

The friend of wisdom is also a friend of myth.

—Aristotle

My mission in life as a storyteller is to share the importance of story and of telling of your stories... In order for our world to be healed, we need to reach back into the past, and reach back to our stories to reconnect and to find those connections through stories that aren't being told now.

—Hohepa Harawira

...Myth also gives expression to the knowledge that we are not lords of ourselves, that we are not only dependent within the familiar world but that we are especially dependent on the powers that hold sway beyond all that is familiar, and that it is precisely in dependence on them that we can become free from familiar powers.

—Rudolf Bultmann

Myth is the foundation of life; it is the timeless pattern, the religious formula to which life shapes itself.

—Thomas Mann

...Stories are important because the circle is not always there for people to share their story. So in meeting somebody new and in them sharing their story; in us sharing our story we have already created a bridge that is safe for each one of us to walk on. And also for us to be able to open and to share what is that gift we are bringing... And every single time that they have shared with somebody and they have also listened and received this story of the other person something new is born out of them.

—Sobonfu Some

In reality, the feral child does not live as a god in the jungle, but as a being rather less than human and not as well adapted as a beast. We are in danger of creating our own feral children when we deny them access to their inheritance of story. When we let them run free with only their minimal animal demands on language, or deprive them of the insights and poetic visions expressed in words that humans have produced throughout human history, we deny them— in the end—their own humanity

—Jane Yolen

The myth as a work of art has as its principal form the shape of drama. So too the human personality: its patternings of impulse express themselves as identities in an internal drama. The myths that are the treasure of an instructed community provide the models and the programs in terms of which the growth of the internal cast of identities is molded and enspirited.

—Jerome Bruner

It is somewhat limiting, I think, to argue that while myth belongs to times past, the psyche still needs myth for its own being. I also think it is limiting to tie myth only to the imagination, literature, metaphor, depth psychology, and the humanities. All those connections are certainly true, but today in a period of cultural chaos and breakdown, there exist perhaps more urgent and pressing reasons for the necessity of what myth provides: we need a sense of myth for our individual and collective equilibrium.

—Robert Sardello

The myth is something that never was but is always happening—the coded DNA of the human psyche calling us to refresh the dream that has been pushed so far away...The myth is always the stimulus, the alarm clock, the lure of becoming. It quickens the heart to its potential and prepares the ground for society's transformation.

—Jean Houston

Our being is in our stories.

—Lynda Sexson

Faery might be said to represent Imagination (without definitions of this word): esthetic, exploratory and receptive; and artistic; inventive, dynamic, (sub)creative. This compound—of awareness of a limitless world and a desire for wonder, marvels, both perceived and conceived—this 'Faery' is as necessary for the health and complete functioning of the Human as is sunlight for physical life...

—J. R. R. Tolkien

Depend upon it, there is mythology now as there was in the time of Homer, only we do not perceive it, and because we ourselves live in the very shadow of it, and because we all shrink from the full meridian light of truth..."

—F. Max Muller

The latest incarnation of Oedipus, the continued romance of Beauty and the Beast, stand this aftenoon on the corner of 42nd Street and Fifth Avenue, waiting for the traffic light to change.

—Joseph Campbell

A myth is like a fulcrum balancing two realities: the external world I meet day-to-day, and the inner psychic world that has its own objective nature, not needing me to exist but is rather working itself through me and that I must come to a fuller awareness of to have a fuller knowledge of what I am.

—Dennis Patrick Slattery

What of the gods? What of the elves?
Gianthome groans, the gods are in council,
The dwarves grieve before their door of stone,
Masters of walls. Well, would you know more?

—"Völuspá," *Poetic Edda*

Introduction:
The Continuing Pageantry of the Powers

> The gods created humanity because they love to hear
> stories.
> —African proverb

It may be a rule of sprawling civilizations that the greater their
craving for power and control, the higher the number of untruths that
circulate. It is not true that our planet's resources are unlimited. It is
not true that quantifying things offers the only, or even the best, way
to know them. It is not true that cavemen coexisted with giant
carnosaurs, that allowing the legalized theft of national treasuries
inflates the generosity of the super-rich, that repressing the rebellious makes them quiet down, or that voting in one bumbling grifter
after another is the best we can do about governing a country.

And it is not true that we can live without myth.

Mythic images surround us. Some are easy to spot: zombie
apocalypse, online avatars, UFOs, New Age, Hogwarts School of
Witchcraft and Wizardry. Angel investors, witching hour, Invisible
Hand, Alpha stock, Omega leveraging, Black Friday. Spacecraft
names like Orion and Hutu. Days of the week, months of the year,
names of planets, signs of the zodiac: all derived from myth.

Less conspicuous myths gleam forth once you peel back the
mundane cover of everyday things. Why store up documents on
your computer when, biting into the edenic Apple of knowledge, you
elevate them into the Cloud like spirits rising into heaven? Few sing
hymns to threshold-crossing Hermes nowadays, but piles of small
rocks stacked into herms decorate many a shoreline. The primal

Earth Mother peers back at us from behind environmentalist slogans about all-giving Gaia. The hundred-eyed watchman the ancient Greeks knew as the Argus lives on in technologies of mass surveillance.

"Coincidence," we might blurt dismissively—in unconscious imitation of the ancient Roman practice of evoking Fortuna, blind goddess of chance.

Focusing upon the storied nature of the living world is difficult from within the industrial belly of our Titanic civilization: we live inside our machinery now, like bacteria in the gut. Yet the simplest remote control commands a greater profusion of shimmering imagery than the strongest amulet of legend. The priestly ritualist formerly covered in feathers now wears a white lab coat. The mystique of material Progress trades in the Golden Calf for the Bronze Bull of Wall Street. Flags are worshipped like religious relics protected from contact with the ground. C.G. Jung believed that for some, UFOs have taken over the role of angels; perhaps their earthly counterparts parade in costume at every science fiction convention. In the United States, standardized tests, spirit-smothering competition, and fantasy-killing curricula loom over rows of students like the shadow of dark Saturn, paranoid eater of children. One of the tests is even called SAT.

Mythic themes and motifs, images and dramas recur again and again. An education in mythology can highlight where they come from, what they seem to want of us, how they react to current events, what they say about our lives, and, perhaps, even how to thread the mechanical Modernist maze and be reborn into a more fluid and Earth-honoring contemporaneity, into ways of living more meaningfully linked to multiple storied lineages.

By following the golden thread of myth, we may yet emerge from Nod and neurosis alike to breathe the sparkling clean air of Xanadu, Tir-na-Nog, Meru, or Avalon, our feet on the ground all the while. Awareness of the web of stories in which we move invites the magic of reweaving them for daily use, thereby reenchanting the world itself for us. "Olympus," Thoreau observed, "is but the outside of the earth everywhere."

THE TALES COLLECTED HERE, some familiar and others told less often, reflect my years of teaching and talking about myth inside and outside the classroom, online and in person, one-on-one and in large groups. The criteria for selection were: Does the tale contain power, juice, and vitality for me and for students who have engaged with it? Is it reflected somehow in the mirror of our time? Is it simple and yet instructive enough to be useful in a graduate or undergrad introduction to mythology? In an educated reader's course of self-education? Does it heighten appreciation for its culture of origin? Do its elements brew blends of cultural specificity and universal appeal?

Some of these tales might read as more folkloric than mythic. Because this book is for an audience beyond the academic, I have not been at pains to observe the slippery, problematic distinction between myth (oral sacred narrative arising from a particular people and place), legend (local anecdote once taken for true), and folktale (story known to be fictional, and with such general characters and settings that the events could have happened anywhere). "The earlier poets and story-tellers," remarked Hilda Ellis Davidson, "would have been unlikely to demand such accuracy and consistency as is required by the modern academic mind."

Instead, myth is treated herein as a poetic, primordial, collective storying fed by a magic circulatory fluid of felt resonance like that which animates legends and fairy tales. Just look at how certain "folkloric" figures—like King Arthur; like Coyote; like La Llorona, the Weeping Woman—come forth in grand mythic proportions while bringing with them the trappings of older deities. Psychologically, it makes little difference whether a folktale, legend, or a myth confronts you once the responsibility for creative engagement knocks on your door to demand entry.

Lore of any kind escapes academic categories when retold from within the great worldwide tradition of storytelling. Its unstoppable vitality yearns to be expressed and elaborated in every teller's voice. In recognition of that yearning, I have retold these stories, as I have in my myth classes, instead of formally anthologizing them. While intending to convey the wonder these stories inspire in me, my retellings preserve the essentials of the events (except where I have shortened very long plotlines) while eschewing pedantic rigor. There is a place for rigor, but as J. R. R. Tolkien and many other myth-loving scholars have pointed out, love of the tale must come first.

> Every account of a mythology—unless it reproduces its sources in the original text and in their fragmentary condition (a procedure, by the way, that would offer the reader merely "dead matter")—must be an interpretation.
> —Karl Kerényi, *Gods of the Greeks*

A telling you read in this book might be different from one you have heard before. Myths come in variants. Also, they sometimes circulate as fragments, and the emphasis details receive depends on time, place, teller, and audience. Many European readers will recognize Prometheus as the god chained to a rock for stealing fire from heaven, for example, but an important result of this—his renewed allegiance to Olympus after his imprisonment—is often left out, especially when the social imaginary favors plots of progress over those of fealty to transhuman powers.

The Reflections section after each myth includes questions to stimulate thinking and feeling, to engage imagination, to highlight parallel events in today's world, and to move around the many levels of myth, including the personal, the familial, the cultural, the ecological, and the archetypal. The Reflections also include help with pronunciation. See Appendix 2 for a glossary of mythological terms.

Asking reflection questions instead of offering hard-and-fast interpretations seeks to counter the assimilationist habit of putting one's own meanings on other people's stories. The Reflections also refer to the myths' cultures of origin.

Before publishing my retellings, I invited critical feedback by people who grew up where some of the tales came from. Members of a myth's culture of origin should have a voice in how we understand the myth. In turning to the Chinese tale of Nuwa repairing the sky, for example, we could interpret the figure of destroyed Mt. Buzhou, whose name means "without completeness," as injured psychological wholeness. But when we know that, for the Chinese, the name of the undamaged mountain implies *collective* effort rather than purely personal self-integration, our appreciation is enriched. To level the mountain, as the monster Gung Gung does, depicts a lethal fragmentation of the relations between heaven and earth, nature and culture. Today he looks less like failed inner wholeness than like mountaintop removal.

At the same time, however, respecting a myth does not require blindly accepting whatever anybody from its culture(s) of origin says about it. We do well to remain open to the complexity of what is brought to the tale by everyone who retells it. For example, the Christian devil is a fairly obvious mythological Trickster, yet he is seldom considered one by traditionalist Christians, as I learned from growing up among them. The more a mythic figure has been literalized and institutionalized, the less flexibility of interpretation that figure tends to receive. Here we can hold open the space of disparate perspectives: "I know you've been taught that the devil is evil incarnate, but what happens if we imagine him, if only for a moment or two, as a Trickster instead?" We should also bear in mind that time shifts how a mythic figure or event is held. The devil seems to have started out as a kind of adversary working, like any Trickster, unwittingly on behalf of the cosmic ecology. The stories shift even more as they migrate into other cultures and find new homes there.

We should also avoid making value judgments about which myths or mythologies are better (more evolved, more advanced, etc.) than others. Like comparing works of music or art across cultures, this gets us nowhere useful and creates unnecessary rancor. Such rankings exhibit their own unconscious mythology, with the evaluator unwittingly possessed by the otherworldly realms, levels, or hierarchies lurking in the background.

My recommendation, then, is not to read each myth for what it means in general (agreement on this is scarce even from within its original culture, let alone from people outside it), but to read for what it means to *you*, for what it brings forth in you, and for how it can increase your appreciation for the culture, time, and place in which it grew as well as for the diverse interpretations it attracts. In truth, we owe these societies our gratitude for their priceless additions to the worldwide treasury of timeless stories.

AS WE WILL SEE, mythic consciousness is much more than an archaic or primitive step to get beyond. We can no more wrench free of myth than we can dispossess ourselves of drama, legend, story, or earthly roots. Remember what Icarus forgot.

My hope for this book is that, in addition to encouraging a revival of mythological inquiry on its own terms and not as a subset of some other field, it illustrates the urgent practicality of familiarity with myth. According to Thomas Berry, we are in trouble as a species, with institutions and ecosystems failing on every side, because the stories for making sense of our place in the world are moribund. Not just their content, however. The means of storytelling has been so totally dominated by the financiers of mass media and politics that we seldom know how to tell our own tales anymore, let alone grasp the relevancy of stories and plotlines of the past that intrude themselves into the present.

Loss of myth means loss of orientation in a bewildering time. Echoing Campbell, Mann, Hesse, Jung, and a host of other mythologists and mythographers, Rollo May compared the state of a mind seemingly swept free of myth to the proverbial house cleansed of an evil spirit—who then returns with seven evil companions. "The more enlightened our houses are," noted Italo Calvino, "the more their walls ooze ghosts." Many mythologies tell of the takeover of entire worlds by forces of gargantuan power and greed imaged as demons, frost giants, Kaiju, Titans, and other rampaging monsters who charge into every void left by disenchantment—"Once upon a time, in a place where nobody believed in demons anymore..." — and who must be dealt with before they wreck everything of value. In our day, the monsters look like malignant nationalisms, fundamentalist ideologies, Frankensteinian tampering with plants and flesh, and totalitarian trade agendas that starve millions. As Novalis observed long ago, when there are no gods, the phantoms reign.

> It seems to me that with the burial of myth, the barn in which the mysterious animals of the human unconscious were housed over thousands of years has been abandoned and the animals turned loose—on the tragically mistaken assumption that they were phantoms—and that now they

are devastating the countryside. They devastate it, and at the same time they make themselves at home where we least expect them to—in the secretariats of modern political parties, for example. These sanctuaries of modern reason lend them their tools and their authority so that ultimately the plunder is sanctioned by the most scientific of world views.

—Vaclav Havel, "Thriller"

The loss of a conscious relationship with myth means more than lacking a charmed picture of the world. At bottom, it signals the loss of stories that make sense of who we are, where we live, what we do, what we should strenuously seek to avoid, and what we might become. Little wonder, then, that the widespread modern hunger for myth swallows counterfeits like those isms and ideologies that promise fixed orientations they never deliver to a world in constant change. Nor do only the uneducated or irrational remain susceptible: as the example of Nazi Germany proved for all time, those most dedicated to objectivity and reason risk falling under the sway of mythic possession. To attain to only the heights of civilization resurrects violent archaic powers in the dark depths of consciousness.

Mythic beings will not stay locked out, pinned down, or confined to a grid. In a rationalist, desacrilized world run by money, propaganda, and hardware, they creep in from the margins and ruptures and edges, disguised as symptoms, nightmares, political upheavals, works of art, comic book characters, moods of enchantment, extraterrestrials, brand names, uncanny dreams. An education in mythology feeds the hungering soul by serving up nourishing images, narratives, timeless motifs, and thoughtful questions in response to the tales that seek us out. When savored and digested, myths become food for the heart, medicine for the soul, and therapy for the imagination.

"All the world's a stage," remarked Shakespeare's magician Prospero. Mythology tells us who the characters are, how they address us, and what that stage is dreaming about.

To briefly summarize what awaits:

Chapter One asks, "What is Myth?" Here you will find various frameworks for understanding the nature of myth, including a sampling of theories and models. This chapter also discusses my own approach to *metamythologizing*: applying mythic tools aware of their own mythological backgrounds as we enter the stories that reach out to us. A longer, more detailed discussion of theories of myth appears in Appendix 1.

In Chapter Two, "Working with Myth," we learn about different ways to handle the stories reflectively, setting aside confining literalistic habits to let the stories breathe. We will also consider storytelling skills and why they matter.

Chapter Three, "In the Beginning," starts the retellings with creation myths. We begin with the theme of birth to arrange the myths here and that follow along the human lifespan.

Chapter Four, "Family Ties," contains stories with something to say about the complexities of family life. How we view it changes with which characters we listen in on.

Chapter Five, "Love and Loss," deals with relationships and romance. A diversity of kinds of love shows up here.

The "Awakenings and Initiations" of Chapter Six lead us through trials and rites of passage. Even the gods must undergo them. Performed well, they bring deep transmutation.

"Heroes and Monsters" of Chapter Seven show up together because the Hero tends to bring forth the Monster or Antihero and vice versa. Where one is found, the other soon arrives.

Chapter Eight contains tales of the "Post-Heroic Journey" that opens just as the Hero's Journey described by Joseph Campbell closes. Stories here follow a sequence of steps from "Landing Here" once heroic tasks end to "Apomythosis," which means how and when the hero turns into a myth.

In Chapter Nine we meet "Tricksters" from several cultures. As figures who bring sex, death, and fire, Tricksters serve as agents of chaos and comedy, especially when life gets too rigid.

Chapter Ten, "Justice and Community," gathers stories that exemplify collective fairness as an archetypal need. From amoeba to

Aether, gatherings of beings into societies mean the arrival of disorder and of creative responses for managing it.

Chapter Eleven, "Nature and Earth," places myths back into the ecological context from which the oldest of them always emerged. Traditional tales (we sometimes forget) come from specific locales and remain flavored by their places of origin even when the tales circulate widely.

Chapter Twelve, "Apocalypse and Renewal," completes the cycle of retellings with tales of the end of worlds. Important to remember what these tales so often suggest: that times of descent are unavoidable, and that they lead to eventual rejuvenation.

In Chapter Thirteen we look at possibilities for "Modern Myths" emerging from our sciences, laws, moneys, machines, and various other appurtenances of contemporary life. Modern myths include *personal myths*, referred to by C.G. Jung as "life myths" when he acknowledged in a letter that he felt confronted and challenged by the ancient figure of Faust the alchemist.

Chapter Fourteen, "Dreaming the Myths Onward," borrows a phrase of Jung's to discuss (as Joseph Campbell did) Earthrise as a mythic image of our time. Unpacking this, we will also consider the possibility that forms of the reappearing gods call once again for a reimagining, this time with the sacred encountered as immanent, embodied, and terrestrial, even when celestial.

Even after this tour, though, we will not be able to claim to understand myth entirely and for good. Ultimately, myth well-coaxed consents to cast flickering lights on mysteries outside our ken. As the old maps warned, "Beyond this point, there be dragons." There always will be however much the maps improve.

Meanwhile, spend enough time around the great stories that forever retell themselves and they stop materializing as symptoms or ailments or futile repetitions. Given adequate space and respect, they gather themselves up, step out from between the covers of books, and walk winged and scaled into the mundane particularities of lives actually lived, belching fire, breathing smoke, leaving a twisting trail of claw marks, and, if they happen to be in the mood, slyly leading the bold adventurer through the maze to the hidden treasure.

Chapter One – What is Myth?

> The moment we abandon this dilettante attitude toward the images of folklore and myth and begin to feel certain about their proper interpretation—the minute we look in them for facts rather than truth—we forfeit our proper humility and open-mindedness before the unknown, and refuse to be instructed, refuse to be shown what has never yet quite been told either to us or to anybody else. And we attempt, instead, to classify the contents of the dark message under heads and categories already known.
> — Heinrich Zimmer, *The King and the Corpse*

In Walked Myth

When asked to define a myth, probably most of us would give one of two answers: that a myth is a lie (e.g., "the myth of the liberal media"), or that a myth is an archaic explanation for some natural event like thunder that science can now explain.

If we are religious, we might define our beliefs as The Truth and other beliefs as myths (lies). For atheists, all religions are myths but, again, one's own standpoint is the true one. This is why mythologist Joseph Campbell joked that one definition of "myth" is "other people's religion."

What such common-sense definitions tell us as offsprings of Modernity is that myth has become a stranger to us. That is why we think of it in such disparaging terms. The dream suffers a similar mistreatment. Something was "only a dream," we are assured, or "only a myth." Even the imagination, a foundational human power, is thus disparaged: "only a fantasy."

This judgment is handed down by the Modernity mindset in which we get stuck: a fundamentalist literal-mindedness to be found wherever opinions, whether scientistic or religious, have rigidified into what artist Bob Miller diagnosed as a "hardening of the categories." For the Modernist worldview, only what is explainable or measurable is real. All else is fluff and fancy (excluding, presumably, the fancy that only what is explainable or measurable is real). In the West, this worldview, coming out of the self-congratulatory historical period known as the Enlightenment, is a reaction against centuries of men in black robes telling the masses that God said the powerful could do whatever they wanted, however harmful to everyone but the elite. And so the cultural pendulum swings.

When we use *theories* of myth, therefore, in order to define what myth is, we run the risk of observing myth from outside, like the shopkeeper in an old Western peering through the blinds at the tall dusty stranger sauntering into town. And from the shopkeeper at the window to the sniper squinting down from behind the rooftop railing, the only real distance is a quick change of roles. Cynically sized up, myth made fugitive is apt to vanish like quiet from a saloon.

Perhaps that is why, at least in the West, we are confronted by so many theories of myth. Myth seems problematic mainly in societies that have lost the knack of mythologizing, of polishing old tales until they glow with entertaining images and handy truths. For storytelling societies, collective stories are important, tradition matters, tellings connect their hearers to nature and cosmos and the Divine and each other, and the quality of our consciousness, personal and collective, is only as clear as our tale-telling is rich, diverse, and abundant.

Although the purely academic study of myth has been one of the least successful of all disciplined endeavors, especially when undertaken to reduce myth to one of its components, we cannot afford to ignore the occasional insights it has produced from behind the blinds and the rooftop rails. These insights complement studies more welcoming, if idealizing, of myth: stranger as savior. If nothing else, a brief consideration of two types of theorizings could prompt us to ask fruitful questions about the living nature of myth.

Two Types of Theories of Myth

Echoing the multidimensionality of myth, definitions of what a myth is abound. The word itself, from *mythos* (plural *mythoi*), meaning a story or telling, points back to divine poetic inspiration, which is one reason hard-headed thinkers like Heraclitus have always sneered at it. Yet Plato found myths useful for philosophizing. In those days, *mythos* referred to a poetic telling in public, not to something symbolic to be deciphered. That came much later. In his *Poetics*, Aristotle used *mythos* to mean the arrangement of events in a story's plot. For Homer and the Greek poets of his time, mythos carried a hint of the ornamental, incantational, and resonant, emphasizing the beauty of the telling. For Hesiod, mythos is the speech of the Muses. By contrast, in Hesiod and elsewhere, *logos*, which we now think of as truth or explanation, carried connotations of dissimulation, seduction, and falsehood.

As Greek fascination with the old forms of the gods faded, skepticism grew. In 530 BCE, Xenophanes wrote of the gods as what we would now call human projections: to a bull, he sneered, the divine would look bullish. Pindar, Theagenes, Thucydides, even Plato treated myth as disreputable. By the time of Herodatus, logos and mythos had traded places. The trend to regard myth as faulty rationality (prescientific explanation for Theagenes, politics for Plato, distorted history by Euhemer, allegory for Porphyrus) was on. Logos ate mythos.

A similar rationalism broke out in India, where materialist thinkers enshrined doubt and reason (600 BCE), and in China (300 BCE), where one day the gods of myth would reappear as ministers and kings. And the same in other societies. Many later commentators would see this as inevitable cultural progress: what science and logos gain, myth loses. Historically, however, it seems cyclical. The old skins wear out, and the heady wine leaks through until new containers are found. (More about this in Chapter 14.)

In times and places where myth has been regarded as strange enough to theorize about, two general groups of theory have arisen. The first we will designate *reductive-literalistic theories* because of their emphasis on parts over wholes and on fixed meanings over the symbolic, metaphoric, or mysterious. This has been the dominant approach in the rationalistic West, and, in folklore studies, sociology, literary criticism, religious studies, and cultural anthropology, it still is. The second group, *holistic-organic theories*, seeks to understand the meaning or value of myth as more than the sum of its discernible elements. The first group is analytic and decompositional, the second synthetic and, at its best, inspirational.

Reductive-Literalistic Theories

This group includes the following theories and theorists:

Myth as superstition or propaganda: Xenophanes, Theagenes, Plato, Pindar, Thucydides, the Charvaka philosophers of India, the Chinese *Heavenly Questions*, Justin Martyr, Tertullian, Cyprian, John Toland, Fourmont, Warburton, Pluche, Voltaire, Pierre Bayle, and the like. Example: belief in a God is merely fear of mortality amplified by the elites who make the myths.

Myth as moral, political, or natural allegory (from *allos*, meaning "Other" made over into Same): Chrysippus, Heraclitus, Zeno, Natale Conti, Francis Bacon, George Stanley Faber, Dupuis, Max Müller, and a host of others. Theorists who view myth as an allegory of natural forces like sun, moon, or storms include Epicharmus, Pythagoras, Müller again, S. N. Kramer, Thorkild Jacobsen, John Tu Er-Wei, Adalbert Kuhn, Sir William Jones, Charles Dupuis, Leo Frobenius, Émile Senart, and James C. Moloney. Example: Odysseus as an ideal Greek.

Myth as pre-scientific explanation: Bernard Fontanelle, E. B. Tylor, James Frazer, Andrew Lang, Marett, Balfour, Horton, Kramer, Bidney, et al up to and through the present. Example: Thunderbird as a mythic explanation for thunderstorms.

Myth as idealization or exaggeration of once-living heroes (*euhemerism*) or events: Prodicus, Euhemer, Hecateus, Herodotus, Confucius, Ennius, Dadu of India, Diodorus, Cicero, Persaios,

Polybius, Strabo, Saxo Grammaticus, Lactantius, Newton, Shuckford, Hume, Herbert Spencer, Robert Wood. Example: Alexander the Great worshipped as a god after his death.

Myth as history itself, if a bit warped: Thomas Keightley, Karl Müller, Otto Gruppe, Jean Bérard, Carl Robert, Martin Nilsson, Edouard Willthis, Robert Graves, Peter Munz. Example: Zeus's marriage to Hera as a faded memory of the patriarchal and military domination of Mycenae.

Myth as code for or remnant of secret esoteric practices, mentors, or knowledge: Giovanni Boccaccio, Marsilio Ficino, Pernety, Waite; more recently, Marie Jones and Larry Flaxman. Example: Hermes as a Greek version of the Egyptian wisdom god Thoth, bestower of mystical knowledge to the initiated.

Myth as primitive thinking: most of the names on this list, and also including Lafitau, Brosses, Van Dale, and Levy-Bruhl. Example: animal totems signifying a pre-logical state of felt unity with the natural world.

Myth as language structures like conceptual opposites or hardened metaphors: Christian Gottlob Heyne, Max Müller, Robert Brown, Angelo de Buernatis, Troubetzkoy, Propp, Greimas, Goldzieher, R. F. Littledale, Smythe Palmer, George Cox, Levi-Strauss, Barthes, Jason, Dundes, Guttgemanns, Althusser, Detienne, Liszka, Schnapp Metz, Mosko, Serres, Calame, Todorov, Sourvinou-Inwood, Hartog, Gould, Gilkey, Leach, and the Barbers. Example: the Oedipus story as a verbal clash between nature and culture.

Myth as dependent on ritual: Jane Harrison, Frazer again, Lang again, Tylor again, Robertson Smith, Cornford, Cook, Murray, Hocart, de Vries, Widengren, Engnell, Preuss, Girard, Mauss, Granet, Genrnet, Lord Raglan, H. S. Hooke, J. A. K. Thompson, Margaret Murray, Gertrude Kurath, H. S. Versnel, Weisinger, Honko. Example: Persephone's descent to the Underworld as a leftover autumn planting rite.

Myth as a social charter of norms in storied form: Ibn Khaldu, Emile Durkheim, Bronislaw Malinowski, Franz Boas, Radcliffe-Brown, Graebner, Schmidt, von Sydow, Obrik, Krohn, Kluckhorn,

Dumézil, Lincoln, Hulkrantz, Van Baaren, Eggan, Toelken, Bantly, Vandiver, and most of today's Western cultural anthropologists and sociologists. Example: the Yellow Emperor of China as exemplary husband and government official.

Myth as culturally influenced semiotics or ideological verbal codes: Karl Marx, Theodor Adorno, Louis Althusser, Bakhtin, Barthes again, Baudrillard, Benjamin, Chomsky, Eco, Foucault, Gramsci, Habermas, Hall, Jameson, Sartre, Lacan, Lyotard, Said, Deleuze, Guattari, Derrida, and the Barbers again. Example: the downfall of the tyrant Erisychthon as a moral and material victory for the working classes.

Myth as an expression of biology: Freud, Richard Payne Knight, Walter Burkert, and Hans Blumenberg. Biogenetic structuralism (Eugene d'Aquili, Charles Laughlin) draws on biology, sociology, cognitive psychology, ethology, and neurology to study myth and ritual as evolutionary survival responses. Example: gods of death as expressions of an innate death drive.

Myth as early philosophy: Rudolf Bultmann, Ricoeur, Langer. Example: Native American tales of emergence from underground as speculations about people's place in the world.

Myth as a sign of prepatriarchal religion, patriarchy itself, or the struggle against patriarchy: Marija Gimbutas, Riane Eisler, Gerda Lerner, Spretnak, Carter, Baring, Cashford, Larrington, Billigton, White, Payne, Liu, Brenner, Vytrovskaya, Weigle, Purkiss, Seller, Caputi. Example: the replacement of earth goddesses with sky gods as male cavalry overran Old Europe.

Myth as outdated, irrecoverable, and irrelevant (mythoclasm): Xenophanes again, Theagenes again, Barthes again, Batto, Mauss again, Voss, Eichner, Goldenberg, Giegerich, Ginzburg, Heller, Manganaro, Dubuisson, and Day: in other words, Modernists and pre-Modernists.

As an obedient child of Modernity, the reductive-literalist approach is stamped by:

- Reduction of myth to one component of it (nature, culture, historical events, allegory, language, pathology, superstition, etc.)

- Externalized and emotionally distancing explanations for subjective experience
- Dualism between nature and culture, inner and outer, observer and observed, and natural and supernatural, privileging one while minimizing or denying the other
- Various modes of literalism, including allegorism, secularism, historicism, and fundamentalism
- Emphasis on the outdated antiquity or primitivism of myth
- Distrust of myths' numinosity: in other words, a fearful rejection that exhibits what Jungian analyst Lionel Corbett refers to in another context as the Scrooge Defense against too intense an emotional charge emanating from spiritual imagery.

This group of theories tries to position itself outside of myth altogether, as though bending over a microscope. Although it captures some details, like the binary themes so beloved of Lévi-Strauss, it generally misses what the tales mean to those who tell them and listen to them, like cetacean biologists who claim that whales breach to remove barnacles while missing their clear enjoyment of the leap. "It is ironic," notes Ruth Benedict, "that the academic study of folklore should have labored through its course under the incubus of theories explaining seven-headed monsters and magic swords as survivals of primordial conditions, allegories of the sun and moon or of the sex act or etiological philosophizing and have ignored the unconfined role of the human imagination in the creation of mythology."

Reductive-literalist theories also underestimate the force with which the old tales can return to life at any time whether or not we want them to. The stranger entering town today, for example, can be an ominous Trickster; as the first line of Ray Bradbury's *Something Wicked This Way Comes* puts it, "The seller of lightning rods arrived just ahead of the storm." We might recall archeologist and adventurer Dennis Puleston, who insisted that the Maya placed sacrifice victims atop the El Castillo pyramid at Chicen Itza to expose them to lightning. His life ended one day when, standing on that height, he was killed by a bolt from the blue.

Holistic-Symbolic Theories

The holistic-symbolic approach also grew up in the house of Modernity, but it ventured out long enough to search for its roots, finding them in imagination, the depths of consciousness, folk storytelling, and the humanities.

Myth as a remnant of a time or place—inner or outer—of lost greatness: Paul Mallet, Hugh Blair, Abraham Anquetil-Duperron, William Jones, Romantics like Novalis, Hölderlin, Creuzer, the von Arnims, Eichendorff, Benfrey, William Perry, G. Schmidt, Mircea Eliade. Example: Avalon as a vanished magical isle.

Myth as storied experience of the sacred: Friedrich Schelling, Friedrich Schlegel, Rudolf Otto, Wach, Eliade again, Cassirer, Urban. Example: a creation story as signifying spiritual awakening.

Myth as psychological: C. G. Jung, Karl Kérényi, Joseph Campbell, Northrop Frye, Fiedler, Lowes, Knight, Murray, Spurgeon, Singer, Hillman, Woodman, Johnson, Miller, Meade, Bly, Jungians in general, and Pattanaik. More reductively: Sigmund Freud, Bruno Bettelheim, Rank, Schneiderman. Example: the drowning of Narcissus as an illumination of narcissism.

Myth as a form of literature: Richard Chase, Lawrence Coupe, Frye again, McCune, Wheelwright, Orbison, Withim, Falck, Tolkien, and Veyne. Example: Gilgamesh as an enduringly entertaining story.

Myth as holistic (whole-person) philosophy: many of the Romantics (e.g., Schlegel and Schelling again), Henri Bergson, Alan Watts, and Lawrence Hatab, Krolick, Scarborough, and Baeten. Example: Inanna's descent to the Underworld as a model for gaining wisdom.

Myth as holistic ritual: Victor Turner, Karen Armstrong, Malidoma Somé. Example: Sir Percival's departure, adventuring, and achievement of the Grail as a rite of initiation.

Myth as an ecological emergent between people and places: Jakob Grimm (to some extent), J. G. Herder, Goethe, Moritz, Sean Kane, Jake Berry, R. S. McCoppin. Example: the stormy weather characteristic of Mt. Olympus in Greece appearing in myth as battles between Olympians and giants.

Myth as expressive of more than one cultural dynamic: Morris Freilich, G. S. Kirk, William Doty, E. J. Michael Witzel, Karen Armstrong, Harvey Birenbaum, Wendy Doniger. Example: Isis as a figure of mercy, norms of motherhood, the maternal side of the psyche, and the beneficence of the Nile River. (Monomythical explanations of myth have generally proven more popular than pluralist.)

Holistic-Symbolic theories are characterized by:

- Interest in the story as a whole
- Focus on what myth reveals about subjectivity and psychic depth
- Application rather than allegory (J. R. R. Tolkien's distinction)
- Tending of many possible meanings (i.e., polysemous)
- Awareness that the inquirer inevitably participates in the myth, even when analyzing it
- Emphasis on the continuing relevance of myth
- Contextualization of the story as involving a larger-than-human world (nature, archetypal reality, realms of spirit).

At their best, holistic-symbolic approaches allow us into the living tale so we can be moved, taught, and transformed by it. At less than their best, they abandon cultural nuances in specific stories to the Nameless, the Whole, the Eternal, the Archetypal, or some other vague all-encompassment.

The two groups of theories are not absolutely distinct; theorists overlap in their approaches. Jung, for instance, might be considered holistic-symbolic in his unwillingness to reduce myth to language or biology, but his eagerness to emphasize archetypes (universal thematic patterns like Death, Rebirth, Solar, Lunar, Initiation, etc.) over obvious cultural factors (patriarchy, racism) betrays a perilous proximity to reductionism. On the other hand, reductionist-literalists

Malinowski and Barthes insist on the vital discursive role myths play in all human culture. David Miller's enthusiasm for myth comes through clearly on days when he forgets to mythoclastically argue for its inevitable loss and decline.

If we look at these approaches through the lens of myth—metamythologically, so to speak—we might glimpse figures like form-fitting Procrustes, stern and structured Saturn, conservative Hephaestus, and monochromatic Aten behind the first, and the likes of generous and earthy Ala, the Muses of inspiration and memory, fluid Yemaya, and artful Aphrodite and her Graces informing the second. An ideally comprehensive approach would delight in visiting the vantage of every mythic power.

Which is why it might get us farther to see these two groups of theory not as opposites, but as differently angled lenses capturing myths at various stages of their maturation.

A Developmental View

Like all living beings, a myth goes through a life cycle: birth through imaginative vision, insight, or dream; adolescence, when the myth spreads and grows through retellings; adulthood, when it assumes traditional, ritual, and institutional forms; and old age, a period of declining energy.

As a myth loses its force, there at the end of its long life cycle, one of five outcomes awaits it:

- *literalization* into ideology, which turns myth and its hosts into zombies;
- *fossilization* into unconvincing dogma or mere belief;
- *fictionalization* by raconteurs and fabulists;
- *intellectualization* when rationalists shrink myth into something boringly formulaic; or
- *revitalization*, which updates the myth and gives it new life, whereupon it starts a new cycle. In no phase does a myth really die.

Theories of myth tend to focus on single phases of a myth's life cycle. Eliade, Cassirer, Frye, the Romantics, and Jung stayed with its fresh and childlike numinosity; Frazer and the poets and so many comparativists, with its adolescence; Levi-Strauss and the linguists, sociofunctionalists, and philosophers, with its adult structural elements; the mythoclasts, allegorists, and euhemerists, with myth already hardened into ideology. So far only a few voices (Vico, May, Holderlin, Herder) have echoed Jung's observations about mythic rebirth: "The most we can do is dream the myth onward by giving it a modern dress." In Chapters 13 and 14 we will see how that works.

From a developmental perspective, then, holistic-symbolic theories come upon myth newly born, in its childhood, or in its adolescence, whereas reductionist-literalist theories study it once institutionalized, aging, or decrepit. The first group catch the butterfly in flight, the second when stuck to a pinning block. Both tell us something about a myth as well as about the myth's inquirer.

What, then, is myth?

Working Descriptions of Myth

> It is because they are alive, potent to revive themselves, and capable of an ever-renewed, unpredictable yet self-consistent effectiveness in the range of human destiny, that the images of folklore and myth defy every attempt we make at systematization. They are not corpselike, but implike. With a sudden laugh and quick shift of place they mock the specialist who imagines he has got them pinned to his chart. What they demand of us is not the monologue of a coroner's report, but the dialogue of a living conversation.
>
> —Heinrich Zimmer

We do not lack definitions of myth. "Myths are universal and timeless stories that reflect and shape our lives—they explore our desires, our fears, our longings, and provide narratives that remind us what it means to be human" (Karen Armstrong). "Myths are original revelations of the preconscious psyche, involuntary statements about unconscious psychic happenings, and anything but allegories of physical processes" (C. G. Jung). "A mythology is a system of images that incorporates a concept of the universe as a divinely energized and energizing ambience within which we live.... And a myth, then, is a single story or a single element of the whole mythology, and the various stories of the mythology interlock—they interlock to be consistent within this great world image" (Joseph Campbell). "Myths are narrative patterns that give significance to our existence" (Rollo May). "The myth as a work of art has as its principal form the shape of drama" (Jerome Bruner).

Verlyn Flieger believes that defining myth is impossible. Unanimity on an exact definition will never occur because it will leave out what someone, somewhere, considers important; too loose a definition will lack enough specificity to be useful. She might be right. To define means to make exact, clear, distinct. *Define* comes from roots that mean to finish, to determine: *de-* "completely" + *finire* "to bound, limit." But myth's deepest thinkers link it to undefinable mysteries. The pinned butterfly no longer lives.

> The mythical gesture is a wave which, as it breaks, assumes a shape, the way dice form a number when we toss them. But, as the wave withdraws, the unvanquished complications swell in the undertow, and likewise the muddle and the disorder from which the next mythical gesture will be formed. So myth allows of no system. Indeed, when it first came into being, system itself was no more than a flap on a god's cloak, a minor bequest of Apollo.
> — Robert Calasso

If not a definition of myth, let us have at least a working *description* (from "write down; copy; sketch").

First of all, a myth is a *tale*. Doty and others have contested this, but in actual practice, myth has been told since the dawn of time as a once-upon-a-time or in-the-beginning, even when it includes lists, genealogies, and temple dimensions. Even in them, the tale is implicit.

A myth is an *entertaining* tale (as Okpewho, Lithui Yang,

Hamilton, Yolen, and Tolkien observe), otherwise nobody would hand it down. Something in it must grab us.

A myth is an entertaining tale that contains *great marvels and mysteries* that *conflict or develop* and are usually personified. Not just a small marvel, like a talking dog. Great marvels, numinous, archetypal, and more-than-human, if not always involving gods.

These marvels infuse the *existential questions* we all face about why we are here, where we are going, birth, life, death, and the Beyond. This makes myth different in degree if not in kind from the folktale or fairytale, as many scholars note: for example Robert Redfield's distinction of Great Traditions from Little Traditions and Martin S. Day's between "grand opera" and "operetta," distinctions akin to those made in many cultures.

Furthermore, by being told and retold, a myth becomes *collective* and *traditional*, and as such, *often believed in*, at least by most, because in myth-friendly cultures, few hearers outside the lore keepers pause to split fanciful from historic or symbolic from literal. ("In all the wild imaginings of mythology, a fanciful spirit is playing on the border-line between jest and earnest."—Bronislaw Malinowski). Nor is that belief strictly literalistic, as in the Protestant query, "Do you believe in God or not?" It is more like "I've been told" or "what the ancestors said."

Even when myth deals mainly with spiritual forces or presences at play, their *relation to the human* is always there, whether in the background or in other myths in the cycle or simply implicit in the telling.

What does that give us? *A myth is a collective, entertaining, and imaginative tale of the existential conflicts and relations between grand, more-than-human marvels or mysteries and human beings, at least implicitly, and as such, is a sacred story believed in by most hearers but held as instructive or metaphoric by wisdom teachers.* To this could be added features noted by other theorists of myth: the stories take place in a timeless present, the marvels and mysteries are often personified and named (unlike folktales and fairy tales that deal mainly in roles), various realms of being are described, spiritual entities are present, and the myths tend to collect in groupings we call mythologies (again unlike folktales, which often fly solo), mythologies often, but not always, tied to important religious rituals.

A shorter description: ***Myths are fanciful collective sacred tales about interactions with and among mysterious beings, forces, or dimensions of existence.*** Shorter: ***Myths are elaborated collective dreams/fantasies/stories***, because they begin, as far as we know, in dreamlike or visionary states that, once described, resonate in many listeners. (We might refer to mythopoetic tellings not yet aged by tradition as *protomyths*.)

Here's another, from my classes: ***A myth is a collective oral mystery story that is traditional, fantastic, highly personified, archetypally rich, once believed in, and often sacred.***

Shorter yet, following J.G. Herder: ***"Myths are personifications of effective powers."***

Perhaps that will do for now. Even if we can't define myth, we know it by how it is told and what we feel in its presence.

Mythologizing and Metamythologizing

As I continue crafting my approach to myth, I feel uninterested in compiling—even if it were possible—a model to fit all contingencies. The assimilationist crusade feels impractical and, frankly, arrogant. "The will to a system is a lack of integrity": perhaps not always as bad as Nietzsche makes out, but when I see this will at work in other fields, philosophy for instance, where in some quarters "integral" seems increasingly to mean "totalitarian," the partiality of so many myth theories suddenly shows a silver lining.

Not every aspect of every theory or model or path to myth will have equal weight for the lover of myth. Although I appreciate my intellectual forbears (many of whom show up in Appendix 1), I do not resonate with all their approaches or ideas about myth. My own seeks to be story- and character-centered, animistic-ecological, developmental-cyclical, archetypally informed, culturally appreciative, and pluralistic of view. The basic medium of myth as I hold it is imagination, not as a shallow making-things-up, but as a deeply creative working-with-and-witnessing. Prompted by personal or cultural events, archetypal structures emerge in the space between the human and the more-than-human and coalesce into stories of marvel. If the medium of myth is imagination, storytelling—through voice, ritual, drama, art, film, some creative medium—is its vehicle. As we will see, symptom and emotional possession are also vehicles, but they operate unconsciously.

While working with myth I observe a distinction between two complementary modes of doing it.

Letting it speak to me, studying its sources, reading it out loud, listening to it, walking around inside it, watching it transform me, appreciating it, inquiring into what it provokes or disturbs in me, sharing insights with other readers, hearers, or tellers of a myth, writing or telling my own versions, designing and carrying out myth-honoring rituals, and other activities mentioned in Chapter 2 are examples of the mode of *mythologizing*. *Mythology*, of course, is the study of myth, although the word is also used for the collective myths of a culture. *Mythography* studies theories of myth and ritual, particularly in written form. *Mythologizing* refers to actively engaging with the tales. Immersion. Not just studying the lake, but swimming in it. (Jung's dictum comes to mind: You can't wash a dog without getting wet.)

Metamythology is when we use myth to think about myth and to comment on what we do. Not "meta" as in "above" or "beyond" (late corruptions of the Greek preposition), but as in μετά- , "beside," "with," "among," "between." This prefix informs words like *metaphor, midwife, metapsychology*, and Plato's *metaxy*, the trans-subjective middle ground in which fabulous daemons hover between us and the great gods of being.

Academically, "meta" also as transdisciplinary, in Alfonso Montuori's sense: paradigm-questioning, self-reflective, inquiry-driven rather than discipline-driven, honoring of imagination and not just Saturnian rigor or Procrustean procedure.

Working metamythologically does not pretend to study the stories from outside their frames. Instead, we move *with* them, noting how abundantly *their content and imagery infuses the very movements of our inquiries about them:* heroic efforts to learn about

Cuchulainn, threshold insights into Hecate, Underworld sojourns on the way to Osiris, runelike scribbles to remind us of watchful Odin. Pretending to be Odysseus by telling a clever lie to hitch a free ride to mythology class is mythologizing. Noticing the heroic tone in one's description of the exploit is metamythologizing. So is seeing where Penelope appears nearby, how a classmate's response reminds us of Tiresias, or when we act more like lost Telemachus than like his swift-footed father. Psychological approaches view the myth as inside us, and at least some of it often is; but metamythologizing views us as inside the myth as well.

When we analyze a myth, we seek something from and in it. Metamythologizing allows us to ask: What does this myth want from me? Why has it popped up here, now? Where in its story is its energy at present? What does it intend? Is it here to bless us, to reveal a truth to us, to seduce us into a new retelling? To demand a symbolic sacrifice? To bestow a precious gift?

James Hillman was brilliant at tracing the archetypes in our activities: the Hero in our activism, for instance, or motherly Demeter in pleas to save the planet. Inspired by this insight, metamythologizing shifts the lens to other entities present as well: the language in which we tell the tale as a mood or spirit within the tale; the surprise of one of the characters at large in the audience, or in us; the settings of our tellings, as when alternations of genre in a student's description of Phoenix imagery in a local city mirrored the two "wings" of the city, one artsy and quirky, the other formal and structured. Can we discern the forests of France through the mythic trees of Arduinna of Gaul, Greek caves of limestone in tales of Hades, pulsations of the Nile in the moods of life-giving Isis?

Here are 20 Metamythological Considerations for your perusal:

1   **Story *precedes* the distinction between mythos and logos**, as Eliade, Cassier, and Chase point out; in fact, mythos and logos are themselves fabled catagories. "If we agree," wrote Dundes, "that a myth minimumly involve a narrative, then we can dismiss all references to 'myth' as a synonym for error or fallacy." "Myths work," adds Laurence Coupe, "according to the imperative of narrative dynamism and

will always evade the stasis of doctrine." Myth is the truth of fact, not fact the truth of myth (Kathleen Raine).

2 **The logocentric fantasy of an original, pure version of a myth is arid and hopeless.** No two tellings are alike, nor should they be. Each telling interprets (Marina Warner, Dennis Tedlock, Dell Hymes, David Aaron Murray, et al). "It is not true that there is some hidden thought or idea at the bottom of the myth, as some in a period of civilization that has become artificial have put it, but the myth itself is a kind or style of thinking. It imparts an idea of the universe, but does it in the sequence of events, actions, and sufferings." So Nietzsche thought.

3 **Spontaneous in origin** (contra Emerson, who thought we could just make up our own), **myth is a living narrative, a storied illumination or "felt logic" of life** (Birenbaum), a storied imaginal weave or net that drifts through the world seeking elaboration and evolution and what Richard Rorty called "inspired readings." It "appreciates" being given a new form that nods to the old even while bearing it in new directions. Zimmer: "Myth is the sole and spontaneous image of life itself in its flowing harmony and mutually hostile contrarieties, in all the polyphony and harmony of their contradictions. Therein resides its inexhaustible power." Fighting off literalistic criticisms of the gods, Sallustius (4th century) wrote about myth, "This never happened but it always is."

4 **Myths (and folktales) demonstrate a persistent autonomy.** They push back against the *mythuse* of bad-hearted retellings. Hitler tried to stage Ragnarok and ended up playing the doomed Fenris wolf. Max Lüthi and Linda Dégh give examples of how *märchen* (fairytales) have survived exploitation, even Disney's, without losing their essence; the same is true of myth. Although myths have been retold and modified numerous times before we even hear them, they retain their power to evoke and instruct. "We all have

a sense of the difference between what the story demands and what the teller of the story or the listener might like the story to be" says Robert Duncan, who adds, "For the Bororo people who live immersed in myth, Claude Lévi-Strauss tells us, the myths themselves are *persons.*"

5 **Myths exhibit a lifespan.** Starting out fresh from dreams, visions, or numinous fantasies that are told and catch on, young myths are vibrant. Mature ones are stable, especially when backed by ritual, institution, or creed. Myths in their prime can hold thought and feeling together for entire cultural groups, at least for a while. Eventually, though, they begin to wear out, like the old wineskins Jesus mentions. They limp along as ghosts of themselves, whether literalized, fossilized, fictionalized, or intellectualized, until a change of relevance revitalizes them.

6 **Theories of myth habitually focus on single phases of a myth's life cycle**: its childlike naturalness and freshness of vision; its sprawling adolescence; its adult responsibilities and norms; or its old-age lameness or crustiness prior to its rebirth through updated tellings that fit the needs of a time. We would do well to keep in mind the entire life cycle of a myth and of its surrounding mythology.

7 **When we fail to respect the story as story, we face a ruined quarry we have mined for what we wanted to dig from it.** As Robert Duncan puts it, "For theosophists, psychoanalysts, and the converts of revealed religions, it is not the story that is primary but the meaning behind the story." But if we show the story respect and hospitality, if we converse with it instead of exploiting it, we open the door for the gods, spirits, daemons, and other presences to walk in, speak to us, and go their way in peace. "Hence the guardian figures that stand at either side of the entrances to holy places: lions, bulls, or fearsome warriors with uplifted weapons," writes Joseph Campbell. "They are there to keep out the 'spoilsports,' the advocates of Aristotelian logic, for

whom A can never be *B;* for whom the actor is never to be lost in the part; for whom the mask, the image, the consecrated host or tree or animal, cannot become God, but only a reference. Such heavy thinkers are to remain without."

8 **Surpassing what is known and customary, myths carry a sense of the mysterious**, uncanny (Freud), the glamorous, the strange, the wondrous, the otherworldly and underworldly. Birenbaum: "Myths often emphasize the very aspects of life that our ethics or our sense of decorum will teach us to shun, such as the grotesque and the violent, the painful, the impractical, the self-indulgent." The mood they evoke flows beyond the confines of literal meaning or belief. Even when they mention facts or linear processes, they do so in service to the feeling they evoke.

9 **Myths are irreducibly complex**, layered by the personal characteristics of each storyteller or writer, cultural interpretations and overlays, linkages to physical places of origin, accretions through time, and foundational archetypal dynamics. None of these dimensions can be reduced to any of the others without degrading the myth—not even to language, for the tale goes on however well or badly it is translated. A myth interpreted in only one fixed way is temporarily drained of life. "A Bantu or Indonesian critic will only be able to wonder: How were the Westerners able to write thousands of volumes on the 'beauty' and the 'eternal values' of *The Divine Comedy*, the work of a political exile, and see in our mythologies and our messianic symbols only a protest of oppressed peoples?"—Eliade.

10 **Neither a Dionysian overemphasis on myth's cultural differences nor an Apollonian agenda of comparisons that flatten can serve to open the tales.** These two gods were, after all, brothers who knew how to work together. For David Miller, the "as if" of myth contains both a connecting word and a difference word. To emphasize difference over unity is the reactive reverse of emphasizing unity over difference. In studying myth we must neither forget the cultural distinctiveness of a telling nor, widening our lens, miss the similarities across tales from a range of times and places. In fact, noting these similarities can further our appreciation of where tales and details diverge. They can also bring new light to old tellings, even for those who grew up hearing them (Doniger).

11 As with art, we cannot make authoritative statements about what myths always mean, either within or across cultures. We can't even say that for a single myth read or heard at different points of an interpreter's life. An old woman with grown daughters might understand Demeter's anguish at losing Persephone very differently than when hearing the story as a high-spirited young woman. False confidence in interpretation should give way to a tentative "This is what the myth brings up for me at this time." For what a myth means to its society of origin, we must rely on the tale-tellers of that society; and even they might not agree with each other.

12 When working archetypally, hunting for images and motifs, we pay less attention to objects and attributes (big breasts = fertility, lighting-throwing = king), which can mislead us, **and more to the styles, flavors, or personalities of gods and other beings.** All-seeing Jupiter, for all his lightning, is nothing in temperament like impetuous Thor, nor is Odin, mobile and tricky though he be, otherwise much like Hermes, Jung, Campbell, and taciturn Tacitus notwithstanding. Ancient Babylonians knew Shamash as the sun, but they prayed to him as a god of justice.

13 Archetypes in myths cannot be accounted for as images of instincts, neurological effects, or cultural memes. They image forces, presences, and situations found ultimately in the world around us, where we too originate. Myth is a connective tissue that links human life to these great ecological (Jacobsen, Keen, Momaday) and trans-cultural forces colored differently for each cultural group. "The imagination, a plastic medium, receives impressions from the archetypal forms of nature, and by an active force realizes those impressions in its own forms, as images, symbols, and ideas" —Lloyd De Mause.

14 By definition, a myth is both collective and multigenerational. A "myth" created out of an agenda of entertainment or personal enlightenment might actually be a *submyth*: a story filled with archetypal motifs but not believed in as sacred or traditional or hallowed by the passage of time and many tellings (Le Guin). However, mythopoesis is ongoing; UFOs as spontaneously emerging "modern myth" (Jung) could be seen as examples of *protomyths* on their way to becoming genuine myths enfolded in arising mythologies.

15 Myths give us insight into the underlying structural forces of a time because, as Jung pointed out, **they express a compensatory response to them.** Think of the powerful goddesses of patriarchal Athens, where women were seldom allowed outside the home. Doty: "Myths (and rituals) may emphasize values and conditions that are just the opposite of what is found in contemporary experience; for example, myths stressing coordination and peace may be prominent during a period of anarchy or warfare." So when we don't like a myth, let's not kill the messenger.

16 Myth does not rigidly separate the natural from the imaginal, cultural, or spiritual. Herder believed myths to be communal poetic philosophy as an embodiment of nature's powers of growth: "...The whole Egyptian mythology bespeaks...the blessing of Earth, the Nile, the animals, men—thereof speaks everything! Onions and Garlic! Mendes and Apis! Man and Woman! Generative vitality was the theme of their mythology, interpreting all..." John Anderson: "The foundational images of our language would have to predate humanity, because for humans to read the environment, to understand and relate to the weather, to other animals, and to the lay of the land, an inherent familiarity with the *lingua franca* of the natural world be necessary." Pauline McLeod: "When you look at the complexity of the culture you realise that language, dance, music and art, all depend on the area of land you lived in. What you would present as an area artform would be the spiritform animals from around your region. Therefore, if you lived in the Snowy mountains—they'd be mountain stories; the desert—desert stories; coast—coastal or ocean stories; islands—island and ocean stories."

17 **Myths reenact themselves in many ways**: by being constellated by outer events and our responses to them; by major life transitions; by gaps or pressures in collective consciousness; by societal blindnesses and injustices that bring the old stories back to life for a kind of unconscious group therapy; by changes in religions and spiritual paths... *The contents of the myths we study becomes, at some point, the process by which we inquire*. Paying heed to the myths and archetypes within our theorizings and applications of myth deepens our appreciation of the tales. (In Frazer's work, for example, we might discern the figure of Attis awaiting sacrifice; in Malinowski's, the dominance of the solar; in Levi-Strauss's, the mechanics of a blacksmith god; and in so many Modernity perspectives, old Procrustes sharpening his ax.)

18 **Myths also come back to life as *personal myths***, or what Jung called "life myths": **myths we are born into and are tasked with creatively elaborating.** Though collective in origin, these myths are personalized in how we reenact them as characters within them. Jung as Faust the alchemist, Freud as King Oedipus, Sir Isaac Newton as Janus, John Keats as Icarus, Percy Shelley as Prometheus, Mary Shelley as Nemesis, Mozart as the divine child Iacchus, Marilyn Monroe as Venus, Martin Luther King Jr. as King Arthur, John Steinbeck as Lancelot, Jim Morrison as Dionysus, Joseph Campbell as Percival, and Ken Wilber as

Hephaestus are possible examples. (See "Personal Myths" in Chapter 13; refer also to my book *Storied Lives*.)

19 Myths and archetypes repeat themselves, but when worked with consciously, their wisdom applied instead of allegorized (Tolkien), **they soften so that the stories they animate sprout new delineations and outcomes.** It's as though they want to be told differently. As Jung and Zimmer have observed, myth offers inexhaustible abundance ever in need of consulting. Herder: "This brings us to another usage: that of adding a new feature so skillfully to the old mythology from the modern age and its customs that the new becomes venerable and the old rejuvenated."

20 Myth worked with consciously brings a lived sense of reenchantment. Engaging with folklore in general and myth in particular opens an experiential portal by which we walk into an animated world filled with powerful presences that enliven and permeate our relations with ourselves, each other, the animate Earth, and the great cosmos in which we float. Ultimately, our very survival as a species might well depend on the quality, humaneness, and spaciousness of our rejuvenated mythologizing.

When my metamythologizing links to my sense of social justice (see "Archetypal Activism" in Chapter 14), I play with the pun of aspiring to "Metis mythologizing." As Bruce Lincoln observes, "The kind of cunning that lets the weak overcome the strong—or, to put it more properly, that lets those whose power rests in their wiles and words overcome those with power of arms and armies—was known as *metis* among the Greeks." Metis, quiet and cunning mother of Athena.

Meta- also relates etymologically to the *mid-* in midwife. How might we midwife the possibilities gestating in myth? We take up that question in the following chapter.

Chapter Two - Working with Myth

> The tale remains patiently in wait for the unsuspecting
> teller to pass by.
> —Herbert Mason

The question of how to work with myth is large enough that I recommend we begin with another: *What prevents us from working with myth?* Seeing our initial resistances to this work will help us move forward into it.

Resistance to Myth

We humans are natural storytellers. To resist working with story and myth requires energy to pit against our natural inclination. That energy is itself mythic: to be more specific, in many cases it is Procrustean, guardian of the inn and assailant of the wayfarer.

Procrustes started out as Damastes, a blacksmith. He wanted to build, mold, and guard things. He was also a bit of a rogue. Like most of us, he feared whatever did not fit his frame.

On that level, resistance to myth is natural. Myth both regulates and disrupts lives, worldviews, even matter itself, as when it shapes armies, cathedrals, and computers. Myth can maim, kill, or rejuvenate. "For healthful I can be," states Mercurius Trismegistus, the mythic god of alchemy, "and also poisonous."

Even so, we are immersed every day (and night) in the currents and waves of the ocean of myth. Our normal propensity is to swim.

But when a culture dominated by rationalism and materialism turns against the imagination, the result is usually the compromise formation (Freud) of an ism, a repressive doctrine of defense.

The isms below are examples of internalized psychological institutions that react on the level of reflex. Each prevents us from tending the living being of myth:

- Ideologism: reducing a myth to a single interpretation, sometimes to grind a religious or political ax. We all do this at some point, especially when a myth first seizes us. Allegory—reducing myth to a moral—is an example.

- Euhemerism: insisting that mythic stories are stories about external human events. In other words, about the known, the safely familiar, the already-experienced.

- Iconoclasm: insisting myths are "wrong" if they are not factual, provable, or authenticated by a sanctioned political, religious, or scientific authority.

- Scientism: reducing a myth to a pre-scientific explanation for some natural occurrence we now understand better. This defense goes with that of

- Evolutionism: making an unwarranted distinction between "primitive" and more advanced myths or mythic systems (e.g., monotheism versus animism).

- Propagandism: using fragments of mythic images to promote group narcissism (e.g., nationalism). For some, their country's flag is mythic.

Take note of what makes these isms similar to each other: literalism, reductionism, fear of myth's numinosity, fear of fantasy, blockage of myth's transformative power, and distrust of myth's subjective pole. All demonstrate a fear of myth similar to fear of the unconscious psyche, of untamed nature's wildness, and of spiritual experience. Fear of what escapes the inelastic frame.

The result of successfully pushing myth out of consciousness (if not out of symptoms, nightmares, wars, market crashes, or interpersonal conflicts) is what Rollo May describes as "loss of myth."

Myths are our self-interpretation of our inner selves in

relation to the outside world. They are narrations by which our society is unified. Myths are essential to the process of keeping our souls alive and bringing us new meaning in a difficult and often meaningless world. Such aspects of eternity as beauty, love, great ideas, appear suddenly or gradually in the language of myth.

"Without myth," he continues, "we are like a race of brain-injured people unable to go beyond the word and hear the person speaking" (*The Cry for Myth*).

Loss of myth means more than a loss of philosophy or belief because the stories provide

a framework of meaning not only for reason, but for experience. They organize how we feel into ourselves, our culture, the world, the universe. Imagine the shock of a person of the Middle Ages transported into our time. Computers and traffic would be the least of their worries;

a set of tools for handling recurring problems. After a high school fight with a bully, I was advised by my grandfather to be patient instead of retaliating: "The mills of the gods grind slow, but they grind exceeding fine" (and they did);

inspiring models of noble poise and action, which is one reason why the suppression of Goddess story and image has been so hard on women in monotheistic societies;

solvents for melting confining categories of race, sex and gender. What sex is Dionysus? Whichever s/he wants to be at the time;

plotlines and images for staying in conscious relation with more-than-human forces around and within us;

therapy for some of our compulsions. When a constellated myth is not met consciously, it can manifest as unconscious ritual;

antidotes to dangerous psychic epidemics (Jung). A

repressed mythology returns as a monster, a fury, a violent ideology that can mobilize millions. To the myth-starved, even destructive stories (propaganda, nationalism, religion hijacked by psychopathy) feel better than no stories;

tools for working with monstrous or demonic defensive figures haunting dream and symptom (D. Kalsched);

pluralities of viewpoints that place us outside our customary categories of thought and value. In myth we find as many value systems as gods and spirits;

fabulous havens against the cold soullessness of materialist Modernity;

cultural roots, values, traditions, celebrations, and wisdom lineages;

glances at future paths, goals, possibilities of doing and being.

> The loss of myth-consciousness I believe to be the most devastating loss that humanity can suffer; for as I have argued, myth-consciousness is the bond that unites men both with one another and with the unplumbed Mystery from which mankind is sprung and without reference to which the radical significance of things goes to pot. Now a world bereft of radical significance is not long tolerated; it leaves men radically unstable, so that they will seize at any myth or pseudomyth that is offered.
> —Philip Wheelwright, "Poetry, Myth, and Reality"

This loss brings a disenchantment that devastates Earth itself. Patrick Curry describes the resulting loss of will to protect what's left in *Defending Middle-earth:*

> No strategy based purely (or even largely) on calculations of usefulness, self-interest or rationality can survive the onslaught of the economic and scientific monologic that comprises "development." Only re-enchantment can

make it possible to realize that this world, its places and its inhabitants are existentially already wondrous—and as such, worthy of the kind of respect and love that doesn't permit their wanton, callous and stupid destruction. You won't fight for what you don't love.

Resistance to myth and the disenchantment into which it sours—which are different from being between myths while seeking those that resonate and instruct—bring to mind the old Greek word *dysdaimonia*: actions out of alignment with the daimonic, the sparklingly mythic, dimension of life. *Eudaimonia*, often translated as "happiness" or "virtue," results when we greet the mythic dimension with openness and hospitality (*xenia*).

Welcoming the Stranger

Books and other resources on working with myth abound; some appear in the Bibliography. Before I add to this array of techniques, let me recommend what may be the most important attitude to inform our work: that of welcoming the stranger.

One mythic basis for this is the tale of Baucis and Philemon, an old, poor couple who were the only citizens of their village to provide dinner and beds to two tall wanderers who turned out to be Mercury and Jupiter. The grateful gods blessed the couple and remade their hovel into a temple. Their xenophobic fellow villagers perished in a flood.

What confronts us in myth, as in fantasy, folktale, and dream, is apt to be strange at first. A feminine figure wearing a necklace of thumbs, a forest dweller sporting a giant penis, a father who eats his children, a giant bird flapping lightning from his wings, and a lover turning himself into a horse to mate with another horse are not sights you see on the street every day. But you see them in myth, and if you read or hear many tales, such figures might start showing up in your dreams as well.

Myth itself offers a helpful response: greet the stranger with respect and curiosity. Receive whatever appears by giving it gracious open-mindedness, even when it seems frightening, and it is apt to bless you with insights not available elsewhere.

Cultural pressures aside, something about myth's yearning to incarnate in new tellings can, if we are not careful, seduce us into interpreting the tales quite literally. But doing so can let all the air out of them, leaving us with flat and boring shadows of themselves. To avoid this, we can cultivate the art of appreciating mythic events, characters, settings, and themes as *symbols*: images that announce or represent something beyond themselves (following Jung, Wheelwright, Ricoeur, Perrin, Yolen, Kawai, and many others). Unlike signs, symbols do not have fixed meanings. Their roots are sunk in mystery. Their potential for illuminating the depths they point to is inexhaustible.

Because mythic symbols are not rational explanations, they must be cajoled into sharing their secrets. Here are some ways to amplify them:

- Describe a symbol (event, character, setting, action, theme: virtually every element of a myth can serve as a symbol) to someone else as though they had never come across it before. What insights does this make available to you?
- Dwell on its details. Do not be in a hurry to interpret it. Ponder it long enough to start knowing it, turning it as you would turn a jewel recently given to you. Listen to it. Talk to it. Describe it vividly in writing.
- Find out what the stories mean to the people who grew up hearing, watching, and reading them.
- Use free associations (Freud) to track what the symbols mean *to you*. When you imagine an amulet, what jumps to mind? Protection? Defense? A family heirloom? Your smartphone? Do this with the symbols that reach out to you, then retell the story through the associations you've gathered. Has your grasp of its relevance deepened?
- As you consider a symbol that stands out, what feelings emerge? Sit with them for a time.
- Check your body to see which parts respond to the symbol as you hold it in imagination. What symbolism do

these enfleshed responses offer?

- Give form to the symbol: paint it, collage it, collect graphics of it, dance it, design a ritual for it. Do this with the story too, or with an aspect of it that strikes you.
- Look for how the symbols are used in other stories and in other mythologies. Where do they show up in literature? In history? Art? Film? Music? Elsewhere? What symbols mean in a variety of settings can shed light on what they indicate in the story you're reading or listening to.
- Enact a scene from a myth, with you and others playing the characters. Feel into the role. What does it bring up?
- Slip into a state of reverie, then summon forth the symbol and allow it to express itself inwardly however it wants. Does it have something to say? To give you? Can you step into the scene with it? Jung called such an exercise *active imagination*.

Suppose I am reading a myth and I come across the symbol of a magic stone. Instead of rushing to interpret it, I might instead walk outside and look for a stone that reminds me of the story stone. To gain a stronger sense of it, I might hold it in my hand, feel its weight and texture, appreciate the colors in it, place it on my desk or on an altar, draw it, photograph it, or make up a story about it. With each respectful move, the stone comes alive for me.

I close my eyes, visualize the mythical stone, and wait for it to speak to me or show me something. What does the stone make of all this? Does it have a name?

Because the story is Irish, I ask someone who grew up hearing Irish lore about magic stones. They tell me about the Blarney Stone of eloquence, of the Lia Fáil stone where the Irish High Kings received their crowns, and of the stony heaps under which People of the Sidhe known as banshees dwell. Strange and wonderful events unfold near stones. To get stoned is to enter an altered state.

As I visualize the stone, I feel my palms tingle, as though my hands hold something solid. Hands for holding; magic in the palms of my hands. No sense of weight pushes my palms down, as though the stone were a burden; rather, my fingers cup spontaneously as though I hold a crystal ball.

A bit of homework discloses that the magic stone is a common folkloric image. Stones are said to be wise, to harbor secrets, to contain ancient knowledge, nature knowledge in particular. They can be still, solid, and unchanging; but "a rolling stone gathers no moss." Centuries of alchemists tried to coagulate the Philosopher's Stone whose radiance (it was said) granted wealth, wisdom, and immortality. Jung saw this Stone as a symbol of wholeness.

Where do stones show up in my life? "Craig," my first name, means "outcropping of stone." What do this mythic stone and I have in common?

I tell the story to receptive listeners. What does the symbol of the stone bring up in them? Not only in them as individuals, but in the group mind?

I return to the magic stone with a network of associations, allusions, images, cultural parallels, sensory impressions, and interesting memories to enliven my feeling for the place in the story held by the stone and, additionally, for what the story might mean to me, and I to it.

Functions, Levels, and Archetypes

Beyond what a myth means, exploring what it does, and on what levels it does it, can also open the door to what wants to come in and converse with us.

Both Rollo May and Joseph Campbell describe what myth does in terms of its *functions*.

May distinguishes between the *regressive* and *progressive* functions of myth. The regressive reveals to us our unresolved wounds and stuck places. The Gnostic version of Eve withdrawing her spirit from her body prior to being raped by archons might sensitize a survivor of sexual abuse to the lingering aftereffects of self-protective dissociation. A student of mine identified strongly with the figure of Percival lost in the woods. The progressive function of myth reveals new goals and directions embedded in the story. Images of happy people living harmoniously together in verdant villages might offer hope that, yes, we can get along with each other and with our still-green planet.

Joseph Campbell has described four other functions served by myth:

- the mystical: myths provoke and express our awe at the mysteries of life;
- the cosmological: myths paint pictures of our place in the world and, in our day, the universe;
- the social: myths embody a culture's norms and values;
- the pedagogical: myths can show us with worthy characters how to grow and learn throughout our lifespan.

To these we might add six more functions:

- the personal: myths reveal a specific story we come in with (see "Personal Myth" in Chapter 14).
- the archetypal: myths show us deep thematic connections across pantheons (more below).
- the chronological: myths can hint at possible futures, blessed paths as well as paths we should not take (Chapters 12 and 14).
- the transrevolutionary: myths can critique our time while suggesting possibilities for transforming it (Chapter 14).
- the ecological: myths reconnect us with the presence of land, nature, and place (Chapter 11).
- the aesthetic: myths entertain, arouse, shift moods and feelings, inspire creativity and art ("Why Storytelling?" below).

These functions also serve as levels on which myths operate. Facing the figure of Athena, we can ask: Who is an Athena in my life, or, Where is she in me (personal)? What happens to Athenas when they stand up in my society (social)? How does she exemplify the archetype of the Wisdom Goddess evident across pantheons (archetypal)? How do her armor and shield reflect the features of the Acropolis (ecological)?

Of the levels above, the archetypal is apt to cause the most confusion. Archetypes are widely misunderstood; Jung's treatment of them varied; they don't sit still long enough to be measured; no standard definition of an archetype has ever surfaced; and the word "archetype" is often used when people mean "mythic image."

Although we can't hope to clear this up here, we can, as a working idea, hold "archetype" to mean a universally recurring grand pattern or motif, one that shows up in our lives, our dreams, our works of art, our relationships—and our myths.

The notion of primordial patterns precedes Jung, as he notes. As an example he cites Plato, who distinguished between the world of phenomena and the grand Ideas or basic patterns behind it. During his plant researches Goethe looked for the Ur-plant, the basic form inhabiting the germinating, flourishing, and decaying vegetation he studied so carefully through direct observation combined with what he called "exact sensorial imagination." Goethe saw each plant as a kind of gesture or style; anybody who has imitated a tree by standing tall and spreading arms wide can get a feel for this idea.

Jung got onto the idea of archetypes by studying Gnostic myths about humans as copies of angelic originals in heaven, by watching his dreams—in one he climbed down into the cellar of an old Roman house and found prehistoric bones there—and by seeing patients in a psychiatric clinic. One of them hallucinated a giant phallic tube extending downward from the sun to blow winds in four directions over the earth. Jung, who had read one of the few books in print that described this image in detail, identified it as a piece of Mithraic mythology. The patient had not owned this book and had probably not read it.

Death, Rebirth, Hero, Seeker, Queen, King, Witch, Mage, God, Wisdom, Justice, Initiation, Strife, Love, Sacred Marriage, Divine Child.... Jung believed that a shared, or collective, unconscious could generate the same basic motifs anytime and anywhere. A bar maid, he commented, could dream of a precise Wheel of Life figure without having seen one. An American barber with little exposure to mythology described to Jung a dream about a man strapped to a fiery wheel, a figure the ancient Greeks would have recognized as Ixion.

Archetypal motifs like these organize human experience even while connecting it to events that include us individually but reach far beyond us. They allow us to see when we stumble into typical, recurrent situations. But we do not directly perceive archetypes themselves (wrote Jung) because, like natural laws that order the physical universe, they are invisible, though discernible by their effects. These include intensely numinous experiences, cosmically themed dream images, sacred figures in art and myth, sudden inspirations, and strongly felt emotional and bodily reactions to synchronistic events: coincidences that feel meaningful, like when you dream about a playful dolphin and see one swim by the next morning while you walk on the beach.

Because they express basic patterns and typical situations, archetypes are more general than mythic images. As an archetype, Rebirth shows up in forms that vary with time, place, story, event, and witness: the Phoenix rising from the ashes; waking up from a coma feeling like a new person; moving into a totally new and vastly more fulfilling career; the death and resurrection of a god. Erotic Beauty looks mythically like Aphrodite, Venus, Freya, Hathor, Oshun, Lakshmi, and their mythic sisters across the world. Trickster flounces forth as Coyote, Hermes, Mercury, Eshu, Ananse, and a multitude of other jokesters, pranksters, and bringers of chaos. Allfather, Allmother, Wisdom, War, Health, Illumination, Death, Wildness, and entire pantheons full of other archetypal beings shimmer forth as specifically imaged goddesses and gods throughout folklore, story, and myth.

Archetypes and the myths in which they clothe themselves tend to power up around certain key life events:

- Developmental milestones like coming of age, middle age, and nearness to death;
- Psychic splits that give rise to self-alienation, trauma, and inner conflict;
- Similar splits in collective consciousness, especially during society-wide disruptions;
- Loss of enthusiasm for traditional symbols and beliefs as consciousness moves beyond them;
- The rise of new symbols and ideas stirring in the depths.

Archetypes presently active in our lives do several things for us:

- They clothe deep psychic processes in forms, faces, and characters we can work with.

- They bring back to us pieces of ourselves, like playful dolphins reminding us to swim along with enjoyment or like heroines reminding us to be bold when we need to.

- They give collective context to what often feel like purely personal struggles. What may seem superficially like a series of failures takes on a different quality when its details parallel the fall of Sophia and the grand creations to which that led. Suffering with a discernible meaning can evolve into a sacred task.

- They reveal the dilemmas and dramas we share with other people, including people of the past, and thereby ease the pain of isolation.

- They reveal solutions to common human problems. Facing the hundred-eyed Argus monster, Hermes displays cunning insight into how to deal with mass surveillance.

- They widen our perspective, from our story being just inside of us to our being inside a larger story.

- By prompting us to research their imaginal expressions, they plunge us into art, literature, history, and other fields of knowledge, wisdom, and craft. As Jung pointed out, an archetypal image left unamplified is as incomprehensible as an ancient baptismal font whose history, origin, and culture remain unknown.

- They reflect deep movements in collective consciousness, as when dreams of a murdered hero hinted to Jung about the onset of World War I (and perhaps II as well).

- They gather up and present to us spiritual imagery bathed in awe regardless of our religious orientation or lack of one.

All these archetypal manifestations gain amplification through the specifying power of myth. Knowing that an illness or conflict partakes of the archetype of Initiation can strengthen our resolve, but we receive helpful tools for managing an infirmity when we can see how it parallels the descent of Ishtar to the Underworld or young King Arthur's chance to pull the sword from the stone.

When exploring the archetypal level of myth, we discern basic motifs across stories, pantheons, societies, and periods of time; but we must not lose our sense of the specificity of each story, including how it is held (if we know) in its culture of origin. As we widen or narrow our focus, we appreciate differences between myths while tracing what they thematically share.

We should also note that surface similarities can deceive. A spiral in one society or subculture might mean something different than a spiral in another. Also, similarities tracked by comparative mythology have limited themselves too often to an objects-and-attributes categorization: of wide-hipped goddesses as fertility deities, of gods with axes or clubs as warriors, of gods of lightning, flood, or rain imagery as divine meteorologists.

In academia, sloppy comparativism is part of why mythological studies have all but vanished. At one time, so much difference-denying universalism held sway that, once the shouts of protest started, scholars familiar with myth grew reluctant to point out cross-cultural parallels for fear of being branded "colonizers."

Archetypes or Stereotypes?

> The problem—at least in its psychological and philosophical form—is essentialism (that is, universalizing). In the name of psychological archetypes, one gets political stereotypes. Archetypalism becomes stereotypicalism, often with regard to race, class, and/or gender.
> —David Miller, "Mything the Study of Myth"

As Robert Ellwood and Charlene Spretnak (to name two among many) have noted, myths and ancient tales do not represent completely natural products of the deep psyche. They come down to us layered with agendas: historical, political, religious; sexist, racist, and imperialist. Generations of feminist scholars have uncovered how socially sanctioned exaltation of masculine deities pushes all other figures—feminine, androgynous, asexual, transsexual—out of public view. Other oppressions run rampant throughout the history of folklore and religion.

Furthermore, labeling a quality or characteristic "archetypal" implies its permanence. What of cultural influences? The "archetypal feminine" or "sacred feminine" described exclusively as dark, receptive, passive, motherly, emotional, and yin reinforces a patriarchal view of women. Nor do the myths themselves agree with it! Try telling Kali, Athena, Eris, Ishtar, or Sekhmet that the essence of femininity is passive. The filter I apply is not to regard as archetypal any quality missing from the natural world we so often forget we're part of. Plants germinate, grow, and die; animals display heroism, maternal and paternal care, leadership, and wisdom; fungi use nets and webs; bacteria sacrifice themselves so their colony will live. Archetypal themes abound around as well as within us: what do they act like outside? At times, not much like what we so often archetypalize culturally.

Another problem surfaces when we focus so much on the archetypal, or what we think is archetypal, that we miss the other levels, the cultural in particular. Jung conducted an entire seminar on the archetypal imaginings of Christiana Morgan without mentioning the current cultural struggles of the African and Native Americans who appeared in her visions and dreams. Or of women; in fact, Jung advised his patient to funnel her immense gifts into being a muse for her male lover.

As repositories of archetypes, myths nevertheless cannot be considered pure sources of wisdom. So many of the myths that have come down to us are laced with mixtures of male privilege, heteronormativity, violence, racism, ethnocentric ignorance, and self-serving propaganda. They are also warnings, for in their brutality and injustice we see our own actions reflected.

The warnings can be misunderstood. To dismiss an unpleasant dream as irrational might ignore an important message, as when, many years ago, I waved off a nightmare of jumping out of a burning building. On the following morning, I joined a psychotherapy center so badly mismanaged that it went out of business not long after I had jumped out of my contract. Our dreams also caution us in symbolic language about our health, our relationships, the times we live in. So do myths, as messengers for entire societies.

When overzealous critics *reduce* mythology to its upsetting imagery or lingering imperfections, they devalue what the ancient stories offer. They miss what is pushing itself upward from beneath myth's often-mucky surfaces. Like the stories' mythusers, those who reject myth altogether shrink it down to ideology. They see only where the stories have warped and degenerated, ignoring what they might have meant to their first inspired tellers. The message in the symptom goes unheeded.

When I was a graduate student, I heard little that was positive about masculine mythic figures. Zeus was reduced to a philandering patriarch, a sign of warlike pastoralists pushing their masculine prerogative. So I was confused when a fatherly figure showed up in my dreams to castigate me for failing to learn from him.

My dad had not been a patient teacher, to me or anyone else. In a dream, I asked "Dad" why he was still coming at me like this. Growing to majestic size and presence, "I am NOT your dad" he informed me in a godlike voice.

I recognized him only after I woke up. Whew!

"Why would my version of Zeus appear in dreams like this?" I asked a fellow student who had participated in years of Jungian analysis. His reply made perfect sense: "Where in your life is *your* authority, your Zeus-like qualities of leadership and command?" The answer was: nowhere. I was in a shy phase then, hiding out, reading, and writing papers instead of sharing what I was learning. Signals that called me into greater visibility, the waiting seeds of my future profession, had gone ignored. Like my dad, Zeus was a bully (I had thought) with nothing to teach me.

The following evening, I summoned up the Zeus-like figure in my mind's eye before going to sleep and said to him, "I'm ready to learn from you." That night I entered the first of many dreams in which a kingly guide no longer argumentative or authoritarian spoke gently to me about stepping out into the world. I followed this advice and began lecturing about and publishing my work. When fellow students asked me to run a study circle, I agreed.

None of these positive developments were served by seeing Zeus only as an oppressive patriarch. That blind spot kept me from connecting with what Jungians refer to as a symbol of the sacred masculine. It also prevented me from healing from my father complex. I had so seldom known good fathering that when the Zeus dream figure told me several months later that my lessons were over, I mourned for weeks, and not only for *his* disappearance. Beneath our mask of male competence churns a river of unshed tears for the generations of wounded fathers who could not fully father us.

How we ideologize myth says more about our own wounds than about the myths that touch them. The flip side of idealizing myth as a source of perfect knowledge is reading it with an ideologically closed mind. Procrustes again. The alternative is letting the stories speak how they want to the welcoming reader, hearer, witness.

Yet myths confront us that *are* tinged sexually, politically, socioeconomically, religiously, racially. Consider Hera, the great feminine pole of the divine, She whose flowing breast milk gave our entire galaxy its Western name. Early Greek writers turned the Queen of Heaven into an insecure shrew worried more about Zeus's philandering than about the order of the cosmos. Judging from the danger posed by some of his offspring, she was right to worry.

A nuanced reading can recover wisdom from the stories by receiving them as many-layered: personal, cultural, and trans-cultural all at once. To a generous openness, each myth carries seedlings of meaning trying to break through and outgrow the ideological crust encasing them. We seek the buried truths while critically aware of their ideological overlay.

Instead of succumbing to easy reductionism, we respect the stories' persistent self-organizing dynamics as their themes pass through time and place to address us. These deep dynamics also spoke to their first tellers and hearers *through their own cultural biases*. The ancient Greeks were patriarchs, so the ultimately archetypal forces that emerge in myth as goddesses like Hera addressed Greek audiences as such, even while pushing them a bit beyond their customary blind spots by presenting strong feminine figures like Athena, Artemis, and unabashed Aphrodite.

While social encrustation shapes a myth's reach, the latter reshapes the former. Even though Hera was widely but wrongly considered a subordinate of Zeus, the ancient stories gave her no nickname comparable to Zeus's "Consort of Hera." (Ginette Paris interprets Hera's jealousy as ultimately dynastic, a concern less about Zeus's affairs than about their impact on Olympus.) Thor might seem an individualistic, musclebound hero type, but he learns from his blunders, and for a warlike culture, the lessons hold lasting relational implications. Our Lady of Guadalupe retains her Aztec characteristics despite the Christian overlay she wears like the star-covered robe draped over her shoulders.

"Myths are metaphors," Joseph Campbell often pointed out; metaphors that symbolize the perennial as well as the transient aspects of life. Mythology is to a time and place what a barometer is to the weather or a seismograph is to an active fault. When deep rumblings sound below the range of audibility, mythic images vibrate and crinkle like the qualities of being they image.

Why Storytelling?

Because it's fun.

Because it helps us get into myth.

Also, because it's effective. "The telling of stories," explains storyteller Gayle Ross, "the desire to share our experiences, is what made us develop into a species with a spoken language. I think everybody has the capability of responding to a story on the deepest level. For that reason alone it's important."

At age one a baby can pretend to put a doll to bed. What does it mean that we spend about half our waking life in fantasy mode by daydreaming on the go, and a third of our entire life asleep dreaming stories? It means we are two-legged procreators and transporters of stories. We are Homo narratus, with fictions that allow us to anticipate before we act and to reflect after we act. Some of these fictions are myths.

Our best facts mean nothing at all without storied frameworks that give them meaning and context. Actions result not from facts, but from what we tell ourselves the facts can mean.

New facts offered without new stories are easily discounted. Changing the story changes what facts can say to us.

Stories allow people to explore meanings and draw conclusions without being preached at. Our spoken examples then lead to listeners' internal conclusions. Nobody is made wrong, yet actions and attitudes change.

Anecdotal stories can disarm the hearer's silent objections by showing how the teller worked through them. Such stories offer more guidance than fixed rules that cannot handle conflict or paradox.

Persuasion and argument push, and people resist being pushed. Stories pull us in. They spread long after the effort required to persuade and manipulate has dissipated. A hearer beaten down with logic will be less reliable than one who makes your story of what you value and why you act their own.

Stories about what's relevant to listeners inspire trust. Honest personal stories make the emotional connection that's required before anything else can happen. As Annette Simmons puts it, "If a picture is worth a thousand words, then a story is worth a thousand assurances." Stories let you demonstrate, not just talk about, your trustworthiness and deep involvement with the topic. Being perceived as trustworthy prompts less push-back.

A story character can present an attitude- and action-changing point of view more effectively than simply making an argument for it. It's hard to empathize with an argument. But who can hear of Inanna's perilous descent without twinges of sympathy for her sufferings?

Stories reach across cultural and political divides, opening common ground where the conservative and the radical, the materialist and the spiritualist, the dreamer and the cynic can meet.

They also allow unexpected, non-linear perspectives not calculable on charts of data. New stories can bring fresh views that shrink problems without having to rationalistically analyze them to death.

Mythic stories are big-T True because, unlike the small-t truths of statistics and surveys, they capture the great multidimensional Truths of our existence. They show what is too complex to be charted. Big picture stories give purpose to frustration and struggle. When I suggested to a depressed religious client that her beloved grandmother newly departed now looked down from heaven, waiting to see what my client made of herself, she decided not to try suicide again.

A single story can exert enormous impact. *Uncle Tom's Cabin* galvanized Union efforts during the American Civil War. The *Kalevala*, an epic woven of folktales, solidified the independence of Finland. *Roots* was the most-watched film of its day. This power of story forcibly contradicts what Tolkien called *Sarumanism:* the belief that only money and might make important things happen.

When President Kennedy stated, "We choose to go to the moon!" the naive thought him blinded by science fiction, ignorant of how symbols and aspirations—not facts and figures—drive us, especially in a "mythless" culture that leaves us with huge voids of meaning. To act differently, people must think and feel differently, and those require new stories that prompt and challenge and inspire.

Inspiration is key. Martin Luther King Jr. did not say, "I am an oppressed victim." He said, "I have a dream!"

Abraham Maslow's Hierarchy of Needs leaves out Fantasy. You can last three hours without shelter, three days without water, and three weeks without food, but you can't make yourself go one hour without a fantasy. Prisoners fantasize. Poor children growing up in a dump play there. We imagine, therefore we are, and vice versa. Maybe that's why we evolved, or why our stories evolved us: not just for our own complexification, but for theirs. Maybe they use us to deepen and proliferate. Maybe our survival as a species now depends on how well we tell our stories.

> At this point, realism is perhaps the least adequate means of understanding or portraying the incredible

realities of our existence. A scientist who creates a monster in the laboratory; a librarian in the library of Babel; a wizard unable to cast a spell; a space ship having trouble in getting to Alpha Centauri: all these may be precise and profound metaphors of the human condition. Fantasists, whether they use the ancient archetypes of myth and legend or the younger ones of science and technology, may be talking as seriously as any sociologist—and a good deal more directly—about human life as it is lived, and as it might be lived, and as it ought to be lived. For after all, as great scientists have said and as all children know, it is above all by the imagination that we achieve perception, and compassion, and hope.
—Ursula K. LeGuin

Before you await myths drawn from many times and places, many sources and cultures. Here are a few more tips for welcoming them in:

- Read each myth with an open mind and heart. Pay attention to what your emotions and your bodily reactions do with the story. Where is the myth in your body? Where does it want to go?
- Read it out loud to a group, then discuss what it means to each of you. Start with the first scene, which evokes the opening mood of the tale.
- Let the myths work on you, greeting each with appreciation and hospitality. Some won't speak to you, at least for now; others will whisper, sing, dance, or shout. Greet them all and allow them room inside your imagination.
- Recreate the myth or a scene from it in the form of a play or ritual that engages fully the senses of all participants.
- Ask yourself periodically: Through which mythic lens do I view this myth? Do I hold it at an Apollonian distance? Nail it down like Procrustes? Wield it like Shango? Care for it like Isis?
- Stage imaginal conversations with the characters and see

how they respond. What do they have to say for themselves? How do they feel about how the tale frames them? What would they like to say to each other?

- See if you can glimpse common ground behind the myth's cultural overlay. Remembering that mythic images are metaphors can help with this.

- Do homework or self-analysis on whatever resonates in the story, on whatever fires you, stirs enthusiasm, bothers you, makes you curious, or has an edge for you.

- Remember the distinction between allegory and application: between jamming a myth into a pre-conceived meaning and, more graciously, allowing its relevance to appear to you.

- Look for thematic parallels between a resonant myth and your life, past or present. How are you living inside the tale? Where do you want to go with it? Where does it want to go?

- Watch for the appearance of mythic figures and situations in your dreams and in synchronistic happenings around you. (Shortly after dreaming about a kingfisher, Jung found one near a lake by his home.)

- Explore within yourself your reactions to other people's interpretations, especially when you find them strange or jarring. Something inside requests your attention.

- Once a myth has opened itself to you (you can feel this happening) and you have explored it for a while, try writing or rewriting it from your own point of view or that of one of the characters. Bring forth the background characters and give them voice. For a more extraverted approach, fashion a ritual or dramatic scene from it and enlist other participants.

- In "Archaic Torso of Apollo," Rilke declared, "You must change your life." What do the tales that grip you have to say about what you can become? Milton Scarborough:

> The ultimate assessment of myth must be of a kind suited to the nature of myth as giving expression to apprehensions of the life-world and as functioning to provide an orientation for living in that world. Within those strictures

> myth is neither true nor false *in a theoretical sense* but viable or not viable for the tasks (both theoretical and otherwise) which confront us. This viability is not determined in intellectual terms but in the very process of living, by whether or not one is energized, whether or not problems are being solved, whether or not life is integrated at a variety of levels, whether or not it is endowed with a significance that pulls one toward the future in hope.
> —*Myth and Modernity*

The appreciative tender of myth should bear in mind King Vikramaditya, who carries the corpse he must cut down from the graveyard tree over and over and over, until he finally perceives the greater truths in the stories told by the spirit who animates the bones slung across his back. Having learned to hear deeply, he overcomes the mythoclastic spell that imprisons and silences the spirits. Once freed, they gratefully divulge their tales.

Chapter Three - In the Beginning

Every culture entertains a creation story. Even the scientific Big Bang account recalls the bursting Cosmic Egg found in myths around the world.

Creation stories answer the questions Why are we here? Where did we come from? How? *Although they answer symbolically and not just literally, they often refract images found within later knowledge. A Kiowa tale depicts this Great Plains people emerging into the world from a hollow log, an emergence through a tree, an archetype that throughout the world reminds us of evolution (look at our taxonomies) and growth of complexity (as with our tree-like nervous systems). In ancient Persia, a myth in which a round sky made of rock crystal came first, followed by water and air and then earth, reminds us of asteroids and meteors that help form planets and that carry the chemical seeds of life. "As above, so below."*

The following creation stories bridge many levels of being, including the metaphysical, the metaphorical, and the ecological, spiritual, cultural, and personal. Read them with one eye on the tale and one eye on the reader.

Creation of the World (Aboriginal Australian)

Pauline McLeod, Aboriginal Australian storyteller:

> Everyone had stories, so it was part of the land, their totem, belief system, culture and the community they'd grown up with.
>
> Where I grew up, the traditional stories were passed on to the children by the females in the community.
>
> Most of the creation stories of the dreamtime are in the general or public storytelling category and are traditionally told, sitting round a campfire. Each region in Australia has their own dreamtime stories of creation — how the animals came into being. I'd say in Australia there would be more than 700 stories about How the Kangaroo Got its Pouch.
>
> We have to bring back the power, the honour and the role of the storyteller in society again. We have to teach ourselves what a storyteller is.

In the beginning, deep within the timelessness of the Dreamtime before time as we know it began, the moon, the sun, and the stars slumbered beneath the earth. So did the Eternals, our ancestors. They awakened one day and decided to surface and emerge.

This they did, and as they roamed around, they wore many different shapes: lizard, emu, kangaroo, even biped now and then, though always a kind of leafy, plantlike biped.

While out on their nomadic sojourns, two Eternals called the Self-Created Ones (*Ungambikula*) noticed some round, featureless beings lying there like lumps of clay no one had sculpted yet. So they dug out their stone knives and set to work. As the heavens sprang into being overhead to light their labors, the Eternals shaped eyes and faces, hands and feet, arms and legs. They worked and fashioned and sculpted until before them stood human beings, brought forth from plants, animals, soil, and the patient arts of the original earthly Powers.

Having done this, the Ancestral Powers and Creators reentered the earth, transmuted into many shapes—plants, stones, birds, creeks, wells, fish—and, having left their handprints and footprints in everything, returned to their peaceful slumber as moon, sun, and stars sailed serenely onward lighting the world from high overhead.

Before resuming their sleep, however, the Eternals had bequeathed to their freshly created children a power akin to their own: *jiva*, the "seed power" by which all doings upon the earth leave their presences written upon it, just as the ancestors had left records of theirs in mountains, oceans, and breezes. Places Dream of these doings. You can see them in the tilt of hillsides, the outline of pools, the contours of rock.

And all of the creation, including human beings, participate in the humming of this seed power: the Dreaming of the Earth and everything walking upon it, flying over it, swimming across it, pushing through it, and slumbering peacefully within it. Those who bend down low enough can sometimes hear this Dreaming.

For Reflection:
- Comment: Because Australian Aboriginal culture reaches back for more than sixty-five thousand years, its sacred stories might well be the oldest in the world. Storytellers sang them long before 1788, when eleven ships under Captain Arthur Phillip brought the first Europeans to Australia. This story, one version among many, tells of the primal Creation of the land out of which many Aboriginal people insist they originated. We pay respect to this ancient and unbroken lineage of storytelling by beginning with one of its better-known tales.

- C. G. Jung advised his students to pay particular attention to how a dream opens because it announces the psychic state of the dreamer. What is the mood of the start of this myth? What is present, and what is absent? If you were there, what would you sense? Would you perhaps see the creation of human consciousness?

- Many myths tell of archetypal creator beings. In this story the creators emerge from the earth and take on the forms of various natural features. What might this suggest or hint about how this myth depicts the relationship between spiritual beings and Earth?

- How do you understand the power that leaves a record of all activities in the places where they occurred? What might be contemporary examples of that?

- In many myths, the creators or ancestors withdraw from their creation. Why is that? What purposes would it serve?

- Comment: In most mythologies the creation of humans follows that of other animals. In this, mythology aligns with evolutionary theory and diverges from thought systems that place humans on top of everything else.

- What might be some contemporary expressions of the Dreaming?

- Joseph Campbell said that myths work not by offering rational explanations for things, but by having an effect on us, by giving us an experience. What is the mood of this myth? What feelings or realizations does it leave you with?

- How might Gary Snyder's statement from *The Practice of the Wild* amplify or affirm this myth:

Recollecting that we once lived in places is part of our contemporary self-rediscovery... Two conditions—gravity and a livable temperature range between freezing and boiling—have given us fluids and flesh. The trees we climb and the ground we walk on have given us five fingers and toes. The "place" (from the root *plat*, broad, spreading, flat) gave us far-seeing eyes, the streams and breezes gave us versatile tongues and whorly ears. The land gave us a stride, and the lake a dive. The amazement gave us our kind of mind.

Brahma Tries On Bodies (Hindu)

Devdutt Pattanaik, Indian mythologist, lecturer, writer, and former Chief Belief Officer at Future Group:

> This diamond-shaped land was described as Jambudvipa [Blackberry Island], the continent shaped like a rose-apple. The Persians called it Hind, located beyond the river Hind, which the Greeks called Indus. It was a land watered by rivers, foremost of which was the great Ganga and its many tributaries.
>
> One is constantly told that all gods are the same, that they are different manifestations of the same truth, yet each deity has very specific offerings: a particular kind of leaf and a specific kind of food: Shiva is offered bilva leaves, raw milk and uncooked food, while Krishna is offered tulsi leaves, butter and food prepared with jaggery and ghee. It is not efficient but it is very effective as the deity's uniqueness is acknowledged.
>
> That no deity can exist without an ecosystem of consorts, children, servants, assistants, friends, plants, animals and minerals is a reminder that nothing exists in isolation. We are part of a web, and depending on the context, one deity becomes more important than the other, more significant than others, but only until the context lasts. Eventually all gods have to go away, thrown into the water at the end of

the *puja*, a ritual known as *visarjan*, until they are needed once again.

Brahman was One and All, and yet Brahman was incomplete.

So Brahman formed an egg. From the egg emerged a lotus, and from it grew Brahma, the Creator.

Sensing a world waiting in the waters of Nara below, Brahma took the form of a boar and plunged into them. To him Earth bowed as he raised her up from the waters.

Assuming a four-headed form, Brahma meditated; and as he meditated — who knows for how long? — a dark body formed around him. From its rectum blew the winds and demons and shadows. When he cast off this body, he hung it on the sky as Night.

Meditating, he took on a body of light. From its mouth emanated the radiant bodies of the gods. When he cast off this body, he hung it on the sky as Day.

In his pure (*sattva*) body he imagined mothers and daughters, and fathers and sons, and these took form as ancestral spirits hovering at dawn and dusk. His cast-off third body opened up those edges of day and night.

His fourth body wore garments of mental energy. While in it Brahma conceived human beings. Opening his mouth, he gave them fire. When he cast off this body it glowed in the night sky as the moon.

His fifth body wore the flesh of light and dark energy. Now he thought of monsters, and so there were. While beholding them, his hair fell out and slithered and crept away as reptiles.

His regained composure brought forth plants, birds, creatures with hooves and without them.

So was the world created, with the Creator within every element, mineral, and living being. Maintained by Vishnu and destroyed at last by Shiva, the world will be remade, again and again, eon after eon, era after era, each eon a mere *kalpa*, a day in the mind of four-headed, eight-armed Brahma.

For Reflection:

- A *kalpa* is 4.32 billion years. Each is made up of a thousand cycles of four *yugas* (eras or ages) of varying lengths: the peaceful and pious Satya, the end-of-the-honeymoon Treta, the Dvapara of decline and illness, and the dark and destructive Kali, at the end of which Lord Kalki, an avatar of Vishnu, rides forth on a white horse to restore the cosmic balance and set rolling a new *kalpa*. According to various Hindu sources, we live in the Kali Yuga that started six thousand years ago. This coincides with the rise of armies and urbanization. Coincidence or synchronicity?

- What parallels can we find between the interplay of dark and light in this very early story and contemporary theories of dark and luminous matter?

- Brahma is often depicted with either four or eight arms that clutch a spoon, scepter, bow, water jug, or string of beads. His four heads continually recite the ancient *Vedas*. He travels by turning into a goose or swan. Why these particular attributes?

- In almost every creation story around the world, dangerous beings—monsters, ogres, demons, malicious gods—hold a place. They belong to the scheme of things. Why? How might one deal with them internally? What amplifies their dangerousness? What diminishes it?

- In another variant of this tale, Brahma divides in two, separating his masculine side from the goddess Saraswati. He is so taken by her beauty that he grows a fifth head to keep an eye on her. When she turns into a cow to avoid him, he becomes a bull, and so on through the creation of all the animals. Offended by this incestuous longing, Shiva uses his third eye to burn off the fifth head and declares that humans shall not worship Brahma. Few do. Does anything in either story identify

Brahma as a Trickster figure?

- Indian lore places much emphasis on the archetype of Wandering. India itself wandered for millions of years before joining the rest of geographical Asia. How might the image of Wandering continue to inform Indian mythology and spirituality?

Separating Earth and Sky (Maori)

Hohepa "Joe" Harawira, Maori storyteller, conservationist, educator, and ritualist:

> My mountains are Putauaki and Mauao
> My rivers are Ohinemataroa and the Orini. My ocean is Tauranga
> My *waka* is Mataatua
> My chief is Toroa
> My sub tribes are Te Patuwai, Te Rangihouhiri and Nga Potiki
> My tribes are Ngāti Awa and Ngai te Rangi
> I am Hohepa Joseph Harawira.

> We come from a very oral tradition. As a small boy I'd go to the *marae* where the *kaumatua* [elders], who were all storytellers, would do their *whaikorero* [speech-making].

> I think that our stories actually have the ability to heal the world, as in different cultures, but somehow children and even a lot of adults have become disconnected from their past, from their stories. And I think that our stories have determined our behaviors as peoples—it doesn't matter what culture you're from.

> My mission in life as a storyteller is to share the importance of story and of telling of your stories.... In order for

our world to be healed, we need to reach back into the past, and reach back to our stories to reconnect and to find those connections through stories that aren't being told now.

"Aroha" means "love," but for we as Maori it actually means a lot more than that: it's about compassion for the environment and understanding the environment. We're all connected to the natural world.

For time out of mind, Earth Mother Papa and Sky Father Rangi embraced as their children stumbled about in the darkness between their ever-clasping parents.

Tired of the cold and the confinement, of making their way through lightless caves and narrow tunnels, the children of Earth and Sky met to discuss what to do about it.

Tu-matauenga, a warrior by temperament, bluntly spoke an idea: "Let's kill our parents."

"No," replied Rongo-ma-tane, his head bumping the sky. "We cannot kill Mother and Father. Instead, we will push them apart and live close to Mother Earth." This plan would make him the god of cultivated food.

Most of them approved, but Tawhiri-matea, god of the winds, snorted. "This isn't necessary, Tane. Are we not safe and protected here? Be careful what you contemplate."

Tawhiri's protest was not popular. "We need room!" cried the gods. "We need space! We need light!"

Very well. Bracing himself, watched by his siblings, Tane put his shoulder against the body of his father Rangi, took a deep breath, and tried to stand up fully.

At first nothing happened. Then Tangaroa, god of the sea and its creatures, joined Tane. As they pushed upward together in darkness, grunting with the effort, Haumia-tiketike of the fern root and wild berry added his shoulder, as did Tu-matauenga, future creator of human beings. But Rangi, still caught in blissful embrace, did not budge.

Finally came Tane-mahuta of the forest, insects, and birds.
Putting his back against Mother Earth, he placed his feet on Father
Sky, took a breath, shoved hard, and kept shoving.

Soon the gods heard a groan rise from trembling Earth as she felt
Sky being forced apart from her. With a mighty roar, Sky flew
upward and away. Light and wind rushed into the space where Rangi
and Papa had held each other for so long.

"Free!" rejoiced the young gods, dancing.

Tane, who loved his mother, decided to give her a new green girdle. On her surface he planted trees but, being new at creation,
placed them upside down, with tops in the soil and roots in the sky.
He considered them. Somehow, they looked funny. The birds and
insects thought so too and did not use them for dwellings. So Tane
upended a huge kauri tree and put its roots in the soil. Immediately
the birds and insects landed happily in the branches and the wind
blew music through the leaves. Ahhh, that was better. Before long,
Mother Earth wore a verdant new garment.

Looking upon Earth, her children saw for the first time how
beautiful their mother truly was. Tears fell down upon her from the
mourning eyes of silver-mist-cloaked Sky: the first rain.

Tane had noticed, though, that Father Sky seemed not only sad
but desolate. So Tane lifted a mighty red sun and a glowing silver
moon and hung them in the heavens. That helped, and at sunset Sky
wore the remnants of a great red robe Tane had given him long ago.

Even so, Rangi looked dark, forlorn, and barren for much of the
night.

"I will find you something else to wear," Tane told his unhappy
father.

Now, at the very edge of the world rose the mountain
Maunganui, and on this mountain lived Tane's brother Uru.
Reaching the Great Mountain, Tane greeted his brother and told him
of Sky's predicament.

"May I have," he asked Uru, "some of your children to light
Father Sky at night?"

Below the two romped Those Who Shine, the eye-shaped children of Uru. At this, they quit playing and rolled uphill toward their

father and uncle.

Uru set a large basket upon the ground. When the Shining Ones drew near, Tane and his brother bent, scooped up an armful of playful lights, and placed them within the basket. Hefting it, Tane thanked his brother and departed.

"Look what I have found you," Tane told Sky. Setting down the basket, he drew forth four Shining Lights and set them in the cardinal directions. Picking out five more Lights, he arranged these in a cross on the breast of Rangi. Others he fastened to his father's robe, and the rest he hung, basket and all, in the sky where we now see a soft white band at night.

Adorned with shining stars, Sky was pleased. So was Earth, who admired him from below.

* * * *

All this time Tawhiri-matea had kept his discontentment over the new state of affairs to himself. When he was good and angry, he opened his fist and unleashed the mighty storm winds as Tangaroa's grandsons Ika-tere, god of fish, and Tu-te-wehiwehi, god of reptiles, played contentedly in the sea.

Birds fled as trees bent and broke in the forests. Then huge holes opened in the wild seas.

"Run to the forests!" shouted Tu as the winds poured forth by Tawhiri gained even more force. Waves rolled by like wandering mountains. "No!" shouted Ika, "we must flee to the kingdom under the sea!" Naturally, oceanic Tangaroa sided with Ika, so when Tu ran ashore, the sea god never forgave him, which is why the sea and the land battle still.

Within the wrecked forest stood Tu-matauenga, straight as a mighty tree. Seeing him, Tawhiri sent a gigantic blast, but Tu was unbowed. Another blast rolled over broken trees and filled the sky with torn-up plants; but when it subsided, Tu stood in the midst of it, arms crossed. Tawhiri gave up and withdrew.

"Henceforth, those who come after me," announced Tu, gazing around, "will not be conquered by the wind. My children will wield power over the airs, the crops, and the seas over which their canoes will transport them. They will fish and plant and gather."

Having given birth thus far only to immortal children, the gods gathered with Tu and bent to work with the soil. From it gradually rose the form of a lovely, black-haired, bronze-skinned woman. When Tane breathed into her nose, she stirred, opened her eyes, and looked up in astonishment at the circle of gods waiting expectantly around her. She sneezed.

After ritually cleansing her, the gods called her Hine-ahu-one, Woman-made-of-Earth. With Tane at her side she gave birth to strong children, all girls. The warrior Tu then fashioned Tiki, First Man, to be with First Woman and people the world with descendants to beautify it even more.

For Reflection:

- Many myths from many lands tell of the separation of Earth and Sky. What does this archetypal act say about how the structures of consciousness unfold?

- Why do the gods not see the beauty of Earth until after her separation from Sky?

- Why does the agricultural god Tane play so large role in the creation of the world?

- Getting the Creation wrong (e.g., Tane planting trees upside down) is a common mythic motif. What might it suggest about the Creators? About the Creation?

- What does Tane's decking out of Rangi with stars correspond to in human life?

- Often in myth a god's apparent evil proves necessary. How does Tawhiri's stormy revolt ultimately serve humanity?

- Why does First Woman sneeze after becoming conscious?

- Comment: The discovery of Mitochondrial Eve, a black woman born in East Africa 200,000 years ago, coincided with genetic research demonstrating that humans come from the Rift Valley in Africa. The wise woman who comes first and acts as mother to us all appears frequently in stories all over the world.

- What do you think of the idea that humans are here to beautify the world?

Sky Woman's Descent (Haudenosaunee)

Kay Olan, Mohawk (Six Nations member) educator and storyteller:

Perhaps you've noticed that the Indigenous tradition of storytelling is not only alive, it is thriving. There is interest in learning and remembering the stories that have been passed down through the oral tradition. It is recognized that there is value in the storytelling tradition and that it isn't just for children.

Some types of stories are told just for entertainment. We need to have fun and laughter in our lives. Other stories are told so that we will always know about our history and our treaties. Some stories describe how the universe came to be and what our relationship is to every part of the natural world... Stories may remind us of how we should interact with one another in order to maintain peace and harmony. They help us transmit values and ideals from one generation to another. The child who misbehaves may be told a story in which the character exhibits the same behavior. In that way, the child learns about appropriateness and consequences, but without undue embarrassment or damage to the spirit. (Adults benefit from periodic reminders of those same lessons, as well.)

Why should we encourage storytelling? Because when we take the time to sit together and tell our stories, we

discover that we have more in common than we have differences. We find that we have similar hopes and dreams
for the future generations. We remember that we can
accomplish much more if we learn to communicate and
work together.

When the girl took the initiative and asked the tribal magician to
marry her, he was skeptical. Given her youth and her story—namely,
that her dead father had recommended the marriage—he decided to
test her.

Once they reached his home, he asked her to grind an immense
amount of corn, which she did. He then asked her to cook it into
mush. Although hot corn burned her bare skin, she did not complain,
not even when the large animals he kept as pets licked the corn off
her with their lacerating tongues.

Satisfied, he married her and gave her home the village gifts of
meat and white corn.

Now, just outside the magician's lodge grew a wondrous tree
whose blossoms glowed with light so bright it lit up the ground all
around. The woman took to sitting under it and conversing with the
spirits nearby. For hours she sat as the tree's gentle light bathed her.

Late one evening, the woman opened her legs to the tree. A
glowing blossom detached itself from a branch, floated downward,
and came to rest on her vagina. The light penetrated her. With a pulse
of joy, she realized she was pregnant.

As her belly grew, her husband's health deteriorated. When his
arts failed to enlighten him about the cause of his illness, he consulted other magicians and healers.

"We cannot cure you," they informed him after examining him,
"but we believe the cause to be your wife." The magician nodded.
He had never understood her great power, and he feared it. Besides,
had her father not been the first of anyone ever to die? The healers
suggested a plan.

One day, therefore, the magician uprooted the Tree of Light. The
hole it left revealed a portal to a world below the world. He called
his wife to see it.

"Amazing, isn't it?" he asked, peering down into the darkness. "Who would have thought an entire world could be below the Tree?"

As they gazed downward over the edge toward a mysterious blue glow, "You could float down there like a blossom," he suggested, "and see what things are like in that world." She hesitated. The glow emanated from far, far below through much intervening darkness.

"You are powerful," he said. "Jump!"

Taking a breath, she crouched, then dove into the dark hole.

She fell.

For ages she fell, and as she fell she forgot her name, her tribe, her past; her father, her husband, her childhood, the shamans she had beaten in contests; even the Tree she had loved and the world from which she descended. (High above her, the council put back the Tree, and the hole disappeared.)

As she fell, timeless and without memory, she sensed the spirits of other beings: Water Bird, Beaver, Turtle. They sensed her as well, and they wondered about her. Reaching a decision, seven Water Birds flapped toward her, put their wings and thoughts together, net-like, and slowed her fall. She slept, spiraling down.

As she slept, Beaver searched the waters below and summoned assistance. Imprinting Sky Woman then with the primal creative patterns his industrious kind used to build dams, he uttered a blessing on her and swam away.

*   *   *   *

She woke to the sound of gentle paddling: *swisssssssh, swisssssssh*. Something solid supported her back. Solid and of enormous size...

Turning over, she looked around and realized where she was: atop a great Turtle swimming a stately pace through the void. The shell edge formed the horizon. Gigantic rowing arms left a long wake behind. *Swisssssssh, swisssssssh*...

With that, Sky Woman's memories returned. She sat up, sorting through them.

When she had remembered herself and found her center, she raised her arms, opened them wide, and sang.

As she chanted, her voice cycling slowly outward like the spiral swum by Turtle, universal patterns of power came into being: as-yet intangible frames upon which an entire Creation would be hung. As she rose, still chanting, and commenced a birdlike hopping dance, the void filled with invisible interstices within the web of forces she wove.

It is ready, she thought. Turtle swam on, a slowly circling continent.

As Sky Woman chanted and walked in a circle, seeds she had carried from the other world fell from her hand. The soil covering the Turtle's back—animals had dived deep to scoop it up from below before depositing it there—accepted the seeds. From them sprouted fruit trees, corn plants, and other growing and nourishing things.

Crouching, Sky Woman drew a long stalk from between her legs. This she straightened and blew on to dry. She waited.

Stooping, she planted the stalk in the soil covering Turtle's huge back.

The first passage of her song made the stalk stand up straight. The second thickened it into a trunk. The third gave it branches reaching out and up. The fourth ignited round blossoms of light hanging downward like ripening fruit.

As the song ended, she beheld a Tree of Light grown from the seed planted within her long ago in a distant place.

She slept beneath the glowing branches, smiling.

When she awoke, she greeted a new daughter given forth from the shining Tree.

* * * *

Though well trained in her calm mother's sacred arts, the daughter grew into a restless dreamer filled with conflicting urges. A time came when she felt compelled to wander farther and farther from Sky Woman.

While on her wanderings, seeking she knew not what, the

daughter came to the Tree of Light, contemplated it for a moment, then lay down exactly where her mother had lain ages ago in another world. Falling asleep, she dreamed of a large, glowing, masculine presence standing beside the tree.

Her eyes opened. He was there.

"You are here!" she said.

"Yes," he acknowledged, "I am here." Some say he was the West Wind.

Beneath and around the Tree they danced and sang together, blending into each other. Then his presence faded, and she went back to her mother's home cured of the urge to wander.

Eventually two male presences grew within Sky Woman's daughter. After arguing with each other about the right way to emerge, one presence came forth from her and stood up near the Tree. But the other, anxious and determined, and closer to her heart, came into the world by tearing his way through her.

Sky Woman found the boys at the foot of the Tree bending in grief over their mother's dead body. "It was his fault," said Bud, the one who had killed his mother. "I tried to stop him"—pointing at Sapling—"but could not." He shed convincing false tears as his mourning older brother remained silent.

She picked up Bud and carried him home. Left alone, Sapling sang his songs of creation to console himself in the dark places.

To the bright Tree Sky Woman brought her daughter's body, which she placed below the Tree while she chanted a dirge. From the body poured the gentle dark of starry Night and the changing seasons that make order in the world.

Sky Woman's grandsons, though of very different temperaments, set about creating animals and plants, insects and brooks, valleys and hills, lightning and snakes, and creatures that walked about on two legs. After cooking these two-leggeds over a fire, the brothers blew into their mouths, and the creatures surged to life.

When Sky Woman finally died, her shining head rose and became the Moon.

For Reflection:

- What attributes identify Sky Woman as a personification of archetypal Wisdom?

- Comment: Often in myth, the human world dawns with the coming of Wisdom in feminine form (Woman-made-of-Earth, Sky Woman, Sophia, Barbelo, Pandora, Nasaba, Eve, Amaterasu, Au Co, Nuwa) or receives culture from her (Ala, White Buffalo Woman, Athena, Minerva, Scathach, Neith, Luonntar, Durga, Brigid).

- Many Wisdom Goddesses suffer a great fall into world, darkness, or matter, after which they bear a dual aspect: Lower and Higher Sophia, for instance, or Medusa and Athena. Kali and Durga. What might this tell us about the nature of Wisdom?

- Why is Wisdom so often related to a Trickster?

- What psychological purpose is served by being severely tested, as Sapling is by tricky Bud? Might this purpose still be served even if the tester bears ill intent?

- What would be a contemporary way of understanding Beaver's primal creative forms?

- Explore the symbolic significance of the Tree motif.

- On one level, this story deals with the well-known patriarchal fear of powerful women. On another, how does Sky Woman's exile lead to a new Creation?

- Seven water fowl catch Sky Woman. What meanings adhere to the number seven?

- Astrophysicists tell of vast frameworks and scaffolds of dark matter holding entire galactic systems in place throughout the cosmos. Remnants of the song sung by Sky Woman?

- Comment: The twin gods who create human beings appear in many times and lands. One god is usually a Trickster and the other a lover of order. Life then unfolds as a play of order alternating with chaos.

Sophia and Her Descendants (Gnostic)

Elaine Pagels, American professor of religion:

> In December 1945 an Arab peasant made an astonishing archeological discovery in Upper Egypt...Word of this codex soon reached Professor Gilles Quispel, distinguished historian of religion at Utrecht, in the Netherlands.... Quispel was startled, then incredulous, to read: "These are the secret words which the living Jesus spoke, and which the twin, Judas Thomas, wrote down." Could the text be an authentic record of Jesus' sayings?
>
> What Quispel held in his hand, the *Gospel of Thomas*, was only one of the fifty-two texts discovered at Nag Hammadi (the usual English transliteration of the town's name). Bound into the same volume with it is the *Gospel of Philip*, which attributes to Jesus acts and sayings quite different from those in the New Testament:
>
> > . . . the companion of the Savior is Mary Magdalene. But Christ loved her more than the disciples, and used to kiss her often on her mouth. The rest of the disciples were offended... They said to him, "Why do you love her more than all of us?" The Savior answered and said to them, "Why do I not love you as (I love) her?"
>
> Another text, mysteriously entitled *The Thunder, Perfect Mind*, offers an extraordinary poem spoken in the voice of a feminine divine power:
>
> > For I am the first and the last. I am the honored one and the scorned one.
> > I am the whore and the holy one.
> > I am the wife and the virgin....

> I am the barren one, and many are her sons....
> I am the silence that is incomprehensible....
> I am the utterance of my name.

> The Nag Hammadi texts, and others like them, which cir-
> culated at the beginning of the Christian era, were
> denounced as heresy by orthodox Christians in the mid-
> dle of the second century....Yet to know oneself, at the
> deepest level, is simultaneously to know God; this is the
> secret of gnosis.

Bythos, "Depth," was one of his many names. No one knew
them all because he was the Ultimate, the cosmic Fathermother
behind everything that would be.

Each of Depth's emanations bore one of his names:
Forethought, Sagacity, Creativity, Silence, Intent, Grace, Love, and
many others. Their assembly filled their continuum, the heavenly
Fullness, with glorious light. But it was static light, for these aeons
floating in their various realms and spheres knew much, but they did
not know who they were.

By the will of Bythos, an aeon in the eighth realm—the realm of
fixed stars—grew dissatisfied with her distance from the Light of
the Ultimate. Her name was Sophia ("Wisdom"). As her dissatisfac-
tion grew, a shadow formed beneath the great curtain that separates
the Fullness from the rest of the cosmos. Sophia looked down at it
and saw her own light reflected in the dark waters below her.

As she approached the light it grew dimmer, as did the light
above her. She lost herself in darkness.

From the shadow emerged a demonic form. Sophia was dismayed to see that her shape-shifting son looked like a serpent with
the head of a lion. Lightning flashed from his eyes. His name was
Yaldabaoth, which means "Child of Chaos," but he also came to be
called Saklas ("Fool") and Samael ("Blind God").

When Sophia thrust him away from herself, he set to work, for
he was an ambitious archon, a ruling power of the world-to-be. He
had seen her light reflected in the waters, and within that light, the

primal images of the Fullness. He would copy these, forming a material universe as a reflection of a reflection.

First, he masturbated into existence twelve other archons; these became the houses of the zodiac. Seven others took up station to oversee the planetary spheres; another watched over the underworld. These in turn "created" other authorities, they thought; but in truth nothing was created freshly because the archons were actually shadows cast by aeons shining in the Fullness like distant beacons.

"I am your God," Yaldabaoth told his follower-creations; "you shall have no other gods before me."

From high overhead, Sophia's voice came down: "You are wrong, Blind God!"

"Come," said Yaldabaoth to seven other archons, "let us descend to the waters below and create a human being, that he may give us light." He wanted no reminders of his origins.

First they created a man of soul: bone, sinew, flesh, marrow, blood, skin, and hair, all of soul. Then they added matter. Finally, at Sophia's cunning arrangement, her son blew into the new man the breath of light and spirit, emptying himself of what his mother had given him at birth.

The man rose up. His name was Adam, meaning that he grew from the dust of the earth. The light of intelligence shone from his eyes. Sophia's divine light glowed within him.

Immediately, the assembled archons feared him for the light he bore. Casting him down, they left him asleep, unconscious and immobile in the darkness of the lowest place in the newly formed world, and went their way.

They did not know, however, about Eve.

* * * *

Anticipating the archontic attempt at motherless creation, Sophia had let fall a drop of her light into the waters below. Of this was born Eve, or Zoe ("Life"), wisest of all created beings and known later as the Instructor of Gnosis for that reason.

Eve came upon Adam lying helpless on the ground and called

out to him, "Adam, live! Rise up off the ground! Wake up!"

"Who calls me?" asked Adam, "and brings me hope in this imprisonment?"

Blinking, he slowly got up and looked at her. "You will be called the Mother of the Living," he said in love and gratitude, "because you have given me the gift of life."

"I am the foreknowledge of the Light," replied Eve, citing her spiritual lineage; "I am the thought of the undefiled spirit. Stay awake, Adam, and always remember: beware of the deep sleep."

Seeing this, the archons, greatly disturbed, sought to rape her, but Eve sheltered herself within the Tree of Knowledge. That is one telling; others say that the archons raped her material body as her spirit withdrew to the heights of the Tree.

When Sophia saw all this, she hurled the archons from the heavens and exiled them to rulership over the world below. They rule it yet. The strongest of them, Yaldabaoth, though depleted, exiled Eve and Adam from Paradise. His archons, known also as the Authorities of Darkness here below, spread the lie that Eve came from Adam's rib, but those who knew better called her the Messenger of Light.

From her descended all humanity, in three groups: Hylics whose consciousness remained bound to material things, Psychics who loved abstractions and beliefs, and Gnostics who sought the presence of divine light.

For Sophia had left sparks of herself within the world she birthed: in matter, in souls, in everything. Seekers who find those sparks of light and return them to the Fullness after the body dies add Sophia's regathered luminosity to the Celestial Treasury.

And all of this came about so the Fullness and its aeons could be complete and lack nothing.

For Reflection:
- What does the word "depth" mean to you?

- Aeons and archons have been described in Jungian terms as archetypes and their power shadows. What does it mean that they don't know themselves?

- What might "the deep sleep" refer to? (Jung referred to the Gnostics as "the first depth psychologists.")

- In some tellings, Sophia is not an aeon but God's feminine pole: First Thought, also referred to as Barbelo ("Fourfold God") and, later, as Anima Mundi ("Soul of the World"). Like the Egyptian goddess Neith, Sophia brought into being a world and its luminous powers. Why would she leave some of her light in the world after its creation?

- When Sophia grew confused, sad, and lost, she passed through three states: materialistic blindness (*hylikoi*), mentalistic abstraction (*psychikoi*), and, as she found her bearings, aware once again of the divine light (*gnostikoi*). These states spread through the Creation into three kinds of consciousness. Where do we see them today?

- How do Yaldabaoth ("yal-DAH-buy-ought") and the Authorities of Darkness serve the long-range purposes of Sophia and Bythos?

- Who or what would a Gnostic identify as the archons of our day?

- Gnostics criticized orthodox believers for being *hylic* (literal-minded, reductive). Where do you see hylicism rampant now?

The Orishas Gain Their Powers (Yoruba)

Wole Soyinka, Nigerian Nobel Prize-winning playwright and novelist:

> The Yoruba is not, like European man, concerned with the purely conceptual aspects of time; they are too concretely realized in his own life, religion, sensitivity, to be mere tags for explaining the metaphysical order of his

world. If we may put the same thing in fleshed-out cognitions, life, present life, contains within it manifestations of the ancestral, the living, and the unborn. All are vitally within the intimations and affectiveness of life, beyond mere abstract conceptualization.

And yet the Yoruba does not for that reason fail to distinguish between himself and the deities, between himself and the ancestors, between the unborn and his reality, or discard his awareness of the essential gulf that lies between one area of existence and another. This gulf is what must be constantly diminished by the sacrifices, the rituals, the ceremonies of appeasement to those cosmic powers which lie guardian to the gulf. Spiritually, the primordial disquiet of the Yoruba psyche may be expressed as the existence in collective memory of a primal severance in transitional ether, whose first effective defiance is symbolized in the myth of the gods' descent to earth and the battle with immense chaotic growth which has sealed off reunion with man...

Orisha lived with his servant in a modest hut. The servant cooked his food and kept things in order, but he secretly plotted to kill Orisha.

When Orisha came home one day, the servant dropped a boulder onto the hut and crushed Orisha to bloody bits. Pieces of him were flung all over the world.

When Orunmila, the son of Father Olorun, arrived to see Orisha, he discovered what had happened. Thinking it over, he picked up a large calabash called Orishanla and began going around the world gathering up the pieces of Orisha.

Those he found he deposited at a shrine in Ife, but many others he did not find because there were so many. These became the Orishas, the deities that each form one living, shining facet of Olodumare, Creator of heaven and earth.

One of the Orishas, Oduduwa, got tired of seeing endless water on every side and went to Orunmila, who advised him to make a sacrifice and, after that, gather up five hundred chains, five chameleons, a hen, and some sand packed into a snail shell. This Oduduwa did.

Climbing down the chains, which were tied to the heavens, Oduduwa spread the sand across the waters. When it had hardened, he put the chameleons on it. They walked gingerly across it and did not fall through it. Neither did the hen. So Oduduwa climbed down from the chains and stood upon the ground at what would be known as Ile Ife, where he made his house.

Aje, the Orisha of prosperity, climbed down the chains to be with Oduduwa on the land. Because of her he attained great wealth.

Next came Ogun and Obatala and the rest of the Orishas, each paying homage to Oduduwa for being the first to make dry land so they could live on earth. With Ogun arrived a new vitality that gave all things the dimension of depth in energetic motion.

* * * *

He was Oko of the Orishas, and he wondered why he always had to go to his brother Orunmila first to accomplish what was necessary. In this he was no different from his sister and brother Orishas nor from the humans they lived with, humans created by Obatala.

"Why is this?" Oko asked Orunmila.

"Because I speak for our Great Father Olorun," replied Orunmila.

"I know, but why not endow us with our own powers and attributes?"

Orunmila said he would ponder it. He pondered it even more after Ogun, Eshu, Shango, Sonponno, Olu-Igbo, Osanyin, and the rest asked him the same question. He hardly ate or slept because of it.

As he walked around and thought, he encountered Agemo the chameleon, who asked him what lay so heavily upon his normally placid brow. Orunmila was known for his calmness.

"I want to do right," he explained, "by my sisters and brothers.

But I do not know how to divide up the powers and attributes fairly. Surely, someone will complain of being slighted." He sighed. Representing the distant Allfather was no easy responsibility.

Agemo spoke an idea. When he had finished, Orunmila thanked him for his cleverness.

Soon messengers visited the homes of the Orishas, telling them, "In five days Orunmila will rain the powers you seek down from the sky onto the fields of the earth. You must be there in the open to grasp whatever falls near you. Each of you will gain something."

The Orishas agreed this was fair and told the messenger to thank their thoughtful brother. The chameleon had advised him well.

After five days, the Orishas walked out into the fields, where the powers fell from the sky onto the ground.

Bold Shango grasped the thunderbolt and grew strong. Oko gained the power to grow crops, Osanyin to cure and foretell, Olu-Igbo to tend the woods and wild places, Sonponno of the wooden leg to inflict smallpox. Rambunctious Eshu seized not only the power of eloquence, but that of converting order and purpose into chaos.

For Reflection:
- Comment: Ile Ife ("EE-lay EE-fay") was founded in 500 BCE in what is now Osun State in southwestern Nigeria. The city is a spiritual center renowned for its works of bronze, iron, pottery, and intricate terracotta sculpture. The Yoruba religion of Ifa embraces oracles and dreams and does not rigidly separate spirit from nature.

- If we thought of the servant of Orisha as a god, what sort would he be?

- What makes Oduduwa ("odd-doo-DOO-wah") different from an autonomous creator god?

- Orunmila ("oh-run-MIL-ah") picking up pieces of Orisha paints in the archetypal motif of the scattered and gathered god (e.g., Isis reassembling Osiris). What are some significances of this motif?

- In his poem "Paradiso XXXI, 108," Jorge Luis Borges

muses, "Perhaps some feature of the Crucified Face lurks in every mirror; perhaps the Face died, was effaced, so that God might become everyone." How might such an incarnation apply to Orisha's dismemberment?

- How does achieving a firm standpoint help create consciousness?

- How are the Orishas like the Gnostic aeons? How are they different?

- The Yoruba precept of *ori ire* refers to when consciousness aligns with one's fate. How does this show up in the Orishas in terms of the gifts they obtain?

- Why is it necessary for the Orishas to claim their own powers? In which of our acquaintances, friends, loved ones do our unclaimed powers await?

A Change of Worlds (Navajo)

Laura Tohe, Navajo poet, Professor of English at Arizona State University and speaker for the Arizona Humanities Council:

> Storytelling is part of the oral tradition of indigenous peoples. Stories impart values, language, memories, ethics and philosophy, passing them to the next generation. A lot of people think of storytelling as just entertainment for kids, but for the Diné [Navajo] it helps maintain tradition and language.
>
> I grew up surrounded by stories and gossip. Some of the storytelling was unintentional...My mother would tell us stories about people she knew and stories that her grandparents told her about Navajo beliefs and creation.
>
> By the 1860s, the Diné had firmly placed their roots in the bottomlands, planted their cornfields and peach

orchards, and raised their flocks of sheep. The canyon [Canyon de Chelly] had accepted the People. In turn, the Diné had found agreement with the canyon, where they could build their homes, raise their families and live a harmonious life based on *hózhó* [beautiful order].

It had been a long climb upward. In the First World, the People had known only darkness and confinement; in the Second, warfare and hunger. They had nearly died.

In the Third, a realm marked off by free-flowing streams and four sacred mountains, the People and their animal and insect companions enjoyed plenty of room. Everyone understood everyone. Everyone got enough to eat...at first.

As time went on, though, and the People multiplied and multiplied, food grew scarce, land diminished, and arguments escalated. Nobody knew how to cultivate and plant. Hunger and fighting broke out and began to spread.

Noting this, the Four Judges who watched over the Third World sent word around that it was time for the tribes to gather. Once they had, discussion began about what to do. How to solve the problem of crowding? Of getting enough to eat?

Eventually, after much speaking, listening, and negotiation, a consensus formed: It was time to leave the Third World they had outgrown.

In those days everyone could fly. Swarms and clouds and hordes of beings darted skyward searching for the opening to the Fourth World. They searched and searched, up and down and around, wings buzzing everywhere, but nowhere could they find the passage.

Just as they thought about giving up, a mighty voice boomed from the East:

"Come here!"

From the West: "Come here!" And the same from the North and the South: "Come here!"

In each place, at sky's edge, a gigantic masked face had appeared.

One group moved toward the face in the East. This group became the Earth Surface People: the Navajo. From behind this mask First Woman beckoned them into the Fourth World.

The Bird People flew toward the face in the South, where First Girl led them into the Fourth World. Even now, birds fly south in winter.

The Animal People ambled in herds toward the face in the West, where First Man guided them into the Fourth World. Their passage was mountainous, and they live up high even now.

The Insect People swarmed toward the face in the North, where First Boy summoned them into the Fourth World. It was cold there, which is why insects bore and burrow in winter even now.

*　*　*　*

Noticing how careworn and tattered her people looked, First Woman taught them to bathe. Then she taught them how to tie back their hair, how to weave clothing for themselves, and how to build six-sided hogans so the People could stay warm and protected. But they were still hungry.

Other people lived in the Fourth World. Among them were the Pueblos, skilled at planting seed to grow corn near the cliffs where they lived. "Work for the Pueblos," advised First Woman, "and they will give you seed for growing your own food." She left.

Doubts arose among the clans. Why had First Woman led them here? Were they better off in the Fourth World? Wasn't this the same hunger problem they had faced before?

In the distance, Coyote had grown aware of their dissent. Taking advantage of it, he sauntered among them and said, "Why work for your food when the Pueblos have plenty to eat? Go harvest it at night, while the planters sleep, and you'll have all you could want."

"We don't steal," they told him.

"Who said anything about stealing?" he replied smoothly. "Just help yourselves to the bottom ear of corn on every stalk. There are plenty of ears; the Pueblos will never notice. Or don't you want to be able to plant your own crops some day?"

This seemed smart, so four waves of volunteers carrying sacks crept into the Pueblo fields and began picking and bagging ears of corn, quietly. Coyote grinned and walked off into the night, chuckling at their folly.

When the first volunteers returned to camp, they poured out their stolen corn ears, only to find them too wet to use from growing near the ground.

The second volunteers poured out stolen ears gnawed by mice.

The third volunteers brought corn ears eaten by worms.

The fourth volunteers brought corn ears covered with mold.

The people harbored unkind thoughts about Coyote, off laughing in the dark somewhere, and decided to invite First Woman back to counsel them. Having stolen from the Pueblos, the people could not work for them. What to do now?

"Let four young women and their brothers proceed in the four directions," advised First Woman. "In exchange for gifts the women will bring back seed corn, and their brothers will bring back the ceremonies for planting." She vanished.

"That sounds like a lot of trouble," came a voice from the edge of the circle. Looking up, the People saw Coyote smiling charmingly at them. But he had mistimed his reappearance, and they chased him away. Now they would heed First Woman's advice.

They sent forth the women and their brothers, wishing them luck, and posted lookouts. Men turned up the soil to prepare it for the seed corn. Then everyone waited.

In four months, a woman and her brother appeared in the east. She carried a basket of white corn. Her brother carried the Seed-Blessing Ceremony.

Then the second woman and her brother appeared in the south. She carried a basket of blue corn. Her brother carried the Corn-Blessing Ceremony.

The third woman and her brother appeared in the west. She carried a basket of yellow corn. Her brother carried the Growing Ceremony.

The fourth woman and her brother appeared in the north. She carried a basket of many-hued corn. Her brother carried the Rites of

Harvest Ceremony.

"Be welcome!" the People greeted them.

"Along with seed and ceremony," the travelers announced, "we have brought you herbs, pumpkins, squash, beans, tobacco, medicine bundles, rain rattles, feathered headdresses, dance robes, and other ceremonial gear." The People rejoiced.

From that time on, women stored seed in the winter and planted it in the spring once the men made ready the fertile fields. The four women and their brothers were remembered with praise and honor, as was First Woman. Coyote they treated cautiously, as a goad to strengthen that which was weak. Everything had a use.

The People remembered all this even after they outgrew the Fourth World and emerged in time into the Fifth.

For Reflection:

- What might be signified by the recurrence of the number four?

- What does it mean to outgrow a world? What if this were done psychologically instead of literally?

- Who or what serves as the Four Judges today?

- Why can't everyone emerge into the Fourth World through the same passage?

- In some versions of this story Spider Woman helps the People weave the baskets they use for stealing corn. Why would she do this?

- Archetypally, First Woman and Coyote could be thought of as Navajo versions of Sophia and Yaldabaoth: Wisdom and Trickster. What are their roles in this tale?

- Why must the People travel to get what they need? What did they learn from this?

- Comment: The People in this tale have no identified leaders, but they get things done even so. The leadership model is collaborative instead of authoritarian.

They only go wrong when they look up to Coyote as a leader.

- The sociopath holding a position of political, religious, or financial power might be thought of as an extreme, unconscious Coyote. What does how consciously and carefully a culture manages such Coyote manifestations tell us about that culture?

- Traditional Navajo think of themselves as children of the earth goddess Changing Woman. She teaches how to adapt without losing one's essence. How does the myth illustrate this adaptability?

- Comment: That First Woman has a second plan for feeding the People after Coyote misleads them demonstrates that not all is lost with the first failure. Young Percival missed an opportunity to claim the Holy Grail, but the second time, after growing more mature, he stepped up and accomplished the deed after all. Difficulties can be initiatory.

Au Co and Dragon Prince (Vietnamese)

Ngoc Binh Nguyen, Vietnamese essayist:

Ask any Vietnamese about the origin of his people, and most likely he will tell you that they were born of a dragon and a fairy ("*con rong chau tien*"). Certainly this is an unscientific explanation, and one that can hardly be sustained or demonstrated historically, yet the power of that myth is such that no Vietnamese, no matter how much scientific training he has received, would ever deny believing in it at least to a certain extent.

Many traditional Vietnamese myths were originally conceived as instruments of protest, as weapons in the struggle against foreign invaders and foreign ideologies, especially the Chinese Confucian ideology. This form of protest is found again and again in later centuries in Vietnamese history...even in the present day with the spontaneous creation of a vast folk literature of protest.

It is clear, even from the very incomplete record of ancient Vietnamese myths, that at one time the ancestors of the present-day Vietnamese asked some very searching questions regarding the nature of the universe and the human condition, both in its universal dimensions and in the dimensions particular to Vietnam. That some of the answers, in the form of myths, were quite successful is clearly evident in some of the tales we have retold.

From the vantage of the thirty-sixth realm of heaven, the newly formed world below looked inviting. The goddesses watched its turnings: blue, white, green, and brown, lit by day by the great golden crow whose wings had shot the stars into the once-dark heavens.

"Let's go see it!" cried Au Co, the youngest.

Turning into dazzling white Lac birds, the goddesses flew down, passing over mountain ranges, vast valleys, verdant forests, and azure seas that captured their bright reflections as they streaked toward a hill and landed. Folding their wings, they walked down to a meadow filled with wildflowers. They danced.

Fascinated by all the fresh-shining newness, Au Co's sister goddesses saw her lift a handful of soil and did likewise, reveling in its fragrance and dark squishiness. Au Co bent to taste some. "Don't!"—but it was too late. The celestial goddess had ingested a lump of earth.

As they considered what to do, the light dimmed as evening came on. It was time to return to heaven. With a rustling snap, they turned back into birds and thrust themselves into the air, flapping to gain altitude. Au Co tried to soar with them, but what was this mysterious heaviness that kept her from flying as high as they?

"Come back!" she called, but they streaked away skyward. She could not follow now that she had tasted of earth.

She landed again, disheartened, and began to weep. And weep. The weeping extended into a trickle, then a stream, then a river.

The river poured into the sea, where living things with shells, fins, claws, and bony joints reported the astonishing development to Dragon Prince, the son of Sea Dragon Emperor. Shapeshifting into fish form, he swam upstream to investigate.

At one point he leaped from the waters for a look around. What he saw amazed him. In the last light of the golden sun crow he saw blue skies, green trees, tall mountains, and wide seas. A new world had been born. How? Who had made it? Reaching a riverbank, he jumped out onto land and, growing arms and legs, turned into a man.

As he walked his wonder increased. The colorful lichens, waving mosses, wildflowers visited by butterflies dancing on the breeze: all this new life and more came from the fresh water whose source he now traced. He walked up a mountain, then stopped abruptly at what he saw.

A weeping woman leaned against a stone. Her long black hair mingled with the waters running downhill from her feet into the sea. Birds and butterflies and other new creations flapped, circled, and soared skyward along the entire meandering path of the river.

"Who are you?" he sang to her, startling her. "Why are you weeping?"

"I am Au Co. I flew down from above with my sisters," she sang in response, "but after tasting of the earth I cannot fly back again." She sniffed. "Who are you? Where do you come from?"

"I come from the sea, where my father rules in his underwater palace. I am Nagaraja, but I am usually called Dragon Prince."

The two sat down together and began to share stories. They talked through the night.

In the morning, the golden crow rose again and sent her warmth across the clear face of the land. The beauty of it blended with new-found companionship to raise Au Co's spirits. How did this stranger, whose past was so unlike hers, whose world must be so different from hers, understand her with such completeness? How did so much of what he told her about his own life stir such deeply powerful resonating responses in her?

As they walked down the mountain hand in hand they noticed the vegetation drying up. "It needs the water of your tears," Dragon Prince noted. "Wait here a moment and I will show you something new."

Bending to the river, he sipped some of it, then dived into the sea. After a time, dark clouds built on the horizon. As they loomed overhead, lit from below by a flash of lightning, fresh water fell in drops on Au Co, on the bushes and trees, on everything. The land drank it in: the first rain.

From the clouds Dragon Prince looked down at Au Co and noticed for the first time how the streams branching from the river formed the shape of her legs. Clefts and ridges radiated down and away from where she sat like the waves of her hair. He flew back to earth and gave her a lotus blossom.

*　*　*　*

For seven thousand years—a handful of days to an immortal span of life—Au Co and Dragon King raised and taught generations of humans as they moved out over the face of the world. Many were as soulful as goddesses and as courageous as dragons; some wore a dragon tattoo to scare off sea monsters and a Lac emblem to symbolize their growing clan. Au Co gave them childcare, song, dance, and the art of weaving, and Dragon King language and fire, shelter and rice, salt, and nets for fishing. And time cycled on.

On a day when the fishers brought in a huge portion, Dragon Prince felt his right arm tingle as though pulled on by an unseen hand.

He sighed deeply. His father was calling him home beneath the sea.

"I am about to become the new Sea Emperor," he explained sadly to Au Co.

"May I go with you?"

"I wish with all my heart that you could, but earth and sea, though their mingling be beautiful, must remain in their separate realms."

He stood looking down into the sea, then met her eyes again. "I will return after the ceremony. Although we dwell apart, we can always come together again."

He kissed her, gazed at her for a long moment, and dove in.

Although earth and sea dwell apart to this day, they meet here and there, now and then, to remember and sustain what they created. You can sense their love and longing when it rains, when the shore greets the tide, when rocks rejoin the sea, and when the rivers run.

For Reflection:

- What parallels can you find between this tale and others in which the archetypal Wisdom Goddess involves herself in the creation of the world?

- Why do so many creation stories involve sacrifice and loss?

- Some of us act as though we can fly away on intuitions and insights without ever tasting the earth. It's as though we have one foot in the Otherworld and go around only partially born here. What were some of your earth-tasting moments, those that brought you down to the ground?

- Why do the contours of the land parallel the features of Au Co?

- What would Au Co and Dragon Prince (now King) have to say about how we've looked after the world they gave us?

- Alchemists referred to the mingling of elements as the *Coniunctio* (Conjunction) and Sacred Marriage of elements. *Coniunctio* alternates with *Separatio*, their separation. Joining and separating: this pulsation if carried forward long enough births the Philosopoher's Stone of health and wholeness, but only if *coniunctio* and *separatio* occurr at the right moments, not too soon and not too late. Do milestone events in life, in history, in the natural world seem to follow this alchemical blueprint?

- When you watch rain moisten the earth or sea waves wash the shore, how does it change your perception to think of them as Dragon King and Au Co saying hello to each other?

Nightfall (Indigenous Amazonian)

Eliane Potiguara, director of the International Indigenous Treaty Council, president and founder of the Network of Indigenous Communication in Brazil, Professor of Indigenous Linguistics, indigenous ceremonialist, poet, and writer:

> We indigenous people, we consider nature as our siblings, sister stone, sister water, brother sky, brother wind, all are our siblings. For us, the indigenous people, all the livings beings are members of our family. The river is a member, God is a member, he is our father, the plants are our members, the birds are our cousins. So if the world starts to understand these family relations, we all will understand that we are all the same since we all are living beings and we all have the ability to think.
>
> My mother, my aunt, and my grandmother were strong women and fought for their beliefs. They passed on to me their spiritual and cultural knowledge, and now that's being invested in the indigenous people's fight.
>
> In the process of oppression of the indigenous people, women suffered the most. But the spirituality of my people is deep and it will not disappear easily.

The word of the indigenous woman is sacred like earth.
And if the word of the woman is sacred then it must be
heard.

The day was unrelenting.

At one time Sun lived on earth with everybody else, even before
many birds, plants, and bugs lived here. When a shaman had cut the
hair of a man so old that his lost teeth numbered the generations he
had seen pass by, Sun had directed the shaman to blow the hair into
the air. With each breath Sun had transformed the strands of hair into
every flapping, soaring, walking, and nesting bird in existence: birds
loud and quiet, bright and dark, plainly colored and iridescent like
the rainbow. Then the old man's bones formed the guava tree, his
fingers the leaves of the tobacco plant, his fingernails cashew nuts,
his toenails corn kernels, his ears sweet potatoes, and his eyelashes
and eyebrows the termites that feed things back into the soil for
rebirth.

The creative power of Sun had accomplished all this and more.
Everything depended upon his light and heat. However, rest from
these he could not provide.

The daughter of the Great Water Serpent who lived deep within
the Madeira River felt concerned about her husband. How hard he
and the other men worked planting and harvesting corn, manioc,
sweet potatoes! But no rest for any of them because, sweating,
weary, and ill, they could find no night to shade them into slumber.

As she considered the too-bright ceremonial headdresses, too-
bright feathers, too-bright leaves, and too-bright surfaces of streams,
the daughter of Serpent remembered a realm of darkness, coolness,
and quiet her father had shown her at the bottom of the river where
he lived.

"You must send three good servants," she told her husband when
he came home hot and exhausted from laboring in the fields, "to go
and ask my father to give us Night, the time of dark and rest."

"Have you been out in the sun too much?" her husband asked.
"Do you need to rest? There is no 'Night,' only the endless day."

"I saw it when I was a child," she replied. "Send the men, and tell them to tell my father that my happiness depends on his granting our wish."

"Very well," said her husband. For she was a woman of arcane power, and her wishes were not to be passed over lightly.

Three servants paddled their canoes to the end of the river where the Serpent lived. Past crocodiles they rowed, past fallen trees, below the glaring arc of the sun they journeyed until they found the Serpent asleep in his hammock of palm fronds. He was difficult to awaken because he had just feasted on a tapir and drunk from a jug of manioc rum.

At length, he rolled over, mumbled, belched, opened his eyes, and sat up. The servants bowed.

"What do you want?" he asked them. They explained.

"Wait here," he said. He slid into the river.

After an hour or so, the servants got nervous and concerned, but here came the Great Serpent with what looked like a large coconut but was actually the fruit of the *tucumá* tree. But this *tucumã do pará* bore a hole in the top sealed with resin.

"Do not open this," said the Serpent as he gave them the nut. "Only my daughter knows what to do with it. If anyone else unseals it, Night will escape and be abroad in the world."

The servants thanked him, boarded their canoes, and paddled off as he wound himself back into his comfortable hammock.

As they paddled, one of the servants heard odd noises from inside the nut: *shay-shay-shay* and *tem-tem-tem* sounds mixed with strangely unfamiliar songs of frogs and crickets. "Listen!" he told the other two as they paused to hear the commotion from within the nut.

"Let's open it," one of them suggested. After a short debate punctuated by croaks and chirps from within the *tucumã do pará*, they pulled up to a shore, disembarked, and built a fire. They held the nut toward it so the resin would melt.

Dark! That was their first impression as the entire world went black around them outside the light of the fire. In a moment, *whooshing* sounds announced the passage of stars out of the opening and into the sky, where they arranged themselves into glittering constellations. From their light the servants saw the dim shapes of night creatures flying out of the nut and into the air. Dew settled on the foliage around them.

From far off, the daughter of Serpent heard owls, snipes, and frogs hooting, chirping, and croaking as bats flitted through the trees. Outside their hut, a canoe metamorphosed into a duck, its oars into fish, its cordage an anaconda. Other objects turned into night animals as well; in great fright the husband watched, eyes popping out, as a nearby basket flowed into the shape of a growling jaguar.

She sighed. "My father," she told her husband, who lay half-risen next to her in a hammock, "has given Night to the servants, but they let it escape into the world."

"How can we live without day?" he demanded of her in fear and despair. He had forgotten his earlier disbelief in any possibility of Night.

"Don't fear," she said, pulling a hair from her head. "With this I will separate Night from Day." She rose. "Shut your eyes and wait." Gradually, snores rose and fell from his hammock. It was the first real rest he had ever gotten.

Just then the guilty servants arrived. Before they could make excuses, she turned them into monkeys that jumped chattering away into the trees.

Through the door she opened flowed Night, wrapping her in billowing blackness. She breathed in fragrant cool air, listened to the sounds of crickets, frogs, owls, bats, and jaguars fanning out through the dark, and lay back again, to sleep soundly.

Upon awakening, refreshed, she threaded the garments of Night through her strand of hair and pulled the thread tight. Leaving one patch of darkness aside, she stuffed the rest of the black bundle back into the nut and resealed the opening.

"Wake up, my husband," she said. "The sun rises, the night beings sleep, the stars withdraw, and the day birds sing." He stirred and turned over.

"From now on," she told him, "Night will alternate with Day. We will work and journey....and love and rest."

For Reflection:

- Purusha (Hindu) the giant Ymir (Norse), and watery Tiamat (Babylonian) transforming their flesh into the world's are three of many examples of mythic beings undergoing all-creating sacrifice. What does this transformation imply about how we story the relationship between deity and matter?

- What point does the myth make about the balance of day and night? What might it tell us about light pollution?

- In what way does the disobedient servants' transformation into monkeys seem fitting?

- How does the Serpent's daughter compare to Gnostic Eve, who awakened Adam?

- What associations does the serpent carry in mythology? What might it refer to in a dream?

- Why does the serpent live in a long and windy river?

- If it's not coincidence that "Madeira" means "mercy," how could Serpent's river have come to possess this Spanish name? Is something about a place smarter than its colonizers?

Chapter Four - Family Ties

Family: the matrix arranged by the Fates for our entrance into life. Human cultures span the extremes of engagement with this matrix, from pretending one's individuality places us beyond all family ties to being unable to see oneself as different from other family members.

Distant or close, fragmented or whole, our families wear the signature of our future—not just past!—connection to that which is other than ourselves. Ahead of us wait new loves, friends, opponents, colleagues, strangers, allies, and perhaps new additions to the family. Behind us, siblings, parents, extended family, generations of family, and ancestors watch over whatever we do in this life.

Hestia, Heart of the Home (Greek)

Eleni Bastea, Greek art historian, architectural historian, writer, and director of the International Studies Institute:

> In an urban history seminar in St. Louis, I ask my students to what city or place they feel most connected. Proud of their adaptability, most of them assure me that they could live almost anywhere, while those from small towns insist that they certainly do not want to go back home. "Where is it that you want to be when you die?" I prod them further, trying to get past their airs of detachment and noncommitment.

> I left Thessaloniki when I was seventeen, yet I find myself going back in spirit whenever I embark on a new project and need an infusion of courage and inspiration—whenever I am searching for a bit of my old self. When I actually visit the city, I realize that I do not know the new generation of its inhabitants—slim girls in black tight pants, cool Eurokids, and recent immigrants of all ages. I secretly miss the close-knit provincialism of the 1960s and 1970s and hold on to the city I remember from my childhood with the stubborn, fixed gaze that former residents share with the elderly. Nevertheless, I claim Thessaloniki as "my town."

Hestia was first to be born of Rhea and Cronus, first to be swallowed by her father, and last to be disgorged by him, rescued by a ploy of her mother and grandmother guiding the firm hand of her brother Zeus.

She was born into an argumentative family. When the twelve Olympians got together they bickered, for each stood for a fixed point of view. Zeus and Hera ruled, Aphrodite seduced, Hephaestus hammered, Poseidon stirred wave and quake, Hermes flitted between Underworld and Upperworld, Apollo made music, prophecy, and healing, Demeter grew grain, Artemis hunted and tended animals, Dionysus celebrated, Athena wove and taught, and Ares warred, often impulsively. Each insisted on their own view of reality, on what was primary: Authority, Marriage, Beauty, Craft, Mutability, Message, Order, Abundance, Wildness, Ecstasy, Wisdom, War. But not in the presence of quiet Hestia. Something about her veiled reserve chastened them.

Little wonder, then, that a dispute about which of them should sit in heaven as part of the Twelve, Dionysus or Hestia, ended with her absenting herself in favor of the drama god. He would fit in much better on bright Olympus than she. Not even enticing invitations by Poseidon or Apollo would budge her. Besides, she had other business on earth.

That business involved dwelling in the center of human life: of the town or temple, where a flame burned in her honor; of the home, at its hearth; and of the heart, the hearth of the human frame. At the still hub of all living things resided the introverted goddess whose presence few now noticed, although in Rome, as Vesta, she attracted crowds of Vestal Virgins known to later times as Roman Catholic nuns. In antiquity, they guarded the sacred fire at the heart of town and officiated the rituals for lighting and maintaining it.

Hestia was quiet but her influence pervasive. Where families gathered for meals or prayer, where supplicants knelt at altars, where exiles sought sanctuary, where meetings opened and closed, Hestia stood in the midst.

When acknowledged, as when a meal's first portion was offered to her, or when a home or temple was built to honor her place, Hestia blessed the participants. When unrecognized, she added no central warmth to the gathering, and its soul departed, empty. To her was offered a portion of every sacrifice to the gods lest its holy action be in vain.

Having been propositioned by gods oceanic and oracular, Hestia had touched the head of Zeus and sworn herself to eternal virginity. At a feast of Rhea, the goddess of domesticity decided to lay down in the grass for a nap; the noise made by whooping satyri and singing nymphae had tired her. Engorged by celebration, Priapus spotted a prone fair form and, approaching the sleeping goddess, lay down next to her. Suddenly, a donkey left near a creek by drunken Silenus brayed so loudly that Hestia woke up, frightened. Seeing her so, a group of outraged partygoers made for Priapus, but he darted through their grasping hands and escaped.

There is a purity, a beingness, a homecoming dwelling within the precincts of Hestia. Her gentle presence holds every silence between caring family members, every quiet space within each home, every still moment in the contemplative heart. For Hestia does not act. She is.

For Reflection:

- We usually think of family dynamics—birth order, for example—as working their way into mythology. But what if it's the other way around? What if they are archetypally patterned?

- Family Systems Theory observes that families hold themselves together by unconsciously assigning and distributing roles like Hero, Lost Child or Exile, Comedian, Peacemaker, Rebel, Scapegoat, Martyr, Beauty Queen or King, Dramatist, Second Parent, and Computer. What was your family role? Did it ever trap you? What other family roles did it collide with? ("Sibling rivalry" often reflects role collision.)

- How does it feel to be an introvert in an extraverted family or culture? What adaptations are necessary in such settings?

- What does it mean mythologically to be virginal? How might this quality make a sanctuary safe?

- Why would Priapus show up when Hestia sleeps?

- Why does a portion of every sacrifice go to Hestia?

- What unacknowledged god stood in the middle of your family of origin?

- Archetypally, Hestia's home-and-hearth sisters include Agnayi, Aspelenie, Ayaba, Chantico, Esta, Fuchi, Hinukan, Mara, Panike, Rhea Saule, Silvia, Tabiti, Vesta. What is the purpose of this goddess force taking on different appearances?

- Western philosophy has swung between viewing our sense of reality as *esse in intellectu* (being-in-mind) and *esse in re* (being-in-things: in the outer). Steering between these, Jung wrote that psyhic life is based upon *esse in anima* (being-in-soul): the sense of reality is rooted in relation to image. However, Socrates said: *esse in Hestia.* Hestia as the essence of things. What do you think?

- Ginette Paris writes that in many homes, Hestia has been replaced by the television or computer monitor, just as fast food counters have invaded Hestia's spot at meal times. Where no flame burns in her honor, fire consumes the hearth, the home, the street corner, even the overheating planet. How can her gentle flame be honored?

Maui Finds His Parents (Hawaiian)

Leilani Violet Hughes, Hawaiian storyteller, *kapuna*, activist, and educator:

> My mother told me this story (I must have been about ten years old): about being taken with her mother—she didn't tell me where, but this would've been on Maui—and she said that when she was a little girl, her mother took her, and told her before they left, and gave her all the instructions: you have to sit quietly, you can't move, if you want to sleep just lie down and put your head on my lap or up against me, but you're not to move, you're not to ask for water, for anything to eat, to leave...

And then they went in, and she said they had a hole dug in this area, and a young banana plant; and all of them started to pray. And then the tree was put into the hole to be planted, and after it was put in there, the prayer continued, and they did it in unison, and then individually sometimes, but it was a continuous prayer.

...And she said she fell asleep, and awakened, and they were still praying, and she noticed that that little banana plant had started to grow. And she watched for a while, fell asleep—and it had grown a little taller...And by midday, she said you could see the bananas were ready to eat.

When Tama heard the unexpected wail of a baby, he went outside his cliffside house near sky's edge to look around on the shore. The wail grew louder as he walked toward a pile of seaweed.

Stooping, he pulled back the fronds. The wail came from a baby wrapped in what seemed to be a woman's hair. His mother's, perhaps? Why would she abandon him like this?

The wail subsided as the baby's cold skin grew warm against Tama's. Only one thing to do. Tama took him home, fed him, and made a hammock for him near the fire.

As wise Tama raised him, teaching him to interpret how birds called, fish swam, and animals walked and climbed, Maui grew rapidly into an extraordinarily strong and outgoing young man. A young man with abundant curiosity.

"Where did I come from?" Maui asked Tama one day. "Who are my parents?"

Tama knew many things, past, present, and future, and these answers he knew as well.

"It's time for me to meet my kin," Maui decided.

Tama nodded sadly. "Yes, it is time. Remember the old man who raised you. And remember that you will enjoy many adventures, see many things, and assist many people until your very last adventure, the one we all finally face. But never mind that now."

He held Maui tightly.

"Now go, my boy. The entire world awaits."

* * * *

"Stand up," she said, "when I call your name. Maui-taha."

He was the eldest. He stood, there beneath the rafters.

"Maui-roto. Maui-pae. Maui-waho." Four boys stood at attention. A soft fire burning behind them spilled shadows around the room.

"Let's dance!" she said, clapping.

From those shadows stood forth a fifth boy.

"I am Maui too," he announced. Startled, everyone turned to stare at him.

"You can't possibly be," said the woman, studying him. *And yet he seems familiar*, she thought. "Where do you come from?"

After all these years of anticipation, he could finally tell the tale to his mother and brothers.

"From the sea," he said, "where waves carried me. The birds and fish were my first family. I was cast upon the waters in a bundle of seaweed tied with my mother's hair." He handed her some. "A wise old magician found me on the shore and raised me, teaching me many things. He also told me where to find you. So I passed over dunes and around trees and across streams to meet you."

After a long silence, "And who is your mother?" she asked him.

"You are, Taranga."

She hugged him.

"Yes," she said, "I am your mother. And these"—waving toward them—"are your brothers. You will be called Maui-tikitiki-a-Taranga" (Maui of the topknot of Taranga). "Welcome home, little Maui!"

It was soon apparent that "little" Maui was a bundle of tricky talents. Whatever his brothers did—running, throwing, swimming, diving, holding the breath—Maui did faster, higher, farther, deeper, or longer. When the creatures of sea and valley and forest spoke, only

Maui knew what they said. After he teased his brothers for being too dull or too slow they sought to beat him, but, summoning the magic Tama had taught him, he always changed into a bird and flapped away, cawing his laughter down at them.

His curious eye noticed his mother's habit of disappearing in the morning and reappearing in the evening. He asked his brothers about this, but they did not know why and did not care. He decided to investigate.

Once he heard his mother sleeping, he filled in the cracks in doors and windows so no light could come in. Then he removed her lovely girdle and apron and hid them under his mat.

In the morning she woke, but because the cracks were filled in, she thought it was still night and went back to sleep. When she woke again she heard birds singing. She opened the window. Daylight! Her girdle and apron were missing, so she drew on a cloak and hurried out the door—with Maui invisible behind her. The cloak made her easy to follow.

At length Taranga ran up to a tuft of grass and pulled on it. Into the opening this revealed she dropped, pulling the grass cover back in place to conceal the hole.

So that was it. Maui returned home, thoughtful, putting the pieces together.

"Our mother visits the Underworld," he told his brothers. "Our father must live down there. Let's go find out."

"Our father," said one brother, "is Rangi in the sky, and our mother Papa, the earth. Who cares where she goes or whom she sees?"

"I do," said Maui.

Taking out the girdle and plucking some feathers from the apron, he put them on, then transformed himself into a pigeon. His brothers watched him fly away.

Maui landed near the tuft of grass. He pulled it up with his beak and darted into the hole.

Down and around he flew through many twisting passages, some wide, some narrow, until he reached the land without sun. Winging through the motionless air, he found a tree and sat on a branch to wait.

He didn't have to wait long. Soon his mother and a man whose features reminded him of his own came along and sat under the tree where Maui perched.

Maui dropped a berry on his father's head.

"A bird dropped it," his mother remarked.

"No," said his father, "it was ripe."

A shower of berries descended on them both.

As they stood, other denizens of the Underworld came up to stare at the marvelously colored pigeon. They picked up stones and threw them at Maui, who came down only at the touch of his father's stone.

The young, black-haired, girdled, brown-skinned man stared up at his father.

"This," said his mother hugging him, "is my youngest, Maui of the sea. Some day he will do great things in the world. Bless him, for he is your son."

Make-tu-tara, shade of the Underworld, blessed his young son with spells that gave him strength and speed and luck. Try as he would, though, he could not remember the spell to guard Maui against death.

* * * *

As Maui lived with his parents, traveling back and forth from Upperworld to Underworld, he noticed food being cooked and carried off for somebody no one ever mentioned. Naturally, being Maui, he was curious about this. He asked.

"Muri-ranga-whenua eats it," he was told.

"And who might he be?"

"Your grandfather."

"Then let me take the food next time."

Instead of delivering it, Maui hid the food basket. And the next one. And the next one.

"I am hungry!" a voice growled through the passages of the Underworld. "Where are my baskets of food?"

Hearing him, Maui moved quietly toward him.

Sensing him but unable to see him in the shadows, the old man sniffed north, east, and south but smelled nothing. He sniffed toward the west.

"Who are you?" he asked. He sniffed again. "Is it my grandson Maui?"

"It is," replied Maui.

"I was going to eat whomever stole my food," the old man said. "What do you want?"

"I want your jawbone. In exchange for it I will feed you."

"Very well," said his grandfather. "Soon you will need it more than I do."

Maui removed the magic jawbone, gave his grandfather the baskets of food, and went home.

He would indeed need it soon, for he intended to lengthen the intervals of daylight. To do that he must trap the Sun and beat him into submission. The Sun's name, Maui now knew, was Tama.

For Reflection:

- Tama in his earthly form might be thought of as an example of the archetypal Green Man, a hardy, nature-loving figure found across cultures and eras. His leaf-framed face peers out of medieval stonework on the sides of cathedrals. Pan, Sylvanus, Al Khidr, the May King, Papa Bois ("bwah"), Robin Goodfellow, Cernunnos, and Jack in the Green are examples of Green Men. Where is the Green Man today?

- The partnership of boy and old man is an ancient motif. Jung referred to the archetype of the *puer* ("boy," usually a divine child figure) and *senex* ("old man," often wise). Where you find one, the other is not far off. The boy brings spontaneity, fresh ideas, a thirst for freedom and a fear of entanglement; the old man stands for order, structure, and loyalty to the community. How do these poles of human experience get out of balance? What realigns them?

- Adoptees who search for birth families sometimes learn that they have siblings they knew nothing about. What is your fantasy about why a mother would keep some children but not others?

- Why is it important, at least for some of us, to know about our roots?

- Why do you suppose the brothers show so little concern about where their mother goes during the day? What other matters aren't talked about in this family?

- Maui's attributes identify him as an expression of the Trickster archetype. How does the presence of a Trickster influence the family?

- What does the jawbone of Muri signify, and why must Maui force him to give it up?

- How is it that Maui must subdue the man who raised him?

The Weeping Woman (Mexican)

Gloria Anzaldúa, Chicana essayist, activist, and poet:

> I am a border woman. I grew up between two cultures, the Mexican (with a heavy Indian influence) and the Anglo (as a member of a colonized people in our own territory). I have been straddling that *tejas*-Mexican border, and others, all my life. It's not a comfortable territory to live in, this place of contradictions.

> Living on borders and in margins, keeping intact one's shifting and multiple identity and integrity, is like trying to swim in a new element, an "alien" element. There is an exhilaration in being a participant in the further evolution of humankind, in being "worked" on. I have the sense that certain "faculties"—not just in me but in

every border resident, colored or non-colored—and dormant areas of consciousness are being activated, awakened.

Down the road, a little ways from our house, was a deserted church. It was known among the *mexicanos* that if you walked down the road late at night you would see a woman dressed in white floating about, peering out the church window. She would follow those who had done something bad or who were afraid. *Los mexicanos* called her *la Jila*. Some thought she was *La Llorona*. She was, I think, *Cihuacoatl*, Serpent Woman, ancient Aztec goddess of the earth, of war and birth, patron of midwives, and antecedent of *la Llorona*... Long before it takes place, she is the first to predict something will happen.

Nobody remembers her name, although it was probably Maria or Laura, while she lived at least.

They do say she was beautiful, though, more beautiful than anyone in the village. Loveliness, passion, and perceptiveness had all found a home in one much-desired if somewhat aloof young woman whose inborn nobility could not be dimmed by the poverty of her upbringing.

The wealthy landowner who rode into the village noticed her immediately.

At first she rejected his advances and said nothing when he greeted her or opened doors for her. After a time, after much persistence on his part, she began to speak to him in rather cold pleasantries.

His smile, his charm, and his position in life eventually wore down her resistance. It was rumored that they saw each other, had fallen in love, were intimate in private places. Somebody thought he saw them holding hands; someone else whispered about a kiss given and received on the fly. When he smiled at her she smiled back.

As the size of her belly grew, so did his promises to marry her.

Despite the snickering around her, many noted her motherly glow, the rose coloring in her cheeks.

When her time came, she brought forth two babies who gave forth lusty cries. The midwife in attendance smiled. Their father held them with pride beaming from his face.

Although their parents had not married, the children saw their father often. He cared for them, played with them, and saw to their every need. She felt grateful for this, but to her smiles and nods clung a noticeable wistfulness. When he was absent, she often looked over the heads of her playing children into the distance beyond the village as though searching the horizon for him, wondering perhaps where he was and what he was doing.

When the villagers noticed an abrupt, desperate sadness in her, they wondered at it until word went around: A man of his station (so he had told her) could not marry someone like her. He was intended for another woman, and soon he would bind himself to her in marriage. But (he explained hurriedly) he would still visit the children and love their mother dearly. Nothing substantial would change.

As the months went on, she grew sadder and more silent. Then the worst news of all landed on her: The father of her children intended to take them away from her to live with him and his new wife.

In sorrow and rage, she brought her children to the river one night. Under the full moon, she held them underwater until they stopped struggling.

For a long while she stared at the still little bodies. From the middle of her own body a cry broke out, "O my children, what have I done? What have I done?"

Villagers up early found her wandering, muddy and quite mad, by the river the next morning. They also found the two little bodies lying under the water. "Where are my children?" she kept crying. "Where have they gone?"

Because of her desperate state, no one thought of holding a trial. Her madness soon claimed her life, some say by drowning. But it did not end there.

Not long after her death, a voice of wailing was heard now and again near the river. One villager said it sounded like a sobbing wind; another, that it wailed loudest under the full moon. Storms and shadows often brought it forth, always at night and always by bodies of water.

Even now, wayfarers out late at night are frightened to come upon La Llorona, the Weeping Woman, the spectral mother in black or white wandering along the riverbank seeking the souls of her lost children, and condemned to do so until she finally finds them.

For Reflection:

- The myth of La Llorona has worldwide counterparts like Medea, the Lamia, and the Crying Wind in Africa. The La Llorona version emerged from Mexico shortly after its conquest by Hernando Cortes, who according to legend abandoned his young lover-translator, the Aztec slave girl La Malinche, for his wife. Women who kill their children are often referred to as "modern Lloronas." What depths of desperation would drive them to do this?

- Sandra Cisneros published an anthology of La Llorona stories called *Woman Hollering Creek*. She and other Chicana feminists have reimagined La Llorona as a figure of self-assertion, as the woman who cannot be silenced and will not be constrained by boundaries of sex or gender or small-town respectability. What then might the voice of La Llorona contribute to culture, community, and consciousness?

- What might drowning one's children mean psychologically?

- What might it feel like to be a child of a La Llorona mother?

- The story of La Llorona spread upward from Mexico and into the Southwest. It always follows in the wake of conquest: of people, of places, of the land itself. Why might that be? What might it herald?

- Gloria Anzaldúa traces La Llorona to the more complete Aztec goddess Cihuacoatl, whose name means Serpent Woman (as does Athena's). With Quetzalcoatl, she created human beings, a partnership that recalls that of Sophia and Yaldabaoth. After the conquest of Mexico and the repression of Aztec religion, Cihuacoatl went underground, to emerge as La Llorona on the one hand and La Virgen de Guadalupe on the other: goddesses dark and bright, the halves of a split archetype (remember Lower and Higher Sophia). What could heal this split?

Papa Bois Grows Up (Trinidad)

Marjuan Canady, producer, director, actress, and playwright:

> Folkloric traditions have survived because of our ancestors. They have also taken on new forms and meanings with the migration of Caribbean peoples throughout the world.
>
> When my mom would tell me the stories, the characters sparked my imagination. The folkloric stories are so magical and full of danger, hope, fears and dreams, all in search of reclaiming memories. This folklore is rooted in the mystery of what else exists in the world. I thought it was important to re-create these stories through illustration because there are so few books geared towards black and brown kids, especially of Caribbean descent.
>
> Through migration and assimilation many of my Caribbean relatives forgot their history or chose to not remember. I see this to be detrimental to preserving our history and culture. I think this is why telling the stories of T&T's [Trinidad and Tobago's] folklore was so impor-

tant to me. There was power in the story. The story is
what got us through slavery, made sense out of chaos and
allowed us to be free and creative in a constricted world.

The hunter found no happiness in town. Too many people, too
much chatter. Too much buying and selling. Too much busyness cut
off from the world of plants and insects, animals and streams. He
longed for what was essential and honest, simple and serene.

Rising early, he made up a light pack, sheathed his arrows,
picked up his bow, and headed for the forest, walking.

The green shadows soothed him. Instead of noisy bickering,
here his ear caught bubbling waters, bright chirps, pleasant winged
buzzing. Slender shafts of sunlight like strings on a magical instrument angled down from tall trees. In a clear stream he washed off
the odor and grime of the town and, naked, walked deeper into the
forest, leaving his garments behind.

After walking down animal trails the hunter came to another
stream and bent to drink. Raising his head, he was surprised to see
a deer drinking from the same waters. When she saw him she lost
her balance and, flailing, fell in.

Seeing that she was sinking, he waded in after her. His strong
arms lifted her from the water and set her on the bank.

"He saved Gionda!" screeched a parrot from the trees. "He
saved the Mother of the Forest!" From around him the hunter heard
a gleeful chorus of chirping, squawking, cawing, and barking—even
the trees seem to wave at him—as the frightened dear bolted and
dashed away among tall trees.

He pursued her but, wearying, gave up and took his rest under
the friendly arms of a large tree. He slept.

As it happened, the hunter had fallen asleep under a sacred tree
inhabited by the spirits of the forest. This was no accident. The forest had known for some time that it needed to bridge the widening
gap between itself and human beings who, lost in towns, were forgetting the life of the wild. What was needed (the spirits decided)
was a being who would bear within himself, in his very blood and

bones, a mix of human and wild.

The hunter was roused by the nose of the deer gently brushing his face. He sat up with an odd feeling that the entire forest watched.

"Do not fear," she told him. "You are safe here."

"You can talk!" he blurted. "Why did you run away from me?"

"Every creature in the forest fears humans now. Even I, who am immortal, do."

"Who are you? *What* are you?"

"I am Gionda. I am the goddess who tends the forest and all who live here."

Looking into her eyes, he felt in his heart what she would say next before she said it:

"...And I am lonely."

He could understand that. "So am I," he said.

He was also getting cold.

She lay down beside him for the night. Her fur and breath were warm.

* * * *

In the morning, the spirits of the forest announced their joining as a couple. Sounds of delight emanated from the crawling, flying, rooting, running, slithering beings of the forest. They came in a procession to congratulate the happy couple...all but Snake, who would now be second in Gionda's heart to some human hunter she had just met. As leaves jostled and blooms opened wide in joy, he alone crept away, bitter and discontented.

Later that day the happy couple stood on a high ridge from where they could see the green canopy of the entire forest spread out below them. Colorful splashes of bright feathers marked out the birds circling high overhead. In the distance a valley cut the land. From here the cut seemed small, almost unreal.

"That," said the hunter, pointing, "is the place of humans from which I came."

"Do you miss it?"

"No. It saddens me, though, that so many cannot appreciate the peace out here. They have forgotten it."

"I am happy you remembered. And that you will stay with me." That night they slept in a close embrace.

The next morning he was surprised to find her gone. At first this did not trouble him, but as the morning passed, he grew aware that the feel of the forest had changed. It no longer felt happy and welcoming. Now, somehow, it was ominously silent and cold, shadowy and forbidding. The hunter did not yet realize it, but his reason for being there was already accomplished.

He wandered around searching for his bride until he spotted Snake.

"Where is Gionda?" the hunter asked him.

"She has left you," replied Snake in a cool, dry hiss.

"Left me! How could that be?"

"Did you really imagine that you, a human, could stay in the forest forever? I hope you had a pleasant visit, but the hard truth is that we don't want you here with us. Can't you feel it?" Not a single chirp or branch stirred in argument. "I will tell her goodbye for you. You cannot see her."

Gionda had gotten up early to meet with the most ancient turtle of the forest. He bore a prophecy for her.

"You," Turtle informed her, "will bear the child who will tend the forest after you. He will grow up strong in body and learned in forest lore. He will know his lineage, and you and your love will be proud of him. His name will be Papa Bois."

Her dark eyes reflected joy. "When will these things take place?"

"The child will enter the world soon, but the prophecy will not be fulfilled until the fruit of the sacred tree glows golden. When it does, I will return and bear you off to a land called Venezuela. Only then will all be revealed."

Her joy quickly turned to agony. Where was her hunter? She sought him everywhere but could not find him.

"He is gone," said Snake. "I tried to stop him, but he was determined to return to the land of people. Good riddance." He slithered away, and so did her happy hopes.

The boy welcomed by the forest grew rapidly. Human from the

waist up and deer from the waist down, he learned from every bird, branch, and patch of soil that mentored him.

When he was old enough to notice the sorrow in his mother, she told him of his father and of his mysterious departure. From the ridge she pointed out the distant valley where human beings lived.

Not long after this, the fruit of the sacred tree turned gold. Up from the deep forest lumbered the ancient turtle. It was time.

Blessing her son and all the creatures of the forest, Gionda climbed onto the turtle's back. The ancient one made for the sea.

Papa Bois watched for a long time as they swam away, and then he turned back to the forest, gaining his balance as he went.

* * * *

"Why have you summoned me?" Snake asked Papa Bois, who noted that the serpent seemed nervous. *As well he should be*, Papa thought. Flamingo had come to him with an account from Grass. Grass sees everything snakes do.

"You know already. *Why did you send my father away?*" The roar echoed all through the forest. Snake cringed. No fancy lie would serve, he knew.

"Because we can't have humans living in the forest, Papa. You know that. First one human, then more, then even more..." Animals curious about the shout ambled up to listen.

Papa Bois could not hold Snake fully responsible, especially since the ancient turtle had told the young tender of the forest about the plan of the elder spirits. Who knew what else they were up to?

"Consider," he told the animals, "how this intolerance has caused my parents such great sorrow. Things should not be like this. From now on we shall judge by actions, not by descent or by how many legs we go around on. And no more secrets! They poison the forest and the heart. Do you understand?"

They understood.

From then on the forest knew peace. It was not a perfect place, nor even completely safe. Creatures died and were feasted upon, their remains gone back to the soil, air, and water. This, though, was the way of things. Even conflict and death served life in an orderly world.

The ancient turtle's reappearance caused quite a stir, but nothing compared to the reentry of the hunter.

He was old now and he needed a straight stick for walking, having left his youth and agility far behind. The forest creatures who greeted him noticed how his black hair had whitened and how his brown skin had wrinkled. He seemed peaceful, though. "I forgive you," he told Snake, who nodded shyly.

"Meet your son!" squawked the parrot whose voice the hunter recognized. With gladness he embraced Papa Bois.

"Where is your mother?" the hunter asked.

"Let me show you something."

Papa led his father to a clear pool. "Look into the water."

The hunter looked down and saw his own face, but young and animated once again. He smiled.

"So will Mother be young," said Papa Bois, "when you meet her again. Our friend Turtle will take you to her now. She awaits you. Please give her my love."

They embraced again, and then the son's strong arms lifted his father onto the back of the turtle. The ancient one headed for the sea.

Papa Bois watched for a long time as they swam away, and then he turned back to the forest. The ground felt solid beneath him.

For Reflection:

- In Greek myth, a hunter out with his dogs spots naked Artemis bathing with her nymphs in a secluded stream. Startled, Acteon turns away to dash back to camp and boast to his comrades about what he has seen, but the goddess splashes him with magical water that turns him into a stag hunted down by his own hounds. How is the hunter in the tale above different in character from Actaeon? How are his actions different?

- Why couldn't the hunter remain in the forest?

- The mischievous doings of Trickster—in this case Snake—invite the reflection that personal failings can serve transpersonal ends. Can you think of when mistakes you've made ramified and mutated in accord with larger purposes visible only much later?

- Beyond seeing into the future, what are Papa Bois and his father doing when they stare into the pool?

- Sometimes myths and fairytales—and for that matter life events—tell of sorrows that never entirely heal. The hunter and Gionda cannot get back the years they spent apart. What might this suggest about the agendas of the gods?

- The departure of Papa Bois's parents could be interpreted as their entrance into the Otherworld. How might their deaths affect their son? Serve his maturation?

- In what ways do nature myth figures like Papa Bois bridge human and nonhuman?

The Strivings of Isis (Egyptian)

Abeer Soliman, writer, storyteller, photographer, and reinterpreter of the *1001 Nights*:

> I admire Shaharazad a lot. She's an intelligent and smart woman, who is telling stories not just for the fun of it, but because she wants to save the life of women from the power of Shahryar, who was bent upon killing one woman every night.
>
> I had to fight hard for my choices. I am a girl from a small village near Tanta who chose not to get married but to live alone in Cairo; who decided that art, in various forms, would be her life's calling.
>
> I adore the art of storytelling, and this is an art that calls

for complete devotion...Storytelling is a journey
between two points, one in which you summon your
skills to bring the audience into another world of secrets
and intimacies.

Every ruler has a blind spot, and that of Osiris was his brother
Set. Even after so much success organizing Egypt and teaching
humans to plant and farm; after marrying his wise and beautiful sister Isis to much acclaim; after sleeping with Nephthys, wife of Set
and mother of dog-headed Anubis; even after all this, Osiris still had
no idea of the murderous jealousy burning in the desert god's admi-
ration-starved breast.

Wrapped in innocence, Osiris attended a large banquet arranged
by Set.

At the height of the festivities, Set unwrapped an intricately
carved wooden chest of superb workmanship. It was built of cedar,
and strangely elongated.

"Whomever can fit inside this cabinet," announced Set, "may
possess it."

It just so happened, of course, that Osiris fit the box perfectly;
his brother had measured his shadow to make sure. Set slammed
down the lid. The partygoers—in actuality seventy-two of Set's
henchmen—rushed forward to nail down the lid and pour molten
lead over it. The seal hardened quickly.

"Party's over," sneered Set as they carried out the box to be
dropped into the Nile River. "Now *I* shall rule."

*   *   *   *

When Isis felt her lover die, her tears ran so fast and full that
they flowed down valleys and plains and flooded the Nile. Even so,
the desert expanded through Egypt, drying out the land.

Summoning wise Thoth and her sister Nephthys, Isis set out on
a search for Osiris so she could give him an honorable burial.

Down the Nile they journeyed in search of the sealed casket,
which had drifted with wave and wind until coming to rest on the

shore near Byblos. As they approached this place, Isis heard stories of a fabulous tree recently seen there, a tamarisk that emitted a heavenly fragrance. Not knowing the tree had grown around the coffin of Osiris, Queen Astarte and King Melkart had ordered the tree cut down and shaped into a pillar for their palace.

As Isis sat on the stump wondering where to look next, a royal retinue approached her. Having heard of a holy stranger arriving in their land, the queen and king decided to personally invite her to their home for a visit. Isis accepted. When the queen's baby squealed in delight to see her and sucked on her finger, drinking milk as one would from a breast, the new parents decided to appoint Isis their royal nurse.

Although the queen and king did not recognize her, Isis was happy with that arrangement, for she had identified the location of her dead husband. At night she chipped away at the pillar in the palace. In gratitude for the couple's hospitality, she also placed their child in a fire that warmed and strengthened without burning.

One night Queen Astarte walked in on her. Shrieking in horror, the queen rushed forward to pull her baby from the fire. She whirled to confront the royal nurse.

Orbiting the pillar in the form a swallow, Isis revealed her identity. "You should have let me finish with the child. He would have become immortal. Instead, he will look ahead to a long, though mortal, life."

"Why are you carving up that pillar?"

Isis told the queen at last about Osiris.

In the morning, the queen and king ordered the pillar split open. Isis removed the casket, said goodbye to them, and went home.

When she had unsealed the box, she was surprised to find the body of her mate perfectly preserved. Was it possible he could be brought back to life? Summoning her powers, Isis bent over him, placed her mouth on his, and breathed deeply into his body. It stirred, and after a moment Osiris opened his eyes and looked up at her.

Because Set ruled now, they hid out in the countryside. But Set knew. The retreating deserts told him that his hated brother had revived.

Waiting until Isis was elsewhere, Set pretended to go out hunting gazelles by moonlight. He tracked his brother through dark marshes and found him. Osiris was sleeping.

This time, Set told himself, he would make a thorough job of it. He tore Osiris into fourteen pieces. Then he transported each piece to a distant region of Egypt.

Once again the deserts expanded. Once again Isis mourned.

It took her and her helpers a long while, but eventually she recovered thirteen of the hidden pieces of her lover and rejoined them on an islet in the Nile. The deserts halted. The last piece, the phallus, she could not recover because fishes had eaten it.

In remembrance of the tree that had embraced her husband, she fashioned a wooden phallus for him. Crouching over him and weeping, she conceived, then summoned the priests to embalm him because his soul had already fled to the Duat.

The expectant mother hid in the marshes of the Nile delta to give birth to her son among the rushes. The name of the hope of Isis was Horus. His eyes blazed as the sun and moon, and he flew like a falcon. "One day," she told him, "you will avenge your father and challenge Set for the throne of Egypt."

These things came to pass, but, by the will of Maat, who preserves the universal balance, there would be no lasting victory. Horus battled Set many times, on one occasion losing an eye even as Set lost a testicle, which is why the deserts are barren. Set's wife Hathor joined efforts with Khonsu the moon god to replace the eye, but Horus gave it to his father Osiris so he could preside as king in the Underworld.

Although bright Horus often won against his dark uncle Set, he never completely did away with him.

For Reflection:
- Comment: The goddess Maat refers to the cosmic order (compare Dharma, Tao, Meh). For the ancient Egyptians, justice and a good life were bound up with

conforming to this order.

- How is it that pseudoinnocence tends to bring about the very disasters it refuses to think about? What motivates it?

- What does it mean that Set measures his brother's shadow?

- Why won't Osiris stay revived?

- In another variant, dismembered Osiris does not lose his penis to the fishes. What is the significance of the wooden model?

- Osiris bears comparison with dismembered Dionysus, descended Dumuzi, castrated Attis, and crucified Jesus. All four are associated with ecstatic states, breads, grains, a rejuvenating female partner, dismemberment, and descent into the Underworld prior to rebirth. What archetype might they represent?

- Comment: The episode of Isis putting the royal child into the fire shows up later in Greek myth as Demeter (in mourning when her daughter Persephone vanished into Hades) bathing the child of Metaneira, the wife of Keleus, in a fire to grant immortality. Why is this procedure interrupted?

- In this story Set appears to be purely evil, and yet he guards the Sun Barge that passes through the body of Nut every day from being attacked by the dragon Apep (Apophis). What other purposes are served by Set? Who is he archetypally?

- The ancient Egyptians appreciated the need for timely mourning. In one of their creation stories, humans arose from the tears of Ra. Words for "tears" and "human" are similar in ancient Egyptian. How does your culture of origin deal with mourning?

- Comment: Egyptian myth is foundational for many later mythologies, including the Greek, Roman, and

Judeo-Christian. You can see this in three versions of the Creation: 1. Ptah the artisan god speaks the world into being ("In the beginning was the Word..."). 2. Thoth, verbal god of writing and Underworld judgment and forerunner of Hermes, creates the Ogdoad, four snake-headed goddesses paired with four frog-headed gods: Naunet and Nu (original waters), Amunet and Amun (air, wind), Kauket and Kuk (darkness), and Hauhet and Huh (spatial infinity). As in Hindu myth, the gods make a lotus blossom from the primeval waters ("the face of the deep"), and when it blooms, the sun god Atum rises. 3. From the ocean Nu rose Atum, who stood (like Ptah) on a raised pyramidal mound called the *benben*. Atum masturbated—or swallowed his own semen and spit forth—aerial Shu and watery Tefnut. Atum also produced Geb (earth) and Nut (sky), separated by Shu after they birthed Osiris, Isis, Set, and Nephthys, an Egyptian Persephone who parented Anubis with Osiris. The supreme solar creator god Ra appears during the Fourth Dynasty.

- Monotheism seems to have started in Egypt, when Akhenaten (Amenhotep IV, 1352-1336 BCE) and his wife Nefertiti worshiped Aten, the sun god with hands. The pharaoh and his followers effaced images of other gods throughout Egypt until his death, when Tutankhamun took over and restored polytheism, but not before (it is thought) the Hebrews in Egypt were exposed to monotheism. How do desert and monotheism go together?

- Comment: Moses is an Egyptian name, and "Red Sea" a mistranslation of "Sea of Reeds." The story of Joseph being accused of raping Potiphar's wife derives from the Egyptian "The Tale of the Two Brothers." The *Book of Proverbs* resembles the *Wisdom of*

Amenenope, and Apep the serpent in Eden. The Christian Cross reflects the Ankh, a symbol of life, and, like Isis, blue-clad Mary flees city life to protect her baby. Images of Isis nursing Horus inspired Madonna and Child imagery in art, but Jesus as a mythic figure stands closer to Osiris.

- Like the early Christians, the earlier Egyptians were fascinated by death and rebirth, which they saw in the growth and death of crops planted between the Nile and the desert. The Pyramid Texts, the world's oldest written mythology, contain a guide to the afterlife. Stars in Nut's night body were the spirits of dead pharaohs risen to join the gods. In the Duat, the *ka* soul of the departed passed among forty-two evaluators to arrive in the Hall of Two Truths to be judged by Thoth, Anubis, and Horus. Thoth weighed the heart of the *ka* on a scale balanced by the white feather of Maat. A clean heart that had lived well received an *akh*, a resurrected subtle body that reunited *ka* with *ba*, the individual part of the soul, and passed into lush and pleasant realms. A cold heart was either reincarnated into a hard life or eaten by the death god Ammut. Osiris presided over all these judgments. How might they parallel internal actions of death, judgment, and rebirth within the psyche?

- Sigmund Freud was fascinated all his life by Egyptian archeology and lore. Why might this be? Witness his first childhood nightmare, a replication of an ancient Egyptian funerary ritual:

In it I saw my beloved mother, with a peculiarly peaceful expression on her features, being carried into the room by two (or three) people with birds' beaks and laid upon the bed. I awoke in tears and screaming and interrupted my parents' sleep. The strangely draped and unnaturally tall figures with birds' beaks were derived from the illustrations to Philippson's Bible. I fancy they must have been gods with falcons' heads from an ancient Egyptian funerary relief.

- What are the long-term results of the strivings of Isis? How do her actions set the stage for an event not mentioned in the tale: the creation of humans by ram-headed Khnum, potter of the gods and deity of the Nile?

- Comment: The land of Egypt (from *Kemet:* "black land" of rich soil) left a deep imprint on its myths. The pyramid and obelisk get their shape from rays of the sun sloping down like stairways to the flat expanses below. The bright sun cast sharp shadows. The Nile floods yearly to give life; the desert desiccates and mummifies. Above, jackals scavenge graves; below, jackal-headed Anubis judges the dead. The thin line between soil and sand, life and death, reaches into polarities like death/rebirth, land/sky, commoners/ Pharaohs, Southern and Northern Egypt. Might dualistic thought, and perhaps myth too, ultimately originate in the land itself?

Short-Tailed Li (Chinese)

Lihui Yang, writer, anthologist, and professor of folklore and mythology at Beijing Normal University, and Deming An, author and professor of folklore at the Chinese Academy of Social Sciences:

> By "Chinese mythology," we mean the body of myths historically recorded and currently transmitted within the present geographic boundaries of China. ...Since almost every ethnic group has its own mythical gods and stories about their creative actions, there is not a systematic, integrated, and homogeneous "Chinese mythology" held and transmitted by all the Chinese people.

Myths in ancient China are preserved in various written accounts, usually in a fragmented form. They were not collected and organized into a single, systematic mythology of China. ....Chinese myths have not suffered what Yuan Ke describes as a complete reworking by literati and others, like Homer's and Hesiod's work, and thus remain in a more or less "pristine condition."

Talented singers or storytellers can also be important bearers of mythological tradition. When the Dong people in southern China offer sacrifices to their ancestors, they gather together to sing songs and dance to entertain the gods.

As a traditional genre that was primarily created in the ancient past and has been transmitted for thousands of years, myth has deeply influenced people's ordinary lives throughout history. It often helps to shape people's attitudes toward the world, provides evidence and reasons for their behaviors, and supplies meanings and models for their current lives.

When Li was born, such was the fire of his dragon self that suckling made his mother faint. Outside, a fierce wind blew gray clouds across the sky until they released a downpour.

Li's father came in soaking from laboring all day in the fields. He took one look at his ugly new son—the last thing the struggling family needed was another child, let alone a child with black skin and a large snout—and hit him with a spade. The blow severed part of Li's tail.

Roaring with pain and anger, Li reared so high that he broke the roof of the house. Shedding smoke and sparks, he leaped upward and flew through the hole. He never looked back.

Eventually Li spotted an inviting river and decided to make his home there. He did not know exactly who or what he was, but he knew he needed to find out.

*   *   *   *

I should go see what that young man is up to mused the old man who lived by the river.

Few wanted to live near a river liable to flood, but the old man knew the ways of land and water and preferred to cultivate the moist soil there.

When the dark youth had arrived and asked for a place to stay, the old man had agreed immediately. The young man was willing to work, but the old man said, "It's up to you. If you'd like to work that's fine. If not, just rest." He seemed to sense that the young one had been through much. Gratefully, the youth did the cooking, gathered firewood, and kept the home clean for the both of them.

One day the old man came home looking tired. He had been trying to clear some land for planting, but trees with large roots stood in the way.

"How about if we switch, Grandpa?" asked the young dark one. "You cook and clean, and I'll go out during the day and clear the land." The old one nodded.

After a few days of the new routine, the old man grew curious and decided to go see how the clearing was going.

As he approached the river, his ears picked up enormous crackings and thumpings. His eyes could hardly believe what they beheld: a huge black dragon wrapping his tail around tree trunks and jerking them from the trembling ground. Boulders and other debris whizzed through the air. The old man retreated before he could be struck by something and went home.

"How did the clearing go?" the old man asked the youth over dinner.

"Well enough, but I think I worked a little too hard at it."

"Yes."

The youth looked at him. "You saw me?"

The old man nodded. "I went out to the fields to see how you were doing. Had to come home, though, so I wouldn't be hit by a stone or stump."

"Now that you know what I am, can we still be friends?"

"Of course we can."

"That is good, Grandpa, because I want to settle permanently in this area."

"You're welcome to keep staying here."

"Thank you, but I think I will live in the river. To do that, though, I need your help. A dangerous white dragon already lives in the river—that is why it floods now and then—and I have to remove him first."

"How could I possibly help you do that?"

"The white dragon and I both need to replenish ourselves during great efforts like fighting. He has hot food and soup down there, but I have only water. If you would prepare large stones and steamed buns and pile them up on the riverbank, then when I reach up you could hand me the buns, and when he reaches up you could hand him the stones. That would really help."

At dawn the next day the young dragon walked into the river, and the battle for it began. All morning huge waves crossed it and steam rose from it. Now and then thrashing scaled limbs and tails broke the surface, sometimes white, sometimes black. The old man threw stones and buns into the river until, by afternoon, the youth triumphed and the river's waters darkened. He emerged dripping and thankful. The white dragon did not.

All this happened long ago, and since that time, Short-Tailed Old Li (as he is now called) has watched over not only the river, but the entire region, even stopping its invasion by hostile forces from other countries.

Although Short-Tailed Old Li never saw his parents again, after his mother died he paid his respects at the grave in Shandong. He does this without fail every May 13th. When he stoops down from the sky it always rains, even during droughts.

For Reflection:

- Some children are simply too much for their overpowered parents. How might Li's childhood have been different had his parents been supported by a network of relatives and friends instead of isolated by poverty and overwork?

- Why would it be important for Li to remember his family even after his time with them was cut so short?

- Li's father's action with the spade foreshadows Li's future involvement with working the land. In a sense, he becomes a tree-removing spade. Which of your early wounds seem to point forward to future involvements?

- Li finds a way to what Nietzsche advised: "He who does not have a good father should find one." How does it help heal Li for his true nature to be witnessed and accepted by the old man?

- Dragons are revered in China as aerial beings of good luck, power, and royalty; emperors were said to descend from dragons. They are numinous creatures of awe and might. According to an old tale, Lord Ye Gao loved dragons so much (he thought) that he filled his home with dragon images and even wore some on his garments. Curious about this, the Heavenly Dragon came to visit him. When faced by a real dragon, Ye Gao fled in terror. What might it mean to be confronted by the powerful energies of the dragon?

- In some Chinese tales, black and white dragons play instead of fighting. How might such play change this tale?

- Why steamed buns? According to legend, *mantou*, a staple in Northern China and a treat in the South, got its name from when Chancellor Zhuge Liang tried to lead his Shu Han army across a river too rapid to cross. A local chieftain told him of a custom: throwing the heads of sacrificial victims into the river to calm it. Instead of killing more men, Zhuge Liang ordered his cattle slaughtered, their meat to be placed into head-

shaped buns and hurled into the river. With its god pla-
cated, the army crossed, and the buns were thereafter
named "barbarians' heads." How does this bit of legend augment our understanding of this tale?

- How would one "feed" a dragon? Weigh one down
  with "stones"?

- In the West, white is often associated with good and
  black with evil. What do these colors signify in Old
  Li's story?

- Who brings the rain in your family? Causes the floods?
  Reacts with overwhelm and anger? Patiently tends the
  soil?

Dumalawi's Magic Family (Filipino)

Jay Menes, Filipino actor, director, artist, storyteller:

> Stories are the building blocks of knowledge, the foun-
> dation of memory and learning. Also, stories connect us
> with our humanness and link past, present, and future by
> teaching us to anticipate the possible consequences of
> our actions.
>
> Storytelling passes on the essence of who we are. Stories
> are a prime vehicle for assessing and interpreting events,
> experiences, and concepts from minor moments of daily
> life to the grand nature of the human condition. It is an
> intrinsic and basic form of human communication.
>
> Storytelling is what happens when a story is told, face to
> face, eye to eye, mind to mind, heart to heart. The story
> is intimately known by the teller, spoken aloud, and
> shared, like a gift, with the audience.

Storytelling is the oldest oral art. Many years ago, when the only form of communication was by word of mouth, stories were the only means of gaining information and spreading news. Stories taught us who we were, where we came from, and how we should relate to each other.

Normally, the birth of a baby gives joy to a couple, and so did the arrival of Dumalawi to his mother Aponibolinayen and his father Aponitolau.

As the years passed, however, the boy's father came to hate him, who knows why. Maybe Aponitolau envied his son's imaginative gifts, for the boy was a natural dreamer. Maybe he envied the boy some of his wife's affection. Maybe the father saw a future in which he would be surpassed by his son.

Whatever the motives, one day Aponitolau looked at Dumalawi, now a young man, and decided to do away with him.

"Let's go into the forest," he said to Dumalawi. "Bring your knife."

Once there, they cut bamboo sticks and sharpened the ends.

"Now," instructed Aponitolau, "the idea is that we're going to throw these sticks at each other to challenge our bravery. You go first. Throw yours at me." He knew there was little chance of being hit.

"I can't do that, Father," said Dumalawi. "You go first."

Aponitolau hurled stick after stick, spear-like, but none of them landed.

"Your turn, son."

"No. I don't want to kill you."

He could not be persuaded, so they returned home, Dumalawi wondering why his father would want to harm him. What had he done wrong? At supper he couldn't eat.

The next day the two went to repair the little house built to shoo away birds and other animals looking for easy food in the fields of crops. When they reached the house, Aponitolau pointed to a patch of ground and said, "When I was a boy I buried a jar of sugarcane wine there. It has been fermenting ever since. Dig it up and we'll drink it."

Once they had drunk three coconut shells of the wine, Dumalawi became drowsy and slept. Summoning magic, his father called up a great storm with powerful winds. They lifted the sleeping son and transported him into the middle of a wide field.

* * * *

When Dumalawi woke, he looked around in alarm. Not a tree, not a house, not a bush or an animal did he see, just a flat field where his father's spell had left him. He was bereft.

After sitting in sadness for a time, he remembered his own powers and used them. Betel nuts sprouted all around him. Soon the field shone as though covered with gold.

"You," he told them, "will be my new companions."

Late at night he moved among them, cutting them into pieces. These he scattered through the field. Satisfied, he went to sleep.

The sounds of talking people and crowing roosters woke him in the morning. He saw groups of people keeping warm around fires lit to fend off the cold mountain air. Rising, he made the rounds to say hello.

After meeting everyone, he returned to Dapilisan, a young woman, to speak more with her. Her look and smile made it obvious that she liked him as much as he liked her, so he asked her parents for permission to marry her.

"But what about your parents?" they asked. "Shouldn't they be involved in this decision?"

"My parents abandoned me. I am alone."

"In that case, we agree."

The happy couple decided to ask everyone to the celebration. "Oil yourselves," Dapilisan told the betel nuts she had summoned, "and go invite everyone to our ceremony."

Still mourning for her lost son, Aponibolinayen felt seized by a puzzling desire to chew a betel nut. Fetching one from a basket, she picked up a knife.

The nut said, "Don't cut me. I bear an invitation for you to attend a grand ceremony."

"For what purpose?"

"To celebrate the wedding of Dumalawi and his new wife."

Dashing out of her home in tearful ecstasy, Aponibolinayen shouted for everyone in the village to wash and prepare for the celebration. The wave of happiness and relief spread rapidly. Soon a crowd gathered near the river to cross over.

When Dumalawi received word of their coming, he gestured, and a group of alligators paddled toward the waiting celebrants like a fleet of small ferries. Soon every villager stood on a ridged back to be carried safely across the water.

Aponitolau shambled toward the river in shock. The news of his son's survival had sent him into a daze. When he boarded an alligator, it shook itself so fiercely that he was catapulted back onto the shore. Dumalawi gestured again, and another gator pulled up to take his father across the river.

The celebration was as grand as everyone had hoped. Dumalawi supplied generous amounts of tasty food, and jars of sugarcane wine provided by Dapilisan refilled themselves. Having been reunited with her son, Aponibolinayen told all the people how proud she was to be Dapilisan's mother-in-law. Aponitolau remained in the background.

"Now," she added, "we will pay the customary marriage price to the bride's family by filling the spirit house"—the small structure built for the after-wedding celebration— "nine times with different kinds of jars." At her gesture the spirits of the springs did her bidding. The spirit house stood so packed with jars that the door could scarcely shut.

At this Dalonagan, mother of Dapilisan, stepped forward:

"We thank you, but there is one other payment we would ask of you."

She summoned a large spider and gave it instructions: "Spin your web all around and through the town."

As the spider went its patient way, crossing here and spinning there, Aponibolinayen summoned the spirits to string the threads with golden beads. When the web was finished, Dalonagan hung her full weight on it. It held her and did not break.

"Thank you," she said. "I am satisfied. Let the celebration recommence!"

When it finally ended, Dumalawi's parents approached to seek reconciliation. They asked if he would come home with them. He shook his head.

"Although I'm glad you came," he replied, "I am staying here with my wife, with my kin, with my new family, and with all my welcoming neighbors."

For Reflection:

- Families that carry a legacy of unresolved pain and fear of change often attack the family dreamers: in this case Dumalawi ("doo-*may*-lay-WE"), a son of a Wisdom Goddess set upon by his father Aponitolau ("ah-poh-*neet*-oh-LAO"), a kind of Noah in Filipino myth. Instead of the blessing of the father this son receives a curse. How does he make something good come of it?

- Dumalawi's father leaves him in a flat, featureless field on his own. What does this correspond to emotionally?

- Before Dumalawi can feel belonging, he must evoke separation by cutting up the betel nuts and scattering them. Why is this?

- The tale contains references to altered states of consciousness. In what ways might the tale be interpreted as Dumalawi's spirit journey?

- Beyond simple retaliation or punishment, what was the alligator that shook off Aponitolau trying to tell him?

- Dalonagan could be considered a counterpart to Aponibolinayen. What is behind her requirement that the strong web be strung?

- Chewing the betel leaves of the areca nut, a fruit of a tropical palm tree, goes far back in time in Oceana and East Asia, where this stimulant has gathered associations of love and togetherness. How are love and nature linked in this story?

- On one level, the town, neighbors, bride, and new family could be understood as imaginary compensations dreamed up by a disenchanted boy trying to escape from a destructive father. In the world of imagination—or the world of online gaming for some young people of today—he receives the love and belonging he cannot find in the outer world. On another level, Dumalawi is an archetypal creator god summoning forth people to inhabit the world. What other levels might this myth disclose?

- What does the lack of resolution at the end of the story say about the resolvability of some deep conflicts that arise in a family?

Hina-uri Lost and Found Again (Maori)

Kiri Te Kanawa, opera virtuoso and author of *Land of the Long White Cloud: Maori Myths, Tales, and Legends*:

> New Zealand is a country of green fields, lakes and rivers, all gloriously beautiful, and one really has to visit to appreciate what they look like.... One of my favorite places was Lake Taupo where I used to love to go fishing and sailing with my father. I love the many Maori stories of fishing and boating adventures because they remind me of those wonderful expeditions.
>
> Late in 1987 there was an enormous gathering of all the Te Kanawas at our ancestral home in Te Kuiti. My father was brought up there and the Te Kanawa's own *marae*, our meeting ground, is situated on a hill outside of town.

The wonderful celebrations lasted for three days with feasting, dancing and singing.... In that warm atmosphere, as we swapped stories and caught up on news of so many old friends, powerful memories of my childhood came flooding back and old familiar stories came to mind.

Two brothers, Ihuatamai and Ihuwareware, were astonished to see a woman-shaped mound of seaweed wash up on shore.

At first they thought she was dead, but her barnacle-covered chest rose and fell, so, unwrapping her, they picked her up and carried her home to warm her by the fire.

The warmth brought her back to life and awareness. As it turned out, she was Hina-uri, the wife of a man turned into a dog by the youngest Maui brother. In her grief, she had hurled herself into the sea and let the waves take her where they would.

"Stay with us," they suggested.

Although she became wife to these brothers, she never told them her true name. Instead, she called herself Ihungarupaea, which means "Stranded-log-of-timber."

When the village leader Tinirau heard of this, he decided to pay a visit. Seeing how young and beautiful she was, "You will be my third wife," he told her. Over everyone's protests he hauled her off to his home.

Seeing her coming, his other two wives, Harataunga and Horotata, felt no sympathy for her, only envy and competitiveness. To her fell the most degrading chores and the smallest portions of the meals they cooked. When their husband was away, they insulted her, and on one occasion they hit her.

Enough was enough. The next morning Hina-uri rose early, walked quietly outside, and began to weave a spell.

The leaves and breezes grew still as she chanted; even the earth seemed scarcely to breathe. Her voice grew louder and louder until, with a defiant pushing-away gesture, she finished the chant.

In Tinirau's hut, Harataunga and Horotata stopped moving, their eyes wide open, and fell over dead, their soles pointed skyward.

* * * *

Maui-mua the Eldest Born missed his sister, but no one could tell him where she had gone. After her husband's awful transformation she had vanished, who knew where.

Who knew? *Perhaps* he *knows*, Maui-mua thought. *I shall visit my ancestor and ask.*

With that, he drew on the magic flowing in the veins of his family. He shapeshifted into a pigeon named Rupe and flew upward, heading for the tenth heaven.

It was a long journey. He stopped at every heaven to ask the way, only to be told no bird had any business being there. "If Tane had meant birds to fly so high, he would have made birds spirits!" Rupe flew on, trusting his instinct, and at length he reached the bright tenth heaven and made his way to its summit.

There Rupe beheld an ancient visage, one few had ever looked upon. A gentle command rumbled from behind the wrinkles and kindly eyes that glowed like stars:

"Bring dishes for our guest." Thus spoke the celestial voice of Rehua.

Once his servants had placed a set of calabashes between them, Rehua shook birds from his long hair. The servants caught the birds and took them away; and at length freshly cooked flesh filled the dishes. This gave Rupe pause—after all, he was in pigeon form—but one should not refuse the food of the gods. (Perhaps this ambivalence is why pigeons of today croak a bit when they talk.)

After an interval of polite small talk, Rupe tentatively approached the topic of his concern. He decided on an indirect question:

"How much news to you receive from the world below these days?"

Rehua smiled. He knew the course of Rupe's thoughts.

"She is on Motu-tapa," he replied, naming the Sacred Isle. "Fly there and listen for her voice."

On Motu-tapa, Hina-uri was nursing her newborn boy, whom she had conceived with Ihuatamai, when she noticed a crowd gathering below a pigeon sitting on a window sill of Tinirau's hut. Arms rose to hurl rocks, a noose, a spear at the bird, but it hopped spryly aside, dodging. She rose with the baby and went over to the spectacle.

As she approached, the pigeon noticed her and, dancing, sang with joy:

> "Hina-uri,
> Hina-uri is my sister,
> And Rupe is her brother,
> But how came he here?
> By travelling on the earth,
> Or flying through the air?
> Let your path be upwards through the air."

Recognizing the voice, Hina-uri replied,

> "Rupe is my brother,
> And Hina his young sister,
> But how came he here?
> By travelling on the earth,
> Or flying through the air?
> Let our path be upwards through the air
> To Rehua."

"Greetings, sister!" he said, studying her. "I take it you aren't happy here?"

"No."

"Then let us be aloft, to fly to a place of happiness." He scooped them up.

Afterwards, Rupe, Hina-uri, and her baby lived happily in the tenth heaven in Rehua's great house. Rupe kept things clean and orderly there, but one day he killed Kai-tangata, a son of Rehua, by accident. Rupe had added a building to Rehua's aerial compound, and this building contained a faulty beam. Kai-tangata leaned on it, and when it sprang back into place, it hit him so hard that he perished.

"He always was clumsy," reflected Rehua.

Some tragedies bring good fortune, however. When the afternoon grows old, the sun shines through the splashed red blood of Kai-tangata. People down below look up to admire the carmine colors of sunset.

For Reflection:

- Comment: In our psychological explorations of parental influence we often neglect that of siblings, yet our bonds with them often outlive our parents.

- How might one's mate turn into a "dog"?

- Why didn't Hina-uri tell her new husbands her former name? Why take on a new one?

- In personal myth work (see Chapter 13), a clear thematic link often surfaces between the names we come in with and whatever names we take on later in life. It's as though all our names color in various aspects of who we really are. What do your past and present names mean to you? What are their etymologies?

- What would be a contemporary psychological example of weaving the incantations that killed Harataunga and Horotata?

- Why all the doubled names and figures in this story?

- Is Hina-uri's brother Rupe a shaman? Why or why not?

- Rehua is a god of healing. What about this family needs healing? (Very often splits between siblings mirror splits running all through the family.)

- Why would Jung suggest that eating strange food in dreams and fantasies means a psychic step forward in one's development?

- What (if anything) might the behavior of Tinirau's people—throwing things at a bird, for example—suggest about Tinirau?

- What might conceiving and bearing a newborn indicate in myth and dream?

- Kai-tangata's name, Man-Eater, actually reflects the behavior of his wife Whaitiri, who was a cannibal. They split up because he refused to eat human flesh, yet the name stuck. What does this say about what our former relationships can leave us with?

- *In The Fellowship of the Ring*, Frodo wishes that his uncle Bilbo had killed the "vile creature" Gollum, who pursues Frodo to take back the Ring of Power. He adds, "He deserves death." The wizard Gandalf replies, "Deserves it! I daresay he does. Many that live deserve death. And some that die deserve life. Can you give it to them? Then do not be too eager to deal out death in judgment. For even the very wise cannot see all ends." How does this thought illuminate the roles of Tinirau and Kai-tangata?

Bujang Permai Dreams Big (West Sumatran)

Murti Bunanta, Indonesian president of the Society for the Advancement of Children's Literature, writer, educator, and storyteller:

> There are four religions in Indonesia: Islam, Christianity, Buddhism, and Hinduism. Nearly 90 percent of Indonesians are followers of the Islamic religion. Indonesia is not, however, an Islamic state. Religious tolerance and freedom of religion are guaranteed by the constitution and ensured by the *Pancasila* creed, so that Indonesians are free to follow their own faith.

Each ethnic group has its own *adat* or local custom which has been passed from generation to generation and influences the practice of religion. Many rituals are still performed and are an integral part of life. These might mark rites of passage, such as pregnancy, birth, marriage, death, anniversary, or circumcision, or they could mark such events as initiating a new building, celebrating the harvest, or honoring one's ancestors.

Traditional storytelling takes place everywhere throughout the archipelago. Each ethnic group has its own art of storytelling. These performances will last hours, beginning in the evening and continuing until dawn. In some cases a performance may continue over several nights.

"They must be dead," said Dahar. His two brothers nodded sadly.

Many days had passed since their mother and father had left to sell the crops they had grown. A flood had wrecked the bridge they had passed over. No word at all since then.

After the period of mourning, the three brothers packed their things and set out at daybreak to make their way in the world. At nightfall they reached an empty hut on the edge of a village. While resting there, they fell to talking about their dreams of the future.

"I want to farm," said Dahar, the eldest. "I plan to find a wealthy landlord and plant cassava, black pepper, beans, and other vegetables there. I will want for nothing."

"I," said Dahir, the middle brother, "will herd water buffaloes for their owner. I will drink their milk and eat their curds and be content."

At first Bujang Permai, the youngest, felt shy about confessing his dream for the future. After prodding by his brothers, he said, "I want to be a king, a good one so my queen and our people will be happy."

This did not sit well with the two older brothers. Was he mocking them? Or just pretentious?

"We did not suspect," replied Dahar, "that when we let you come along we were in the presence of royalty."

Rising quickly, the two tied Bujang Permai to a post. "Enjoy your reign over this hut," said Dahar, and with that, the two left their younger brother.

The brothers entered the village and began asking for work. Soon they were put in touch with a wealthy farmer who after speaking with them decided to hire them.

The overjoyed brothers bedded down in the hut he made available for them, but sleep eluded them. They felt guilty about leaving behind their younger brother. What if something bad happened to him while he was tied to that post? He must have learned his lesson by now. They decided to get permission in the morning to go back for him.

Unable to escape, Bjuang Permai had fallen asleep. In a dream, an old man in white with a beard that reached to the ground told him not to try to follow his brothers. "I will free you and leave you with seven sacred palm leaf ribs. Care well for them: they can revive the dead. When you awaken, pick up the leaves and follow the bird who will guide you. Here are the spells that make the palm leaf ribs work...."

When he woke, he found his bonds removed and the palm leaf ribs on the ground next to him. As he picked them up he heard the song of a bird call from outside the hut. He set out, following the bird wherever it flew and sang.

Not long after his departure, Dahar and Dahir entered the hut to free their brother and found him gone. After looking around for him, they sadly gave up and went back to the village to farm and herd buffalo.

* * * *

After three months of forest travel, guided by the bird, Bujang Permai came across a dead macaque. Reciting spells, he brushed the small body with the palm rib leaves and it stirred and sat up.

"Thank you," said the macaque. Small fingers handed him some incense. "Burn this if you ever need me, and I will come." The monkey darted off, glad to be alive.

Bujang Permai went on until he spotted a dead firefly. He revived it, and it too gave him incense. So did a restored squirrel, an ant, and an elephant. He was glad to have these friends of the forest.

After three years of travel he entered a village. While mingling with its people he picked up some local gossip. The king, he was told, had a daughter who was dying, and no one could cure her. Weary from travel, Bujang Permai found a comfortable tree just beyond the village and rested.

From there he said hello to a passing minister of state. The man looked worried. "I am searching all over this land," he confided, "to find a healer for the king's daughter, Princess Nilam Cahaya, but she is close to death and no one has been able to cure her."

"Let me try."

The minister had noted the stranger's rumpled hair and dirty garments, but he was desperate. "This way," he said.

As they approached the palace, a cry of grief went up from the people around it. "The Princess is dead!" someone moaned. The minister put his hands over his face.

"This is no time to give up," said Bujang Permai. "Bring me to her."

He stood over the lifeless princess for a moment as her family eyed him in astonishment. Who was this drifter?

"Everybody out," he said.

Once they had gone, he recited the spells and brushed the princess with the palm leaf ribs. Her eyes opened.

"Thank you," she said, sitting up. "You who have awakened me shall be my husband."

The king had promised this, so he could hardly go back on it. But he could delay it.

"I would ask three tasks of you," he told Bujang Permai, "before the wedding goes forward." They were: a small hill to be leveled, betel leaves to be plucked from a fragile vine-wrapped tree, and the

Princess herself to be picked out of a group of forty similar-featured and -dressed young women. "In the dark," specified the king.

That night, Bujang Permai burned incense.

The elephant and his burly friends made short work of the small hill, and the squirrel and macacque raced around the dying tree and got the betel leaves picked in no time.

Entering the dark room filled with Princess lookalikes, Bujang Permai waited until his friend the firefly landed on the nape of her neck. He took her hand.

The king need not have worried about his new prince, who made wise decisions, sought advice from the princess, judged fairly, and saw to the heart of complicated problems. His wisdom grew as the years passed.

When the old king died, the people embraced Bujang Permai as their king and Nilam Cahaya as their queen.

*   *   *   *

Although he had reached the summit of his dream, Bujang Permai liked to mingle with the people to hear their talk and gauge their mood. In the marketplace he overheard a farmer selling corn and, next to him, a herdsman with curds to sell. The men looked familiar. *Was it possible?* he wondered. *After all these years?*

"I will buy your corn and curds," Bujang Permai told them. "Please bring them to the palace tomorrow."

The following day, the farmer and herdsman delivered their goods as promised. They were surprised when the king invited them to stay for a meal and talk a bit.

"So are your parents still around?" the king asked after a time. "If so, they must be proud of how hard you work."

"We thought they had died," said Dahar as Dahir nodded. "A flood struck our village and washed out the bridge, but we found out after we had left that a neighbor saved their lives." The king was hard put to conceal his joy at this welcome news.

"Unfortunately," said Dahir sadly, "soon after that, we lost sight of our younger brother. We looked for him but could not find him."

Dahar nodded.

"A pity."

The king surprised them again by proposing to build their long-suffering parents a large new home. He would meet the brothers there when it was finished. They left almost too speechless to thank him for his grand favor on behalf of their humble family.

On the day the house stood ready for occupancy, the king made his way there and greeted the brothers and their aging parents. They gazed at him with awe and gratitude and thanked him again and again for his generosity.

"May I borrow that room for a moment?" he asked, pointing. "I wear these royal garments a lot and would like to get out of them." Once alone, he changed into old clothes of the cut he used to wear as a child.

When he came among them again they nearly fell over in astonishment. "Bujang Permai! You are here!"

After the joyful shock had diminished somewhat, his brothers begged his forgiveness. "We are so very sorry. We went back for you but could not find you."

"I know," he told them, "and I forgive you. What matters now is that we are reunited, that the past is gone, and that we three brothers obtained exactly what we dreamed of."

For Reflection:

- The motif of the visionary mistreated by siblings is a common one, as Cinderella, Psyche, and Joseph of the many-colored cloak could attest. What are the underlying family dynamics?

- How is it that, symbolically, the touch of a palm leaf could revive the dead?

- What are some psychological counterparts of a visitation by a deity in the midst of difficulties? Do the difficulties themselves somehow constellate the way beyond them?

- Why does the helpful deity appear here as an old man?

- What does the story say if we consider the revived animals aspects of the protagonist? What does it say if we think of him instead as *their* instrument?

- Although he went on a long journey of initiation, how does Bujang Permai fit the King archetype better than the Hero archetype?

- What does he learn from the three tasks imposed by the old king?

- Many of us might blame or laugh at the officials who fail to recognize the healer in the dusty drifter's garments, but might one of *his* life lessons be about aligning how he presents himself (Jung would say: his *persona*) with who he really is?

- What might healing the sick princess in the heart of the kingdom symbolize?

- What does it mean to follow one's bird?

Chapter Five: Love and Loss

Love and loss: how often they go together in life, in fable, in myth....

In myth love is primal and primary. It creates the cosmos and binds it together into a whole. Love is so comprehensive a force that no god claims it as sole specialization: all gods are involved in it in their own way.

Love is so open to a variety of expressions that in myth, everybody can love everybody. Gods change sex and gender at will, often just to be with each other. Heterosexuality sheds heteronormativity to take its humble place as one of many possible configurations of love and sex and eros.

Willingness to love, of course, means willingness to lose the beloved. In myth as in everyday life, love always comes with risk and often requires sacrifice.

Shaktishiva

Leela Namboothiripad (Sumangala), Indian writer, public relations officer, and storyteller:

> Usha [eldest daughter] made me an author. As a young girl, she wanted to hear a new story daily, while having dinner. I narrated stories from the books in my library. But when that got exhausted, I started writing stories for her.

> My first story was about a day in the life of Kurinji, the cat. In fact, a cat at our home was the inspiration. Cows, dogs, crows, squirrels...all the creatures in our neighbourhood became characters for my stories. They all thought and talked like human beings. Usha was eight then, now she is 61! Later on I had to come up with more stories for my younger children, Narayanan and Ashtamoorthy.

> My first work, *Kurinjiyum Koottukarum* [the story she first wrote for her daughter], was published in 1965 and I wrote for the magazine for many more years. It was not to make money. Rather, I enjoyed what I was doing. I realised that it was what I was destined to do.

The cosmic brow of Brahma crinkled in loneliness.

To Brahma's surprise and delight, a being sprang forth from that furrowed brow. Before the god stood Ardhanarishvara.

On the being's left side Brahma noted feminine curves, a rounded breast, a blue lotus suspended from the neck, and an arm with a hand holding a mirror. This half shone with golden light. The right half, glowing white, bore an erection, a muscular chest, a jeweled serpent at the neck, and a hand raised to offer a blessing.

Above broad shoulders draped with dhoti and sari, the Third Eye burned and beamed with such radiance that Brahma's admiring gaze turned aside.

"I," announced Ardhanarishvara, "am Prakriti and Purusha, Shakti and Shiva, left and right, life and death, creation and destruction, motion and rest, becoming and being, nature and void, energy and consciousness, many and one. I make the infinite finite."

Awed and inspired, Brahma went without nourishment and warmth and embraced the ascetic way for a few millennia. Perhaps for longer, or not, for Time did not yet exist.

"I am pleased," Ardhanarishvara told a much thinner Brahma, "that you have embraced the holy disciplines. I will repay them by giving you many companions, for I know of your great loneliness."

Down the middle split the god until two gods stood facing Brahma: Lady Shakti and Lord Shiva, Becoming and Being, Creativity and Rest.

They embraced each other lovingly and with great passion.

From Shakti ran forth three humming Threads along which the cosmos unfolded: Order, Movement, and Obscurity. From Shiva reached forth the mighty frame of Consciousness to hold it all. Thus threaded and framed, the universe shimmered into manifestation as they held each other tightly.

With this inspiration, Brahma descended to earth and opened like a clam into two sacred beings: Satarupa and Manu, who gave birth to all the burgeoning, scheming, fighting, and loving dynasties of human beings. In a later incarnation, Manu, tipped off by Vishnu, would save humanity from a terrible flood.

Shakti and Shiva yet long for each other. When they embrace, they remember that they are each other. As Ardhanarishwara they ensoul the world through which the lives of all beings cycle without end.

For Reflection:

- Mythology is rich in transgender deities: not only Brahma and Ardhanarishvara ("ard-hah-NAR-ish-vara") but Prajapati, Dvaya-Prithvi, Vishvarupa, Vaikuntha-Kamalaja, Atum, Purusha, Hermaphroditus,

Agdistis, Mercurius, Dionysus, Hymenaius, Kami-Musubi no Mikoto, Tiresias, and many, many others. What does gender and sex fluidity in myth suggest about how the Divine manifests in human beings? What patterns might this fluidity offer for human love?

- Why do some divine beings temporarily divide into multiple forms?

- Ardhanarishvara's inspiration of Brahma signals the motif of creation carried out in accord with a sacred archetypal blueprint. What would a sacred blueprint look like in oneself? In a family? A nation? Humanity?

- Comment: When this god presents her/himself as potentially halved, the Shakti/Prakriti side symbolizes the intelligence and creative wisdom embodied in the cosmos. In Hindu thought this embodiment of divine power partakes of the Three Gunas symbolized as threads that parallel Creation (*sattva*), preservation (*rajas*), and destruction (*tamas*). The threads recall the three Fate goddesses of Rome (the Fata), Germania (the Norns), and Greece (the Moirai: Clotho the spinner, Lachesis the allotter, and Atropos the Unalterable who cut the thread of life in due time).

- What does it mean for a god to perform austerities like an ascetic? Can gods learn?

- We usually think of self-division as pathological, but in myth it sometimes serves creative purposes. How might this be true inwardly? Culturally?

- Flood stories are common around the world. What might they signify psychologically?

Apollo and Hyacinth (Greek)

Giorgos Seferis, Greek poet, diplomat, and Nobel Prize winner:

In the tightly organized classical tragedies the man who exceeds his measure is punished by the Erinyes. And this norm of justice holds even in the realm of nature.

...When autumn approached, when there would be a rather strong wind, and the fishing barges would have to sail through rough weather, we would always be glad when they were at last anchored, and my mother would say to someone among the fishermen who'd gone out: "Ah, bravo, you've come through rough weather"; and he would answer: "Madam, you know, we always sail with Charon at our side." That's moving to me.

I don't consider that Aeschylus was making a propaganda play by putting the suffering Persians on stage, or desperate Xerxes, or the ghost of Darius, and so forth. On the contrary, there was human compassion in it. For his enemies. Not that he's not of course glad that the Greeks won the battle of Salamis. But even then he showed that Xerxes' defeat was a sort of divine retribution: a punishment for the hubris that Xerxes committed in flagellating the sea. Since his hubris was to flagellate the sea, he was punished exactly by the sea in the battle of Salamis.

Apollo tried not to love the beautiful young man. Was not Phoebus a god of healing? But no ambrosial magical medicine sufficed to cure his longing for Hyacinth.

No one is certain who the boy's parents were. Some say the Spartan king Amyclas and his wife Diomede; others, Oebalus or Eurotas. Be that as it may, his handsome features, fair face, and muscular body beneath his purple robe caught the eye of far-seeing Apollo one day.

Soon, Phoebus was seen teaching Hyacinth archery, then lyre-playing, then chariot-riding. "Be sure to come visit me," Apollo told him after showing him how to drive.

Soon the smitten god's affection flamed with such obvious light that it made the gods smile to see him carrying Hyacinth's fishing nets and gathering his hunting dogs for him. (Taking advantage of this, newly born Hermes made off with distracted Apollo's cattle, walking backwards in reversed shoes to hide the direction of the tracks.) Watching his beloved try the art of prophecy, Apollo felt tears of joy in eyes shining below his neglected hair.

Apollo was not the only one struck nearly mute by young Hyacinth, however. From afar, Zephyr the West Wind observed all this and grew jealous. He could do nothing, though, because Hyacinth clearly preferred Apollo's presence to all others.

Hyacinth seemed to excel at whatever he turned his hand to, including sports. Whenever he trained, he had only to turn his head to see his biggest heavenly fan admiring him from the sidelines.

On a sunny, breezy day, the two went out to practice throwing the discus. They walked off from each other to make room. "Like this," said Phoebus, putting his legs, back, and arm into the throw as the disc shot from his hand.

At that moment, alas, envious Zephyr, having inhaled, blew the discus off course. Hyacinth was already running to retrieve it when it struck his forehead a sickeningly solid blow.

Apollo ran toward him even as he went down, but he was dead by the time the god arrived at his side. Beyond the reach of all healing, the soul of Hyacinth had fled to the world of shades.

Apollo held him and wept in great wrenching heaves of sorrow. "I am so sorry, Hyacinth," he said when he could speak. "My error has stolen your youth and your life. Where did I go wrong? Was it wrong to love you, teach you, play with you? I wish I could die in your place so that you would awaken and smile once again."

Laying the body back to the earth, he kissed it and placed his hand over its heart. "I cannot revive you, but I shall celebrate your life and your death in song. And I will use my powers to make your memory rise up and blossom like Spring itself."

As he spoke, the blood of his beloved gathered itself up into a purple flower. On its lovely leaves were inscribed "Ai, Ai," the sounds of sorrow made by bereft Phoebus, who watered it, like repentant Zephyr, with glittering teardrops.

For Reflection:

- What does it mean to be pursued by Apollo?

- Apollo is called Phoebus because of his sunlike character, and yet he is never lucky in love. For example, Daphne, whom he pursued, turned into a tree to avoid him. Why would someone spurn Apollo?

- *Hyacinthus* is Greek for a different flower, possibly the larkspur. What qualities are both flowers known for?

- How could the west wind's love turn so easily to a desire to kill the beloved?

- From the standpoint of the Fates, why did Hyacinth die?

- Why can't Apollo, a god of healing, revive Hyacinth?

- Why does Apollo see the death in terms of his own failure rather than as an accident?

- We tend to think of falling and being in love as permanent, perhaps because we feel the force of the Fates in it. What does this story suggest about time and love?

Oisin's Last Journey (Irish)

Liz Weir, Irish storyteller, librarian, and writer:

> My mum was pretty good at telling stories and I used to hear about her adventures; they [her family] lived in different places in the world. Also, there was no TV when I was growing up until I was eight or nine, and so families talked to each other.
>
> In 1985 I started an adult storytelling group at the

Linenhall Library called The Yarn Spinners, and I had a dream that one day there would be story telling groups all over Ireland. That dream has sort of come true; there are now the Tullycarnet Yarn Spinners, the Dublin Yarn Spinners, the Cork Yarn Spinners, there's a group in Castlerock now as well.

When we started off the Troubles were at their height, and somebody would get up and tell a story about an Orange Lodge dinner, and somebody else would tell a story about going to Mass. The fact was we were all listening to each other's stories, and respecting each other's stories, and I think that's very important. If you listen to someone's story, you're giving the utmost respect.

It was not easy to join the Fianna.

To become one of the wandering warriors who defended the High Kings of Ireland required extensive training and perfect success passing difficult tests. If you swung spear or sword unsteadily, broke a branch underfoot while running through the forest, fell into the hands of pursuing warriors, failed to leap over a bough at eye height or roll under one at knee height, or sustained a wound while standing in a hole warding off spears with a wooden shield, you were out.

You had to live off the land, hunt silently and expertly, track an animal—or a man—rapidly without stirring a bough. You had to give up loyalty to your home clan and pledge your life to the king you defended, fighting by the side of your hereditary enemies when the king required it. And you had to be a poet: not a mere versifier, but educated, enchanting, and eloquent.

Oisin was not only Ireland's greatest poet, he was the son of Fianna leader Fionn mac Cumhail. Before he was born, Oisin's mother Sadbh had been turned into a deer by an evil magician; when Fionn let her go during a hunt, she changed back into a human and bedded down with him. He stayed with her until the magician, whose name was Fer Doirich, changed her back into a deer. She walked into the forest again, but not before giving birth to Oisin, whose name means "Little Fawn." As a young man, Oisin still bore the lock of hair where his mother had licked his forehead.

When he applied to the Fianna, he expected and received no favoritism for being Fionn's son. He trained hard and possessed the three ideal qualities of a Fian: strength of limb, purity of heart, and agreement of speech and act. Passing all tests, he joined the Fianna, with whom he faced much danger and undertook many adventures.

One afternoon, after an unusually bountiful if wearying hunt in the forest, Oisin's fellow hunters felt so tired that they left him and his three dogs to look after the game and went home. He sat wondering what to do when a strange sight gave him pause.

As far as he could tell, in the distance was a being with a pig's head and a woman's body. She approached. Not wanting to be rude, Oisin stood but shifted his gaze to the pile of game at his feet.

"A pity to leave all this," he said, "but I have no way to get it back to camp."

"I can help you carry it," said a pleasing feminine voice. "Tie it up into two bundles. I will shoulder one and you the other."

Oisin did this, and they went off into the forest together.

The day remained warm even as the sun dipped toward the invisible horizon. The walk was a long one. Finding a large rock, "Let us rest," suggested Oisin.

They sat. When she fanned herself with her top to cool herself, Oisin glimpsed a comely form beneath.

"How came you to bear the head of a pig?"

"My father, the king of Tir na Nog, the Land of Youth, was told one day by a druid that he would be supplanted by a son-in-law. Fearing this, my father touched my face with a magic wand, and this was the result. The druid told me, though, that if I married a son of Fionn mac Cumhail, I would get my original head back."

"Our meeting is no coincidence, then," stated Oisin, glancing over at her.

"No. It's not as though you're hard to look at or talk with, though."

"What is your name?"

"Niamh of the Golden Hair. Are you sure you want to go through with this?"

He smiled. "And miss the chance to see your original face?"

* * * *

No sooner had the druid spoken the rites than sea-green eyes set in a lovely face looked steadily back at him. "Thank you," she said.

"My pleasure."

"But, my love," she continued, "if you want to stay with me, we cannot remain here." At this a white horse approached, neighing as it caught sight of Niamh. It lowered its head to let her hand rest upon its nose.

"This horse," she introduced them, "brought me here from the Land of Youth. Are you willing to ride there with me? You will love it there, and you shall never grow old."

"I will follow wherever you go."

Bidding goodbye to his sad father, and waving farewell to his loyal Fian brothers, Oisin mounted and rode off with his bride.

The scenery quickly grew unfamiliar. Past shimmering peaks and plateaus of dream they rode, traversing meadows of bright grass under golden suns and bright moons and strange constellations.

"I do not recognize these places," remarked Oisin.

"We ride between the worlds, love," she replied, her arms around his waist.

In the courtyard of her father's castle they dismounted and asked to see him. He came running, a look of joy upon his face. To Oisin's surprise he knelt to Niamh:

"I apologize," he told her, taking her hand and kissing it. "I should never have inflicted that spell upon you. Please forgive me."

"I do," she said. "Please meet Oisin, my husband."

The three talked long that evening while enjoying a celebratory feast in honor of Niamh's return and marriage. At a suitable moment, the king brought up the matter of the succession:

"The seventh year is upon us," he told them, "and tomorrow the champions assemble to see who can run the fastest."

"Surely that is not what decides who claims the throne?" said Oisin.

"No, it is a preliminary. An important one, though."

Oisin had not joined the Fianna by disliking tests. On the following morning he outran his competitors and reached and sat down in the designated chair on the hill before anyone else could reach it.

After that, no one would compete for the office. When the old king passed away, Oisin was crowned.

*   *   *   *

Oisin was happy in the Land of Youth. He hunted in green forests, fished in clear streams, and composed songs of love to make his wife happy. The game was plentiful, the sun bright, the breezes never frigid. Nobody aged, grew sick, or died. Laughter was abundant.

Oisin was happy except in his dreams, which were filled with the faces of friends, family, comrades in arms, places he had known. How long had he been gone? About three years, he figured, judging from the pangs of homesickness.

"I want to go back for a visit," he told Niamh one day. She shook her head.

"You have been away for longer than you think. There is nothing and no one there for you anymore."

"I must see for myself. Just one visit."

After a long, thoughtful, and rather ominous pause, she whistled. Her white horse ambled up.

She kissed Oisin but looked worried as he mounted.

"Be sure you never, ever, dismount while you are there," she warned him with a serious tone. "If you set foot on your native land, you will die."

"I'll be back," he said and rode off. She gazed after him for a long time.

When he reached the vicinity of his father's home, he found nothing but wreckage long overgrown with moss and vines. Puzzled, he rode in widening circles but saw no familiar landmarks. What had happened?

"You there," he called to a man walking up a trail. "Where is Fionn mac Cumhail? Where are the Fianna?"

The man looked at him as though he were crazy.

"You must be from elsewhere," the man said after a pause. "The Fianna are long gone, and old Fionn has been dead for three hundred years. All that remain of any of them are legends."

How could this be? Oisin wondered. His friends, brothers, family: all passed away into oblivion?

I will ride to Tara, he decided, *and ask the High King himself.*

On his way there he was about to pass a gang of men making a road at Gleann-Na-Smól when one asked, "Would you help us lift this big stone out of our path and into the wagon?"

A Fian always responded to the call of service. Oisin dismounted, took one step, and fell to the ground. In three minutes he aged three hundred years.

As the astonished workmen gathered around, a priest came up and knelt, looking down at what seemed like a skull with white hair. The wrinkled mouth wheezed.

Quickly, Oisin told his story to the priest, who said, "I will remember it."

As the darkness closed upon him, Oisin's last thought was of Niamh.

For Reflection:

- What does it mean to be loved by a goddess? To love a goddess?

- Why a pig's head? Does it have to do with Oisin ("oh-SHEEN") being mothered by a doe?

- Fionn mac Cumhail ("finn mac cool") ate of the Salmon of Knowledge and became one of the Fianna's greatest heroes. His son Oisin seems to follow in his footsteps (as will Oisin's son Oscar), but only to a point. Beyond loving Niamh, why is Oisin so willing to give up a heroic life and family legacy?

- What would Jung say about Tir na Nog ("TEER nah nohg")?

- Unpack the symbolism of being crowned.

- In what ways is the imaginal journey to the Land of Youth literalized and commercialized in your culture?

- Heraclitus wrote that one can't step into the same river twice. Can the gods really know this truth of our mortality, or only mortals?

- Why was Oisin safe so long as he stayed mounted?

- How would you interpret Oisin's stay in the Land of Youth: getting lost in fantasy? Mystic journeying? Should he have gone there at all? Would you have?

- In a Russian tale of Ivan Savelevich, the protagonist, who winds up with a *rusalka*, a river fairy, is never able to return to his homeland, not even for a visit. How is this different psychologically from Oisin's fate?

- King Arthur's knight Ewain ("You-when") falls in love with the magical Lady of the Fountain, but, with help from a lion, he brings her to Camelot instead of remaining permanently in her realm. Speculate on why Ewain is able to bridge the realms instead of ending up like Oisin.

- Another contrast: A Maori tale tells of the chief Tura marrying Turaki-hau, a woman of the Aitanga (Fairies), who tells him she must die when she gives birth to their son. He prevents her from dying but must leave the Otherworld and grow old in this one until his son, now a man, fetches him back. What principle of exchange between worlds does this imply?

Izanagi and Izanami (Japanese)

Hayao Kawai, Jungian analyst, clinical psychologist, writer, and head of the Japanese Agency for Cultural Affairs:

> Reality consists of countless layers. Only in daily life does it appear as a unity with a single layer which will never threaten us. However, deep layers can break through to the surface before our eyes. Fairy tales have much to tell us in this regard: the mansion that suddenly appeared and the beautiful lady who lived there are good examples of that type of experience. Heroes of fairly tales often encounter curious existences when they have lost their way or when they have been left by their parents.
>
> I try to make it clear that the main thrust of Japanese fairly tales [and myths] is aesthetic rather than ethical. Japanese fairy tales convey to us what is beautiful instead of what is good.
>
> The image of the sole ego and its integration was born of Western Christian culture, while Japanese can imagine the existence of multiple egos. This multiplicity may be more effective and flexible vis-a-vis future society which will include more diversity. Isn't having all kinds of consciousness—including senex, puer, male and female—the very way to establish wholeness?

His beloved was dead.

In the primal time, the two of them had stood on the celestial floating bridge while he, Izanagi, stirred his jeweled spear in the watery chaos. Glistening drops falling from the tip formed Onogoro, the first island. They coupled there.

She, Izanami, gave birth to the islands of Japan and to their valleys, hills, rivers, waterfalls, trees, winds, and rice. A new world was growing into being before their eyes.

But then Izanami gave birth to the dangerous fire god Kagutsuchi, and by doing so was burned by his flames. In anger, Izanagi slashed him with a sword, and the flying splashes of blood took heavenly form as the Milky Way.

Deities continued to pour from the womb of Izanami, but the strain of it all was too much for her, and she finally lay back lifeless. Izanagi wept as her spirit fled down to Yomitsu Kuni.

"It cannot end this way," he said to himself. "I will go down after her and bring her back to life."

He found her shade standing near the entrance to the Underworld. She was difficult to make out, but he sensed her familiar presence. They greeted one another.

"I have come for you," he said.

"I will see if the gods here approve of releasing me," she told him, "but I have eaten Underworld food, so it is unlikely." Sensing his frustration with the darkness: "Please do not look at me while I am about this."

Yearning to see her, Izanagi waited until she lay down to sleep. Then, disregarding what she had told him, he ignited a torch so he could gaze upon her. To his horror he beheld decaying, maggot-covered flesh. She woke suddenly at the light.

"You have shamed me!" she cried. He dropped the torch and ran. Behind him, she summoned an army of ghostly hags and warriors to pursue him.

Led by Ugly Night Spirit, they howled as they came, gaining on him. As he ran he pulled the right and left combs from his hair and dropped them. By the time Ugly Night Spirit reached them they had shot forth into appetizing grapevines and bamboo shoots. The monster forgot about his prey and stopped to stuff them into his mouth.

Izanagi fled so rapidly that he reached the surface in time to roll an enormous boulder over the opening to block the world of the dead from reaching that of the living. As he wedged it in place, he felt Izanami's dark presence approach the barrier and stop.

"I want a divorce," he called out.

"If you do not return, I will slay a thousand of the living every day until you do." And so death came into the world.

"Very well. I will raise up a thousand and five hundred every day." And so life replenishes what dies.

To purify himself from contact with the dead, Izanagi bathed in a stream. Deities emerged from his cast-off clothes. From his left eye the sun goddess Amaterasu shone forth, from his right eye silvery Tsukiyomi the moon, and from his nose emerged tricky Susano.

"You will inherit the world," he told them. "Rule it wisely."

For Reflection:

- Izanami means "She Who Invites," and Izanagi "He Who Invites." What do they invite?

- The motif of the woman asking her mate not to look at some aspect of her hidden life, and turning away in shame when he does, occurs frequently in mythology, Japanese mythology and folklore in particular. What might it signify?

- In a Greek myth, Orpheus loses his wife Eurydice to a poisonous serpent bite. Following her into the Underworld, he plays his lyre so beautifully that he persuades Hades and Persephone to release her back to life, but on one condition: that as Hermes guides them up the steps to the daylight, Orpheus not look back at her. Just before they reach the surface, the sound of her footsteps behind him stops; he turns to see if she is still there, and her spirit flies back down below. Never at peace with this, he plays sad songs on his lyre for the rest of his life. How are the Japanese and Greek versions of this widespread tale different?

- When Hades abducts Persephone, she solidifies her tie to the Underworld by eating a pomegranate seed. Izanami too eats in the nether realm. What does it mean to ingest the food of death?

- What is the symbolic significance of grapevines and

bamboo shoots?

- Can you think of a time when you unwisely went back to a former lover, or tried to, and all hell broke loose? What constellates this commotion? What is its message?

- What happens to us when we fail to mourn a loss and instead maintain a fantasy (usually unconscious) of getting back or restoring what we lost?

- Widely considered the first true science fiction novel, Mary Shelley's *Frankenstein* is told by a doctor in pursuit of the old dream of immortality. What can his story and the tale of Izanagi and Izanami tell us about the consequences of such a pursuit? (In the inaccurately titled 1994 film *Mary Shelley's Frankenstein*, the doctor tries to revive his betrothed after the monster kills her. It doesn't work out well.)

Aphrodite, Persephone, and Adonis (Greek)

Constantine Petrou Photiades Cavafy, Greek poet and journalist:

> On hearing about powerful love, respond, be moved
> like an aesthete. Only, fortunate as you've been,
> remember how much your imagination created for you.
> This first, and then the rest—the lesser loves—
> that you experienced and enjoyed
> in your life: the more real and tangible.
> Of loves like these you were not deprived.

By the time Aphrodite found the infant beneath the myrrh tree, his history had already grown complicated.

His mother Myrrha, daughter of Cinyras, the King of Cyprus, had boasted of being more beautiful than Aphrodite. The goddess of beauty and sexual love reacted to this act of hubris by inflaming

Myrrha with a desire for her own father. Dressing up as an erotic priestess, Myrrha lay with Cinyras and conceived Adonis.

When the king realized why she was pregnant, he drew his knife and ran after her until, panting, she asked the gods for help. They converted her into a myrrh tree; and Cinyras, disgraced, killed himself.

In pity, Aphrodite picked up the parentless child and carried him down to Hades, where she persuaded Queen Persephone to raise him. She handed him over with a certain reluctance. He radiated a refreshing, giggling joyfulness.

After a span of years, Aphrodite recalled the pretty baby and came calling to ask how he was doing. Adonis, now a handsome young man, looked back at her and smiled.

Wow, thought Aphrodite, who had been nicked by an arrow of her son Eros.

She had never been known for indirectness. "Would you like to come with me?" she asked him, smiling back. He blushed, warming her blood even more.

"Or would you like to stay with me?" asked Persephone in a jealous tone.

"*I* found him!" insisted Aphrodite.

"And *I* looked after him while you were out chasing other prey...."

To Adonis's confusion, the argument got very ugly indeed. Aphrodite's eyes emitted red and gold sparks; Persephone's throne vibrated as the caverns around them rumbled.

"Stop this!" called down a deep masculine voice. A peal of thunder cracked and rolled as an eerie white light filled the cavern.

"Adonis," declared Allfather Zeus, "will spend four months with Persephone, four months with Aphrodite, and four months with whomever he chooses."

The goddesses agreed. The mutual glare subsided. Adonis sighed with relief.

Once in the world above again, the young man found the charms of Aphrodite so irresistible that he spent the other four months with her too. This did not make Persephone happy, but there was little she could do about it.

*   *   *   *

When Adonis, a shepherd, was not with Aphrodite or tending his flocks, he loved to hunt. Knowing this, she began to accompany him. Soon, however, she sensed that spending so much time with him took her away from her divine responsibilities.

Growing aware that erotic connections were failing in heaven and on earth, "I must leave your side for a time," she informed him; "but remember this: Beware of any animal that charges you without fear." She kissed him and vanished.

He made his way deep into the forest, following a set of unusually large tracks until he heard a grunting snuffling. Looking up, he beheld the biggest boar he had ever seen. What a prize it would make!

Disregarding Aphrodite's warning (what did she know about hunting anyway?), he lifted his sharpened spear and leaped forward just as the boar charged him.

No one ever found out Who wore the flesh of the boar. Some guess Artemis, who held a grudge because of Aphrodite's indirect responsibility for the death of Hippolytus, who spurned love in favor of hunting and horsemanship and was trampled by his own horses. Others point to Ares, who saw much less of Aphrodite after she rediscovered Adonis. Still others suggest Apollo, angry for Aphrodite's blinding of his son, Erymanthus, who spotted her making love with Adonis one day.

Hearing Adonis cry out, Aphrodite dashed back to him, but it was too late. The boar had castrated him, and he lay dying in agony. Even as she clasped him to her, his spirit fled to the Underworld. Weeping, she turned the drops of his blood into blooming anemones.

Naturally, Persephone was very happy to see Adonis again, but she frowned when Aphrodite appeared. "I'm here to bring him back," she stated.

Persephone glared at her. "A bit too late for that."

The fighting started again. Again, the Allfather made a decision:

"I will restore Adonis to life," he said, "on one condition: that he spend six months with each of you to preserve the balance." They agreed.

You might have noticed the ever-cycling absence and abundance of vines and grains through the seasons of the year. You can tell by these when Adonis is visiting Aphrodite and when he stays below to be with Persephone.

For Reflection:

- Adonis resembles the earlier Phrygian shepherd god Attis, a consort of Cybele abandoned in infancy. While marrying a king's daughter, he was driven mad by Cybele and castrated himself under a pine tree, although a Lydian version tells of his castration by a boar. In another variant, he made love to a river god's daughter and was turned by Cybele into a fir tree. Archetypally, he reappears as Osiris, Orpheus, Iacchus, Dionysus, and Jesus ("I am the vine, you are the branches"), born in Bethlehem ("House of Bread"). Why is this grain and vine god always symbolically dismembered and reborn?

- Aphrodite and her sisters across pantheons (including Venus, Astarte, Lakshmi, Enya, Inanna, Freya, Yao Ji, and Xochiquetzal) are often known as love goddesses, but as this tale makes clear, their style of love is primarily aesthetic, concrete, and erotic. *Every* goddess and god demonstrates their own style of love. How is Persephone's different from Aphrodite's?

- Why does Zeus intervene? Patriarchal pushiness, or something more?

- How might one respond to being pulled on by two different but equally demanding archetypal principles?

- Why a boar?

- What ultimately stabilizes the three-way relationship?

Hi'iaka Teaches Pele a Lesson (Hawaiian)

Lopaka Kapanui, Native Hawaiian storyteller and haunted locale tour guide:

> I have to tell the story that's appropriate with the location, you know, no matter what it is…. People have to know about the physical, the geographical history of that place, and the spiritual history, why it's haunted. But before I begin any tour there's a protocol where you have to do a chant in Hawaiian that asks for permission and where you announce your intentions to the unseen.

> I ask permission of each spot we go to, and I do it every time.

> Considering the condition of the world and how we're so caught up in the media and music and all this other stuff, we've forgotten as human beings how to talk to one another, and communicate instead of doing it through text messages and through email and instant messages. We've got to get back to this one-on-one face-to-face communication, and I think the best way to propagate that is through storytelling.

"Don't disturb me," Pele told her sisters, "or I'll burn the place down."

They knew she meant it. Even the skies and clouds attended when Pele's hot flows of lava steamed across the islands, remaking them, before pouring into the sea with a loud hiss.

The Pele who lay down in her cinder-rimmed cavern—red eyes, smoking hair, fire-blackened skin—was not in appearance the comely young Pele who awakened as a spirit in Kauai to watch the dancers at the festival there. Entering the sacred hall, she glanced around the room. Her eye immediately fastened on the young chief

Lohi'ai. Between them an invisible flash of lightning crossed the room.

Making their way to each other, they sat down among the celebrants and spoke over the music:

"Care for something to eat?" he asked, waving his hand at delicacies on nearby tables. She shook her head.

"You clearly aren't from here," he noted.

"No, from much farther...."

Eventually they moved their conversation into his home, where they talked and flirted for hours. In spite of himself, the normally self-controlled chief found his heart swelling for her. It was as though he had known her always, yet he had just met her.

When he gestured to his sleeping mat she shook her head.

"I will bring you to Hawaii, my home," she said. "Only then."

He kissed her goodnight and she walked out into the night. Once beyond the circle of firelight she drifted into dark mist and floated home.

Lovestruck Lohi'ai could not get Pele out of his mind. He waited....and waited...and waited. Then he looked for her. Then he sent servants to look for her. Try as he would, though, he could not find her. She must have been playing with him, he decided. She was gone.

His servants found him dead, therefore, swinging from the ridgepole of his home. Cutting him down, they wrapped him in his robes and mourned the end of his short life.

Pele slept on. So long did she sleep that finally Hi'iaka, her favorite sister, decided to awaken her. She chanted over Pele's pale form until the goddess opened her eyes and sat up.

"I met the most beautiful man..." Pele muttered. Turning to her sisters, she asked, "Who among you will go to Kauai and bring Lohi'ai to me?"

They were silent. Much danger awaited out there — and here as well, for Pele's jealousy was legendary.

"I will go," said Hi'iaka, the youngest.

"Very well," said Pele. "But be warned: you are not to touch him, not to seduce or be seduced by him. You have forty days to bring him here."

"I agree," replied Hi'iaka, "on two conditions: that I go on the journey with special protection, and that you will not harm my friend Hopoe by burning up her lehua groves while I'm gone."

"Agreed," said the goddess prone to unpredictable fiery outbursts. Receiving a powerful blessing from her, Hi'iaka set out with Palauopalae of the Ferns and, meeting pale Wahine'oma'o on the way, went forth into territory controlled by demons, dragons, sea serpents, and various threshold guardians. She of the Magic Skirt slew them as they attacked her and, with her two former lovers mopping up stray threats, went her way.

Upon arriving at the village in Kauai, she learned that the chief had died of love-struck grief for the mysterious woman who had visited him at the festival.

"Take me to him."

Kneeling over him in the mountain cave where they had placed him, Hi'iaka chanted until his soul, thin and wan, at last reentered his body.

I can see why Pele likes him, she thought as she worked through the night to restore the chief of the island. Even in uneasy slumber he held the bearing and magnetism of one born to stand out.

* * * *

As they approached Hawaii on the return trip, Hi'iaka felt an ominous sense of concern. Because of the restoration ceremonies they had not been able to keep the forty-day time limit. That was bad. She hoped Pele had stayed in a favorable mood.

"Wait here," she told Lohi'ai and dashed forward to look upon the lehua grove where her friend resided.

She topped a rise and saw before her blackened desolation. The full retaliatory fire of Pele had burned the ground, the trees, and what remained of poor Hopoe. Smoke rose from piles of ash where greenery had grown.

This was too much. Returning to Lohi'ai, Hi'iaka took his hand and led him to a height upon Hahoalii she knew to be regularly observed by Pele. They sat under a surviving lehua tree to rest.

As Pele and her other sisters watched, Hi'iaka put a wreath around the handsome chief's neck and leaned toward him provocatively.

"Isn't it nice here?" she asked, placing a palm on his thigh. "Such a view, and best enjoyed in good company." His heart beat rapidly. On the journey an attraction to her had added itself to his gratitude. He leaned toward her as her arm went around his neck.

"Look!" cried one of Pele's sisters, "she's kissing him!"

Pele pretended to turn away, trying not to look.

"They're laying back in the grass!"

She growled. The ground beneath them rumbled.

"They—oh my..."

Her eyes turned red. "Burn them!" she roared. Nobody stirred. Fine. She would.

Seeing fire and smoke streaming downhill toward him, Lohi'ai guessed what had happened and uttered his death chant. As he finished the lava poured over him, killing him. Hi'iaka uttered a cry of grief.

Pele wasn't through. She had raised enough fire to incinerate the entire island when the god Kane swept down and stood before her with a palm held out toward her. He had always been able to talk her into calmness, and he did so again.

Gradually, the fires subsided, and the smoke dimmed and dispersed. The red glow left Pele's eyes. She exhaled deeply and sat down with her sisters.

Just then a magician of renown walked into view. He had been with the travelers. He climbed down to where the sisters sat and faced Pele.

"What do you want?" she asked.

The magician was not deflected by the abrupt question. "To know why my friend Lohi'ai has had to die twice."

"Twice? What do you mean? When was the first time?"

"He died once already at home, pining for a lovely visitor. Hi'iaka revived him."

Pele looked at her.

"It's quite true," Hi'iaka said, bolder after all her adventuring.

"We were late because it took so long to bring him back to life. And you have killed him again."

"You broke your vow! I saw you lie down with him!"

"I was paying you back for killing my friend Hopoe and burning up the grove."

Pele ground her teeth. She hated it when one of her rages turned out like this.

"Let us summon my brother Kane-milo-hai," she suggested.

By then, Lohi'ai's spirit had flown far out over the sea; but, coming fast in a shell canoe, Kane-milo-hai caught it in his magical net and brought it back to Hawaii.

It took time for him to melt the hardened lava around the body and breathe life and spirit back in, but at length, and with the magician's help, Lohi'ai sat up again and blinked, gazing around.

"You must choose," Pele told him. "Which of us do you want to be with? Me or my sister Hi'iaka?"

"Hi'iaka," he said, looking fondly at the youngest sister, who looked fondly back.

Pele sighed. "This isn't the first time my anger has driven everyone away," she muttered.

"Not everyone."

Looking up in surprise, she saw an alluring smile on the magician's face. It made him very handsome.

For Reflection:

- It's striking how often mythic characters personify natural forces. The lava of volcanic Pele ("PAY-lay") endlessly creates and reshapes Hawaii as her younger sister Hi'iaka ("hee-ee-YAK-ah") manages the clouds above and the hula dances below. Hopoe ("hoh-POH-eh"), whose name means "to encircle," looks out for the trees and their groves, and Lohi'ai ("low-HEE-aye") might be thought of as the spirit or soul of Kauai (possibly meaning "Around the Neck" like an arm, and nicknamed "Beautiful Island"). What does the story reveal, then, about the ecology of Hawaii?

- Many families include a reactively angry person who bullies and dominates others. Living with such a person feels like having to walk on eggshells in constant fear of setting off an explosion. Does Pele remind you of anyone in your past or present relationships? Of yourself at times?

- Is it possible that Pele favors her youngest sister because Hi'iaka is the only one who will stand up to her?

- What might Lohi'ai's change of affection from Pele to Hi'iaka say about the relational consequences of rage?

- Those of us who harbor anger but fear it often subtly and effectively impel outbursts in others. Could Hi'iaka harbor unconscious anger of her own toward her friend Hopoe? Was mentioning her to Pele a set-up for incineration?

- Sometimes feeling drawn to someone is the deep psyche's way of bringing people together for some kind of soul work. What could Lohi'ai's and Pele's attraction to each other—literalized into romantic longing by both—have made possible that would not have happened otherwise?

- The idea of bringing someone back from death is literalized today in body-freezing schemes and efforts to upload and virtualize consciousness out of the body. What does resurrection mean psychologically?

- What lessons might angry Pele learn from how events turned out?

Guinevere and Arthur (French, English)

Graham Langley, British storyteller, folklorist, educator, arts activist, and promoter:

My first intention when starting into storytelling was to tell traditional English tales…received from my father and others. But things got skewed and I gathered repertoire like a rolling stone.

The experiences in many folktales have at one and the same time an individual and a universal meaning. It is this link between individual response and universal meaning that gives traditional tales their power as a teaching tool.

A lot of old stories have some wonderful truths in them for adults as well as children. And almost anyone can tell a story. It doesn't cost and it is interactive.

I have a great appreciation of the creative capacity of all people—not just children. Storytelling inspires them, allows them to speak—to know what they say is valued.

When she heard the clop-clop-clop of hooves, she knew somehow it was Arthur. His armor creaked once as he dismounted.

She stood, took a breath, and held herself erect as befitted a queen. A soft knock on the heavy wooden door. *An oddly gentle sound to announce so absolute a liege*, she thought.

"Come in."

He did, bowing.

"My lady." He had removed his helm so they could look each other in the face. Even so, she was never sure of the color of his eyes.

"My lord."

After a moment of silence, he said:

"I have come to take my leave of you. I do not know how much news you have here, but Mordred has gained control of Camelot. I ride now to meet him in battle. I have a feeling I won't be back."

She nodded. Mordred had made his move almost as soon as the

king and his men had departed to run down Lancelot. Arthur had returned post haste from France to the Land of Logres to defend what was left of his kingdom.

"What are your chances against Mordred?" she asked.

"I do not know. Many knights have already fallen. Gareth... Gaheris... Gawain... Lamorak.... Dinadan.... Agravain...." He shook his head sadly.

"May God grant you victory."

"Thank you, milady."

"....and me forgiveness. I am sorry."

He stared. "For what?"

"For Lancelot. For running away. For all of it."

"God give you peace," he said, "but it is I who am sorry."

He began to pace, and Guinevere nearly smiled. An old habit of his when he felt uncomfortable. She waited while he assembled his thoughts.

"From the time I drew the sword from the stone," he began, "duty obsessed me. I was so young and confused. 'Take charge,' Merlin told me, but I didn't know how. My father was dead, and everything was falling apart.

"So I fought and rallied men and tried to keep alive the vision of Camelot. When you brought us the Round Table so we could all assemble as equals, I included you in our knightly meetings, but not in my innermost stronghold"—he pointed at his heart. "The drawbridge stayed up and the gates closed."

He cleared his throat. "And then Lancelot came. He was so good, so strong, so chivalrous, a better man than even Sir Tristam. Our ideal, on the back of a horse. Our truest brother. How could you *not* love him? He was there in the flesh. And I? I was chasing my vision."

He finished one circle and began pacing out another. "When the rumors began, I ignored them. How naive I was, but not only about the two of you. In my innocence, I let everyone else carry the sides of me that did not fit my notions of the dutiful king: Lancelot my passion, Gawain my impetuosity, Galahad my piety. Agravain my discontent. Mordred my malice...

"When I finally admitted to myself what was happening, I turned against my former friend and cast him out of the kingdom. I paid no attention while Mordred, who seemed an ally, worked against me. Worst of all, I let Mordred and Agravain convince me that a private matter was a crime against the state. It was Mordred's idea to ambush Lancelot, and hot Gawain's to war upon him; I went along with all of it, refusing to back down even when I wanted to because king and law must always be right.

"All I saw was principles, not people; and in forsaking people I turned away from principles, from good counsel, from Camelot, our dream of unity, and from you...."

His pacing had brought him back in front of the queen. He looked her in the face again and saw the tears in her eyes.

"You were always so insufferably *good*, Arthur," she told him. "Even as a young man you were. But how can one stay married to the sun?"

He nodded. "So here I stand, the dutiful king, as everything I fought and bled for falls into chaos beneath the ruddy dragon on my battle standards, and speak of this to the one person I should have confided in all along. I am most heartily sorry, Guinevere." He took her hand, kissed it.

After a long silence, he walked toward the door, but then stopped and turned back to her with a rueful, self-deprecating smile that tore her heart:

"You know, I've often thought that, when history was done with us, I could be, not the king of Camelot anymore, not the shining example for all to behold, but just your husband, and you could be, not the great queen, not the wise woman of the realm, but just my wife. We could go away together and laugh at whatever people said and wrote about us. So much for dreams, eh? So much for dreams..."

After the door shut she stood staring at where he had been.

As he had spoken, a stirring, a warmth, had broken out unexpectedly in her heart. She had always admired him, the visionary, the leader, the brave warrior, the charismatic speaker; but it dawned on her that she actually loved the man she had never suspected lived inside the robe and breastplate of the king.

How did I not see him? she wondered. Had he hidden himself, as he had said, or had she never really looked? And now, he — a man after all — was leaving her, with nothing left for him but to die for his falling kingdom....

She pulled open the door and ran out across the flagstones. A sharp, chill breeze stirred her white mendicant's robes.

"Arthur!" she called to the armored horseman rapidly receding. "Arthur!"

At this distance she could not see his face or what expression he wore. Certainly, he could not hear her above the gallop and the wind.

For a moment clouds parted, and a ray of sunlight gave her the last of him she would ever see in this life: the red dragon flashing on the crest of his helmet as he rode away to war.

For Reflection:

- "So many scholars have spent so much time trying to establish whether Arthur existed at all," wrote John Steinbeck, "that they have lost track of the single truth that he exists over and over." That a certain Artorius Castus in England tried to fight off the incoming Anglo-Saxons does not diminish the mythic power of Arthur, a reluctant king struggling to unite polarized realms of experience: his two families, allies and enemies, land and society, feminine and masculine, indigene and colonizer. What can Arthur tell us about the struggle between being true to a vision and finding balance?

- Guinevere starts out in myth as the White Woman, a nature goddess of ancient British lore. Janet Rich and I have both emphasized her affinity with Sophia and her other sisters of the feminine Wisdom archetype. How does this tale paint her differently than critics who blame her for the fall of Camelot?

- What can possession by a vision do to one's humanity? How does this impact others?

- What does the Round Table brought by Guinevere symbolize?

- To Geoffrey of Monmouth's inventions and collections we owe most of the details of the Arthur Cycle of myths originating in Wales, with the addition of Grail and Lancelot by Chretien de Troys ("KRESH-en day twah") and the touches added by Sir Thomas Malory. All three blurred the academically drawn line between myth, folktale, and fiction. Is there a real difference?

- Why might these stories have gained such prominence just when the supposedly universal church had grown infamous for its corrupt politics, continual wars, and crookedly obtained worldly wealth?

- In *The Idylls of the King*, Tennyson portrays Arthur as dangerously naive and pseudo-innocent. Where do you see that psychology abroad today, collectively? Why does it so often constellate disaster?

- Arthur kills Mordred at Camlann but sustains a wound so severe that three wise women appear and transport him to Avalon. Once he heals, he will return again when most needed. What is the mythological necessity for his status as "the once and future king"?

Skadi Dumps Njord (Norse)

Ola Henricsson, Swedish musician, storyteller, and educator:

> It has been 12 years since I am into story telling in Sweden and about three years back we tied up with Kathalaya [the House of Stories in India] for the exchange of experience and knowledge. India and Sweden have many similarities. For example, people of both the countries enjoy stories told in any form no matter where they come from. It was these similarities that

helped me connect with India and I joined hands with
Kathalaya.

Stories help students imbibe language skills, life skills
and help them gain knowledge on history, life stories
and on various subjects that they learn as part of daily
school lessons. One chemistry lesson was supposed to
be on carbon. So I told the students a story about a diamond from South Africa, which ended up being brought
to England to be part of a crown. Not only did the students ask about diamonds and structures, they also started questioning about ownership and why jewels can't be
given back to the countries they come from.

It all started when tricky Loki told Idunn of some magical apples
he had found in the forest. "I bet they compare with yours," he confided with a wink.
"I bet they don't," she retorted, stung.
"Only one way to find out. But perhaps you'd rather not..."
When the youth goddess carried her apples into the forest to
make the comparison, Pjazi the giant flew down in eagle form and
seized her in his talons. He carried her away to Pyrmheim, his
stronghold in Jotenheim, the realm of the giants.
With the apples went the immortality of the gods. Turning gray,
they soon discovered that Idunn was last seen with Loki.
"Where did she go?" they asked him.
"How would I know?"
"Oh, you know all right. You probably arranged it."
"How little you think of me, dear family!"
"Less every day; and if you don't bring her back, slow torture
and death await you."
 Begging the use of Freya's magic cloak, Loki shapeshifted into
a falcon.
He flew until he reached Pjazi's great hall at Prymheim. In he
soared through an open window.
Loki had gotten lucky: Idunn was there by herself. He turned her

into a nut, scooped her up, and beat his wings as rapidly as he could for Asgard, the home of the gods. He did not get away unseen, however.

Seeing him coming with eagle-formed Pjazi in pursuit, the gods prepared a pyre, and waited.

Loki dashed over it and landed safely. As Pjazi circled in behind him, a torch descended on the pyre. The resulting blaze roared skyward to neatly catch the eagle, which burst into flame and landed a charred corpse.

*   *   *   *

Now, Pjazi had a daughter named Skadi. When she heard that the gods had killed him, she dressed for battle, picked up her weapons, and journeyed to Asgard. Once there, she demanded an immediate audience.

"I have come," she told the gods, "to avenge the death of my father."

The gods took her in—warrior stance, solid muscle, strong chain mail, shining helmet, deadly scowl—and decided to settle with her.

"Here are my terms," she stated. "First, Odin will place my father's eyes in the night sky, that they might shine forever as brilliant stars. Second, you will make me laugh. Third, I will choose a husband from among you."

Once Odin had relocated the eyes of Pjazi to the heavens, Loki appeared with a length of cord. Tying one end to his testicles and the other to the beard of a goat, he pranced around with the bleating animal until Skadi burst out laughing.

To pick a husband, Skadi was informed, she could look only at the feet of the male gods assembled for her inspection. Their faces were covered. Up and down she went until she came to a pair of feet so shapely they could only be those of handsome Balder.

"That one," she said, pointing.

Njord uncovered himself. She sighed but nodded. At least his feet were comely.

Unlike the Aesir gods, Njord was of the Vanir, an older order.

The Aesir and Vanir had fought long ago until, weary of the bloodshed, both sides had agreed to exchange of three permanent hostages. With his children Freyr and Freya, Njord went to live with the younger Aesir in Asgard, the realm of the gods within the Nine Worlds supported by the giant tree Yggdrasil.

Njord dwelled in Noatun, a many-halled palace that shone with his immense prosperity. He lived near the sea because he oversaw its winds, its waves, and the fishing, trading, and sailing undertaken by mortals. Skadi, however, always lived in the wintry mountains, where she could ski, bow-hunt, and look after the animals.

They decided on a compromise: they would live nine winters in Prymheim in the mountains and nine in Noatun.

They tried, for a certain fondness and warmth grew with their being together. But Njord complained, "I hate these mountains. Nine nights was all I could stand. And those howling wolves! I prefer the songs of swans."

Skadi complained, "Neither could I stand the sounds of the sea or the irritating screeching of gulls. Who can sleep with that noise?"

So saying, Skadi left for her mountain home, and perhaps she remains there, skiing and hunting, just as Njord keeps an eye on wave and wind.

For Reflection:

- The giants are to the Norse gods as the archons are to the Gnostic aeons, but giants and gods often interact. What does that indicate about their mutual identity?

- What does it mean that a threat to the vitality of the gods brings together Skadi ("SKAH-thi") and Njord ("NEE-yord")?

- What sort of event could parallel a conjoining of sea and mountain? ("Skadi" could be a root of the later word "Scandinavia.")

- How would you interpret the gods' regaining of the apples of youth?

- Balder is a solar god. Why might Skadi prefer him to

watery Njord?

- If nobody is to blame for the failure of this relationship, why didn't it work out?
- Archetypally, who is Skadi? Who is Njord?
- Why does Skadi need to laugh?

Vertunmnus Woos Pomona (Roman)

Italo Calvino, Italian writer, journalist, novelist:

> Myth is the hidden part of every story, the buried part, the region that is still unexplored because there are as yet no words to enable us to get there. The narrator's voice in the daily tribal assemblies is not enough to relate the myth. One needs special times and places, exclusive meetings; the words alone are not enough, and we need a whole series of signs with many meanings, which is to say a rite.

> Myth is nourished by silence as well as by words. A silent myth makes its presence felt in secular narrative and everyday words; it is a language vacuum that draws words up into its vortex and bestows a form on fable.

> Shakespeare warns us that the triumph of the Renaissance did not lay the ghosts of the medieval world who appear on the ramparts at Dunsinane or Elsinore. At the height of the Enlightenment, Sade and the Gothic novel appear.

> So here we are, carried off into an ideological landscape quite different from the one we thought we had decided to live in, there with the relays of diodes of electronic computers. But are we really all that far away?

Soil, root, pollen, leaf, blossom, vine, twig, water, sunlight, seed, and fruit: these elements of growth filled up Pomona's world. She especially loved the fruit trees in her orchard. Not for her the wild places of Diana or Pan.

Although the trees and bugs enjoyed her attention, the fauns and satyrs and other would-be suitors did not. She did not notice how many admiring fans stared in her direction, but when they hovered too near her orchard, she never failed to eject them.

One of them was Vertumnus, but, cleverer than the rest, he had devised ways to get near her. The afternoon might find him hauling a basket of corn, evidently a farmer, or lugging a heavy scythe on one shoulder. Under a morning sun he could seem a herdsman just come from yoking oxen. Evening might see him a weary shepherd strolling home, or a soldier on leave, or a fisherman after a day on the river. She gave him friendly greetings without ever suspecting the ardent longing concealed by his disguises.

Pomona looked up one day to see an old woman limp into the orchard. A hat covered her gray hair. Leaning on her staff, she looked around.

"What a lovely garden you keep! Such abundant vines and lovely round vegetables." She gave Pomona a friendly but rather lengthy kiss and sat down under an elm. Pomona sat beside her.

"Just look at this tree," the old woman continued, "so beautiful with the vine snug around it. A perfect couple, tree and vine, are they not? They support and need one another; neither could grow without its mate.

"I am elderly, my dear, but I have good eyes and a good mind, so let me presume to advise you, may I?" She went on without waiting for a reply: "I have seen you, who tend what is young and fresh and growing, spurn suitor after suitor. Will you not heed the lesson of the elm and vine? I can understand wanting to wait for the proper mate, but if you wait too long, Venus will not take kindly to it."

Pomona looked thoughtful. The old woman went on:

"Being watchful, I have also noticed one called Vertumnus, the most serious of your many admirers. He is no drifter or satyr or other questionable creature, but a man of seasons and green growing things. He understands the secrets of abundance and bringing forth just as you do. Who better to select as a mate?

"Between you and me," she confided, "I am here to plead his case. He is somewhat shy. Perhaps you will accept his proposal if it comes from me rather than from him."

The old woman adjusted her hat and went on:

"In this he is not entirely unlike Iphis, a young man of common roots who fell in love with Anaxarete, a noble lady. Her nurse, her maids in waiting, and letters and garlands from his own hand pleaded his case, but she remained as cold as a winter gale and even mocked him for loving her.

"When he could no longer bear his longing or her cruelty, he hung himself from her gate post. It chanced that the funeral passed her home; and when she heard the mourners' cries, she looked out and saw his poor pale corpse on a bier carried by sorrowing friends. At that moment Venus chose to exact her vengeance, and Anaxarete stiffened into a stony statue as still and cold as the body of her former suitor.

"In any case, let us hope that you accept your best admirer so the winter winds may never blight your fruit trees or wither your colorful blossoms. At least let him make his petition!"

So forcefully did the old lady speak these last words that her hat fell off, breaking the shapeshifter's concentration. His features flowed into their natural form: a face bronzed by the sun and lit by admiring eyes. The old woman's cloak dropped from arms sculpted by planting and gathering. A necklace of blossoms circled his neck. His curly hair reminded her of plant tendrils.

Pomona took Vertumnus by the hands as the two rose from the ground and stood close. She smiled at the slow dawn of hope on his nervous face.

"Why didn't you just say so?"

For Reflection:
- What is lost when we hook up instead of courting?

- In the end, what charms Pomona about Vertumnus?

- Pomona is a hamadryad—a wood spirit—and Vertumnus an example of the archetypal Green Man. Who are we mythically in each other's tales? Do we ever partner with someone without participating in an archetypal backstory?

- Could the vividness of falling in love indicate meeting a partner who plays a character in our personal myth? What if falling in love is more mythic than personal?

- A woman with Pomona (for example) as a personal myth would be inclined to involve herself romantically with a character in the Pomona story. In that case her partner would fill that role, but without necessarily having it as a personal myth. And the same with her role in her partner's story. But for his personal myth to actually be Vertumnus—in other words, for each to be the mated figure in each other's myths—is rather rare. Might this be what we refer to as a soulmate relationship?

Chapter Six - Awakenings and Initiations

These tales focus on the simultaneous awakening to self, world, and other people and beings.

Awakening goes hand in hand with initiation into full psychological maturity. Myth can tell us what initiation looked like to people who came before us or who are among us even now, bringing folk together to witness the necessarily painful transition into adult personhood.

A culture that lacks means of initiation risks regression into a culture of neurotic children in adult bodies. The mature awakener, the true elder, is the most precious resource we have for personally and collectively growing up. In the absence of the awakener, our woundings must stand in as our initiators.

Sedna Lets Go (Inuit)

Uvavnuk, Inuit shaman and oral poet:

> The great sea
> frees me, moves me,
> as a strong river carries a weed.
> Earth and her strong winds
> move me, take me away,
> and my soul is swept up in joy.
> —translated by Jane Hirshfield

"You will marry," ordered Anguta, her father. "I will find a handsome hunter for you."

"I will not," replied Sedna.

One hunter after another visited the camp and pleaded for the beautiful woman's hand, but she ignored them all, staring down into the sea and brushing her shining black hair.

The last of the series of suitors showed up in fine furs, long legs, and strong boots. "My home is grand and comfortable," intoned his easy, confident voice. "Plenty to eat, there, too. I will take care of you and your family when your father is old," his mouth promised beneath a beaklike nose and small, bright eyes. She had trouble seeing the rest of his face because his hood cast a shadow over it.

Impressed, Sedna's family arranged the match. The hunter paddled off to his island with his silent new wife seated in their kayak. Her eyes never left the water.

"What is this?" she asked when he showed her his home. All she saw was a nest and some black feathers atop of a high cliff.

Turning around, she opened her mouth to say more but stopped. He had removed his hood and was peeling off his thick jacket and pants. His head was black and his legs spindly. His laughter cawed.

He was a raven.

"You will eat fish," he told her. And she did, lots of them and little else.

When her father heard her cries of distress on the wind, he realized he had made a terrible mistake. Boarding his kayak, he paddled off in search of his daughter, following the sounds of protest she made.

When he reached the island, the raven was out catching fish. Sedna boarded quickly and he rowed them away homeward.

The raven returned to find her gone. He immediately gathered his friends to go in search of her.

As Anguta rowed, he noticed the sea getting up, swells lengthening rapidly. The wind blew with ever-growing fierceness. He turned and saw a cloud of ravens flapping their wings to raise the angry waters.

The heavy storm that rolled in tossed the kayak around like a toy. He had never known so rough a ride.

Two in one boat cannot survive this storm, he thought. Reaching around, he picked up Sedna and hurled her overboard.

The storm did not diminish; the ravens kept flapping. Leaning over, he saw his daughter clinging to the side of the boat.

"Let go!" he called.

"No!" she shouted back.

With a spasm of terror, he drew his hunting knife and slashed at her fingers. One severed joint exploded into a multitude of fish, another into walruses, others into seals, porpoises, and whales.

Sedna let go and sank in the darkness.

As she sank, she too transformed. Her body expanded, and her hair grew longer, resembling ropes of seaweed. Her legs joined, then lengthened into a long fish tail. By the time she reached the bottom, the creatures of the sea, spawned from her bleeding digits, welcomed her as their mother and leader.

Not long after her descent she met Qailertetang, the goddess of weather, and fell in love.

Now they share a home in Adlivun, the place of watery depth. Sedna guides the creatures of the sea, and her partner moves the clouds and rains.

On occasion a shaman sends his spirit down to visit Sedna, especially when game is scarce. The shaman speaks graciously to her and combs and braids her hair. The hunter Pinga visits her too, often bringing along spirits new to the underworld.

As for Anguta, it is said he paddled safely home, but this seems unlikely because today he sits in judgment of the dead whose souls end up in Adlivun.

For Reflection:

- For many daughters, the unavailability, selfishness, or even violence of the father feels dismembering. In the German fairy tale "The Handless Maiden," a father chops off a daughter's hands to exchange her for wealth offered by the Devil. After gaining silver hands through her own efforts, she gets back her natural ones again, but Sedna does not. What is the meaning of this loss?

- Why would a Trickster figure like Raven kidnap Sedna?

- Why does she call out to her father for help even though he let her be taken away?

- In the myth of Persephone, Hades abducts her, much to the sorrow of her mother Demeter. Zeus arranges a compromise: every year Persephone will spend three months in the Underworld and nine in the Upperworld. As a result, she becomes the goddess of spring and the queen of Hades. Are Persephone and Sedna victims or initiants?

- Why does Sedna's life change once she finally lets go?

- Shamans who visit Sedna aren't merely in search of game for their hunters. Their clan, they believe, has gone temporarily out of balance with the natural world. The visit seeks to restore the balance by showing appreciation for the sea goddess. Do you think the natural world notices when we fail to appreciate it? If so, how would it act?

Mataora and Niwareka Bring the Markings (Maori)

Jenny Bol Jun Lee, Maori scholar, writer, and researcher:

> "Rona," a spontaneous rendition told in *te reo Maori* (Maori language), was one of the first traditional *pūrākau* [sacred stories] my daughter heard as a child. As a four year old, she learnt that Rona lived with the moon. She understood that Rona was a space traveler, and when the moon was full and bright, she could see Rona clutching to a *ngaio tree and taha* (calabash). Rona's entrapment on the moon serves to remind people of the power of *atua* (gods), if we should cause offence.

> *Pūrākau* such as "Rona" continue to be a feature of our family's everyday talk as we struggle to sustain Maori language as a first language, and inculcate Maori cultural values, beliefs and worldviews to our children. *Pūrākau* range from stories about the creation of the world, people and the natural environment to historical events and particular incidents.

> Maori narratives, including *pūrākau*, offer huge pedagogical potential that can cut across the regulatory confines of time and space. Categories including age, gender, subject, institution, geographical and tribal boundaries may be mediated in the pursuit of *pūrākau* that encourages lifelong learning and cultural development.

Mataora woke from a dream in which he battled enemies while a circle of pale women laughed at him.

"Who are you?"

"*Turehu*," they said.

He frowned. Underworld spirits outside the door of his hut! Long-haired and clad in seaweed. Was he awake? Yes.

"Who are *you*?" they asked. "A man? Or perhaps a god?" They giggled.

"Can't you see I'm a man?"

"If you're a man, where are your tattoos?"

He pointed to the marks on his face.

"They're only painted. They rub off."

"How else would they be put on me?"

"How else indeed?" murmured a tall woman who caught his glance.

"Well, then, would you like to come in and eat?"

They preferred to stay outside, and to eat raw fish.

After the meal they danced. His eyes kept meeting those of the tall woman. They smiled at each other.

"It is not good," he said when they finished, "to be single and a chief. Might I ask for a wife from among you?"

"Which of us would you choose?"

He pointed out the tall woman. "You."

"I agree. My name is Niwareka." They pressed noses together to seal it.

The spirit women left, dancing.

"Where are they going?"

"Back to Rarohenga, the Underworld, where my father Ue-tonga reigns."

"I hope you will be happy up here with me, Niwareka."

* * * *

At first it was so. Their love deepened as they got to know one another.

But Mataora had a temper. On one occasion, it got the better of him and he struck her. She was stunned.

Ashamed of himself, he left to be by himself for a time. When he returned, she was gone. *Serves me right*, he thought.

Knowing she had gone to Rarohenga, he sought passage there to make amends. He stopped at the House of Four Winds and described her to the Underworld Guardian.

"Yes, she came by all right. She was weeping."

Mataora hung his head.

"You can follow her down," said the Guardian, opening a door onto a black tunnel, "but only if you have courage and resolution."

"I will go," said the chief, and he stepped forward.

After a long walk through darkness, berating himself as he went, Mataeora emerged into a vast underground realm. Below a distant roof of rock, hills bracketed streams flowing through trees and reeds and winding through little villages. No sun or sky shone above his head; everything, even the grass, glowed with its own uncanny light.

Continuing on, Mataora paused occasionally to ask directions to the village of Ue-tonga until he came to a group of huts. In front of them an elder who could only be Ue-tonga himself bent over a man lying face-up on the ground. Mataora heard a faint but rhythmic tapping sound.

Moving closer, he was astonished to see the Underworld chief cutting lines with a chisel and hammer into the young man's face. As Mataora walked up, Ue-tonga laid the tools aside and applied pigments to the markings he had made.

"That looks painful," he stated. "Up above we paint the designs."

Ue-tonga reached up and smeared Mataora's facial markings.

"Down here, we make sure they last. Permanently." He pointed at the markings etched into his own face long ago.

"I would like a design like yours."

"Very well. Lie down."

Mataora swallowed and took a breath. With the first gouge of the chisel the sweat broke out all over his body. He bit his lip to keep from moaning aloud each time the hammer hit the chisel.

As blood ran over his face, a familiar rage rose in his chest. He wanted to lash out in pain at Ue-tonga, at the Underworld, at everything for hurting him so much. As the rage crested, he realized he had never really ridden it like a canoe over a strong wave: he had always escaped it with fists and blows. Hurting under the chisel forced him to ride it.

Being able to do this gave him a kind of fierce joy within his pain. Niraweka's younger sister heard the man being tattooed start singing out: *Niwareka, where are you? Niwareka, I came here for you....*

When Ue-tonga finally rubbed in the paint and let Mataora sit up, his face was so bloody and swollen that nobody recognized him but the tall, still woman sitting before him. They embraced with gladness.

"What do you plan to do?" Ue-tonga asked as he put his tools away.

Mataora spoke: "To return to the Upperworld together."

"I have heard the Upperworld to be a place of darkness. A place where some husbands beat up their wives."

A shadow of shame passed over Mataora's swollen face. He thought of paddling over waves. "There will be no more beatings. Ever." Niwareka pressed his hand strongly.

"No, there will not be," said Ue-tonga, "because if there were, you would never see her again." Mataora knew that he meant it.

When they reached the House of the Four Winds, the Guardian wanted to know what was in Niwareka's bundle.

"Just some clothes," she lied.

"No. You carry the garment of Te Rangihaupapa," he replied, pointing at the cloth that bore the border pattern worn by women elders in Rarohenga. "Because you have tried to deceive me, the way to the Underworld will be closed forever now except to spirits of the dead."

When he turned to hang up the garment he had confiscated, the couple slipped by him and ran free across the Upperworld as the gate slammed shut behind them.

From that time forward, Mataora, now a man of peace in deed as well as word, passed on his knowledge of the permanent markings to be carved on the faces of fiery young men. Niwareka taught women how to weave the colorful borders that gleam on the cloaks of the elders.

For Reflection:

- In more cultures than not, tattooing connects to the

need to get initiated into adulthood by the elders. Where no such elders are available, the urge usually remains unconscious and is symptomatically acted out. Why is conscious initiation necessary for full psychological maturity?

- Why is Mataora ("mah-tah-OR-ah") initially drawn to Niwareka ("NEE-wah-ree-kah")? Why is she drawn to him?

- Having a bad temper is often seen as an isolated state, but it is actually symptomatic of a lack of emotional maturity. In patriarchal societies, this lack becomes very dangerous, especially to women who learn through abuse that a perpetrator's regrets do not end it. What does Niwareka's decision to leave her husband after his first assault suggest about her boundaries and self-esteem?

- Michael Meade observes that the fires burning in young men must be added to the hearth of the community; if they are not, the flames will burn down the community. In what ways does being initiated by a male elder help Mataora learn to hold his fire? How might he educate other men about holding theirs?

- What would happen to the armed services of a nation if all the young men received genuine initiation before reaching the age of enlistment or draft?

- Why is Niwareka's lie to the Guardian a mythological necessity?

- Why is it crucial for the elders of a culture to remain in close contact with its less mature members?

Ishtar Encounters Ereshkigal (Mesopotamian)

Simin Behbahani, award-winning Iranian poet:

Old, I may be, but, given the chance, I will learn. I will begin a second youth alongside my progeny. I will recite the Hadith of love of country with such fervor as to make each word bear life.

I feel for my people, the language, the ability to write about them through cultural bonds. The creativity in me comes from them, and I want to share it.

Notwithstanding my age, I have almost never had the possibility to raise my pen without being worried by censorship. Under both the previous and the Islamist regime censors would read every text, and every writer would always have this sentence in mind: Do not write this, we will not let it be published. But the true writer must ignore these murmurings. The true writer must write.

To stay alive, you must slay silence . . .
To pay homage to being, you must sing.

"If I'm not back in three days," Ishtar instructed her lady in waiting, "tell the other gods to send for me." The Underworld descent is easy once it begins. The difficulty is in resurfacing.

She kissed her lover Dumuzi goodbye and departed, heading down.

Soon she stood before the gates of Irkalla. She knocked loudly.

"What do you want?" asked the gatekeeper.

"I am here to attend the funeral of my sister's husband Gugalanna," she replied. Ishtar had sent Gugalanna, the Great Bull of Heaven, against proud Gilgamesh, but the hero and his beast friend Enkidu had killed the bull. "Go and tell her."

When Ereshkigal heard who was at the gate she was livid. Through stiff lips she said, "What is *she* doing here? Surely she isn't visiting to take a casual look at how I weep for the babes who cannot live rich full lives? The lovers who part and never see each other alive again? —Tell her she may enter, but in full accord with how we do things down here."

"You may come in," the gatekeeper informed Ishtar, "but, as with everyone else who enters here, you must divest yourself of every earthly accouterment."

At this, the first gate, Ishtar handed over her crown, under protest; at the second, her earrings; at the third, her necklace; at the fourth, her breast jewels; at the fifth, her girdle of birthstones; at the six, her wrist and ankle bangles; and at the seventh, her garments, protesting all the way.

Naked, she walked into the presence of her dark older sister, who looked her up and down in fear and anger.

"Unleash upon her," Ereshkigal ordered Namtar, her gatekeeper and vizier, "the sixty infirmities inflicted upon the dead to punish them for their earthly transgressions." Ishtar's nude body convulsed as diseases of eye, arm, foot, face, and heart covered her from the top of her head to her heels.

When she glanced up in horror at her sister and lurched forward to protest, Ereshkigal glared with the full force of her killing stare, and Ishtar died.

*   *   *   *

Up above, all the living beings that normally procreate suddenly stopped. The female and male of every kind—insect, four-legged, winged, two-legged—looked at each other with indifference.

"The plants aren't even breeding," Papsukkal complained to the moon god Sin. "Soon no one will be able to eat."

Ishtar's servant had raised the alarm when the goddess was overdue, but nobody stirred. Only now did the gods grow worried about her absence. They decided to take steps.

From the dirt beneath his fingernails, crafty Enki, Ishtar's father, fashioned two sexless beings. Equipping them with the food and water of life, he sent them down to Irkalla to revive the goddess, whose corpse had been hung on a hook to rot.

Ishtar's brother Ea assembled Asushunamir, the most beautiful male (except for a single blemish) to be found anywhere, and sent him down as well.

"The most handsome man in the world has come to visit you," the gatekeeper reported to Ereshkigal.

"Well, show him in!"

Distracted with anticipation, she did not know that Ishtar had been taken down from the hook on which her body had hung for three days.

"Welcome!" called Ereshkigal, advancing to meet her handsome guest. His muscular body wore nothing but a loincloth. "How nice of you to visit me down here. Please be comfortable. My, my, you are a nice-looking man...."

Once they had gotten warm and cozy on her couch, Asushunamir said, "Before we go farther, I would like to make a request of you. Will you give me one little, unimportant thing?" His smile softened her heart.

"Whatever you like. What is it?"

"Ishtar's body."

"An odd request, but yes, certainly."

Her astonishment at seeing Ishtar suddenly walk in was heightened still more when the grimly powerful Annunaki filed in behind her. They formed up in one solemn body of seven to utter a pronouncement.

"As the Judges of the Dead," they intoned, "we approve the departure of Ishtar, now revived, from this realm of death." Ereshkigal opened her mouth to protest and closed it again. No argument would sway them, even down here in her home. "However, she must fulfill one condition: upon reaching the world above, she must find someone to replace her presence down here."

"Agreed," said Ishtar.

As she and the Judges left the chamber, Ishtar to recover her garments, bangles, girdle, breast jewels, necklace, earrings, and crown on her way out, Ereshkigal turned back to Asushunamir.

"Very clever of you," she observed with a smile. "But at least I still have you to enjoy."

At this she removed his loincloth, and gasped.

"You're a eunuch!"

*   *   *   *

As Ishtar approached the Upperworld, a wave of intense coupling swept across the land.

"Welcome!" said her servant, her brother, and a crowd of friends and admirers—even her hairdresser—still wearing the garments of mourning.

There was one notable exception.

Upon a jeweled throne sat Dumuzi. Garbed in celebratory finery, he laughed merrily from the center of a circle of lovely young girls. Evidently the party had been going for some time.

When he saw Ishtar he gaped, momentarily speechless. Then:

"I can explain—" holding up one hand.

"You're about to take a trip," Ishtar cut in, eyes burning. "No time for explanations."

"A trip?"

"Yes, a trip. A long one. I hope you enjoy yourself—in Irkalla."

She glared at him with the full force of the killing stare she had learned from Ereshkigal, and Dumuzi died.

For Reflection:

- Why would Ishtar need to be initiated?

- Why are initiation rituals so often painful or risky?

- What does it mean that Ishtar's sister Ereshkigal does the initiating?

- What do seven gates signify? Why must Ishtar strip?

- In one variant, the two beings sent to revive Ishtar moan in empathy when Ereshkigal is sad. Why would an Underworld goddess need empathy?

- Comment: The Babylonians knew Ishtar as Inanna. She was worshiped with erotic fanfare in her cities, which is why the Bible refers to "the great whore of Babylon." An ancient story describes how Inanna appropriates the arts of urban skill and craft from her father Enki, who warns her that civilization will prove a very mixed blessing indeed.

- Why would the gods ignore the initial warning about Ishtar's absence?

- The image of the constellation Taurus derives in part from Gugalanna. Ishtar sends the heavenly bull against Gilgamesh after the hero spurns her advances. How does that connect to her reception in Irkalla?

- How is Ishtar different after her Underworld initiation?

- Comment: Scholars have argued that the shepherd Dumuzi's trip to the Underworld inspired the story of Christ's descent into Hell. Suspension on the cross echoes Ishtar's three days on the hook.

The Humbling of Indra (Hindu)

Vijaydan Detha, Rajasthani poet and writer:

I am less of a story-writer and more of a story-teller.

We come from the community of *charans*, who professionally sang praises of their feudal lords and sometimes criticised them.

My village was my university, and my literary education, if there was any, came from rural women who always had so many interesting stories, anecdotes and wisdoms to share... Unlike conversations of men, who were corrupted by their travels outside the village and their interactions with different people, quirky feminine gossip was such a landmine of interesting ideas.

During my schooling in Jodhpur, all our teachers were from Hindi-speaking states and we would be severely reprimanded for speaking in our native language Rajasthani. Experiences like these made me think of writing in Rajasthani.

When I returned to the village, I realised language is made not by professors of linguistics but by the illiterate rustic folk. I learnt the art of language from them.

After losing his palace for sixty-thousand years, Indra was understandably keen on refurbishing it. But in his eagerness he forgot how he lost it the first time: by neglecting Earth, who warned him he'd lose everything, and by forgetting to respectfully greet his guru Brihaspati, who cursed him to be a beggar until he had begged and prayed enough.

Back in charge now, and somewhat full of himself after hurling a thunderbolt that incinerated a giant serpent, Indra ordered the celestial architect Vishwakarma to restore the palace for him, there atop the cosmic mountain.

At first the building went well. After a time, though, Indra, who supervised the repairs, slipped into oversupervising. To his suggestions and commands he added complaints and scoldings.

Sick of this, Vishwakarma went to see Vishnu.

"Nothing is good enough for him," complained the architect. "He's after me all the time. And he wants so much that I can't get to other projects. His was supposed to be finished millennia ago, but it drags on and on. Is there anything you can do?"

The next day, a shrewd-looking boy with blue skin was admitted to see Indra. "This is your palace?" he asked the sky god, waving an arm in a small circle.

"Of course," replied Indra, looking proudly around at it. "Who else could have built such a grand place?"

"Yes," the boy went on. "Certainly no other Indra ever enjoyed a palace as fine as this one."

Pause. "What do you mean, 'no other Indra'? There have been others?"

"Oh yes, many, many others. The worlds governed by Indras are as the eyeblinks of Brahma. As well count the grains of sand on a beach or the drops of water in the sea."

As they spoke, a line of ants crossed the floor. The boy giggled at them.

"What is funny?" asked Indra, quite angry by now.

"Do you really want to know? Perhaps not."

"If I didn't I wouldn't ask, would I?"

"Well, what's funny is that line of ants. Do you know who they were?"

Glumly: "No."

Merrily: "Indras who have risen and then fallen, risen and then fallen. Reborn now as ants. What will it take for them to learn?"

Just then an old yogi was admitted. Naked but for a dirty loin-cloth, he clasped a banana leaf parasol.

"Greetings, O yogi," said the blue boy before Indra could speak up. "Who are you, and why does your chest bear a half circle of hairs?"

"Greetings," replied the yogi. "Call me Hairy. I have no home or family; instead, I wander and meditate on the passing of time. Half the hairs have fallen out of my chest, you see. Each goes when an Indra dies and his kingdom vanishes. Won't be long before all the hairs are gone. So why make a fuss about anything?"

"What am I to do?" Indra asked them.

"Go bathe in a river," the boy suggested. "Cleanse yourself, and perhaps you will see that you already have everything you need."

The blue boy and Hairy smiled at Indra, who recognized them just before they disappeared: Vishnu, who preserves the order of the cosmos, and Shiva, who dances it into nothingness.

Indra was alone, seated on an elaborately decorated throne in the center of an elaborately constructed palace. A palace he no longer craved to expand. He summoned his architect.

"Thank you for all you have built and restored," he told Vishwakarma. "The place is perfect." Vishwakarma bowed, greatly relieved, and left.

When Indra's wife Indrani came home, he related to her all that had taken place.

"What now?" she asked him. "More asceticism? More monster-slaying?"

"No. In all these lifetimes I have always tried to be more than I am. For once I'm going to do something different. I'm going to bathe in a river, attempt to manage a kingdom wisely, and learn to be a good husband. I'm going to try to be what I am...while there is time to."

For Reflection:

- Indra's archetypal counterparts include Zeus, Jupiter, Enlil, Dagda, Baal, Marduk, Olorun, and Perun, among others. Indra is widely thought to be one of the more narcissistic gods. How can having a higher view lead to inflation?

- What might be an ecological lesson taught by this myth?

- Why would Vishnu appear as a boy and Shiva as an old man?

- Across pantheons, archetypal alter egos of the divine architect Vishwakarma include figures such as Daedalus, Amatsumara, Goibniu, Cinyras, Kurd-ala-Wargon, St. Joseph, Weyland, and Vulcan. Daedalus built the labyrinth that held the Minotaur and was trapped in a tower until he escaped on makeshift wings. Hephaestus lived alone inside a mountain. What makes the architect so easy to isolate or trap?

- What are the secret fears that drive controlling, micro-managing bullying?

- Self-improvement, which goes by many names—self-realization, enlightenment, etc.—is normally considered a good thing. How might it feed narcissism?

- Why do inflation and deflation tend to alternate?

- How is it possible to learn a crucial life lesson at great personal cost and then forget it again? What would it take to remember it?

- What might suggest that Indra really got the lesson this time?

Psyche and Cupid (Greek, Roman)

Diana Bertoldi, Italian-Scottish game warden, naturalist, and storyteller:

> Tales have been told for thousands of years, and each story becomes alive and changes with gestures and words of the storyteller.
>
> "Let your heart do the talking" told me once a wise man. This is what I try to do every day, telling dark and cheerful, strong and delicate tales, to adults and children.
>
> With stories we can go far away, each tale is a wonderful journey in a land of magic, and when words fade away, only the wonder of heart remains, and we keep it with us forever.
>
> Working as a game warden and wildlife manager for many years helped me to develop my instinctive love for Nature....My major aim now is to take adults and children back in touch with wildlife and nature through storytelling.

Certainly, the youngest daughter of the king and queen was beautiful, no doubt of it. But no merely external beauty could summon such devotion that blissful men walked before her strewing flowers in her path—and neglecting the rites of Venus, who grew angry.

"This is unlawful," she told her winged son Cupid. Pointing at Psyche, who beamed to receive another round of worship as her sisters looked on with bitterness, Venus ordered her son to inflict on the girl a passion for some low, ugly, ignoble being. "That should bring her down to mortal size again."

Accordingly, Cupid went off to the two fountains flowing in his mother's garden. Dipping one vase into the fount of bitter water and one into the sweet, he flew down with them into the bedchamber of Psyche. She was sound asleep.

A few drops of the bitter water moistened her lips. She moaned in her sleep, frowning. The touch of Cupid's arrow in her side woke her. Although he was invisible, she seemed to stare directly at him, so disconcerting him that he scratched himself with the arrow.

He stared at her. He had never appreciated how beautiful she was. Guilty for his actions, he hastened to flick some of the sweet water into her hair before he departed on distracted wings.

Once the bitter water of Venus had touched her, no suitor would approach her. Everyone still admired her beauty, but none would marry her. Smiling quietly, her sisters went off with their new husbands. Psyche found herself alone.

Seeing this, her worried parents decided to consult the oracle of Apollo at Delphi.

After making pilgrimage to that holy place, they left their question about Psyche with a priest, who took it to the Pythoness, who sat in the presence of Phoebus. His reply startled them: "Your virgin daughter will wed no man, but a monster not to be resisted by either gods nor mortals. To meet him, she must go atop the mountain."

"You should have grieved," Psyche told her distraught parents, "when people mistook me for Venus. I go now to meet my destiny."

Following a brief wait on the mountaintop, Psyche let the wind Zephyr lift her up and carry her to a dale filled with flowers. After resting there, she woke and entered a grove of tall trees.

Within the grove bubbled an enchanting fountain in front of a sumptuous palace. Entering, she marveled at the vaults and arches, the golden pillars, the paintings depicting wondrous animals and colorful scenery. Gleamings of gems and lustrous metals winked from within cupboards and behind half-open doors. It was a house of treasures.

"And all of this is yours," came a group voice from an unseen source. "We are your servants, here to obey you in all things. We have prepared a bed of down for you, a bath, and your supper." After a nap and the bath, Psyche beheld a table loaded with delicacies and wines. The sounds of song and lute pleased her ears as she ate.

He came to her in the night as she lay in bed. She could not see him, but his chest, his lips, his caresses were certainly not monstrous. She had never imagined how an unseen, unknown lover could arouse such passionate response in her. When she woke in the morning, relaxed and blissful, he was gone.

And so it proceeded, this strange romantic encounter. Soon she asked him to linger, to spend the day with her, to let her look upon him, but he would not.

"Are you not happy here?" he asked. "Do I not love you dearly, and you love me? Do you not have everything you need and desire?"

"Everything except being able to see you."

"If you saw me, you would see, perhaps, an object of either fear or veneration. All I ask for is your love, and for you not to try to see me."

He also wanted her all to himself, but he consented at last to allow her sisters to visit. Zephyr brought them in from the city.

Psyche showed them around the magnificent palace. Unaware of their envy, she heard their dark warnings, but not the malice behind them.

"The people of this valley," they told her, "say your invisible husband is plying you with delicacies to fatten you up and devour you. And do you not remember the oracle that described him as a monster?"

"But now that I'm here, alone with him, what should I do?"

"Obtain a sharp knife and a lantern, and hide them. When your husband sleeps, open the lamp and see for yourself who he is. If he is a monster, cut off his head."

One night, then, when she heard him sleeping, she rose quietly, armed herself with knife and lantern, and crept to his side of the bed. She uncovered the lantern and stared down at him.

If a monster, he was certainly a beautiful one. His golden hair, shining now in lamplight, curled down behind rosy cheeks. On his shoulders folded white wings with shining feathers. His chest rose and fell peacefully. She leaned closer for a better look.

As she leaned, a drop of hot oil fell from the lantern onto his bare shoulder. He woke with a jolt and stared at her through dilated pupils. In one bound he leaped from the bed to the window. As he exited he spread his wings to catch the air.

Psyche grabbed his right leg and found herself tumbling through the window to the ground.

"Is this how you repay my love?" he called down to her from the top of a cypress tree. "I disobeyed my goddess mother to be with you, marry you, and give you everything you could have wanted. Now, I must leave you." He darted away.

Cursing her curiosity, Psyche got up and turned to reenter the bedchamber. It was gone. Treasures, palace, fountain: all gone.

At this, Psyche threw herself into a river running nearby, hoping to drown herself, but the river lifted her in watery arms and placed her on one bank. Looking up, she saw Pan sitting nearby teaching pipe music to the nymph Echo.

"I'm sorry to see such a lovely young girl in so much suffering," he told Psyche, "but drowning will do you no good. No. Instead, send prayers of adoration to Cupid, that he may hear your summons and come around."

Overcome with sadness, she stumbled away from the riverbank through the now-empty field. If she was to have any chance of making things come out right, she had to draw at its source the poison that had killed her marriage.

In the city, Psyche's sisters fingered the gemstones she had given them and hoped their sister would die of grief.

Psyche came first to one, then the other, to apprise them of the dismal outcome of their advice. Now fully alert to their malice,

Psyche added a twist: "....And when Cupid flew away, he told me that because of my disloyalty, he would now wed you instead of me. Zephyr's wind will carry you to him."

Pretending sympathy until Psyche had left, each sister climbed the mountain to the topmost rock. Each asked Zephyr to waft them to Cupid, that he might accept them as his loyal wife. Each leaped from the rock expecting immediate transportation; and each gyrated through empty air and fell screaming down the cliff to her death.

*   *   *   *

Psyche roved the land in search of her husband. Perhaps she could explain her sisters' plot to him and be forgiven.

She spotted a temple on a mountain peak. Could he be there? She climbed despite her weariness and entered, surprised to see sickles, hoes, and ears of barley and wheat dropped into an untidy heap. *A shrine should not be left in this disorder*, she thought, and placed everything in neat piles.

"Thank you, my dear," spoke Ceres as she entered the sacred area. "In return, let me tell you that a white tern found Venus upon the seas and told her about your tryst with Cupid. She is furious and quite determined to put you through your paces. I appreciate your labors, but you need to think about yourself now."

"Generous Ceres, may I please hide here until the wrath of Venus has passed?"

"No, Psyche, you may not hide, but go to your trials with my blessing."

Onward she went until a grove in a valley disclosed another shrine. This one had been carefully kept by devotees who left offerings, among them gold-lettered ribbons pinned to trees and doorposts. This must be the orderly house of Juno. Falling to her knees before the altar, she prayed for relief.

"I'm sorry," said Juno, standing briefly before her, "but I cannot give you sanctuary, only a blessing and good wishes as you head into further trials."

After a period of reflection, Psyche realized she could not

escape the eye of Venus. *I might as well seek her out*, she decided.

As it happened, Venus was waiting for her, having been told by hawk-eyed Mercury of Psyche's reluctant approach. The door opened, and the servant Consueto pulled her in by the hair.

"About time you visited your mother-in-law, isn't it?" asked Venus sweetly, looking her up and down. "Before we chat, why don't my maids Sollicito and Tristie look after you?"

When they had finished maltreating her, the servants brought in large heaps of lentils, beans, chickpeas, poppyseeds, millet, and barley, all of which they threw on the floor in a giant mess. "Sort them out—by tonight," Venus called over her shoulder as she departed.

All this time an ant had watched Psyche suffering. In sympathy, it summoned a workforce of ants. "Laborers of Terra," the ant told his fellows, "help this girl with the task set before her."

By the time Venus returned, the ants had sorted everything and vanished. The goddess was not impressed. "Someone helped you," she sneered. "At dawn I will have another task for you."

The following morning Venus showed her a grove filled with a multitude of horned sheep covered with golden fleece. The horns looked very sharp. "Those sheep are mean," remarked the goddess, "and their bite is poisonous. Nevertheless, you must bring me back a tuft of their golden wool." She turned away.

Psyche was again thinking about trying to drown herself when a nearby reed spoke up as a gust of wind passed through it: "Psyche, do not give up. Wait until the heat of day diminishes and the sheep grow calm, then hide under the plane tree. Go to the grove next to this one, and you will find golden wool tangled in the foliage and there for the picking."

"Next," said Venus, her hands full of shining wool, "you must climb that mountain peak and fetch me some water from its springs." She handed Psyche a crystal jar. "The only problem is that to get up there, you must cross the marshes of the Styx. Which are deadly. And guarded by poisonous snakes."

As Psyche approached the Styx, she heard its dark waters calling out discouragements: "It's hopeless! Turn back! Beware! You will fail!" She stood stock still, paralyzed.

An eagle flew down and landed beside her. "Hand me your jug," it screeched, extending a claw. Flying over dark waters and past lunging serpents, the eagle dropped, scooped a jarful of water, flapped higher, circled, and returned to Psyche.

"Obviously benign powers are looking out for you," said Venus as she picked up a small box. "I have a final task for you. Yes, this is the end of the road. Journey down to the Underworld, find Proserpina, and give her this box, telling her that I desire a one-day supply of her beauty cream." She handed the box to Psyche, smiled, and left.

This was it, then. *Might as well go down there quickly*, Psyche thought. She climbed a high tower and prepared to jump.

But the tower spoke from beneath her:

"Why give up now? This is your last trial, the occasion for your final effort. No time to despair! Jump and your soul will be severed from your body. You must find another way down."

"What way?"

"On the border with Sparta you will find Taernarus, a vent down into the Underworld. Take with you sweet barley cakes baked in wine and two coins held between your lips. First you will meet a lame driver leading a lame ass carrying logs. The driver will ask you to pick up some logs that have slipped from the ass's back. Ignore him and say nothing. Coming to the river Acheron, allow the ferryman Charon to take one coin from your lips for his fare. He will carry you across the dark river. As he does, an old man will float up and ask you to drag his corpse into the boat: do not. Once you have crossed, some old weaving women will ask you for help at their loom. Ignore them too. The driver, the old man, and the weavers are agents of Venus sent to distract you. Keep going.

"At the gateway to Hades you will see an immense hound with three heads. He will bark ferociously. Offer him one of the sweet cakes and pass.

"Now you will meet fearsome Proserpina, queen of the dead. She will ask you kindly to sit next to her and share her meal. Don't. Sit on the ground and ask for coarse bread. After eating it, tell her of your errand. Take the filled box from her and go, giving the second cake to Cerberus as you pass him again. Allow Charon to take the second coin to ferry you across the Acheron, and return to Venus with the box.

"And this above all: do not open it."

Psyche found the vent, descended to the Underworld, avoided all the traps, paid Charon, fed Cerberus, received the box from Proserpina, and made her way back again.

As she walked the ways of daylight once again, she began to wonder what was in the box.

Beauty cream for Venus? she wondered, bewildered. *Why would the goddess of beauty need beauty cream?* It must be an extraordinarily potent substance if even fair Venus wanted to possess it.

Psyche began to think of Cupid. Would he even speak with her? Might her chances improve if she wore a dab of whatever was in the box? If she took just a little, Venus would never know....

She opened the box. In it was nothing but a small black cloud: the deep sleep of Hades. It poured into her nose and mouth. Her last sensation was of lying down for a long, long rest.

*   *   *   *

Cupid, having recovered from his burn, and tired of being penned up in Venus's house, flew out the window and went looking for Psyche.

Spotting her body lying on a path, he came down to her. She wasn't breathing.

The sleep of Hades! He brushed it from her lightly and put it back in its box. A prick from one of his arrows woke her.

"You always were a curious one," he said as they embraced briefly. "Now back we go to complete your task for my mother."

As Psyche made her way to the goddess, Cupid left to ascend to the gates of heaven, where entered and sought out Jupiter himself.

"What does it take for a grandfather to get a visit from his grandson?" the god asked, embracing Cupid. "Although your arrows have never been far from my tender hide," he added, winking. "What brings you here?"

Cupid told him.

Jupiter turned to his winged messenger. "Call an assembly of all the gods." Mercury darted away to do it.

They came, some grumbling, some late, some wanting answers right now and getting none, but they came. At length Jupiter addressed them:

"You all know," his voice boomed, "that Cupid here has enjoyed free play among most of us for many centuries. The time has come for him to settle into adult responsibilities; and to do that, he must take the hand of the woman he loves."

"But she is MORTAL!" screeched Venus.

"Not for long," replied Zeus. Picking up a cup, he handed it to Psyche, who was ushered into their presence by Mercury. "Drink of this cup, and you shall join us in immortality and Cupid in divine marriage."

And so it was.

The wedding celebration outdid itself in cheerful spectacle. Juno and Jupiter sat together drinking heavenly nectar. Merry Bacchus poured wine and joined his lyre-playing brother Apollo in musical revelry. Venus danced alluringly with the Muses as her chorus while Mercury watched, eyebrows raised, in grinning admiration. Pan played an accompaniment on his syrinx. The Graces raised their hands in blessing, the Seasons poured colorful flowers down from above, and Vulcan busied himself cooking up a fine dinner with grains and vegetables provided by Ceres.

Psyche and Cupid clasped each other, enjoying a secret that would not be one for long: she was pregnant. She smiled to reflect that the presence of her daughter, named Voluptas, or Pleasure, already made herself felt in such festive joy.

For Reflection:

- Comment: When Freud proclaimed Eros (the Greek name for Cupid) a foundational drive of the psyche, he dipped into a long tradition. Plato himself had praised Eros at length in his Dialogues. In some myths,

Eros/Cupid was the first god to emerge from primal Chaos.

- If drinking the bitter water of Venus translates psychologically into a long romantic dry spell resulting from offending the goddess, how might one gain access to the sweet water?

- How does Psyche's state of innocence jeopardize not only her, but her marriage?

- A literal interpretation would view Venus as merely jealous or vindictive, as Cinderella's and Vasilisa's stepmothers seem to be, but what if Venus acts here as Psyche's initiator? ("Hubris" was the Greek term for arrogating to oneself the qualities of a god/dess.)

- Think about an initially perfect-seeming but actually unconscious (sightless) relationship in your past. What was the lamplight or oil burn that broke the spell?

- Why do Ceres and Juno refuse to grant Psyche sanctuary?

- Comment: Consueto's name refers to Habit, and those of Sollicito and Tristie to Melancholy and Sorrow.

- Why is the Underworld journey necessary for Psyche?

- It could be argued that Psyche failed to be initiated because she received outside help every step of the way, but what if part of the trial included learning to draw on the ant, eagle, etc. within herself as personal capabilities?

- Psyche's allies include nature beings. What does this suggest about the psyche's relationship to the natural world?

- Joseph Campbell referred to acts like Psyche's opening of the deadly box as the motif of the One Forbidden Thing. Should she have done it?

- What does it mean that Psyche and Cupid marry?

Moses and Al Khidr (Muslim)

Rukhsana Khan, Muslim writer and storyteller:

> I initially came to the whole process of story via the
> writing. It took me close to ten years to establish my
> ability to conceive, develop and then write down a good
> story. It was only after my first five books had been con-
> tracted and were in the process of being published that I
> discovered storytelling.
>
> Initially I looked at storytelling as a means of promoting
> my books. In the process I found a complete and sepa-
> rate art form that has claimed me on its own merit. I do
> use storytelling techniques when presenting my books to
> audiences. I never 'read' my stories, I storytell them.
>
> Societies are in a constant state of flux. Members move
> between communities and with this comes the cross-pol-
> lination of ideas. Over time cultural norms must change
> and adapt as a result of this.

"There is One who is wiser than you."

So Moses heard from above, or within, after believing himself
uniquely gifted by Allah. After all, did he not enlighten others by
teaching them? Did he not prophesy? Could he not work miracles?

Nevertheless, "Who is he, that I may learn from him?" Moses
asked Allah.

"Carry a live fish in water on your journey. Where the fish vanishes, your teacher will appear."

Moses went forth with a young companion carrying the fish.
After going a long stretch, they came to a place where two seas met.
Here Moses decided to rest and promptly fell soundly asleep.

Once he had awakened, they continued on until morning. At

length, Moses found himself ravenously hungry. "Shall we eat the fish?" he asked.

"I'm sorry I forgot to tell you," confessed his traveling companion, "but at the place where we stopped, the fish jumped out of the water and ran into the sea."

"That is the place we seek!"

They retraced their steps. Where the seas met stood a robed and hooded man, waiting.

Moses approached him and greeted him:

"Peace be upon you. I believe Allah has taught you things I need to know. May I follow you?"

"You will not be able to bear with me," said the hooded figure.

"I can if Allah wills it."

"Very well. Come with me—and do not question me about anything you see me do."

They proceeded until they came to a destitute fishing village, where the hooded teacher paused. Moses expected him to offer the poor fishing folk something they could use. Instead, Al Khidr kicked a hole in the bottom of their only remaining boat.

"Surely this is an evil deed!" blurted Moses.

"I told you that you would not be able to bear with me."

"Sorry."

"Let us go on."

They walked until they came to a boy in the road. Without so much as addressing him, Al Khidr gestured, and the boy fell over stone dead.

"What have you done?" cried Moses, appalled.

"I remind you one final time not to question me."

They went on until they came to a town. By then Moses was very hungry, but when he asked the people for some food, they gave him none. As they walked through the town, Al Khidr approached a wall about to collapse. He gestured and it stood straight again.

"Surely," said Moses, "you could have charged them something for straightening their wall."

"Now," said Al Khidr, "we must part; but before I go, I will enlighten you about what you have witnessed.

"An official had been dispatched to assess the fishing village for taxes. Because the fishers had no money to pay him, he would have taken their boat, starving them. The hole made the boat worthless to the official, and the fishers will easily repair it and be able to sustain themselves.

"The boy was on his way home to treacherously murder his parents. They will be better off without him, and their next child will bring them divine favor.

"The wall was owned by a faithful father and two orphaned boys. Had the wall fallen, selfish neighbors would have made off with the treasure below it. Now the boys will gain strength and come of age before they find the treasure, nor will they be deprived of it."

With that Al Khidr departed, and Moses went his way a wiser man.

For Reflection:
- This tale, which appears in the Quran, contains far earlier elements and reads somewhat like a folktale. Are there significant differences between folk (or fairy) tales and myths?

- It's not only the self-deluded who get inflated. Very often the possession of great gifts brings with them an enlarged sense of specialness. How does Allah's intervention via Al Khidr act as a course correction?

- What was lacking in Moses that he would need initiation from an archetypal Trickster?

- When the fish vanishes and Al Khidr appears, it's as though the fish turned into him or went looking for him. Why? What might this suggest about how we exchange our sources of nourishment once a true teacher appears?

- What is symbolized by the juncture of two seas?

- Why must Moses retrace his steps?

- What might idealistic reformers and political activists learn from this story?

- What does the story suggest about the transience of the teacher-learner relationship?

Mary Magdalene Shares Her Vision (Gnostic)

Stephan Hoeller, Gnostic bishop and author:

> Gnosticism is the teaching based on Gnosis, the knowledge of transcendence arrived at by way of interior, intuitive means....Gnosticism expresses a specific religious experience, an experience that does not lend itself to the language of theology or philosophy, but which is instead closely affinitized to, and expresses itself through, the medium of myth.
>
> Indeed, one finds that most Gnostic scriptures take the forms of myths. The term "myth" should not here be taken to mean "stories that are not true", but rather, that the truths embodied in these myths are of a different order from the dogmas of theology or the statements of philosophy.
>
> Myths, including the Gnostic myths, may be interpreted in diverse ways. Transcendence, numinosity, as well as psychological archetypes along with other elements, play a role in such interpretation. Still, such mythic statements tell of profound truths that will not be denied.

"....In the end, will matter be utterly destroyed or not?"

"Everything, every form, every creature," replied Jesus, "connects to everything. In the end, all will dissolve together into their root elements."

"You have told us almost everything," said Peter. "Tell us one more thing? What is the sin of the world?"

"There is no such thing as sin. You *create* sin when you fail to pursue the good within your own nature." Peter frowned. Jesus went on: "You get sick because you love that which deceives you. Reflect on this, and remember how I told you to seek contentment of the heart."

To those present—Mary of Magdala, Peter, his brother Andrew, and Levi—Jesus gave his final blessing, for after being crucified he had returned to teach them all he could, and now it was time to depart:

"Peace be with you! Acquire my peace within yourselves!

"Guard yourselves against deceivers who point over here or over there to indicate my return—for the image of true humanity lives within *you*. Follow it! Those who search for it will find it.

"Go forth, share the good news about the Kingdom of Heaven, and do not get caught in rules and laws, or one day they will dominate you. Farewell."

When he vanished, the male apostles wept. "How are we to announce this good news?" they asked. "Look at what they did to him! Surely they won't spare us."

Mary stood up and gave each of them a kiss. "Do not let your hearts be irresolute. His grace will be with us whatever befalls us. Instead of weeping in distress, we should celebrate how he has united us and made us true human beings."

Peter found his voice:

"Sister, we know he loved you more than any other woman. Did he tell you anything that we have not yet heard?"

"Yes, because I saw him in a vision.

"When I greeted him, he said, 'How wonderful you are for not wavering at my appearance. Where the mind is, there is the treasure.'

"I asked him, 'Do we see visions with the soul or with the spirit?'

"'Neither,' he replied; 'visions are seen with mind, which is between soul and spirit.'

"'Why are you here?' I asked, to which he replied, 'To tell you of the ascent of the soul through the heavenly realms.'"

Peter and Andrew frowned. They had never heard the Savior

touch on this.

"To reach the heights," explained Mary, "the soul must face seven evil Powers, one after the other as it rises. The first Power the soul encounters is the archon called Darkness. The soul must hold to the Light within the Darkness to move beyond this Power.

"The second Power is Desire. To transcend Desire the soul must distinguish between what is surface and what is true self.

"The third Power is Ignorance. Here the soul must be free from judging.

"The fourth Power is zeal for death, the fifth the lure of the flesh, the sixth the foolish speech of the flesh, and the seventh the speech of the wrathful; all these are manifestations of Wrath. To bypass them, the soul must know its own liberation from ignorance, desire, time and its forgetfulness, and every archetype, however high above; and it must rest and receive in silence." The vision had ended here.

After a moment, Andrew looked at the others. "Say what you will about this, I do not believe the Savior taught these things to her. These are strange ideas."

"Are we to believe," asked Peter, "that he spoke in private to a woman about things he did not teach us? Are we to be taught by her, then? Did he choose her over us?"

Seeing their ignorance, Mary wept for them. "Peter, what do you imagine, that I thought all this up? That I lie about the Savior?"

"Peter," said Levi, "you have always been full of wrath. You contend against Mary as though you were one of the evil Powers. If the Savior believed her worthy, who are you to reject her? He knew her well. That is why he loved her more than us. Because of that, we should be ashamed of ourselves. Let us put on the perfect Human, as he taught us, and go tell the good news, making no rules or laws apart from what the Savior said."

Levi left to begin preaching. After a while, the others went out too.

For Reflection:
- Comment: This tale circulated before the rise of institutional Christianity, so it is not alternative or revision-

ist. It reflects the Gnostic belief in Mary Magdalene (from *Magdala*: "fish tower" or "drying rack") as the true inheritor of the inner teachings of Jesus. As he tells her in another Gnostic source, "Mary, thou blessed one, whom I will perfect in all mysteries of those of the height, discourse in openness, thou, whose heart is raised to the kingdom of heaven more than all thy brethren." In another he calls her "the fullness of all fullnesses and the perfection of all perfections." In the *Pistis Sophia* she asks more deep questions than the other disciples together. In the *Acts of Philip* she disguises herself as a man so she can teach and baptize while evading the authorities. In the *Gospel of Philip* she is referred as the *koinônos* of Jesus, a word that means partner, companion, or consort. In the gospels included in the Bible, Mary is first of all to announce the Resurrection; a later tradition calls her Apostle to the Apostles.

- Where else in the spiritual traditions of the world can be found the image of all things being interconnected? Of all forms passing away?

- Jesus — who makes no mention of hell or damnation in this tale — describes sin as an inauthentic *relation* rather than as an evil *substance*. Why is this idea radical? Why would self-appointed religious authorities consider it heretical?

- What are the implications of Jesus commanding the apostles to find true humanity within themselves instead of waiting for him to return?

- What does it mean to be possessed by an archetype, and how is it possible to be liberated from it?

- Many Gnostics believed that the hardening of Jesus' teachings into archontic laws and literalisms was coming true all around them as orthodox elements of early Christianity gained political power in the Eastern

Mediterranean, Northern Egypt, and, eventually, in Rome itself. What does this tale suggest about the archontification of the early church as founded, not by Mary, but by Peter, who cut off a slave's ear, betrayed Jesus with silence before the cock crowed, fell asleep in Gethsemane, and was called "Satan" by Jesus in the *Gospel of Mark*?

- Levi has often been understood as a name of the apostle Matthew, but here he seems to be a man of faith apart from the other apostles. Perhaps his story was written out of the Bible because he sided with Mary. (In other Gnostic sources Mary complains to Jesus that she fears Peter because he hates women and has no comprehension of the inner teachings.) Who resembles Levi today?

- Although the vision of ascent can be interpreted as the soul's path after the body dies, how might we hold it psychologically as a guide for dealing with inner and outer manifestations of malevolent powers?

- Otherworldly belief stories have been criticized by George Orwell, William James, and many others as failures to confront problems in the daily material world. However, scholar Karen King writes that the dialogues in the Gospel of Mary, a source of this tale, "instruct the reader in the truth about the very nature of Reality by contrasting it with the deception that characterizes life in the world...a biting critique of how power is exercised in the lower world under the guise of law and justice." Additionally, "The mythic framework of the *Gospel of Mary* allows the spiritual, the psychological, the social, the political, and the cosmic to be integrated under one guiding principle: resistance to the unjust and illegitimate domination of ignorant and malevolent Powers." How else might myth constitute a quiet but potent form of resistance to injustice?

The Awakening of Siddhartha (Buddhist)

Sita Brand, Buddhist actor, producer, storyteller, and owner of Settle Stories:

> I grew up in Bombay, and in India, everything is stories. There's always some cultural festival taking place and there's always a story behind it. There's always a story being told to you.
>
> These old folktales like Cinderella or Little Red Riding Hood, or the other versions of them, you can find them the world over. Take Cinderella, there's a Vietnamese version and various north African versions, a North American version, a European one ...
>
> One of the wonderful things about stories is the way, within that safety net, you can explore those difficult feelings and experiences you wouldn't want to in real life. And once you've come to terms with them and found a way through them, that allows you to put them to rest.

He sat down under the fig tree and let the remnants of his life drop away. Childhood as a young prince, marriage to Yasodharā, fatherhood, departure, years of yoga and ascetic austerities, journeying, arrival here in this isolated spot: the memories floated through the detached consciousness he first tasted while watching his father farming. When they drifted on, still he sat there under the friendly tree, waiting. He would not rise until he understood the truth of his existence.

As he sat, he grew aware of motion in the distance. After a time he could make out what it was: Mara approaching with a heavily armed host of warriors.

The god of illusion rode on the broad back of an elephant, an army of demons marching behind him. Steaming tongues hung from mouths like black gashes filled with glistening fangs below eyes glowing like hot coals. Soldiers with the heads of donkeys or lions carried axes and swords dripping with blood.

They were coming for Siddhartha.

"Let me at him first!" some shouted; "no, I will kill the monk first!" "My eyes will burn him to cinders!" "I will drink his blood!" Laughter.

Deep in meditation, eyes open but gaze soft, Siddhartha did not move.

At a gesture of Mara's, terrific winds swept in to uproot trees, knock over cattle, and destroy entire villages. The ground shook.

Siddhartha did not move. No wind touched him.

Torrents of rain obliterated hillsides and filled valleys. Choking rivers of mud flowed by, carrying all within their lethal grasp.

Siddhartha did not move. Not a drop fell upon his robe.

From the rear of the oncoming army, armored demons unleashed a cloud of arrows that whistled as they pierced the sky. Closer at hand, troops hurled great rocks at the still form of Siddhartha, who did not move as rocks and arrows alike changed into falling flowers that came to rest on the ground around where he sat beneath the tree. To Mara's fury, he saw a faint smile on the face of the meditating man.

At another gesture from Mara the entire army charged forward, swords and axes raised, cries of battle tearing through the air. This mighty force ran straight into the shield of light around Siddhartha and bounced. Swinging weapons changed into flowers fluttering down atop the layer of petals already on the ground. Stunned, the demons backed away and ran off, grunting.

From around the halted elephant stepped the three lovely daughters of Mara: Tanha, Arati, and Raga. Smiling, they danced before Siddhartha, revolving their hips in sinuous circles as their naked arms beckoned him to bed. They pouted prettily when he took no notice of them. They evaporated like the demons.

At this, Mara rode up close and looked down through slitted eyes.

"By what right," he called, arms crossed, "do you sit there under that tree like a lord?"

"By right," replied Siddhartha calmly, "of my strivings for awakening over many lifetimes." They had come back to him in all their banality, terror, and glory as he sat beneath the tree. "By right of having identified the truth of suffering, the cause of suffering by craving, the cessation of craving, and the path of liberation."

"I too have striven, as my minions will verify. But who will vouch for you?"

In response, Siddhartha lifted his right hand and placed it gently on the ground.

"*I, Earth,*" rumbled a powerful voice from below, from all around, "*have seen this man in service over many previous existences up to now, when he surpasses all living men in wisdom and generosity. I will vouch for him.*" Silence.

Then Mara slid down and walked up to Siddhartha.

"All right," he said in a reasonable tone. "No more tricks. Just tell me one thing. After all your striving, all your effort, and all your contemplation, why not just go on to Nirvana and final peace? Why bother to stay and teach? Do you really imagine that people want to be enlightened?" He chuckled. "No indeed. They are but children and fools who want comfort, enjoyment, and somebody to look up to and be led by. A few want worldly power; others, lavish garments and gems; still others, beautiful lovers. And that's about it. Why would you even consider sticking around on *their* behalf?"

For a long while Siddhartha thought it over as the waters of Mara's floods receded, soaked up by the earth. The sun warmed the tree behind him. Its leaves rippled in the breeze.

How much had humanity really changed over time? How far had people in general, aside from the occasional exceptions, proceeded along the hard-to-find and harder-to-accomplish Eightfold Path of enlightenment? Was there any signs of real progress at all?

And were there not many Buddhas and boddhisattvas devoting entire lifetimes to the salvation of all beings? What was one man's effort, however sustained, by comparison? Would it make any real difference to the cosmic depths and heights if he did go his way in eternal peace, forsaking the world of material being with its clinging delights, ignorant leaders, and passive led?

At length Siddhartha made his reply:

"I will stay and teach," he stated, "because some will understand."

Shaking his head, Mara vanished.

Siddhartha got slowly to his feet. He patted the tree, looked around, and chose a direction. He walked.

After walking most of the day, he met some officials of a nearby kingdom. As they greeted each other on the road, the officials noted a strange look and light hovering about the half-smiling traveler asking permission to teach at court.

"We would like to know who you are first, for you glow strangely and your voice, though mild, carries great power. Are you perchance a god?"

"No."

"A demon, then?"

"No."

"Some other elemental power?"

"No."

"....Or a worldly authority going about in humble guise?"

"No."

"Oh. Well. Then, may we ask: just what are you?"

Siddhartha's smile might have been tinged with sadness; then again, it might not. His clear brown eyes neither squinted nor drooped, but held steady. His voice was quiet, friendly, and calm:

"I am awake."

For Reflection:
- Origin stories of the Buddha say the sight of illness and death triggered his quest to understand life deeply. How would they prompt such seeking?
- Symbolically speaking, why would he pick a tree to sit under?
- How would you describe his relationship with Earth?
- Why do myths collect around actual historical figures?

What do the myths add to how we receive what such people stand for?

- Some complain about the difficulty of meditating in noisy surroundings. How does Siddhartha manage it?

- Mara trying to tempt the Buddha has often been compared to Satan tempting Jesus with power and fame. Why are these Trickster temptations mythically necessary?

- For his last temptation Mara employs what might be called the Voice of Political Pragmatism, the voice that so often refers to the public as "the masses." Dostoevsky's famous Grand Inquisitor in *The Brothers Karamazov* uses the same voice to rationalize controlling people for their own good with "miracle, mystery, and authority." What view does this attitude imply about human nature? What is gained by seeing people this way?

- The names of Mara's daughters mean Craving, Boredom, and Passion. In other versions of the story, two other daughters show up: Fear and Pride. Why are they seductive? What distinction might be made between feeling these impulses and identifying with them?

- What is the difference between "some will understand" and going on a mission to awaken all of humanity?

Toán and the Whale (Yurok)

Kathy Wallace, Yurok and Karuk oral traditionalist, basketry expert, assistant lecturer for the American Indian Studies Department, and Cultural Liaison at San Francisco State University:

> Because I'm from an area that was not impacted as soon as a lot of areas in California, even though our ceremonies were outlawed, even though we had the boarding

experience and a lot went underground compared to the other tribes in the state, we kept a lot of our traditions alive and going.

Within our tribe we have cultural committees and we have natural resources committees, and we have lawyers, and we have people who can contend with all the different problems and have the expertise. But like I said, sometimes for some tribes in the state that is not the case at all.

Basically we are taught that if you have a gift, you're supposed to use it; and if you can, you teach it. It's not something that's sitting static there, it's not something you own yourself. You need to give it away, spread it around. When you really think about it, that's a form of resistance. Making it a living thing, instead of something dead and spoken about in what happened a long time ago or what we used to do. It keeps us alive.

Redwood on stone. The sturdy four-sided house named Pekwoi had sheltered many generations of well-respected family, but with the world tilted out of balance, trouble was coming for lovely thick-haired Nemen and her parents and grandparents.

It arrived when she fell in love with a young man who lived in the village of Kotep. His family was poor and almost invisible; hers, prominent and well-known. When she swelled with the new life in her belly, her lover promised to work faithfully for her father, but Nemen's shocked family would have none of it. In fact, they confined her to Pekwoi.

No one knows what happened to her lover after he went away in sorrow. After he left, they kicked her out for good.

In desperation, she moved in with Huné, mother of her vanished lover. Huné had little enough to share—a bit of food, a dilapidated house—but she cared for Nemen as though for a daughter of her own. Her love spilled over onto the baby, happy Toán, who came into a troubled but warm little world.

A year after Huné died, families headed upriver to participate in the World Renewal dance. Nemen had not planned to go, but friends of hers paddling by shouted invitations until she agreed to show up later.

When she did, with her baby and herself neatly groomed, everyone welcomed her and her son—except her family. Looking across the fires that lit the way for the dance teams, she saw them deliberately ignoring her.

When no one was looking, she slipped away into the night, weeping bitterly. The patter of salty teardrops woke little Toán, who wondered at his mother's sadness.

She put him down so they could walk together. She had selected this trail around Kewet Mountain because few used it and she did not want to be seen. Reaching Fish Lake, she made camp and they bedded down for the night.

Normally, the shamans and the dancers kept the world in balance, but odd things could happen when it tipped. One such imbalance had raised the ocean so high that it washed a young whale into Fish Lake.

This whale, whose name was Ninawa, heard Nemen talking to herself in her sleep and understood at once why she cried. Nemen's sorrow moved her so much that she decided to do something to help mother and son, both abandoned. Laying across the water, Ninawa willed them to walk across her back on their long way home.

Nemen tidied up in the morning, fed her son, and broke camp. Seeing adventurous Toán climbing up onto what seemed an enormous wet log, Nemen followed him across.

* * * *

Nemen's father's father had seen everything: his granddaughter's rejection and exile, her relocation to the shabby house by the river, the death of Huné. It was not his place to advise anyone directly, so he didn't. Instead, he simply showed up with his woodworking tools one day in front of Nemen's house and began fashioning a large box.

When Toán ambled over to watch, he offered to help his great grandson make his own box. When it was finished, Toán put bird feathers in it.

As the boy got older, his great-grandfather suggested he stop collecting feathers and go in search of birds. In reply to Toán's puzzled stare he crafted a bow and some arrows, showing how it was done, and then taught Toán how to use them.

His great-grandson was a natural. He brought back birds, then fish, then many other game animals as he learned their paths and tracks, their places of rest and gathering, the kinds of weather that helped him hunt, the asking of permission of the game to sacrifice itself to his arrows, net, and knife. By the time the old man died, Toán was the best hunter in the entire region.

In sorrow for the passing of the man who had taught him so much, Toán sought out Fish Lake and, alone, went to sleep there, noting that the log he had crossed over so long ago was gone.

In a dream, Ninawa the whale came to him.

"Remember," she asked him, "that trembling underfoot when you crossed the big log? I was that log. The ocean washed me into that lake."

"Why are you no longer here?"

"The Inland Spirits carried me away to a larger lake. It is a not place for humans to behold."

"Why are you visiting me, then?"

"Because I remember when, after your mother made camp, how confused you were by her weeping. I heard because, like her, and like you, I too know what it is to be cast out of a family. I decided to see if I could help the two of you.

"Toán, like us, the winter moons are outcasts, the children of lonely parents. Yet they bring the rains that grow the green, blooming life through all the warmer months. I decided that you too should have the strength of the winter moons. As you walked from my tail to my head, I sent my power into you for a blessing."

"To what aim?"

"So that when you come of age, you, the exiled son of an exiled mother, will be the greatest and most successful of all the sons of Pekwoi.

"Remember what your great-grandfather taught you. Remember your mother's lessons in manners and in the ways of the sweat purification. Pray to the winter moons. Dance to keep the world in balance. And don't forget that once you walked on Ninawa's back."

Toán remembered. Even after his fame spread, his wealth grew and circulated, his uncle invited him back to Pekwoi to live, he married the village woman he loved, he took up his position as head of Kotep, and he invited his aging mother to live with his wife and children, he remembered.

"Welcome home," they greeted Nemen.

He danced with the villagers and the shamans, and the world came back into balance.

In a distant boat-shaped lake far inland, Ninawa's huge tail struck the water with a satisfied slap.

For Reflection:
- What could be the mythic purpose or meaning behind this series of exiles? What is gained or served by them on the personal level? The collective? The archetypal?

- What does this story suggest about imbalances within the self, the family, the tribe, and the natural world? What does it take to correct these imbalances?

- What predisposes a family of one social class to look down on people of another social class? Why were Nemen's parents outraged?

- The nuclear family has been pointed to as a model family, but everyone suffers when the nucleus splits, or when parents receive insufficient emotional support. How does the extended family structure support Nemen and her son in spite of their being outcasts from their nuclear family?

- What strengths come from being a conscious outcast?

How is culture served by those who identify as outsiders? How does one know when the status of outcast no longer serves?

- How would you describe the great-grandfather's mentoring style with his grandson? Why are his family interventions not more vocal and active? Should they be?

- How might Toán have ended up without an attentive great-grandfather, a pious mother, and a strong connection to the natural world to educate him? Where do the neglected and ignored Toáns end up today?

- In 2011, a 45-foot gray whale swam into the estuary near the Yurok village of Requa. She survived for two months before beaching herself and dying. Yurok Janet Wortman said about this, "She would just swim back and forth right in front of you and at one point go like this, like she was waving at us. Silly me, I waved back. It was like she was there to see people. She went back and forth. It was almost like she was going, `Here I am, you guys. Can you see me?'" Some passersby played flutes and violins for the whale as she floated under the Highway 101 bridge over the Klamath River. After she died, her calf swam out to sea. The Yurok took this event as an indicator of a dangerous loss of balance in the world. Why? And why else would the myth recur?

Chapter Seven - Heroes and Monsters

The archetypal Hero tends to be a loner, eloquent, physically brave, initially impulsive, brooding, reckless, suspended between self-indulgence and self-renunciation, torn between cynicism and idealism, intensely ambivalent about being in the limelight, many-named, often cross-dressed or humorously attired, equipped with unusual transportation, more comfortable with being a follower than a leader, a mother's rather than a father's child, challenged in knowing when to withdraw from a bad situation, and death-seeking when failing to live up to high ideals.

In myth, not all heroes transform, but a key task of the archetypal Hero is to make the transition from an external hero of force to a self-reflective cultural hero of wisdom and principle.

Perceval Seeks the Grail (French)

Albert Camus, French novelist, playwright, and philosopher:

> If one believes Homer, Sisyphus was the wisest and most prudent of mortals. According to another tradition, however, he was disposed to practice the profession of highwayman. I see no contradiction in this....

> If this myth is tragic, that is because its hero is conscious. Where would his torture be, indeed, if at every step the hope of succeeding upheld him? ...Sisyphus, proletarian of the gods, powerless and rebellious, knows the whole extent of his wretched condition: it is what he thinks of during his descent. The lucidity that was to constitute his torture at the same time crowns his victory.

> Then a tremendous remark rings out: "Despite so many ordeals, my advanced age and the nobility of my soul make me conclude that all is well." Sophocles' Oedipus, like Dostoevsky's Kirilov, thus gives the recipe for the absurd victory. Ancient wisdom confirms modern heroism.

Perceval's eyes were half-closed from fatigue, but they were open enough to take in the most strongly defended castle they had ever beheld. Powerful turrets surmounted smooth, thick walls whose arrow-deflecting curves might have been turned on a lathe. A mighty drawbridge sealed off the structure from attack of any conceivable size.

Not that Perceval planned to attack anyone. He could barely sit on his horse.

"Lo there!" he hailed a squire stationed near the drawbridge.

"Who goes there?"

"Sir Perceval of Camelot. I seek lodgings for the night. A fisherman directed me here."

With a ponderous clanking, the drawbridge ascended to let him ride into the castle.

Once inside, he entered a grassy courtyard and dismounted. The knights and squires who greeted him there smiled in friendliness, but Perceval thought he caught a mood of sadness.

After they removed his red armor, washed the dust of travel from him, and draped a silk cloak around him, attendants led him to a chamber of candlelit tables laden with food.

There he rested in conversation with other knights until a well-dressed attendant entered and addressed him in a supercilious tone: "Would His Majesty care to be shown into the presence of his host now?"

"Pray do not take offense," cautioned the knights who had seen Perceval's balled fist; "he is but a jester accustomed to making merry with guests."

Thrusting away his anger, Perceval walked into a hall lit by chandeliers of every conceivable size and form. His gaze swept past what seemed to be a hundred couches covered with rich quilts, candles without number suspended from wall niches, and lush round carpets underfoot. Three cavernous marble fireplaces emitted pleasing aromas.

Although all present were well-behaved, Perceval spotted an occasional glance directed at him by women and some of the men. He knew that glance, for God had made him an uncommonly handsome knight, as his wife Blancheflor was fond of noting.

Through an ornate entrance limped an old man on the arms of two attendants. In spite of the warmth he wore a fur jacket covered by a long black cloak. On his gray hair perched a crown-shaped fur hat bearing a single ruby.

When he had been seated, he gestured for Perceval to join him. "Welcome to Castle Corbenic," he called just as Perceval recognized him as the fisherman who had directed him here.

Before the small talk Perceval always dreaded had gone very far, a strange procession entered the hall: two squires bearing candelabra on either side of a third squire holding a shining white lance. Silence spread through the hall as they passed directly in front of

Perceval and his host. Drops of blood fell from the tip of the lance.

As the squires crossed the hall, a group of laurel-crowned maidens in green dresses brought in bright candles in gold holders. In their center advanced a woman in white holding a glowing chalice. With her every step, beams of candlelight flashed from its rim and handle. Behind her, other maidens carried items Perceval took to be sacred objects: a book, a broken sword, a silver platter....

As they too passed near Perceval, he yearned to ask the lord of the castle what it all meant, but Gornemant, Perceval's mentor in arms and etiquette, had chided him for always asking too many questions. He held his tongue. The room dimmed as the maiden with the chalice left the hall.

Dinner was served, but with a polite but discernible unhappiness now evident. Had he committed some faux pas? Tact had never been his chief gift, Perceval knew. He learned that his host had been stabbed in the groin long ago, a wound that had never healed, and that his castle sat in a diseased countryside, but little else.

Eventually, he was escorted, politely if rather coldly, to his room. He lay down gratefully in a large bed, drew the covers over himself, and slept soundly.

He rose the following morning with an odd silence around him. No one came to wait on him. He dressed and walked from room to room but found no one present. Everyone, it seemed, had left the castle. He wondered why.

Arming himself, he greeted his horse in the courtyard. He could think of no reason to stay and saw nobody to thank, so he saddled his mount, got up, and trotted across the drawbridge. Behind him it lifted, drawn by invisible hands, and sealed the entrance again. He shook his head and rode on.

He had not ridden far when he came upon a pale maiden seated upon the ground. Her thinning hair had once been rich and brown. In her bloody lap she held a dead knight in dented armor. Tears glistened on her contorted face.

"What happened?" he asked, dismounting and sitting down beside her.

In answer, she could only sob. Perceval held her hand and waited. It took time for her to gather herself enough to speak clearly.

"Who are you," she asked, "why are you here, and where are you headed?"

"I am Sir Perceval of Camelot, and I was trying to get home to see my mother when a fisherman directed me to a fabulous castle. I spent the night there."

"Do you not recognize me? Perhaps not; the years have not been kind to me. I am your cousin Sigune."

"Sigune!"

"Yes, and our meeting can be no coincidence. —What did you see in the castle?"

"Many wonders. A great hall lit by three fireplaces, and knights who seemed sad. A strange procession passed by, with a squire carrying a bleeding lance and a maiden in green carrying a glowing chalice."

"Do you know what you saw?"

"No. I did not ask."

"Why not? You beheld two surpassing wonders of the world: the spear that pierced the side of Christ, and an even greater marvel: the Holy Grail into which His blood poured out on the day He was crucified. Were you not curious about such wonders?"

"A mentor once told me I asked too many questions."

"Oh, Perceval! To be wise requires knowing when *not* to follow even the best advice. Had you asked the right question, the Fisher King whose castle you visited would have been healed of his wound, and the terrible waste spreading through the region been halted."

He had wondered why things around here looked so dreary, lifeless, and dark.

"Furthermore," Sigune went on, "your trip is for naught. Your mother—Aunt Herzeloyde—died of grief not long after you left home to find the court of King Arthur."

He put his hands over his eyes. *Can this day get any worse?* he wondered. Despite all his efforts and accomplishments—striking out on his own, training in knighthood, defeating the Red Knight who had shamed King Arthur's court, marrying Blancheflor—he was the same innocent, bumbling boy he had always been. The greatest of all holy mysteries had been within his grasp, and he had lacked the wisdom to recognize it. What a fool he was.

After parting from his cousin, Perceval long sought the Grail Castle but could not find it. Every time he thought he got close, some lout of a knight would rise up to challenge him. As a result, a long line of prisoners ended up in Camelot swearing their loyalty to King Arthur. One of these was the Haughty Knight who had slain his cousin's friend.

"I'd like to know," Arthur told his court, "who that knight in the red armor is so we could invite him to the Round Table."

*   *   *   *

Had his cousin come upon Perceval five years later, she would scarcely have recognized him again.

Years of fruitless search had hardened his body against the elements, sharpened his knowledge of the forest, and seasoned out his innocence. With it had gone his idealism and most of his faith. He could not remember the last time he had been shriven or prayed in a church. With twisted creatures and evil knights patrolling the swelling darkness abroad in the land of Logres, pleas for divine help seemed pointless. For every highwayman he trounced, two more waited for him down the road. Trees died and streams dried up regardless of whom or what he defeated. The land would not be healed through contests of arms.

Spending time with a hermit living on the edge of the Wasteland felt like the first comfort in a long spell of inner and outer aridity. Without a hint of judgment, the hermit suggested that Perceval reflect more deeply on why he had failed at the Grail Castle.

By the time the young knight went his way again, his faith had not returned fully, but his heart was open again. He felt ready to go back at last to Camelot.

After doing well in a tournament there, it pleased him to see the surprised expressions all around when he removed his red helmet before the court. After the unveiling he was asked by the king himself to join the fellowship of the Table Round. The rite of passage in which he took the oath to serve God, king, the poor, and the helpless revived his weary soul. He rode forth again.

All Round Table Knights know adventure in plenty, but Perceval's doings gained in complexity and depth. Instead of rescuing maidens and fighting foes, he found himself engaged with increasingly symbolic endeavors: retrieving a magic hound and stag's head, mending a broken sword, recognizing an enemy knight as a friend, helping his wife expunge a recurrent evil at her castle. Once he played chess against an invisible opponent—and lost. On another occasion he accepted a maiden's request to convey a magic ring to the Grail Castle once he finally found it again. *If* he found it....

By the time five more years had passed, he reflected: *I have just begun to understand what I thought I knew well but did not know at all: the true flower and essence of knighthood.* Every wayward event reminded him now of the root meaning of *knight:* "to serve."

At the top of Mount Dolorous he hitched his horse to a peculiar pillar seemingly installed there for just that purpose. As he tied the rope, the voice of an old man drifted over his shoulder:

"I always thought you showed promise."

Perceval turned and beheld a short, white-haired gnome of a fellow in a hooded gown as deep and dark a blue as the pre-dawn sky. Stars cavorted on a matching cap. He leaned upon a long, gnarled staff whose end bore a playful wisp of faery light.

Merlin smiled. "What has happened to that blundering bull of a boy peeling potatoes in King Arthur's kitchen?"

"He grew up, I guess."

"I guess he did. Do you recall the first time you saw a Round Table knight?"

"Yes. Three of them riding by our home. I saw the light reflected off their shields and thought the riders were angels."

"Your dear mother tried to keep you from knighthood, God rest her soul, after your father and brothers, all knights, perished in battle; but the call to deeds was stronger. Are you ready to take the next step along the way?"

"Frankly, I don't know what the next step is, let alone where the way leads. I have searched for the Holy Grail for ten hard years without success. My armor is dented, my sword is pitted, and my horse is old and tired. My heart is weary with what I have seen; the land itself is bleeding. —Do you know where the Grail Castle stands? Does it really exist, or did I just think I was there once?"

Merlin chuckled and skipped a little jig. "Why, the Grail Castle stands over here and over there, near the sea or in the air, high and low, above and below, everywhere and nowhere, without and within—and always where you least expect it."

He threw back his head and emitted a falling series of barking laughs, making a downward scooping gesture with his left hand as he did this. He melted, and with him everything else: hill, grass, bushes, post, horse, even the sky, all streaming down into a polychromatic puddle that built itself back up into flagstones, rugs, couches, pillars, fireplaces, candles by the hundreds, the wounded Fisher King at his side, knights looking on, and a procession of maidens and squires bearing sacred objects.

Vanished Merlin's voice whispered like a breeze: *"This time don't blow it."*

One of the objects was the Holy Grail. A lady in green held it out—within reach.

Perceval stared at it with wordless longing. It was the loveliest, most precious thing he had ever seen.

As he stared at it, he remembered his oath, his wanderings. He remembered lessons painfully learned along the way: from brushes with death, from other knights, from mentors, from prayer, from his wise and loving wife. And with a surge of humility leavened with pride and loyalty, he remembered King Arthur's dignified response to a visiting knight's saucy question about those who sat at the Table Round: "The best men in the world."

Perhaps he would lose his chance again, and for the last time; but he would do it striving to be a true knight.

Turning aside from the Grail, Perceval bent to the Fisher King, took his hand, and asked:

"What ails thee?"

A sudden blaze from the Grail lit the room brighter than if a stroke of lightning had fallen. No concussion followed, but as Perceval's eyes cleared, he saw the Fisher King standing straight up before him without assistance. Everyone cheered.

"What ailed me," said the king, "has been healed at last. I most heartily thank you — grandson."

As they embraced, clear beams of sunlight shone on the plains beyond the windows. In place of barren ground and twisted trees, Perceval now saw strong trunks and grassy hills. Chirping birds filled the bright air as deer dashed by. The scourge had been lifted from the land. His heart began to soar.

"Grandson?" he asked.

"I am descended from Joseph of Arimathea," replied the king, face smooth now with the lines of pain gone at last, "who caught the blood of Jesus in yonder cup and brought it here to the Land of Logres. You too are of his lineage, which means that when my time on earth is ended, you will be the next Grail King, with happier responsibilities than my own have been."

"How did you come to be wounded, Grandfather?"

"Like so many of the men in our line of Crusaders, I spent my youth in recklessness and violent foolishness. While out in the woods I tasted salmon flesh that was not meant for me, and a fiery thrust deprived me of my manhood. Until now, grandson. Until now."

"I have so many questions — "

"In good time. For now, you have more pressing business."

"What is that?"

"Hadn't you better go home and tell your wife?"

For Reflection:
- Comment: Like many other key elements in the Arthurian tales, the Fisher King begins in Welsh mythology. In the *Mabinogion* he is known as Bran the Blessed, a giant king who gives his daughter Branwen in marriage to Irish lords and then attacks them when they mistreat her. Mortally wounded, he asks that his

head be buried in London, where King Arthur eventually finds it. The men who transport the still-talking head pass some time in a magic castle. Bran's life-reviving cauldron, destroyed in the war, returns as the Holy Grail.

- Another Grail echo shows up in the Irish Dagda's pot of food, the inexhaustible Undry; and another in the witch Cerridwen's pot. Why is this archetypal Grail so difficult for mortals to obtain?

- What indications reflect pre-initiated Perceval's psychological immaturity?

- What is the symbolic import of the Grail King being a fisherman? (He parallels the Irish hero Finn mac Cumhail, who ate the forbidden Salmon of Knowledge.)

- Why does Perceval fail during his first visit to the Grail Castle?

- Lady Herzeloyde tries so much to protect Perceval from even seeing a knight that when he finally does, he is overcome with a desire for knighthood. How did she set him up for this, and by doing so obtain exactly the result she most dreaded?

- How does Perceval overcome his mother complex (or does he)?

- What do the years of search teach Perceval about true knighthood (and maturity)?

- The saints of many faiths describe spiritual states of inner aridity. John of the Cross, for instance, compared them to green wood being consumed by fire. What purposes are served by such painful states?

- What do you suppose convinces Merlin to help Perceval find the Grail Castle?

- Why is "What ails thee?" the right question?

- How might "Crusading" be linked to the wounding of the masculine in Perceval's family line?

- What does this tale tell us about the relationship between our health and that of the land?

Princess Bari Revives Her Family (Korean)

Shin Bum Shik, Korean Minister of Culture and Information:

> A nation without her myths is solitary, a land without its legends is barren, and a people without their folktales are devoid of creative power.
>
> In every corner of our beautiful land we have a good many grandiose legends. They have never been dead; they have always been alive in our hearts. And our folktales, an inexhaustible source of interest, are a good manifestation of the creative imagination of our forebears who taught themselves to help themselves. folktales, therefore, have served as a good companion of our people in our jealous vigilance for our independence.

When the prince reached a marriageable age, his father the king sent a trusted court lady to ask the best soothsayer in the kingdom how to find his son a wife.

"If the prince marries in a bad year," said the soothsayer, "he will have seven princesses but no male heirs. If he marries in a good year, he can expect seven princes."

When the king heard this, he let his impatience make the decision: his son would marry as soon as possible so he could get busy producing an heir.

At length the prince became the king. One of his first acts as king was to get his fortune read. "Unfortunately," said the soothsayer, "you married in an inauspicious year for sons, so all you can expect are daughters."

The new king sneered at this prediction and went his way. What could mere oracles tell him anyway?

Six princesses later, the king wasn't sneering, nor was he so young anymore. How could this happen? Was he cursed to die without an heir? Who would look after the ancestral shrine? Had he committed some terrible injustice in a past life?

When the queen became pregnant for the seventh time, she dreamed that a blue hawk sat on her right hand, a white hawk on her left hand, and a gold turtle on her lap. The sun and moon shone light on her shoulders. Blue and gold dragons twisted themselves around the ceiling beams of the room in the dream.

"Surely," said the king, "this must mean that a prince will be born to us." He sent for a reading on this, but to his intense disappointment, the soothsayer predicted another daughter. And so it was.

At first the king wanted to place his seventh daughter for adoption, but the queen objected. Then he tried to abandon his daughter in the back garden, but crows and magpies descended and covered the girl protectively with their wings.

"All right," decided the king; "I will give her as a sacrifice to the Dragon King in the sea. I owe him a gift anyway."

The girl was placed in a jade chest with a bottle of her mother's milk, a note stating when she had been born, and a lock shaped like a gold turtle. The Minister of Education picked up the chest and took it down to a river that fed into the sea. As the grass and birds looked on, he set it in the water.

A sharp clap of thunder rang across the land as a turtle surfaced, nosed the chest onto its back, and swam off.

The Buddha and his followers were walking near the East Sea when they spotted mist and clouds rising. Drawing closer, they saw gangs of crows and magpies darting and circling and cawing. Closer still, and they saw the jade chest. Retrieving it, the Buddha opened it and found the girl.

"A boy," he mused, "might have made a disciple." Instead, he brought the girl to an old man, Birigongduk, and asked him and his wife to adopt her.

She was remarkably quick, the girl, learning reading, writing, and the sky and land sciences on her own.

"Where are my birth parents?" she asked those who had raised her.

"We are," they replied, surprised.

"Impossible," she said, "you are too old."

"Heaven and earth are your parents," they said.

"Heaven and earth are everyone's parents," she said. "Try again."

"You are a magical child," they said. "The paulownia tree on the hill is your mother, and the giant bamboo in Cholla your father."

Her "father" was too far away to reach, but she visited the tree with respect three times a day from then on.

*   *   *   *

Several years later, the king and queen grew ill. When the healers could do nothing, they consulted a soothsayer.

"By discarding your daughter," the oracle informed them, "you have also thrown away your lives. You will both die on the same day because of this evil act."

Not long after this prophecy, the king and queen shared a dream. In it six blue spirits flew down toward the royal couple. "Because you abandoned your daughter," they announced, "we have come to remove your souls from the world."

"Is there nothing we can do," asked the royal couple, "to go on living?"

"You must go and find your daughter and bring her home. Then you must take the Elixir of Life from the mountain of the goddess Samshin and the Medicine of the hermit who guards a certain shrine."

When they woke up, the couple hurriedly sent out the Minister of Education with official letters and seals, vials of blood drawn from the parents' hands, and some of the girl's baby clothes.

The magpies and crows arrowed to give him direction along the way, and the grass leaned forward when he kept to the right path. At length he reached the home of Birigongduk and his wife.

Greeting the young woman, he told her of being sent by her birth parents. At first she did not believe him, not even when he presented the letters, seals, and baby garments. But when he drew blood from her ring finger and set it on a tray with the blood of her parents, all ran together and joined into one red pool that emitted a little cloud.

"I will go and see for myself," she told him.

"The royal palanquin awaits to bear you there," he replied.

"No. I will ride my own horse."

Swinging herself up onto the horse's back, she decided she would need a new name. *Let it be Princess Bari,* she thought. It meant "Princess Letting Go."

Naturally, her parents were delighted to see her. But after the tearful reunion, the problem of retrieving the Elixir and Medicine remained. "Who will retrieve them?" asked the king anxiously, looking around.

Six of his daughters made excuses not to go. They were spoiled and valued only their own skins.

"I will get the Elixir and Medicine," stated Princess Bari.

"How may we thank you, daughter?" asked the deeply moved Queen.

"You carried me in your womb for nine months," replied the princess, "and then labored to bring me into the world. That is thanks enough."

Donning the clothes of a young man, she picked up a walking stick and set out into the West.

* * * *

The Buddha was out teaching in the countryside.

"Why have you come here?" he asked, curious about Princess Bari's strange clothes.

Bowing, she said, "I, the Crown Prince of Korea, seek the medicine that will cure my ailing parents."

The Buddha was not fooled. Peering at her, "I recognize you," he said, "the daughter of the king who has no princes. I found the jade chest that contained you and brought you to the couple who raised you. I will help you now as well." He gave her an amulet to shake in times of difficulty.

When she came to land's end, she halted and looked across the sea. How to cross it? She shook the amulet and the sea disappeared.

As she walked she passed near tall cliffs. A rumbling alerted her to an oncoming avalanche. She shook the amulet and the debris fell on either side, missing her. She continued.

After a long walk, she was stopped by towering castles of iron and thorn. She shook the amulet and a castle door opened.

Beyond it stood a shrine. She approached and spotted its attendant: a hermit so scary-looking he was ugly as well. Marshaling courage, she greeted him, bowed, and told him of her mission.

"Did you bring any money to pay for these healing things?" he asked.

"No."

"Very well," he said, peering at her. "To pay for them you must chop my wood for three years, light my fireplace for three years, and fetch me water for three years."

She sighed and agreed.

At the end of the first three years, she knew all to be known about trees, axes, plant lore, woodcraft, and handling tools; her hands were strong and her arms firm from the labor. After three more years, she knew firecraft intimately, and in another three, the ways of water and its many uses.

"Now," said the guardian when she came to him for the Elixir and Medicine, "because you have chosen not to disclose your true identity all these years, I require one thing more: that you marry me and give me seven sons. *Then* I will give you what you ask for your ill parents."

So the princess learned the ways of married life and of raising children. And she learned something else, or at least suspected it: that her hermit husband was a hidden god.

After dreaming about two broken chopsticks left in a silver bowl, she went to him. "A dream has informed me that my parents are about to die," she said. "I have done all you have asked of me. I need the Elixir and Medicine."

Her husband looked very sad.

"You shall have it," he said. "You have more than earned it. The water you carried for me is the Medicine you seek, and the wood when properly prepared will give you the Elixir."

She turned to fetch them; but:

"Before you go, please consider the eight of us who love you and will miss you when you have left. You are free to return to your parents and your kingdom, but would you consider taking us with you?"

"Yes," she said. "You and my sons may come with me." He bowed his head in gratitude.

Upon nearing the kingdom, the princess told her traveling family to stay outside the royal precincts until she had a chance to explain who they were. Her husband and sons melted into the forest.

She continued on to the home of her parents. The presence of a crowd of mourners there told her the news before anyone could speak it: the king and queen were dead.

Bending over the bodies lying in state, she poured the Elixir into their eyes and pushed the woody Medicine through their skin down to bone. She waited.

After a moment, the couple opened their eyes, astonished to see the crowd gathered around them. "What are all these people doing here?" asked the king. "What did we miss?"

"There is something I need to explain to you," said the future Queen Bari, smiling and thinking about her husband and seven sons.

For Reflection:

- Why do the kings ask for oracular readings and then disbelieve them?

- Sometimes what is thought of as personal conflict or trauma actually originates in previous generations; sufferers live out the original wound unconsciously but symbolically. What are the emotional legacies handed down through this royal family?

- How does the name of the princess reflect the healing this family needs?

- In the film *Whale Rider*, a family charged with continuing the line of chieftains receives a girl rather than a boy. If a family can be said to have a fate, or guiding spirits, what do they intend by arranging this?

- Why was it necessary for Princess Bari to be separated from the court?

- One read would view the princess as a compliant victim of patriarchy, and yet after her abandonment, her Underworld journey, her years of training, and her creation of a family, she enters full adulthood initiated, centered, highly skilled, reconciled to her family, and prepared to take over a kingdom. What other purposes do difficult rites of passage serve?

- People who acquire psychological or spiritual gifts often seek to improve or evolve their own families. By contrast, the princess goes away, works on herself, makes her own way, and returns as a healer only after finding the proper uses of her medicines. Nor does she try to change her six useless sisters. What about her is authentically rejuvenating? What does her example suggest about the effect we can have on our families?

- What could the hidden god's arrival in town signify?

Thor Attends a Wedding (Norse)

Lene Andersen, Danish folklorist, archivist, and research librarian:

> A new interest in oral storytelling has emerged in Denmark over the last 20 years. Performances of oral storytelling take place in cafes and libraries. There are courses where the participants are taught how to tell a story; there are storytelling circles where storytellers practice storytelling together, and books are published with instructions on how to tell a story. Storytelling fes-

tivals where storytellers perform stories are regularly arranged.

The storytellers' use of historical narratives gives the impression of a romantic rather than a historicist approach. By altering the old stories and relating them verbally, the storytellers aim to make the old written stories relevant to the audience, and thus to pass on the essence of the stories to the present. In so doing, some of them point out that they are doing the same as the old traditional storytellers, who also created their own variants of the stories of oral tradition.... The past is gone forever, and the storytellers do not seriously wish themselves back in time – but they long to change the present a little.

"WHERE IS MY HAMMER?!"
The roar blew through Asgard with a little less volume than a thunderclap. The gods seated around the council table flinched in unison.

"Thrym has it," Loki said in a small voice. "You must have left it at his feast."

Anywhere else, the sound might have been rocks grinding together, but in Asgard it could only be Thor's teeth clenching in frustration.

"How do you know this?"

"When I realized it was missing, I borrowed Freya's falcon dress and flew shapeshifted to the house of Thrym. When I heard him brag to his hounds that soon they would wear collars of Asgard gold, I asked him outright what he would demand in exchange for Mjollnir." He paused.

"Well?"

"The hand of Freya." Fair Freya, the spell-weaving goddess of love, beauty, and oracular wisdom.

"Freya marry a giant? Never!" The gods nodded.

"Unless...."

"Unless what?"

"Unless one of you puts on Freya's veil and dress and, through my magic, appears as her at Thrym's door."

"Who would do such a thing? It's ridiculous!"

"How much do you want your hammer back?"

"We agree," intoned the gods, rising quickly. "Thor lost his hammer, a precious tool used not only for his own activities but in defense of Asgard. He should stand ready to do whatever it takes to win Mjollnir back from the giants, for his sake and ours." They adjourned before Thor could muster an argument against Loki's plan.

"You'll need a garland of flowers to wear over your veil, and some pretty rings—"

"Shut up!" Thor paced in thought, sorting alternatives, but it was useless, Loki knew. He would do it.

"So what's your plan, Loki?"

"I will change your appearance such that you will seem to be Freya. Thrym will be fooled and will invite you into his hall. When he asks to join in marriage with you, he will place Mjollnir in your lap. The rest I leave to you."

He turned to go, but Thor reached out a meaty hand and spun him around.

"No, no, Loki, you will go *with* me." The front of Loki's tunic crinkled as Thor's fingers clenched on it. He went on:

"I think you're responsible for this. I think you're doing it to make a fool of me. Maybe I should just kill you now and—"

"And lose your hammer forever?" Loki replied quickly.

"You're coming with me." It was not a request.

"Very well. I'll notify the household of Thrym that we accept his offer."

"Yes."

"And don't skimp on the perfume and jewelry."

"Grrr."

*　*　*　*

"Enter, lovely Freya and her bridesmaid!" beamed Thrym as he came to the door to greet them. With lusty approval, his giant's eye noted the veil, garland, blond tresses, wide shoulders, housekeeper's keys, and bright red dress.

Swift messengers riding to Jötunheim had delivered notice to begin wedding preparations. At Thrym's hall, guests now gathered—giants, mostly—as vast quantities of butchered meat were laid steaming upon the brightly covered tables.

Thrym tried to lift the veil for a kiss, but at the last moment Loki's hand rested on his shoulder. "We in Asgard are bashful about kissing in public," he murmured. "Let the veil stay until after the wedding."

"Yes, dear," said Thrym's mother, "leave the veil be. The gods are known for their refined ways." She took "Freya" by the hand and led "her" to a table to be seated. Thor's eyes burned beneath the veil. Thrym sat on one side of him and Loki on the other.

The first course was fish. Thor was hungry and ate eight salmon straightaway, as an appetizer. Ignoring Loki's foot presses, he started in on an ox. To the amazement of the giants, he consumed the entire beast.

"These goddesses may be refined," whispered one giant to another, "but their appetites be as mighty as their powers are told of."

"Poor Freya," said Loki to Thrym. "Hasn't eaten for eight days for pining for you."

"Ahhh...."

Thrym waved, and servants brought barrels of mead to the table. "Have a drink, my dear," and Thor drank. Three barrels.

"Maybe," whispered a giant to Thrym's mother, "it's for the best that we never managed to pluck brides from the heights of Asgard. We'd go broke feeding them." She frowned as she looked ahead to centuries of anxiety about how much food to prepare for her new daughter-in-law.

"Why are her eyes so red?" asked Thrym as the veil slipped momentarily and was replaced.

"The dear has hardly slept for wanting to be here with you.

—Well, that was a grand and filling meal! Perhaps it's time now for the ceremony?"

The Norse custom was for the couple to sit close together, whereupon the man would place a symbol of his love, commitment, and worldly possessions into the lap of his soon-to-be-wife.

Resting his hand on "Freya's" thigh, Thrym drew forth Mjollnir as agreed and laid it gently in "Freya's" lap.

A very large hand emerged from within a red sleeve and curled firmly around the haft of the hammer.

"Thank you."

The masculine rumble startled everyone except Loki, who quickly darted to one side as he felt the spells he had cast sputter and give out. The giants gasped as the veil fell off.

In one blurred motion, Thor sprang to his feet and swung the lightning hammer into a nearby wall. Screams echoed throughout the hall as the wall burst into fragments of stone and came down. An ominous grinding creak told Thor's ear that the roof, deprived of support and starting to tip, was about to collapse. He shoved Loki ahead of him.

As they emerged into the fresh air, the entire hall fell down with a series of booms and crashes on top of the shouting giants.

Without looking back, the two visitors from Asgard strode down the road, Loki gathering up his bridesmaid's skirts and Thor taking care not to snag his red dress.

This is how Loki and Thor won back the hammer Mjollnir, and how Thor came to be the patron god of vulnerable women forced to endure humiliation at the hands of tyrannical men.

For Reflection:
- Jung and others compare Thor to Zeus, perhaps because both throw lightning, but Thor clearly belongs to the Hero archetype rather than that of the far-seeing, all-knowing, and often distant Heavenly Father. Why is comparing mythical attributes like lightning so alluring to theorists?

- Many of the world's hero figures encounter humiliating situations. An example is Lancelot being forced to ride in a dwarf's pillory cart in order to rescue Guinevere, who then spurns him. Why must heroes go through this?

- Heroes and tricksters are also known to cross-dress on certain highly charged occasions. Why?

- Mjollner ("MULE-ner") means "masher." With this powerful gift of the dwarves Brokkr and Sindri, Thor does much more than smash a few giants or trolls: he also breaks down the walls that imprison cultural values. (His oracular wife Sif's name means "affinity" or "connection.") When he throws the hammer, it gives off lightning, strikes its target, and returns to his waiting hand. How might we understand Mjollner symbolically, and what does it mean for a giant to gain control of it?

- When the gods head to Asgard for a meeting, they usually pass over Bifrost ("BAY-vurst") the rainbow bridge—except for Thor. He takes the low roads, traversing valleys and wading through streams. The ostensible reason is that he's too large to fit on the bridge, but why else?

Dobrynya Nikitich and the Dragon (Russian)

Svetlana Boym, Professor of Slavic and Comparative Literatures at Harvard University:

I take walks on the Charles river as a part of a daily ritual. I photograph whatever catches my eye, or I just walk camera-free, making mental notes on pictures not taken. On a breezy March day I see only shadows on the river surface, separating and touching each other, escaping my viewfinder.

I persist and follow a few dry tree branches in the sky-water. My memory card is filled with crooked abstractions in black, white and blue, phantom limbs without roots. At home, while saving the images to my computer, I see something I haven't noticed before. A face made of litter and light is staring back at me.

After a thousand photographic takes, captured over a period of two months, I manage to find ten faces. Who are they? Pentimenti for an unknown creation? Drowned characters in search of an author or some winking imaginary friends? Did I conjure them into existence or did they find me?

Some day, warned the mysterious voice, *Dobrynya Nikitich will kill you*. So uttered the oracle to the dragon Zmei Gorynytch.

Dobrynya Nikitich was one of the *bogatyri*, the elite knights of Prince Vladimir of Kiev. He could read, sing, play chess, conduct diplomacy, and fight. He had beaten the Mongol chieftain Batur.

Today, though, from the dragon's point of view, the famous bogatyr lolled ineffectually about, naked in a river. The day was warm, the water deliciously cool. Cool enough to drown out his mother's words of warning: "Don't you go into the Sorochinsk Mountains or bathe in the Puchai!" *Bah*.

Smelling smoke on the breeze, Dobrynya looked up—to see a green monster standing between him and his sword and clothing sitting on the riverbank. His horse had run away.

"Now then," rumbled the dragon as sparks tumbled out of her nose, "what am I to do with you?"

In answer, Dobrynya ducked beneath the water and swam hard for the opposite bank.

Here he surfaced, waded ashore, and picked up what he had glimpsed from the other side: a magician's hat filled with sand. The hat's edge was sharp enough to draw blood from a probing finger.

Shaking water and a booming nearby told him that the dragon had leaped to this side of the river. A fanged head dropped toward him as he turned.

He slashed with the hat. The severed head dropped into the river.

When the dragon was down to one remaining head, he leaped upon its back and raised the hat again.

"Stop!" she pleaded. He felt her body shift as she tried to balance herself with most of her heads gone.

"Why should I? You tried to kill me. No doubt you've been more successful with others of my kind."

"Because if you spare me, I swear I will never attack a human being again."

Dobrynya thought it over, then diplomatically accepted this and let her go, dismounting.

The dragon rose into the air, and, beating its wings heavily, flew off to Kiev.

Zabava, the niece of Prince Vladimir, looked up when the big shadow fell upon her. In an instant giant jaws grabbed her up and hoisted her, screaming, into the air.

The next time Dobrynya reported for duty, the Prince asked him:

"Remember that dragon you released unharmed?"

"Yes, Prince Vladimir."

"It just made off with my niece."

For a moment, Dobrynya's normally smooth expression cracked in astonishment. He opened his mouth to reply, but the Prince got there first:

"You made a deal with the dragon, I believe. So I'll make one with you: in exchange for the privilege of continuing to breathe, you bring back Princess Zabava. Clear?"

The knight found the lair by riding a clever old chestnut mare. Old, but speedy. Soon he was among the fire-breathing young of Zmei Gorynytch.

The mare trampled them as they went, but so many bit her that her strength began to leave her.

When she grows tired, his mother had advised, *brush her flanks with this silken whip*. He did this and she stood straighter and stepped stronger once again.

They entered the cave and confronted a dragon greatly enraged by the deaths of her offspring.

"This is how you keep your bargain, O man?" the dragon complained, snout glowing red.

"You broke the bargain by abducting the Tsar's niece. Either you release her to me or I will come and get her."

"I will not give her to you."

Dobrynya had fought dragons before, but not like this one. It took him three utterly exhausting days, and many strokings of the silken whip, before he could finally plant his spear in the scaly hide.

As he pointed the horse toward overjoyed Zabava, he faced a new problem: they were stuck fast. The blood of the dragon had pinned them to the ground like glue.

"Earth!" called out the tired bogatyr. "Will you please drink up this blood and free us?"

Once the ground lost its sticky red sheen, horse and rider proceeded to the rear of the cave, where thankful Zabava mounted in front of him.

As they rode back to Kiev. Dobrynya relished the thought that he would continue to breathe.

For Reflection:
- Comment: Often compared to King Arthur's knights, the fabled Bogatyri serving Vladimir Bright Sun included Ilya Muromets, who after thirty-three years of inactivity slays an outlaw sorcerer of the forest; Dobrynya Nikitich, dragon-killer and diplomat; young Alyosha Popovich, who defeated enemies through trickery; and Vasilisa the Beautiful, who, having been initiated by the witch Baba Yaga, rescues her father and her future husband the Tsar. Some of the Bogatryi are thought to be loosely based on actual people.
- Why do things go amiss with Dobrynya?
- Why a hat as a weapon?

- How would you describe the images of the feminine in this tale?
- "Zabava" means "fun, distraction, entertainment." How does knowing that influence how we understand what unfolds?
- According to Joseph Campbell, part of the Hero's task is to develop a sense of individuality. Here, though, individuality seems to be part of the problem. What does Dobrynya learn by the end?

Bhima Swarga (Balinese)

I Nyoman Sumandhi, Balinese puppeteer and folklorist:

> I was born in Bali, Indonesia, December 31, 1944, in a family of *dalangs* or traditional Balinese puppet masters. My father was a famous dalang, and I have followed in his footsteps. Becoming a dalang involves a mastery of traditional Balinese music, dance, and choreography, as well as the repertoire and theatrical techniques associated with the *wayang kulit* or shadow puppet theater, which is regarded as the pinnacle of the arts in Bali.
>
> In Balinese culture, dalangs are masters of a world inhabited by our puppets and we are the gods that animate them. Since they rest between each play, I bang on the box to wake them up and then I arrange them on either side of me with the heroes on my right and the villains on my left. You can also tell the different characters apart by their shapes.
>
> We need our performing arts for these ceremonies. You don't want to have audio cassettes or videotapes. In rit-

ual contexts you need the real performances! In Bali this will not change.

"Something terrible just happened," King Pandu told his two wives.

"I was out hunting and shot two deer as they lay together in love," he went on. "At least they seemed to be deer, but in actuality they were a priest and his wife disguised so they could be together in peace. The priest has cursed me such that the next time I make love I will die. So now I must live in chastity."

As it happened, Pandu's wife Kunti had received a special blessing while a young woman: the power to call forth a god to make love with. But she could use this power only five times. Now four, because she had once summoned Surya the sun.

He was followed by Dharma the cosmic law, Bayu the wind, and Indra the thunderer. Pandu's other wife, Madri, grew envious.

"May I please use the last summons?" she asked Kunti, who agreed.

Because Madri had only one chance, she decided to summon two gods, the Aswin twins, to double her pleasure. Kunti wished she had thought of that.

One day the king was watching a sunset when he felt overcome by desire for Madri. They lay down together, loved together, sighed in satisfaction—and Pandu flopped over dead.

In remorse, Madri took her own life, leaving Kunti and her retinue to raise five sons.

"Mother, why do you continue to weep?" asked Kunti's son Yudhisthira, whose father was Dharma. His brothers looked on with concern.

"I keep having nightmares in which Pandu and Madri suffer the tortures of the Land of the Dead. Something must be done for them!"

After a long silence, "Since when are we Pandawas silent?" asked Bhima, proud son of Bayu. "I'll free our parents, and let no god or demon stand in my way."

Up to the night before Bhima's underworld journey, the festivals and musicians rolled on continuously. Crowds turned out to join the shadow puppet plays, the rituals and dances, as clouds of pungent incense wafted skyward. The preparation culminated with an unexpected blessing as the strength of Kunti, the intelligence of Yudhisthira, the decisiveness of brothers Nakula and Sahadewa, and the agility of brother Arjuna poured into Bhima's already powerful body. He felt like a god.

The next morning Bhima departed, taking as traveling companions two clowns: Twalen and his son Mredah.

* * * *

They faced many obstacles on their way to Swarga, the Plane of Transition between worlds. The first, a river bulging with hungry crocodiles, terrified the clowns. Bhima merely pointed at the beasts, said, "Here are our brothers; stay close by," and boarded a big croc who was happy to be recognized as kindred. He carried the three safely to the opposite bank, where they disembarked and continued on.

They reached a mountain pass that led downward into what seemed to be staging areas of judgment and punishment. A pig gnawed the body of a man who in life had been a butcher who cheated his customers. Demons threw sufferers into a huge cauldron bearing cowhead handles; other demons stoked a fire below its iron belly. A folk healer who had overcharged, a couple who had stolen rice from the hungry, an avenger who had used poison, a farmer who had built over a sacred grove, a hunter who had killed elephants just for fun: all were recorded in the book held by the demonic overseer Suratma and sent for punishment. A huge gnarled tree with sharp blades for leaves hung over the ghastly scene.

This was Yamaloka, kingdom of the death god Yama.

The clowns trembled in terror, but Bhima's keen eyes took stock, eventually spotting the bare-chested demon Jogormanik instructing souls who had fulfilled their terms of judgment. They were now bound for heaven.

"Let's find the center," said Bhima.

On the winding downward path they turned a corner to find Jogormanik barring their way. His muscles rippled.

"You aren't due here yet," the demon stated. "You are still living. Who are you and why are you here?"

"I am the second son of the Pandawa family. My name is Bhima, and I have come for the souls of my father King Pandu and my stepmother Dewi Madri."

"You can't disturb the order of this place. Go away while you still can."

Bhima didn't move.

"Very well," sighed Jogormanik and raised his hand. From behind him sprang a horde of armed demons grinning like angry dogs. They attacked.

Some fell to Bhima's club, whistling as it swung through the air. Others fell to the spear and arrows of Twalen and the long knife of Mredah. Jogormanik and his account book lay still, victims of Bhima's strong arm.

"What now?" asked the clowns, considering the bodies.

"Now we wreck the place." Bhima reached forth and with a great heave overturned the boiling cauldron, freeing those cooking within it. "Overturn everything!"

As he put out fires, disarmed demons, and nodded to grateful souls released from torment, he scanned the area for his parents but did not see them.

Meanwhile, the demon Nirganetra was busy informing Yama of these events. Yama's face turned red.

"Bring him."

Bhima and Twalen strode into Yama's palace and stood before its ruler. Mredah waited outside.

"I order you to leave my kingdom at once, Bhima of the Pandawas," said Yama.

"I will not until I free the souls of my parents."

"Then you and your servants will die."

Bhima and Twalen turned away.

Once outside they faced an army of demons with Yama, mounted on a spotted elephant, at their head. "Charge!" called Yama.

To the death god's bewildered eyes it looked as though Bhima were everywhere at once, dodging, stabbing, twisting, breaking necks, knocking down whole ranks of demons. Arrows and sword points bounced damaged from his body. The clowns were in furious motion too, mopping up what remained of the attackers.

If I wait any longer he will liberate every soul! thought Yama as his face turned black. He placed his crown of battle on his head and leaped from his elephant into the fray. Steam poured from his ears.

He reached for Bhima, but the son of the Pandawas gripped Yama's throat first and squeezed. Yama fell to his knees.

"Let me go!"

"Bring me my parents."

Yama gasped as the powerful fingers opened. Veins bulged across his face. He pointed to a nearby cauldron filled with smoking lava.

When Bhima overturned it, he saw among the souls pouring out his beloved parents still caught in an embrace. He picked them up in his arms and nodded to the clowns, who bowed in respect to the royal couple.

Time to return to the upperworld, Bhima realized, before Yama changed his mind.

"Why are they so quiet?" whispered Twalen on the way back. He nodded at the couple.

"They cannot yet speak, for they have not come fully back to life," said Bhima. He led their relatively quiet sojourn home.

There, the overjoyed queen and her sons paid homage to Madri and Pandu, who seemed to appreciate it but said nothing. Queen Kunti understood. She turned toward Bhima:

"My son, you must make one more journey before these souls can enter heaven. You must go there yourself and bring back the Tirta Amrta, the water of immortality."

* * * *

When Bhima and his retainers reached heaven, the gods met in council to discuss this disturbing event.

"The water of immortality," intoned Siwa of the four arms and open third eye, "is not meant for humans, least of all humans who have been down to Yamaloka. We must stop Bhima from having his way here. The peace of heaven must never be disturbed."

Bhima and the clowns met the armed gods of heaven as they had met the demons below. Magic edges, spears, and arrows glanced from them harmlessly.

"Summon Bayu," ordered Siwa as the sounds of battle faded from the skies.

A golden halo clung to Bayu's approaching form. The clowns were amazed at how closely father and son resembled one another. The two stood face to face.

"I'm disappointed in you," said Bayu. "None but the gods may drink the water of immortality. You have disturbed heaven for nothing. You must go home now."

"I am sorry, Father, but I cannot obey."

"I command you to obey!"

Bhima raised his great club. The clowns watched in horror.

Seizing his son's rising arm, Bayu sent a blast of force through him. Bhima shook for a moment and collapsed to his knees. By the time he lay sprawled on the ground he was dead. Bayu vanished.

The heavens dimmed. Stunned, the clowns picked up Bhima's body and carried it off to watch over it.

As days of mourning passed, the saddened clowns noticed how depleted the gods seemed as they shuffled through heaven. Even the light was gray.

Twalen and Mredah kept the death watch over their fallen lord. Occasionally they dozed off. They had been through much.

One evening they woke suddenly to see a shining white cloud descend from the starry sky. Rays of light emanated from it, some touching the body of Bhima as the cloud moved toward him. The face of a god formed within its bright swirls.

"Bhima," rumbled the voice of Sanghyang Acintya, head of all the gods, "you must arise. Let your strength be known once again."

Bhima sat up blinking. When he saw the shining face and realized what had happened, he knelt respectfully. "Thank you," he murmured as the cloud dispersed.

He stood up and saw the clowns. "Let's go. We have something to find."

The gods soon realized they could not stop revived Bhima this time. "Let him find what he seeks," advised Bayu in council. "The highest god is on his side. Not ours." And so it was.

Back on earth, Pandu and Madri drunk from a winged goblet and regained voice and life. Bhima smiled. Embraces and kisses descended upon the awakened couple.

"There seems to be some of the water left," Mredah whispered to his father. "Who gets the rest of it?"

"Quiet!" Pause. "I wonder if they will store it somehow...."

Behind them, the reborn couple said their goodbyes. After so much suffering and suspension and renewal, they longed mightily now for the heights of heaven.

"Cherish each moment," they advised, "work hard, learn much, play much, love much. Do not forget your dreams."

Gazing into the water of immortality, the clowns saw the couple reach the eastern heavens, the celestial home of contemplative souls. Sanghyang Acintya himself stood there to welcome them.

In front of Madri and Pandu materialized the winged cup bearing the water of immortality. It would be their heavenly refreshment.

When their eyes finally came back into focus, the clowns realized that everyone had left the palace. Before them sat a brass bowl filled with ordinary water.

For Reflection:
- What did Pandu really do to bring the curse down upon him?
- What could it mean to make love with a god? With more than one god?
- Might the image of shadow puppetry give a hint about Balinese ontology? (The Balinese pay careful attention to dreams.)

- Why do exaggerated speech and action so often characterize the hero?

- How do the sufferings and regrets of the dead parents follow their children? How does the hero redeem them?

- What is significant about Bhima referring to creatures like crocodiles as "brothers"?

- What do the father and son clowns suggest about Bhima's father complex, if anything?

- How does Bhima come to see that souls other than those of his parents need liberation from eternal punishment?

- Why is Bayu (Vayu in India) the only god who can kill Bhima? Why does he do it?

- What does Bhima learn from his death and rebirth? What do the gods learn from it?

- In an Arthurian Cycle story, Sir Galahad finds the Holy Grail and vanishes into heaven with it. In the Balinese tale, the cup of immortality nourishes the souls of Madri and Pandu in heaven. What is the difference in this detail?

Sigurd and the Ring (Icelandic)

Halldór Laxness, Nobel-winning poet, essayist, and novelist:

> I am thinking of all those wonderful men and women, the people among whom I grew up. My father and mother, but above all, my grandmother, who taught me hundreds of lines of old Icelandic poetry before I ever learned the alphabet.

> My thoughts fly to the old Icelandic storytellers who

created our classics, whose personalities were so bound
up with the masses that their names, unlike their lives'
work, have not been preserved for posterity. They live
in their immortal creations and are as much a part of
Iceland as her landscape. For century upon dark century
those nameless men and women sat in their mud huts
writing books without so much as asking themselves
what their wages would be, what prize or recognition
would be theirs. There was no fire in their miserable
dwellings at which to warm their stiff fingers as they sat
up late at night over their stories. Yet they succeeded in
creating not only a literary language which is among the
most beautiful and subtlest there is, but a separate literary genre.

"Let me tell you a story of treasure and loss," said Regin to his
foster son Sigurd.

"One day I, a smith, my brother Otr, a shape-changing fisherman, and Fafnir, the strongest and meanest of us, stood near a waterfall. Otr had changed into the form of an otter so he could catch a
salmon.

"Along came Odin, Loki, and Hoenir of Asgard. As we stared at
them, Loki picked up a rock and hurled it at my brother Otr, killing
him.

"As the gods began to skin him, we laid hands on them and
demanded that they compensate us for Otr's death. 'We want,' we
told them, 'an otter's skin filled up with golden treasure.' They
agreed to this, so we let them go.

"To meet our demand, Loki netted the dwarf Andvari, who had
changed into a pike, and forced him to hand over his hoard. Andvari
tried to keep a magic ring for himself, but Loki demanded that too,
whereupon the dwarf warned, 'This ring Andvaranaut, meaning
Andvari's Gift, will bring death to whomever owns it.' The ring
could make gold and was therefore worth more than the rest of the
treasure.

"Knowing the ring was cursed, Loki gave it along with the hoard to our father Hreidmar the dwarf king.

"He didn't hold it long, though. Possessed by greed, Fafnir killed him, took the ring and the hoard, and turned himself into a dragon to guard it. That's the story."

"I will kill Fafnir and liberate the treasure," replied Sigurd.

Twice did his foster father attempt to forge him a sword, but both times Sigurd snapped the blade while testing it. So Sigurd went to his mother Hjordis:

"Is it true that you still keep the fragments of my father Sigmund's sword Gram?"

"Yes," she said. "I will give them to Regin so he can make you a new sword."

This time the anvil and not the sword split in half.

Sigurd tested Gram again by slicing King Lyngvi in half for killing his father, cutting Lyngvi's brother in two, and dispatching most of their fighting men.

"Now I'm ready for the dragon," he told Regin.

"Good. Your father is avenged, and mine shall now be as well."

As advised, Sigurd looked for the dragon's track near water. When he found the signs of the beast's passage, he dug a trench.

As he worked, a hooded old man walked up and, fingering his beard, asked Sigurd what he did. Sigurd told him.

"You must dig other trenches to hold the worm's blood," Odin advised.

Trembling ground warned him of the dragon's approach. As the shadow of its bulk passed over him, Sigurd, who lay in the ditch, took a firm grip on Gram and stabbed upward.

The dragon shrieked, its heart pierced, and rolled over, spasming. Sigurd got to his feet and stood over the dying beast.

"Who are you that have killed me?" panted the dragon.

"Sigurd, son of Sigmund."

"You have won my hoard, but it will be your death. Leave while you can." He grew still as Regin came up and congratulated Sigurd on his brave act.

Seeing the trenches full of dragon's blood, he stooped to drink.

Then:

"Now roast the heart over a fire so I can eat it."

As the flames warmed the bloody flesh, Sigurd poked it with a finger to test whether it was cooked enough. When he placed the reddened finger in his mouth, he realized that the birds nearby were speaking in a way he could now understand.

"Eating the heart would make Sigurd wise," remarked one nuthatch.

"Wise enough to know," said another, "that Regin plans to betray him for the treasure."

"Sigurd should cut off his head," said a third, "and take the treasure for himself."

"Then he should saddle his horse and go to Hindarfell, where sleeping Brynhild awaits," twittered a fourth.

Sigurd did these things, followed Fafnir's track to the hoard, loaded it up, admired the ring for a moment—what a prize!—and departed on Grani, a horse given to him previously by a bearded old man.

* * * *

On a mountain wall built from battle shields he found the sleeping woman. Gram slicing through her chainmail armor awakened her.

"Are you Sigurd, descendant of King Volsung, and is that the sword Gram?"

"I am, and it is. You are Brynhild?"

"I am."

"How did you come to be here?"

"Two kings decided to go to war with each other. I backed one, but Odin favored the other. When it was over, he pricked me with a thorn. I went to sleep." The short cadence of her replies matched her hard beauty.

They stayed together, and from Brynhild he learned etiquette and proper speech, the arts of healing, and the lore of the runes. For this he pledged himself to her, chaste shield maiden though she be, destined to marry fair Gudrun though he be, and gave her Andvaranaut.

It was a pleasant sunny day to bathe in the Rhine, or would have been if the queens had not argued.

"I am so glad I ended up with King Gunnar," remarked Brynhild. "His manhood and valor surpass that of every other man living."

"Except that of Sigurd," Gudrun shot back, "killer of Fafnir and hero of a hundred battles."

"Gunnar rode through a wall of fire to be with me after I had refused all other suitors."

"*Sigurd* rode through, in disguise, on Grani! Did you not know?" Brynhild paled.

Gudrun went on relentlessly: "Gunnar's horse would not bear him through. My mother Grimheld provided the magic." *She also provided the draught to make Sigurd forget* you, she thought with lingering bitterness.

"It is not true."

"It is, and I can prove it." She held out her hand to display the golden gleam of Andvaranaut. "Your ring is a fake. Sigurd traded rings with you when he courted you."

There are some arguments that should perhaps be lost rather than won. When the bloodbath was over, the dead included Sigurd, stabbed while sleeping by the sword of Guttorm, Brynhild's brother-in-law; Guttorm, killed by Gram with Sigurd's last living act; Brynhild, who in sorrow and guilt stabbed herself to death; King Atli, who had married Gudrun to possess the treasure, had killed her brothers-in-law Gunnar and Hogni for it, and was stabbed by her when drunk one evening; and the two sons of Atli and Gudrun.

As for the treasure and the ring, Gudrun had made sure they reached the bottom of the Rhine, where they would trouble no more the living...unless found again one day.

For Reflection:
- Comment: It's easy to confuse the various versions of this time- and culture-crossing tale. The Völsunga Saga

originates in Iceland and was committed to paper around the 13th century. From there it emigrated into Germany and became the story of Siegfried, Brunhild, and Kriemhild in the *Nibelungenlied*, a poem composed near the Danube to describe the doings of the mythical Nibelungen family of Burgundians who had landed at Worms. Richard Wagner drew on and altered these stories for his operatic (or "dramatic" as he preferred to call it) *Ring* cycle, during which he kills off not only Siegfried et al but some Rhine Maidens and even the gods before burning down Valhalla.

- Many of the male heroes and kings of Sigurd's family have names that contain the word "victory," but they come to violent ends. Why?

- It would not be too much to call Siegfried the German Hercules. Yet C. G. Jung dreamed early in his career that he helped kill this revered figure, and in his *Red Book* he claims that the Hero must die for the depths of the psyche to become conscious. What does he mean?

- What does Brynhild's bragging about Gunnar really say about their relationship?

- Sigurd serves Fafnir and other enemies with symbolically retributive violence. This is often true of Heroes. Another example is Theseus stretching Procrustes on his own lethal bed. What does this tell us about the Heroic sense of justice?

- Why does Andvaranaut exist, and what ultimate purposes does it serve? Does it have any positive attributes, or is it only and irreversibly destructive?

- Where do we see the magic ring operating today?

- Once Wagner had plundered the Sigurd tale for his own purposes, Hitler enlisted Wagner's music for his own political and military purposes. The Japanese government did the same with the fairy tale of the hero

Momotaro (Peach Boy). American conservative politicians and clergy cite Moses to encourage young men to fight the latest resource-rich enemy. What makes heroic myths so easy for dictators and warlords to hijack? How might this be prevented?

- When asked if *The Lord of the Rings* were based on Wagner's *Ring* cycle, Tolkien replied that being round was all the rings had in common. Yet many elements of the tale of Sigurd appear in Tolkien's trilogy: not only the ring that cannot be worn, but the reforging of the king's broken sword, the one-eyed opponent (Odin), the dwarf miners and smiths... Does Tolkien reinvent these mythologems, or does he use them as raw material for a work that remains quite his own creative project?

- In a letter to his son Christopher, JRR Tolkien said, in reference to World War II, that although he hoped that Hitler would be defeated, one cannot use the Ring of Power to fight the Enemy without becoming the Enemy. He also worried about what the Allies would do with their mechanized might after the war. Where was his intuition pointing?

Sacrifices of Jangar (Mongolian)

Chao Gejin, Mongolian professor of folklore and Director of the Institute of Ethnic Literature:

> Mongolian *tuuli*, or epic poetry, the most important genre in Mongolian literary history, is a vast tradition of orally composed works. Accompanied by musical instruments such as the *tobshur* and the *choor*, *tuuli* relates these nomadic peoples' glorious past: their ideal heroes—the bravest hunters and herdsmen—and their ideal world—rich pastures, open steppes, decorated

yurts and palaces, beautiful maidens, and swift horses. The heroes keep and guard these riches, perform deeds in defense of their holdings, and, more importantly, acquire new herds and new nomadic territories.

Mongolian epic is not a historical record, but represents a kind of historical spirit. Thus, the *manggus* represents everything of a negative nature rather than a particular historical villain or a particular social evil. The hero is not a historical hero per se, but rather the embodiment of the dreams, ideals, and aspirations of the Mongolian nation.

"What is the matter, Jangar?" asked Aletan Qieji. "Why are you so downcast? Why do refuse toasts and dances?"

The great midsummer Naadam Festival was supposed to be a celebratory occasion, with its games, dances, and horse races. It was held in Bomba, the center of an ever-expanding territory crowned by an ever-growing Golden Palace.

Yet the khan of Bomba felt surly. He finally spoke:

"Do you know of Sanale, out by the Abuhun Sea and the west foot of Xijier Mountain?"

"Certainly."

"Well, he sits on a throne of eighty prize camel hair cushions. He wears a gown of seventy layers and armor eight layers thick. His helm is made of gold, and he rides a rare red horse."

"And so?"

"And so he's also ambitious, and he troubles the prairie herdsman near him."

"I will go and speak with him," replied the minister, who, though old, looked out of eyes like a snow leopard's above a beard divided like an eagle's wings. The wrinkles above his eyes resembled wrestling bulls. Placing a gold helmet on his head, he picked up a mace, settled his bow on his back, strapped his sword on his left thigh, and stalked forth.

After hearing nothing for six months, Jangar dreamed of the minister riding smiling toward him. He woke knowing there had been trouble.

Saddling his horse, he gathered a band of warriors and rode forth to the camp of Sanale, who was rude. Blades came forth.

The two fought until Sanale saw a ray of light emanating from Jangar's back. Putting down his sword, he surrendered, and Jangar enlisted him.

Aletan Qieji belatedly reappeared, having been injured by Sanale, but his battle wounds healed quickly. Sanale's territory became Jangar's.

Every time the khan sat on his forty-four-legged throne and got drunk with his men, there in the fabulous nine-colored palace, a foreigner would arrive to announce a new challenge. He had, in fact, fought monsters (the many-headed *mangguses*) as well as more mundane tyrants since age three.

Jangar was the son of Ujung Aldar Khan, son of Tangsag Bumva Khan, son of Tahil Zul Khan, who had led the people to Bomba before being buried one day by an avalanche. Tangsag Bumva had worked himself to death fighting livestock-killing weather. Ujung Aldar had grown so preoccupied with his long-awaited new son that he neglected his duties until the monster Goljing noticed, attacked, and killed him and his wife.

Before he died, though, the khan placed a piece of white jade in his little son's mouth, sat him on the horse Aranjagaan, gave him the ancestral spear Aram, and ordered the servant Menhbayar to help the child escape. This was done, but Menhbayar was killed in battle.

In a cave in Big Black Mountain, Jangar sucked the white jade for nourishment. Then he began to cry.

Mengen Xigxirge was out hunting when he noticed the fine lone horse grazing. Curious, he approached, and as he did he heard the boy's cry.

"Your name," he told the boy, "shall be Jangar."

"Yes," said the boy, "for I will be master of the world."

At this, Mengen Xigxirge feared that this powerful child would grow up to displace the hunter's son, Hongor. *Better not bring him home*, he thought. He left some food and water before departing.

Thus abandoned and alone again, Jangar stepped outside the cave. He threw back his head and burst forth with a roar that echoed for miles around.

Responding to this distress, wolves gave him their milk, and deer brought him fruit. From the eagle he learned to hunt, from the antelope how to run, from the tiger how to growl.

In a dream an old man appeared as Jangar slept under a tree and taught him about his lineage. When he woke he also remembered lessons in magic and fighting.

He mounted Aranjagaan. He was ready.

He returned to Bomba, where he killed the monster Manggus Goljing.

From the roof of his palace he declared himself khan, bidding everyone to return. They were safe now, he told them. This was how grand new days came to Bomba.

When local chief Shar Durgeng tried to raid the newly liberated land, Jangar threw him from his horse and threatened to break his back. Shar Durgeng sued for peace and paid his tribute.

Hearing news of this, Mengen Xigxirge decided to amend his decision to spare the uncanny infant he had left in a cave long ago. He challenged Jangar to a wrestling match.

It was a fierce fight. Mengen would have beaten the khan had Mengen's son Hongor not pleaded for his life.

Enlisting Mengen as kin, Jangar also agreed to a campaign against Mengen's enemy Altan Gheej. In return, Mengen's wife Zulzandan adopted the young ruler.

*   *   *   *

Clever Altan Gheej of the poisoned arrow, Drunken Shar Durdeng, ambitious Sanale of the crimson horse, strong-armed Sabar, Jaan Taij Kehan, Khan Wuchuuhen Tib, Tyrant Hiyalgan: with every challenger of Jangar either killed or converted into a vassal of Bomba, that territory increased in size, just as its opulent palace gleamed in ever-brighter splendor. A suggestion went around that the palace soar high enough to touch the very clouds.

"This," warned enemy-turned-adviser Altan Gheej, "can bring no good to Jangar Khan or to Bomba. The Khan is human: he should not strive to compete with Heaven. He belongs down here, on earth, with us."

Within the towering palace, decked out in a lush robe and a jade-studded fox fur cap, Jangar toasted and was toasted by his inebriated men, who sat in seven rings around the khan, Hongor at his right in the place of brotherly honor. Even Aranjagaan wore a golden halter and silver rein.

"No good will come of all this drunken feasting," complained adviser He Jilgan as yet another challenger came forth to deliver a tyrant's threat.

And still the palace soared. Below its rising spires and gold-plated tiles, eighty-four halls gleamed with paneled ivory. Each hall framed red columns bearing colorful paintings masterfully inlaid with threads of silver and gold. Folding screens depicted battles won by Jangar. His portrait stood in the palace's very center, surrounded by portraits of his ministers.

The khan's young wife outshone even the palace. Avai Gerel of the cherry lips, black hair, and white teeth wore brocade, red ribbons, and a pair of gold earrings worth seven hundred good horses. In a sweet voice she sang songs that birds chirped to accompany.

Why, then, was Jangar so unhappy that he rose one day, saddled Aranjagaan, and left Bomba with Hongor in charge, to the dismay of everyone who knew? Once disbelief wore off, panic spread behind him.

*   *   *   *

Seeking to get away from those he had left stunned and dismayed, Jangar rode east, coming upon and then climbing mountains of marble. There he got lost in a large basin until he released the reins so Aranjagaan could choose their way forward.

They came upon a golden palace on a green mountain. Unlike his own back in Bomba, this palace was quiet and hidden.

Dismounting, Jangar walked through the front gate, saw an inner window, and peered through it at a young woman embroidering a tobacco bag. At her waist hung a yellow handkerchief similar to one Jangar's wife had given him for victory and luck.

"Hello," he said as he bounded into the room through the window. His cupped hand prevented her from screaming. "Do not be afraid. I am Jangar of Bomba." She took his hand from her mouth.

"Why are you alone here?" he asked.

"My father is hunting and my mother is visiting my ill grandmother. —Are you truly Jangar?" He nodded.

"My name is Oyontsetseg," she said, looking directly at him. She smiled as he pulled out his own yellow handkerchief.

"Flower of Wisdom," he repeated her name as they walked to the lakeside...

When they had lived for some time in the house of stone he built there, she asked him why he had left Bomba.

"To find peace," he told her, "from the endless rounds of duty and responsibility, detail and procedure. From everyone wanting something from me. From ceremony and politics. From the confines of court life." She touched his callused hand.

Three years later, Shovshuur, the young son of Jangar and Oyontsetseg, came home with Aranjagaan and a new red pony. At first Jangar thought Shovshuur (whose name means "Little Wild Boar") had taken the pony from someone, but the boy handed over a feathered black arrow that could only have come from Altan Gheej.

A band of passing warriors formerly of Bomba had asked Shovshuur about his mount, but the child had been too ignorant of his own past and parentage to answer their questions.

Holding the arrow, "Let me tell you where we come from," Jangar told him, and spoke at length.

When he had finished, Aranjagaan whinnied. Jangar went out to him.

His horse opened his mouth and, to Jangar's surprise, chastised him at length for neglecting Bomba, his wife, and his duties. "After you left," the horse finished, "Bomba fell to Shar Gurguu, and his invaders destroyed the Golden Palace and drove your people into the Gobi Desert." He had heard this from the other horses.

Jangar told his wife and son to wait for him with her uncle until he could put things right again in Bomba. He promised to return.

Saddling Aranjagaan, he rode for home.

* * * *

On the way he met an old man who told him more about Bomba's fall.

Hongor had tried his best to defend the realm. Overwhelmed at last, had been captured and imprisoned in the underworld below the Red Sea.

Jangar decided to rescue his friend-brother first, then reassemble the elite Ih Bataar warriors to retake Bomba from Shar Gurguu. He rode on again for the coast.

Jangar located the entrance to the Underworld after a long search. He sent his horse back to the old man's shabby home. Down into darkness he climbed on a sturdy rope of camel hair.

As he descended, Shoyshuur tracked him to where the old man lived. Aranjagaan had just come trotting up. After making friends with his father's horse, the boy got on him and rode rapidly away, letting his wise mount cross seven mountains and three rivers before reaching the Gobi.

When the ragged refugees of Bomba saw Aranjagaan, they wept, thinking Jangar dead. Shovshuur identified himself.

"My father," he told them, "has gone to rescue Hongor, but I mean to strike at the source of the trouble and end the mass murder and banishment. Who will come with me?"

It took time to muster men, but eventually a refugee army approached Bomba. Shar Gurguu laughed and came forth with his fighters. As they assembled in neat formations, the waves of furious outcasts piled into them.

At the height of the melee, Shoyshuur held down Shar Gurguu with one hipbone and pushed his head into the sand until he surrendered.

Warriors spurred on by Aranjagaan's whinnies had rushed the palace and driven out the invaders. Once captured, they agreed to a change of loyalty and were spared.

"Let the people know," Shovshuur told overjoyed Altan Gheej, "that they may now return to Bomba. The trouble is over. It is time to rebuild."

* * * *

Jangar parted his lips to let the jade in his mouth illuminate the winding tunnels. He slipped past two door-guarding demons and, guided by advice from two boys, he made his way toward his imprisoned friend, pausing only to rest and to free the daughter of the god of mercy from several demons, one disguised as an old woman.

After hauling her upward with a rope, the boys lowered it and invited Jangar to come up next. He saw no other way around. Up he would go.

As he hovered in the dark, they cut the rope, dropping him into the bottom of a cave. The impact broke his right hip and stunned him. He lay there a long while.

When he came to, a female mouse was biting his leg. His swat broke its back.

Its cry brought a male mouse carrying a piece of green leaf. She nibbled on it and got up, restored. Then she bit Jangar again.

His next slap broke her left hip. He waited for the male to bring another medicinal leaf.

Jangar took it from him. The mouse scurried away for another leaf. Jangar took that one too, and several more.

He ate them and felt his bones knit and his health return. As he recovered he fed bits of leaf to the female mouse.

He followed the mice out of the cave. They led him to a tree whose branches were heavy with magic leaves. He gathered a bundle and proceeded onward.

When he met up with the boys again, they apologized for cutting him loose. Demons had starved them, and they were afraid he would eat the food they had scavenged. He gave a healing leaf to the woman they had pulled up from the cave (her legs were paralyzed) and went on.

After passing a red door he met three lovely women who told him where to find his brother. Descending further, he allowed them to lead him through a hall full of demons and monsters, some of which he killed with his sword.

A skeleton was all that remained of Hongor.

Weeping, he put the bones into his deerskin bag and made his way back to the world above.

On the shore, the surf roaring behind him, he arranged the bones in their proper places and covered them with the magic leaves. He sat down there and recited the name of the Buddha, over and over, from dawn to dusk.

Hongor finally sat up, restored, just as rain began to fall.

"I am sorry," Jangar told him, helping him up. "Let's go home."

Upon reaching Bomba they were startled by joy. The land was healing, the people had returned and were rebuilding, and horses ran happily through the grass. Fragrant smoke from cooking stews drifted skyward through the clear air.

People rushed out to greet the weary travelers. Jangar was relieved to see Avai Gerel smiling in the company of Oyontsetseg. The two stood together like sisters, his wife the elder by one year.

A great feast commenced to welcome Jangar home, give proper greeting to his new son and wife, and celebrate the return of the long-suffering people of Bomba. Stringed music accompanied the sounds of dancing and revelry. A soft rain moistened the land.

As the feast drew to an end, Avai Gerel ordered the Golden Palace rebuilt.

For Reflection:

* Comment: This excerpt comes from a tale that achieved its fullest forms at the end of the 1800s. By then, generations of *jangarqi* storytellers had passed it on from much earlier. No one knows exactly where in

western Mongolia it originated. It is usually recited as
a heroic epic poem.

- How are the traumatic deaths of Jangar's father and
grandfather reflected in his own life?

- Why do the challenges always occur when Jangar and
his men are partying?

- How does court life in Bomba foreshadow its capture
and fall? Why does collapse so regularly turn out to be
the fate of empires?

- Was it necessary for Jangar to leave Bomba?

- Mythologically and psychologically, who is
Oyontsetseg? Why is it important for Jangar to form a
relationship with her?

- What is the significance of the hip bones?

- How is Shovshuur different from his father? How do
his priorities differ?

- Beyond having to rescue his brother, why did Jangar
need to visit the Underworld? How did the visit transform him?

- By the end of this excerpt, has Jangar learned whatever
he needed to learn after the capture and restoration of
Bomba?

- Is the rebuilding of the Golden Palace at the end a positive outcome, or a warning? What would you predict
for the rest of the tale: happily ever after, or more troubles to face?

Nafanua Fights Back (Samoan)

Albert Wendt, West Samoan novelist, poet, writer, and English
professor:

...My grandmother used to tell us *fagogo*, traditional stories, and she would stop if she realized we were getting bored and falling asleep; she would wake us up by saying, "Wake up or the story will not continue"....If she found you getting bored, she would switch the story, she would go off on another tangent. Even though a *fagogo* has a set form, she would go off onto another subplot. She would say, "Well, remember this other story," and off she would go, and then come back to the main story. Or she would start singing a song. The supposedly "postmodernist" mix is not new.

In many ways, my *imaginary* family are more real to me than my *real* family. When I say that to my students, they look at me and ask, "What do you mean?" My answer? "Look, the most influential people who ever existed on this planet have been imaginary people." If you look at all the stories of our culture, the oral traditions, at the stories of *atua* and mythological heroes and creatures, they are absolutely crucial in shaping our ways of thinking and behaving and dreaming.

Nobody knew quite what started it, the war, but everyone knew what fueled it: greed for land, for ever more land. Fought between two sides of the island of Savai'i, the War called Climbing East and Climbing West wasn't good for anyone. No war is.

It was especially hard on Falealupo people. If Chief Lilomaiava found anyone from the west on his side of the island, his men forced the visitor to climb a coconut tree upside down. The alternative was decapitation.

When Falealupo chief priest Tai'i was forced to hang upside down from a coconut tree or else lose his head, his sigh reached so far that they heard it down in Pulotu, where Nafanua lived with her father Saveasi'uleo. Tai'i was Nafanua's uncle and her father's older brother.

Falealupo was dear to Nafanua. It was her father's place: the place of he who had searched for a baby born prematurely in the shape of a blood clot and buried in the ground by her mother. That baby was Nafanua, whose full name Nanaifanua means "Hidden in the Earth."

"Our people in Falealupo are enslaved and persecuted," she complained to her father. "I can hear them calling out in their agony, and so can you. I must go to their assistance."

"Very well," replied Saveasi'uleo. "Before you depart for Samoa, chop down the *toa* tree and make weapons with it."

Nafanua found the tree standing over a dark shore of the realm. With one powerful sweep of her hand she knocked it down.

Returning a few days later when it had dried, she bent to carve the wood into four deadly weapons. She spoke to herself as she worked: "The first club is called the Ulimasao. It shall be my paddle." She sawed. "The second club is the Faauliulito, for the use of my allies." She chiseled. "The third club is the Tafesilafai. I wield it only against enemies, for it is deadly." She polished. "The last club is the Faamategatau. I will raise it in victory on the day I restore order to all of Samoa."

As she gathered up her clubs she noticed cowry shells all around the *toa* trunk. She spoke as though to herself: "The cowry shells live but the *toa* tree is dead."

"Now," advised her father before her journey, "it is most important that you remember this: When your enemies pull back to the stone wall at Salega, you must halt your pursuit."

"Why, father?"

"Because you will have reached Fualaga, the village of Chief Seali'itumatafaga, your mother's sister's son, and your kin deserve respect."

*   *   *   *

It was a long, wearying journey from Pulotu to Samoa. Days of paddling with Ulimasao through the undulating seas finally ended with Nafanua's arrival at Taliifiti Falealupo. She flexed her strong but tired arms, secured her boat, and lay down on the beach to sleep.

She was still sleeping when Chief Matuna and his wife came along. Who was this, they marveled, lying near the entrance to the Underworld? A ghost? A woman? A goddess? They walked over and woke her up.

"Greetings," they said to her as she sat up. "You're all wet!"

"I am newly arrived from Pulotu," she explained, "to lead the defense of Falealupo against further injustice. It's time to organize everyone for a common effort."

"We have few battle-ready men left. Chief Lilomaiava has enslaved them and ground them down with forced labor. Where will we find more?"

"Do not worry. I will command spirits who will assume the form of cicadas and dragonflies. They will be our allies. Here, this is your weapon"; and she handed them Faauliulito. "Use it against those who resist you, and spare those who ask for mercy."

The Matunas went forth around the village to announce the call to defense, but the weary villagers shook their heads; a few snickered. So long had they been mistreated by the warriors of the east that their fighting spirit was gone.

It was most discouraging, the couple told Nafanua when they returned with a report.

"We don't need them," she replied. "Just be on the far side of that road"—she pointed it out—"by tomorrow afternoon, and take on whomever comes down it. I will be on this side. If any of your opponents run over here, don't follow, for I will deal with them. You will handle anyone from over here who crosses to your side. Under no circumstances are you to leave your side of the road."

They looked scared. "Do not worry: all will be well," said Nafanua.

On the following afternoon, the frightened but determined chief and his wife were heartened to see the great cloud of an aerial army of dragonflies and cicadas buzzing toward them, a formation that poured over the land and darkened the sky.

Just in time. Here came their enemies: warriors led by Chief

Lilomaiava stalking down the road in formation, grimacing and carrying war clubs worn by frequent use.

With a cry of defiance, Nafanua whirled into them. The Matunas leaped after her as bodies began to fly off the roadway.

Surrounded by the buzzing insects that flew into the eyes, mouths, and nostrils of the eastern warriors, the couple gave a good account of themselves, beating their way up the road through the ranks of their opponents. Now and then they stole a glance at Nafanua, who bludgeoned dozens to death with single swings of her whistling war club. She quickly cleared the road around her and advanced on bewildered fighting men whose eyes rolled with terror at her approach. Those who asked for mercy she spared.

The Matunas were so caught up in battle they forgot Nafanua's warning. They strayed from their path to pursue a fleeing warrior when they entered the deadly radius of Nafanua's hissing weapon. It flew as though of its own mind; and they were instantly turned to stone. (It is said they yet guard the roadway.)

From the height above the Pa o Fualaga, Nafanua halted to look down on the carnage she had wrought.

The enemy army had fragmented in disarray. She felt tempted to pursue them, but her father's warning passed through her mind just as a gust lifted her coconut-leaf tunic.

Looking upward, the eastern fighters glimpsed her breasts and gasped. They had been destroyed by a woman! In shame, they surrendered immediately. The war was over.

Representatives from all over Samoa soon arrived to ask for a share in the new post-war government. They brought Nafanua offerings of food and moved her house to a place of honor in Falealupo.

She asked the chiefs there if any cared to swim with her. Those who complained that she could hold her breath underwater far longer than they were chastised and sent on their way; those who held their peace received influential postings.

Under the new program of shared governance, some petitioners became village leaders, some regional heads, some reservists, some official peacemakers and restorers of justice, and some caretakers of the forest.

The people called her Toa Tama'ita'i and celebrated their new-found peace.

Nafanua raised Faamategatau in victory.

For Reflection:

- Nafanua, also called Toa Tama'ita'i ("Warrior Princess"), is worshipped on the western side of Sava'i at Falealupo, where tradition places the entrance to the world of the dead. Why would reconnection with that world, or visitation from one of its emissaries, herald a time of peace?

- What is the significance of the punished priest being the brother of Nafanua's father? Besides kinship, why would this incident trigger an Underworld response?

- Why would that response arrive in the form of a female warrior?

- How might failure to respect the archetypal-mythical dimension of war make literal war more likely to break out?

- Why is respect for boundaries emphasized throughout?

- Why cicadas and dragonflies?

- Why were the Matunas turned to stone?

- What is Nafanua really saying with the breath-holding contest?

- This retelling appears here in the chapter on heroes. What difference would it make to the story to consider Nafanua an archetypal war goddess instead? Or an Underworld goddess?

- Comment: For his efforts to safeguard the Samoan rainforest, ethnobotanist and ethnomedicine expert Paul Alan Cox received the title of Nafanua in 1989 from the chiefs and priests of Falealupo. In 1997 he received the Goldman Environmental Prize.

- "The cowry shells live but the *toa* tree is dead." What might this mean? Could it refer to the courage needed to make hard decisions?
- Think about Nafanua's name. Does being at odds with her mean being at odds with the natural world?

The Death of Cuchulainn (Irish)

Maeve Binchy, novelist, playwright, columnist:

> I was the eldest child of two nice people who loved each other and told me I was the nicest girl in the world. It made me happy and confident. When my sisters came along, I had to share being the best girl in the world, and that was the best gift, the sense we were great. We were sure of an audience of five, we all listened to who my mother met when she went out, what my father did in the law courts all day, the dramas, old farmers fighting with each other. My life was full of stories.
>
> In my stories, there's no makeover. The heroine does not become beautiful—my God, Miss Smith, you're beautiful when you take off your glasses. You're not changed by any one outer thing, certainly not by one guy swooping in and taking you away.
>
> No one's life is ordinary. We're all the heroes and heroines, with fate or flaws to beat.... A streak of toughness combined with optimism is a good passport through life. The winners are the ones who get on with it.

"I want that bull," stated Queen Maeve of Connaught. It was not a request.

Her messengers nodded and departed for Ulster.

It had started with King Ailill's contemptuous hint that the Queen's wealth derived largely from marrying him. When they got out of bed to compare what they owned, Ailill came out ahead by only one bull, Finnbhennach ("White-Horned"), a fertile beast born into Maeve's herd but unwilling to be owned by a woman.

Very well. To even the score, she would obtain Donn Cúailnge, the Brown Bull of Cooley, a stud so renowned that even the Morrigan had entrusted to him her prize heifer.

Donn belonged to Dáire mac Fiachna.

"The Queen," her messengers told him, "offers you land in Connaught, and fifty heifers, and a chariot, and...friendship." Wink. "In return, she asks only the loan of your fine bull for one year, after which she will return him, with interest." Dáire agreed. He saw the messengers well-fed and plied with strong drink.

Too strong, perhaps. A drunken voice came to him on the breeze: "A good thing he agreed to the deal! The Queen would have taken the bull regardless, but this way is much less bloody."

When Maeve heard that Dáire had angrily called off the deal, she sent out a call for the invasion of Ulster. The king did likewise, to support her. He wished now that he had never taunted her.

This should be a handy victory, thought Maeve. She had heard of the curse of Macha against the warriors of Ulster. For making her run a horse race while pregnant (they had heard of her legendary fleetness of foot and wanted to see it themselves), Macha had inflicted upon them the pains of childbirth in their hour of preparation for battle. War-hardened men who had joked about the trials and duties of motherhood found themselves rolling on the ground groaning with false labor pains.

* * * *

The boy's name had been Sétanta, but after he killed the smith Culann's ferocious guard dog in self-defense and offered to watch over his house, he was called Cuchulainn, the Hound of Culann.

Son of the god Lugh and the charioteer Deichtine, nephew of King Conchobar of Ulster, he displayed remarkable strength and

intelligence early on. At seven he had equipped himself with the
weapons of his uncle in accord with a prophecy by the druid
Cathbad, which began, "He who bears arms this day will attain great
fame..." The boy ran off before he could hear the rest: "...but will
live a short life."

His rage was legendary. When the *ríastrad* came over him, his
body vibrated within his straining skin, sinews stretched from forehead to neck, as calves and heels traded places with toes and shins.
One eye enlarged as the other sank; his cheeks swept back to reveal
teeth, jaws, gullet, lungs, and liver; his hair stood up in spikes; and
his strength surpassed that of an entire troop of fighters. So dangerous was he even after battle that his Aunt Mugain devised the solution of forcing him into nine barrels of cold water, the first of which
exploded into steam on contact with his overheated skin.

After his military training by the crone Scáthach, Cuchulainn
won the hand of Emer by storming her father's fortress and carrying
her off. Another woman, Aife, bore him a son, Connla, but upon failing to recognize him, Cuchulainn killed him. He also killed the sons
of challengers he had fought; and these acts would catch up with
him.

The queen first heard of him from the soothsayer Fedelm, who
warned her that Cuchulainn would perpetrate a great slaughter
among her fighting men. She ordered the march on Ulster anyway.
What could one seventeen-year-old do against thousands?

They approached in unopposed while Cuchulainn lay blissfully
in the arms of a lover. The Red Branch fighters writhed on the
ground in agonies of false childbirth.

When Maeve's army entered Ulster, the air overhead buzzed
menacingly. Scores of men fell over, their foreheads bloody with
missiles cast by an unseen sling. At the peak of the confusion, a single form stood up on the heights of Slieve Foy. His long wind-blown
hair flapped brown around his shoulders, red at his neck, and gold
on top. Seven pupils gazed out of each eye toward the men of
Connaught gathered below. The invaders were surprised by how
short he was.

At this point the queen had lost quite a few men, not only to the young warrior but under the angry hooves of Donn, who had been warned by a crow to escape with his herds. She offered the young warrior a truce in exchange for lands, treasure, and women.

He produced a counter-offer: he would rely on single combat, one champion a day. In return, the queen would remain at this ford and refrain from removing any cattle until he was dead. She agreed.

One evening after a day of hard fighting, Cuchulainn looked up to see a beautiful young woman walking toward him. Her garments shone with the light of many colors. When she came near he greeted her and asked her name.

"I am the daughter of the Eternal," she replied, "and your great deeds have mightily moved my heart. I would be with thee, Cuchulainn. I have brought my treasures and my cattle."

He sighed. "I am quite busy just now."

"I know. You could benefit from my help."

"I'm not doing all this just for the sake of getting laid."

After a silence, "Very well," the woman answered in a tone as cold as winter. "If you will not accept my love, you will have my hindrance instead." The first time he had encountered Morrigan, she seemed a woman in red driving a heifer across his territory; when he drew his sword against the intruder, she changed into a crow sitting on the branch of a tree. Today, he again had failed to recognize her.

The next day Cuchulainn fought Loch, who had called him a "beardless youth" and had blackberry juice rubbed into his face. As they clashed, a red-eared heifer knocked into Cuchulainn. He recovered his balance at the cost of a cut and broke the heifer's leg. While wading into a stream, a red eel got between his legs. He tramped it, but again he was cut, and again when a red wolf bit his sword arm. He struck its eye with a stone from his sling and kept fighting. Loch finally fell before a spear thrust.

Weary, Cuchulainn made his way from the field, walking until he came across an old woman, blind and lame, milking a cow with three teats. She gave him three drinks of milk. "May you be healed for this kindness," he told her. Her blind eye opened, the bruise on her head faded, and her broken leg straightened.

"You once told me you wanted naught to do with me," she said.

Looking more carefully, he realized her wounds to be those of the animals which had attacked him earlier. "Had I recognized you," he said, "I would never have healed you."

"Prepare yourself for the bloodshed to come."

Maeve stood at the ford and decided she had lost enough warriors. She sent in Fergus, one of her greatest, an exiled Ulsterman. Nobody could stand against Fergus.

But when he walked onto the field, he saw his stepson and knew he could not fight with him. They stood sadly together.

"I will leave the field to you," Cuchulainn said at length, "but you must do the same for me at the proper time." Fergus agreed, and the younger fighter withdrew.

The next day Cuchulainn fought mighty Ferdia at the ford to be named after him.

The son of Damán and step-brother to Cuchulainn had not wanted to fight his best friend. He was there because Maeve had shamed him into it. Both had been trained by Scáthach. They possessed equal strength and skill. Ferdia was angry because the queen had told him that "Cuchulainn says you're no match for him."

They fought at the ford for three endless-seeming days, dodging, striking, panting, and bleeding. The men of Connaught watched in horrified fascination. Again and again, Cuchulainn landed blows that would have carved a lesser man in half, but his opponent was covered in magic armor no sword or spear could dent.

Finally, as the Ulster champion grew tired, his guard dropped briefly. Ferdia's sword shot forward and pierced Cuchulainn's chest. He fell.

But he fell still clutching Gae Bolga, the spear whose full power he had not wanted to unleash. He hurled it, and magic struck magic as the spear cut Ferdia's armor, entered his body, and spread its barbs into every muscle and joint.

In sorrow, Cuchulainn retired from the field.

He woke still collapsed on the ground, but somewhat stronger. His father Lugh had visited in the night and brought healing to his many wounds.

By morning, the men of Ulster, still recovering from their *ces noínden* pangs, entered the field to oppose Connaught. Many died, particularly the youngest, as Cuchulainn observed from a distance. Too young to be afflicted by the curse, they arrived before the older soldiers. Mere boys armed with swords and spears lay in red death in great numbers.

Cuchulainn felt the frenzy come over him. He slew hundreds of his opponents before his aching wounds halted him.

Now Fergus led a charge. Seeing him, Cuchulainn made his way across the field and faced his step-father:

"I remind you of your promise. You must withdraw."

Fergus nodded and led his men off the field.

Maeve knew she and Ailill could not win now against Ulster. *But at least I have the Brown Bull at last!* During the fighting her men had captured Donn.

Leaving the field to the oncoming Ulstermen, she had the brown bull sent back to Connaught while she organized an orderly retreat. It would be a long march back.

Donn Cuailnge crossed the path of Finnbennach at Athlone and gave three ground-shaking bellows. The white bull bellowed back. They hated each other. They had once been battling swineherds, then worms eaten by two cows. Reborn now as bulls, they continued their snarling, stamping, biting feud at the hill called Tarbga.

After a fight lasting a day and a night, the brown bull headed back home with the entrails of the white dripping from his horns.

He reached Ulster, shook his head, moaned, fell over, and expired.

* * * *

Maeve and Ailill made peace with Ulster, but they did not forget Cuchulainn. Nor did Morrigan. Nor did the sons of the men he had killed.

Nor did the three daughters of Catalin, whose sons and grandson were slain in the recent fighting. Maeve sent them to Scotland to study the arts of magical deception.

Cuchulainn feasted in Emain Macha when the noise of screaming and the fires of war ignited in Ulster, or so it seemed. Against the advice of the druids who saw through the spell, and despite the bloody tears of his horse Liath Macha and the wine offered by his anxious mother to calm him down, Cuchulainn mounted his chariot and drove out to meet the invaders.

On the road he passed a young woman of the Sidhe washing bloody armor in a stream. A bad omen.

He drove until he saw three one-eyed crones eating cooked dog on spits of rowan. "Sit and eat with us," they called out. He politely refused, but they jeered at him: "What, too good to eat with us? Can't be bothered to keep company with three old women?"

This was a problem. Just as his son had been forbidden to reveal his own identity, Cuchulainn was forbidden to eat the flesh of hounds—but also forbidden to refuse hospitality when offered.

Seating himself, he took some meat in his left hand and ate a small bite. Half the strength flowed out of the left side of his body. He could almost hear the Morrigan laughing on the wind....

Weakened but resolute, Cuchulainn drove on until he came to a stretch of road where a group of men stood waiting for him. With a sense of finality, he recognized them. Three were the surviving sons of Catalin. A fourth was Lugaid, son of slain Cu Roi. They were there to kill him.

The men locked shields, but Cuchulainn's chariot drove into them and broke through. He turned and attacked.

As he reached from the vehicle to slice off heads and limbs, a druid standing off to the side called out:

"Lend me one of your spears, or I shall make fun of you throughout all Ireland!"

"Never let it be said I am not generous"—and the spear ran through the druid's head and cast him down.

Waiting for this, Lugaid pulled it forth, hefted it, aimed, and threw it at Laeg. The point entered the driver's stomach.

A second druid called out: "Give me your spear, or I will speak badly of you!"

"I never refuse a well-met request"—and it flew from his hand

and impaled the druid. Lugaid jerked it free and threw it at Liath Macha. The horse went down heavily, though not before kicking two nearby enemies to death.

"Your spear, or your name shall be ruined!"—and Lugaid, having pulled it from its bleeding target, hurled it straight at Cuchulainn.

The assassins and Maeve knew the prophecy that the three spears of Cuchulainn would each slay a king. Liath Macha, king of all horses, lay dead, as did Laeg, king of all charioteers. Cuchulainn, king of all champions, fell disemboweled from his chariot.

He picked himself up and, trying to hold back his insides, staggered to a nearby lake to wash himself and take one last drink. To a stone pillar he lashed himself with his belt. He would die on his feet, his sword in his hand.

As the light left his paling face, his enemies held back, wanting his head but still fearful and wary. Only when a crow landed on Cuchulainn's cooling shoulder did they dare to draw in close.

For Reflection:

- Comment: The *Táin Bó Cúalnge* (*Cattle Raid of Cooley*) is the hub of the Rúraíocht, the Ulster Cycle of Irish myth. Its variants descend from oral tellings going back at for perhaps two millennia.

- The wounded Brown Bull's wanderings translate into many Irish place names. *Bóthar*, the Irish word for "road," contains *bó*, which means "bull." The word also appears in Ardboe, Drumbo, Drumshambo, Inishbofin, and Lough Bo. Cattle represented wealth, and raids for cattle were usually more initiatory of young warriors than outright violent. What might the bull signify archetypally?

- What qualities does Cuchulainn share with the other Heroes in this chapter?

- Why does he reject Morrigan? What does it look like today to turn away from the bidding of an archetypal summons?

- Why is the threat of being shamed or spoken badly of so compelling to Cuchulainn?

- According to Joseph Campbell, the Hero undergoes an Underworld descent and returns, transformed, with some great Prize for his culture. Is this true of Cuchulainn? Why or why not?

- When Lugaid cuts off Cuchulainn's head, the dead warrior's sword falls forward, severing Lugaid's hand. Conall eventually avenges Cochulainn. In retaliation for the murder of his mother, Furbaide places a hard piece of cheese in a sling and kills Maeve as she bathes. But none of these vengeful acts halts the coming bad fortune of the Red Branch of Ulster. What does this story suggest about the nature of violence?

- As an Irish Venus or Aphrodite, Maeve makes her own way. Married off to Conchobar by her father Eochaid Feidlech, she is unsatisfied with the marriage and leaves it. She requires that her future husband lack jealousy because she knows she will have other lovers. In a realm run by men, she succeeds by assertiveness, trickery, boldness, sensuality, and violence. Is she amoral? If not, what kind of morality does she observe?

- The Persian hero Rostam kills his son Sohrab, and Herakles kills his own family. How might Cuchulainn have averted the death of his son? His own tragic death? What are his fatal flaws?

- Why do blood feuds go on, generation after generation, when they obviously never resolve anything?

Chapter Eight - The Post-Heroic Journey

Joseph Campbell's Hero's Journey unfolds the archetype of Initiation in phases that take the seeker into the Underworld, where a treasure hard to attain is found, and then back out again.

The Post-Heroic Journey envisions what happens after. It unfolds in these phases, each illustrated by a tale below:

Landing here. *Fully arriving home. After great deeds are done, the Hero who survives them finally returns.*

Facing mortality. *The Hero faces death many times, but facing gradual decline culminating in life's ending is a different challenge.*

Enduring disenchantment. *How to live once the magic of the great Heroic Journey wears off?*

Learning limitations. *How to bear them once the divine sources of help go away?*

Reimagining relationships. *Learning interdependency, intimacy, companionship.*

Dispensing the boon. *Setting loose the beneficial effects of whatever has been heroically attained.*

Enjoying life. *Learning to have fun and laugh.*

Mentoring new heroes. *Being a model; offering wisdom.*

Apomythosis. *Campbell believed the Hero's Journey to include Apotheosis, or divinization, but this happens to many mythic figures (see Mazu's story later). Apomythosis refers to conversion into legend while the Hero still lives, sometimes with her or his consent.*

302

The Return of Odysseus (Greek)

Nikos Kazantzakis, Greek writer:

> What I felt was simply that Odysseus's selfhood widened as he advanced, that it smashed each and every mold — individual self, family, nation, race, species, organic being, universe. I felt him continually identifying with the fearful, indestructible, and totally mysterious *elan* that appears on our planet in the form of Life. Odysseus...sensed that *elan* acquiring consciousness, creating eyes with which to see, ears with which to hear, a heart with which to experience joy and pain.
>
> Although I can tell you what position I take, Odysseus passes beyond me. That is why Odysseus, transcending nationalistic limitations, is a citizen of the future commonwealth (*of each and every future commonwealth*). The Cretan glance does not mean that we dispense with the Western-Eastern civilization of ancient Greece. It means that we synthesize all that and, primarily, the gushing of *new elements* inside us, so that we may experience a fresh conception of life that is broader, nobler, and more responsible.

The first sound Odysseus heard upon awakening was the gurgle of waves over the shore.

He opened his eyes and sat up under an olive tree where Phaeacian sailors had left him, laying him down gently, still asleep and wrapped in linen, on a rug spread beneath his tired body. Lavish gifts from his friends sat grouped around the trunk of the tree.

He stood and looked around. Thick fog prevented him from seeing little besides the shore, the tree, a cave beyond. His palms slapped his thighs in frustration.

"Where am I?" he asked out loud. "Yet another place of hungry, evil, murderous creatures? Why have my new supposed friends not carried me home as they had promised?"

As he sorted through the gifts, wondering whether to hide them or not, a slender young shepherd materialized out of the mist. Odysseus noted a spear, sandals, a heavy cloak. He decided on a tactful greeting, at least until he learned more:

"Friend, you are most welcome. I hope you will show due consideration to me and to these, my possessions, for I am but recently cast upon this shore and do not know my way around here yet." He continued, "What place is this, and what manner of men live here? Is this an island or the shore of a larger land?"

"It is a rugged isle you have come to, stranger," replied the shepherd while leaning on his spear. "A narrow isle, too, but not without riches of corn and grape watered by fog and rain. There is good pasturage here as well."

Some of the tension left the strong but battered shoulders of Odysseus, master of sea ways and land ways.

"I am glad to hear this," he said in a smooth tone, "for I have traveled much since slaying Orsilochus, son of Idomeneus of Crete, after he tried to steal the booty I took away from the Trojan War. I killed him with my spear before he could rob me and make of me a slave. From there I sought escape on a vessel of the Phaeacians, whom I paid well, but the wind came up and drove us here by night. From sheer weariness I fell asleep, and woke to find the sailors gone. They must have left me here with my goods and sailed on for Sidon."

Coming up close, the shepherd smiled and touched him in friendliness. The smile remained, but the face flowed and the garments rearranged themselves, hung long, brightened. Standing taller, encased in light, a gray-eyed goddess in silvery mail chuckled at him as the fog swirled around her.

"Few could surpass you, Odysseus, in either cunning or guile. Not even here, it would seem, do you feel safe enough to drop these trusty old tools of yours." The musical voice of Athena chided him even as he blinked at her in astonishment.

Suddenly, a wave of anger broke over his face.

"I used to believe you were on my side, Goddess. But after we sacked once-proud Troy and sailed away, a god scattered our ships to the four winds, and I have been in peril ever since. For these eighteen years I have tried to get home, only to be seduced by dangers in comely form, attacked by monsters, set upon by ghosts in the Underworld.

"I have struggled and schemed and cheated and killed; I have destroyed cities and sailed past shores uncounted; I have lost all my men, every last one of them. I have been shipwrecked, rescued, and shipwrecked again, and I stand before you lost and bewildered, the fate of my family still unknown to me.

"Where have you been?"

"At your side, son of Anticleia and Laertes, ever at your side. I saw to your survival; I arranged your rescues; I made sure the Phaeacians bound up your wounds, let you rest, and favored you with gifts and transport. I saw when you met the shades of Agamemnon, Achilles, your own mother; when you consulted Tiresias.

"You did not recognize me, O clever Odysseus, because I sometimes held the shape of crewman or islander, porpoise or bird. But through it all, I, the daughter of Zeus, looked out for you."

She lifted her strong arms. "And I am looking out for you now."

The fog rolled back to reveal a familiar harbor, a vaulted cave near at hand, and forested Mount Neriton in the distance. His eyes opened wide.

Against all odds, in spite of all sorrow, death, and heartbreaking loss, he stood again upon Ithaka. He was home.

Speechless, he knelt, bent down, and kissed the blessed earth.

For Reflection:

- Odysseus stories precede their distillation in Homer's famous epic. In them the hero wanders over land and sea before coming home: a long initiation. What is involved in the transition from a heroic to a post-heroic psychology?

- What role does a Wisdom Goddess play in this transition? What does it mean to be favored by Athena?

- Why is the fog necessary?

- Trauma survivors often learn to dissimulate and stay wary because of what they have been through. How might these once-necessary defenses work against the survivor? By wearing a disguise, what is Athena trying to tell Odysseus?

- After the Phaeacians drop off Odysseus, Poseidon, the god who sent him all over the Mediterranean to lose some of his hubris, turned them and their ship to stone for countermanding his will. What happens when pleasing one archetypal presence (e.g., Athena) means angering another? What are the options available?

- Comment: Finally coming home sounds like "happily ever after," but, cautioning Odysseus against complacency, "Be of good cheer," Athena advises him, "hide away your gifts for now, and let us think together about how to recapture your home from the suitors who have shamelessly invaded it." In some ways, the struggle never ends.

- In *Waiting for God*, Simone Weil wrote: "We feel ourselves to be outsiders, uprooted, in exile here below. We are like Ulysses who had been carried away during his sleep by sailors and woke in a strange land, longing for Ithaca with a longing that rent his soul. Suddenly Athena opened his eyes and he saw that he was in Ithaca. In the same way every man who longs indefatigably for his country, who is distracted from his desire neither by Calypso nor by the Sirens, will one day suddenly find that he is there." What does it mean to come home? Is it a purely inner state? What about family, relationships, sense of self, of place and time?

Gilgamesh Grows Up (Mesopotamian)

Hassan Blasim, Iraqi writer, poet, and filmmaker:

> I'm interested in the rhythm of stories, because I really care about the rhythm – like in a film. I don't want it to feel boring. It's a change in the rhythm, to put the story to another person. And also maybe because, in Iraq, everyone wants to tell a story – because they have lived through forty years of violence.

> All the stories come in more of a picture form for me. When I sleep I have many dreams; one day in Helsinki I went to the doctor and said, 'I dream a lot, am I normal?' and he said, 'It's okay, you're a writer, just use it!'

> I'm like the other five million Iraqis who are outside Iraq. We dream of a safe country where human dignity is not violated, either directly through violence or through rigorous physical and intellectual control.

Enkidu, his once-enemy and now-friend, was dead. Gilgamesh held him and wept.

Then the hero who had planned the great city Uruk, raised zig-gurats, dug wells, planted gardens, and killed monsters removed his royal robes, put on animal skins to look more like his hairy dead friend, and set off to seek Utnapishtim, holder of the secret of immortality.

As he made his way through the wilderness, he reflected on the irony of it all.

Because he had enslaved men, ravished brides, and worn out his subjects with hard labor, the gods had sent the mighty beast Enkidu to put Gilgamesh in his place. After fighting they had become fast friends who scorned city life for adventuring. Together, they destroyed the forest demon Humbaba and, against the advice of the elders of Uruk, carved up the tallest cedar into an enormous gate and a raft on which to float home. Together, they killed the Bull of Heaven sent by enraged Ishtar after Gilgamesh refused her seductive invitation.

The gods then inflicted an illness upon Enkidu, that child of the wild tamed by an erotic priestess, and now the true brother of Gilgamesh lay lifeless. "So now I must become a ghost," Enkidu had said at the end, "to sit with the ghosts of the dead, to see my dear brother nevermore!"

As I will I be too some day, unless... So mused Gilgamesh as he neared Mt. Mashu. Unless he found the mysterious wise one who had survived the last great flood.

While traveling he kept watch over his dreams. They had always advised him. A dream had heralded the coming of Enkidu, the battle with Humbaba, the wrestling match with the Bull of Heaven. He remembered part of a premonitory dream of Enkidu's and shuddered:

On entering the House of Dust, everywhere I looked were royal crowns piled in heaps...

Mt. Mashu stood so high and deep that it guarded both heaven and Underworld. The sun rose on one side and set on the other. Upon the shoulders of stone at the gate of the mountain Gilgamesh saw two giant scorpions rise and point their tails at him.

"Why have you come here, O part-god?" asked one as he drew near and halted.

"To ask my ancestor Utnapishtim about the secret of life and death." His voice might have trembled a little.

"This no mortal has ever done. You would cross the mountain through twelve leagues of darkness so black none can see."

"Even so, come what may, I must go through. Let me pass."

"Very well. The gate opens to you."

The creatures stood aside, and Gilgamesh made his careful way down the Road of the Sun into the blackness.

After what seemed an interminable march he emerged into a dazzlingly sunlit garden filled with flowers colored like lapis lazuli, carnelian, hematite, ruby, and emerald. A curve of blue sea swept away over the glimmering horizon.

The veiled tavern keeper Siduri locked her door and gate.

"I am not here to rob you," he called out, "but if you don't open your door I will smash it down and walk through anyway. Do you not recognize me? I am Gilgamesh."

"You do not look like Gilgamesh. Your cheeks are sunken, your face is sad, and you wear a travel-worn animal skin."

"I have fought with Humbaba, grappled with the Bull of Heaven, and lost my best friend to death. I've wandered ever since. Why should I not be sad?"

"Where do you go, then?"

"To seek Utnapishtim. Can you tell me the way?"

"No mortal has ever gone to him, Gilgamesh. To reach him, you must fight the stony beings of the wilderness, then cross the Waters of Death. Only Urshanabi could help you do that. Why not instead savor the things of life? Why not dance and make music, play with children and enjoy the company of a loving mate?" He turned away.

Gilgamesh found Urshanabi the ferryman near the river and told him where he desired to go.

"Unfortunately, the stony things you just smashed held the ropes we need to cross the Waters of Death. Go into the woods and come back with trees carved into punting poles."

He did this, and they set out over the river, with his skins serving as a sail. When they came to the Waters, Gilgamesh fended off the dead who tried to board the ferry.

On the far shore the ferryman let him off near an old man staring out over the river.

"I am Gilgamesh," said the traveler after a long silence. "Where might I find Utnapishtim?"

"I am he whom you seek. What do you want?"

"Not to die."

Another long silence.

"Has it not occurred to you," Utnapishtim asked, "that all your labors and seekings bring you closer to death even faster? Life is like a short reed snapped off by that which it never sees. The strength and beauty of youth fade inevitably. How long do our houses stand? Do our contracts endure? Do our brothers enjoy their inheritance? Would you gaze upon the face of the sun itself? How alike are the sleeping and the dead. The gods established Death and Life, but they have not disclosed the secrets of either."

"Then how have you survived?"

"Long ago the gods decided to have an end to humanity altogether. Ea warned me about this before the great flood, giving me enough time to build a large boat. I put my family and the seed of every living creature aboard and set sail as the rains poured down over the lands, erasing them. When the waters receded at last, the gods repented and promised not to destroy humankind again. For witnessing all this, I was granted the boon of immortality."

As though to himself, "How can I get you to return home?" Utnapishtim mused. Then:

"You have traveled far, but to continue you must be alert. Can you stay awake for a week?"

Gilgamesh sat down, nodding, and fell asleep.

"Look at him," said the old man as his wife walked up. "He wants to be immortal, but he can't keep his eyes open for even a moment."

She nodded. "Let him return safely."

"I will. —Bake him a loaf of bread for each day he sleeps and make one mark upon this wall."

Seven days later, the old man touched Gilgamesh, who started and opened his eyes.

"My wife has baked you seven loaves, but they rotted as you slept. Only one is fresh. Can you not see what is written on the wall?"

Gilgamesh hung his head in despair. "What am I to do?"

"Tell him about the plant," said his wife. Utnapishtim was immortal, but he had been human and still felt pity. He nodded.

"Gilgamesh. After you have cleansed yourself and put on your kingly garments once again, go to the middle of the river. You will find at its bottom a rare plant like a boxthorn. Pick the plant. If you can carry it home, you will achieve what you seek."

Thanking him, Gilgamesh bid the ferryman to row him out. He

then attached large stones to his feet and plunged into the water.

When he reached the bottom, he untied the stones and, holding his breath, sought for and found the plant the old man had described. He picked it and swam with strong strokes to the surface, where he reboarded the ferry in jubilation:

"I have found it! The plant of immortality! When I get home I will ask some old men to eat it and see if they grow young again."

That night Gilgamesh and the ferryman camped on the bank of the river. As they slept, a snake smelled the appetizing odors of the plant and slithered close, sniffing. It slid in silently and went off with the plant.

After a taste, it left only its skin behind for Gilgamesh to find the next morning. A great cry of grief echoed across the river.

"What am I to do now, Urshanabi? I have accomplished nothing! Through my misdeeds I even broke the markers that would guide us home." Tears ran down his nose and cheeks.

Even so, the ferryman brought them home.

"Look at the wall around Uruk," observed Gilgamesh as he blinked at the city with different eyes while the ferryman watched and listened. "Consider the solid foundations, the meticulous brickwork, the intricate organization, the orchards, the gardens, the soaring Temple of Ishtar.

"Perhaps this wonder of a city will stand...for a time."

For Reflection:

- The tale of Gilgamesh, the oldest and most complete early hero figure in the West, was carved into tablets found in the ruined library of an Assyrian king at Nineveh across the river from Mosul, Iraq. The Assyrian Empire fell when, having been weakened by expansionary and aggressive kings, it was attacked by the peoples it had subjugated. How does this history reinforce what the tale suggests about the impermanence of heroic kingship?

- How might Gilgamesh provide the prototype for the colonial settler who sets out to conquer a continent, only to end up disenchanted?

- Jung interpreted Enkidu as the shadow of Gilgamesh. What does it mean that Gilgamesh befriends him?

- Why is Gilgamesh punished for failing to love Ishtar? (Siduri, whose name means "young woman," can be thought of as a byform of Ishtar, as can the erotic priestess who tamed Enkidu.)

- Part of the hero's task is to overcome his own impulsivity. What helps Gilgamesh do this?

- The universal flood shows up in many, though not all, mythologies. Utnapishtim's story antedates Noah's. What could such a flood symbolize, collectively?

- Just as Lancelot does not win the Grail, Gilgamesh fails to obtain the plant of immortality. Was there any real chance that he could? What does his failure teach him?

- The archetype of Initiation unfolds in three stages: Departure, Crisis, Return. At the end of the story is Gilgamesh a fully initiated hero?

- Comment: The serpent and the hero often appear together, as when Thor wrestles a world-circling snake. The serpent seems to represent knowledge gained through a difficult initiation (no wonder so many people fear snakes!). One can imagine the snake slithering off to teach Eve and Adam in the Garden of Eden...

Ditaolane's Departure (Sotho)

Napo Masheane, Sotho poet, playwright, director, and artist:

> Before anything I am Napo Masheane a Mosotho girl raised by Basotho so I carry within me the Sotho lan-

guage wherever I go. My tongue represents its customs and rituals.

I was exposed to African literature at a very young age. By 12 or 13 I was already reading *Things Fall Apart* by Chenue Achebe. My father, a visual artist and teacher, always brought books home. I also read a lot of Sotho novels that my Mom would recommend.

I use my work to re-write the lies of our history. I celebrate our scars and joys. I heal wounded hearts. I appreciate sisterhood, spirituality, my ancestors and the God whom I wear her face every day.

The screaming of many throats tearing the air told the pregnant woman that something horrible approached.

She wasted no time smearing her body with ashes and crouching in the calves' pen. She wished she could help her fellow villagers, but saving her son was paramount.

It was called the Khodumodumo: an ogre whose head swayed above the treetops as the beast rolled through the mountain pass eating whatever living beings it could scoop into its cavernous mouth: people, cattle, fowls, goats, even dogs whose barks were abruptly silenced by death.

She held her breath when a dark, shapeless mass blotted out the sky. The ogre bent toward her property, searching for more food. Its eyes saw what seemed to be a stone sitting in the pen and moved away. It made for the pass again but could not get through because of its swollen belly.

In the pen, labor pains rippled through the woman's lower body. It was time.

She squatted and pushed hard, and out emerged a glistening baby boy.

She wiped him off and left him on the ground for a moment while she looked around for bedding for him.

She returned—and stopped, staring. Where a baby had cooed lay a man.

One strong hand clenched two spears. A knife hung at his waist. A necklace of divining bones lay strung across his muscular chest.

"Sir, do you know where my child has gone?"

"It's me, Mother. I'm your child."

"How can that be?"

"It's true. —What is going on out there?"

She told him about the ogre.

"Let us go and look at it."

They left the pen and climbed a wall around the path. From the top they saw the hill-sized ogre lurching here and there as it struggled to get out of the valley.

They returned to the pen, where the man, whose name was Ditaolane, sought a handy stone. On it he sharpened the tips of his spears.

"Time to go hunting," he told his mother as he left the pen.

When the Khodumodumo spotted him coming, it opened its mouth wide and lunged for him, but he was already around it sinking a spear into its side. The ogre's scream sounded across the valley.

The beast turned toward him but again he dodged and thrust in the second spear. The body toppled, hit the ground with an impact that shook it, and expired.

He had pulled out his knife and set to work cutting open the ogre's flesh when a muffled voice called out, "Don't cut me!" He tried another section of flesh but another voice cried out when the blade slashed someone's leg. The third time produced the lowing of a cow. He continued to cut, avoiding spots beneath which a goat bleated, a hen cackled, and a dog barked.

When he was finished, the valley's eaten but undigested humans and animals staggered forth rejoicing from the well-flensed carcass.

For his act of heroism, Ditaolane was appointed headman of a village. He received enough cattle as gifts to make a herd, and enough marriage propositions to fill a home with grateful wives.

But the man whose leg he had cut never forgot the injury. The leg healed, but the outrage did not.

This cunning man played upon the envy of his fellow villagers by making insinuations—never open accusations—about their savior:

"With all those wives it's a wonder he gets anything done."

"Wouldn't you like to have half that many cattle?"

"Is it me, or does he seem rather bored with us unheroic types now?"

"I wonder at times about his mother's strange story about his birth..."

Before long, he had stirred up so much envy and fear that people began talking openly about how to get rid of Ditaolane.

The bones he wore on a necklace warned him. On one occasion, he managed to avoid falling into a pit concealed with dry grass. On another, he escaped a crowd that had gathered to throw him into a fire; they threw in one of their own conspirators instead.

When they tried to trap him in a cave set on fire, he materialized in their midst, shaming them. When they tried to push him off a cliff, another man fell. With powerful healing magic, Ditaolane brought him back to life.

This only increased their envy and distrust, however. And when he saved people eaten by the monster Kammapa by cutting open its intestines from within, the envy and distrust again multiplied.

Weary of their hostility, Ditaolane finally let them kill him. When they did, his heart burst out of his silenced chest, sprouted wings, and flapped away as a bird.

They watched in awe as it receded from their view and was never seen by them again.

For Reflection:

- For the hero who expects only a hero's welcome, an encounter with envy and paranoia can be shattering. What does this South African story tell us about heroism's emotional impact on a community? (In my counselor days, a male client told our men's group that he had seen a man hitting a woman and gone to her assistance, only to have both of them round on him.)

- What could the hero have done in lieu of accepting power, cattle, and wives while still respecting the community's need to recognize his achievement?

- Psychoanalyst Erich Fromm coined the term "group narcissism" to describe a field of mutual unconsciousness in which people feel egotistically proud of being members of a particular group. The group can be of any size: a work unit, a family, a neighborhood, a nation. To offend the group or its symbols (flag, religious icon, holy book, etc.) is to offend the members. How does well-intentioned Ditaolane inadvertently offend his village?

- What sorts of in-groups need out-groups, or outsiders, to scapegoat?

- Why do we nurture grudges? What does holding a grudge do to us psychologically? How do we get free of them?

- Comment: Although poison is not mentioned in this myth, many myths and legends do portray the dark power of unchecked insinuation as poisonous. In Tennyson's *The Idylls of the King*, this kind of poison helped destroy Camelot.

- Melanie Klein uses the word "spoiling" to denote acts with which the envious ruins other people's pleasures or achievements. Spoiling allows revenge on the object of their envy. What are examples of spoiling have you suffered?

- Ditaolane is a classic hero, a miraculously born monster killer moved by his disenchantment into a post-heroic phase. What were his options, if any, other than letting himself be killed?

- Why does his heart fly out of his chest?

Oonagh Protects Her Husband (Irish)

Mick Moloney, Irish folklorist, scholar, and musician:

> When I came to the United States in 1973, I had no idea
> there was this huge repository of Irish American songs.
>
> The Irish were one of the first ethnic or racial groups to
> constitute the wretched of the earth in America. The life
> expectancy of Irish immigrants working on canals and
> building railroads was very low, something like 7 to 10
> years, and there was a tremendous amount of anti-Irish
> sentiment and discrimination.
>
> It's high time, really, that the Irish-American song tradi-
> tion was highlighted. I'm not talking about the nostalgia
> you hear in Tin Pan Alley songs, either, where Ireland is
> painted as this paradise that, frankly, many Irish immi-
> grants in the mid-19th Century wouldn't recognize or
> recall. I'm talking about songs focusing on the key role
> the Irish played in fighting America's wars and in creat-
> ing America's infrastructure: roads, canals, dams, rail-
> roads, buildings.

I wonder how my wife is doing? thought Finn MacCumhaill as
he paused from his labors on the Giant's Causeway, an enormous
stony bridge from Ulster to Scotland.

He turned and walked toward Knockmany Hill, telling himself
it would be good to see Oonagh; but in truth he was, for the first time
in his life, afraid.

He and his companions built the Causeway to meet
Benandonner, a legendary Scottish giant who wanted to challenge
Finn. At first the rumors about this giant did not bother Finn: oppo-
nents always boasted of their doings before they met face to face.
Benandonner, it was said, could beat any giant in the world. He had
flattened a thunderbolt like a pancake and put it in his pocket. He

had jumped up and down and caused an earthquake.

Finn disregarded the gossip until he saw what seemed to be a large hill on the other side of the Causeway. Gradually, he realized that the hill was Benandonner, waiting for him.

Fighting giants was one thing, but fighting a hill-sized giant quite another.

Oonagh must be lonely for me by now, thought the legendary head of the Fianna as he opened his front door and greeted her with a kiss that echoed through the trees.

"I'm just fine, love," she told him as she ran a hand through her golden hair. "Keepin' meself busy. What brings you home early?"

"Oh, just because of missing you, my love, just because of missing you."

Oonagh's eye and ear missed nothing. She decided to wait him out.

"It's Benandonner," he admitted with embarrassment. He told her about the pancaked thunderbolt, the earthquake, and the hill.

He placed his thumb in his mouth, a habit from when he had burned it while cooking the Salmon of Knowledge for Finnegan the Druid. Tasting the Salmon fat on his thumb had given him the gift of prophecy.

"He is coming," Finn stated. "He will be here by tomorrow. If I run away, I'll disgrace myself. If I fight him...."

"Leave him to me."

* * * *

Oonagh opened the door after Benandonner's spear butt nearly beat it in.

"Yes?"

"I'm looking for Finn MacCumhaill," rumbled the giant.

"He's away hunting, but would you like to come in and wait for him?"

"Yes."

"But before you do...well, the wind has gotten up a bit cold, if you take my meaning. When that happens, Finn always picks up the house and turns it away from the wind. Would you mind?"

After an uncomfortable pause, the giant put his arms around the house (barely) and, with a great heave, managed to turn it out of the wind. He stood up panting.

"I appreciate it. Now would you mind doing me another favor? You might have seen that pebble lyin' at the bottom of the hill over there. We've had dry weather and little water, but Finn says the rock covers a fine spring. He was going to break open a space for the spring but he's not here. Would you be able to do it?"

She took him down the hill and showed him. To his dismay he beheld a huge slab of solid stone. With a painful effort, he opened a gash (now called Lumford's Glen) but cracked his right middle finger doing it.

"Thank you ever so much. Won't you come in now?"

The sweating giant entered the hall and looked around.

"Go ahead and put down your spear over there next to Finn's." She pointed to a tall fir tree topped by a boulder. He stared at it for a moment. *Finn could wield that thing?*

"What is this?" asked Benandonner, pointing at a block of oak as large as four chariot wheels.

"Finn's shield. —Have a seat at the table here and I'll bring you some of the griddle cakes I make for him. He loves them."

The giant rested from his labors while the sizzle of cooking bread and fat wafted from the kitchen. Soon Oonagh appeared with an enormous plate of cakes and set it on the table.

Benandonner eagerly bit into one and howled in pain.

"Owww! Blood and fury, here's three of my teeth missing! What is this you served me?"

"I'm so sorry," she replied courteously. "Finn likes his bread rather chewy." The cake concealed an iron griddle cooked inside it. He found the bacon no easier, perhaps because it was nailed to a block of timber.

"I see my baby is awake. I had better feed him."

She gave the "baby" a cake with no griddle baked into it. To the giant's surprise, the large mouth beneath the charming blue bonnet ate the entire cake at one go. A thumb replaced the cake.

"This is Finn's son?" asked the giant, marveling at the size of the form beneath a dress as large as a bedsheet.

"Yes. He's just a little lad compared to his father, but he'll have plenty of time to catch up. —There there, sweetness. Would you like another cake?"

Suddenly Benandonner seemed eager to leave. Oonagh showed him out.

As they passed through a garden, she pointed out a group of boulders as tall as the giant.

"It's a pity Finn isn't here. You and he could play catch with those stones."

"Catch?"

"Yes. He uses them for exercise."

The sooner I'm back in Scotland the better the giant thought. He thanked her for her hospitality.

"Will you be calling on Finn again? I'm sure he'd like to meet you."

"N-not any time soon." He hurried away.

As she turned back home, her husband dashed past her, stripping off bonnet and sheet as he ran. With the giant heading out over the Causeway, Finn's injured pride made him scoop up a handful of earth and hurl it at Benandonner's retreating back. It missed, but when it landed it created the Isle of Man. The hole left by Finn's scooping hand became Lough Neagh.

Benandonner's huge fist pounded the Causeway as he went, destroying it behind him.

Oonagh stood staring after Finn, a smile of affectionate irony on her face.

"You're welcome," she said.

For Reflection:

- Comment: The Giant's Causeway is a series of hexagonal basalt columns formed sixty million years ago by volcanic upheaval on the northeast coast of Ireland. The columns look like stepping stones. Similar columns stand at Fingal's Cave on the Scottish Isle of

Staffa ("Pillar Island").

- The hero constellates the monster. How is Finn responsible for the appearance of Benandonner?

- Finn's prophetic thumb warns him that he will encounter Benandonner but does not tell him the outcome. Why? What are the limits of intuition?

- How does Oonagh ("OO-nah") make use of the same fear in Benandonner that troubles Finn?

- What is slyly hinted at by her plan to make Finn appear as a baby?

- What qualities make Oonagh the hero of this tale?

- The tasks Oonagh sets before Benandonner might be compared with the labors of Hercules imposed by Hera. What do these tasks teach the giant about himself?

- Myths often explain features of the land as sculpted by giant beings. How do the natural forces responsible connect with these mythic beings?

Manawydan Versus Llwyd (Welsh)

Owen Staton, Welsh actor, police officer, and storyteller:

> Tales had always held an interest for me. As a sixth-form student, I clearly remember reading a book on *Rumours And Oddities Of North Wales* whilst on a field trip to Nant Gwyrtheyn and the other students got drunk around me.

> At the turn of the millennium, when millions were starting to discover the myths of old, the steel industry in South Wales was really starting to suffer, like the fall of Rome so long before: a once-mighty colossus on the

coast of Wales was falling into ruin. I decided to take one of the few lifeboats and jump ship.

Terrified of tale-telling alone, I wrote a small play about competing storytellers telling old Welsh myths, cast three performers including myself and off to Scotland we went. It worked. I had found my voice, and Owen Staton, police officer, father and part-time actor became Owen Staton, police officer and storyteller.

It's tough, but the time between times is short, the veil between our world and the world of stories is only thin for a small part of our lives. I recommend anybody to step through it. You never know what you will find on the other side.

It was not long after the wedding of Manawydan and Rhiannon that Pryderi, King of Dyfed, decided to visit the mound of Gorsedd Arberth.

Pryderi was a trifle drunk with celebration, but the older couple heard him out with gratitude. He had brought them together.

Both had known hard times. Rhiannan, his mother, had been married to Pryderi's father Pwyll after a difficult courtship. Then their baby disappeared. Rhiannon was framed for his murder and forced to wear a horse collar and sit at the castle gate for all to see. She was fully cleared only after her blond baby—not dead but stolen out of his crib—had grown up with Teyrnon, who had found him as an infant lying abandoned near a stable.

As for Manawydan, he, a son of Llyr, had been deposed from the throne of the Isle of the Mighty (known one day as Britain) by his traitorous cousin Caswallawn. Manawydan had been a wanderer since the burial of his brother Bran's head until Pryderi asked him to live in Dyfed.

"My father climbed that mound," Pryderi said to his mother, smiling. "He met you there. What say we go and see what it's doing?" Gorsedd Arberth, the Hill of the Immortals, was in the habit of coming and going. When present it stood as a high knoll reached by a grassy path. Whomever reached the top would see marvels.

Pryderi, his wife Cigva, Rhiannin, and Manawydan found the hill and made their way to the top, where they sat down to wait for adventures. The moon rose above them as they chatted.

They jumped when a bolt of lightning rent the sky overhead. As the thunder rolled and boomed, a thick mist descended.

It lifted gradually to reveal a very different Arberth than the one they had just walked through. Where crops and forage had grown stretched a great wasteland. The sky was clear of the smoke of cook-fires and chimneys. Pryderi's great hall looked abandoned.

"Let's go see what happened," suggested Manawydan. They walked down the hill and through the fields until they reached the hall.

Exploring it revealed no presence, not even that of a chicken, and no signs of where all the people had gone.

With hunger and thirst on their heels, they decided to live off the land for a while. By day they took fish from the streams and honey from hives, and at night they bedded down under the bright stars.

For weeks of this rough living they kept each other company, but a day came when Manawydan stated what all of them had thought but not spoken:

"My companions, it is time we went in for something more secure. The land has given generously to us, but we can't keep on like this. We need to make a living."

"How?" asked Pryderi. "We have no money."

"Let us go to Hereford. If people still live there, we can learn a trade and support ourselves that way. I have some knowledge that should help us."

People indeed still lived in Hereford. Once there, Manaywydan used a technique he had learned for coloring saddles and sold some. Soon they operated a successful saddlery.

It was so successful, in fact, that it took business from the established saddleries. Angry tanners and saddle-makers began making threatening remarks.

"Let's fight them."

"No, Pryderi, there are too few of us. We need to move on to the next town."

"What will we do there?"

"Make shields."

"Do we know how?"

"We can learn."

In the next town Manawydan applied a technique he had learned in his fighting days and turned out shields that were both beautiful and strong. When envious shield-makers turned against them, they moved on again and crafted luxury leather shoes with gold buckles. Again they were forced to move on.

"I'm tired of this," said Pryderi, who as was used to royal treatment. "If the people in town reject us, let us return to Dyfed and live off the land again."

Manawydan felt concern about this course of action, but his three companions favored it, so they packed up their materials and revenue and headed back to Dyfed.

*   *   *   *

While out hunting one morning Manawydan and Pryderi watched as their hounds entered a thick stand of trees and ran out again barking furiously. The barking turned frantic as an enormous white boar poked its tusks out of the bushes, darted at the hounds, and ran off.

The pursuers dashed on through the woods until the boar broke from them and ran over a ditch and through the gate of a tall fortress. The trees around it stood in its shadow.

"Whose hall is that?" asked Manawydan as they considered it.

"I know these woods well, yet I've never seen this fortress here before, or a boar that acts so oddly."

They waited for some sign of the hounds, but all remained eerily silent.

Pryderi stepped forward. "If they won't come back, let's go get them."

"Let's not."

"Why not?"

"Because I suspect that whatever power made this castle appear also spun the enchantment we've been living in all this time."

"What more could they do to us if we enter?"

"I do not know, but my instincts say not to advance."

"I won't stand by while some arcane force threatens my kingdom."

"Our wives are waiting for us."

"Then let only one of us go in. I will. If I don't come back, please look after both our wives." He marched scowling over the ditch and walked through the gate.

He found himself in a spacious hall empty except for a large fountain on a marble platform standing in the center. Chains suspended from the fountain's bowl held a large gold cup. The sound of flowing water reminded Pryderi of his thirst. He advanced and stepped up onto the platform.

As he picked up the cup he froze solid with his mouth still open in surprise.

Outside the hall, Manawydan waited all afternoon for him. When his friend failed to appear, he decided to be prudent and return to camp.

He informed the women of what had taken place. Cigva burst into tears.

"Why did you leave my son in there?" Rhiannon demanded as she held her weeping daughter-in-law.

"I told him not to go in. Would you rather we both failed to return?"

"If you won't go after him, I will. Where is the fortress?"

He told her, reluctantly. She left, pushing angrily through the trees.

When she saw the battlements in the fading daylight, she increased her pace. Over the ditch and through the gate she strode until she saw her son by the fountain.

"Pryderi! Why are you still here? We've been terrified for you!"

As she approached she saw that he did not move. He must be stuck.

She reached for the gold cup to free him and froze.

A bolt of thunder cracked over the forest.

The fortress disappeared.

*   *   *   *

"Where could they have gone?" asked Cigva through her tears.

"I do not know."

"I would rather die than live without Pryderi."

"And I miss Rhiannon. Let us return to town and take up shoe-making again until we devise a plan for rescuing them."

"All right."

Again, they were successful. But before the other cobblers could turn against them, Manawydan and Cigva had saved enough money to buy seed. This they took with them back to Arberth.

Manawydan sewed the seed in three nearby fields. They cared for the soil until the green shoots came up and grew into ripe ears of wheat.

But on the morning he went out to harvest the wheat, Manawydan found earless stalks in the first field. On the second morning he found the same in the second field.

"Don't be discouraged," he told Cigva with a smile. "Whoever made off with our wheat must now feel assured that the third field will provide."

At midnight, the ears of wheat began to tremble as though ruffled by the wind. Manwydan darted from his cover at the edge of the third field and ran toward a wave of mice caught in the act of gnawing off the ears of wheat.

He let all but the slowest and fattest get away. Grabbing that mouse by the tail, he dropped it into his glove and stuffed it into his pocket.

Atop Gorsedd Arberth, the morning sun lit a small wooden scaffold. Manawydan finished constructing it just as a robed man walked up the path to the top of the hill.

"Good morning, Traveler. From where do you come?"

"Good morning. I come from Lloegyr, where I composed songs

in its cities."

"Odd," said Manawydan.

"Why odd?"

"Because besides my friends, I've seen no one here in seven years."

"There is a first time for everything. —What are you making there?"

"A gallows. I mean to hang a thief."

"What thief?"

Manawydan drew the mouse from his glove and held it by the tail.

"This thief."

"You're going to hang a mouse?"

"I am."

"It seems a mean thing to do to such a little creature. Would you consider freeing it for a coin or two?"

"No. I mean to hang it."

"Ah, I see. Very well. Good day." The robed man walked away.

A druid approached as Manawydan fastened the crosspiece. After a similar conversation and a larger offer of money, the druid went his way.

As Manawydan fitted the noose around the mouse's neck, an archdruid walked up at the head of a crowd. This man offered not only money, but all the wealth held by his entire following. Manawydan shook his head and prepared to hoist the mouse.

The archdruid begged him to stop: "I will give you anything you ask for."

Manawydan paused. "Anything?"

"Anything."

"Very well. In return for the life of this mouse, I want Rhiannon and Pryderi."

"I agree!" Empty air hung where the crowd had gathered.

"I'm not finished. You must also lift the spell you have cast over Dyfed."

"Agreed!"

"And I want to know this mouse's true identity."

"My wife."

"And who were the other busy mice?"

"My people. Her pregnancy kept her from getting safely away."

"And who are you?"

"Llwyd son of Cil Coed."

"Why did you cast that spell and imprison my companions?"

"I did it because Pryderi's father and Rhiannon trapped my father Gwawl in a badger bag and beat him." Gwawl had been a less than savory rival for Rhiannan's hand.

Manawydan almost smiled. Gwawl had gotten off light with just a beating. Pwyll had been Lord of the Underworld.

"Did not your father promise no vengeance in return for being released?"

"He did, but his descendants did not."

"My last condition is that you will forswear vengeance against me and mine in return for your wife."

Llwyd agreed and raised one arm, and Rhiannon and Pryderi shimmered into being.

She advanced. "I was wrong to say what I did to you," she told Manawydan.

"And I to insist on entering the fortress," added Pryderi.

"In this world events must run their course as best they can."

"About my wife?" asked Llwyd pointedly.

"Ah." Manawydan removed the noose and gently set the mouse on the ground. As she scampered toward her husband she grew into a woman who threw her arms around the archdruid's neck.

After they had faded from view, the three remaining on the mound saw Cigva waving from a great hall crowded with festive celebrants. Smoke curled lazily once again from the sturdy chimneys of Arbeth. Verdant crops filled the fields. From somewhere below came the neigh of a contented horse.

For Reflection:

- Comment: Manawydan ("man-uh-WUH-dan"), a character from the *Mabinogion* ("maa-bin-OH-ghee-on") collection of Welsh myths, finds his parallel in the Irish

Manannan ("mah-nah-NAHN") and in the Arthurian Merlin. The Isle of Man is named after him. He is normally classified as a sea god, but his archetypal style is that of a Magician. (Perhaps that style appears here and there in the comedy *Waking Ned Divine*. It was filmed on the Isle of Man.)

- Rhiannon's Roman name was Epona, the source of the word "pony." As a goddess of horses and childbirth she parallels the Greek Artemis, patron of the natural world. Why would such a goddess she get together with Manawydan?

- How do they complement one another? How is their relationship different from that of Pryderi ("pruh-DAIR-ee") and Cigva ("SIG-vah")?

- Pryderi's father Pwyll ("poissh" with air blown between the back of tongue and the roof of the mouth) was king of Annwn ("AH-noon"), the Underworld of Welsh myth. Why would Rhiannon have married *him*?

- Most mythologies lack the absolute monotheistic dualism between this world and the Otherworld. One is out walking when the magic knoll or castle appears. Jung would probably see this as easy entrance into the collective unconscious. What else might it represent?

- Pryderi, whose name means "loss" because of his having been abducted at birth, strikes the pose of a Hero, whereas Manawydan, a fighter when younger, now offers a post-heroic way of dealing with matters. Has he lost his nerve, or does his faith in patience and hard work suggest something deeper?

- Pryderi and Rhiannon are action-oriented, but they end up immobilized. What does that look like in daily life? What does it mean to fall under an evil spell?

- Why must the trio learn to make saddles, shields, shoes, and wheat? How is this different from the style of the wealthy magician Llwyd ("LOO-EED," spoken as one syllable with breath blown through the L) and from grasping for the cup of gold in the fortress?

- What does seeing the land of Dyfed ("DUH-ved") as an empty waste when it isn't one suggest about the power of warped perception?

- What flaw in Llwyd makes it possible for Manawydan to trap him?

- An old image of the Gallic magician-god Ogmios (kindred to the Irish Ogma, inventor of writing) shows long chains of precious metals running from his tongue to the ears of his followers. His eloquence binds his listeners. Why does Manawydan's plan work better than simply fighting Llwyd?

Nekumonta's Plea (Haudenosaunee)

Maurice Kenny, Mohawk poet:

> If we take a deer down, we give something back to its spirit—tobacco, something—because it's given us so much so we can survive.... John Mohawk feels the same way. Peter Blue Cloud feels the same way. So if I take something out of a culture, even a small rhythm for a poem, I must give it back. I am *compelled* to give it back, and I think that's a problem with present-day Anglo writers. They don't think that way and they *must*. They must find out where it came from and then give it back.

> We don't know our place, and in my creative writing classes that's what I teach, place. The central object is your place and everything comes out of there. Your style comes out of there, your rhythm, your diction, your image, it all comes out of place. It must. Where else can

it come from? Your voice is your place.

Nekumonta, mate of Shanewis, could look back on many actions that had demonstrated his courage, to his satisfaction and that of the people. When younger he had taken many risks and, the watchful world having been kind, survived to see them acclaimed. He walked, not with hauteur, but with the confidence of having settled accounts on many occasions. Sometimes with the patient talk of skillful negotiation, and sometimes with strength, speed, and boldness when the words were done or insufficient.

He wished a good fight would settle this account. The people were dying.

His eye moved wearily across the snow-covered winter ground. Under it slept his parents, his sisters, his brothers, and many kin. The plague had struck without mercy. Only a handful of villagers were left. His own wife lay trembling and pale beneath the furs he had covered her with. His heart clenched with grief when he thought about her.

None of his skills availed him now. He must find a cure, and for that he needed help.

Pulling the furs up higher to keep Shanewis warm, and leaving the rest of the food for her, he pulled on his snowshoes, picked up his staff, and went forth.

He searched all day through the snow for herbs that would bring his people healing. No hint of green poked above the white covering. Branches of big trees sagged beneath its wet weight.

For three days he searched, and then he spotted a snowshoe rabbit.

"Brother!" he called out to it. "Where are the healing herbs planted by the good spirit Manitou?" But the rabbit did not know and hopped away. Nekumonta shuffled on.

His weary steps brought him to a brown bear's den. He halted and called out over the chilly wind, but the bear was asleep, waiting for winter's cold to end.

A deer darted by, but it did not pause when he asked for a path to the herbs. Nor did the squirrel. Nor did the birds or any of the other creatures he addressed.

Finally: "Manitou!" he called out to everything around him: the snow, the air, the silent forest, the ground below, the sky above. "Help me heal my people!"

Overcome by hunger and despair, he sank down to the ground and fell asleep.

The deer and other animals stood close to him, keeping him warm with breath and heat of body. They remembered his many kindnesses over the years, among them his love of flowers and trees and his refusal to hunt lightly or for sport.

And Nekumonta dreamed...

Sweet, liquid voices murmured his name, over and over. Then:

Seek after us, Nekumonta! Keep looking for us! Find us, the Healing Waters, and Shanewis and your people will live!

He woke and looked around. The animals had gone, and he saw no waters, but his inner ear remembered. *Release us!*

He looked down. Was it from there the voices called to him?

Taking a grip on his staff, he pushed the snow aside and dug into the moist earth.

After a time, water began to well up in the hole. He dug more and a tiny spring emerged. Where it touched, snow melted and green appeared. It gave him quiet joy just to look upon the trickle of bright liquid.

Taking clay from the ground nearby, he pushed it into the shape of a jar. It would do. He filled it and ran back to the village.

Shanewis, barely breathing, was nearly gone. He trickled the sacred water between her cracked lips until she fell into a healing slumber and the lines of illness went out of her face. He could see the return of health flowing across her skin and sinking in.

He took the waters from dwelling to dwelling. Everywhere he went, the people rose, restored to life.

For Reflection:
- What shift in consciousness does the crisis of the plague require of Nekumonta?
- How does his culture support it?

- Comment: "Manitou" is often translated as "Great Spirit," but the Mohawks were not monotheists. They believed—and many continue to believe—everything to be animated by intelligent sacred power of infinite expressions, not separate from the world, but throughout it and of it.

- Comment: Estimates of how many Native American people died of diseases brought by incoming European colonists invading North America reach 90% of the indigenous population of 18 million living north of Mexico. Smallpox arrived as early as 1520. Many of the diseases were brought by accident, but some were introduced deliberately.

- Can you think of a time when nature, animals, or elements returned a kindness you had shown them?

- Nekumonta finds the source of healing for his people by listening to the depths of the world. How is this different from mechanistic and anti-animistic cultural views and take matter for a lifeless resource? What might be some implications in terms of how we relate to nature and Earth?

Jonah Flees His Calling (Jewish)

Joel ben Izzy, Jewish author and storyteller:

> Like any tribe of people, when you all live together, you sit around and you tell your stories. But when you suddenly get dispersed—like, say, the Babylonian exile—there's even more desire to hold on to the stories, to reach out and grab them and try to get them exactly right. To get their messages right ... though of course those change with the setting, with the values of the tribe. But there's a need to make sure stories keep getting told.

There are many people who for whatever reason have been turned off to Judaism, but will sit down and listen to a story. It can absolutely be a way back.

Storytelling is the most human of the arts—it's between a teller and the audience. I think especially as the world gets more high tech, people are also becoming more hungry for that. People are realizing that the acts of talking and listening can be spiritual, can be healing.

They say when the heart overflows, it comes out through the mouth.

"Go to Nineveh and preach to them," said the Voice that was more than a voice. "Its people have departed the way."

Jonah headed for Joppa instead to find a ship bound for Tarshish. He had heard of Nineveh, and he earnestly hoped the wicked city would fall, just as it deserved. Let them perish of their own injustices.

He quickly located a ship and reserved himself a space on it. As the bow divided the salt-laden waters, he looked back at the harbor with satisfaction. So much for Nineveh!

Soon the wind got up and the sails began to flap. Dark clouds drifted in and gathered overhead. Jonah didn't like the expressions on the faces of the seasoned sailors. He went below and fell into a deep slumber.

He was oblivious to the growing swells that nearly stood the ship on its bow and stern. Canvas disappeared from the wind-whipped masts. Panicking men clung to whatever they could to keep from being washed overboard.

Jonah opened his eyes to see the captain shaking him roughly.

"We are in peril!" he shouted into Jonah's face. "Call that God you say you talk to and see if he can help us!"

Jonah came up on the heaving deck to the realization that the sailors, who had cast lots, blamed him for the storm. "Who are you?

What country are you from? Who are your people?"

"I am a Hebrew," he said. "I worship the God who made both land and sea."

"What should we do to calm the sea?"

Jonah too believed the storm was his fault. If everyone perished it would be on his head. He couldn't live with that.

"Throw me into the sea. The storm is because of me."

Just as they hurled him over the side, a whale surfaced and opened its mouth. Jonah tumbled in. The mouth closed and the whale sank below.

The clouds dispersed and the waves shrank at once. "Let us worship his God," someone suggested, and they did.

Jonah spent a cramped and smelly three days in darkness. He used the time to pray. He had thought he was a dead man, but God had sent the whale to preserve him.

After three days, the stomach of the whale gave a great heave. Jonah flew out of its mouth and sprawled on dry land. He blinked and looked around him.

"Now go and preach to Nineveh," said God. Jonah got up and headed for Nineveh.

The city Jonah found stretched so far that three days were needed to walk through it. "In forty days," Jonah preached to those who gathered, the words appearing in his consciousness, "this great city will perish and all its inhabitants with it unless you turn aside from violence and repent in sackcloth and ashes."

The Ninevites declared a fast, covered themselves in ashes, and prayed for atonement. Even the animals wore sackcloth. So did the King as he sat praying in the dust.

In forty days the city remained standing. Its chastened and now peaceful inhabitants rejoiced in great relief.

Jonah did not. He was outraged that God had let them off.

"Didn't I tell you this would happen? Now none of them will be punished. I know you are gracious and compassionate, slow to anger and abundant in love, but I'd rather you just killed me, for I can't stand to see these people any longer."

"Is it just," God asked, "for you to be angry?"

Jonah was too furious to reply. He built himself a crude shelter east of the city and sat down in it.

While he sat there fuming, God caused a plant to grow rapidly. Its broad leaves gave shade from the hot sun. But at dawn, a worm chewed on the plant and killed it. Unprotected from sun and the scorching wind, Jonah grew faint.

"Get it over with and kill me."

"Is it just for you to be angry about the plant?"

"Of course it is. I'm so angry I wish I were dead."

"You felt concern about this plant even though you did not grow or tend it. It grew overnight and died overnight. And should I not have concern about the great city of Nineveh, a city of more than a hundred and twenty thousand people who didn't know their right hand from their left?"

For Reflection:

- How is Jonah's initial state of mind similar to that of the yet-to-be-repentant Ninevites?

- How does judgmentalism lead to self-alienation and unwise action?

- What is Jonah so reluctant to face in himself that he prefers death?

- According to Joseph Campbell, it's possible to put off the Call to Adventure that brings on the Hero's Journey, but only a few times. After that the Call gets louder. What does this look like psychologically?

- The Hero's Journey includes an Underworld encounter in which the Hero wins a boon, treasure, or insight. What did Jonah win?

- In alchemical lore, when nearly completed the power-ful Philosopher's Stone began to radiate its healing powers (*proiectio* and *multiplicatio*). When the Hero brings the boon, it proliferates and multiplies. Why would someone feel reluctant to dispense the boon?

- The name "Jonah" means "dove." What is the significance for this story?

- How does a violent society suffer perdition?

- The Torah states that the person who repents stands higher in the eyes of God than the one who never left the path. The rabbinical literature calls such a person the *baal teshuvah*, the Master of Return. Why is such a person so highly prized?

- Abraham Maslow coined "Jonah complex" to indicate the refusal of our calling. It is not our darkness we fear (thought Maslow) so much as our potential for greatness. In what ways have you succumbed to this complex and avoided invitations and challenges at which you might have excelled?

Balarama's Revels (Hindu)

Ashok Vajpeyi, Hindu poet, literary critic, and lecturer:

> Love is a very inclusive, all-encompassing theme. While the main body of Hindi poetry engaged itself with social reality, I chose the marginalized areas of love, eroticism, and the geography of the inner and personal....
>
> I've used many concepts of Hinduism in my poetry, such as rebirth, no beginning - no end, and life-after-death. This is not so much to affirm them as to use them to explore the reality and life of our time, our innermost anxieties and aspirations, and create resonances. Hinduism is not homocentric: it believes in the unity of all beings; it posits a nature without evil; there is no original sin but play and "lila" [the play of the gods]; it has many gods; it locates the sacred and the divine in the earthly and worldly.

The demons are out of hand again, Vishnu said to himself. *Time to send down assistance....*

Drawing forth two strands of hair, one white and one black, Vishnu impregnated Devaki with them. She in turn gave the strands to Rohini so a mortal would bear them.

When her time came, fair Balarama was born first, and dusky Krishna a little later.

The boys grew up in Mathura, on the banks of the Yamuna. Vasudeva fathered them. Behind Krishna stood the heavenly presence of Vishnu; behind Balarama, whose name belled forth his great strength, Ananta Sesha, the mighty serpent upon whom Vishnu sat. Krishna was of mild disposition; Balarama had a temper. Krishna carried musical pipes, Balarama a heavy mace. They herded cows together and they looked out for each other, each in his own way, just as they always had in other forms and lifetimes.

Balarama's heroic exploits burst forth when he was still a child, threatened by a demon in the form of a donkey. When it tried to kick him, he seized the asura's leg, whirled him around, and hurled the body into a tree. When another asura tried to make off with him, he struck his would-be kidnapper in the head and killed him. He threatened to topple the town of Hastinapura with a plow, felled the deceitful gambler Rukmin with a swing of the club, killed the monkey-formed rapist Dwivida with a punch to the forehead. Yet in the great war between the Pandavas and the Kauravas, he used his strength to refuse to take sides even though he had trained some of their warriors.

Krishna had many wives, Balarama only one: tall Revati, the daughter of a king. But they both enjoyed the company of the gopis.

One day a sweet scent rose from a forest in Vrindavana often visited by the brothers. Balarama entered and saw wine falling in glittering drops from the trees. Varuni invisibly dispensed liquor emanating heady aromas because her consort Varuna wanted the amusement of seeing Balarama drunk.

Shapely cowherds standing under the trees sipped in transports of joy. Seeing Balarama, the gopis circled him alluringly, hung garlands of flowers around his thick neck, and chanted pleasingly for him. A fine day to drink wine and enjoy such luscious feminine company. His eyes fluttered in happiness. Unseen Varuna smiled.

Only one thing was lacking: the coolness of nearby water on such a warm day.

"Yamuna!" he called out. His deep voice bounced through the woods. "Yamuna, come over here and refresh us!" But the river did not budge.

He opened his eyes fully in annoyance and shouted, "I will teach you a lesson in manners! You will come whether you want to or not!"

Grasping his plow, he ran it under the ground now here and now there, separating the surprised river into branch after branch and stream after stream.

If this went on, she would end up as nothing but scattered rivulets. The river formed herself into Yami and addressed Balarama as he plowed back and forth:

"Lord, please stop. I am sorry I offended Your Greatness and Your Infinite Power. I was distracted and have now come back to my senses. You who support the All, whose strength and wisdom are Infinite and widely cherished, please accept my apologies and set me at liberty."

At first he held himself aloof; but the wine, the lovely curves of the gopis, and the capital-letter-packed praises of the river's desperate flattery worked on him until his bad mood faded.

"Well...." he said, setting aside the plow and removing his blue tunic. Yami sighed in relief. "Just remember your place."

And with that, he dove in. The gopis followed him, laughing and splashing.

When he emerged once again, restored and relaxed, a gold necklace was placed around his neck.

"Ahhhh," he said, and the gopis smiled. "Let the revelry begin!"

For Reflection:

- Comment: The winding Yamuna, or Jamuna, is the largest tributary of the Ganges. Its meanders and branches have been thought to mark Balarama's drunken plowings. According to legend, the river parted respectfully on the night of Krishna's birth as his father Vasudeva approached to carry him across.

- Heroes tend to be very serious. Balarama can be, but he has learned to play at least once in a while. At the end of his life and career he sits by the ocean in meditation until his consciousness passes out of his earthly body and into all things. How do you suppose he learned how to play?

- Balarama and Krishna can be thought of as expressive of two different archetypes: the Hero and the Drama (or Ecstasy) God; Krishna has often been compared to Osiris and Dionysus. Why would these archetypes manifest as brothers?

- How might a boundless capacity for enjoyment and fun constitute a meaningful response to a worldwide takeover by asuras (demons)? What might we learn from this?

- Why did the river ignore Balarama's first demand?

- Balarama's club, lion skin, powerful physique, fiery temper, and association with plow, wine cup, serpents, bow, and arrows also show up in Heracles. How might we learn whether these parallels are archetypally independent appearances or a cultural diffusion, perhaps from India to Greece? Does it matter?

The Ascent of Heracles (Greek)

Tryfon Tolides, Greek poet:

Calling

Come to the point where, finally, you are lost,
wayside-sitting, wind-gazing, train-whistle-listening,

if you want to converse with the invisible presence,

continual, sustained, indwelling, be lost,

be abandoned, so that the heart, the mind, as big
as God, come to the place where you are lost,

so that all your days and the shuttering of each day's
light and the blue magnetic incomprehensible

jumping and motionless blue of twilight and the fine
blackening after, around the incomprehensible

waiting and breathing of trees with their delight-inducing
cloud-depths and freedom-shapes and darting birds,

happen in pure glory, in ineffable joy of consciousness,
so that your senses overfill to beautiful muteness,

so that mere being becomes the form of your praise.

He had survived Hera's lethal snakes, the Dryopes, deadly giants, the Bebryces; Termerus, Alastor, Cycnus, Antaeus, the Molionides; slavery, twelve brutal Labors, and more. But he would not survive this.

When did the end begin? With his birth? With the two-fisted crushing of Hera's serpents? With the poisonous Hydra, whose blood tipped the hero's arrows? With four-legged Nessus, who made the mistake of trying to rape Deianeira as he rowed her across the Evenus River to meet her husband? From the bank, angry Heracles responded to this attack on his bride by shooting the centaur with poisoned arrow.

"I would beg your forgiveness," gasped Nessus to Deianeira as the ferry headed in, "by offering you my blood. It is a powerful love potion that will aid you well should your husband ever stray." She quickly collected some of the dark fluid and hid it away, just in case.

While Heracles served the Queen of Lydia in expiation for yet another murder, Deianeira grew suspicious at his long absence. That lovely young Iole, won by him in an archery contest, was now his concubine did not make her feel better. She remembered the blood of Nessus and poured some on one of her husband's ceremonial tunics.

"Please take this to Heracles," she instructed Lichas, her herald. *That should bring him around again*, she hoped.

But Nessus had lied. His blood was not a charm: it was an incendiary, full of the fiery blood of the Hydra.

It was time, Heracles thought, to begin Zeus's sacrificial rites.

As soon as the hero put on his tunic it began to burn him. He tried to pull it off, roaring, but it stuck. He threw Lichas into the sea, but nothing would stop the pain of his crisping skin.

In agony, Heracles sent his nephew Iolaus to ask the Delphic Oracle for advice. Iolaus had helped him against the Hydra by cauterizing its heads as Heracles lopped them off.

"He is to build a large pyre on Mt. Oeta," intoned the entranced Pythoness, "and await the will of the gods."

Deianeira received word that she had inadvertently killed Heracles. In sorrow and shame she hanged herself.

To his mourning son Hyllos Heracles gasped, "Please marry Iole when you come of age and look after her for me." Hyllos agreed.

Pain-wracked Heracles carried out the oracle's instructions.

"Would you light the pyre?" he asked his friend Philoctetes. "To you, the incomparable archer," he groaned, "I give my great bow and poison-tipped arrows."

Philoctetes watched as the mortal body of his friend burned away. With a crack of thunder, a cloud gathered around the smoking bones and lifted the spirit of Heracles to Olympus.

There his deeds were celebrated even by Hera, who had tested him so sorely.

By the will of Zeus, Heracles married Hebe, the goddess of eternal youth, and thenceforth lived aloft with the gods.

Finding no bones, the mourners of Athens worshipped Heracles as divine.

Years later, during the Trojan War, an arrow from the bow of

Philoctetes brought down Paris of Troy.

For Reflection:

- How does Heracles bring about his own demise?

- When one defeats an enemy, is the victory ever permanent? Does it not always carry repercussions that push for a later tragic reversal?

- What poisons relationships?

- Hercules was given his name, which means "Glory of Hera," in an attempt to placate her. It didn't work. Why do Heroes so often have mother (or stepmother) problems?

- What are the points of irony in this part of his tale?

- *Apotheosis* derives from a Greek word that means to become divine. History and myth from all over the world offer many examples of queens, kings, and heroes attaining to divinity at life's end. Beyond idealizing heroes by making them into gods, what purposes are served by apotheosis? How might the gods (however understood) benefit from the transfiguration of a hero into one of their number?

- Hercules goes to some trouble to build his own legend. Aside from mere vanity, how might finally setting loose a legend gathering around oneself constitute a final developmental task, perhaps that of separating oneself from the still-living myth?

Chapter Nine - Tricksters

What would we do without Tricksters? Live in a world narrowed by our own overly rigid attitudes, routines and beliefs. When things get too constricted, when procedures displace creative acts, when authority clamps down on spontaneity, Trickster appears to loosen up the order of the day by spreading disorder and chaos. People with an absolute notion of Truth, whether it be religious, philosophical, or scientific, make particularly inviting targets.

To do this, Trickster flirts constantly with losing balance. It is of the nature of this archetype to bring fumbling, comedy, exaggeration, and accident in service to a higher or deeper sense of life. New possibilities grow in the crevices opened by the unexpected antics that appear out of nowhere.

Chameleon Outwits Ananse (West African)

Sobonfu Some, West African (Dagara) ritualist, author, and educator:

> I come from Burkina Faso, one of the smallest countries in Africa, about the size of Colorado and my tribe, the Dagara tribe, lived in the southwestern part of Burkina Faso.
>
> ...Stories are important because the circle is not always there for people to share their story. So in meeting somebody new and in them sharing their story, in us sharing our story, we have already created a bridge that is safe for each of us to walk on. And also for us to be able to open and to share what is that gift we are bringing.
>
> That is what is so beautiful in this time when it's possible for people to basically be able to travel everywhere. To meet new people and to share their story. And every single time that they have shared with somebody and they have also listened and received this story of the other person something new is born out of them. A new level of their gift begins to shine again.

The wealth of tricky Ananse the spider did not stop his eye from wandering to Chameleon's nearby fields.

The two lived next to each other. Ananse labored little because he could afford to hire workers and seed. Chameleon was poor and did the work himself.

Although Ananse's fields normally flourished, the rain had fallen this year only on Chameleon's fields, nourishing them into abundant greenery. Dust blew across Ananse's.

"How much will you take for the fields?" Ananse asked Chameleon in a tone of false friendliness.

"They're not for sale."

"I'll give you a lot for them. More than you realize."

"They're not for sale." Chameleon knew why Ananse wanted to buy.

One morning Chameleon came into his fields to see Ananse harvesting crops in them. He angrily chased out the spider. To his astonishment, Ananse took him to court.

"I can prove the fields are actually mine," the spider told the judge. Taking him into Chameleon's fields, Ananse pointed out the presence of his own footprints there. Many footprints: not for nothing did Ananse's name mean "spider." Chameleons leave no footprints. The judge awarded the fields to Ananse.

This isn't over, thought Chameleon.

Returning to his remaining fields, he dug a hole that looked small and placed a roof over it. Under this concealment he kept on digging until he had hollowed out a vast network of underground warrens. None of this showed above the surface.

Chameleon then collected some flies and stuck them onto vines he wove into a cloak. He put on the cloak and walked across the fields until Ananse spotted him.

"Good day," the spider greeted him. "I hope we can still converse in spite of what happened in court. —Say, that's a splendid cloak." Rainbows of light bouncing from the wings of the invisible flies gave off the appearance of magnificence. "May I trade you something for it?"

"Yes. Since I lost my fields I have been short of food." Chameleon pointed to the small-seeming hole in the ground. "I will give you my cloak if you fill that hole with food."

"Agreed. In fact, I'll fill it doubly full."

After giving the cloak to the judge as a gift of thanks, Ananse worked to fill Chameleon's hole with food. The task dragged on week after week. By this time the spider knew he'd been fooled, but unless he wanted to be taken to court himself, he had to fulfill his part of the trade.

As he labored, he was startled to see a naked judge striding down the road toward him. The expression on his face was not pleasant to see.

"Where is your cloak?" Ananse asked him.

"You know where! The cloak was woven of vines with flies stuck to them. When the vines rotted and broke, the flies flew off and left me naked in plain sight of everyone!"

Tricked twice over! Ananse opened his mouth to explain but the judge cut him off:

"You will IMMEDIATELY return to Chameleon the fields you tricked him out of—AND you will give him the choice selection of your own fields." He stalked off.

Ananse finally finished stocking Chameleon's cellar and slunk on home.

Chameleon took possession of dry new fields, but a thick cloud formed above them. For the first time in a long while the falling rains moistened and refreshed them back to life. The harvests would be immense now. Certainly far larger than Ananse's.

As the downpour went on, Chameleon's smile widened into a grin. Then he laughed.

For Reflection:

- Ananse (known as Aunt Nancy in the African American South) performs tricks on other beings in many tales, but in this one he is out-Trickstered by Chameleon. What does Chameleon learn from Ananse that allows the poorer landowner to prevail?

- What does Chameleon teach Ananse about the nature of surface and depth?

- What does the judge learn from being left naked?

- Sometimes tricky family therapists ask clients to do more of a symptomatic behavior so it will destabilize the family on purpose. Why?

- It is typical of Trickster to bring about a new balance without intending to. Because of this, a superficial reading can mistake Trickster for a purely evil being. (The Norse Loki, the Egyptian god Set, the Gnostic

Demiurge, and the Devil in Christianity might be examples.) What credit should Ananse be given, if any, for triggering a reorganization of land and influence?

- What can the easy manipulation of Ananse's large appetites tell us about our own?

- Who or what besides Chameleon ultimately benefits from his change of fortune?

- How does Nature comment on the new balance between Ananse and Chameleon?

Ame-no-Uzumi Draws Out Amaterasu (Japanese)

Haruki Murakami, Japanese novelist:

> Myths are the prototype for all stories. When we write a story on our own it can't help but link up with all sorts of myths. Myths are like a reservoir containing every story there is.

> I'm always interested in people who've dropped out of society, those who've withdrawn from it. Most of the people in *Kafka on the Shore* are, in one sense or another, outside the mainstream.

> During the four years of writing *The Wind-Up Bird Chronicle*, I was living in the U.S. as a stranger. That "strangeness" was always following me like a shadow and it did the same to the protagonist of the novel.

> We have a sane part of our minds and an insane part. We negotiate between those two parts; that is my belief. I can see the insane part of my mind especially well when I'm writing—insane is not the right word. Unordinary,

> unreal. I have to go back to the real world, of course, and
> pick up the sane part. But if didn't have the insane part,
> the sick part, I wouldn't be here.

Amaterasu the sun goddess was a father's daughter. By contrast, her younger brother Susano-wo the storm god sorely missed their mother Izanami after she had gone to the Underworld. He cried until his beard reached his chest—and until his father Izanagi had heard enough of this wailing.

"Go to the Underworld, then," he told his son.

Susano-wo wanted to see his heavenly sister before his departure. Forgetting the long-standing enmity between them—she the dutiful daughter, he the disobedient son—he approached her directly.

Amaterasu saw mountains trembling in the distance and knew that Susano-wo was coming. She quickly bundled her hair like a warrior and armed herself with bow and arrows. Her battle cry of defiance called across the sky, shook snow from peaks, altered the flow of winds.

Brother and sister faced each other across the River of Heaven.

"I just want to visit," he assured her.

"Prove it."

"Let us engage in a contest to see who can birth other beings."

Amaterasu took his sword and broke it into three shards. These she washed in the Well of Heaven before chewing them up. From the mist she exhaled sprang three goddesses.

His turn. Rinsing, digesting, and blowing mist from her necklace formed five gods, one of them the ancestor of the coming emperors.

"These five gods," she told him, "are mine because born from my belongings. The three goddesses are likewise yours."

"As a male who birthed goddesses, I won the contest, it would seem."

The goddesses lived on earth to aid with navigation. The gods lived in heaven as prototypes of the five peoples of Japan.

This victory did not satisfy stormy Susano-wo for long. She had

.never taken him seriously. So he blew his breath-wind fiercely over Amaterasu's rice fields, wrecking them. When that got no response from his sister, he hurled a flayed piebald into her weaving hall. The dead horse caved in the roof and propelled a shuttle into the groin of an attendant, Waka-Hiru-me, who died.

Such was Amaterasu's sorrow and rage that she retreated to Ama-no-Iwato, the Stone Cavern of Heaven, to be alone. Darkness fell in heaven and on earth.

The eight hundred gods assembled to decide what to do to about this catastrophe. They went to the cave in one group and stood outside.

One among them, Ame-no-Uzume, moved forward until she stood at the mouth of the cave. The gods grew silent. A glow from deep inside signaled the presence of the sullen sun goddess.

Ame-no-Uzume danced. How she danced! She danced so hard and so ridiculously, pulling on her nipples and waving around her genitals, that the crowd of gods burst into laughter.

A petulant voice emerged from the cave: "What is so funny?"

Ame-no-Uzume stopped dancing to answer:

"We are all happy because a goddess even nobler and more beautiful than you has just arrived here." The gods held a mirror near the cave mouth.

When Amaterasu looked out, she indeed glimpsed the light of divine beauty. This aroused her curiosity. She emerged fully from the cave. To her surprise, she saw her own face reflected in the mirror held up by the gods.

She looked around at them. Everyone smiled and bowed.

* * * *

In heaven, Izanagi had had enough of Susano-wo's foolishness and banished the storm god to earth.

Susano-wo wandered aimlessly through Izumo until he came to the headwaters of the River Hi. There he noticed chopsticks floating down the river. He was lonely, so he went upriver until he met an elderly couple who sat weeping next to their daughter.

"Who are you?" Susano-wo asked them.

The old father spoke:

"I am Ashinazuchi, and this is my wife Tenazuchi and my daughter Kushinada-hime."

"Why are you so sad?"

"We had eight daughters," they told him. "Yamata-no-Orochi, the Eight-Forked Serpent, has eaten seven of them and is about to eat the eighth." He nodded sadly toward the young woman.

"What does the serpent look like?"

"It has eight heads, eight tails, and fiery red eyes. Moss clings to its body, which is eight valleys and eight hills long. Cedar and cypress trees grow on its back."

"I perceive that your daughter is a goddess. Will you offer her to me in marriage if I help you?"

"Yes, if you too are a god."

"I am, one descended from heaven."

Susano-wo turned toward the young woman. "I want you with me during this battle."

She nodded and became, temporarily, a jeweled comb for his hair.

"Now," he told her parents, "build a fence with eight gates, each with eight platforms. On each place a vat of sake, which you will refine eight times. Then wait." This they did.

Soon the curious serpent flew down and dipped its head into a vat to drink. Then it drank from the next, and the next. When it was finished, it lay unsteadily down on the ground, where it gave a prodigious belch and fell into a drunken slumber.

Susano-wo leaped forward with his sword drawn and hacked the serpent into pieces. The River Hi ran red with its blood.

When the storm god cut the fourth tail, his sword broke against something very hard. He reached into the flesh and split it apart. Within it glittered treasure: Ame-no-Murakumo-no-Tsurugi, the Sword of the Gathering Clouds of Heaven.

With Tenazuchi and Ashinazuchi looking on, Susano-wo and Kushinada-hime sealed their marriage with sacred vows.

The next time the storm god visited his sister he had little to say for once, but his gift of reconciliation was worth many times many words: the great sword he had taken from the dragon's tail. She accepted it with thanks.

For Reflection:

- Comment: "Amaterasu" means "Shining in Heaven." "Susano-wo" means "Swift Impetuous Male Augustness." "Ame-no-Uzume" is "Heavenly Frightening Female." "Ashinazuchi" is "Foot-Stroking Elder," and "Tenazuchi" is "Hand-Stroking Elder"; both are earth deities. Their daughter's name, "Kushinada-hime," means "Wondrous Inada Princess." "Waka-Hiru-me" means "Young Noon Female" and probably indicates a maiden form of Amaterasu.

- Jungian analyst Hayao Kawai compares Amaterasu to Athena inasmuch as both are luminous father's daughters capable of acting as warriors. In what ways are both distinct cultural expressions of the archetype of Wisdom?

- What are some cultural implications of revering Wisdom as a primary deity? What might be some shadows?

- This story exerted so much influence down the centuries that three of its key symbols—sword, mirror, and jeweled necklace—became the Imperial Regalia of Japan. What psychic structures parallel these important symbols?

- Athena, a weaving goddess, also invented the bridle. A piebald is hurled at the loom of Amaterasu. Why a piebald?

- Two tricksters appear in this myth: Susano-wo and Ame-no-Uzume. Both surprise Amaterasu, if in vastly different ways. Although these Tricksters do not meet in the story, how do their actions play off each other?

- In Greek mythology Demeter, a grain goddess, mourns

and withdraws after losing her daughter Persephone to Hades until the nurse Baubo performs a dance so funny that the sight of the old trickster's jiggling breasts and bottom makes Demeter laugh. This myth and the Japanese tale above seem not to have influenced one another directly. What archetypal dynamics or truths do they express in common?

• Mythic groupings of eight are known in mythology as *ogdoads*. Probably the earliest known were the eight deities worshiped in Hermopolis in Egypt more than four thousand years ago. In Gnosticism the Eighth Realm is the sphere of fixed stars beyond the planets. What do the eights signify in this tale?

• What does Amatersu realize when her own face looks back at her from the mirror?

• Why does Susano-wo decide to reconcile with Amaterasu?

Coyote Steals Fire (Shoshone)

Ramona Wilema, Shoshone tribal elder, educator, crafts expert, and storyteller:

> My dad was the best storyteller. Sometimes, he would tell us funny stories or scary stories at night before bed, so after he was done, we would run into our rooms and pull the covers over our heads. And before we knew it, we were sound asleep.
>
> He was a Bannock medicine man and would take me out on a horseback ride and tell me to jump down and study this or that plant and remember what it looks like and how to use it.

As the story goes, long ago, the animal people were starving to death. The squirrel happened to be the chief. So all the animal people came to the squirrel and asked him how he can save the people from death. So the squirrel in all his wisdom came up with the idea, they would have to dance all night and do the prayer dance. The coyote was the camp crier. He was ordered to announce the dance, so he did. All the animal folks came out to dance....

...In the morning when the sun came up the chief commanded the dance to stop. Chief said "Look, everybody, look." The people saw the mustard seeds growing and all over ready to collect. Chief said, "Get your baskets and beating sticks, collect the seeds." They all collected the seeds in rock bowls and made seed pudding. And all the people were fed and survive.

It was like Coyote to involve others in his own problems: in this case being cold. Whatever he did, he couldn't seem to stay warm. Nor had he gotten much attention in a while.

"Let's travel south to the dry desert lands," he told the animals, "and meet the people living there so we can steal their fire. You've had enough of being cold, haven't you?" He meant himself.

"Yes."

"Then I'll pick three of you, and down we go to see what we find."

Stinkbug, Packrat, and Porcupine accompanied Coyote on his long walk south. They saw the terrain and the weather change as they trudged onward: more severe, more mountainous, and, finally, warmer.

Campfires glimmered on the horizon. Coyote made his plan.

"I need a disguise," he said thoughtfully. "My reputation has undoubtedly preceded me." He ripped off long slices of juniper bark, bundled it, and contrived himself a wig. He put it on.

"Doesn't it look good?" he asked, posing.

"Sure," said Packrat. "Sure." The other two were silent.

"Then let's go into camp. Follow me."

By the time they arrived, the encamped desert people circled the fire in a merry Round Dance. Coyote and his three companions sneaked their way in and joined unobtrusively.

As they swung around the fire, some of the girls noticed Coyote's elaborate wig and Porcupine's quill dress. Seeing this, Porcupine strutted proudly. Coyote winked and the girls giggled. Stinkbug heaved himself up and down to get their attention, but they ignored him.

Following the plan he had laid out, Coyote danced his way in shrinking spirals that brought him closer and closer to the fire. At dawn when the dance ended he quickly leaned toward the flames.

"Look!" someone called out. "It's Coyote by the fire!" The wig gave off a dull thud as it ignited. "He's stealing it!"

By the time the group realized what was happening, Coyote and Packrat had dashed out of the circle and were running for the hills, Coyote with sparks streaking from his head. Stinkbug and Porcupine made a break for it but were too slow. Many hands reached out and halted them in their flight.

Additional runners took off after the two remaining fugitives, one short and the other with a glowing head. Packrat ran faster. The runners closed in on Coyote.

"Here, take the fire!" he shouted and threw the burning wig at Packrat, who tucked it under his belly and kept going just as the desert people grabbed Coyote.

Packrat ran through the desert and kept running as the mountains passed. He ran by bushes and trees and plateaus and rivers. When boughs and branches hung low he scuttled under them. He ran until he reached his nest.

A hot ember was all that remained of the fire Coyote had handed off to him. He set it on the ground, fed it twigs, and blew on it until it yellowed and whitened and flames sprang up once again.

"I have brought you fire," he told the circle of animals curiously watching him work. "Bring something that burns and take your share." They did this.

Eventually, handed off from animal to animal, fire spread throughout the world.

As for what happened to Stinkbug, Porcupine, and Coyote, the desert people let the first two go because they were accomplices who had done nothing worse than dance for a bit. Coyote they kept longer, but eventually they let him go because he talked his way out of captivity. Old Coyote can talk his way out of just about anything.

When he got home, he wasn't cold anymore because fires glowed cheerfully all over the land.

For Reflection:

- Stories about the Trickster Coyote have circulated in North America for thousands of years. Like other Tricksters, Coyote brings fire, sex, and death into the world, always with his characteristic fumbling. Possessing the wisdom to insist that death be permanent, he howls when he loses his own son; he asks Worldmaker to undo mortality, but it's too late. Why would Coyote the animal provide a pattern for Trickster stories?

- What do the three animals that accompany Coyote have in common?

- Why must Tricksters steal fire? Why can't they just ask for some?

- The fire-stealing relay race shows up frequently in Native American myth. What does it suggest about the deeper purposes behind the theft and who will benefit?

- Why are mythic Tricksters almost always egotists?

- Coyote's actions in this story are mild compared to some accounts (those of the Maidu of California, for instance). What is served by Tricksters indulging in outrageous behavior?

- In a Shasta myth Coyote fools a devil that eats people.

He spreads pine pitch over his own furry chest and suggests that they eat each other. Invited to eat first, the devil slices off some skin and recoils at the bitter taste. For his turn Coyote cuts out the devil's heart and lungs and throws them onto a fire. How might this method be useful in dealing with a psychological complex?

- Compulsive hoarding is diagnosed as a mental disorder. What does Packrat tell us about the "fire" that might be concealed in the belly of hoarding?

- Comment: When Prometheus steals Olympian fire for humanity, Zeus orders him chained to the Caucasus, where by day an eagle or vulture eats his liver and by night the organ is regenerated. After Heracles or Chiron lets him down (the stories vary), he wears a laurel wreath and a rock with a chunk of the Caucasus for a stone to signal his allegiance to Olympus. But Coyote never repents.

Eidothea Guides Menelaus (Greek)

Nikos Dimou, Greek writer, columnist, philosopher, poet, and talk show host:

> Modern Greeks will always suffer from knowing what the ancient Greeks accomplished, which we can neither forget nor surpass. My theory is that the Greeks suffered culture shock when they were catapulted from feudal conditions to modernity within the space of a few years in the 19th century. Being caught somewhere between east and west, ancient glory and present poverty, between orthodoxy and enlightenment, has left the Greeks with an identity problem. That's what makes them unsettled and uncertain to this day.
>
> Unfortunately, though, not only does the word "democ-

racy" come from Greek, but also the word "chaos."

We like to live beyond our means. You see this zest for life if you read *Zorba the Greek* — we want to have everything, enjoy everything. The tendency to overdo things is also closely connected to a tendency toward repression. Greece is the home not only of democracy, but also of tragedy. The tragic hero is a person who over-reaches himself, and violates the natural order of things.

Restless Menelaus wandered along the shore of the island of Pharos. He had a lot on his mind besides the heaps of food his empty belly craved.

His Spartan warriors and Greek allies had won the Trojan War and retrieved his wife Helen, only to be blown off course by a foul wind and stranded on this island. How could they get home to Lacedaemon now? Would victory bought so dearly after years of bloodshed sour into desolate, hungry defeat here for the courageous survivors? He shook his head.

I told my men not to bother me here, he thought angrily as he saw a figure advancing toward him. Soon, however, his squinted eye made out fluttering robes rather than rags and a step more graceful than that of any man. He stopped and stared as waves spread along the shoreline.

"King Menelaus" spoke an amused feminine voice as the figure walked up. Clear eyes looked frankly into his. "Have you taken leave of your senses?"

He was too astonished to reply. She came closer.

"Do you revel in your misfortune? Do you not know that your men are losing hope?"

"I do not revel, and I know about my men. At this very moment they bait hooks to fish for what dinner they can capture from the unforgiving sea. We are not here because we wish to be. Evidently I offended a god, and now I am becalmed." She nodded.

"You are obviously their kin," he observed. "How can we make amends, find a fair wind and sail home?"

The plaintive sincerity of his tone seemed to move her. Her face softened.

"I am Eidothea, daughter of Proteus. He often visits this place in his service to mighty Poseidon. He knows the depths and the visions they hold. He can tell you how you got here, how to get home, and, beyond that, how things fare in the homeland from which you sailed so many years past."

"He will help me?"

"Not voluntarily. First you must capture him."

"How am I to do this? I'm just a mortal man."

"There is a way. At noon when the west wind blows, my father comes ashore and lies down to sleep with the seals in caves with entrances like arches. I can show you where. Here is what you must do...."

The next day old Proteus pulled himself out of the gray ocean. As he came ashore, the water fanning off his broad back, a small fleet of sea creatures followed him into the caves. Once there he made his way among the seals, taking note of them like a shepherd looking over his sheep. Satisfied, he lay down with a sigh and closed his eyes.

Four of what had seemed to be seals lost their skins as four men, one of them Menelaus, leaped to their feet and ran toward the sleeping form of Proteus. They piled into him just as he woke up and tried to rise.

Three sailors held down his arms and legs as the king pushed down his chest.

Again and again an arm or leg slipped through hands coarsened by oars and ropes and was repinned. "You can't get away," Menelaus told the struggling god.

"Once you come out from under the skins," Eidothea had instructed him, "go straight for him and hold on no matter what he does or what shape he assumes."

"I appreciate your help, Goddess. Does your arsenal of magic include any specifics against the stench of newly flayed sealskin?"

"I will rub ambrosia under your noses. That should help."

Menelaus looked down into the face of a roaring lion. Its dripping teeth glistened inches from his nose. He ignored them and held on.

Dragon, griffin, sea serpent, leopard, boar, and many other a dangerous beast glared back at the king. Menelaus found himself holding a geyser, a bonfire, a tree trunk, a column of wind; then a procession of gods: Zeus, Poseidon, Hera, Athena.... Men he had killed at Troy came back to life to threaten him. Hector swore at him, Pandarus aimed an arrow at him, Deiphobus mocked him: "I will be the next to take Helen!"

Helen's face appeared, pleading; then Odysseus, lost like himself and asking for directions; then Patroclus, accusing: "Why did it take you so long to bury me, Menelaus?"

"You can't get away, Proteus," Menelaus muttered through clenched teeth as he bore down even harder. "I will not let up until you advise me."

At length Proteus, tired out, resumed his normal form. His daughter had advised Menelaus that he could now release the god, so he did. They all got up.

"Son of Atreus," asked the Old Man of the Sea in a tone of complaint, "who taught you how to trap me? What do you want?"

"I am sorry to have handled you that way, old sage," the king told the ancient one, "but my men and I are becalmed here. You probably know that; you know many things. *I* need to know three things: which of the gods I've offended, how to appease them, and how to get home. Tell me."

"King Menelaus, you have angered Aphrodite, Artemis, Apollo, Ares, and all the gods that favored Troy over Sparta and Greece once you and your army attacked that fabled city and sacked its holy temples. This and much death are what your wounded pride has wrought."

The king nodded.

"To appease the gods and to return safely home, you must return to Egypt and sacrifice cattle in their honor. Here are the specifics...."

After completing the list he went on:

"I see an additional question in your mind."

"Yes. Did the rest of the fleet make it home?"

"Most, but not all. Mighty Ajax met his death at his own hand. He lost a competition for the magic armor forged by Hephaestus."

"Ajax!" He recalled a man of such girth and bearing that three large men could not be seen if positioned right behind him.

"That is not all. Your brother Agamemnon was slain when he reached home by his wife Clytemnestra and her lover Aegisthus. His fleet was becalmed as yours was, and the wind came up only when he sacrificed his daughter Iphigenia to appease the angry gods. Clytemnestra arranged his death in revenge for the loss of her daughter."

Menelaus did not so much sit down as fall down. Tears poured over his face and into the sand as he lay there wishing he were dead.

He had no idea how much time had passed—probably only a few moments—when the voice like waves washing rock stirred his spirit once again:

"Son of Atreus, leave off mourning for now. You must go home. Once there you might find the killers and punish them; or you might find them dead already at the hand of your nephew Orestes. Either way, you will have a funeral to attend."

Menelaus made himself sit up, then stand up.

"What of wily Odysseus? Did he at least get home?"

"He has not. He remains on the island of Calypso, who keeps him there. And there he will stay until Hermes orders her to release him so he may continue his own journey home."

Now Menelaus understood why Eidothea had mentioned the need to be apprised of current happenings. He turned away on the assumption that the telling was over, but Proteus spoke once more:

"King Menelaus, go home with Helen and put the state in order. Rule long and well, and at life's end the gods will bear away you and your wife to the pleasant fields of Elysium at world's end. There you and Zeus's daughter will find eternal rest after your earthly labors, with your brow cooled by the pleasant western breezes."

The king's eyes opened in surprise. His best hope had been to find the way home. The god he had wrestled had given him an unexpected gift. He bowed as Proteus sank beneath the wine-dark sea.

Menelaus turned to his three men.

"Tell the others to prepare to sail. We are going home."

For Reflection:

- According to myth, the Trojan War broke out when Eris, the goddess of discord, rolled an apple inscribed with "To the Most Beautiful" into the presence of Hera, Athena, and Aphrodite. They asked Paris, Prince of Troy, to decide which of them deserved the apple. He picked Aphrodite, who allowed him to abduct Helen . Her husband Menelaus ("men-uh-LAY-us") of Sparta and his brother Agamemnon went after her with an army. What could it mean that a war fought by human heroes actually begins between deities? What are mere humans to do about archetypal conflicts?

- The name "Eidothea" means "Image of the Goddess." Her imaginal style points to the Trickster presence she shares with her father. Why is she willing to help Menelaus?

- What does the king learn by having to imitate a seal?

- Why does it take exactly four to hold down Proteus?

- Jung, who made a great deal of the number four and of psychological types, interpreted Proteus as a personification of the unconscious: slippery, many-faced, dynamic, hard to pin for long. Menelaus would then be someone looking for answers from the unconscious. How would the picture change if we thought of Proteus as the spirit of the sea itself? The elements addressing the king through his own associations and fantasies?

- Tricksters often act as psychopomps that connect the ego to the depths. What comes up from the depths of Menelaus as he struggles with Proteus?

- This tale brings to mind Jacob's struggle with the angel he encountered at the ford of a river: although injured, he exclaimed, "I will not let you go until you bless me!" (As a result, Jacob and all his descendants received the name Israel: "Struggles with God.") Menelaus too is wounded by the news Proteus gives him. What is the relationship between the wounding and the blessing?

- A surface read on this tale would pick up on the folly of going to war for envy and outraged honor (narcissistic injury). But as an old Gnostic story attests, Helen is much more than a beautiful woman: she is Wisdom in the flesh. The entire tale could be read, then, as a Greek parallel to the fall of Sophia. What would it look like to woo Wisdom peacefully?

- Why did Proteus throw in the gift of telling the king his life would end well?

- Comment: Obeying advice from Apollo, Orestes slays his mother Clytemnestra and her lover. For doing this he is hounded by the Erinyes ("air-IN-yees"), vengeful Furies who pursue him to the edge of madness. Athena intervenes to stop the pursuit. As a result of her arguments for justice on behalf of Orestes, the Erinyes undergo transformation into the Eumenides, the Kindly Ones who will now be honored publicly in Athens. With this, the curse that plagues the house of Atreus all the way back to Tantalus, who killed his son Pelops to mock the gods, comes to an end.

Lu Tung Pin and His Magic Oil (Chinese)

Eva Wong, writer, translator, and Taoist master:

When I was growing up in Hong Kong, my grandmother told me many stories about the Taoist immortals. We'd sit cross-legged on her bed together and while she sewed, she would tell me how Iron Crutch Li got his name, how Fan Li and Hsi Shih helped the king of Yueh defeat the kingdom of Wu, and how Mah Ku saved the people of her town by imitating the crowing of roosters.

The immortals are very much a part of my culture. The Chinese people's belief in immortals goes back to the ancient times of prehistory and legend, centuries before Taoism became a philosophy and a spiritual tradition.

Taoist immortals have been role models for the Chinese for centuries and have represented everything that we value as a culture. Now, as more non-Chinese are beginning to embrace Taoism as a spiritual tradition, the immortals have taken on an even more significant role: they have gone beyond being cultural symbols of the Chinese to become universal examples of spiritual attainment.

Lu Tung Pin liked to travel in disguise to test the honesty of people on Earth. It was always his joy to give to those who had integrity the understanding of the Tao and the chance at immortality.

One day he decided to sell oil. Dressing himself up accordingly and carrying his barrels, he set off to find anyone who would accept his measure of oil for a fixed and fair price.

At first he was very hopeful and journeyed to a nearby city to sell his wares. The first house he approached was a grand place, and he knocked at the main door. The doorman opened it and scowled.

"What do you want?" he demanded.

"To sell you a little oil," replied Lu Tung Pin.

"Then get around to the back door. Only gentlemen come through this door." And so saying, he kicked Lu Tung Pin down the stairs.

Picking himself up, Lu Tung Pin trudged around to the back door. But the doorman had already told the kitchen staff about the oil seller who had come to the front door. When Lu Tung Pin knocked, he was treated as a joke and the trash was tipped over him.

He was tempted to level the house and everyone in it. But he decided to leave them to their own foolish ways.

Next, he tried to sell his oil in the marketplace. Everyone wanted to barter with him, but when he told them that the price was fixed, no one would believe him. They were sure that he was trying to trick them, so they would not buy.

Lu Tung Pin soon tired of the city and thought that he might be better off in a smaller locale. He travelled to a nearby town and found a tidy-looking house.

Remembering his painful experience in the city, he knocked at the back door. A friendly young woman opened the door and asked what he was selling. He told her he was selling oil.

A gruff voice sounded from within the house:

"Who is at the door?"

The young woman looked frightened and said it was an oil seller.

"Tell him to come in" ordered the voice.

When Lu Tung Pin came inside, he saw the biggest man he had ever seen, seated at a table.

"How much are you charging for your oil?" asked the man. He told him.

The large man frowned and said, "I'll give you half your price."

When Lu Tung Pin refused, the man stated, "Then I will take it anyway," and he rose to his feet with a menacing look.

Lu Tung Pin was not sure what to do. He could see the woman was very frightened, so he decided to face up to this bully.

Pulling out his fly swatter, Lu Tung Pin waved it in the giant's direction. With a loud bang, the giant disappeared.

Bowing politely to the terrified woman, he made his way out of the house and decided that perhaps the town was not the right place for him either. He went to the local village.

But he fared no better there. People tried to trick him or simply ignored him.

Eventually, after weeks of wandering and trying to sell some oil, he came at last to an isolated country lane. As he passed a tiny tumbledown farm, a woman ran out to him:

"Please, sir, may I buy some oil from you, for I have almost none left?"

Lu Tung Pin hesitated. He was afraid that the woman would not have enough money to pay the fair price. But he had to stick to what he had agreed to with himself. So he named the price.

To his delight, the woman agreed and ran back to get the money.

He followed her and saw the poverty of her house and little farm.

As she collected the coins, Lu Tung Pin took a few grains of rice and threw them into the well. Then he turned, received the money, and gave the woman her oil. With that he wished her well and went on his way.

Later that day, the woman went to draw water from the well—and found that the well did not give her water, but wine. She drew another bucketful. More wine! She soon discovered that whenever she drew water, she got wine.

Within weeks she opened a wine shop. People came from miles around to buy her wine, for it had a most wonderful taste.

Soon she was able to rebuild her farm, and within a year or so, she was one of the wealthiest people in the area and much sought after by the local eligible bachelors. And all this came about because she had integrity.

For Reflection:

- Comment: The Eight Immortals of Taoism appear in shrines and figurines throughout China. Symbolic of the eight primal trigrams of the ancient I Ching, they travel the world inflicting lessons and getting into mischief. This tale concerns Lu Tung Pin, a popular Immortal ever armed with sword and fly swatter and associated with medicine, aid to the poor, and the Taoist "Elixir of Life," a kind of liquid version of the Philosopher's Stone sought by the ancient alchemists.

- What do the repeated rejections of Lu Tung Pin and his oil say about what Lionel Corbett refers to as the Scrooge Defense, a defensive warding off of the sacred when it appears? Why are we so often afraid of it, especially when we expect to be delighted with it?

- Why would the gods be curious about what goes on in human life?
- Why a fly swatter?
- What Trickster qualities are apparent in Lu Tung Pin? How would you compare him to other Tricksters in other cultures?
- Why does Lu Tung Pin insist on sticking to his price for the oil? What does it mean to buy the oil at a fair price?

Quetzalcoatl Sees Himself (Aztec)

Sergio Cruz Duran, Mexican mythic artist:

> Mythology has left a powerful legacy in Mexico, going back as far as the ancient Toltecs, Olmecs, Aztecs and Mayans. It has survived for more than twenty generations through paintings, sculpture, crafts and stories. Like all great systems of thought, mythology aims to understand the world, to raise consciousness and to enable humankind to move closer to the creator.

> Central to this philosophy is the concept of duality, by which opposite principles struggle not to override each other but to generate movement in a spiral, changing the world and renewing life at a cosmic level. The principle of duality is personified in Quetzalcoatl, who is represented by the plumed serpent, symbolizing both the earthly human condition (the snake) and the divine condition (the bird): the symbol of humankind and its possibilities.

Mythology is the realm in which reality and imagination meet, where future and past make the present, where humankind and god make a person, where body and spirit make the heart beat. Mythology in Mexico—like the Mayan pyramids still partially buried under masses of rubble—once uncovered, still dazzles us with its beauty.

"Tell him," said the stranger, "he has a visitor who will show him his own flesh."

The palace servant relayed this odd request to Quetzalcoatl. He stroked his white beard for a moment, then: "Show him in."

If the visitor were awed by the four-sided, four-colored palace crouching over a river, he did not reveal it. Dressed in black and yellow, he stood calmly holding something covered in a rabbit skin. He was difficult to see clearly: wherever he moved he seemed blurred by a cloud or shadow that was itself invisible. He might be young, but then again, he might not be.

"Tell me," Quetzalcoatl addressed him, "how might I see my own flesh?"

In answer the visitor pulled aside the skin to reveal an obsidian mirror. He held it forth. "See yourself as you are seen!"

The Lord of the Morning Star and Master of the City of the Sun peered into the surface and was startled to see a wrinkled, skeletal, sore-covered visage looking back at him.

After a lengthy pause: "How can my people look at this face and not feel frightened?"

"Here," said the visitor, "drink this," and he unstoppered a flask and handed it over.

"What is it?"

"A brew that will make you feel better." Actually, it was a potion distilled by the goddess Mayahuel, the spirit of the maguey plant.

Quetzalcoat sipped gingerly, liked what he tasted, sipped a little more, then more... He never noticed when the stranger departed.

"Quetzalpetlatl!" he called out, "you have to try this!"

Soon brother, sister, and servants were all roaring drunk on the potent beverage. The party lasted well into the night.

At dawn, the aging king woke to find himself in the arms of his sister.

"I am old," he wept, "weary, and no longer fit for a responsible position. I duped the dark gods of Mictlan and fashioned human beings out of bones wetted with my blood. I baited the sea monster Cipactli so we could carve a world from her body. I replaced ritual sheddings of blood with offerings of butterflies, flowers, and jade. I oversaw the arts and many crafts, devised the calendar and reading, brought maize here to be grown, and even returned the dead to life. But now it is time for me to go."

He removed his conical hat and his cloak of shining quetzal feathers and rose...

As he flew off to the east in his plumed serpent form, his tears falling into the sea far below, the palace he had set alight burned and smoked and hurled the sparks of its destruction high into the air.

The visitor watched him go. "Now," chortled the dark wizard Tezcatlipoca, "we'll have us some sacrifices for real."

For Reflection:

- Quetzalcoatl ("KETS-awl-COH-ought") was known to the Mayans as Kukulcan and to the Quiché of Guatemala as Gucumatz. He has also been compared to the Greek trickster Prometheus. What trickster qualities does he display?
- What can be made of "show him his own flesh" and the symbolism of the mirror?
- Is the desire for literal bloody sacrifice characteristic of the Magician archetype that shows up today as the scientist and technologist and yesterday as the war-supporting priest? Or is it a secondary quality?
- Comment: Tollan ("Among the Reeds") might have been a pre-Toltec city later replaced by Teotihuacan. It could also be generic for a mystical city.
- A historical parallel has been suggested for this myth:

the rise of a military class seizing power from the relatively peaceful Toltec priesthood. Does the elimination of symbolic sacrifice usher in literal sheddings of blood, as Jung speculated in his *Red Book*?

- How might understanding Quetzalcoatl's archetype (Trickster) allow Tezcatlipoca to manipulate him?
- Comment: It has often been said, and written, that Hernando Cortez was able to conquer the Aztecs because they took him for Quetzalcoatl. The notion of the god's return seems to have been a fabrication of the conquistadors and the Catholic Church, however. Cortez overran the Mexica because he forged alliances with their enemies, used military technologies unknown to the Aztec warriors, and directed at them a level of brutality far beyond their experience. Also, his men carried lethal pathogens into the New World. These incursions may have been responsible for as many as 90 million deaths.
- Why did Quetzalcoatl really depart? Was he forced out, or was it truly time for him to leave?
- One interpretation would be that Tezcatlipoca ("Smoking Mirror") tricked Quetzalcoatl out of his kingdom. Another would be that the mirror trick was the trigger for the old king's realization that it was time to go. How else might the departure be interpreted?

Eshu's Cap (Yoruba and Santería)

Yinka Tutuola about his father, Yoruba novelist Amos Tutuola:

> Whenever he was on annual leave (before he retired from government work) he would travel to his village with an old Pye reel-to-reel tape recorder; we used to go with him if we are on holidays, and there he collected

stories of all kinds. At nights in the village, he would buy palm wine to entertain his guests who would be competing to tell the best stories they could. He would record these stories still very late in the night.

...He seemed to me to have lived two kinds of lives. While one was real, factual physical life, the other was fictional, folkloric and mythological.

All his novels are written demonstrations and extensions of his sense of humor, for he saw and believed himself to be an entertainer (as a storyteller) rather than a writer. Actually it was for lack of audience at his workplace that made him turn to writing out the stories on paper. Humor was not peculiar to him alone; rather it is a Yoruba character—a way of talking, passing messages, teaching morals, warning, and so on.

The two friends were so close that they dressed alike, spoke alike, and went everywhere together. "We will be friends forever!" they declared to everyone who would listen, and to some who did not care to.

"Do not forget to make sacrifices to Eshu," the orderly god Ifa reminded them. They shuddered. Eshu, they knew, was the clever crossroads god of fortune, decision, and messages from the other spirits, but also of the unexpected. For he made trouble. Had he not disrupted even the heavens by making sun and moon trade places? They decided to forego the sacrifice ritual. *Some things were better left alone...*

One day they were laboring away on a farm when a wayfarer wearing a jaunty cap walked between them.

"Who was that man in the red cap?" asked one friend, straightening from his work.

"What red cap?" asked the other friend, puzzled. "It was white."

"It was red! Where do you keep your eyes, anyway?"

"Where do you keep yours?"

After arguing for a while they settled back to work.

The man returned, walking between them once again, smiling and nodding at each, but without turning his head.

"I am sorry," said the first friend. "I see now that the cap was indeed white."

"What do you take me for? Obviously the cap is red. Why are you trying to make me look like a fool?"

He reached out and pushed his friend, who pushed back. The pushing escalated into a brawl, the first ever for the lifelong friends. The man with the cap chuckled as he vanished into the distance.

After the two had given each other a thorough pummeling, they lay panting and bloody in the field they had cultivated.

Ifa approached. "Look at you two," he said scornfully. "Stop that fighting and go make a sacrifice to Eshu. It was he who walked by in a two-colored cap, red on one side and white on the other. He has made fools of you both."

The two friends, now much ashamed, walked off to make the overdue sacrifice.

For Reflection:

- What would be a contemporary way of understanding why a god would require a sacrifice offered by reverent human beings?

- Comment: *Ifa* is not only the name of a god of order, but of a West African religion thousands of years old. Ifa is animistic and Earth-honoring, and its practitioners show deep respect to their ancestors. It has been in continual evolution; one of its branches, Santería, blends Afro-Caribbean traditions with elements of Catholicism. It is particularly strong in Cuba and flourishes in other parts of the world.

- From the opening chapters of Shelley's *Frankenstein*, the reader feels suspicious of the all-bright, shadowless idealization in the doctor's description of his too-perfect family. (She tips us off when the doctor mentions as an aside that he has a temper but does not know why.) Is a similar pseudo-mutuality evident in the friendship in this tale?

- Why would a Trickster god seek to disrupt what seems to be so harmonious?

- Why do Eshu and Ifa go around together? (Think of the red and white on opposite sides, but coloring the same cap.)

- Might small sacrifices and acts of reverence prevent big sacrificial tragedies?

Nasreddin Hodja (Turkish / Islamic)

Elif Shafak, Turkish novelist, speaker, and scholar:

Migrations, ruptures and displacements have played a crucial role in my personal history....

My grandmother's understanding of Islam was not particularly anti-mainstream but from there, in the years to follow, I could find a gate open to heterodox, heretic interpretations of monotheist religions. Swinging between these two interpretations of Islam, while swinging between two grandmothers, I learned at an early age that every text is open to different interpretations and even the same God has more than one face.

How can people be so sure of their own truths? How can you put a full stop after every sentence? We should talk with three dots . . . at the end of every sentence, leave a door open, a door open to the stranger, to the foreigner, to the one I have not met yet because that person can challenge my truth, my reality. I adore and respect fluidity in both writing and being.

"Great Allah," said Hodja one day as he sat beneath a tree. "Why is it that You grow enormous watermelons on weak vines, yet put walnuts on strong trees?"

As he thought about this, a walnut fell from the tree and bounced off his forehead.

"Ah," he said, rubbing his head. "It is good. Had You thought my way instead of Yours, I would be dead now."

* * * *

On his first day as village *imam*, Hodja was expected to lead the service at the mosque. Those gathered there looked at him expectantly. But he did not know how to address them and had not worked on any sermon.

"Do you know what I am to speak to you about?" he asked them.

"No, we don't," they said.

"If you don't, then I have nothing to tell you." And with that, he left.

The next time he was expected to speak he asked, "Do you know what I am to speak to you about?"

Recalling his abrupt departure, they said, "Yes, we know."

"Good," said Hodja; "if you already know, then I don't need to say it." And he left.

They thought they were ready for him when he stood up a third time and asked his question. By agreement among themselves, some said, "Yes, we know," and others said, "No, we don't know."

"In that case," he said, "those who know should tell those who don't," and with that, he left.

* * * *

The Padishah emerged from the forest, where he had been hunting.

His horse was startled by Hodja and his donkey. The sudden halt threw the Padishah from his horse.

He got up, unhurt but enraged:

"You idiot! I will have your head cut off!"

"My king," replied Hodja, "why would you want to behead your humble slave?"

"Because you appeared and brought me misfortune."

"My Padishah, you appeared and brought me even worse luck. You fell off your horse, but my head will fall from my shoulders because of it. Who then was the worst omen, you or me?"

* * * *

Hodja was with Timur when the conqueror's men dragged in a drunken warrior. The man could scarcely stand.

"What do you want us to do with him?" the men asked Timur.

"Three hundred lashes with a cane."

Hearing this, Hodja laughed.

"What is so funny?" barked Timur.

"I laugh," said Hodja, "because either you have never been lashed with a cane or you don't know how to count."

* * * *

A beggar with a piece of bread stole into an inn. Spotting a simmering pot of soup, he held the bread over it so the rising steam could flavor it a little.

The innkeeper caught him and dragged him to Hodja, who served as the local *qadi*.

"He stole some of my soup!"

"No I didn't," replied the beggar. "I was just smelling the steam."

"Then you must pay for smelling it," insisted the innkeeper.

"Then," Hodja told him, "as the judge of this case, I will pay you myself because this beggar obviously has no money." Taking two coins from his pocket, he banged them together and put them away again.

"I thought you were going to pay me?"

"I have paid you," said Hodja.

"But you did not give me the coins!"

"You wanted to charge for the smell of soup. I have paid you with the clink of money."

*   *   *   *

While serving as *imam* in a distant town, Hodja learned of a custom there. After saving up enough of their gold coins to fill a pot, citizens buried it in their garden. Every year they dug up these pots, admired the gold in them, and buried them again.

Hodja filled a pot with pebbles and buried it.

"That makes no sense," some of the citizens told him. "Why bury pebbles? You are supposed to bury gold."

"As long as you won't spend it," Hodja replied, "what's the difference?"

*   *   *   *

One evening Hodja was surprised and disturbed to see the image of the full moon floating in his well. "The moon has fallen from the sky!" he exclaimed.

He darted into his home and returned with a rope and a hook. Tying them together, he threw the hook into the well and began hauling. The rope came up steadily until the hook caught on the side of the well.

Hodja heaved on the line as hard as he could.

When the hook suddenly came free, he flew backward and landed hard, stunned. When he finally opened his eyes, he saw the moon in the sky high above him.

"Well, I may have gotten hurt," he told himself, "but at least I got the moon back up there where it should be."

*   *   *   *

"We'll make a bet with you," said some of Hodja's friends who knew of his habit of challenging people. "If you can stay outside all night"—it was October and cool—"without a fire or a coat, we will make you a sumptuous dinner feast. If you cheat or quit early, though, you not only forfeit the meal, you must treat us to it."

"Very well," said Hodja.

After a few hours of evening cold, Hodja felt his body begin to shiver. His fingers and toes became numb. *Should I quit?* he wondered.

Just before giving up he spotted the glow of a candle in the window of a far-off house. Concentrating on the flame made him lose himself in fantasies of sitting comfortably next to a cosy fire.

His imagination kept him warm until daybreak, when he told his friends how he had succeeded.

"Sorry," they said, "but you cheated. You were supposed to do it without help, and that includes help from a candle flame."

After arguing with them for a time, Hodja agreed to make them dinner.

But when they came to his home and sat down to eat, they saw no food.

"Where is our dinner?"

"Cooking," said Hodja reassuringly.

After chatting for a couple of hours, their growling stomachs made them ask what was taking so long to prepare the food.

"Follow me," said Hodja, rising, "and I will show you."

In the kitchen they saw a cauldron hanging over a single flickering candle. They turned to him in irritation. "How is one little candle supposed to cook an entire pot full of food?"

"Why shouldn't it? The mere sight of one little candle kept me warm throughout a night."

For Reflection:
- Comment: Nasreddin ("Victory of Faith") Hodja ("Teacher") is thought by some to have been born in 1208 in the Central Anatolian village of Horto before moving to Aksehir. As *imam* he led prayers in

mosques, as had his father, and as *qadi* he served as an Islamic judge when he wasn't tending his small farm. His aphoristic wit appears in hundreds of short tales. Nothing ever robs him of his Trickster sense of humor.

- These tales blur the distinction normally made between folklore and myth. Does it matter? How does Hodja himself keep to the shifting middle space of things?

- Does a myth's historical origins make it any less mythic?

- What does the last tale say about the use and misuse of vision and imagination?

- Tricksters all over the world cause trouble in service to bringing forth a lesson, a new possibility, or a deeper harmony. How does Hodja do this?

Narada Gets Jilted (Hindu)

Ram Krishna Singh, poet, academic, critic, and reviewer:

> Sex is a very vital presence in our life; it is a major constituent of our body and mind. We can't deny it. When God created us as male and female, he created sex and wanted us to live in harmony. God didn't deny coitus. We are flesh in sensuality and there is divinity in it.
>
> I am also inspired by human body which is the best picture of human soul: I glorify it. We are flesh in sensuality and there is divinity in it. It is ever refreshing to me to express love and sex, the internalized substitute, or antidote, to the fast dehumanizing existence without and ever in conflict with my search for life. It helps me enlarge my self to the universal sameness of human feelings.

Cracks

The cracks on the parapet
have widened for the peepal
to stay green for once
rains too want us to drench
our heads and feel one
with cool wind
in a dark corner
shed fears and enjoy love

"There are two of you," King Ambarish pointed out, "but I have only one daughter. Which of you should she marry?"

They sat in the king's court in Ayodhya: the king himself, the wandering sage Narada, and wealthy, mountain-dwelling Parvata.

They were speaking of surpassingly lovely Srimati, who as the daughter of the host had washed their weary feet, whereupon both guests promptly fell in love (or at least lust) with her.

The king felt caught. He did not want to anger Narada, who traveled between the worlds and was a devotee of Vishnu. But neither did he want to displease Parvata, friend of mighty Indra.

In this case the smart way was the right way: his daughter should decide.

"I should be the one," Narada was saying, "because I am the elder."

"But I was the first to ask," argued Parvata. "It should be me."

"Friends," the king said, "we will hold a *swayamvara* so my daughter can make her own choice. Please return tomorrow morning."

"That makes sense," said Narada; "a night of reflection will turn her toward the wandering musical sage who has mastered the *veena*."

"Yes, let her decide," said Parvata; "she will pick the younger and more handsome suitor."

Hmmmm, thought Narada, alarmed. What if Parvata was correct?

Narada soon reached Vaikuntha, the celestial home of Vishnu the Preserver. The Great One agreed to see him.

"Lord," Narada pled, "you know I am your most devoted worshiper, and that I never ask for anything." Vishnu made no comment. Narada went on: "I am in love with Srimati, King Ambarish's daughter. Tomorrow she will choose her man during a *swayamvara*."

"That is just," murmured Vishnu.

"Yes, Lord. But her other choice is Parvata, handsome young friend of Indra. I am concerned that she might favor the fading bloom of looks over the abiding wisdom I could offer her."

"I see. Since it is her decision, what do you expect of me?"

"Please make Parvata appear to Srimati as a monkey so she will choose me instead."

Vishnu pondered for a moment, then: "Very well."

"Thank you, Lord!" Narada clapped his hands in glee and vanished.

Vishnu smiled.

Not long after, Parvata appeared. Vishnu agreed to see him.

"What can I do for you?"

"I have just met the woman of my dreams...."

Eventually he got to the request: "Please make Narada look to her like a bear so she will choose me."

"Be it so," said Vishnu, trying not to laugh.

*   *   *   *

Narada and Parvata waited nervously in a beautifully flowered and decorated hall for the selection ritual to begin. They sat near each other on sumptuous thrones. A crowd of visitors and retainers slowly gathered.

At last the king brought in his radiant daughter.

"Here are two noble rishis waiting for your decision," he said as she came up, her eyes lowered, her hands covered in flowers. "Please hang a garland around the neck of the man you choose to be your husband."

She slowly raised her eyes, then gasped as the smile fled from her face.

"Daughter, what is wrong?"

When she could speak, the words tumbled out: "There are no rishis here! Why, Father, have you brought a monkey and a bear to woo me?"

"What monkey and what bear?"

She gestured at the two men. As she did, a third walked up from behind them.

Something has gone very wrong, thought Narada. "Which of us do you choose?" he asked.

"I chose the man in the middle," she said. "The quiet and radiant man in gem-studded garments." This man smiled as though he knew her completely. She smiled back.

"What kind of trick is this?" Narada angrily demanded of the king.

Realizing that these angry rishis were capable of cursing her father, Srimati told them, "I think you will agree to this, in all fairness: I will throw my garland, and whomever of you catches it will be my husband." They nodded.

The garland landed on the shoulders of the man between them, a "man" the king now recognized.

The garlanded one and Srimati vanished, but not before the two startled suitors recognized him.

"I guess that settles that," remarked the king with some relief.

This time Narada and Parvata together requested an audience with Vishnu. It was granted.

When they stood before the Lord, Narada posed but a single question for both of them:

"Why?"

"Because you bragged about having conquered Kamadeva, the god of love, through meditation and austerities; and now Love has conquered you. Did you not recognize his presence? His power?"

Narada, for once, was silent.

"Because you have not one wife but sixty, as you go around telling all the gods and everyone who will listen. Do you really need one more?"

Vishnu turned to look at Parvata and continued:

"Because the king's daughter was actually Lakshmi, my mate, reincarnated so we could be together again. Did neither of you investigate to learn anything about this mysterious daughter: who she was, how she came to be born, what her interests were, what she truly wanted?"

The two jilted rishis looked sadly at one another.

"Excuse me now," Vishnu told them. "My bride and I have things to do."

Back on earth they finished their conversation:

"At least we didn't end up as enemies," Parvata reflected. "If nothing else, we are joined by our mutual disappointment and humiliation."

"Perhaps we had it coming. What do you plan to do now?" Narada asked him.

"Go back to my mountain and manage the rain. You? Any plans to find a suitable mate?"

"No, I'm done. It's the single life for me." After the sixty divorces were over with, anyway...

And so it was; but forever after, humbled Narada also praised the primacy and excellence of knowledge of the heart, without which even the most learned see little.

For Reflection:

- Comment: In Indian sacred lore, and the *Mahabharata* in particular, the trickster Narada ("nah-RAHD") knew all of history and science, ancient wisdom and spiritual teaching. A master of the stringed *veena*, he sung and chanted to Vishnu, who had awakened him. He remembered everything and was a master of logic, yoga, cosmology, and the arts of war. He also spread many rumors, seldom kept anything in confidence, and caused much trouble, though usually to good effect. One of his titles was Kalaha-Priya, "Lover of

Quarrels." In some tales the rain god Parvata is his nephew.

- How is it that, at least in this story, love can make fools of even the rishis and, in other stories, even the gods? How does it influence Vishnu?

- What does it mean archetypally that Lakshmi, goddess of love, beauty, and good fortune, is the consort of kingly Vishnu?

- In some versions of this story, Narada curses Vishnu to be separated from his wife until a monkey comes along to end the separation. When the demon Ravana captures Sita, an avatar of Lakshmi, Vishnu needs the assistance of the monkey god Hanuman to bring her back. Could this mean that Narada has the last laugh after all?

Chapter Ten - Justice and Community

We usually think of justice as a cultural construct, and its principles do indeed vary widely across cultures. But the basic premises of fairness and equality extend to the animal kingdom. Even bacteria have been seen sacrificing themselves to protect a colony from toxins.

English etymology distinguishes between the cultural construct of morality, *which refers to tradition, and* ethics, *which at root point to where the horses come home at night.*

Below the personal and the cultural, then, perhaps justice is Justice, an archetypal dynamic or presence; and perhaps the myths of many lands show its expressive forms down through human time.

Adapa Foregoes Immortality (Mesopotamian)

Dunya Mikhail, Iraqi poet:

> The way that things come to mind, I feel that they are more as fragments. They are strange. They don't come in order anymore, so the happy moments and the sad moments climb over each other: our home in Baghdad with the roof where we would sleep summer nights and we would go down when we the sound of the siren; the simple heater in the middle of our living room that was called Aladdin, and, on it, that pot of tea with cardamom.

> And I remember my father dying in front of my eyes. I remember the windows of our classrooms shaking from explosions. You know, the war was like the norm.

> I feel that I woke up from a dream, and going back to Iraq is like asking me will I see the same dream if I go back to sleep? It's strange.

> But I keep contact to maybe have some trace of that old dream or experience. And I find that Iraqis all have one dream, and that is to live a normal life and to die a normal death.

Adapa, King of Eridu, first man created by the sea god Ea and observer of divine statutes, was sailing one evening in the Persian Gulf when the south wind saw him out on the water.

Gathering itself powerfully, it blew hard enough to capsize the boat and throw Adapa overboard with a splash.

Adapa was furious. "Take that!" he shouted and broke the south wind's wing.

The wind failed to blow for seven days. The sky god Anu summoned his servant to ask him about this.

"Adapa became angry and injured the south wind."

"Bring him."

Before this meeting Ea hung a robe of mourning on Adapa and gave him counsel:

"When you approach Anu's door, you will see Tammuz and Gishzida standing there. They will ask you for whom you mourn, because of the garments you wear. Tell them you mourn their absence in your country. Flattered by this, they will then be willing to speak favorably of you to Anu.

"Be careful, however, because when you stand before Anu, they will also bring you the food and water of death and set them before you. Do not drink or eat! But when they bring you garments, put them on and anoint yourself with the oil they offer."

When Adapa arrived in heaven, he saw the gods before the door, spoke with them, and was shown in to see Anu, who asked:

"Why did you injure the south wind?"

"My lord," the king explained, "I was out fishing to catch offerings for your temple when the wind rose up and threw me into the sea. I became angry at this and struck. That is what happened."

Tammuz and Gishzida nodded, as though to say: *He is being truthful.*

Noting this, Anu nodded in satisfaction.

"Why has Ea revealed to humanity," he mused to himself, "which he created impure, the heart of heaven and earth, and even knowledge of the name he has given to them? What can be done about this?"

He turned to a servant: "Bring the food and drink of immortality as well as garments and oil."

He was astonished when his visitor accepted the latter but not the former.

"Why do you not partake of what I make available for you?"

"Because Ea, who created me, told me not to."

"Very well," he sighed. To the gods: "Take him back down, where he will live out his mortal existence. —And bring me Ea."

Who left the presence of Anu looking glum in soiled mourning garments.

For Reflection:

- Comment: This myth comes down from the 14th century BCE, when the Kassites ruled Babylon. The tablets on which it was written are fragmentary.

- Why would the south wind knock over Adapa?

- Tammuz (Dumuzi) is a food, revelry, and shepherd god similar to the later Dionysus; Gishzida (Ningishzida) is an Underworld god. Why Tammuz and Gishzida as guardians?

- Ea, also known as Enki, is a Trickster god (as well as father of Ishtar). Why would he deceive Adapa? (A possible parallel: "Behold, the man is become as one of us, to know good and evil; and now, lest he put forth his hand and take also of the tree of life, and eat, and live forever; Therefore the Lord God sent him forth from the garden of Eden" — Genesis 3:22-23.)

- Because he is wise, devout, and clever, Adapa receives an invitation to immortality but refuses it. Only because he was tricked by Ea, or is there a higher logic to why he should return to the world and continue his devotions and his rulership? Why (as Anu wonders) did Ea make humans mortal to begin with? What choice would you have made?

- What does this tale reveal about relations between the gods and humanity?

Nuwa Repairs the Sky and Earth (Chinese)

Aku Wuwu, Yi poet, translator, literary critic, and a professor of ethnic literature studies at the Southwest Nationalities University, Chengdu, Sichuan Province:

I have a responsibility and purpose on behalf of my own
descendants to leave behind this generation's literature
and knowledge...I also take up this generation of Yi
people's difficult life—facing the disappearance of their
history and culture, their heavy spiritual burden, their
floating spirits—and want to give them a picture of
themselves and their spirit.

from "Soul of the Felt Cloak":

The makers of traditional cloaks are wise—
The felt pleats they fashion are like our land.
Wherever Nuosu people go they are enfolded
In the mountains and valleys of their native land.

And the wisdom of the grandfathers' generations
Lives in the trees and vegetation that cloak the ridges,
And lives in the rise and fall of the waters in the valleys,
And lives concealed in the pleats of the felt cloaks
That the generations of today continue to wear.

We embrace the soul of our native earth,
We embrace the wisdom of our ancestors,
We press them within the felt of the cloak,
To warm us forever—our eternal, black banner.

"You have lost," stated Zhu Rong to his combative son.

They had fought across the sky for many days. Father and son
landed on earth, where Gong Gong the red-haired sea serpent had
triggered one devastating flood after another.

Riding in on a tiger of enormous size, the armored fire god Zhu
Rong had wielded his mighty sword with deadly effect. Gong Gong
lay spent and wounded; the throne of Heaven was secure against his
reckless ambitions. After this, yet another triumph (for Zhu Rong

had helped separate earth and sky and had established the order on which the world depended), he rode back to his home up above.

But Gong Gong was humiliated and enraged. He reared up again and crashed his head against Mount Buzhou, one of the pillars supporting the heavens.

As the stone crumbled, the entire sky tilted northwest. The world, also knocked askew, sagged to the southeast, where rivers like the Yangtze and Yellow run even now.

The land below broke out in fires and floods. A Black Dragon ate everyone in its path. The Nine Regions knew no peace, and civilization descended into ruin.

The sea serpent slithered away laughing.

Nuwa heard the noise and came to investigate. She found a world collapsing into chaos.

Long, long ago, when everything was fresh and moist from a recent flood and Ao the turtle swam the South China Sea carrying new lands on his broad back, Nuwa, daughter of giant Pangu, lived with her brother Fu Xi on Kunlun Mountain. When the mist collected in a sign that they should mate, they did, hiding their faces behind fans woven of grass.

From her grew animals and humans fashioned from yellow clay reinforced by ropes. From him descended cooking, hunting with iron tools, fishing with nets, the institution of marriage, and the I Ching oracle to advise generations of leaders and their counselors.

The people on earth prospered—until Gong Gong knocked it all out of balance.

Nuwa picked up five colored stones and melted them into a patch for the skies. You can still see some of her patching when the clouds turn colorful.

After applying it, she cut off Ao's legs and braced up the heavenly corners. Because she placed the shorter legs in the east, the sun, moon, and stars still rotate toward the northwest.

Nuwa returned to earth, where she killed the Black Dragon, laid down reed ashes to halt the floods, and cleared away the wreckage so the land could regenerate itself.

Once again it served as an abode to all the rejoicing living things wise Nuwa had created long ago.

For Reflection:

- Why do orderly parents so often raise disorderly children?

- Entire mountains are now being destroyed to dig up coal. If we look at extractive industry as a contemporary Gong Gong, then air pollution and the social and ecological chaos that results from it correspond well with our tale's account of damage to the skies and destruction on earth. What would a helpful Nuwa ("noo-WAH") look like today?

- *Buzhou* means "not full" or "incomplete." What about Gong Gong was empty or incomplete that led him to smash Mount Buzhou?

- Melting magic rocks and making use of animal parts identifies Nuwa as first among alchemists. China is the home of the philosophy of the Five Elements worked with in transformative healing practices. In alchemy the number five holds the significance of the Quintessentia, the Philosopher's Stone that arises when elementary forces are combined in new patterns. Many of the adepts of alchemy advised that nature could only be transformed beneficially by nature. What could this mean in our day? What would those alchemists, or Nuwa, have made of geoengineering?

- Nuwa understood archetypally is a Wisdom Goddess like Sophia, Athena, Neith, and many others. Can Wisdom can save us from destroying earth and sky?

Neamlau Confronts Nzambi (Congolese)

Kama Sywor Kamanda, Congolese poet:

I was born in a family where my relatives were very concerned about educating children and providing them with an extensive knowledge. Poetry was part of our daily life. Therefore, we have been able to learn about African and non-African traditions.

Exile suffering has influenced my literary work. I still believe that men must resist all forms of violence against people. I have lost everything in the struggle, but poetry writing has saved me from sinking down to the abyss of hopelessness.

The poetic feeling is a universal truth. Therefore, whatever be his style, ethnicity, nationality, style of writing or language of expression may be, the poet touches the human being in its deepest spirituality. Without poetry, there is no religious belief because religion needs words to express the mystery of the world and of the origins.

Nzambi Mpungu created the land, the waters, the animals and insects, but she left one thing out: the drum. How could people dance without the drum?

One of her creations, Nchonzo Nkila, was a small bird with a long tail that rhythmically beat the ground. This sound made people want to dance—and gave the bird an idea.

So he invented the drum. When people saw it and he played it, they danced until they fell down from sheer happy exhaustion.

Nzambi, who lived nearby, heard the beating and understood its meaning. *I wish I had a drum*, she thought. *I and my people could dance too.*

"Why have I, who created the world," she asked her companions, "no drum while a little bird over there can play on one whenever he likes and make people dance? Antelope, go tell that long-tailed bird I want his drum."

"No," said the bird to Antelope. "She can't have it."

"Why not?"

"Because I'm using it."

"But she, our Mother, gave us everything, including the materials you used to build your drum. You owe her a lot, you know."

"I know. But I don't owe her my drum."

After listening to the drum for a while, Antelope asked if he could play it. Nchonzo Nkila handed it over to him.

Antelope played it a few times and ran away with it.

This proved a bad idea for Antelope. Once the bird's people had caught him, they skinned and cooked him. Kivunga the hyena collected some of Antelope's blood and showed it to Nzambi. Nchonzo Nkila played on.

The next to try for the drum was Mpacasa the wild ox. He soon joined the pot with luckless Antelope as the drum beat on over the roar of the cookfire.

"Would someone," cried out Nzambi in grief and frustration, "go and get me that drum!"

After a moment of silence, "I will," volunteered Mflti the ant to the relief of all present who had wondered what being cooked and eaten would feel like. "I'm small. They won't notice me."

Though small, Mflti was clever and very strong. He waited until everyone at Nchonzo Nkila's village lay snoring in sleep. He stole into the bird's house, hefted the drum quietly, and slowly bore it out the door and back to the village of Nzambi, who was delighted to see the drum.

Nchonzo Nkila woke to the sound of drumming booming from the village next to his and knew immediately that Nzambi had found a way to steal his drum.

Summoning the bird people, he told them what had happened; all came to hear except Mbemba, the pigeon. They talked it over and decided to send Nzambi a messenger to bear their demand: that she select a place to meet to submit the situation to tribal law.

Nzambi sent back a message suggesting they meet in Neamlau's village the next day. Neamlau was an official widely known for his fairness.

At the meeting Nchonzo Nkila spoke first about the making and stealing of the drum.

When he had finished, Nzambi explained that those she sent to request the drum had been eaten (Kivunga confirmed this) until Ant retrieved it for her. "I made everything. Don't I have a right to this drum as well?"

Neamlau and the other elders retired to consider the case. Nchonzo Nkila and Nzambi sat waiting and avoiding looking at each other.

Neamlau returned and spoke:

"You have asked us to render a decision in this matter. Here it is:

"Nzambi was wrong to take the drum from Nchonzo Nkila. We respectfully acknowledge her to be the mother of all us, of the land, of everything, just as Nchonzo brought forth the drum. But in our case Nzambi gave us the ability to make free decisions. What we make is ours, just as we are hers. If she had made the drum it would be hers, but she did not: Nchonzo made it. So she has no right to it. If she means to keep it she must pay its maker for it."

Once Nzambi and Nchonzo had thanked Neamlau with customary gifts she paid the bird for the drum, which settled things.

So this is why people all over the world can dance and drum.

For Reflection:

- Nzambi can be held as one of the archetypal Wisdom Goddesses who create and educate. Her sex changes with the telling: sometimes male, sometimes female. Why would having a drum be so important to her?

- Do you think animals ever make music? They seem to enjoy it at times. (A musician in Canada used to play his guitar to orcas who swam up to the dock he sat on and listened intently.)

- In the film *The Weeping Camel*, a Mongolian medicine man and music teacher drapes a stringed instrument over the hump of a camel to help her heal from the trauma of giving birth. The wind playing the strings seems to soothe her. Can you imagine who the first musicians might have been and how the sounds of the world inspired them?

- Parts of Africa rely on a restorative justice model based on tribal laws. Instead of putting people in jail, the community works to address the injustice and heal the wounds it left. What would have happened to the community if Neamlau had tried instead to arrest, imprison, or exile Nzambi or Nchonzo?

- In *Answer to Job* Jung makes a remarkable statement: "The encounter with the creature changes the Creator." Jewish legends tell of rabbis who rise up to heaven to chastise God for turning a blind eye to injustices committed on earth. How is Neamlaw's way of dealing with Nzambi different from staying in a child-parent relation with her? How does she ultimately benefit from his judgment?

- Notions of determinism echo religious traditions that view the gods or the God as all-powerful. How does this tale address the problem of free will?

- What might the drum as a character have said about all this commotion and how things were settled?

The Rejected Gifts of Star Maiden (Indigenous Amazonian)

Maria Clara Sharupi Jua, Shuar poet and translator:

> I write to enable the world to hear the voice of the Shuar people. This is a voice of the jungle, the mountains, rivers, birds, plants, insects, trees, and the sacred waterfalls that are born of our mother and sister earth and are one with the cosmos. I want to convey the wisdom of my ancestors and the orality of my culture that inhabits every syllable I put into writing. While as humans, our

blood is all the same color, our voices are the hues that matter, because they uniquely adorn our language.

From "Like Red-Hot Lava":

I want to bathe your soul
in the dew of my waters
an alphabet of vowels
where one enters and is never forgotten
I want to be the wind
to appease the raging waves of the sea
hands that caress the volcano
and douse the fire of your words
Poison to calm the wrath of Iwia
the tears that fill your childlike eyes
revealing myself and erupting like red-hot lava
to roll like a stone turned to fire
into your salty arms

In the days when no one knew how to grow plants for food and corn was considered dangerous to eat, two brothers listened to their father tell the stories of the river village people.

One brother, Acauá, a bold hunter given to bragging, wore a necklace of jaguar claws and of the many animals he had killed. The other brother, younger Caué, followed sunbeams and the growth of trees in the forest. He spoke seldom.

But tonight he had a question:

"Father, what is that bright star? I wish I could touch it." He pointed.

"That is Star Maiden," his father answered. "It is said that if you wish for her company long enough, she will come down and be with you."

She never had, though.

The two sons went to sleep thinking about Star Maiden.

The following day, after hunting together, the brothers cooked an armadillo, gathered brush for beds, and lay down to sleep, planning to return to the village in the morning.

They did not sleep long. The sound of steps woke them.

"Who is there?" called Acauá, trying to hide his fright.

"It is I, Star Maiden."

In wonder the two sprang up expecting to see a beautiful young spirit. In the light of the fire an old woman with white hair smiled at them. Her skin was as wrinkled as tree bark.

"Get lost," said Acauá and turned angrily away. Tears ran down the woman's face.

"Would you be *my* companion?" asked Caué.

"Yes," she said, her tears stopping, "but I will live inside a gourd and will only come out at night."

In the morning they entered the village and sought the hut of their father. The older brother scolded his father for the idea of calling down Star Maiden, but the younger said, "She agreed to be with me. She's in here." He set down the gourd and opened it.

An opossum jumped out of it, ran across the father's shoulders, leaped onto a nearby maize plant, and tossed corn to the old man. Then it changed back into a woman.

They remained silent as the woman who had been a star and then a taboo animal told them how to make maize cakes from a taboo plant. Acauá walked out in disgust and fear.

The next day Star Maiden went forth into the forest to prepare other good, if unfamiliar, foods for the people. She sought seeds so she could teach them how to plant and stones for building an oven for cooking the foods.

After she was gone six days, her mate-to-be worried about her and went looking for her even though she had told him not to seek her.

He walked through the forest all day and came upon a faint trail that looked recently made. This he followed to a clearing where, to his surprise, he saw sweet potato plants, papaya, melons, beans, pumpkins, yams, cotton, banana, and tobacco, all planted in concentric circles.

As he stared, so did others' eyes: those of friends of his older brother. They had followed him quietly and at a distance. When they saw the plantings, they ran back to tell Acauá about them.

Caué's eyes blinked, once, twice, thrice. Was he seeing correctly? He stepped forward to greet what he believed would be an old woman and found a young one instead.

"Yes," she laughed, "it is I, Star Maiden. I was testing you and your brother. I am planting all this in return for your kindness and so your people will not go hungry any longer."

He bit into a melon and savored is sweet tang. He couldn't wait to return to the village and tell the people about all this bounty.

When the two returned, however, they found their hut burned down and Caué's father sitting outside the ruins weeping.

Acauá and his friends had entered the hut seeking the secret of the gourd. They broke it, pushed the old man aside, and set the hut on fire.

Star Maiden spoke to Caué and his father:

"I want the two of you to come with me to the stars. No villagers will harm you there; no fear or anger are to be found there. And everything I would have given your people here I will give to you up there."

For Reflection:

- What is it about social change that so often prompts violent resistance?

- If the brothers represent two factions in a society, how might they be described? What are their archetypal stances? How is each useful under certain circumstances?

- How is Star Woman like other Wisdom goddesses in the world's myths and lore? How is she different from them?

- What psychological consequences might follow from the absence of the brothers' mother? What kind of relationship do you imagine each had with her?

- What could be the cultural implications of holding the cosmic and the ecological together, as this tale does?

- Why does Star Maiden insist on breaking taboos?

- Comment: This tale contains hints of Amazonian ecological wisdom. They include evening planting to dis-
  courage pests, concentric circles for companion planting, banana plants to lure caterpillar-killing wasps, and
  biologically diverse combinations.

Lady, Serpent, and Song (Korean)

Kim Hyesoon, South Korean feminist poet:

> The first Korean poem is "Gongmudohaga." A woman
> cries sadly and sings when she sees her crazy husband
> with gray hair cross a river. Another woman called
> Yeook sees this and writes this down. This feminine per-
> sona (and her sorrow) are the contents of Korea's first
> poem. Thus, Korean poetry starts with two women's
> emotions. Under the influence of this beginning, emo-
> tions and longings for love are the main ideas of Korean
> poetry.
>
> And in Korea's creation myth, a bear called Woongnye
> and a tiger challenge each other to eat garlic and worm-
> wood. The tiger fails, but the bear succeeds. This bear
> becomes a woman. She gives birth, but never turns up
> again. Women in Korean myths disappear after giving
> birth. The reason they were born is to produce sons. But
> there is one myth where no female disappears. It is a
> fable of the foremother of shamans. Baridegi was the
> seventh daughter of a king and was abandoned because
> she was a girl. After she came back from a pilgrimage to
> the world of the dead, she saved her father and became
> the foremother of exorcists who help lead those who
> have died into heaven.

As a fine-featured woman of surpassing beauty and powerful influence, Lady Suro usually got what she wanted. But when she pointed at some pink azaleas and called out, "Will someone go and pick me some of those colorful flowers?" nobody stepped forward at first.

The flowers bloomed on a seaside bluff near the T'aebaek Mountains, where the retinue of her husband, Lord Sunjong, had paused on their journey to Kangnung and the governorship awaiting him there.

Lady Suro repeated her request. The flowers and the bluff had utterly entranced her. Now she was angry that no one would climb the cliff for her. Was she not a royal personage?

Well, then I'll do it! thought an old man passing on the road. He let go the rein of the cow he'd been leading and started up the cliff face. Anxious eyes followed his progress.

He had seemed frail and old, but he made it to the top, gathered some azaleas, made his way carefully down the cliff. Everyone sighed with relief.

He walked over to the lady, bowed, and sang this as he held out the pink flowers to her:

By the deep-red rocks
The cow let go;
If you will not be shy of me,
Please accept these flowers plucked for you.

She accepted them with thanks, and the retinue passed on. The old man took up the reins of his cow and led it down the road.

They stopped at Imhae Pavilion, again near the sea, to eat a meal. Lady Suro got up and wandered among sea-washed rocks along the shore.

This greatly concerned her husband. "My lady, please come away from there!"

She ignored him, entranced by the swirling waters below.

"Go and bring her back," Lord Sunjong told some servants.

As they walked down to her, giant bubbles broke the ocean surface not far from the Lady Suro. In an instant a giant sea serpent with a neck as tall as a waterspout reared up and snatched her off the rock.

It happened so rapidly that the next sound the servants heard was a thump as Lord Sunjong sat down hard on the ground in shock. Nobody knew what to do.

Just then another old man came walking up.

"I wouldn't lose hope over this," he told them. "The ancients said that the voices of many people brought together could even melt iron. Gather up all the people of the neighboring villages. Take them down to the beach and sing out together while pounding the shore and the hills with sturdy staves. The serpent will not resist such a public outcry."

Lord Sunjong gathered the people as directed. This is the song they sang to the serpent:

Sea spirit, sea spirit, let Lady Sura go.
How great the crime of stealing someone's wife.
If you refuse to give her back,
We will haul you out of the sea, cook you, and eat you.

Upon hearing this the serpent reared forth again and set Lady Suro back on the rock.

"I apologize," said the serpent to Lord Sunjong before it slipped below once again.

They asked the lady how she fared. She was dazed, but as in a dream rather than from being seized.

"The palace below the surface is beautiful beyond words," she said. "Seven treasures illuminate it; food prepared in it rivals anything served above the sea."

She told of many other wonders as they continued onward. For seven days her dress emitted a pleasing fragrance.

Whenever Lady Suro passed through mountain valley streams or along coasts, water creatures made a grab for her. Always an old man appeared to tell people how to get her back again.

<u>For Reflection:</u>

- It would be easy to think of Lady Suro as yet another egotistical ruler angry at the frustration of her whims. What other interpretations might work here?

- If this tale were a dream, ordering the flowers to be plucked and standing too near the sea would have prompted the serpent's seizure of Lady Suro. Why do you suppose it happened?

- Who mythologically is the old man who keeps appearing? Why does he lead a cow?

- Why does it require a community to secure the return of Lady Suro?

- What did Lord Sunjong learn about leadership from this event?

- It is trendy to think of natural forces as what should always be obeyed, aligned with, or harmonized with. In part this eagerness reflects a reaction against the ongoing industrialized destruction of the ecosphere. What (if anything) does the tale suggest about our relations with the natural world, at least in certain situations where our idealizations of it fail?

- Some of the more sensitive and dreamy among us both enjoy and suffer from an unusually strong connection to Spirit, including Spirit in the natural world. Are Lady Suro's abductions an inevitable trial in her life? If not, how could she tend the natural world without being abducted by it?

- Is Lady Suro a shaman?

Ishum Calms Erra (Mesopotamian)

Kamin Mohammadi, Iranian journalist, travel guide, author, and photographer:

Iran today is caught between its ancient traditions and modern desires, a repressive religious regime and a young population clamouring for freedom. The Iranian language is full of poetic turns and elaborate courtesies, an emotional language made for love, yet the people that speak it can be imprisoned for loving in any way other than within the sanctity of marriage.

...Iran has a history of nearly 3,000 years, and once boasted the greatest empire in the world. 2,500 years ago the Persian empire stretched from Europe in the west to the Indus in the east. Invaders, who included Alexander the Great, the Muslim Arabs, Tamerlane and Genghis Khan, left deep impressions but also presented opportunities for Persian culture to assimilate what newcomers offered and emerge more Persian than ever. (Alexander the Great's adoption of Persian dress was regarded with deep suspicion by his Greek followers.) The graceful indirectness of Persian manners reflects this instinct for survival in an insecure political landscape.

"Ishum, I am going into the open country to fight. I need your encouragement, and I want you to guide us. Your light will be as a torch for me."

"Weren't you just in bed with Mami?"

"My seven great weapons called me forth. They said, 'Erra, stop dawdling in your lover's arms. Prepare your weapons, leave your house, and go forth onto the battlefield! Are we to sit around eating women's bread? To succumb to fear and childishness? A war is a fitting festival for young men! If they fight, no one will vilify them for cowardice or lack of honor. Besides, there are too many people abroad in the world as it is; their noise deprives the gods of sleep, and the cattle run everywhere. Let us forsake the bread and beer and comfortable rooms and pitch our battlefield camps. Let us make such a fierce noise that gods and kings tremble and nations bring tribute. Let the seas roll and the trees shake and the mountains crumble and the reeds fall down with the mighty sound! We your bows and blades gather dust and rust with lack of use.'"

"Erra, this will not bring honor to the gods, but trouble to them and to you. You would massacre entire countries to satisfy this crimson urge. Will you not come to your senses?"

"Why should I? In heaven I am a wild bull, on earth a lion, in the country a king, among the gods fierce, among cattle the smiter, in the mountains the wild ram, in the groves a strong-bladed ax. I blow like wind, I rumble and see far. As for the gods, they don't battle, so why should people respect them? Marduk is lazy and neglectful. I will kill his black-haired people. Watch as I confront him through his statue now."

"I will follow you to his palace..."

*   *   *   *

"Marduk! I, Erra, have come to Esagila to confront you. I would like to know why the royal finery of the king of the gods is so dirty, and your crown tarnished. Don't you realize that a grimy statue risks plunging the world into disorder?"

"Erra, there was a time when I, Marduk, brought the great flood that made the very heavens tremble. The face and garments of my image shone, and all who beheld it—those who survived the calamity—felt awe. Where are the gods whose job it is to maintain my image?"

"Yes, where are they?"

"A day is coming when I shall rise from my dwelling and undo the control of heaven and earth alike. The waters will rise again over the land, day will diminish into darkness, storms will cover the stars, and an evil wind will obscure what can be seen. Demons will seize the unprepared, and the gods will trample on living things."

"Until that day dawns, noble Marduk, I will rule Babylon while you get your statue refurbished. Then I will prepare a noble house for it and station Anu and Enlil on either side of its doorway."

Erra and Ishum departed to converse elsewhere.

"So not even Ishtar can talk you out of this, Erra?"

"No, Ishum. As for the rest of the gods, they fled at my approach."

"Even now they convene. Ea will see you humbled, he says."

"It is they who need humbling. Just look at 'mighty' Marduk. Off visiting his tailor! He does not deserve to rule."

"But why, Erra?"

"Because the men of today ignore me and hold me in contempt, I will give them a lesson they will never forget. —Now quit arguing. I must prepare my dawn attack upon Babylon."

*   *   *   *

"Well, Erra, I see that in Marduk's absence you have leveled Nippur."

"I did. I put to death young and old alike, killed babies in their cribs, made grieving fathers bury their fallen sons. The righteous and the wicked lay in stinking heaps together. Those homes I did not destroy I left for invaders to occupy."

"You have put them in their place with a fist of iron, and the governor of Babylon is no more. Marduk heard of all this and fled. Now that you rule heaven and earth, mountain and sea, with even the gods afraid of you."

"I told them it was my nature to cause war. When I am angry I slay right and left, hew down orchards, scorch the earth, and roar like a hungry lion."

"What will you do next with your great power?"

"I will spread civil war across the earth, and I will attack the seats of the gods. None will be spared, and all dissent will be silenced. What will you do, Ishum?"

"I will punish the nomadic killers of Mount Sharshar for their incursions by destroying their base of operations with no loss of life. This action will end quickly. The priests will soon enter your temples once again to make offerings."

"That is a good plan, Ishum. Better perhaps than universal strife."

"I think so."

"Perhaps if I leave off further aggression in Babylon, the nation will recover and be ruled by a new king one day..."

"It seems likely."

"...And the king will worship me."

"Yes."

"Perhaps they will grow strong once again, and tend the fields, and draw fish from the sea, and trade with neighboring lands."

"Perhaps they will, Erra."

"Peace after all has its uses....so long as people remember the gods."

For Reflection:

- Comment: The manuscript for this tale was found in the same wrecked library in Nineveh that held the tablets for the Gilgamesh tale.

- Although the war god Erra uses his supposedly rusting weapons as an excuse to fight, might some truth hide in this claim? (My book *In the Thick of Things* argues that a gun—named after the lethal Valkyrie Gunhilda—is a hardened piece of deadly psychology that "wants" to kill.)

- Erra compares war to a festival. What does this say about the lack of peaceful festival and communal celebration in warlike cultures?

- Kabit-ilani-Marduk, the author of this eighth-century text, claimed that he received the entire poem in a dream. If so, what out-of-balance personal or collective attitude might the dream have tried to compensate? (His society was an empire.)

- What are some basic differences between how Erra and Ishum conduct battle?

- "War is human nature" is a justification that stretches back to the beginnings of organized society. James Hillman claims the same of the war gods: "Mars has no eyes" he writes in *A Terrible Love of War*. Although tribal skirmishes are undoubtedly as old as humanity, the best archaeological evidence available shows no institutional warfare—no troops organized under officers—prior to ten thousand years ago and the beginnings of urbanization and monocrop agriculture. Why do you suppose this kind of warfare begins with agriculturalization?

- What makes war attractive beyond its potential material gains?

- Why do the gods seem to need embodiment in forms like statues?

- This tale depicts Marduk, the god who killed the sea dragon Tiamat and made the world from her flesh, as enfeebled and out of date. What happens to a god in decline? Where does its numinosity go? (By the way, *tehom*, "the deep" over which God moves in Genesis, and the serpent in Eden are both related to Tiamat, the first etymologically and the second symbolically.)

- Erra's complains that people do not remember him. Do times of peace that fail to give the war god his due actually increase the chances of war? William James wrote about the need for a "moral equivalent of war." How might we salute the Warrior archetype without dispatching and risking the lives of literal soldiers?

- How does Erra's counselor Ishum succeed in calming him down?

Rousing Gesar (Tibetan)

Tsering Wangdu, Tibetan bard:

> I had a very long dream. The whole dream was about the story of Gesar. After that, I continued wandering for many years — until 1957 when I started a family and became a herder in the Tangla area of Qinghai Province. Every so often, I told stories to the villagers there.
>
> I'm old, but I'm not old-fashioned. As long as something is good for the preservation of Gesar culture, I'm in favour of it. The Gesar story must be passed on to every generation to come.
>
> Now, there are more and more people interested in Gesar, but for the most part its impact is limited to academic circles.... Another fascinating aspect of Gesar is the interaction between the performer and the audience. If it were possible to record the scene of the performance, it would aide research into Gesar. Performers wear armor, hold whips—it's as if Gesar himself has come down to the realm of humanity.

It was a happy, prosperous time for the kingdom of Ling. Starting out fatherless and in lowly origins, its ruling king, Gesar, had proved himself by restoring justice and dignity to the lands under his jurisdiction.

His list of accomplishments was long. Having won the horse race that placed him rather than his envious uncle Todong in charge of the kingdom, Gesar had fed the poor, organized the Thirty Companion warrior band, humbled invading enemies, eradicated monsters, thwarted assassins, won the hearts of the people, taught them the Dharma, saw them instructed in meditation, and promoted the wise and the brave.

It had not always been so. At one time the earth was wounded, its oceans, lakes, and rivers full of illness. The air was noxious with smoke and poison. Fish were malformed, forests were dying, and birds fell from the sky. Phantoms and evil spirits patrolled lands in which people wandered, lost, rootless, cut off from their homes and families. Some drifted around like zombies with dead eyes. Wealthy lords ruled them from behind high golden walls, and violence raged unchecked. In village and country alike, wisdom had been made to flee before deceit, greed, and naked exercises of brutal power.

Exiled by his uncle to a life outdoors among animals and trees, young Gesar woke in his tent to a vision of Padmasambhava, who had come long ago from India to bring the Buddha's teachings to Tibet.

After they had greeted each other, the great teacher told Gesar just how things stood in the world. Then:

"Even as demons overrun the kingdom, your uncle Todong has his envious eyes fastened on your throne."

"What must I do?"

"You cannot fight demons from within your own walls. You must go out into their realm and confront them there. You will be misunderstood for this, and your opponents will take advantage of it. Onlookers will perceive you as strange, deceptive, confused, and even cruel. You cannot be deflected by this. If your kingdom and the world are to be made whole, you must unseal the weapons hidden in the crystal cave of Magpel Pomra, open the teachings hoarded by Tirthika priests, distribute them to everyone, and then face the four demons on their own ground."

"I will," Gesar replied, standing.

"You must go forth without delay, for your time is now come."

And so with the backing of the land, its people, and the gods, Gesar became king and married wise and faithful Sechan Dugmo.

There have been wise kings who looked more like beggars or outcasts, but Gesar, who had been exiled in his youth along with his mother to live with wild animals, now cut a splendid figure. When he sat on the jade saddle and rode Kyang Go Karkar, the wind horse who not only ran but flew, his crystal helmet blazed, his chainmail glimmered over his armor of gold, his silver shield reflected the light of sun and moon, and the tiger skin of his quiver of deadly arrows set off the leopard skin bow case. To see him draw forth his diamond sword was to taste mortality.

* * * *

One winter night, as a crescent moon looked down from above, Gesar woke to sense his sister, the goddess Manene, in his heart. She had ridden a moonbeam down from the sky.

"Brother," she said from inside him, "even with your armor of gold, starry chainmail, lightning sword, windy horse and arrows; with your queen, generals, advisers, soldiers, and followers, you remain subject to distraction, appearance, and transience. For this world is like an ever-changing forest in which clouds alternate with clarity, night with day, sun with moon, predator with prey. Love turns to selfishness, wisdom to scheming, prosperity to greed, justice to violence. Even your brilliant kingdom will rise and fall, as will your wisdom, power, and authority. No gain lasts; no accomplishment remains stable. They require unceasing effort.

"From the four corners beyond Ling, the demons await their chance to sack your kingdom and run loose through the world. The time to confront them has arrived."

Gesar roused his army and rode forth.

In going after the first demon, Lutzen, Gesar acted on an impulse that would serve him well forever after. Instead of simply slaughtering the defenders of the demon's realm, he called out to them:

"What has Lutzen ever done to deserve your loyalty? You are the sons of gods! Wake up to who you were born to be! Throw off your fear of punishment and come with me." Many did.

He did likewise with the second ring of defenders; but the inner ring were demons beyond the reach of reason or conversion. After dispatching them, he cut the thirteen heads from the giant black demon and turned his attention to the next...

The last, Shingti, demon of the south, was the worst. "He recognizes no gods," Gesar told his warriors and new allies, "no ancestors, no beliefs, no laws, no mercy; just relentless consumption and accumulation. He sits on his bloody throne draped with a human skin, never satisfied with what he has and always reaching out for more. He can seem indestructible; but if we stand together, united, we will show ourselves beyond even his capacity to eat us."

Two messengers of Shingti entered the demon's palace to inform him of the army waiting in the plain.

"They can't stay there without paying me rent," he growled through coal-colored teeth. "If they don't, I will grind their bones into dust."

King Gesar did no harm to the messengers who relayed this to him. Instead, he thanked them; "but tell him that the land is not his, for it belongs to the people. Unless he gives it up and allows his daughter Metok Lhadze to marry my Uncle Todong, I will take him and his army to pieces."

For bringing this warning to Shingti, the messengers were flayed to death with golden whips. "The law of things," shouted the demon to his army as he hit the men again and again, "is that only two kinds of things exist: what is mine and what is not. The first must increase at the cost of the second! No wealth, no field, no pleasure or pain, no dream, no possibility, no thought shall remain beyond my grasp!"

That night Gesar dreamed of a tiny, silver-armored warrior on horseback, white streamers flowing from his helmet. "Onward!" he spurred the dreamer. "Onward!"

The next day, half the king's forces forded a river upstream. The king led the other half across an iron bridge. This vast pincer closed on the demonic defenders, charged, and proceeded to pulverize them.

Looking upward, Gesar saw Shingti climbing a magic ladder to escape into the clouds. The king flew after him on Kyang Go Karkar. Horse and rider shifted, rising, into the form of a turquoise dragon with eyes of obsidian and talons like the iron of meteorites.

Those talons cut the ladder like scythes mowing wheat. The demon screamed and plummeted to the ground far below, where he landed with a crash that made the earth shake. Gesar was right behind him.

When his tired warriors came up after their victory, they beheld the strange sight of the demon's skin staked out on the ground with four spears. "When this dries," Gesar explained, "this skin, which belonged to an evil beast, will nevertheless offer a potent antidote and medicine."

Back at home again, he ended the ensuing celebration with an invitation to all:

"Let those of us who can now seclude ourselves and meditate."

* * * *

It was a day late in autumn when Gesar announced his final departure. He felt complete.

He sang to his people that

> "You need have no doubt, hesitation, depression or fear, for nothing has power over you.
>
> "What belongs to goodness is yours everlastingly.
>
> "Your feet are restored to you.
>
> "Your legs are restored to you.
>
> "Your body is restored to you.
>
> "Your voice is restored to you.
>
> "Your words are restored to you.
>
> "Your perceptions are restored to you
>
> "Your mind is restored to you.
>
> "Your awareness is yours again.
>
> "Your power of movement is yours again.
>
> "Your power to live is yours again.
>
> "Guard this goodness and make use of it, and do not forget it when darkness comes into the world once again. What happens to you is your path."

Even now, when looked for in the sun, Gesar is there; in the moon, Sechan Dugmo; in the stars, all who helped and followed them; and in the winds, Kyang Ko Kar Kar. All are ever-present even as the seasons go round and the years continue their patient cycle.

For Reflection:

- Comment: The Epic of King Gesar ("guess-AHR") reaches back in its various versions to at least the eleventh century, around the time a second wave of Buddhism entered Tibet. It could be much older. Padmasambhava, also known as Guru Rinpoche, came from what is now Pakistan. Some consider Gesar to be his avatar. The epic is popular throughout the East, especially in China and Mongolia. Its full length is over a hundred volumes: about twenty million words. It continues to be recited and sung.

- The descent or arrival of a demigod, hero, king, or queen is a frequent mythological motif; Gesar has often been compared to King Arthur. One legend says that Gesar was sent by Amitabha Buddha because Tibet was ransacked by warlike demons. Where is Gesar today?

- The Ladakhi version of Gesar's name is Kyesar: "reborn, newborn"; also, "anther" or "pistil." Could Gesar be a cultural pioneer plant?

- In *The Idylls of the King*, Tennyson clearly believes that Arthur's goodness and blindness to shadow forced others to carry the darkness and violence that finally toppled Camelot. Why did that not happen to Ling?

- How is Gesar's approach to fighting demons different from simply killing them?

- What are examples of his success in making opponents into allies? How does he do it?

- In the Foreword to *The War Song of King Gesar*,

Chögyam Trungpa states, "When we talk here about conquering our enemy, it is important to understand that we are not talking about aggression. The genuine warrior does not become resentful or arrogant...The armies of Ling fought many wars, killed hundreds of thousands of people, and looted treasure after treasure through their skills in warriorship and their mystical power. But the sole goal was to eliminate the sources of suffering and suppression of people, and to spread and protect wealth, peace, freedom, and the Dharma for all, equally." Is this different from any other justification for warfare?

- He also claims (as do other Tibetans) that Gesar was a historical personage. Why would this matter?

- The *War Song* and other Buddhist tellings would turn the epic into an extended allegory in which demons stand for fears or desires, etc., all in confirmation of Buddhist doctrine. How might this diminish the story? What renews it?

The Fifth Province (Irish)

Eamon Kelly, Irish actor, author, storyteller:

...My ears were forever cocked for the sound that came on the breeze. It wasn't the Blarney Stone but my father's house which filled me with wonder. Neighbors and travelers were attracted like moths around a naked flame into his and my mother's kitchen.... [It had] all the rude elements of the theatre; the storyteller was there with his comic or tragic tale, we had music, dance, song and costume.

The storyteller in the kitchen, at the drop of a hat he'd tell a story. But actually, what has happened, and it happened unknown to me, is that I have to make it live for two hours in front of an audience and on a stage. I wasn't by a fireside anymore.

On radio, where I told the stories first, it didn't demand that. I was nearer to the fireside and it is still the best medium for a storyteller because, as he paints the verbal picture, the person who doesn't see can fill in the background for it wonderfully well.

A great lot of the detail which I would fill into a story is very true. I can even hear voices, almost. Strange the things that stick in one's mind, you know. Possibly, very important things were just passing by, floating by and I didn't notice them at all. It selects, you see. It holds onto some things dearly, just holds on to them and other things it dismisses.

When the Tuatha de Danaan, the Children of the goddess Danu, first arrived in Ireland, their king Nuada asked for half the island. The current occupants refused. These were Firbolg, who had themselves come to the island to escape Greek oppression. Five Firbolg couples had landed in five different parts of Ireland and gone on to found a society.

The Firbolg were a sturdy folk who fought bravely at the First Battle of Mag Tuired, but the Tuatha defeated them even though Nuada lost his right hand to the sword-wielding champion Sreng. Morrigan slew the Firbolg king Eochaidh. The Tuatha gave their defeated foes Connacht and settled down to stay.

The mutilated could not be king in those days, so Nuada stepped aside for Bres, son of the goddess Eriu and the Formorian prince Elatha, who floated to her one night on a silver boat. The Formori were a goat-headed race of one-eyed giants who preceded even the Firbolg. Ireland, the Land of Abundance, owes its name to Eriu.

Bres ruled badly. After forcing the Tuatha into slave labor to pay tribute to the Formori, he suffered greatly from the skilled tongues of Tuatha satirists. Bres was replaced by Nuada, who now wore a silver hand thanks to the ministrations of the healer Dian Cecht.

"What can I do?" Bres asked his father Elatha. "Will you help me?" He meant to raise the Formori and punish the Tuatha de Danaan.

"No. It is wrong to seek by force what you couldn't keep fairly."

Nevertheless, Bres enlisted the champion Balor and assembled an army.

The Tuatha champion was multitalented Lugh the Bright and Long-Armed. He was actually Balor's grandson through his mother Ethniu, whom Balor had locked up in a glass tower scaled by Lugh's father Cian. Balor would have drowned Lugh, but he was rescued by the witch Birog, who had let Cian into the tower. Lugh was raised by Tailtiu and Manannan, whom the Welsh call Manawydan.

Amazed at the passivity of the long-suffering Tuatha, Lugh took over as their commander.

"It is better to fall in battle," he cried to his troops, "than to live under bondage! Rally and fight for your liberty!"

When the Tuatha took the field against the Formori, their champion Balor opened his great eye and looked at Nuada. Warriors held open the eye that killed everything it saw. King Nuada withered and died.

At this Lugh loaded his sling and let fly. The stone pierced the eye, shot out the back of Balor's head, killing him, and mowed down the warriors just behind him. The Tuatha rallied.

A band of retreating Formori managed to steal the magic harp of the Dagda, a big-bellied Tuatha armed with a club and the Undry, a cauldron of never-ceasing abundance. A few plucks of the harp had lined up the Tuatha for battle, but its music could do much more. With it the Dagla could order the seasons, heal wounds, replace sorrow with contentment. Its notes reminded the hearer of family ties, enduring friendships, laughing children, companions lost in war, sweet times gone by.

The Dagda, Lugh, and Ogma of the strong arms entered a banquet hall in search of the harp. At the Dagda's call, the oaken instrument encrusted with jewels leaped from the wall it had been hung on and dropped into the hands of its rightful owner. The first chord plucked from the harp reduced the thieves to tears, the second to uncontrollable laughter, the third to snoring sleep.

Outside on the battlefield, the Formorians began to wonder why the swords and spears of their enemies remained sharp and plentiful while their own blunted and ran out. They could not see Goibniu the miracle smith feverishly forging and sharpening weapons, Luchta the carpenter cranking out spear shafts, or Credne the brazier hammering rivets and sockets.

Nor did the Formori grasp at first why their own warriors died but those of the enemy returned the next day. Dian Cecht, his two sons, and his daughter Airmed had charmed the well Slaine into which they cast the bodies of fallen warriors, who emerged healed and whole. Ruadan (who was actually the Dagda's grandson) decided to pretend to be a Tuatha warrior. He asked for a sharpened spear, then stabbed Goibniu. The smith pulled out the spear and hurled it back at his attacker, killing him. Goibniu then dropped into the well and emerged whole as the keening of Ruadan's mother Bris echoed all over Ireland. Ochtriallach rallied Formori warriors to fill the magic well with stones, but too late to turn the tide of battle.

The victorious Tuatha drove the Formori army into the sea.

Bres, who survived, agreed to make amends by promising everbearing fields, ever-flowing milk from the cows, and knowledge of how to farm. The Dagda took over as leader.

The Tuatha then established their capital on the Hill of Tara, where one day, after the coming of human beings, the High Kings of heart-shaped Ireland would rule the island.

Tara stood in the Province of Midhe, the center of Ireland, the site of reconciliation. Connacht in the west served as home to druid and wise folk, Ulster in the north to brave warriors, Leinster in the east to prosperity and trade, and Munster in the south to those skilled at crafts and horsemanship. The Fifth Province, home of leadership and discussion, beat steadily as the heart of the heart, the place of dialogue beyond conflict. Had not the Morrigan herself announced the time of peace?

This is what she prophesied as the clash of arms went silent throughout Ireland and peace crept back onto the green island:

> Peace up to heaven
> Heaven on earth
> Earth below heaven
> Everyone strong.
> The land a full cup:
> Brimming with honey
> Abundant mead
> Summer in winter
> Shield of spear
> Spear of fort
> Fort standing ready
> Turf for lambs
> Woods for beasts
> Antlers high
> Grain in fields
> Nuts on branches
> Branches heavy
> Drooping with fruit
> Wealth for a son
> Son for a home
> Back of a bull
> Bull and boar
> Wood from trees
> Trees for fire
> Fire on the cliffs
> Cliffs shining bright
> Fish in rivers
> Hostel by the river
> Welcoming and roomy
> Grass growing in spring
> Many horses in fall.
>
> A bond with the land
> Land of long hills

Rugged headlands flowing
Stories honor the land.
"What news?"
"Peace up to heaven."

For Reflection:

- Some scholars interpret the replacement of Firbolgs and Formori by the Tuatha de Danaan ("TOO-ha day DAHN-ahn") as an echo of the Gaels replacing the original tribes in Ireland. This may be true at the human, cultural level, but what is going on archetypally when one race of gods supplants another? (The battlefield name is Mag Tuired ("moy-TUH-rah"): "Plain of Pillars.")

- In what way does the loss of the war god's hand foreshadow the replacement of Nuada ("Noo-AH-dah") by the genial Dagda ("DOY-dah")? (In Norse mythology the war god Tyr ("teer") also loses his hand.)

- In the first battle, Morrigan ("mor-EE-ann") kills the Firbolg king Eochaidh ("OH-kheh," with the "kh" something like the "ch" in "Chanukkah"). Why would a witch goddess do this? (She shows up later in the Arthurian cycle as Morgana le Fay.)

- For what purpose does the enslavement of the Tuatha by Bres ("bresh"), who makes a bad king but a good agricultural god, unwittingly repeat the Tuatha oppression of the Firbolgs?

- The evil eye is a frequent motif in folklore. What psychology does monocular vision imply? (According to a legend, when Balor fell, the eye on the back of his head burned a hole in the ground that filled with water to become Loch na Súl, or "Lake of the Eye.")

- Eriu, Balor, Dagda, and other pre-Christian Irish gods come forth arrayed in nature imagery. What does this suggest about the early Irish relationship to land, nature, and place?

- When Lugh knocks on the door of the great hall at Tara, he asks the doorman for admittance: "I am a poet." Tara doesn't need a poet, replies the doorman. Lugh then asks: What about a war chief? A wheelwright? A blacksmith? A swordsman? A harpist? A wizard? Each time the doorman rejects him until Lugh asks, "Who is here who can do all of these?" That gains him entrance. Lugh is sometimes compared with wily Mercury the Trickster, but what other archetypal presence might be his? (London, town of many ancient oracles, might have been named after Lugh.)

- Ochtriallach ("OOCH-three-ah-lock") leads the attack on the well of healing. Who are his counterparts today?

- The Dagda's harp could be thought of as a character in the myth. Why does it have two names: Oak of Two Meadows and Foursquare and True?

- *Coicead*, the Irish word for "province," also means "fifth." "The notion of a 'fifth province,'" wrote Mark Patrick Hederman in 1985, "is an aesthetic analogy which describes a space which is neither physical, geographical, nor political. It is a place which is beyond or behind the reach or our normal scientific consciousness. It therefore requires a method and a language which are *sui generis* both to reach it and to describe it." According to former Irish president Mary Robinson, the ancient idea of the Fifth Province is about openness, tolerance, conflict resolution, pluralism, and acceptance of difference. *Midhe*, pronounced "meath," means "center." The Fifth Province is an example of a mythologem being updated and retold. How can it continue to be retold without losing its connection to the land itself?

- Morrigan prophecies a time of peace that evolves from the founding of the postwar Fifth Province—but she also speaks a prophecy of apocalypse: what determines which will hold sway?

> I shall not see a world
>
> Which will be dear to me:
>
> Summer without blossoms,
>
> Cattle will be without milk,
>
> Women without modesty,
>
> Men without valor.
>
> Conquests without a king. . .
>
> Woods without mast.
>
> Sea without produce. . .
>
> False judgments of old men.
>
> False precedents of lawyers,
>
> Every man a betrayer.
>
> Every son a reaver.
>
> The son will go to the bed of his father,
>
> The father will go to the bed of his son.
>
> Each his brother's brother-in-law.
>
> He will not seek any woman outside his house. . .
>
> An evil time,
>
> Son will deceive his father,
>
> Daughter will deceive . . .

- This striking contrast of visions suggests a choice of paths, one peaceful and one ruinous. How has this choice played out in Ireland? How does it play out today in the world at large? What would Morrigan say about this contrast?

- What does this myth suggest about the influence and importance of stories and storytelling?

The Domestication of Rübezahl (German)

Richard Hacken, European studies bibliographer, translator, and librarian:

> My family name "Hacken" is also the German infinitive, hacken, meaning "to chop"...
>
> Through the centuries, forest motifs have evolved to support various social, political and cultural themes and counter-themes. The imagined forest is a contradictory forest. To early Germanic tribes, the forest was an object of worship – a temple of holiness – while to others it was the home of evil and danger....
>
> ...It has been the asocial haunt of wild men, sociopaths and thieves, but it has also been the stage for social justice. It has been a moral exemplar but also a place to avoid. The woodlands have been seen as a source of industrial materials; or they have been a place of rest and recreation. The forest has been a source of food and medicine on one hand, and a venue of death on the other.
>
> The structure of a tree has been the well-rooted inspiration for branching charts such as family trees, grammar trees and hierarchies. German anthologies have been literally called "forests." And most recently, in echoing the famous claim of Thoreau that "in wildness is the preservation of the world," Germans, and not only the German Green Party, have increasingly seen the forest as both barometer and fount of ecological salvation.
>
> We often say that we can't see the forest for the individual trees. Yet a forest is more than any given number of

trees. It is a collective noun, a landscape that subsumes every fern, butterfly, tree, rock, soil type, underground ore deposit, clump of lichen, fallen branch, shrub, insect and wild animal within it. Woodlands provide potent and vivid symbols of life, death, regeneration, social process and collective identity.

"What in the world happened up here??"

Whenever Rübezahl came up from underground, which he did every now and then for a break from the halls of glittering treasure, the streaks of minerals in stone, the rubies and diamonds, and the bustle of other busy gnomes, he liked to watch the birds and other wild animals of the forest, even the hunting wolves. He liked the rain on his skin, the whoosh of the wind through the thick tree branches, the banging of stones he rolled down the hills just for fun.

This time, though, he looked upon a changed landscape.

The forest was gone. Those who had cut it down and taken it away as lumber lived in villages full of thatched-roof cottages with smoking chimneys, each lined up on a road. He saw oxen grazing behind slatted fences, high hedges masking fronts of homes, dogs running across square meadows.

Although none of these small two-legged human beings had thought to ask whether he or the other beings of the forest minded the encroachment, he decided to get to know them better. He changed his appearance into that of an old human field hand and walked down to the homestead of his new neighbors.

Once he had gotten to know this farming family, he cultivated, planted, and grew crops for them. At first they were amazed by the height of the plants and the loads of plentiful vegetables he brought forth, but they wasted so much of what the good earth provided that he couldn't bear to work for them any longer. So he moved on.

He worked for another neighbor as a shepherd. He led the sheep to pleasant pastures, kept careful track of them, and never lost one to a wolf. But their owner kept trying to lower his pay, so again he moved on.

For the local judge he caught crooks and kept the roads safe from thieves and highwaymen until he realized that the judge was himself a thief, at which point the judge had him jailed. Changing his form, Rübezahl poured himself through the keyhole like gas through a pipe and escaped.

"So that's what they are like," he muttered to himself as he headed back underground. He decided, though, to have one more look around.

The daughter of the king visited a meadow in the forest to pick wildflowers with her friends. Finding a flower-decked marble pool one hot day enticed her to go for a swim.

As she entered the water, nymphs pulled her down out of sight. The grotto vanished back into forest. The king grieved when he heard about it.

Once underground, the princess, now wrapped in satin, listened as Rübezahl in the guise of a handsome prince told her about the vast jewel-packed palace all around her. She had been frightened at first, but now...

Had Rübezahl thought about himself, he might have felt wonder at how human he had become. Before he had been content to appreciate. Now he must possess...

At first, despite her capture, getting to know him and this glittering place was fun. Then, having moved beyond the glow of adventure and attention, she became despondent. *She must be lonely for the company of her own kind*, Rübezahl realized.

He went out into the forest, dug up the roots of some radishes, carrots, and turnips, packed them into a basket, and brought them to her.

"Take this wand," he said, "and touch them, and they will become your friends."

She tapped a turnip, and up sprang the likeness of her friend Brunhilda. More friends followed, and even a dog and a cat.

Problem solved, thought the gnome.

The princess noticed, however, that her "friends" gradually looked increasingly pale and haggard. Soon they could not even speak anymore. In the end, they were dried-up roots.

"I will bring you fresh ones," Rübezahl told her. He went out, but he came back with a sad face. "The radishes, carrots, and turnips have all been gathered in for the year by our neighbors," he said. "I am sorry. I will plant new vegetables so you can have new friends in the spring." She turned away.

While waiting for the spring and wandering about alone, she thought more and more often about Prince Ratibor. They were supposed to marry. He would be in mourning for her now, she realized. *I have to get out of here*, she thought. *My charming captor lets me walk up above now and then, but never very far. And he pushes me to marry* him.

One day, when spring was finally blooming overhead, she appeared to him in bridal dress. A veil hid her frown.

"My love! Are you ready to wed me?" Rübezahl asked eagerly.

"Yes, but we must have guests. So pick me turnips so I can transform them." He left to gather them.

Now alone, she pulled forth a turnip she had picked during a recent walk. When she tapped it with the wand, it turned into a neighing horse.

She leaped upon its back and rode out to meet the prince. A magpie converted from a root had delivered to him the message to await her.

Rübezahl returned to find her gone. He guessed what had happened and took winged form so he could survey the countryside. From above, he glimpsed her form on the back of a cantering horse.

He smashed together two clouds to form a thunderhead. *If I cannot be with her, I will electrocute her!* But the clouds had their own mind and dissolved into rain. They wet roads, hedges, orchards, and meadows where once a forest had stood.

The underground palace he had conjured for her was now a lonely place. He stamped his foot three times and the palace crumbled to dust. All that remained of her presence was a few of her footprints in the sand.

For Reflection:

- Comment: This tale originates in the German and

Czech mountains. Although sometimes considered a mountain storm being, Rübezahl is a gnome: monstrous demons who guard underground treasure. Gnomes are similar to the Greek Cabiri, whose hands were tongs for metalworking, and to those German Kobolds who, though smaller, inhabited mines. A hotel in Bavaria is named after Rübezahl.

- Swiss physician Paracelsus linked the gnome to alchemy. In active imagination, Jung was told by gnomelike beings to stop working so much on himself consciously so the unconscious could build something new. Does something similar happen in this tale? What alchemical images haunt this tale?

- What does the princess learn during her captivity? How does she apply it?

- What might the imprisonment of the princess in the magic palace signify psychologically? What might her escape signify?

- How is the princess different at the end of the story than at the beginning?

- What would a Rübezahl complex be like? How the princess deal with hers?

- Ecologically, what could Rübezahl's reaction to unchecked development be symbolic of? Might he be the genius loci of the place itself?

- How are the injustices committed in this tale ultimately rooted in what happens to the forest? How is the hewing down of the forest linked to the fate of the characters in the story?

- Should Rübezahl have refrained from direct dealings with humans?

Chapter Eleven - Nature and Earth

Myths always originate in specific geographic locales. As originally local stories, they continue to carry the traces of where they came from. We tend to forget this, especially when reading is our primary relation to myth.

However, myths also describe the characteristics of the cosmos.

What if the gods are actually personifications of those living characteristics? Not only Sun, Moon, Earth, Sky, etc., but also Wisdom, Trickster, and Depth? What if all gods and spirits and powers everywhere are abroad in the world all around as well as active within?

Pahto the Lawgiver (Yakima)

Katrina Miller Walsey, Yakima storyteller:

> My name is Katrina Miller Walsey. I'm a member of the
> Yakama Nation. My Indian name is Yut-te-le-low-wit.
> With my job I do a lot of storytelling. We have done sto-
> ries; they're from the Pushami storybook and we do
> some about the beavers, the big frog, and these stories
> are of the landmarks that are within the Yakama
> Reservation, or that we can see. "Oh, that's where it
> came from"—and so we can see how the animals had
> made these landmarks.
>
> Long ago the animal people were here before us and so
> these two beavers, they didn't like each other very much
> and they're looking around for what they're fighting
> about.... Pretty soon they made it all the way down to the
> Yakama Valley. And they made a river. And do you guys
> know what river that is? Yakama River! So that's how
> the Yakama River came down from Cle Elum is because
> these two big beavers were fighting and they still
> weren't done fighting. They came to the ridge. Since
> they were fighting so much they broke through that
> ridge and broke it through and it made a gap. Do you
> guys know what gap that might be? Union Gap!

No one on two legs knows how it started because no humans
were around to see it. Perhaps Wasco was jealous of Pahto's affection for Sun. Perhaps it was something else further back.

Whatever it was, the two mountains stood near enough each
other that Pahto was in striking range. Wasco leaned over and, blowing her top, knocked Pahto's head into flying boulders and tumbling
rubble.

Then Wasco took all Pahto's belongings: bears, deer, elk, salmon, trout, pine nuts, huckleberries, and, in short, everything living that Pahto had tended on her ample flanks. When it was over, the headless mountain stood stripped.

This made her sullen. From her emanated supercharged summer thunderstorms throwing gigantic bolts of lightning, heavy winter snowfalls, and spring floods that dug at the ground and washed away plants and animals alike. By the time our ancestors arrived on the scene, they couldn't live in the flooded valleys, near the raging riverbanks, or on the denuded mountain slopes.

All this time the Creator had been watching. Knowing that the newcomers could not survive if Pahto remained wounded, and feeling sorry for her too, the Creator gave her back her bears, deer, elk, salmon, trout, pine nuts, huckleberries, and much more besides. With her thus restored the people moved in around her.

She was still headless, however, so the Creator gave her White Eagle for a head.

Healed Pahto became a source not only of life and growth, but of wisdom and law. Into her ears the offspring of White Eagle cried news of whatever they saw around the world. On her flanks flourished the humans she looked after. Past and present, high and low, inner and outer revealed their movements to her mind.

Wasco saw her regenerated sister standing in the sunlight with eagles circling her summit and knew the attack had been futile. She would never do it again.

For Reflection:
- Pahto is known today as Mt. Adams in Washington, and Wasco as Mt. Hood. Both are glaciated, potentially active, many-layered volcanoes in the Cascade Range of Washington state. Mt. Hood was named after Admiral Samuel Hood; two U.S. Navy ammunition ships have also been named after him. The aggressiveness of Wasco seems to be reflected even in its later, European name. Mt. Adams was named by accident; the name had been intended for Mt. Hood but landed

on Pahto instead. Coincidence, or an underlying myth-ic-geologic wisdom rooted in the presence of the land?

- Does the all-too-human relation between unanswered injustice and lingering resentment somehow find pro-totypes in the pre-human natural world? Does restora-tive justice?

- Aldo Leopold coined the phrase "thinking like a moun-tain" in his *Sand County Almanac*, the same book that discusses the value of land-centric ethics. "The cow-man who cleans his range of wolves does not realize that he is taking over the wolf's job of trimming the herd to fit the range. He has not learned to think like a mountain. Hence we have dustbowls, and rivers wash-ing the future into the sea." How do we think like a mountain?

- What eagle-like qualities does Pahto gain from the Creator?

- What allows us to translate injustice into a source of wisdom, farsightedness, and care?

- What effect does Pahto's transformation have on her former attacker?

Aristaeus and the Bees (Greek)

Kiki Dimoula, Greek poet:

> My homeland is more the neighborhood of Kypseli, biographer of almost my entire life, assisted by its co-biographer Pythia Street. I lived there as a child, as a married woman, and as a mother; my present solitary home is just two steps away. That street corroborated all that my inner Pythia prophesied and all that it could not, leaving me thus totally unprepared.

I write very rarely. Only, in fact, when the sheet of paper suffers an existential crisis and threatens, if I don't surrender to it, to bury me alive under its whiteness. Looking back over my own youthful efforts, I realize how often emotion monopolized them, leaving the deeper, essential residue lying stagnant.

Life's essential length is only a few pages long, as succinct as a line of verse and as brief as the title of a poem.

People say to me, "It's a consolation." And I wonder how I can console them because I myself am inconsolable. I would be very happy if one of my poems suddenly offered someone a shady rest stop, a breather in our interminable march under the murderous, scorching heat of the superfluous.

Aristaeus was a boy born of a courageous shepherd and a god, and nursed by the Seasons and by great Gaia. Like most bright boys, he found himself devoted to many different activities at various times.

Just now his passion was keeping bees, an art he had learned from the nymphs who had nursed him. He loved to watch bees at work in the hives he built for them. Their humming always pleased him. Now and then he wrapped himself in protective leaves and extracted sweet yellow liquid from the dripping honeycombs.

He came home one day to find his hives empty of bees. At this he burst into tears. He sought the sacred fountain in which his mother lived.

Cyrene had fought a lion to protect her flocks. She had been loved by Apollo himself. She knew everything. She came forth from the waters and sat by him.

"My son, you must have a talk with Proteus," she said. "Here is how you catch him...." The two then poured a libation onto the altar of Poseidon.

Proteus awoke on the beach to find his arms chained to the ground and a shepherd standing over him expectantly.

"Who are you and what do you want? And how did you know to bind me like this?"

"Never seen a blue beard before. —My mother, the naiad Cyrene, told me. She knows everything. I am Aristaeus, and I have a question for you. Where did my bees go?"

Proteus sighed. "They died of sickness and hunger, for you have angered the nymphs of sad Orpheus, husband of his lost bride Eurydice. When you chased her, she ran and failed to see the poisonous serpent at her feet. She is now a shade in Hades. The nymphs have cursed your bees because of this."

He remembered a lovely woman he had glimpsed one day and pursued until she ran out of sight. She had died because of it! Because of him. Remorse made his heart ache.

"How can I remedy this?"

"Pick four choice bullocks from your herds on the heights of Lycaeus and the same number of unyoked heifers. Set up four altars by the shrines of the nymphs. Upon these altars sprinkle the blood of the sacrificed oxen and cows whose bodies remain in the grove. At dawn give Leith's poppies to Orpheus as a funeral offering and apology, sacrifice a black ewe, and revisit the grove, where you will honor Eurydice by slaying a calf."

Aristaeus followed these instructions exactly. To his joy he saw swarm after swarm emerging from the carcasses of the butchered cattle. The bees hung in buzzing bunches from the branches of the trees.

For Reflection:

- The father of Aristaeus was Apollo, who left. The boy was raised by Chiron the Centaur, who taught him the arts of healing. How would it have impacted Aristaeus to be the son of an absent father and raised by a wounded one?

- How would you describe the character and behavior of

Aristaeus, whose name contains the same root as "aristocracy"? How is he different after visiting Proteus?

- Eurydice becomes an Underworld goddess like Persephone when she dies and descends. Her husband Orpheus, a god of the lyre, follows her down but is unable to bring her back. What is the nature of the misdeed committed by Aristaeus against Eurydice?

- Myths eternally recur as responses to blind spots in collective consciousness. Colony Collapse Disorder caused by widespread pesticide use in warming environments has decimated bee colonies all over the world. How might the blunder of Aristaeus parallel one of our own?

- Why a sacrifice to Eurydice?

- Why *four* oxen and *four* cows? Why a black ewe and a calf? What is Aristaeus really sacrificing? (In another variant, Proteus tells him to sacrifice a young bullock just getting his horns.)

- If nymphs personify the aliveness of creeks and streams, in what state of health are these beings today?

- Comment: The story of King Erysichthon complements the Aristaeus myth appropriately. The king cut down the sacred groves of Demeter, after which he was cursed by Nemesis with a hunger so insatiable that he ate all the food in his kingdom, then his subjects, then his family, and then himself.

- Given that raising cattle in huge feeding factories contributes substantially to global warming, what might the advice to sacrifice tell us about how to bring back the bees?

- Another story has it that an older Aristaeus goes to Ceos to build an altar to Zeus Icmaeus (Moist Zeus) to relieve a drought. Where is Aristaeus today?

The Island of Peace (Haitian)

Charlot Lucien, Haitian artist, poet, cartoonist, and storyteller:

> My father, who used to be an agronomist, dragged us —
> me and my two brothers — all over the place in the coun-
> try to do outreach and education with folks, and that's
> how I got to know the country.
>
> ...I found that the best way to revive or express or
> process those memories of Haiti was through story-
> telling. So I incorporate both folktales as well as social
> storytelling which is based on my observations of Haiti
> as well as cultural challenges that Haitians here have to
> experience, dealing with displacement, language barri-
> ers — French, English, and Creole, languages that they
> have to process — and different kinds of cultural influ-
> ences, both from Europe and from the US here.
>
> Haiti is an agricultural country, so "green" is literally
> what I see, although we do have to deplore huge defor-
> estation issues now, it's literally an ecological disaster.
> But in my memory, my father, again, was an agronomist,
> so green is what I lived in or lived with: the plants, the
> trees, the mountains....And green is also the color that I
> use as background of many of my paintings, so green to
> me is: well, that's my color.

Ever since Christopher Columbus (whose eyes, it was said, bled
continually) brought slavery and hunger to Haiti, the island has suffered one calamity after another. Revolutions, invasions, coups, dic-
tatorships, earthquakes: Haiti, whose name means "mountainous
land," has seen them all down centuries of struggle for independence
from domination by aggressive outside powers.

During the worst of it, native priests draped an altar with white cloth and sent up a prayer to Damballah Ouedo, father of the Loa spirits and of the creation. They asked for relief from conflict and violence.

"Cilla," he said to one of his wives. "Please take to my people the secret of peace."

The Master of Waters called forth a whale. This would be Cilla's ride down to Haiti.

The whale swam slowly through the sea, moving with such lulling rhythms and gentle plashings that Cilla could not help falling fast asleep. It was a long trip.

The whale pulled up near Port-au-Prince and stopped, waiting for Cilla to rise and disembark. She did not.

The whale was afraid to interrupt Cilla's sleep, so it waited. And waited. And waited...

The whale waits still, with Cilla curled up asleep on its back, but it waited so long that they've changed into Gonave Island. On a clear day you can gaze seaward from Port-au-Prince and glimpse the island's mountains forty miles to the west.

Although Cilla has not yet awakened to give the people of Haiti the secret of peace, it makes itself felt to some extent. Runaway slaves found sanctuary on La Gonave. Colonizers avoided it for centuries; pirates made a base there, but then left.

True, it lacks freshwater and is now underpowered and overgrazed, but these problems continue to make it unattractive for exploitation. People who visit sometimes feel a strange calm descend. Peaceful gatherings do well there.

No one knows when Cilla will awaken, but when she does, she will be well-rested.

For Reflection:
- Fringed by reefs, La Gonave ("gah-NAHV") is roughly thirty-seven miles long and nine wide, hilly and mostly of limestone. It is one of many "sleeping lady" rock formations found around the world. Why do so many people see such shapes?
- Because myths circulate widely, we tend to forget that

they start in particular places. Olympus would be unthinkable without the Acropolis. How does this myth connect to the physical nature of the island?

- Why is it that places so often evoke highly specific states like anxiety, vertigo, calm, or enlightenment?

- What do you imagine the secret of peace might be?

- California appeared as an island on maps for centuries after cartographers knew otherwise. Depicted in fiction as ruled by a warrior queen, the Isle of California withstood invasion for centuries before the Spaniards, who lost many ships off the coast, finally landed successfully. The Americans personified the state as armored Minerva on the Great Seal of California. Do some places repel colonizers? Resist mistreatment? (See my Animate California Trilogy and my book *Terrapsychology* for more about the power and presence of place.)

- Global Renewable Energy, Ltd. plans to develop the island into an industrial city, cruise ship port, and golf course complex, with rustic-seeming waterfront "villages" for tourists, resorts, casinos, and an international airport. If Cilla awakened, what would she think of these developments?

Oceanic Mazu (Taiwanese)

Lung Yingtai, Taiwain Minister of Culture:

> With traditional value structures relatively intact, Taiwan has been able to develop modernity well rooted in its own tradition... Beginning in the 1950's when China closed its doors to the outside world, the literature of Taiwan became the source of inspirations for Chinese living in Hong Kong, Macao, Malaysia and Singapore.
>
> In an open society, art has its own idiosyncratic charac-

ter which resists the will to shape from authorities. In a Taiwanese temple, it's not unusual to see a Taoist deity sitting side by side with a Buddha and a Christian saint; likewise, art in Taiwan is also rather laissez faire. While respecting the autonomy of the artists, the Ministry of Culture provides all sorts of incentives as well as subsidies — sending artists abroad for international exchanges, supporting the publication of authors, encouraging digitalization and the transformation to the new media, etc.

Is Kafka's *Metamorphosis* political? Is *Le Petit Prince* political? Is Laozi's *Tao Te Ching* political? If what we mean by being "political" is an expression of attitude about life, yes, art is always political. If being political narrows down to a focus on public issues or management of the masses, then I would say not all art is political.

She was Lin Yuan's sixth daughter and seventh child, born on the twenty-third day of the third lunar month. Her name was Lin Mo-Niang, "Silent Girl," because she emerged from the womb without crying.

Sometimes those born with a special gift or affinity come to it late, as though it needed extra time to deepen and develop. Lin Mo-Niang was a late swimmer even though she grew up on Meizhou Island surrounded by water. By her teens she swam like the fishes caught by her father and brothers.

She also possessed a kind of oracular knowing about rough seas and storms. She often stood on the shore, her red garments a guide to boats sailing through the strait lying between the island and the mainland. Many a grateful sailor saw her even in inclement weather, waving to signal the way to safety through driving rain and wind.

It was said she also came in with the gift of healing, that she was a devotee of kindly Guanyin, and that she saved several officials from a marauding sea serpent. Perhaps her true father was a dragon.

By age 16, Lin Mo-Niang knew she would not follow in the footsteps of marriage. She would be neither wife nor mother.

When she was 28 years old, an unusually powerful typhoon rumbled in while members of her family were out fishing in the strait. The strengthening winds roared through the rafters and bowed over trees outside. Everyone thought the missing fishermen were done for.

Everyone but Lin Mo-Niang.

Accounts differ about what happened next. Perhaps, somehow, all are true.

Some say that she lay down and went into a deep trance. By reaching with her spirit across land and water with the power of her prayers, she rescued three of her brothers, carrying them against all the powers of storm and wave and sea, before her concerned mother noticed her lying unnaturally still and awakened her. To Lin Mo-Niang's sorrow she could not save the fourth brother, and he drowned.

Others say that when her family despaired, she left the house, ran down to the shore, dove into the raging sea, and swam out to save her father and brother after their boat fell apart in the storm. But she perished in this brave attempt, and her body washed up later on Nankan Island.

Still others say she succeeded in her rescue, and that she rescued many others, and that, on the ninth day of the ninth lunar month, when her time on earth was over, she climbed a mountain and ascended into the heavens to become immortal Mazu, who calms the stormy seas, protects sailors from shipwreck, looks after dying children, restores health to the sick, brings rain to farmers' crops, preserves their plants from hungry pests, and catches bombs in her skirt to guard the people of Taiwan.

In paintings and murals Mazu wears a red or golden robe; in sculpture, the jeweled robes of an empress with a staff or tablet in her hand. On either side of her stand Thousand Miles Eye and With the Wind Ear, demonic generals who agreed to work for her after she vanquished them.

Mazu welcomes the immigrant and the traveler even when no

one else will. To this day her worship bridges the gap between the island and the mainland.

For Reflection:
- Saving lives is usually considered heroic, but what about Mazu's patience, her certainty about the direction of her life, and her compassion in healing others? Her willingness to risk becoming a ghost rather than an ancestor by refusing to start a family?

- What would be a psychological read on saving people from drowning?

- In Taiwan, red holds associations of happiness and luck. What else might it symbolize?

- To a literalistic mind, the various versions of a story cannot all be true. To a mythic consciousness, however, they all can be in a metaphoric sense. In most versions of this myth, Lin Mo-Niang descends into the depths and then rises to the heights. What might this indicate?

- Comment: Worship of Mazu extends to at least 1500 temples, three religions, twenty-six nations, and two hundred million people throughout East Asia and far beyond. An island, a city (Macao), and even a TV series have been named for her. During the Cultural Revolution in China she was worshipped underground and often at great personal risk. In an age of fortified borders and nationalist jingoism, she remains available to welcome the immigrant, the wanderer, and the exile.

Rakhsh and Rostam (Persian)

Vesta Sarkhosh Curtis, Curator of Islamic and Iranian Coins at the British Museum and Joint Editor of *IRAN, Journal of the British Institute of Persian Studies:*

Persian myths are traditional tales and stories of ancient origin, some involving extraordinary or supernatural beings.

The geography of this region, with its high mountain ranges, plays a significant role in many of the mythological stories... The myths which appear in the part of the *Avesta* known as the *Yasht* include some tales of very ancient pre-Zoroastrian origin, probably belonging to the pagan Indo-Iranian era. They describe the heroic deeds performed by the gods, kings and warriors against both supernatural and human enemies. Many of these myths reappear in the *Shahnamen (Book of Kings)*, an epic in rhyme by the poet Firdowsi, which was completed in AD 1010. The *Shahnameh* in particular plays a crucial role in Persian life and culture, not only because of its considerable literary merit, but also because of its importance in preserving the myths and history of a very distant past in the Persian language.

Stories from the Rustam saga were very popular for the decoration of tiles. By the end of the nineteenth and the beginning of the twentieth century a genre of paintings by folk artists, the so-called qahveh khaneh (coffee house) paintings, were also reproducing scenes from the *Shahnameh*. In all these ways, Persian myths continue to prove their relevance to the beliefs, social attitudes and tastes of the Iranian people today.

Rostam used a simple test to see if a horse was strong enough to bear his burliness: he pushed a hand down on its back. If it gave way, even a little, he moved on to the next.

He had tested in all the herds in Zabulistan and was frustrated. Could no horse living carry him forth on his mission?

Perhaps *this* colt could? Rostam had just spotted him standing behind his mother, a powerful, slim-waisted, lion-like mare whose ears stabbed out like unsheathed daggers. The colt resembled her in build but carried a long, proud tail as he walked on hoofs that gleamed like steel. Rostam's eye noted a saffron coat dotted with sunlike spots of rose. Sharp black eyes gazed steadily from an alert head. The colt stepped lightly but looked to be stronger than an elephant.

Rostam uncoiled his lasso and threw it, and the mare charged him. He opened his mouth and jaws and from the bottom of his belly emitted an echoing shriek like a lion's roar. She stepped back, startled, as he made his way closer to the colt.

Rostam stood next to him and pushed down with one hand on a sturdy back that did not move. The horse did not even blink.

"How much do you want for the horse?" Rostam asked the herdsman. The man took a moment to answer. He was still surprised that this white-haired stranger had been able to get near the colt, let alone touch him.

"This colt is worth all of our country. If you be Rostam, he of whom I have heard, then take him—his name is Rakhsh—and go relieve the sorrow of Persia."

"Thank you. I will do that."

The army of the Turks was overrunning the country when Rostam appeared, mace in hand, on the field of battle. Rakhsh bore him so close to the enemy shah that Rostam pulled the man from his horse and hurled him to the ground in disgrace. After that the Turks sued for peace.

Rostam's next mission was to rescue his liege, the reckless shah Kay Kavus, a lesser son of a wise and peaceful king, from the White Demon of Mazandaran.

"You would think," Rostam said to Rakhsh, on whose back he rode, "he'd escape from anything with that flying throne of his. Well, maybe the eagles that pull it got tired." The horse snorted.

After riding all day, Rostam dismounted in a field of reeds. Setting his sword nearby, he made himself comfortable on a patch of ground and drifted into sleep.

The cooling body of a lion lay nearby when Rostam woke. A large chunk had been bitten out of its back.

"I appreciate this," he told Rakhsh while waving a sword-callused hand at the body, "but this mission is too important for you to risk your life that way. You should have awakened me." It had not occurred to him to make sure he slept far away from any lion lair.

* * * *

Sometimes a sickly branch grows from a good root. King Qobad ruled with integrity, but Kavus sought slaves and booty. He sat on a golden throne propped on crystal legs and collected horses and drank too much wine.

Kavus heard demons disguised as minstrels sing alluring songs about Mazandaran and decided he must conquer that country. His nobles disagreed, but not even wise Zal could enlighten the shah.

"Never mind, I will go do it myself with the mightiest arms and army in the world," boasted Kavus.

Initially, he won; but after looting Manzandaran for a week, he faced twelve thousand angry demons and was decisively defeated. In prison he ate bran, drank no wine, and enjoyed no treasures.

He did manage to dispatch a messenger to Zal. The note acknowledged his foolishness and Zal's wisdom.

"You had better go and retrieve him," Zal told Rostam. "Go with great care, and beware the wiles of evil Ahriman, whose dark minions are everywhere."

The way was hot and difficult, and soon both Rostam and Rakhsh found themselves parched, so much so that Rostam's tongue swelled within his mouth. He dismounted and prayed for help and was delighted when a ram appeared. It led him to a thirst-quenching stream where the two drank their fill as Rostam splashed cool water over his overheated horse. Rakhsh snorted with relief.

"No more fighting without me," Rostam told him as he bedded down for the evening. "Wake me if anything interesting happens." Rakhsh nibbled grass and pretended not to hear.

The dragon who lived nearby saw them from across the plain

and decided on a meal. From snout to tail, its length spanned more than that of a dozen elephants. Rakhsh saw it coming and pawed the ground loudly to wake Rostam. The dragon turned invisible.

"What is it?"

The horse looked across the plain, but nothing stirred there.

"You woke me for nothing." He released his sword and turned over.

The dragon reappeared. Rakhsh pounded the ground near Rostam's head.

"What?"

He saw nothing.

"Why don't you sleep at night, Rakhsh? If you wake me for nothing again I'll cut your legs off."

The dragon drew so close Rakhsh could see the flames on its breath. He whinnied loudly and woke Rostam once again. So near was the beast that even in the dark, trained eyes picked out a dragon-shaped outline of nothingness.

Rostam drew his great sword and faced it.

"Tell me your name," he called out.

"I own this place," growled the dragon, "and the sky above it. Eagles do not fly here, nor does any beast escape. Tell me *your* name."

"I am Rostam, son of Zal, son of Sam, of the family of Nariman."

Now visible, the dragon leaped at him.

Rakhsh fastened his teeth in the dragon's shoulder, halting it. As the monster rounded to bite the brave horse who would not let go, Rostam sprang forward and swung his blade under the scaled neck. The dragon's head bounced away as the long serpentine body shuddered and collapsed. Fountains of poisonous blood splashed over ground, grass, and defenders, who quickly found a clear stream in which to cleanse themselves.

"Enemies are many and years growing fewer," reflected Rostam as he remounted. "May the Great God see us through this journey."

Many indeed were the enemies: a pretty wine server who turned out to be a lethal hag; a band of marauding horsemen; a mounted demon war chief; hellishly possessed guardsmen; and the helmed and armored White Demon, whose heart and liver Rostam cut from the cooling corpse.

Once freed, Kavus and his Persian soldiers joined with reinforcements to regroup and attack the armies of Mazanderan again.

Reins released, Rakhsh carried Rostam into the fray. His spear pierced the armor of the enemy king, who quickly used magic to turn himself into a boulder of granite. Rostam jumped to the ground, hefted the boulder, carried it, and set it down before the Persian shah.

"Change back," Rostam told the rock, "or I will shatter you."

The king blinked to behold his champion holding the arm of the defeated Mazanderan.

* * * *

When Rostam's half-brother Shaghad asked to marry the daughter of the king of Kabol, the court felt trepidation. Shaghad was strong, a good rider and skillful warrior, but the astrologers predicted a dark future for him. The king ignored them and blessed the marriage.

Now that Shaghad was his son-in-law he felt safe discontinuing the tribute of cow skin paid annually to Persia.

He was wrong. The Persian court demanded the tribute be paid with no further delay.

"It's my brother's fault," Shaghad told the king. "Always the one to search for glory; always the one to look down on others. Let us discuss how to rid the world of him."

Rostam was delighted to see the brother he hardly knew ride into his camp one day.

"How goes the world with you?"

"The King of Kabol just insulted me at a royal banquet," Shaghad complained with assumed bitterness. "He drank too much wine and went on about what he called our lowborn family."

"I will make him pay for that and seat you on his throne, brother."

"Your reputation is such that if you merely threaten him, he will apologize."

The king of Kabol sent a messenger inviting Rostam to parlay on neutral ground.

They met there, and the king removed his boots and turban and bowed low. "I was drunk. Please forgive me."

"I forgive you. It is over."

"Thank you. Will you feast with me today and hunt with me tomorrow? I know a place nearby with open country and plenty of game. I would be honored if you accompanied me there."

Rostam's hunting party approached a plain recommended by the king. Below the wide sky the riders searched for their quarry.

Without warning, Rakhsh grew tense and reared.

A touch of his rider's whip prodded him reluctantly forward— to lose his footing as his forelegs plunged through what had appeared to be brush. As they went over the edge, the cover fell and Rostam saw swords and spears just before they pierced man and horse alike. The king's men had placed them in hidden pits dug to trap the hero.

Rostam looked up and saw his brother's gloating face. "The heavens have finally dealt justly with you," Shaghad called down. "After all the blood you've spilled, your own now enters the ground." The king's face appeared beside him.

"My son Faramarz will avenge me upon you, evil king," Rostam shouted upward.

To Shaghad he said, more gently, "Please grant me a dying request. String my bow and place it by me with two arrows so I can ward off any lions that come looking for easy prey."

His brother complied. Rostam quickly notched an arrow and shot, pinning him to a plane tree.

And so three died together: bold Rostam, teacherous Shaghad, and ever-loyal Rakhash, who perished trying to save his friend.

For Reflection:
- Like many a hero, Rostam encounters—constellates, perhaps—enemies with attributes like his: the lion, the

white-haired demon, the glory-seeking brother. Through it all, Rakhsh (whose name means "luminous") remains a loyal and, at times, wiser companion. How do you suppose the horse views their relationship? What would he say about it?

- Rostam, the son of Rubadeh and Zal, braves seven key trials and serves five monarchs. Like Thor and other archetypal Heroes, he breaks down borders that divide people from each other. Why would a Hero serve an undeserving monarch? Would horse sense prevent this?

- Comment: In wandering bands of horses, the lead mare stands at the head, with the stallions in the rear ready to drive the other horses to safety while the mare confronts the danger.

- Horses are renowned for their loyalty to us and to each other. A legend says that to find the most loyal, the Prophet Muhammad loosed a hundred thirsty horses near an oasis and blew his horn. The first five to return, the honorable Al Khamsa, gave rise to all the Arabian breeds, including those that fed Bedouin children with their own milk. Why are horses so loyal?

- An Islamic tale relates that Allah ordered the South Wind to condense so He could make fine horses from it. He hung happiness from their forelocks, made them fast in retreat and in pursuit, and placed riches on their backs and flight in their legs. What do this image and the myth of Rakhsh and Rostam tell us about the archetypal qualities of the horse?

- The word "nightmare" recalls old legends of the intuitive and intelligent fright of horses. Are nightmares sometimes inner warnings of our horse sense about our straying into dangerous situations?

- Traumatized combat veterans, sexual abuse survivors, prison inmates, drug addicts, and people with many other kinds of emotional wounds have found healing and strength by spending time (not necessarily riding) in the presence of horses. Why would this be?

- How else might horses act as emissaries between us and the natural world?

The Plants Make Medicine (Cherokee)

Lloyd Arneach, reservation-born Cherokee storyteller:

> We would sit and listen to them: Uncle George would tell a story, and Uncle Dave would tell a story, and it was like watching a tennis match going back and forth between them. And without realizing I started learning the stories. "Tell the story about how Bear lost his tale." "Tell about Spear Finger." "Tell about the animals' ball game."
>
> And eventually, there was a lady who came to the Cherokee—not Cherokee, she had actually come up from Alabama. And she realized the young people were not learning the old stories of our people, so she gathered a small group of us together and had us learn a story well enough to tell it. And then normally once a weekend during a month in the winter she would take us out to outlying communities, and we would share stories.... She was instrumental in getting a lot of us to learn the old stories well enough to tell them to a group of people.
>
> I feel blessed because of all the stories that would come to me.

You know, humans and other animals used to talk to each other. Talk to and listen to each other. They were neighbors and family, and they acted like it.

Then the humans began to kill their kin for skins and food and trophies of the hunt. It was easy: the humans just walked right up, slew their former friends, and took their flesh, their skin, their bones, even their heads.

At first the animal people were bewildered. Then they were shocked. Finally, they got angry. They met in councils to discuss this threat.

After gathering the bears, White Bear said, "I know you all want to make war on the humans. But consider this: they have spears and bows for killing. How can we stand against them?"

"We'll make our own weapons!" someone roared. This seemed like a good idea until someone else growled, "We can't. Our claws get in the way." Younger bears voted to remove the claws, but the older bears said, "No, we need them for fishing and climbing."

In the deer council overseen by Little Deer, no talk surfaced of fighting the humans, but the deer people agreed that every human wanting to kill a deer must either ask the spirit of Little Deer for permission or apologize humbly after the deed. Humans who failed to do either would suffer aching bones and joints, permanently.

The reptile and fish people agreed to transmit to humans frightening nightmares filled with serpents. The insect and bird people agreed to spread various diseases among the heedless two-leggeds.

However, the plant people, who were listening to all this animal talk, saw the issue differently. It was wrong, they believed, to harm humans for killing for food. The animals did that themselves, and look at all the green things they ate. Nor did the plant people appreciate all the talk about poisoning humans or infecting them with horrible diseases. (At this point the bear people were still arguing about what to do next. For all anyone knows, they still are.)

"This is what we will do," the plants decided in their generous, earthy manner, "we who are so accustomed to giving, nourishing, and providing. Each of us will be an antidote for one of these ailments. When the humans get sick, we will serve as their medicine."

For Reflection:

- Although it's not mentioned in the myth, what do you suppose changed for humans that we became so reckless in our killings off of animals? How, perhaps unconsciously, do we suffer for it? What does it do to earthly ecosystems?

- Over the past few years, quite a few stories of animals harming humans have circulated in the news. Is it possible that such encounters constitute an instinctive and natural response of some kind to the ongoing destruction of habitat?

- Why did the animals not take council with the plants?

- Comment: As more and more forests are mowed down, more and more unseen cures go with them. It is possible that human industries are destroying today the remedy to an illness that will inflict itself upon millions of us tomorrow.

- California is the only state in the U.S. with an extinct animal on its flag. The last California Grizzly was shot in Tulare County in the 1920s. What might be the underlying meaning or message brought by the persistence of the imaginal bear now that the flesh-and-blood grizzly can no longer speak to us?

- The common image of evolution is of an upward, progressive movement from "lower" to "higher" forms of life. In this myth, however, it is the lowly plants who feel the most compassion for humans. How would you interpret this?

- Many specialists in plant medicines maintain that plants are not only active bringers of healing, but mentors and emissaries who speak to us in our visions and dreams about our relations with the natural world. How might this be explored?

A Family of River and Stone (Bulgarian)

Krassi Zourkova, Bulgarian novelist:

I grew up in a tiny town in the Balkan mountains where, if you opened the window at night, you would hear crickets and frogs. It was magical. I think that's when my fascination with Bulgarian folktales began. The *wildalones*, in particular, are extraordinary creatures who are vicious by nature but are also susceptible to falling in love, like all of us.

...The everyday can be quite bleak as it is. Art nowadays, literature included, has a penchant for showing reality in its most gruesome, ugly, hopeless. I believe art can be more than a mirror to our grim predicament. It can—and should—give hope, capture the good in us, guide us.

Rila always was willful. Especially when she married Pirin. Her parents disapproved, but she married him anyway.

They disapproved mainly because they knew nothing about him. He came from an unknown family living in lands far away. Rila was their only child.

"Forget it," they told her. "You cannot marry a man we don't even know."

Instead of ceremonies to celebrate the joining of two families, instead of the blessings of proud parents, an elopement.

Eventually, the strong-willed young couple had rebellious children of their own to deal with. Two of them: a girl named Mesta, and a boy named Iskar. They fought a lot.

"Won't you help me with them?" Rila asked her husband, but he spent most of his time out hunting.

"I need to make sure we can eat and be warm," he said sternly. "The rest is up to you."

Isolated, alone, and with rowdy children to deal with: this was a recipe for disaster.

The next fight pushed sad Rila over the edge.

She raised her hands and intoned, "Let you be separated so you never see each other again. Let people fear and run from you. Let frogs, fish, and lizards run over you. Let me turn to stone so I will not have to shout at you anymore. Let trees be my children, and my body be soil and stone. Let my tears rush forth into springs. And let my husband Pirin become a mountain, tall, apart, and silent."

And so it was. The parents grew and hardened into mountains, and the children subsided into running rivers, Mesta hissing southward through the hills to lift her father's mood, Iskar leaping wildly northward and down to the Danube until he was halted by a dam.

For Reflection:

- Comment: Bulgaria occupies the western side of the region known in ancient times as Thrace, the homeland of mythic Orpheus and Eurydice and of Bendis, the Thracian Artemis. Thrace in turn was the goddess daughter of Oceanus and Europa. Bulgaria bridges Greece to the west and Turkey to the east. Metals and gems have been worked there for at least six thousand years.

- Why is there so little support today for the frustrations of mothers left alone to deal with their children?

- A modern and rather anthropocentric way of viewing the relationship between myth and place would see the myth as a purely human invention to explain the features of the place. But what if this is backwards, with the story suggested by the character of the land?

- Rila is the highest of the Balkan Range that divides much of Bulgaria. To what extent might family and even societal conflicts be pre-reflected in the contours of the places where they occur?

Yosoji and the Girl in White (Japanese)

Ueda Masaaki, Japanese Professor Emeritus of Kyoto University and Chair of the Association for the Study of Sacred Forests:

> In Japan, divinities might be of mountain, sea, or river. People find divinities in nature. This religious faith still exists. I think then that we can understand shrines as points in which nature, divinity, and human beings come into contact.
>
> In the collection of Japanese classical poetry known as the Manyoshu, compiled in the 8th century, the kanji we now use to write jinja or yashiro (two words for "shrine") were both pronounced "mori," which means "forest." This suggests that since antiquity Japanese people have believed that forests were places where divinities were enshrined.
>
> In Shintoism we see divinity in everything—it's pantheism. Through this pantheism it is possible to coexist... Shintoism has a belief in symbiosis that includes not only coexistence but creating and producing together. We call this "tomomi."

Like many in the village of Kamiide, Yosoji's mother was very sick with smallpox. He was worried about her. He went to consult with the magician Kamo Yamakiko.

"What can I do?" he asked the older man. Yosoji was sixteen.

"Find a stream flowing from the southwest side of Mt Fuji. Near the source you will see a shrine to the God of Long Breath. Draw water there and bring it back for your mother to drink."

At the place where three paths cross, Yosoji stopped to consider which to take.

A girl in white came out of the forest and walked up near him.

"Follow me," she said. "I know why you are here."

She led him through the forest to the stream pouring from a cleft in a rock. There, she bade him drink the clear-running water and to fill a gourd with it. Then she led him back to where they had met.

"Meet me here again in three days because you will need more water."

He bowed deeply, thanked her and went home.

After five visits to the shrine and the healing waters, he was relieved to see his mother growing strong and healthy once again. So did the previously ill people of his village.

For this he received much praise, as did the magician, but Yosoji remembered the girl and wished to thank her more than he had been able to.

By now he could find his way to the stream and the shrine, but when he got there, he saw that the water had dried up.

After a moment or two, he knelt in prayerful gratitude. Then he got up.

The girl was there, smiling.

"I cannot begin to thank you enough for what you have done for all of us," he said. "May I know your name?"

Her only answer was a smile and a wave of a branch of camellia. As she did these things, a cloud descended from the forested side of Mt Fuji, gathered around her, and lifted her into the air. She floated away toward the sacred mountain

Yosoji knew then who she was. He knelt again, facing the mountain, and whispered:

"Thank you, Mt. Fuji."

In answer the camellia branch landed beside him.

He took it home and planted it.

It grew into a tall tree. Dewdrops from its leaves were said to restore vision.

For Reflection:
- Features of the land personify as characters in many myths and legends. In animistic cultures this is seen as

quite natural, a blessing from the place itself. More than one shaman has dreamed about being summoned by a mountain. (My books *Terrapsychology* and *Rebearths* offer everyday examples.) What kinds of worldviews preclude such an intimate view of the soul or spirit of place? What kind embrace it?

- A story persists in Hawaii that when people get lost, they should take a nap so Pele, the volcanic goddess of the islands, can appear in their dreams to give them guidance. Why would a place help us?

- Comment: The year 1025 saw a severe smallpox outbreak throughout Japan.

- Ueda Masaaki distinguishes between folk Shinto and the official sort hijacked by the Japanese military for use during World War II. Why is co-option of religions so common throughout world history? What makes them attractive to ruthless opportunists?

- Mt. Fuji contains hundreds of monasteries and has been a site of contemplation and spiritual activity since antiquity. What about sacred places enables them to act like spiritual emissaries and locales for transformative reflection?

Cangjie Discovers Writing (Chinese)

Ming Di, poet and translator:

> ... Political tragedies impact me from very early on but how to turn the emotion into power in poetry is hard— I didn't have the strength to do so until I reached middle age...

> In recent years I try to look beyond the political events and look more into myself and into ancient history and

mythologies—modern history is too distant for me to grasp the true meaning and too close to get the true essence either.

...Poetry writing is not as simple as black or white, male or female. Voices of poetry are as rich and complicated as a full spectrum of colors, full wavelengths of lights; translators navigate in the sea, face the waves and cross them. Translation broadens the view, the vision, the horizon— that's how it affects my own poetry writing.

Cangji made a useful historian and scholar for the Yellow Emperor. He had four eyes, four pupils, clear intent, and a sharp mind. And he was willing to try out new ideas.

Which is just as well, because the Emperor came to him one day in a state of frustration:

"I am sick of the *quipu* method of trying to convey information by tying ropes in knots," he stated. "Would you attempt to invent something better?"

Cangjie went to one of his favorite places to think—the bank of a river—and sat down. This time, however, his pondering failed to produce anything worthwhile, so he decided to forget about it for now and go hunting on Mount Yangxu.

He had not been there long when he noticed a tortoise crawling by. The pattern of veins across its back got his attention.

Watching them, he imagined patterns and relations between them. They were not just lines on a shell: they were images.

He quickly found other examples of orderly patterns: the flights of birds, the meanders of streams and rivers, their branchings and spirals, the rise and dip of the land, the stellar constellations up above. All things, it seemed to him, spoke silently in a common language of pattern, image, configuration.

He began to draw images. Each time he finished one he went out looking for more. He studied the roundness of sun and moon, the angles in birds' claws, the netlike connections in the webs of busy spiders.

When he finished, he had a language of characters to show the Yellow Emperor.

"Congratulations! These are splendid! Please show them to the premiers of the nine provinces so they might learn how to write them."

In this way writing came into the world.

For Reflection:

- Go outside and look for primary patterns: spirals, circles, angles, nets. How many can you find? It's surprising how much of the world's amazing fractal complexity derives from a relatively small number of basic forms.

- What is the relationship of such form-images to archetypes?

- Did the natural world teach humans how to write?

- Why four eyes and four pupils?

- A document from the Warring States period (475 – 221 BC) reads: "When Cangjie created the characters, millet fell from the heavens and ghosts wailed in the night, and as human wisdom increased, the virtue of humankind diminished." In his book *The Spell of the Sensuous*, David Abram argues that writing began a long development of conceptualization that eventually separated humanity psychologically from direct conscious contact with the natural world. What do you think of his argument?

- Given the knack for reading patterns that appears in every human cultural group, is there really such a thing as an illiterate society?

Chapter Twelve - Apocalypse and Renewal

Apocalypse *derives from a Greek word that means an unveiling of what has been hidden. In many mythologies the world ends when the formerly unseen comes to the surface to battle with the dominant gods. The old ruling principles give way so the new ones may rise.*

Collapse and destruction represent only half of apocalypse, however. As the tales below suggest, the other half is renewal as a new order of things, even a new world, rises from the wreckage of the old.

If we face apocalypse consciously, we journey toward new adaptive possibilities for living. We also dream the gods onward by giving them a modern form, as Jung suggested. But if we refuse to face apocalypse at all, we risk being caught in a literal, disastrous ending.

The Visitors (Anatolian)

Hera Buyuktasciyan, Turkish (Armenian/Greek) artist and story-teller:

> When you tell the story it's not your story, it's someone else's story, so you don't carry the responsibility of the whole thing.
>
> From their childhood up until they died, they [grand-mother and her friends] would come together to have coffee. And every week, without exception, they used to share the same story with the same words, same sentences. This was really amazing me a lot. It's not the story but the way they did the storytelling. It's like it stuck in their mind, and the memory is a kind of instrument, which is playing non-stop in the mind.
>
> Wherever I go, I'm a type of Other. What does it mean, a community? What does it mean to become part of a community; is it necessary or not? It's not only about an identity-based community. A bazaar space, a gallery, an opening, creates a community also. Wherever people come together it creates a community. But at what point do you become a part of it?
>
> Water, it makes connections. And it's not only used to be exiled or leave somewhere. It could also be used to come back to the dock again.

Daylight was just giving way to twilight as the two tall, hooded strangers walked into the Phrygian village and knocked on the door of a large, freshly painted house with a neat garden inside the sturdy fence. They sought lodgings for the evening.

Their murmured request was answered by the door closed in their faces. They went next door, knocked, and received the same treatment.

Having knocked on every other door in the village, they approached a small, dilapidated hovel and rapped on the weather-beaten door. It opened to reveal the kindly features of an old woman and an old man. Their garments had seen better days.

"Yes?"

"We are looking for a place to stay for the evening. May we enter?"

"Come in." The door opened wider to admit them.

After making sure his guests were comfortably seated, Philemon went out back to kill and dress a goose. Only two were left, but obligations were obligations. At least no one would go hungry tonight.

They cooked and dined in the same small room. Here Baucis poured out some of the last wine left and served it to the hooded visitors with plates of bread and cheese. She could not see the visitors' faces well, but they accepted the cups and plates with polite thanks. She sat down to chat with them.

A loud squawk interrupted the conversation. The goose selected by Philemon slipped from his grasp and ran into the house. Before he could catch it, the bird threw itself into the lap of the tallest of the visitors, who laughed and petted it.

"Do not take the life of this poor goose," he requested in a courteous baritone as his companion nodded. The old man entered the room and, hearing this, looked over at his wife for her response, but she was staring at her cup of wine. Somehow it had refilled itself. More than once...

The meal was sparse, but the conversation pleasant. The wine never ran low.

"And now," said Philemon when they had finished, "we would be happy to show you to your room. We know traveling can be wearying, although we haven't done it in some time now."

"Actually," said the smaller visitor as both stood up, "there is something *we* would like to show *you*."

Their hoods fell back to reveal glowing faces, one wiry and clever, the other magisterial and strongly marked. The visitors suddenly seemed much taller and broader. Light filled the room.

With a jolt Baucis and Philemon recognized their faces from the images on sacred statues. The couple knelt together. Before them stood Mercury, messenger of the gods, divine trickster, psychopomp, governor of commerce, giver and taker of knowledge, and master of the mysterious craft-science of alchemy. At his shoulder towered the taller figure of Jupiter the Allfather, omnipotent king of heaven and earth.

"Please forgive us for serving you such simple fare," muttered Baucis from behind hands raised in devotion, as were her husband's, "but we had none better, O gods."

"Forgive you? You have blessed us and shown us every hospitality. Please rise now, gather a few of your possessions, and ascend the hill behind your home. A flood is coming to consume this entire village."

Without a word the couple rose, packed a few simple items, and left for the pathway up the hill. They climbed until they stood at the top an arrowshot above the village. They turned to look back down upon it.

The flood had struck while they climbed. Not an expensive house, well-kept yard, or professionally trimmed orchard had been spared. A bog sat where the village had been. An eerie quiet prevailed. The trickle of receding waters was the only sound to reach their ears.

Looking about, they spotted where their hovel had been. A gleaming temple lavishly decorated with carved pillars stood in its place.

They walked down to it, faced Mercury and Jupiter, and bowed to the gods.

"Ask for whatever you wish," said the god with wings on his feet.

"May we remain here and guard this place?" They had talked on the way down the hill.

"You may. Furthermore, when you reach the end of mortal life, you will be transformed together into intertwining trees, one linden and one oak, and shade the entrance to our holy temple."

<u>For Reflection:</u>
- Although the Roman poet Ovid clothed this myth in Roman garments, it probably sprang from Phrygia in what is now central Asia Minor. Göbekli Tepe, an immense shrine of stone carved by hunter gatherers nearly twelve thousand years ago, stands unearthed in Southeast Turkey. To the northwest, Çatalhöyük was raised as one of the oldest settlements in the world. Farther northwest at the Golden Horn stands Istanbul, the site of former Constantinople. Could something about Asia Minor welcome residential temples?
- What does it mean to lock out the gods? Why could this be cataclysmic?
- What are some of the deeper implications of showing hospitality to the strangers who knock?
- Why Mercury and Jupiter and not some other gods?
- Why an oak and a linden?
- In Goethe's *Faust II*, the alchemist Faust offers Baucis and Philemon a farm if they will agree to move so he can develop their land. They will not: their ancestors are buried there. Agents of Mephistopheles (the Devil) arrive to relocate them, and during the confrontation they die. Where does this happen today?

The Cosmic Hunt (Sami)

Elina Helander-Renvall, Sami scholar, author, and storyteller:

> Sami mythology is a local expression of a larger pattern of ideas, knowledge, beliefs, rituals, legends and symbols. Many myths are connected to shamanism.

According to the Sami worldview, nature and the entire world are alive. This explains the existence of many spirits and divine beings. These spirits reflect the consciousness, creativity, and purpose of the cosmic world that we live in.

Regardless of how we define myths, the myths are available to us. In their daily lives, people often search for explanations for their existence and identity, for the origins of their activities, for the plans of gods, and for certain truths to emerge. Myths are able to give answers that modern knowledge systems cannot afford to give. In postmodern times and beyond, myths help to stretch the boundaries of the prevailing worldviews and modes of thought.

Although Diermmes has the entire sky for his hunting grounds, he follows only one animal: the golden-antlered reindeer Meanndas-pyyrre.

At one time Diermmes hunted and fished down here. His steps left valleys in the ground next to the trees that fell over wherever he walked. He makes Thunder, the giant sound that follows the lightning whose arrows he shoots from his mighty bow. In his other hand he grasps the rainbow. He stands larger than ten gigantic fir trees.

Now he hunts in the sky, and his dogs run baying before him.

Meanndas-pyyrre wears a coat of shining silver on his snowy body beneath his coal-black head. Do not look into his eyes, or they will burn you. His pantings deprive you of speech; his running deafens every ear. Fortunately, he too is up in the sky.

So are others. Favdna hunts Saarvva the Elk up there. Galla and his sons also chase the Elk.

One day Diermmes will close to within arrow range of Meandas-pyyrre. He will draw an arrow on his bow and set it loose.

When the first arrow lands, mountains will crumble and rivers will run backwards, upstream. The rains will stop falling, the land will dry out, and the lakes and the oceans will be empty.

When the second arrow lands, what mountains remain will boil where new mountains will rise. Ice thought eternal will melt, and the North will burst into fire.

When the dogs seize the celestial reindeer, and when Diermmes draws his knife and stabs golden-antlered Meandas-pyyrre in the heart, then the world will have run its course. The stars will fall from the sky. The moon Aske will dim and turn black. The sun Beaivvas will go out. Ash will cover the earth.

For Reflection:

- Comment: Favdna is known to Western astronomy as Arcturus, Saarvva the Elk as Cassiopeia, Perseus, and the constellation Auriga, and Galla as Sirius. The Mesopotamians linked Arcturus to Enlil, sky father inventor of the mattock. The Greeks placed him at the knee of the constellation Boötes the herdsman and also described him as a leader of hunting dogs. Perseus, a monster-killer, flew the magical winged horse Pegasus. The crook of Auriga resembles that of a shepherd or goatherd. Cassiopeia spurned Apollo and was therefore cursed to utter warnings no one believed. It would seem, then, that many motifs found in the Sami myth also show up in other pantheons concerning the same stars under different names. (Diermmes is not a star or a constellation but a lightning-limned hero god like Thor.)

- Comment: The Sami (formerly called Lapps or Laplanders) are indigenous Europeans who live across and around the borders of Norway, Sweden, Finland, and northern Russia. Traditionally, they trap, fish, hunt, and herd goats and reindeer. Today's Sami live in step with modernity but resist agriculture. They are and always have been a peaceful people. Christian missionaries have had little luck influencing them. Their culture remains intact and vital.

- What does it mean for gods of the earth (associated sometimes with the past or present) to move to the heavens (future)?

- Why golden antlers? What is the hunter really hunting, collectively?

- The Wild Hunt is a motif found throughout Northern Europe. In one version, Wotan leads the slain across the sky with their dogs and horses. The Hunt presaged a catastrophe. Does the Sami myth imply that the catastrophe is inevitable, as natural as the hunt itself?

- Jung interpreted apocalyptic myths as signals of the collapse of old "gods" or ruling principles: the wearing out of old archetypes as collective consciousness outgrows them. What can such an interpretation tell us about this myth?

- Given the disastrous effects of global warming, might this myth contain an element of foreshadowing, a message from the collective unconscious or even the world unconscious? Is it coming true literally?

- Where is the image of renewal in this myth?

The Wooden Ones (Mayan)

Victor Montejo, Mayan anthropologist, poet, folklorist, author:

> I grew up speaking Popb'al Ti', and I went with my mother to various Maya ceremonies and festivities.

> I learned the names of the sacred places and the stories of our culture heroes, like Q'anil, the Man of Lightning. We learned all these stories from the elders, who passed on to us through the oral tradition the knowledge of the world around us and the greatness of our people.
> I received my basic education at the seminary, which

was run by Benedictine priests. I learned a great deal there, but the distance from my family and the culture shock of being in a different town where the spoken Maya was different from my language gave rise to some adjustment problems... It was at this school that I discovered world literature and found in ethnohistorical books such as the *Popol Vuh* and the *Annals of the Kaqchikels* that these ancient stories bore great similarity to those in the oral tradition in my small village.

This was the beginning of my interest in writing and of my strange dreams. In one dream I found myself in the middle of a cornfield showing the people (the corn) books on whose covers my name appeared as author.

"Earth!" called out Plumed Serpent, Hurricane, Newborn Thunderbolt, and Raw Thunderbolt.

In response, the land and its mountains and valleys rose from a mist and solidified. The waters receded. Sky and land drew apart.

"It is turning out well," Plumed Serpent commented as he surveyed their work. "Let us populate this place with birds, jaguars, deer, pumas, snakes, and other beings." They came to be as he spoke. "And let them all have homes," and they did, some high, some low, some near water, some among bushes and trees.

The Maker, Modeler, Bearer, and Begetter soon noticed a certain silence in this world. Nobody spoke.

So the Creators said, "We made you and named you. Name us and praise us."

From the freshly made world and its creatures burst forth a cacophony of chirps, whistles, barks, growls, roars, hisses, and wingflaps—but no names. The Creators were not happy.

"Let us try again, and this time we will make a giver of praise, giver of respect, nurturer, and provider."

They tried....and tried. After many false starts they finally asked

Grandmother Day, Grandmother Light, Possum, and Coyote for assistance.

Again words of power brought new life into being.

The manikin-like creatures possessed round heads, two arms, and two legs, all made of wood carved from reed and coral tree pith. They could speak and breed, and they did.

They bred so many children that the world was soon filled up with wooden people who rushed to and fro and spoke a lot. But they spoke with nothing in their hearts. Their minds remained dark and barren of knowledge. When bad things happened to these people they did not weep; when good things happened they felt no joy. They didn't feel much of anything.

Nor did they remember their Creators. They walked all over the world oblivious to its beauties, delights, and foundations. They felt no curiosity about the gods who watched them. They did not hear the language of the animals, of things, of the world. They had no idea where they came from, and so neither could they know where they were going.

When it started to rain and did not stop, they scarcely looked up from their activities.

"You hurt us," said the turkeys and other animals the wooden people had consumed, "and ate us. Now we will eat you."

"You made us chase sticks," said the dogs, "and beat us when you wanted and starved us. Now we will chew on you."

"You rubbed us raw," said the grindstones; "you burned us black," said the griddles and cooking pots. Water jars, hammers, axes, houses, harnesses, blocks of stone, trees sawn for lumber, and many other things joined the chorus of protest against the thoughtless exploitations perpetrated by the wooden ones.

The wooden people sought safety from the rising waters by seeking the tops of roofs and the insides of caves, but the roofs collapsed and the caves spit them out again. Trees they tried to climb threw them off. The animals chewed and stung them, the pots burned them, the headstones carved for forgotten ancestors fell on them and crushed them.

The people ran, but there was nowhere to run: the entire world had set itself against them. Although numerous, they perished one and all. When they were dead, outraged objects smashed their faces, and outraged animals ate the remains.

The waters receded. Chirps, whistles, barks, growls, roars, hisses, and wingflaps sounded once again throughout the slowly drying world.

"Let us try again," mused the Creators. "This time we'll use corn."

For Reflection:
- The universal flood is one of the most frequent mythological motifs in the world. What does it indicate culturally? Psychologically?
- Why would the gods need praise and remembrance?
- The manikins were the proto-humans who came before us, but are there not eerie similarities between their behavior and ours?
- Why were the wooden people eradicated? What did they do or not do that led to their demise?
- What could it mean that the things of the world possess speech and sense? How could we grasp this in contemporary terms and concepts?
- Does it ever feel to you like personal objects—computers, cars, doors, appliances, etc.—have suddenly turned against you? How do you explain that to yourself?
- Why corn for a creative substance?
- Do you think a new sentient species will come after us? What might it be like?
- The canard that most of the Mayans perished despite their highly advanced civilization has circulated for decades in and out of academia. Recent studies suggest that only the Mayan upper classes disappeared. Could this myth have foreshadowed the mysterious disaster?

Danced Premonitions (Korean)

Kim Kyung Ju, Korean poet:

> Outside you could be a respectable citizen, but as soon as you walk into an internet cafe you are the devil incarnate with Devil 666 as your handle. When our previous president committed suicide, it was a reflection of the reality that we are not a united country or people, that we are really isolated from each other and have dangerous and violent sides to ourselves. We suffer from dissociative disorders, where our awareness, identity, and perception of reality often disrupt and break down. Of course I'm not only talking about Korea. All industrialized societies have these problems.

> Yes, I want to talk about the world as a ghost, to create the atmosphere and point of view with the feeling that I am dead. Realism talks about the world as we see it. For example a ninety-year-old lady crosses the road when the signal is red. So she probably knows and senses the rules but is no longer interested in them. She is living in her own world beyond reality. I am interested in capturing that world.

When King Hon'gang got in his carriage and left the capital for a trip, music wafted over a kingdom of prosperous cottages under clear skies. But as he stopped to rest on the way home, clouds gathered overhead and a fog rolled in, a fog so thick it hid their roadway.

The king asked his oracle about it.

"It's the changing of the dragon of the Eastern Sea," the man said. "It will clear if we do what is appropriate to do."

The king promptly ordered that a temple be built there for the dragon.

The clouds parted and the fog cleared, which is why that place is known as Kaeump'o, Port of Opening Clouds. The dragon and his seven sons sailed down from above and landed near the carriage to thank the king with music and dance.

Ch'oyong was one of these dragon sons, and he decided to go with the king back to his court. The king gave him a beautiful wife and made him a minister.

Unfortunately, the wife was of such beauty that she caught the eye of the Demon Spirit. He seduced her one night in human form right before Ch'oyong came home.

The upset husband responded by composing a song-dance on the spot:

> In the bright moon of the capital
> I enjoyed the night until late.
> When I came back and looked in my bed
> I saw four legs in it.
> Two are mine,
> but the other two: whose are they?
> Once upon a time that was mine;
> what shall be done, now these are taken?

He then withdrew quietly, wondering what to do.

The Demon Spirit took the initiative and came to see him.

"I slept with your wife," he told Ch'oyong, "and yet you did not show anger or become violent. I am impressed. So much so that whenever I see a likeness of your face anywhere, I will avoid it from now on."

When they learned of this, citizens of the kingdom posted images of Ch'oyong's face on gates throughout the kingdom to keep misfortune at bay.

One day the king decided to honor the Eastern Sea dragon even more. He ordered built a temple called Manghaesa (Sea View Temple) on the eastern side of Yongchu (Spirit Eagle) Mountain. Then he went out again, this time to P'osokchong (Abalone Stone Pavilion).

When he arrived there, the spirit of South Mountain appeared to him. The spirit's name was Sangsim (Fortunate Manifestation), and it danced.

"Is it not wonderful?" the king asked his attendants, but they were puzzled because they could not see the spirit. So the king imitated the dance for their benefit, and they passed it on to the people. They call it the Reign Dance for Sangsim. He also had its movements carved in stone, after which it became known as Frosty Beard Dance.

Traveling again, the king visited Kumgangnyong, Diamond Pass, where the spirit of the northern hills showed up to dance the Jade Blade Clasp.

During the banquet at the palace, the earth spirit came to perform the swirling steps of the Earth Elder.

The mountain spirit performed the last dance at the banquet. The name of the dance, roughly translated, means, "Those Who Rule with Wisdom Understand and Flee in Great Numbers."

"Aren't these dances marvelous?" said the king, the ministers, the attendants, and the people. "They must be a good omen for us!"

They said these things just before the kingdom fell.

For Reflection:

- Comment: This tale comes from the Silla Kingdom period (57 BC – 935 CE) in Korea and has been performed ever since.

- Some who hear this story wonder why Ch'oyong is so passive when he sees his wife in bed with a demon. How would you interpret his behavior? Does it reflect a passivity at large in the kingdom?

- Is the demon truly grateful for Ch'oyong's lack of anger, or is he ridiculing him?

- Is it enough to honor a synchronicity, dream, or sign, appreciating it for its own sake? James Hillman called for honoring each dream image entirely on its own terms. But what if it is actually a warning to change course?

- In 2011, Steve Jobs, a founder of Apple, died of complications of islet cell neuroendocrine tumor, a curable illness if treated in time. For nearly a year he ignored medical treatment recommendations and tried a fad diet instead. He also consulted a psychic. Around the world, people frequently perish from "spiritual" cures that do not cure. Does the myth address this issue?

- The final catastrophe is preceded by a number of appearances of spirits who dance, first at the coast on the edge of the kingdom, and finally in the very heart of it. Where did the people go wrong? Could they have prevented the outcome?

Re Reorders the Cosmos (Egyptian)

Ahmed Abdel Mu'ti Hijazi, Egyptian poet, professor, author, critic, and editor:

Portrait

Who is this drunken man,
the one who tilts his cup to savor the last drop
His face is in
the light
asking forgiveness of the dark
The redness of his eyes pours over the walls
He pleads for another cup
He bows down intoxicated, singing like a bird,
as if, nightly, he were acting out the debt of his fate
for a creditor behind the veil...

Once Set had killed Osiris, murder was loose in the world, and humans began to partake of it.

This greatly displeased old Re of the silver bones and gold flesh. He oversaw a Golden Age coming to an end, and humanity, born from one of his tears, along with it.

"I cannot look at this anymore," he told the other gods. "They would do away even with me! To seize the throne upon which I guide the world!"

"If you wish to punish them," said Nut, oldest of all of them, "summon Hathor."

Hathor was therefore apprised of what was afoot on earth. So great was her rage that she changed into the form of lethal Sekhmet.

"I will take care of it," she growled.

She descended to the desert where the plotters for divine power had gathered, then wreaked fearful slaughter among them with claws sharper than hardened metal.

Watching the blood fly, Re grew nauseous and sad. He had not created these foolish people to have their end come to this. But now that Hathor-Sekhmet was among them he could not halt her frenzy with words.

He quickly summoned messengers and dispatched them to Yebu to bring him great quantities of red ochre.

When it arrived, he ordered priests to grind it while maidservants crushed barley for beer mash. He mixed them.

He went out very early the next morning and poured the red beer over the fields to the height of three palm trees. Then he withdrew once again to the heavens.

Sekhmet woke and, seeing the mash, took it for blood and lapped it up in great quantities. She became cheerful and lapped up more...and more...and more until she was so drunk she could not continue the slaughter.

She lost her catlike shape. As Hathor once again, she heard herself emit an inebriated "Moo" before she passed out. (Some of the human survivors remembered forever after to include beer in their ceremonies.)

"What will you do now?" the gods asked Re. "There aren't many of them left, but they still need you."

"I don't care. I've done enough for them. It's time for me to retire." He summoned Nut, who came in the form of a great cow.

The human survivors who cared about the greatness of Re took up bows and arrows to finish off the Sun God's enemies.

"I appreciate this," he told them, "but I'm still leaving. Farewell, my children, and if you ever wish to praise Me, look to the cosmos."

So saying, he ascended on the back of Nut, who rose and expanded until she was a sky filled with blessed realms, Fields of Offerings and Reeds for the dead, Thoth posted aloft to represent the light of Re in the darkness, a rejuvenated Earth under Geb's wise care, the Infinite Ones to oversee all, and glittering new constellations.

For Reflection:

- Comment: This story is found in the *Book of the Heavenly Cow* (1323 BCE) that only exists now in fragments found in Egyptian tombs. A first fragmented version was discovered in the burial chamber of Tutankhamun. A reference to Re's ascension has been found in the Pyramid Texts.

- What would be some contemporary examples of coveting the throne of Re?

- Is all human suffering somehow foreshadowed in Re's tears?

- Hathor could be thought of as an Egyptian Aphrodite (or vice versa). Why would human usurpation of Re's power and authority upset her so much?

- How is it ironic that beer, a grain product with which Fertile Crescent civilization began, should be an antidote to humanity's demise?

- Why does a Golden Age so often alternate with one of decline?

- Brian Swimme and others rely on Thomas Berry's idea of a New Story for humanity, one that emphasizes appreciating the beauty and grandeur of the cosmos. Is it possible that such a New Story might include reimagining a very old story like this Egyptian myth?

For the ancient Egyptians, the stars were close, living presences.

The Fifth Sun (Aztec)

Miguel Leon-Portilla, Mexican anthropologist and historian:

> My uncle was Manuel Gamio, the founder in Mexico of modern archaeology, as well as cultural anthropology. He introduced me to Teotihuacán, where he had done a great deal of work and where he discovered the Quetzalcoatl pyramid. I would also accompany him to Cuicuilco and other archaeological zones.

> I found questioning like that of the pre-Socratic Greeks: "Do we really speak the truth on earth? To what place will we go where death does not exist?" Questions of this type are so beautifully expressed in Nahuatl [Aztec] poetry.

> [from *The Broken Spears: The Aztec Account of the Conquest of Mexico:*] "Ten years before the Spaniards first came here, a bad omen appeared in the sky. It was like a flaming ear of corn, or a fiery signal, or the blaze of daybreak; it seemed to bleed fire, drop by drop, like a wound in the sky. It was wide at the base and narrow at the peak, and it shone in the very heart of the heavens."

It all began with Ometeotl, divine source of difference and order.

Female, male, and neither, Ometeotl the Self-Created produced the Tezcatlipocas, the Four Directions that oversee the quarters of heaven and earth. White Quetzalcoatl, the advocate of humans, watched over the west; red Xipe Totec, the farming and springtime god, the east; black Tezcatlipoca, the conflictual change god, the north; and blue Huizilopochtli, the war god, the south. It was in these four directions that the gods stretched the vanquished sea monster Cipactli to unroll the fabric of the Creation.

The gods decided next that a cycle of Suns was needed to bring light to everything. Each Sun would blaze as a world, a deity, and an era.

Black Tezcatlipoca served as the first, but Cipactli had eaten his foot and lamed him, so he shone rather dimly. Furthermore, Quetzalcoatl had never gotten along with him. The Plumed Serpent raised his stone club and knocked the First Sun out of the sky. In retaliation for this demotion, Tezcatlipoca ordered jaguars to eat all the people in the world.

The gods created more people and hung Quetzalcoatl in the heavens to be the Second Sun. But this second race of people forgot the gods in time and stopped praising them and praying to them. For this, Tezcatlipoca turned them all into monkeys. This upset Quetzalcoatl so much that he raised a great hurricane and blew them all away.

When he stepped down, Tlaloc the rain god shone as the Third Sun. After it hung for an era Tezcatlipoca seduced his wife, the erotically gifted Xochiquetzal. Tlaloc went into mourning and neglected his duties, and a drought dried out the world. So ardently did people pray for rain that Tlaloc got sick of hearing their pleadings and rained down fire upon them. From this world's ashes the gods built a new world.

Tlaloc's second wife Chalchiuhtlicue served as the Fourth Sun. A goddess of rivers and sacred waters, she possessed a tranquil temperament that fluctuated when something bothered her—like Tezcatlipoca's claim that she only pretended to be tranquil and kind to win praise. She cried for fifty-two years, and the people below perished in the deluge. Quetzalcoatl traveled to Michtlan to retrieve their bones so he could resurrect humanity. The bones were broken, but Cihuacoatl, called Snake Woman, ground them into meal to be mixed with the Plumed Serpent's blood.

These people awoke (some say) to see Huizilopochtli the

Warrior burning above them as the Fifth Sun, but others say that when the gods gathered in Teotihuacan to make a new Sun, proud Tecuciztecatl stepped forward to volunteer for the glory of it. The second choice was quiet and humble Nanahuatzin. He was sick and old.

The gods purified themselves and faced the fire into which they must leap to become a Sun. Tecuciztecatl was afraid to enter it, so Nanahuatzin walked into it and blazed with light. For his courage he was renamed Tonatiuh: Sun Shining With Light.

Tecuciztecatl, shamed by this, jumped in as well. Now two Suns glared in the east.

The resulting flood of light and heat threatened to consume the world, so the gods threw a rabbit at Tecuciztecatl to make him dimmer. He became the Moon. You can still see its rabbit mark if you look on a very clear night.

Unfortunately, neither Sun nor Moon would move now. They stood still in the sky as rivers dried up and the parched land stopped bearing plants. The gods looked at each other. What should they do?

"We too must sacrifice ourselves," they decided. One by one, they offered themselves to the obsidian knife of Ehecatl.

Aided by the spiritual power of their blood, he blew forth a wind so great it pushed Sun and Moon across the sky.

But Ehecatl cannot keep this up forever. He needs the help of priests who offer up the blood and hearts of the sacrificed in remembrance of how the gods gave up their own lives that the world and its creatures would go on.

When this nourishment stops, the Fifth Sun will go out, the Moon will go out, the envious stars will win their long war against bright daylight, and earthquakes will destroy the world.

For Reflection:

- In Aztec cosmology the four directions—Quetzalcoatl ("ketz-al-COH-aht"), Xipe Totec ("ZSHEE-pay TOH-tek"), Tezcatlipoca ("tez-cat-lee-POH-kah"), and Huizilopochtli ("hooee-tzil-oh-POHCH-tlee")—are themselves divine beings. But the fifth direction, the center, corresponds to the Pleiades (Tianquiztli) star cluster. Its passage over the zenith at midnight marked the beginning of important Sun-renewing ceremonies. What psychological dynamisms might be involved in an otherworldly emphasis in contrast to experiencing *this* world as holy?

• The stretching of the sea monster Cipactli ("see-PACKT-lee") invites comparison with Marduk's dismemberment of Tiamat. The Aztecs and the ancient Babylonians both explored the heavens astronomically. What else might they have shared in common?

• The mythic motif of the sacrifice of the gods shows up in many forms around the world. What does it mean? Why are humans expected to honor and imitate it?

• Each Sun involves a god sacrificed in order to become a ruling principle of that era. Why must each cycle end?

• An alternate version of this myth portrays Huizilopochtli as the Fifth Sun. What could it mean for the ruling principle of a cycle to be a war god? (Huizilopochtli's influence increased as the Aztecs built and expanded their empire.)

• Symbolically, why would a rabbit help dim the second sun into a Moon? (Tecuciztecatl: "teh-koo-seez-TEH-cat.")

• How do the Fifth Sun and the Moon balance each other as cosmic principles?

• Only the Fifth Sun—Nanahuatzin ("NAH-nah-hoo-AHT-zeen"), the Sun of our time—requires all the gods to sacrifice themselves, with Ehecatl ("eh-HAY-cat") as their priest-executioner. Why must this be?

• Jung believed that literal belief in a mythology kept it alive. But what if literalism actually sends it into decline as people forget that myths are wisdom stories and not factual accounts? What if sacrifice to the ruling gods had been held as a metaphor instead of as a bloody necessity to be carried out under a priest's direction?

- Aztec stories and carvings contain no mention of a Sixth Sun. What might this imply about our cycle?

The Final Rectification (Zoroastrian)

Niloufar Talebi, Iranian and British multidisciplinary artist, writer, and performer:

> My areas of interest far surpass things Iranian, but regarding drawing inspiration from Iranian culture in my recent projects despite having formally studied Western literature, art history, and performance, there was an aha moment when I discovered the platform my unique access to both cultures furnishes. ...Many of my projects are somehow about fusing and reimagining the things I learn in my inquiries into Iranian culture.

> I did not set out to start from Yalda, but at some point in the research, when the story was forming, I realized that it is all about LIGHT, the yearning for light, and the celebration of its birth.

> In the early stages of my research into Iranian philosophy, I came across the concept of *Mana*, which is the Persian (and Oceanic) term for the divine life force that embodies everything in the universe, and then *Ahsha*, which is an Avestan term for truth/existence in Zoroastrian theology, whose realm is fire. While Mana and Ahsha are not personified in their traditions, I

reimagined them as characters by marrying their philosophical concepts with human characteristics.

Ātash Sorushān (Fire Angels) refers to the role both Mana and Ahsha played out, angels with a message of purification and peace, ending a world and beginning a new one. Mana and Ahsha begin under the assumption of difference, and through the power of transformation, end by realizing their sameness.

The winter sun will remain unseen, the days grow shorter, the crops fail, the soil's fertility begin to die. Some people will mislead one another; some wrongly amass great fortunes; and most will go around without gratitude for anything, even for the Creation itself. Twisted creatures will rain down from the darkened skies.

The end has been a long time coming. In the first age, good and evil were separated and the world made good. In the second, evil invaded the good world and began to take it over. In this, the third age, the final battle will commence.

For the third is the age in which the prophet Zoroaster declares Ahura Mazda, known also as Ohrmuzd, to be the unborn Spirit, the creator and upholder of Truth (*Asha*), and Angra Mainyu, known also as Ahriman, to be the ultimate enemy of Truth.

This third age will know three prophets. The first, righteous Aushedar, will be born of a virgin as a descendant of Zarathustra. The second, Aushedar-mah, will be born like the first. So will the third, Soshyant, Bringer of Salvation, who comes just when the monster Azhi Dahaka breaks loose from his prison on Mt. Demavand to destroy water, land, and plants.

Soshyant leads the army of *yazatas* to victory against the demonic *daevas*, not through physical might alone, but through sacred ritual carefully and piously enacted. As this occurs, Vohu Mana (Good Mind) defeats Aka Mana (Evil Mind) and Angra Mainyu himself is thrust by Ahura Madza back into the realm of darkness from which he will never again emerge.

At a signal from Soshyant, the dead will rise, resurrected.

Rivers of molten metal melted by *yazatas* Airyaman and Atar will then flow down from the hills and mountains over the earth. Whether living or dead, those who walk through the burning liquid undergo separation: the good feel it only as warm milk and are saved, but the evil shriek in agony. Valleys rise and mountains fall as the evil ones caught in magmatic rivers fall downward to join Angra Mainyu.

As the currents and streams of metal reshape and purify the earth, Soshyant sacrifices an ox and mixes it with *haoma* to make an elixir of immortality. Those who drink it will live in perfect bliss, their spirits returned to restored bodies breathing in a world restored to goodness, a world without sickness, evil, or death. No one will hunger, sorrow, rage, or suffer. Uniquely and together, the resurrected will stand forth in the Light.

For Reflection:

- Comment: That a man named Zoroaster (also called Zarathustra) was born in Iran around 628 BCE does not detract from his mythic endurance. Probably a priest, he claimed to have received a vision from the god Ahura Mazda, the father of the *Spenta Mainyu* (Holy Spirit), and preached reform rather than the overthrow of the polytheistic religion of his time and place. The *Gathas* also mention several of the *amesha spentas*, immortal beings similar to angels. Zoroaster's ministry emphasized justice, truth, piety, and righteous thinking and living to his *ashvan* (followers) up to and beyond the Frashokereti, the final Rectification at history's end. He also emphasized a primordial choice for humans: to follow death or life.

- Christian borrowings from Zoroastrianism become obvious when reading the *Book of Revelation*, yet each religion maintains its own distinctive cosmological principles and daily practices. The release of evil forces previously imprisoned recalls the word "apocalypse," which means to loose what was bound and to reveal what was hidden. What are the clearest parallels between the two eschatologies?

- Zoroastrianism and the Manichaeism it inspired are usually considered dualistic, but if the good and evil mentioned in this story are deliteralized and not held as substances, what are the psychological implications?

- Comment: The Zoroastrian teaching of a world mixed with good and evil followed by a separation of the two (recall the sword-wielding mouth of the Savior in *Revelation*) followed in turn by a physical-spiritual mixture foreshadows a similar emphasis in Western alchemy, where the great opus begins with darkness and *massa confusa*, proceeds to *separatio*, and ends with *coagulatio* and renewal.

- What is the relevance of destroying evil with ritual rather than violence?

The Soul-Sparks Return to the Fullness (Gnostic)

Birger Pearson, Gnostic scholar and professor of religion:

> In the case of Gnosticism, Gnosis is the very basis of salvation. One comes to Gnosis by having it revealed to that person, and through that revelation one is awakened from ignorance, from sleep, or from drunkenness, which are various metaphors that are used for the state of the human being before he or she received Gnosis.
>
> Once Gnosis is revealed to that person and is accepted by that person, it's ultimately the basis for integration into the world of the divine from which that person had originated.

Sophia fell, bringing with her the light bequeathed her from the unknown and unknowable Depth above.

"I am the First," she said as Protennoia, "the Thought that dwells in the Light. I am the movement that lives in the All, She in whom the All takes its stand, the first-born among those who came to be, She who exists before the All." She would also be known to the light's inheritors as Eve, Norea, Mary Magdalene, Barbelo, and Zoe, whose name means Life.

The light spread downward through her tricky and ambitious son Ialdabaoth, the lower god who created the world. From him it blew, inadvertently, as a breath-spark of animation into Eve and Adam, and from them into other Messengers of Light. It could be that some of the sparks penetrated into the heart of matter itself, there to slumber until the time of great awakening.

Be that as it may, the Gnostikoi who discover the light within themselves bear it upward when they leave their mortal bodies behind to take on their stellar form. Soaring beyond the archons, each of which they bewilder by displaying a cipher and uttering words of passage, they fly beyond the sphere of the planets, beyond the sphere of the fixed stars, beyond the Kenoma (Emptiness) and its Boundary, and into the Pleroma, the Fullness from which all things emanate.

Once there, they enter the Treasury of Light, where the ultimate God without name, sex, or attribute gathers up the homecoming soul-sparks. Here at last do the Gnostikoi see the full face of the Divine.

The Apocatastasis, the Great Restoration, will then be complete. The helpful aeons will be at rest in the Pleroma, the kenomic spheres will disappear, and the world will come to an end.

For Reflection:

- What light does this shed on the fall of Sophia?
- What do you make of the idea that only those with conscious Gnosis will be saved, with the rest condemned to nonexistence?

- Although the word "apocatastasis" seems to derive from the Babylonian image of the universe ending once all the planets have fully cycled, it is ultimately an archetypal motif. In Acts, Peter uses it to refer to the restoration of the Kingdom of God. What might it mean on the level of a renewal of consciousness?

- In his novel *Childhood's End*, Arthur Clark imagines a final harvesting of psychically gifted humans into a vast alien Overmind. Edward Edinger speculated that every act of human consciousness augments the collective unconscious. Could this be why we are here?

- If we imagine Ialdabaoth as a forerunner of the Christian devil, how does it sit to consider that some Gnostics believed even he would find salvation in the end?

Ragnarok (Norse)

Jónas Hallgrímsson, Icelandic poet and naturalist:

from "Iceland":

Iceland, fortunate isle! Our beautiful, bountiful mother!
Where are your fortune and fame, freedom and virtue of old?
All things on earth are transient: the days of your greatness and glory
flicker like flames in the night, far in the depths of the past.
Comely and fair was the country, crested with snow-covered glaciers,
azure and empty the sky, ocean resplendently bright...

Snorri's old site is a sheep-pen; the Law Rock is hidden

in heather,
blue with the berries that make boys—and the ravens—
a feast.
Oh you children of Iceland, old and young men together!
See how your forefathers' fame faltered—and passed
from the earth!

Everyone knew it was coming: the gods, the giants, the Einherjar warriors feasting with Odin in Valhalla while awaiting the final battle. Odin himself had known since leaving one of his eyes in wise Mimir's well in exchange for prophecy and runic knowledge.

It started with animals changing their paths and habits. Rodents that gathered nuts in late spring, for example, buried them earlier than usual. Then the weather altered. Sunlight darkened. Frosts fell with more damaging severity for three long winters.

Fighting broke out across the bewildered world. Hordes died of hunger. Ties of loyalty and kinship drowned in blood.

Gods, giants, Einherjar, animals, plants, and skies felt it coming. After millennia of imprisonment, powers long bound were breaking free.

Loki had finally gone too far. After his brother Balder, beloved of the gods, dreamed of his own death, his mother Frigg made everything in heaven and on earth promise never to hurt her favorite son. Everything so promised except the lowly mistletoe plant.

Loki was envious of bright Balder and crafted an arrow of mistletoe, which he brought to a game in which the gods amused themselves by throwing dangerous objects at their supposedly invulnerable brother. Loki gave the arrow to the blind god Hoder, deity of winter, who shot Balder with it. To everyone's shock he died. Odin mated with the giant Rindr, who a day later gave birth to the marksman Vali, who killed Hoder.

Hel agreed to release Balder from the underworld if Frigg could convince everything in the upperworld to weep for him. Everything did except the giant Pokk, who was actually Loki in disguise. *So much for wise, fair, gracious brother Balder*, he sneered internally.

For this the gods bound him to a rock with a chain woven from the entrails of his son Narfi. Skadi set a serpent to drip poisonous venom into his face. Loki's wife Sigyn held forth a bowl to collect the venom, but whenever she turned to empty it, some dripped on him from above, causing him to writhe in agony and the world to tremble.

After millennia of this torture, Loki figured out a way to break free. After that he traveled to Jotenheim and consulted with the giants about a final attack upon Asgard.

Loki had not been the only one bound. Ages ago the gods had chained up the gigantic wolf Fenrir, who bit off Tyr's arm; cast the serpent Jörmungandr into the sea of Midgard; and sent Hel down to Niffelheim. All three were children of Loki and the giant Angrboda, She Who Brings Grief. They were confined because a *völva* seeress had predicted that they would bring trouble to the gods.

The convulsion with which Loki freed himself shook the ground so hard that Fenrir broke free as well. Jormundgandr writhed and flopped onto the land. Hel remained in charge of Niffelheim, but her hellhound Garm broke his bindings and howled. Crowings shrieked from the throats of three roosters in three worlds.

The Aesir sat in council one last time as the Einherjar sharpened their swords and axes and the dwarves shut their stone doors and the world tree Yggdrasil gave a shudder that shook the Nine Worlds.

In Midgard the daylight turned dark as Fenrir opened his vast jaws and swallowed the sun even as his brother Hati swallowed the moon. The stars went out. Trees fell over, crevices opened, and mountains toppled. Entire populations fled for their lives.

The ship Naglfar slipped its moorings and set sail at last. Built out of the fingernails and toenails of the dead, it was steered by the giant Hrym. Behind him, rearing Jormungandr blew toxins into air and sea and Fenrir emitted flames from his nostrils. The very sky split in two.

On land, mounted Surt waved his sun-bright sword and led an army of giants out of fiery Muspelheim. They traversed the worlds on a march straight for Bifrost, the soaring bridge leading to Asgard.

Heimdall, the watchman who never slept, saw them coming and blew his mighty horn to alert the gods: time to assemble for battle.

The oncoming giants crossed Bifrost, which shattered into rainbow fragments behind them, and formed up in the plain of Vígríðr, Battle Surge. Loki, Fenrir, Jorgmungandr, and Hrym joined them there as Odin led the Aesir and the Einherjar onto the field. He wore a gold helm and rode his eight-legged steed Sleipnir.

Odin raised his spear Gungnir and charged Fenrir as Thor lifted his hammer and ran at Jormungandr. Surt cut weaponless Freyr. As the Vanir god fell to the flaming sword, Garm leaped upon Tyr and both died together, as did Loki and Heimdall.

Odin's son Vidarr saw Fenrir swallow his father and sprang forward. Gripping the wolf's upper jaw, he planted a boot on the lower jaw and heaved. Fenrir's jaws broke apart and he died with Vidarr's spear in his chest and Odin in his cavernous stomach.

Thor swung his hammer and crushed the skull of Jorgmungandr, but not before being sprayed with venom. He took nine staggering steps and fell dead to the ground.

Gods were fighting giants on every side and dying with them when Surt swung his sword in a wide arc. Its fires poured forth to ignite the entire world.

It burned as it sank slowly into the sea. Heaps of ash that were the fallen bodies of gods, giants, and humans hissed as the waters closed over them.

* * * *

In time a new earth rose from the calming waves.

Self-sown crops and fresh green forests dotted the land. An eagle circled over a waterfall. High above, the daughter of the sun devoured by Fenrir lit a world cleansed of the evils of its violent past. A gentle breeze caressed its lovely face.

Back when the long winters had set in, two humans, Lif and her mate Lifþrasir, saw what was coming and hid in the Hoddmimis woods sheltered by Yggdrasil, the tree that stood even as the worlds fell. The couple now came forth to drink the dew and turn their wondering eyes on the new lands and seas they had inherited.

In the field of Idavoll, the Plain of Splendor that sat where Asgard had stood, the surviving gods gradually gathered together. The first to arrive were Odin's sons Vidarr and Vali, Thor's sons Modi and Magni, who brought Thor's recovered hammer with them, Hoder and Balder, reunited in the Underworld and finally released from it, and Hoenir, who had helped Odin create human beings.

They sat in the field and conversed about many things: Ragnarok, the doings of gods and giants, the origins and uses of the runes. As they talked, someone spotted gold glinting in the grass: game pieces the Aesir gods had once played with.

One day survivors of Ragnarok would live in the gold-thatched hall Gimlé, whose beauty outshone the sun, as newly built temples across the land received blessings for the gods. Today they were content to sit outside and speak of what had happened, and of how the new cosmic game might be played.

For Reflection:

- "It started with animals changing their paths and habits...Then the weather altered." It has been said we live in apocalyptic times, with global warming the most urgent of many crises all hitting at once. What is the underlying meaning of apocalypse?

- What would a conscious Ragnarok be like instead of an unconsciously enacted one?

- Why must the gods (ruling principles) suffer death? ("Ragnarok" means "development or fate of the gods.") Do they truly die? Why couldn't they and the Einherjar ("AYN-her-yar") stop it even though they foresaw it?

- Jung often wrote about uniting the opposites, but in this story (as in Jung's own journals) the opposites united cancel each other out: Thor and the Midgard serpent, Odin and Fenrir, Loki and Heimdall, etc. Why must they meet at all?

- Who in the myth really set Ragnarok in motion?

- What do repression, oppression, and rigid restraint always engender?

- Jung wrote an article, "Wotan," in which he argued that Wotan (Odin) had returned to life in the collective German psyche just before World War II. He linked Wotan to battle frenzy. But Wotan/Odin is not primarily a battle god; rather, he is a father god like Dagda, Indra, and Zeus. Even so, Jung was right about the Norse mythological imagery in Nazism. Some of it was deliberately manipulated, but the rest could not have been: Hitler's first name meaning "wolf," for example. Could WW II have been a mini-Ragnarok?

- An Indian myth relates that when the fourth *yuga* ends this cycle of universal time, Vishnu will appear as bow-wielding Rudra the storm god and subject the world to a protracted drought, after which it will be incinerated by the sun in preparation for the next *yuga*. Why apocalypse by fire?

- What if the surviving gods didn't really survive, and Gimlé is actually the afterlife?

- What do the recovered game pieces suggest? If gods (and humans) are game pieces, who after all are the players?

Chapter Thirteen - Modern Myths

Can Modern Myths Exist?

On July 30th, 1958, this melodramatic headline appeared in the *Washington Post:*

Flying Objects Real, Psychiatrist Insists

The psychiatrist referred to was C. G. Jung, who had said that UFOs were "not mere rumor" and that the US Air Force was spreading panic by withholding information about them. *Dr. Jung Declares Flying Saucers Are Real* blared the *Meriden Record* on the same day. The *New York Herald Tribune* got on the little green bandwagon: *"Flying Saucers Real," Psychologist Jung Says*.

Not exactly. Jung was not going around claiming that extraterrestrials were flying about in the atmosphere, although he did confess to being intrigued that a UFO could throw back a radar echo (he must have read this in some report or other). What he meant was that flying saucers were *psychically* real: real as collective visions, as mass-psychological claims. Which was not, of course, as exciting as a world-famous psychiatrist coming out for hovering ovoids and hissing death rays.

In the same year, 1958, Jung published *Flying Saucers: A Modern Myth of Things Seen in the Skies*. He wrote:

> In the threatening situation of the world today, when people are beginning to see that everything is at stake, the projection-creating fantasy soars beyond the realm

of earthly organizations and powers into the heavens, into interstellar space, where the rulers of human fate, the gods, once had their abode in the planets.... Even people who would never have thought that a religious problem could be a serious matter that concerned them personally are beginning to ask themselves fundamental questions. Under these circumstances it would not be at all surprising if those sections of the community who ask themselves nothing were visited by `visions,' by a widespread myth seriously believed in by some and rejected as absurd by others.

Had myth been declared dead prematurely? Could there be such a thing as a "modern myth"?

Mythographers, sociologists, and anthropologists of the more strait-laced sort would say no. A story doesn't get to be a myth until it has been around long enough to collect generations of retellings and a certain degree of tradition, reverence, and belief. But as we have seen, a stone without moss is still a stone. Myth is not just traditional tale-telling: it is a basic structure of mentation, reflection, and culture-making. Modern myths pass the Duck Test: If it looks like a duck, swims like a duck, and quacks like a duck, then it is probably a duck. If we must, let us dub it a protomyth and wait a few centuries to see if it takes.

Another question: Can a modern myth be cut from wholly new storied cloth? In his flying saucer book Jung referred to extraterrestrials as "technological angels." Yesterday they wore wings to fly; today, a wavery glow as they accelerate heavenward. In ancient Greece they would have been seen as aerial daemons. Well?

In this chapter we consider several candidates for modern myths and contemporary mythic motifs. Let us see if we find any new inventions among them.

In what follows, I will skip the work of substantiation in favor of suggesting possible mythic structures, images, and parallels. Readers interested in substantiating should look back to the criteria of what identifies a myth (Chapter One) and then investigate how many apply to each modern myth candidate when studied in greater depth.

Techno-Amulets

"With this smartphone," I told the audience as I held up an iPhone, "I can do things Merlin could not do: change my shape (at least online), summon food, tell the weather on the other side of the world...."

The audience consisted of coders, programmers, and other IT professionals drawn to the event by the Highground Hackers, a San Francisco advocacy group interested in high-tech solutions to social ills like gun violence.

Whenever Apple updates its phones, customers form long lines and even camp out waiting for the new models. It is shallow to claim that these eager people are empty and have no lives. They are not really awaiting a few extra seconds of processing speed or a few more gigabytes of memory. They are lining up for new talismans with magic powers.

As far as the deeper layers of the unconscious are concerned, where a dream feels real when we're in it, a smartwatch is an amulet, and a tablet a scrying pool. No wonder they are spellbinding. The Apple logo itself hints at the forbidden knowledge of lost Eden. Microsoft's less potent mythos is that of peering at life through a window; the very name Microsoft would make a Freudian analyst chuckle. No wonder their sales periodically sag.

It is said that in times gone by, powerful rabbis scooped up clay and chanted over it, raising it up into the shambling form of a humanoid without consciousness, a servant who carried out orders literally. They called this being a golem. Set one loose, and the only way to turn it off was to draw a certain mystical symbol upon its forehead: a big problem if the automaton was too tall to reach. Today we call the golem artificial intelligence, robotics, and digital cybernetics. The monitor into which we peer is a glass and metal face that peers back at us. Some of us call the golem a smarthouse and live inside its belly.

If we consider science and technology through an eye for myth, we might ask: Which myths operate in our innovations and e-ideologies? Is AI a form of techno-resurrection, an ancient dream given new digital life once again? Is the "selfish gene" idea beloved of Richard Dawkins—every gene for himself and Darwin take the hindmost—actually a kind of genotheism, with one bio-power to rule them all? As global temperatures rise perilously high, who will stand in for Hou Yi, the moon goddess's heroic husband, who shot down the extra suns sitting like birds in trees now become spindly smokestacks?

Which gods inhabit our machines? Jung thought of trains as modern dragons and airliners as giant prehistoric birds. Cars look like animals: two front lights for eyes, grille for a mouth, wheels for legs: unconscious motorized theriomorphism. "Electricity" gets its name from the Greek word for both amber and its goddess, Elektra, many-armed nymph of storm clouds. The ill-fortuned ship *Titanic's* name recalls the Titans, those hubristic monsters locked up in a box at the bottom of the abyss by order of Zeus. The gun recalls Gunhilda, the Norse battle goddess; "bullet" derives from *bull*, not the quadruped but the papal edict. Gun is also a reckless Chinese war god.

The problem with being unable to recognize the archetypes in our equipment and its ideologies is in how they have their way with us, often destructively. Procrustes has broken loose in psychology, a field once known as the study of the soul and now a soulless mechanization of mass-mindedness. His minions lurking in the American Psychological Association designed torture regimens for the second Bush Administration; with a nod of approval from President Ares, the beds of the infamous innkeeper rematerialized as waterboarding racks. This was no mistake: ever since Francis Bacon called for the rape and torture of Nature by the scientist, the treatment of living beings as machines to be taken apart and studied has delighted sadists posing even to themselves as ardent seekers after knowledge.

The alternative to all this darkness would be a conscious remythologizing of what we do and intend. When we use clean energy and transportation, for instance, we trade in the Underworld gods of extraction and burning rivers (the Greeks called theirs

Phlegethon) and hidden wealth ("plutocracy" derives from Pluto) for the abundant sun god Helios, the persistent wind god Aeolus, and pulsing Poseidon and his wife Amphritrite, among others (and from other pantheons too). Gaia is not just a Theory, but the maternal originator and supporter of all the life we know. Shall we not come fully home once again to Earth, not as wasteful and spoiled adolescents, but as responsible psychological adults?

Media Magic

The Bill Moyers documentary *The Power of Myth* made millions aware of how closely the first Star Wars films followed Joseph Campbell's conception of the Hero's Journey.

Since that time, mythic stories have lit up every conceivable medium and venue: not only film and television (*Game of Thrones*, *Once Upon a Time*), but theater, literature (including science fiction), painting, computer gaming, in-person storytelling events, and even comic books brought to the silver screen.

Shortly before the First World War, JRR Tolkien, a philologist by profession, caught the wave of enthusiasm about folklore introduced by the Brothers Grimm. Why, he wondered, did not England have a distinct mythology like Germany, Greece, Egypt, Ireland, and, since the publication of the *Kalevala*, Finland? Sure, there were King Arthur and his Round Table, but they were British rather than English and, what was dramatically problematic, overtly Christian and therefore allegorical rather than truly mythic. (Tolkien was a devout Roman Catholic; his criticism was aesthetic rather than religious.)

Taking his cue from the poet of Beowulf and from Elias Lönnrot, collector-author of the *Kalevala*, Tolkien created what he called his legendarium: an intricately and spaciously imagined world of fantasy, with its own cosmology, cosmogony, and intergenerational hero tales. From this emerged *The Hobbit*, *The Lord of the Rings*, *The Silmarillion*, and a number of shorter works, some unfinished. If he could not furnish England with a traditional myth, he could at least compose one.

Not *invent* one, however. When asked where the legendarium

came from, Tolkien said: from the Elves. In his imagination he had heard them speaking Elvish.

Jung heard imaginal speech too, and at about the same time. Although the two men did not study each other's work (Tolkien knew of Jung's but not in detail), each produced and illustrated with art his own remarkable "Red Book" of visionary encounter, Jung's red leather tome known as *Liber Novus* and Tolkien's fictional one as the *Red Book of Westmarch*. Both books are packed with imaginal figures inhabiting realms (Faerie, the collective unconscious) recognizably fantastic and even Gnostic. Both witnesses ("authors" seems the wrong word) wrote down what these figures told them. Tolkien did not try to interpret their communications. When Jung tried to analyze two of these figures, Philemon and Salome, as psychological principles, Philemon replied, "We are real and not symbols." (For more comparisons, see Becca Tarnas's dissertation *The Back of Beyond: The Red Books of C. G. Jung and J. R. R. Tolkien*.)

Since its publication in 2009, Jung's *Red Book* has sold millions of copies. Tolkien's *Lord of the Rings* was the most popular book of the twentieth century; since the invention of print, it has been only less popular than *A Tale of Two Cities* and the Bible.

Peter Jackson's film remakes of Tolkien's books have netted nearly six billion dollars in revenue worldwide. If we add Star Trek, Star Wars, and Marvel's run of films, the amount of time and money spent on them surpasses calculation. For fans who wait in long lines, attend conventions, and purchase nobody knows how many plastic phasers and lightsabers, these fantasy-based productions are not just fictional creations: they are beacons of belonging and hope for an age of chaos and alienation.

Jungian scholar Sonu Shamdasani claims that Jung's *Red Book* introduces a new myth for our time. Dr. Lance Owens makes a similar claim about Tolkien's legendarium. Are these works indeed foundationally mythopoetic?

Myths in the traditional sense are anonymous creations, but they must have started with some one story, the telling of which underwent countless elaborations. The Melanesian cargo cults and the American Ghost Dance are relatively recent examples of how a vision led to a story and then to ritual and myth. Visions come from visionaries strong enough to tell others what has been witnessed. Therefore, the fact of individual "authorship" in the case of the two Red Books does not necessarily rule out the dynamic of myth creation at work. Owens argues that both are examples of how myths originate.

The question of modern myth creation hinges in part on whether myths require belief. At least some of the members of a society do believe its myths as though they were histories, as geneticist Spenser Wells learned when he tried to tell an Aborigine that all humans originated in Africa, whereupon the offended listener insisted that his people had always lived in Australia. Some Native Americans display a similar rejection of the theory of Beringia, a land bridge between North America and Asia, in spite of support for this theory from genetics, archeology, geology, and biogeography. The stories that say we were here forever are taken literally.

However, a certain number of elders, shamans, and medicine people always recognize the symbolic nature of their society's sacred stories, even telling them on occasion with a reminder not to regard them as factual. Tolkien emphasized the power of myth as a story capable of setting up "secondary belief": not just suspension of disbelief (Coleridge), but temporary acceptance of the rules and laws of mythic reality for purposes of appreciative participation. Lihui Yang points out that myths endure in part because they entertain while saying something meaningful about how we live.

Even so, we know of no ancient myths that were not taken as actual by large numbers of their tellers and listeners. More accurately, these traditional stories arose in societies that did not separate literal from symbolic truth, so the question did not arise back then.

When you put a modern translation of an ancient myth next to *The Lord of the Rings* or Star Trek, the felt difference is obvious. Nobody believes or has believed that Frodo or Kirk were ever real. Their origins are clear rather than lost in generations of retellings. Yet, they inspire and ramify somewhat like myths. Ursula K. LeGuin calls such as they *submyths:* mythic in feel and image, but aesthetically, spiritually, and traditionally inferior to genuine myths.

Myths or not, are they new? Only in the sense of contemporary authorship and interpretation. It looks as though both Tolkien and Jung tuned into a Gnostic layer of collective consciousness awaiting resurrection and new expression. Tolkien is not thought to have studied the Gnostic myths extensively, but Jung's work has demonstrated that such conscious knowledge is not needed for archetypes to resurface. If all of mythology were wiped out at a stroke, he speculated, it would reinvent itself in a generation. Jung's own *Red Book* is packed with Gnostic imagery, as Lance Owens points out in his introduction to Ribi's *C. G. Jung and the Tradition of Gnosis*.

If Tolkien, Jung, and the filmmakers and novelists do not offer new myths, they do make available retellings of ancient but newly activated mythic plots and motifs for people thirsty for what organized religion unadapted to the times cannot give them.

Myths in Money and Politics

It might be somewhat arbitrary, at least in the United States, to discuss myths in money apart from myths in politics because at the national level, our politics are determined by money. We are, in fact, a plutocracy ruled by Pluto, god of death and hidden wealth: a plutocracy pretending to be a democracy. Our customary political campaign trinity is not Father, Son, and Holy Ghost, as theocrats maintain, but Ares the reckless war god and his sons Phobos (Fear) and Deimos (Terror). In their service our Hero complex seeks to extend our police and surveillance state—call it the New Argus after the hundred-eyed watch-monster—all across the globe. Meanwhile, Pluto demands subsidization of the fossil fuels that are turning our planet into Tartarus.

Money did not always bear such darkness. After centuries of barter and trade, in 2000 BCE someone in China thought up the idea of circulating metal markers instead of actual goods. By 806 CE, the markers were replaced by paper. During the Renaissance, the introduction of Arabic numbers made accurate bookkeeping possible, and by 1436, Gutenberg's printing press standardized paper money.

With the Age of Exploration and colonization, however, money began to grow more and more ethereal as well as disconnected from actual labor and tangible goods. As this happened, finances gained a psychological vocabulary, with money a kind of fantasy person capable of depression, recession, inflation, and deflation. Consulting a Misery Index might lead a financier to an analyst and to a prescription of an After-Hours High to ward off the Summer Doldrums. In the States, Thanksgiving is followed by Black Friday.

As money dematerialized, its institutions took on the aspect of corporeal life, with corporations gaining the legal status of persons. Freeways and turnpikes gained the term "artery," with time-lapse video revealing oddly synchronized pulsations and flows of traffic through the body of the metropolis. Business models are now described as "ecosystems." Today Ray Bradbury might have penned *I Sing the Body Transnational.*

Meanwhile, the mythology cast out by the Enlightenment reappeared as bulls and bears, witching hours and castles in the sky, scalping and capitation, and unicorns spotted in the Silicon Valley over which angel investors have been known to soar. The bronze bull guarding Wall Street resembles the bull god Moloch of the insatiable appetite for bloody sacrifices of the young, the aged, and the infirm. Beware the reach of the Invisible Hand of the Market.

Not even holidays are exempt from the relentless ideology of unregulated capitalism. Santa Claus goes back to the Norse god Freyr as well as to Father Christmas, true, but the marketers provided red-nosed Rudolph to sell Coca-Cola.

Resacrilizing and making conscious our relationship to money could begin with studying its mythology. In ancient Rome, money was not kept in banks, but in the temple of the goddess Moneta. The Romans also knew the lesson of the Wheel of Fortuna: what goes up inevitably comes down.

Religions and Cults

When my students tried to argue that the terror group ISIS was misnamed, I pointed out that benevolent Isis could get angry; that she controlled canals, a military goal of the other ISIS; that, like them, she sought to give birth to a Redeemer; that fire and dismemberment were part of the story she shared with Osiris and Set; and that we might expect some violent reaction after centuries of bombing, desertifying, and colonizing what was once an edenic garden. That which we cast out stages a return as symptom, nightmare, or catastrophe. "The unconscious turns toward us," wrote Jung, "the face that we turn toward it"; and so indeed do the gods and even their altars.

In the West, we wonder why young people rush to join brutal terror groups like ISIS, which promise the glory, belonging, and purpose our crumbling and soulless secular institutions eradicate, even though the promise is never made good and the recruits always victimized. It's sobering to realize that religious fundamentalists and militant atheists have at least one important quality in common: aggressive literal-mindedness that hardens ideological stances, destroys imagination, subverts empathy, and obliterates dialogue.

When the big myths fail, pseudo-myths rush to fill the gaps. What was once called the Golden Age is rewritten by conservatives as the 1950s in (white) America. Techno-redemption would stop global warming, end crime, and spread wealth with a click. But the Icarian pseudo-myth of Progress leads inevitably, time and again, to deflation and descent.

Pseudo-mythology shows up in the kind of New Age posturing that stops self-inquiry with pleasant affirmations, touts positive thinking for "manifesting" positive results, and even blames people for their own misfortunes (e.g., "you must be off your path"). To consider the world a gigantic blackboard for one's personal edification reflects a Divine Child view of spirituality. In 1984, psychotherapist John Welwood coined "spiritual bypassing" to illuminate the narcissistic defense of taking refuge in light and cheer to avoid the hard work of building character, facing one's weaknesses, managing sadness and anger, and making responsible and practical choices: in other words, achieving psychological adulthood.

Bypassing can include barging into experiential spirituality without the support of a tradition or discipline. Too often this brings what Stan and Christina Grof call *spiritual emergency*: the psychological breakdown of an identity faced with an onslaught of impulses and images emanating from the depths. Cultures that recognized these visionary manifestations provided safety, stability, and support for the recipients. Today the visionaries are liable to be hospitalized. Spiritual adventurers might do well to recall the lesson of Ye Gao.

Not all New Age spirituality bypasses or looks schizotypal. Behind the chants and the clouds of incense we can discern the thoughtful recognition that powerful spiritual forces move below the surface of contemporary change. We can also find many re-dreamings of ancient mythic figures into modern guides: gurus into Ascended Masters, gnosis into channeling, angels and daemons into UFOs. New wine needs fresh bottles.

To the degree that traditional religion can stay open to such re-dreamings, it too can vivify itself. Some dismiss the figure of La Virgen de Guadalupe as a ploy by the Catholic Church to attract followers in Mexico, but to her devotees she is an olive-skinned representation of the Mother of God. It remains to be seen whether other empowering feminine images of the divine find similar acceptance.

Culture and Academy

Once upon a time widowed King Akademus abducted wise Helen, later of Troy, to be his young bride. This brought the mighty brothers Castor and Pollux down on him in short order. Hand her over, they demanded, or we will level your city.

"You can find her at Aphidnae," he told them. For some reason he was venerated forever after as a savior of Athens, perhaps by followers who forgot that he had caused all the trouble to begin with. In any case, this episode set a precedent: future invaders of Attica spared the olive grove where he had kept his intended wife. In honor of it and in recognition that it was sacred to Athena, Plato called the school he founded there the Academy.

Since that time, academia has often been the cultural arena and boxing ring for two other mythic brothers. When Apollo rules, scholars look for single causes of complicated events, explain life with monolithic models, compare religions, philosophies, and entire societies, and invent grand theories of everything. Like Apollo and his silver bow, they try to hit their targets from a distance, without direct involvement. When Dionysus rules, the grand certainties of

Modernism and Structuralism give way before the fragmentary standpoints of Postmodernity and Poststructuralism. Now everything (note the contradiction) is partial, provisional, experimental. Now variety trumps unity. Every point of view is relatively valid except an encompassing one. The language of order, framework, and system retreats before that of rupture, transgression, and dissolution.

We academics tend to enlist with one brother against the other while forgetting a lesson of Delphi, where the Oracle of Apollo prophesied for two thousand years: when Apollo wanted to sojourn elsewhere, he asked Dionysus to stand in for him. They are not opposites, as Nietzsche thought: they are brothers who know how to work together, fashioning form to suit impulse and stoking passion to fire form.

When they don't work together, when we forget the lesson, they act rigidly and dogmatically, swarming each other as worthy Dionysian demands for diverse course offerings degenerate into Apollonian political correctness. As they fight, other gods enter the arena: our old friend Procrustes fingering his ax, indigenous Coyote setting fires, Gong Gong accepting lucrative grants to level mountains for coal, and even stern Saturn imposing his leaden will on the competitive SAT test: Saturn, the god who ate his own children.

What richness could a mythic-archetypal approach bring to our scholarly efforts? We might then realize that each suitable way of doing research (for example) must find its own altar. *Puer* explorers who open up new fields of inquiry cannot be held to the standards of *senex*ian fact-checkers and verifiers. If we seek possibilities of renewal in social situations of marginalization and death, we had better consult our Osiris powers of discernment, fairness, and night vision. If we look for what habitat or planet need from us, we might make use of Gaian modes of inclusion and balance. Studying rigidified political structures might require tricky Eshu's propensity for shaking things loose. For deep psychological research Robert Romanyshyn recommends Orpheus as guide for our descents into the Underworlds we encounter (*The Wounded Researcher*).

The question is: At Whose altar do we stand just now?

Space, Time, Number

In grade school I was introduced to a universe made of particles whose effects, even when invisible, were discernible and calculable, at least to some extent. It was in many respects an Apollonian universe of luminous matter seen through telescopes and spectrographs; a universe of organization and principle; a universe regulated by laws we would fully understand one day.

In the early 1900s, Bohr, Planck, and Einstein had begun to complexify that regularity. In their wake bobbed the fractal nature of the cosmos (a cosmos of rough edges, not neat Euclidean lines), Chaos and Complexity Theory, irregular groupings of entire galactic clusters, mysterious black holes, theoretical wormholes, visible exoplanets ("strange new worlds"), invisible mega-lattices of dark matter and energy. What a shift: from a largely comprehensible if very large place, the universe was now much stranger, much less predictable, mostly dark, and, ultimately, beyond human powers of observation. So often psychologists have tried to make psychology be like physics; but now it was as though physics had discovered its own version of a cosmic unconscious of unknowable depth and extent.

Even our creation story began to change. The opening of a bright cosmic egg is a familiar image in many mythologies; so is the motif of the Divine Parents as creators. No sooner had Stephen Hawking compared the question "What came before the Big Bang?" to asking what was north of the North Pole than new observations and mathematics hinted at the presence of vast interdimensional membranes ("branes"), two of which touched long enough to spark our daughter universe. Streaks of light where none should have been hinted at universes other than our own, even prior to our own. String Theory recalled the Fates and Norns and other mythic weavers of destiny.

Mythology had always suggested that not only Space, but Time too was irregular. Experiments backing Einstein's theories showed Time to be fluid, relative, even changeable, especially near the speed of light. Instead of Time and Space, physicists now spoke of *space-time*, a single fabric unfurling from the singularity with which it all began. Ancient Greeks had known Time as Chronos, a three-headed serpent. The Romans knew him as lion-headed Aion. Jung believed that moments of time possess their own unique qualities. Something in us must agree: why else so many mythic names of numbers, holidays, days of the week, planets and asteroids, constellations and galaxies?

What about time and number? Why the "superstitious" intensity of ends of millennia, 2012, solar eclipses, Friday the 13th? What do they have in common? Liminality. Transition. They all mark thresholds of time.

Concerns about particular numbers tend to vary from culture to culture, but fear of death shows up in many. In China and Japan, buildings go up without a designated fourth floor because the word for "four" sounds like the word for "death." The number 17 is unlucky in Italy because Roman numeral XVII can be rearranged to VIXI, "I have lived" (and soon won't). The number 26 is unlucky in India because the giant Gujarat quake, the 2004 tsunami, and terror attacks in Guwahati, Mumbai, and Ahmedabad all struck on the 26th of the month.

In many cultures, 13 is unlucky. It too has liminal qualities. It is the first *emirp* ("prime" spelled backwards): a prime number that when reversed is a different prime. (The next is unlucky 17.) Its emphasis in English shifts from last syllable to first depending on where it appears: by itself "thirteen" is pronounced thir-TEEN, but THIR-teen in "1300." In the Tarot deck, the 13th trump is Death. Because a solar year carries just over 12 lunations, the thirteenth month of the lunar calendar is smaller than the others. In the Middle Ages a year with 13 full moons instead of 12 confused the calendars of Christian monks. A torus can be sliced into 13 segments with three plane cuts. The three fastest horses in a race can finish 13 different ways, taking ties into account. Bell numbers count up the ways a mathematical set can be partitioned into nonempty subsets; 13 is the third.

No one knows quite how Friday the 13th got its evil reputation. In Zoroastrianism, the 13th day of the year is unlucky, a doorway to potential evil. Jesus, who died on a Friday, was betrayed by Judas, often referred to as the 13th disciple. The trickster Loki, the 13th guest in Valhalla, was responsible for the death of the bright god Baldur and the onset of Ragnarok. According to legend, King Philip IV of France ordered the arrest and execution of the wealthy and powerful Knights Templar on Friday the 13th, October 1307. Fear of Friday the 13th is called "triskaidekaphobia." Alfred Hitchcock was born on Friday the 13th, and on that day in 2029, an asteroid will pass close by Earth.

Then there was Apollo 13....

What an unlucky mission. Liftoff was at 1300 hours and 13 minutes. Before then, one astronaut had been replaced because of illness; after launch, a center engine unexpectedly cut off. Before the flight, and for the first time ever, the three-man crew recommendation by the NASA Director of Flight Crew Operations had been rejected by management. Three other astronauts were selected; their weightlessness training was finished in 13 days. They rode skyward on Saturn V boosters 111.3 meters tall. A helium disc burst, but it was a minor problem and wasn't paid much heed.

On April 13th, 1970, pressure in an oxygen tank popped the bolts from a 13-foot section of outer aluminum panel. The oxygen valves on numbers 1 and 3 fuel cells closed, leaving them three minutes of feed line air. The line from number 1 tank ruptured, spewing oxygen to spew into space for 130 minutes: "Houston, we've had a problem," a statement later misquoted. Jim Lovell's heart rate reached 130 beats per minute. (His wife Marilyn had felt a premonition of disaster and lost her wedding ring down the sink drain. She eventually found it.)

As the crew shifted from the heroically named *Odyssey* command module to the humbler lunar module *Aquarius*, the flight plan was changed into the shape of an infinity symbol: the astronauts would circle the Moon from a distance and come home.

By fitting a square peg into a round hole, Mission Control engineers devised a makeshift oxygen scrubber for the endangered crew, who referred to it as "the mailbox." But did they get the mythic message?

As the capsule fell toward Earth, the communications blackout aroused anxiety by taking 33 seconds longer than expected. The mission insignia of three flying horses might have seemed just then like a shared three-person nightmare.

Once the men were safely home, a Cortright Report was issued in June to analyze the mission. It contained five chapters and eight appendices.

In an attempt at lightening what could have been a tragedy, Grumman pilot Sam Greenberg made out an invoice to North American Rockwell, Pratt and Whitney, and Beech Aircraft to bill them for towing the spacecraft to the Moon and back. The amount came to $400,540, the numbers of which happen to add up to 13.

A cash discount payment option cut the grand total to $312,421.

Personal Myths

> There is some one myth for every man which, if we but knew it, would make us understand all he did and thought.
> — William Butler Yeats

In the English translation of his *Memories, Dreams, Reflections*, Jung announces that he will tell his "personal myth." But there is no personal myth mentioned in the heavily edited book.

However, in a 1942 letter to Paul Schmitt, Jung writes that

> ....All of a sudden with terror it became clear to me that I have taken over Faustus as my heritage, and moreover as the advocate and avenger of Philemon and Baucis, who, unlike Faust the superman, are hosts of the gods in a ruthless and godforsaken age....To the extent that I harbour a personal myth of this kind you are right in nosing up a "Goethean" world in me.

Imagine Faust the alchemist eager for the wisdom of the depths as Jung, who researched alchemy and esoteric knowledge; Faust's homunculus as Jung's boyhood manikin; Faust's palace as Jung's lakeside tower; Mephistopheles as the shadow; the realm of The Mothers as the collective unconscious. Sabina Spielrein as the unfortunate Gretchen. These and many other parallels link Jung, author of *Modern Man in Search of a Soul*, to the legendary German wizard who sold his own soul for knowledge.

Although it has become psychologically fashionable to speak of rewriting or replacing one's "personal myth," it is nothing we invent or plan for. We seem rather to come in with it. Even our names can reflect it. *Carl* refers to a free man, *Gustav* to a royal staff like that which Philemon gave him in an inner vision (Jung called this staff "the key of symbolism"), and Jung to "young." Behind him stood the immortal seeker who wrestled with God, conjured spirits of earth and air, and struggled to unify the "two souls within my breast." Both enjoyed a moment of supreme beauty shortly before shuffling off the mortal coil.

Faust's tale is a tragedy. Jung's life was not because he lived his myth consciously, and by doing so he softened, transformed, and responded creatively to it.

What about Freud, born into a family of sons named after kings? He seems to have hit the nail on the head by writing to Wilhelm Fleiss about realizing that "I am Oedipus," a figure far older than any Greek play. Oedipus did not realize that his own actions endangered Thebes; Freud misinterpreted his dreams about poisoning his female patients. Like Oedipus, the boy Freud overheard a prophecy of his own greatness; and like Oedipus, Freud grew up in a problematic and emotionally incestuous relationship with his mother, who idolized her "Golden Sigi." Oedipus was riding a chariot when he came across the father he would kill; Freud bore a lifelong fear of trains, and one of his famous cases analyzed a boy's fear of horses — as told by the boy's father. A medallion Freud received for his fiftieth birthday showed Oedipus solving the riddle of the Sphinx. Oedipus fathered two boys and two girls, as did Freud, with another girl, Sophie, dying in young adulthood. He referred to Anna as "my Antigone"; after being interrogated by the Gestapo (a Nazi Cleon), she led Freud out of Vienna just as Antigone led Oedipus out of Thebes.

Personal myth: where ancient tales find renewal in contemporary lives.

In my book *Storied Lives: Discovering and Deepening Your Personal Myth* I speculate about the personal myths of the following public figures besides Jung and Freud: Harry Houdini (Mercury), Joan of Arc (Athena), Mozart (Iacchus), Sir Isaac Newton (Janus), Mary Shelley (Pandora), George Washington (Saturn), George W. Bush (Ares), John Denver (Icarus), Phoolan Devi (Durga), Jodie Foster (Persephone), James Hillman (Lucifer), Timothy "Speed" Levitch (Mordecai the Vovnik), Marilyn Monroe (Venus), Princess Diana (Diana-Artemis), Oprah Winfrey (Queen Calafia), Al Gore (Merlin), Sean Connery (Zeus), Maeve Quinlan (Queen Maeve), and Dr. Martin Luther King Jr. (King Arthur). I have also written an online article on "Sir John of Steinbeck" and Lancelot du Lac, who was knighted on St. John's Day.

Here I would like to add a few names to the list:

Perhaps we should call it Trickyleaks, because to a locked-up security system kept from public view, potential Russian spy Julian Assange brought the retribution of Hermes, who delights in taking down what is ponderous and rigid.

Was President Obama actually President Apollo, the Olympian god who loves harmony and who kills from afar with silver arrows? Obama succeeded in pushing through healthcare reform where the Clintons failed: naturally, for Apollo is also the god of medicine as well as of sudden death. His style is one of distance, his reserve legendary.

From a distance, the stage-managed feats of bare-chested Vladimir Putin look like those of a would-be Hercules, but his myth is probably someone more Underworldly, someone who plagiarizes freely, arranges criminal back-door deals, initiates digital attacks on elections, and makes his opponents disappear. Putin is undoubtedly on good terms with Hades....

Where injustice predominates, we should expect the appearance of Athena to deal with it. In the U.S. Congress she might like

Elizabeth Warren, who refuses to run the polis instead of Zeus but who relentlessly holds it accountable.

Icarus showed up once as John Denver, but he also reappeared as former test pilot and visionary Gene Roddenberry, who in Hollywood made creative use of his aerial impulses. He referred to *Star Trek* as a "wagon train to the stars," but after he died, the stars were pulled down to sit on the wagon train of spinoff after spinoff. Later producers like Rick Berman departed drastically from Roddenberry's course set toward a peaceful future; they even found a bust of Roddenberry and wrapped red fabric around its eyes.

Lancelot rides ludicrously into literature in "The Knight in the Cart," where he was subjected to public ridicule, much like fallen champion Lance Armstrong and his bicycle.

A friendlier Hades than Putin might have animated the life and career of Christopher Lee, who before entering the grave played Saruman, Count Dooku, Scaramanga, Dracula, and a host of other Underworld figures—and who turned Christmas songs into his own heavy-metal parodies, served as a Royal Air Force intelligence officer who survived a bombing attack, and escaped several other brushes with death. On one occasion a volcano exploded a few days after he had hiked on it.

Although seeking the myths behind public lives can afford a measure of amusement, seeking our own myth serves the practical and serious purpose of enlightening us about some of the strengths and shadows hanging over much of what we feel, perceive, and do. A personal myth repressed can turn rigid, dangerously so, as in the tragically terminated lives of Phoolan Devi and the Princess of Wales. When acknowledged, it makes sense of what seems chaotic to us about our own existence and offers possibilities for imaginative elaboration. "What's my myth" is really another way of asking, "What is the story of my life?"

Some suggestions for discovering your personal myth (see *Storied Lives* for more):

- Acquire a basic education in mythology. It's difficult to identify a myth if you haven't read many myths. Pay special attention to the ones that seem to fall synchronistically into your lap.

- Look for mythic motifs throughout your life. What themes and images recur? What stories and films drew your enthusiasm in childhood? What were the circumstances of your birth? Any odd event twists or anecdotes there?
- Examine your first dreams and memories for mythic images, themes, and characters.
- Take note of the objects, images, and animals you collect.
- Look for a mythic background to important events in your life.
- Look up the etymologies of your names for clues.

> In the Dagara tradition, you own your name up until the age of five. After the age of five, your name owns you. Your name is an energy; your name has a life force. It creates an umbrella under which you live. That is why it is important to hear the child before they giving him or her the name, because the name must match the purpose. My name, Sobonfu, means "keeper of rituals."
> — Sobonfu Some

Be aware too of *mythic resistance*: a certain anxiety about being inflated or burdened by what you discover. What helps with this resistance is to note and respect it, to consider the possibility that everyone has a mythic self as a link to the transpersonal dimension of life, and to reassure yourself that the story doesn't have to end the same way (and shouldn't). A personal myth presents the opportunity to step into a tradition and continue its lineage as only you can carry it forward.

"The More That Things Change...."

We have found no completely new myths abroad. Instead, we

see, inside us and on every side, retellings or reactivations, whether submythic or protomythic, of old myths that never die but do take on contemporary forms. New content, if old structures.

This would not surprise Jung. He spent most of his career tracing stories, fantasies, images, and dreams, all of which show up in past and present events, to archetypes. For Jung, all myth, modern or otherwise, is ad hominem because psychological. His speculations that archetypes transcend the psyche arrived late. Even so, for Jung archetypes do not evolve or multiply.

The genius of Nature makes do with a limited number of primary patterns that when combined and recombined result in infinite diversity. Look how often the spiral has been reused, and the hexagon, and the branch. Go outside and look around. You will probably find, at most, twenty or perhaps thirty such patterns. If they are truly the foundation of existence and consciousness, and therefore of myth, then a periodic recycling of mythic stories and plots should come as no surprise. As the French proverb tells us, "The more that things change, the more they stay the same."

However, Hermann Hesse insisted that every great truth is subject to reversal. The more things stay the same, archetypally rooted and mythically cyclical, the more they change, diverging into ever-renewed intricacies of creative tale-telling as life repeats the grand themes by which we make our way through the world, looking up now and then to see and perhaps to feel the embrace of cosmic structures—and stories?—we have only begun to fathom.

Chapter Fourteen - Dreaming the Myths Onward

> Gods that are dead are simply those that no longer speak to the science or the moral order of the day—like Michelangelo's and Newton's God, for example, whose hypothetical act of creation occurred at some moment in an imagined past no longer recognized... Every god that is dead can be conjured again to life, as any fragment of rock from a hillside, set respectfully in a garden, will arrest the eye.
>
> —Joseph Campbell, Prologue: *Historical Atlas of Mythology*

We have seen how myths and protomyths arise autonomously, usually in response to massive ruptures or transitions whether personal or collective. We have also discussed individual and small-group work with myth.

In this final chapter, we consider several possibilities for the creative elaboration of myth—applied mythology—on a large, even planetary, scale: an experiment awaiting its time. Perhaps that time is now.

Eradigm Earthrise

On Christmas Eve, 1968, the astronauts aboard Apollo 8 watched in awe and rapture as Earth floated above the lunar horizon. They took photographs and sent them back home.

These images would be appreciated by more eyes than any other pictures ever taken. Joseph Campbell referred to Earthrise as the basis for a new planetary mythology.

Looking back, can we discern large historical movements that begin with a core archetypal image surfacing from collective consciousness? An image elaborated into mythologies, institutions, values, industries, and worldviews, gathering up, expressing, and institutionalizing the aspirations of millions of people before gradually losing numinosity and giving way to the next captivating image? If possible, such an inquiry might give us a transpersonal view of the underside or inner meaning of history, including hints about where we find ourselves, why, and where we are headed.

To more clearly highlight this theoretical grand movement, consider the idea of *eradigms*: collective worldviews that capture and organize entire historical periods, and that draw their influence and authority from a central myth-generating archetype.

Using this lens to look through time, we might discern four of these eradigms: Mother Nature (the earliest), the Heavenly Kingdom (rising during the Agricultural Age), the Big Machine (Scientific and Industrial Age), and, most recently, Earthrise.

Each eradigm corresponds to an onset of massive and prolonged changes in collective consciousness, changes that reach across entire nations and continents. Unlike Joseph Campbell's schema of animal (prehistoric), planting (Neolithic), sky-based (Bronze Age), and human-centered (Axial Age) cultural developments, eradigm shifts do not signal an evolution or progression; rather, they mark gradual colorings in of human experience. Older eradigms remain active, although numinous for fewer adherents as time goes on.

When aligned with consciously, eradigms announce new areas for learning and dreaming; but when acted out unconsciously, they power virulent agendas of domination and control. The ideal would be to remember and live what is of worth of previous eradigms as we enter each new one: in our case, since 1968, Eradigm Earthrise. Returning to the sources of elder wisdom and value in an ancient eradigm would constitute remembrance, then, rather than regression. It may be that those who fail to embody the learnings from older eradigms are most at risk for possession by the newest. Think of Descartes the wanderer fascinated by the Big Machine eradigm but never really at home on generous Mother Earth.

Rising and falling eradigms represent the plate tectonics of collective consciousness. Their movements down the ages may well chart the individuation of the human species, with societies charged and permeated by a new eradigm expressing (though not always responsibly) its force for change while more mature societies provide a reservoir of stability even as they too evolve in their own way.

An activated archetype is known by what it attracts mythically, imagistically, thematically, and emotionally; and the same with an activated eradigm:

<u>Attributes of the Mother Nature Worldview:</u>
- Myths rooted in sacred nature; plant, animal, weather gods.
- Highly developed/differentiated awareness of natural world, resources.
- Kinship with animals.
- Relation to Earth as child to mother.
- Often matriarchal.
- Individual important as community member.
- Emphasis on tradition, ancient ritual, ancestry.
- Ceremonies for initiation into adulthood.
- Absence of organized warfare.
- Craft technology.
- Polytheism; paganism.
- Dream as a source of insight and wisdom.
- Story- and land-based.

Some key Mother Nature figures/events:
- Stone Age (Homo sapiens rises 200,000 + years ago).
- Worldwide migrations begin (50,000 BCE).
- First small villages (25,000 BCE).
- Cave paintings at Lascaux (16,000 BCE).
- Neolithic (10,000-3300 BCE).

Transitions to the Heavenly Kingdom worldview in cultures influenced by it:

- Smithing and increasing complexity in crafts.
- Writing, mathematics, and various technologies arising from the Agricultural Revolution.
- Earth goddesses replaced by sky gods.
- Centralization of power.
- Soaring populations near agricultural areas.
- Urbanization.
- Power hierarchies.
- Specialization of roles, labor.
- Organized warfare: troops under command of officers.

Attributes of the Heavenly Kingdom:

- Mythic hierarchies of gods; a separate Otherworld.
- Sharply defined gender roles.
- Divinization of leaders, who are seen as gods or as appointed by gods.
- Chiefs and priests on top, peasants below.
- Institutionalized religion.
- Religion allied with force (via priests and war chiefs).
- Rising importance of money.
- Matter/earth seen as lower, suspect, unimportant.
- The Otherworldly emphasized to followers as elites gather power in this world.
- Age of Empires, empire psychology.
- Age of Exploration: Columbus, Cortez, Pizarro, etc.: the quest for rejuvenation (for homecoming!).
- Consciousness paradigms: dualism, with spiritual pole uppermost, and idealism.

Some Key Heavenly Kingdom figures/events:

- 9000 BCE: monocrop agriculture and urbanization.
- 2400 BCE: Sargon I conquers Sumer, founds the first empire. Ningal the moon goddess flees war-torn city of Ur.
- 2,000 BCE: the first metal money.

- 1800 BCE: mythical Marduk, builder of Babylon, among the first definable battle heroes; his spear is named "Security and Obedience"; he slays the feminine Tiamat.
- 1350 BCE: Akhenaten (Amenhotep IV) of Egypt ignites monotheism by declaring the sun to be the One God.
- 700 BCE: consolidation of empires, urbanization, Hebrew prophets. Zoroaster, dualism, good vs. evil.
- 5th century BCE pre-Socratics: everything made of *arche*, one substance/essence/principle.
- 428-348 BCE: Plato's dualism; Greek rise of critical thinking.
- 500 BCE-33 CE: Buddha, Lao Tze, Chuang Tzu, Master Kong (Confucious), Jesus.
- The legalist wing of Christianity claims descent from Peter and becomes dominant.
- Heavenly Kingdom vs. Mother Nature: missionaries war on and convert pagans across the world. Rise of Islam. Religion becomes an antidote to urban fragmentation and cosmopolitan anxiety by offering a universal creed and sense of belonging. Emphasis on individual salvation.
- 1000: world population soars as agriculture improves, as does trade; cities and towns enlarge, guilds of workmen, a merchant class; a rise in the desire for learning and founding of universities.
- 1215: first version of the Magna Carta (Great Charter) limiting the authority of King John of England and paving the way to constitutional government.
- 1227: Temujin (Genghis Khan) dies after uniting Mongolia and instituting the Yassa, a written legal code.
- 1321: Dante publishes the *Divine Comedy*. Its imaging of Hell will persist for centuries.

Transitions to the Big Machine worldview:
- 1346: the Battle of Crécy marks the beginning of the end of chivalry as the longbow conquers armored troops.
- Johannes Gutenberg's printing press. Other inventions

move from East to West: the compass, allowing vast sea journeys; gunpowder; the mechanical clock.

- Aristotle's rediscovered emphasis on logic, empiricism, and natural science.
- Islamic manuscripts circulating in Europe include chemist and polymath Abu Jabir's experimental methods and ideas: start of the scientific method.
- Aquinas: nature as grasped by reason can teach us appreciation of the divine. Reason can serve faith.
- Scholasticism sets the stage for the ascendancy of reason and abstract science.
- 1216: the Hostmen of Newcastle monopolize coal.
- Father William of Occam (1285-1348).
- The Italian Renaissance.
- Henry VIII's 1536 disbanding of monasteries.

Attributes of the Big Machine:
- Mechanism as a mythic force.
- Atomization.
- Skepticism.
- Abstraction.
- Totality.
- Quantification.
- Rationality/reason.
- Homogeneity.
- Resistance to religious authority of every kind.
- Atheism as the sense of the sacred retreats and humans attempt to master natural laws.

Some Key Big Machine figures/events:
- 1400s: Filippo Brunelleschi and Leon Alberti of Florence invent linear perspective.
- Scientific and philosophical revolutions: Copernicus (published 1543), Galileo (looked through his telescope in 1609, de-celestialized the heavens, said science should be quantitative), Bacon (1620: science should eliminate sub-

jective bias), Descartes (1637, *Discourse*: "I think, there-fore I am...").

- 1602: the Dutch East India Company becomes the first to issue stocks and bonds.
- 1611: Shakespeare writes and acts in *The Tempest*, a theme of which is the end of the age of magic.
- 1648: The Peace of Westphalia (in eastern Germany) initi-ates the rise of the nation-state.
- 1687: Newton founds modern physics by publishing his *Principia Mathematica*.
- 1765: Scottish engineer James Watt designs an improved commercial steam engine. The Industrial Revolution is funded in part from treasure looted from the New World.
- 1793: Eli Whitney's cotton gin invented to clean cotton; idea thought up by Catherine Littlefield Greene.
- 1828: death of Shaka, who united the Zulus.
- 1848: Engels and Marx expose what Richard Tarnas calls the "social unconscious" in *Das Kapital*.
- 1859: Darwin's *Origin of Species*. Oil discovered at Titusville in Pennsylvania.
- 1860: American Civil War.
- 1867: the Meiji Restoration ends the feudal shogunate and begins to modernize Japan.
- 1879: Wilhelm Wundt sets up the first psychological labo-ratory (in Leipzig). William James at Harvard.
- 1885: Karl Benz puts a combustion engine into the first automobiles.
- 1886: *Santa Clara County v. Southern Pacific Railroad*.
- 1906: Standard Oil Company under John D. Rockefeller: rise of monopolies and globalization.
- 1909: the Haber-Bosch process pumps nitrates from poison gas into the soil to grow monocrops.
- 1914: World War I puts a bloody end to Enlightenment optimism and faith in disembodied reason.
- 1920: the dividing up of Iran and Iraq by oil-thirsty Britain and France galvanize Arab nationalism and Muslim jihad.

- 1940s: World War II; weapons research; existentialism's emphasis on death and alienation.
- 1944: Breton Woods conference founds the World Bank and the IMF for international borrowing.
- 1945: atomic weapons tested at Trinity and dropped on Hiroshima and Nagasaki.
- 1950s: Cold War, nuclear threat.
- 1966: Chinese Cultural Revolution.

Transitions to the Earthrise worldview:
- 1850s-80s: Pierre Janet works with dissociation, hysteria, founds a psychology of the unconscious.
- 1866: "ecology" coined by Ernest Haeckel.
- 1900: Freud publishes *The Interpretation of Dreams.* The cries of women diagnosed with "hysteria" in Europe herald the return of the repressed (the feminine, the unconscious, the body) and the first significant crackings in the Big Machine.
- 1903: *McClure's* praises the U. S. web of trolley lines, a network of clean energy connections.
- From Newton to relativity (1905) to quantum physics: a massive erasure of scientific certainty (e.g., most mathematical laws apply only to linear systems).
- 1910: field theory, Gestalt psychology, liberation movements, "depth psychology" coined, stirrings of environmentalism in U. S.
- 1913: Bohr model of the atom as a solar system of nested, interdependent bodies. Jung starts his "confrontation with the unconscious."
- 1920: 19th Amendment gets the vote for women. Equal Rights Amendment proposed in 1923.
- 1921: Mohandas Gandhi assumes effective control of the Indian National Congress.
- 1920s: postmodernity starts in the art world, picks up speed after WWII.
- 1945: founding of the United Nations.

- 1953: Simone de Beauvoir publishes *The Second Sex*.
- 1955: Teilhard de Chardin's *The Phenomenon of Man* argues that everything, even matter, has a "within" or interior.
- 1960s: Goddess movement; experiments in alternative spirituality, deep ecology, psychedelics.

Attributes of Earthrise:
- Information as the "solar energy" of institutions (Margaret Wheatley).
- Networking rather than hierarchy.
- Polycentricity.
- Ecosystem view of nature.
- Reconstructive postmodernity.
- Egalitarianism.
- Valuing of indigenous knowledge.
- Holism emphasized more than parts.
- Participation more than distance; "objectivity" seen as a fantasy.
- Working practices over grand narratives.
- Process over fixed structures (e.g., the personality as a self-structuralizing flow, not an object).
- Quality over quantity.
- Creative conjoining of the organic with the inorganic.
- Wisdom of the body and of nature.
- Experimentation in lieu of certainty.

Some Key Earthrise Figures/Events:
- 1960s: Civil Rights Movement; Women's Rights; Gay Rights; spread of Far Eastern spiritual practices; Vatican II.
- 1962: Rachel Carson's *Silent Spring* reinvigorates the environmental movement in the US.
- 1969: humans land on the Moon, see the Earth as a whole from space.
- 1974: the Chipko movement in India.
- 1970s: deconstructive postmodernity.

- 1980s: globalization, casting the dark spherical shadow of Earthrise.
- 1988: Vandana Shiva publishes *Staying Alive*.
- Earth Charter (1997), ecopsychology, greening of world religions, Chaos and Complexity Theory.
- Earthrise consciousness paradigms: systemic emergence, panpsychism.
- More: ecoliteracy, sustainability, Macy's Great Turning, Gaia Theory, ecospirituality....

Eradigms are the largest earthly archetypal currents we can see in historical action. The study of this, *eradigmatics*, would explore how archetypal images at the core of each eradigm ask to be dreamed onward into new cultural stories—in other words, new myths—that make sense of our place in the world. Eradigmatics would also study how adherents to previously emplaced eradigms create massive push-back against new eradigms unless their values and stories are somehow integrated into the cresting archetypal wave of cultural transmutation.

Before new myths can appear, however, the old ones must lose their potency. When these myths have served eradigmatic purposes, structuring huge reaches of human cultural experience through the power of collective story, their loss precipitates a mood of apocalypse. And when the need for descent—conscious letting go of outworn values, institutions, dogmas, and other sources of collective meaning—is not acknowledged, it turns the apocalypse literal.

The Meaning of Apocalypse

> In the present century, when man is actively destroying countless living forms, after wiping out so many societies whose wealth and diversity had, from time immemorial, constituted the better part of his inheritance, it has probably never been more necessary to proclaim, as do the myths, that sound humanism does not begin with

oneself, but puts the world before life, life before man, and respect for others before self-interest...
—Claude Lévi-Strauss, *The Origin of Table Manners*

According to ancient Norse mythology, Ragnarok, the Fate of the Gods, announces itself with two eerie worldwide shifts: animals everywhere change their food-gathering patterns, and weather turns unpredictably catastrophic. Soon Loki the Trickster breaks free of his bonds, as do the hellhound Garm and the monstrous wolf Fenris. The giants arm themselves and march on their opposite numbers: the mobilizing gods of Asgard so soon to perish in combat with their mortal enemies.

As we watch massive shifts of climate, habitat, animal behavior, and soil quality creep across our damaged planet, virtually every institution founded on the grandiose separation of nature and culture, self and world, trembles in anticipation of a collapse of unsustainable dualisms. Government, science, education, finance, security, law enforcement, healthcare, religion, energy, communications, transportation, infrastructure, agriculture: all face the overwhelming ecological debts coming due as species vanish, global temperatures rise, ecosystems succumb to industrial poisons, social systems die back with them, and vital resources like food, water, and cropland disappear. In storms, floods, melts, and droughts we have begun to see the first flickerings of this global turbulence.

In public presentations, I have started referring to the systemic breakdown of institutions founded on outdated Big Machine principles as "apocalyptic failure." Much of the official effort to minimize or mask that failure merely demonstrates what Jung identified long ago as *regressive restoration of the persona*. In the vernacular: whistling past the globalized graveyard.

Apocalypse is cyclical. Every now and then moribund cultural structures die out, and the altars and temples of the ruling gods fall. Whether human consciousness evolves collectively or not is open to debate—Heraclitus is said to have referred to history as "a chaotic pile of rubbish"—but it certainly never stands still. The problem is when we cling to toppling structures instead of letting go of them so we can build more adaptive ones. Then what should be an apocalypse of social and psychological transmutation, a series of inward descents to match the reinvention of outworn social systems and institutions, degenerates into literal catastrophe. What we do not face emotionally we act out literally.

The death of the gods or of God said to characterize Modernity (and the Big Machine Eradigm) are actually periodic occurrences. In the first dream of which we have a record, as told by Adduduri, overseer of the palace of Mari in Mesopotamia, "In my dream I had gone into the temple of the goddess Bellit-ekallim; but the statue of Bellit-ekallim wasn't there! Nor were the statues of the other divinities that normally stand beside Her. Faced with this sight I wept and wept."

She was not alone in her grief, not was Bellit in her demise. Zeus and Hera fall before Greek rationalism. Osiris, Attis, Re, Baldur, Dionysus, and Jesus all die and are resurrected. Psyche, Heracles, and many others achieve apotheosis after death; Anu gives way to Marduk (who gives way to Erra), Dyas to Indra (who gives way to Trimurti), Rangi to Tangaroa. Long after Julian the Apostate received word that Apollo would utter no more oracles at Delphi, long after Thor's sacred oak fell in Fritzlau in 723, Swinburne's "Hymn to Proserpina" lamented the passing of the pagan gods, as did Heine's 1853 essay "Gods in Exile."

The gods of the Romans gave way to Jesus and the saints. Nietzsche declared the One God dead: "And we have killed him." Spirituality lives on. It's worth remembering that in ancient Greek, *theos* meant an event, not a personality.

"Apocalypse" also brings an unveiling of what was hidden or unrealized. Descent is only half of apocalypse; the other half is renewal. After Ragnarok, Earth rises reborn from the dark primal waters as a new race of gods trickles through green groves and sacred sites. A similar post-disaster renewal shows up in other apocalyptic mythologies.

Behold a historical cycle. Every now and again, collective consciousness moves to where then-current forms of the gods cannot follow. Values change, habits change, old institutions die, new ones rise—and the statues and icons, texts and tales that served previous generations of the pious feel silly or irrelevant, at least to some. The old wineskins wear out. In myth this looks like deicide. In Modernity it looks like secular materialism and atheism. "Where there are no gods," wrote Novalis, "the phantoms reign." So does apocalyptic failure.

But as Robert Calasso observes in *Literature and the Gods*, "Loss precedes presence: every image must abide by this rule." As we will see below, Jung provided visionary verification. Every now and then the gods seem to die, only to return once they receive new forms, new interpretations, and new altars. Art, dream, fantasy, imagination, and storytelling open the doors of divine reentrance. Then the pageantry of the powers continues.

Old Stories Retold and Renewed

On every side, old myths receive new interpretations.

There is nothing new about this. Most major myths and folktales include variants. Odysseus took many forms before arriving on paper, and his journey never ended. In literature, Marlowe's Faustus goes to hell; Goethe's ascends into heaven; Mann's loses his mind; Jung's turns into a depth psychologist.

Today, though, in what is perhaps an Earthrise twist, the boldly creative make conscious use of story variants in order to raise voices pushed out of public discourse. Dionysus appears as transsexual, Thor as female. Dark sorcerers and wicked witches express suppressed points of view. Lakshmi comes forth bruised in campaigns against domestic violence, La Llorona as the woman who will not be silenced, and Princess Bari in service to the self-image of Asian women rebelling against Madison Avenue standards of beauty. A group of San Francisco Bay Area feminists held a ritual to put the head back on decapitated Medusa.

If we imagine a myth as somehow wanting to be creatively elaborated, we are at liberty to do so with the tales that speak to us. Simply rewriting the myth destroys its integrity, however. The art and craft of mythic elaboration requires preserving the spirit of the original tale while taking the plot in a novel direction, bringing forward backstage characters, and opening up new points of view.

Some years ago, I felt irritated with the story of how Paris of Troy, pushed by Hera, Athena, and Aphrodite to decide which goddess was the most beautiful, chose Aphrodite, giving her a symbolic apple in exchange for the (temporary) hand of Helen of Troy. A young man's error! I asked myself how, having reached middle age, I would have dealt with the dilemma he faced. I wrote about it to explore what a post-heroic form of masculinity might offer the situation:

PARIS' DILEMMA REVISITED

One day late in the spring, a teller of tales was out walking in the hills alone. Twists of scrub and sandy ditches wound around ridges of rock. It was here, Heaven decided, that the trap would be sprung.

Upon rounding a shoulder of stone, he beheld a sight that nearly overwhelmed his startled senses.

Three mighty goddesses stood squarely in his path. So bright was the glorious glow of their faces and robes and hands that he could scarcely see to keep his footing. He halted.

"Whoa," he muttered.

When his sight had returned somewhat, he bowed politely to these three goddesses. But he did not kneel.

Hera spoke first as befitted the Queen of Heaven:

"Greetings, O reweaver of ancient stories," she intoned, her voice causing the ground to tremble slightly below his feet. "We are here to make you an offer no mortal could refuse." She handed him the reddest, fullest, most perfect apple he had ever seen. She had gotten the apple from Eris, goddess of strife.

"You," Hera went on, "will give this apple to the most beautiful of the three of us. It is your decision. We will now speak on our own behalf." Drawing herself up, she said, "If you choose me, I will give you power."

Aphrodite let her robe slip slightly. "I will give you the most beautiful woman in the world," she murmured, turning one perfectly shaped leg slightly outward.

Athena spoke last. "I will give you unconquerable wisdom," she said as the sunlight shone blindingly on her breastplate. Her voice recalled that of a bugle.

The storyteller thought for a moment, then addressed them in the same order:

"Hera, I know the power you offer me is not the vulgar kind, for you stand for more than your Lady Macbeth-like shadow. You are Sacred Marriage, Holy Commitment, and Fidelity in all things. I cannot refuse that."

To Aphrodite he replied, "The gods themselves could not resist your charms, for your beauty and grace are what make existence worthwhile. No man breathing could deflect what you offer. I won't even try."

To Athena: "What teller of tales could refuse the gift of wisdom? No more could I, who am so poor in it despite all my years of tongue-wagging."

Remembering fallen Troy, he then said to the three:

"Because you have placed me on the horns of such a dilemma, I exercise my right—for to challenge the gods is a human prerogative—to raise the stakes still higher by meeting you with a counter-offer. It is this: If I resolve the dilemma, then I claim a gift from each of you, the friendship of all of you, and the enmity of none of you. Do you agree?"

"We agree," they said in unison, a lovely-terrible choir.

"Very well. Before I proceed, I will name the gifts. From you, queenly Hera, I require the gift of your good counsel in every gathering I assemble that meets with your approval. Beyond this, your signal when the inevitable befalls me and I fail to be a good leader." Hera nodded, her shoulders straightening her robe of interwoven stars.

"From you, beautiful Aphrodite, I require the gift of reminders to appreciate the lovely moments I encounter, and your momentary frown at the ones I bypass forgetfully." Aphrodite nodded, the fabric of her shimmering tunic like unto silver mist.

"From you, wise Athena, I require the gift of discernment of every opportunity to add to what little wisdom I now possess, and your admonitory trumpet call when I fail to learn what I need to know." Athena nodded, the butt of her spear scraping slightly against an armored instep.

"Very well," said the storyteller, drawing in a deep breath. "The way out of a dilemma is to take it firmly by the horns — or to be more exact, to take it deep within..." he raised the apple "...and digest it."

With that, he ate the apple.

Respecting its status as a token of marriage, its sweetness as its juice bathed his tongue, and its symbolization of knowledge taken deep inside, he ate slowly, relishing every bite, and gained three mollified goddesses as his teachers.

—Imagine what internationally networked teams of storytellers could do, especially if they wrote about myths of our time!

Whoever speaks in primordial images speaks with a thousand voices; he enthralls and overpowers, while at the same time he lifts the idea he is seeking to express out of the occasional and the transitory into the realm of the ever-enduring. He transmutes our personal destiny into the destiny of mankind, and evokes in us all those beneficent forces that ever and anon have enabled humanity to find a refuge from every peril and to outlive the longest night.

— C. G. Jung, "On the Relation of Analytical Psychology to Poetry"

Bridging Science and Myth

In his book *Dream of the Earth*, Thomas Berry writes, "We are in trouble just because we do not have a good story. We are between stories. The old story, the account of how we fit into it, is no longer effective. Yet we have not learned the new story." He adds: "The universe is a communion of subjects, not a collection of objects. And listen to this: The human is derivative. The planet is primary."

His belief is that we have gone from the institutionalized Middle Age myths of Christendom to a state lacking grand narratives that explain who we are, where we came from, how to cherish our ailing planet, and what kind of cosmos we live in.

Taking up this idea, Brian Swimme writes and speaks about a new, scientifically based, wonder-arousing Universe Story that fulfills these ancient needs for meaning and orientation. Richard Tarnas describes a "participatory" worldview that eschews the entrenched splits of the past (self-world, nature-culture, etc.) to recognize our involvement in whatever we perceive. The work of Jorge Ferrer extends this into transpersonal psychology and calls for varieties (plural!) of spirituality informed by individual experience but rooted deeply in relationships and community.

All of these views, interpretations, imaginings, and framings—we could include Sean Kelly's Planetary Era, Joanna Macy's Great Turning, Marna Hawk's work with eco-regenerative practices, and Gaian research methodologies—read like many New Stories, not just one: many new mythically charged tellings unfolding in the polychromatic light of Earthrise. Not a monolithic new mythology for the planet, then, let alone one thinker or guru self-authorized to figure out the universe for us, but instead, many fruitful examples of what Jung referred to as dreaming the myth onward by giving it a modern dress. A dreaming all the richer for involving myths and archetypal motifs from all around the world.

In *The Universe is a Green Dragon*, Swimme describes ten powers of the universe, powers to be found in seamless, generative operation everywhere we look:

- Centration: the power of concentration and exhilaration; think of all the centers around and within us (core of an apple, of the sun; a hearth; the inside of a vessel).

- Allurement: the power of attraction, of how things hold together (e.g., gravity, the strong and weak nuclear forces).
- Emergence: the power of creativity in service to new forms of complexity and order.
- Homeostasis: the power of maintaining balances (e.g., metabolism).
- Cataclysm: the power of breakdown and destruction.
- Synergy: collaboration; mutually enhancing relationships.
- Transmutation: change in individuals (atoms, plants, individuals) as shaped by community or context.
- Transformation: change throughout the whole of a system, society or community, often sparked by change in an individual member.
- Interralatedness: the systemic and interactive mutuality of every particle and system.
- Radiance: the power of energy and light, like that of the stars and the galaxies made up of them.

After a discussion with Brian about how mythology and science might meet instead of opposing each other, it occurred to me to flesh out his Powers of the Universe schema with gods whose jurisdictions matched those Powers:

1. Centration

Deities of hearth, home, central fire: Agnayi, Aspelenie, Ayaba, Chantico, Dimste, the Domovoi, Esta, Fuchi, Hestia, Hettsui-No-Kami, Hinukan, Mara, Panike, Rhea Saule, Silvia, St. Brigid, Tabiti, Vesta.

2. Allurement

Deities of attraction: Alilat, Anadyomene, Anaisa Pye, Anat, Apostrophia, Aphrodite, Ardwisur Anahid, Asherah, Astarte, Astghik, Atargatis, Benten, Branwen, Cliodhna, Dahud-Ahes, Dione, Enya, Erzulie Freda, Freya, Genetyllis, Hannahannah, Hausos / Eostre / Ostara, Hebat, Inanna,

Innin, Ishtar, Kishijoten, Kubaba, Kythereia, Lada, Lakshmi, Marwe, Medb/Maive, Mullisu, Ninlil, Oshun, Pelagia, Phra Naret, Qetesh, Quetzalpetlatl, Rati, Sauska, Sina, Sonhwa, Tlatzolteotl, Turan, Vanadis, Venus, Xochiquetzal, Yao Ji. Could also include Aengus, Amor, Anat, Anteros, Bes, Chin, Cupid, Eros, Hap, Himeros, Kaamdev, Kama, Konisalos, Lonoikiaweawealoha, Mabon ap Modron, Maponos, Min, Musubi, Orthanes, Pothos, Priapus, Semara, Shukra, Tychon, Vertumnus, Yarylo, Xochipilli.

3. Emergence

Deities of birth and emergence: Adam Kadmon, Amma, Amenominakanushi, Atum, Autogenes, Brahman, Bumba, Chuku, Dainichi Nyorai, Ebenga, Gayōmart, Hundun, Kunitokotachi, Mbombo, Nana-Baluku, Onteotl, Pangu, Phanes, Protennoia, Protogonos, Purusha, Sophia, Tan'Gun, Tuisto, Unkulunkulu, Ymir, Yuanshi Tianzun. Could also include doorway/portal deities like Cardea, Forculus, Ganesha (as Parvati's doorkeeper), Janus, Qin and Yuchi, Quirinus, Sarutahiko Ohkami, Shentu / Yulu, Terminus.

4. Homeostasis

Deities of justice and structure: Adrasteia, Aidos, Alastor, Cecrops, Dike, Eirene, Eunomia, Forseti, Furies/Erinyes, Gugurang, Invidia, Istanu, Justicia, Kettu, Mesharu, Mitra, Nanna, Nemesis, Pahto, Rashnu, Saturn, Shamash, Shapash, Suratama, Sydyk, Themis, Utu, Varuna, Yudhisthira.

5. Cataclysm

Deities of destruction: Agrona, Alala, Ares, Belatucadros, Bellona, Bhishma, Brunhild, Camulos, Chihyou, Enceladus, Enyo, Eris, Erra, Goumang, Grid, Guan-di, Gun, Hachiman, Hippolyte, Huizliopochtli, Intarabus, Jarovit, Kartikeya, Kibuka, King Mark, Ku Ka'ili Moku, Kumara, Lludd, Maris, Mars, Michael (archangel), Muireartach, Nanghaithya, Neit, Nermain, Net, Ningirsu, Nodens, Nuada, Perun, Romulus, Rudianos, Rudra, Saxnot, Skanda,

Smertrios, Svantevit, Teutates, Tūmatauenga, Tyr, Yan Di.

6. Synergy

Deities of pregnancy and birth: Ajysyt, Artemis, Belet-Ili, Bes, Diana, Eileithyia, Haumea, Hathor, Heqet, Ixchel, Lucina, Maia, Meskhent, Mylitta, Nekhebet, Nixi, Pukkeenegak, Renenet, Sar, Serket, Tauceret.

7. Transmutation (what changes the individual)

Trickster deities of transformation: African Hare and Turtle, Agemo, Agni (as psychopomp and messenger and fire-bringer), Ahriman, Aillen, Ame-no-Uzume, Anansi, Angra Mainyu, Arvernus, Aunt Nancy, Bakotahl, Baubo, Bobbi-bobbi, Botoque, Brahma (as creator of all, who tried to seduce virginal Saraswati; his hair fell out when he botched the first creations; farted out the demons), Bricriu, Budha, Burat, Cagn, Chikapash, Chimata-no-Kami, Chiyou, Coyote, Dagonet, Dxui, Ea, Efnysien, Eidothea, Ekaga, Elegba, Enki, Eshu, Ekwensu, Gizo, Glooskap, Gong Gong, Hahgwedhdiyu, Hahgwehdaetgan, Hanuman (e.g., he got the ketaki plant to lie for him), Hermes, Hlakanyana, Ialdabaoth, Iambe, Iblis, Ikaki, Iktomi, Iris, Iubdan, Ixtab, Juha, Kamapua'a, Kavya Usanas, Khnum (as psychopomp and creator god), Kitsune, Kokomaht, Kukulkan, Kwatee/Kivati, Leprechaun, Lilala Humba, Liulei, Loki, Lu Tung Pin, Malsum, Manabozho, Mara (Hindu), Masau'u, Maui, Mercury, Mireuk, Mouse Deer, Mredah, Murile, Nanabozho, Narada, Ngai/Enkai, Obatala, Oxumare, Pa Pandir, Prometheus, Pinga, Pushan, Quetzalcoatl, Ratatosk, Raven, Rübezahl, Samael, Seth/Set, Silde, Sisyphus, Suirenshi, Sungura, Susano, Ti Malice, Tshakapesh, Turms, Thoth, Tirawa, Ture, Twalen, Ushvas, Veeho, Veles, Wakaboko, Wakdjunkaga, Wichikapache, Wiisagejaak, Wihio, Xian, Yurugu, Wisagatcak.

—Could also include witches (Argante, Baba Yaga, Banba, Cailleach, Cerridwen, Chedipe, Circe, Elphane, Empousa, Graeae, Hekate, Jenny Greenteeth, Kundry, Lamia, Lilith,

Lorelei, Macha, Mader Akko, Mallt-Y-Nos, Maria Prophetissa, Medea, Morgana le Fay, Nicevenn, Pasiphae, Prothyraia, Rangda, Scathach, Sirens, Syn, Taweret, Witch of Endor) and wizards (Cangjie, Cathbad, Curoi, Faust, Fintan mac Bochra, Gwyddion, Idris, Kothar wa-Hasis, Klingsor, Kullervo, Legba, Llwyd ap Cil Coed, Manannan mac Lir, Manawydan, Math ap Mathonwy, Melampous, Merlin, Onikoso, Philemon (Jung's version), Simon Magus, Sukkayurae, Sukunabikona, Tezcatlipoca, Three Magi, Vainamoinen).

8. Transformation (what changes the whole)

Deities of education and wisdom: Akanidi, Amaterasu / Wakahirume / Ōhirume, Andraste, Aponibolinayen, Arachne, Ataensic (Sky Woman), Athena/Medusa, Au Co, Ayida Weddo, Bagalamukhi, Barbelo, Belet-ili, Belisama, Bhairavi, Bhuvaneshvari, Brigantia, Brigid, Buto, Catalina, Chalchihuitzli, Chandi, Chhinnamasta, Chimalman, Cihuacoatl, Coatlique, Durga, Eredatfedhri, Eve, Fatima, Gayatri, Guadalupe/Llorona, Guanyin, Guinevere, Helen of Troy, Ilmatar, Kali, Kannon, Kabyeeb, Kokyanwuuti, Lin Mo Niang (Mazu), Luonnatar, Mami, Marcia Proba, Mari Urraca, Mary, Mary Magdalene, Matangi, Mawu, Maya, Metis, Minerva, Neith, Nintu, Nisaba, Norea, Nuwa (Nu Gua), Nzambi, Oyontsetseg, Pandora / Anesidora, Phra Mae Kuan Im, Prajñāpāramitā, Prakriti, Princess Bari, Salome, Sapientia Dei, Saraswati, Savitri, Sekhmet, Senuna, Shatarupa, Shodashi, Sophia, St. Barbara, Star Woman, Sulis, Tanit, Tara, Tripura Sundari, Uma Haimavati, Vajrayogini, Wadjet/Nekhbet, White Buffalo Woman, Yemayo, Yennenga, Xuan Nu, Zhinü, Zihong Jiemei, Zhi Nu.

9. Interrelation

Deities of care (usually clothed in earth imagery rather than cosmic): Akakallis, Ale, Anchiale, Anna Perenna, Aruru, Baigal Ekh, Bestla, Ceres, Chloris, Chrysothemis, Cybele,

Demeter, Feronia, Flora, Gefion, Gerd, Grýla, Gula-Bau, Heidi Gammu, Hipta, Isis, Khesana Xaskwim, Ki, Konohanasakuya-hime, Leizu, Meret, Mokosh, Nantosuelta, Nehellenia, Nikkal, Ninhursag, Ops, Oxum, Pachamama, Pomona, Rana Niejta, Rhea, Saranyu, Shala, Siduri, Sita, Tailtiu, Togorsh, Toyo-Uke-Bime. —Deities of divine marriage: Aditi, Akka, Alusina, Asase Ya, Asherah, Barginj, Frigg, Hathor, Hera, Indrani/Shachi, Ixchel, Juno, Leto (introverted), Luna, Modron, Morgan, Morrigan, Nasilele, Nokomis, Oba, Olokun, Parvati, Sachi, Sarpanitu, Sol and Luna, Taishakuten, Uni, Xi Wang Mu.

10. Radiance

Deities of radiance: Ai, Amitabha, Apollo, Atepomarus, Balder, Belenus, Dainichi, Dawn Star, Fu Hsi/Xi, Grannus, Horus, Hu, Logos, Lugh, Mahavairochana, Maponos, Mithra, Narayana, Nuadu, Orunmila, Pak, Resheph, Saoshyant, Savitr, Sodong, Vairocana, Vindonnus, Yi, Zhu Rong. The deities of Transformation above are also known for being radiant.

Aside from the question of whether more Powers exist (Wildness, Spacetime, Plenitude, Harmony, Nature, Craft, Depth, Animation...?), the advantage of this pairing is that it reveals the mythic background of a set of contemporary scientific concepts. In other words, it stories them, and by doing so invites our wonder at them while revealing the archetypal and mythic motifs within/below our scientific ideas.

It also raises the question of whether the gods and heroes of myth are actually closer to us than we might realize.

The Silver Chain: Gnosis 2.0

Silver Chain is how I conceptualize a particular mythic-animistic tradition in continual mutation from antiquity forward into the present. The ongoing recovery of Gnostic texts, the popularity of Gnostic studies, the proliferation of alternative spiritualities, the publication of Jung's *Red Book* and, before that, Tolkien's (a part of which we know as *The Lord of the Rings*), the renewed interest in nature myths around the world: all attest to this underground tradition's resurgence as membership in traditional religions plummets.

Jung wrote about his take on the Perennial Philosophy (and spirituality) even before Aldous Huxley, who maintained that an unbroken, cross-cultural esoteric tradition stretched from antiquity into modernity. This core represented an underlying link between religions around the world. Taking a cue from Goethe and Ficino, Jung believed in a fabulous Aurea Catena, a "Golden Chain" of perennial esoteric praxis going back through Hermeticism and alchemy to the ancient Chaldeans and Egyptians.

But what if we could glimpse the subtler light of a more lunar, less literal, more intuitive tradition, passed on, not in an unbroken line, but through what surfaces now and then from the depths of culture and consciousness: an Argentum Catena or Silver Chain of images, teachings, and practices involving our psychospiritual relations with a lively, animate world? A tradition never in the spotlight, murmuring instead like a quiet stream flowing through cracks in ideological dams that split self from Earth and spirit from matter? A tradition that keeps psychodynamics and ecosystemics together while shining reflective lunar light on their interplay through time and place.

Of course, esoterica lives all over the world. What characterizes the Silver Chain is its location of spiritual power in the natural and the material as explored by the imaginal and the symbolic. Reaching back to ancient shamanism and nature art, the Argentum Catena includes such figures as Adduduri of Sumer, Aesara of Lucania (her book *On Human Nature* envisions the mind as an arena of interactive forces not confined to the human interior), the philosopher Celsus, alchemist Muhammad ibn Umail ("Turn the gold into silver"), Abu ibn Arabi, Paracelsus, Marsilio Ficino, Margaret Cavendish, Goethe, and, more recently, physiological researcher and nature mystic Gustav Fechner, Hermann Hesse, Henri Corbin, and, to some extent, Jung, Hillman, and certainly Jane Hollister Wheelwright (see *The Ranch Papers*). In my classes I look at four

Western expressions of this tradition: Gnosticism, alchemy, depth psychology, and a personal form of spiritual gnostic ecopsychology I refer to as *terragnosticism*.

What makes the Silver Chain different from so many other esoteric traditions is the mighty figure that binds the links: the World Soul. The Gnostics knew her as the primal self-reflection of the unknown and ungendered God. "I am the First," she declares in the *Trimorphic Protennoia*, "the Thought that dwells in the Light. I am the movement that lives in the All, She in whom the All takes its stand, the first-born among those who came to be, She who exists before the All." She has also appeared as Protennoia, Eve, Norea, Mary Magdalene, Barbelo, Zoe, and Sophia, who breathes soul into all the living.

Gnosticism was forced underground by what hardened into the early Christian Church, attacked by it partly because of a reverence for wise goddesses. Gnostic myths told of powerful archons on the loose: male sub-gods, or "Authorities of Darkness," that ruled the world and worked to keep us all asleep and unaware (and, in our day, funding wars and buying things we don't need).

Sophia resurfaced as a key figure in alchemy, a wisdom tradition born in Egypt and evolved in the Middle East when shut out of Europe by popes and bishops afraid of the alchemical preoccupation with ensouled matter. If everything is enspirited and the Kingdom of Heaven all around us, as the *Gospel of Thomas* says, then we need beg for no keys to get in. Alchemists found magic and meaning even in dungheaps and dark corners. They took seriously the parable of the rejected stone that in wise hands could serve as the cornerstone. "Our gold is not the ordinary gold" goes one of their famous sayings. Another warns of literalism and reductionism: "Beware of the physical in the material."

Like the Gnostics, the alchemists knew that to find Sophia, one must turn away from public spectacles and dazzling venues and seek her sparks of light in the dark, where most fear to look. For adepts cooking and praying at their laboratory altars, the darkness within and in the world blended into one shadowy realm where animated beings and forces held sway. It was possible to glimpse them through *vera imaginatio*, the true imagination, not to be confused with making things up. The alchemists had in mind what Henri Corbin would describe one day as the *imaginal*, the realm of suprapersonal images he had come across in the writings of the Sufi mystic Ibn Arabi. This mystic's visionary encounter with the beautiful figure of Wisdom inspired alchemists, Christian mystics, and European troubadours. Dante's longing for Beatrice recalls this numinous Islamic motif.

Jung saw all this as psychological activity projected onto matter through chemistry. Blackening meant descent, depression; whitening reflection, purification; yellowing dawning insight; and reddening passionately embodied attainment announced by the Coniunctio, the marriage of "opposites" in the individuating psyche. In both alchemy and Gnosticism he saw the ancestry of his own version of depth psychology.

Jung's influence on the Silver Tradition has been a mixed one. Many of us who have heard of Gnosticism and alchemy as wisdom paths owe this to Jung's work on them. His psychology updated both of them. But it also makes the double move of subjectivizing spiritual work while taking soul out of the world. If that world seems animated, Jung believed, only our projected human psyche makes it so. What is of value remains inside us, with outer events important only insofar as they serve interiority.

In fact most, perhaps all, of Jung's original key ideas look like psychologized translations of Gnostic concepts and images. "Archetype," "syzygy," "shadow," "projection," "image," "wholeness," "unconsciousness," and "Anthropos" are Gnostic terms. Individuation is the psychological counterpart to Gnosis. In making these translations Jung reified intuitive, subtle, and lunar layers of consciousness arrayed all *around* us into solar theoretical constructs *inside* us: exactly what Ibn Umail warned against, comparing such an introverted approach with hiding *inside* the brain and the Stone instead of working on its trans-psychic refinement for eventual use out in the world. Jung did likewise with alchemy.

Even so, Gnosticism and the Silver Tradition embedding it received a fresh retelling by Jung. During that retelling he performed an operation of epochal consequence.

Jung Transforms Gilgamesh

Liber Novus, otherwise known as Jung's *Red Book*, was finally published in 2009 after decades of understandable resistance by Jung's family. The book contains descriptions of inner visions that assailed Jung from 1913 to 1917 as well as startling images painted by him.

In one vision, tended in active imagination, Jung looks up to see the fearful approach of Gilgamesh. This giant being, whom Jung refers to as Izdubar, says he seeks to reach the moon and thereby gain immortality. When Jung explains that the moon circles the Earth and is unreachable, Gilgamesh accuses Jung of poisoning him, smashes his own ax, and collapses. Realizing that this god is actually a piece of psychic reality (Jung had not yet found the word "archetype"), Jung shrinks him down into an egg and walks off with him: "Thus my god found salvation...He did not pass away, but became a living fantasy, whose workings I could feel on my own body..."

Later, Jung kneels and chants over the egg until it emits smoke — and flame, judging from the painting adjacent to the text — and opens. From this emerges a healed, reborn, a blindingly shining god who rises in the east like the sun. Jung reels from the emotional sacrifice this requires of him.

In times gone by, Gilgamesh was believed in as a literal god. Jung updated the god's imaginal manifestation by *framing it as a* psychic *event!* Understood psychologically, the gods are archetypes: the structural foundations of the psyche.

Jung observes that the sun of the depths cannot rise until the old form of the Hero is slain. If we fail to do this, we slay each other, as was shown, tragically, by the outbreak of World War I. Jung's replacement of old symbolic wineskins with new allows the archetypal image of the Hero — Gilgamesh is a Heroic god — to evolve. In Jung's consciousness, the heroically murderous but ailing god changes into a luminous solar being, a healed and healing source of interior insight. The implications for peace studies and for the rejuvenation of religion are profound.

This updating of god to archetype formed the experiential basis of Jung's later comment, "The most we can do is to dream the myth onwards and give it a modern dress. And whatever explanation or interpretation does to it, we do to our own souls as well, with corresponding results for our own well-being." Jung used this insight to study the evolution of the Western image of God.

A limitation in Jung's daring reinterpretation of the sacred lurks, however, in the risk of internalizing the sacred to the detriment of its external expressions. The numen is demoted to a psychological operation. The goddesses shrink down into animae, the gods into animi, and the heroes into functions of a hardy ego consciousness. Jung's repeated claim that he dealt only with *psychic* realities because he was an empiricist and not a metaphysician cannot avoid this risk because he has already declared the outer world devoid of any sentience or meaning not bestowed by the human psyche. The result of this premise is a reinforced disenchantment with a world deprived of its spirit. Perhaps Gilgamesh was right about being poisoned.

Throughout Jung's work he certainly emphasizes the need to stay consciously engaged with the outer world. But he also thinks that our sense of the world as animate and charged with images comes from us and not from the world. This passage from *Psychology and Alchemy* is characteristic of Jung's habitual introversion on this point:

> Everything unknown and empty is filled with psychological projection; it is as if the investigator's own psychic background were mirrored in the darkness. What he sees in matter, or thinks he can see, is chiefly the data of his own unconscious which he is projecting into it.

Nor did Jung ever change his pairing of archetype with instinct. For Jung, archetypes are imagistic expressions of biological impulses within our bodies. "Like the instincts," Jung states in the chapter he wrote for *Man and His Symbols* shortly before he died, "the collective thought patterns of the human mind are innate and inherited... We can identify them even in animals, and the animals themselves understand one another in this respect, even though they may belong to different species." In the same chapter he continues:

> There are no longer any gods whom we can invoke to help us. The great religions of the world suffer from increasing anemia because the helpful numina have fled from the woods, rivers, and mountains, and from animals, and the god-men have disappeared underground into the unconscious.

From where they occasionally raise an outer ruckus, as Jung acknowledges in his work on synchronicity; but even then it's a matter of an archetype *influencing* outer events, not of founding or underlying them. As early as his doctoral dissertation Jung interpreted mediumistic manifestations like ghostly rappings on walls and tables as exteriorizations of complexes triggered within seance participants. In old age he changed his mind about ghosts always being complexes, but not about the primacy of the inner world or the psychic silence of the natural world. He acknowledged at most a probable if invisible bridge between psyche and matter.

By explaining divine images and influxes psychologically as activated archetypes, Jung gave us a modern way to connect immediately and intimately with the sacred dimensions of our interiority. He also updated how we think about the gods, and by doing so furthered their continuing incarnation. Although Jung's subjectivizing of them has proven one-sided, disenchanting, and deanimating, we can still make use of his tools and ideas for dreaming the gods onward, creating for them renewed and ecologically relevant vehicle-forms and thereby reanimating the world with their presence.

Because, under the eradigmatic light of Earthrise, what if the world around us brims with archetypes?

Archetypes of Place, Earth, and Cosmos

Saundra Wolfe assigned our permaculture class an exercise: "Go outside and find all the basic patterns you can, then come back and we'll discuss the functions they serve in nature."

Locating curves, spirals, circles, nets, branchings, polygons, and other primal shapes, I wondered how anyone could miss the presence of archetypes out here. Mandalas everywhere, and none of them projected. Yet some Jungians still maintain that archetypes are exclusively human.

These natural forms affect us below the level of consciousness. We climb mountains to find peak experiences, seek deserts for spiritual purification, swim rivers to catch the flow of life, and drop into valleys to descend into ourselves. *Terrapsychology* is the systematic exploration of these inner-outer parallels.

Dig out a map and look at Washington D.C. Observe how the Potomac River runs north and branches to enfold the city, held as though near a fallopian tube in a womb. Virginally named Maryland and Virginia squatted like expectant midwives on either side of the newly born District of Columbia as the bald head of the new Capitol emerged. With Father Washington standing by proudly, the architect who platted the city named its birth canal radii the L'Enfant Plan after himself. A height restriction still in effect prevents tall buildings there from growing up. The District has yet to achieve full statehood, and only a third of its residents can read. The womb image holds not only for the local geography, then, but for the human cultural life it contains, including *les enfants terribles* of emotionally stunted politicians obsessed with sexuality, rape, and birth control. No wonder the press calls it the Beltway Bubble. Perhaps we should rename the city Wombington.

Paris a brain, with the longitudinal cerebral fissure of the Seine dividing the city's cultural hemispheres. Revolutionary Moscow and its hub of rivers caught in the geographical-psychical motif of a revolving wheel. The great African Rift Valley the earthly vagina that birthed humanity. New York City the chancy wheel of the goddess Fortuna, whose statue goes by the nickname Miss Liberty thanks to Irving Berlin. Estuarine San Francisco the altar not only of nature saint Francis, but of his Greek brother Dionysus, genderqueer god of drama, ecstasy, altered states, and edge places. The mythically informed eye of terrapsychology traces how features of the landscape align, archetypally and folkloristically, with the doings of the dwellers there.

Many of the indigenous yet inhabit a spiritually animated world. All our ancestors did before the Agricultural Revolution split cultivated from wild, a wound widened by the Industrial Revolution. As David Abram notes, indigenous cultures that preserve their traditions hold their storytelling as an expression of the place where the events occurred. Nodding to this elder wisdom, terrapsychology uses contemporary concepts to substantiate deep connections between who we are and where we are.

Furthermore, place presences seem nested. Who is California? She appears on our State Seal as Minerva, the Roman Athena. Her name comes from a word that means "female successor." This is relevant. From the steep seaside cliffs to the Cascades, eastern Sierra and southern deserts, she stands armored; dozens of submerged ships carrying would-be invaders lay in ruins along the coast. San Francisco represents her cosmopolitan enthusiasm, San Diego her borderline defensiveness (the city is split by caverns), and Los Angeles her projected Emerald City idealizations and nightmares, especially after the ancient Los Angeles Basin had risen like a stage from the depths of the Pacific. Native people sojourned there to receive spiritual messages long before Hollywood encased its stars' hands in asphalt.

Widen the lens. California is the Athena of the *Americas* whose name refers to "great power" and to "master craftsman": we are here to work, South and North alike. The alchemists would have said: to labor at the opus of matter's transmutation. Is Europe Europa, carried away to crown-wearing greatness on the back of the king of the gods? Names are revealing; "Africa" might derive from the Egyptian "Motherland." And so with the other places, cities, countries, bioregions, continents, all arrayed as presences across the face of still-beautiful Gaia, which is why all mythologies speak of earth goddesses by whatever local names.

And why stop there?

New places away from Earth will bring new dreams and stories, some with familiar faces. Astronaut Don Pettit says that while on Earth he often dreams about flying. "I just kind of lean back, and I'm floating around the room, not like Peter Pan, but—because if I say that, then some of my colleagues will put my face on a Peter Pan and tape it to my office door. But anyway, it's sort of like Peter Pan." In space, though, he dreams about walking in woods and fields of grass.

Before Charles Duke flew to the Moon, he dreamed of driving there in the same place he would visit in the Lunar Rover, as he mentions to an interviewer:

> I: During an excursion with the lunar rover, you found yourself driving in a place you had seen in a dream before your flight?

> D: Well, yes. In my dream John Young and I were driving the lunar rover up to the north and we as we came across a ridge, there was a set of tracks out there in front of us. We asked Houston if we were allowed to follow the tracks. Houston said yes. So, about an hour later we found another lunar rover with two guys on it that looked like me and John. I felt kind of comfortable. I took parts from this other vehicle, to show to the people down at Houston. Now, when being actually on the Moon, we were going north towards our objective which was North Ray crater and as we went over the hill, I recognized, generally, the little valley that I've seen in a dream before. But in the dream there was a set of tracks. Of course the tracks were not there! It was so vivid.... Yeah I've seen this before, or something very similar in the dream I had. The dream was so vivid that when we were landing I looked out of the window to the north to see if there were any tracks on the surface of the Moon! The landscape was very similar to what I have seen in my dream.

> I: Do you have any explanation for the whole story?

> D: I think it was just a coincidence. And I cannot say it was exactly like the dream. On the Moon every land-

scape is more or less the same.

In myth, the reflective Moon mirrors many things to us. Time does not flow straight there. In some stories, souls pass through the lunar sphere on their way elsewhere.

If we journey farther outward, past Mars (where a giant dust storm obscured the war god's face when the first Gulf War broke out in the desert), past asteroids and planets, we find the fringe of the Local Bubble that encapsulates our solar system. Here we float not far from a fertile supernova. In other words, we find ourselves just outside a stellar nursery.

That nursery is held within the arms of the Milky Way, a gigantic spiral of stars and dust. Astrophysicists say that spiral galaxies usually live longer because their spin funnels gaseous nourishment to their stellar systems. Furthermore, these galaxies, each embedded in a vast framework of dark matter, continue to create, evolve, and self-organize. Is not the spiral also an ancient religious symbol? A symbol Jung interpreted as the path of individuation, a path not linear but circular and three-dimensional?

Ours is one of many galaxies held by Local Group and Virgo Supercluster and, from still farther afield, unimaginably farther, a universe now reimagined by physics as a "daughter" who formed when vast multidimensional "parent" membranes came close enough to spark a Big Bang...

This kind of mythic imagining is different from that in which the gods stand behind or above places, objects, and natural forces. The difference is twofold: thanks to Jung we can imagine gods and spirits as archetypes moving *within* us while appreciating divine family resemblances across pantheons; and we respond, terrapsychologically, to places and natural forces *as* archetypes. In other words, we picture no separate wind god: the wind *is* a "god," and the same with all the other divine powers of earth and sea, sky and cosmos. A cyclone develops an "eye" that looks down upon the soils and waters over which it crosses, a mobile, stormy point of view.

We find this nature link in myth (see Chapter 11) and its commentators. Harvey Birenbaum, for instance: "Athene is not just a dramatic way of saying 'wisdom,' or Apollo 'truth.' There is something alive and personal, dramatic and mysterious, in wisdom and truth, in warfare and in love, in thunder and in flood, that the gods speak from to manifest its nature." For R.S. McCoppin, the vines on trees, the abundant growth, *are* Demeter, just as the sea is Poseidon: "Whenever we find ourselves at places that hold their own myth, the land reveals itself, for those who look closely, as the myth itself." Robert Stange: "The gods do not 'represent' or 'symbolize' elements of our world—they are our world." Lawrence Hatab: "The *moods* of spring and winter, the sense of revitalization and joy followed by the sad closure of the winter months—these are what present the existential meaning of the seasons... At some point, one may sense that the gods *are* this quality of life. the myths are their means of revelation." Even Plotinus: "On the other hand, to despise this sphere, and the gods within it or anything else that is lovely, is not the way to goodness... For how can this Kosmos be a thing cut off from That and how imagine the gods in it to stand apart?"

Archetypes and myths not connected to particular places connect instead, then, to the entire cosmos and live all through it, everywhere. The grandfather gods like Zeus, Odin, Olorun, and Vishnu are abroad and above as the higher view of things. Of course they are sky gods, for they are Sky. Sophia and her sisters—Barbelo, Sophia, Eve, White Buffalo Calf Woman, Sekhmet, Amaterasu, Andraste, Athena, Saraswati, Anima Mundi—pervade the cosmos as its all-animating, all-creating Wisdom. The Hero is its eloquent strength, Wildness its untamed Artemisian integrity, Trickster its rupturing, transitional chaos. Whenever subatomic particles wink into existence, rush together, liberate their energies, and vanish back into the cosmic foam, Lakshmi and Aphrodite and their sisters rise again from the waves, from the nucleii of atoms to trans-galactic lattices of dark matter and energy, Beauty holds it all in balance. Beauty knows this, and knows it clearer, perhaps, when we reflect that knowing back to her.

And (coming back to the ground) why not just call the fruitfulness of Earth (otherwise known as Arda, Terra, Ala, and Gaia) by holy names like Demeter, Sita, Flora, Pomona, or Pachamama, with a contemporary understanding of them not as otherworldly mega-people somewhere *behind* the crops and plants, but as Fertility itself a sentient earthly abundance, imaged, animate, and fully capable of response?

If most viscerally felt Earth to be one vast temple, its destruction would halt overnight. The alternative is Mordor, the Upperworld leveled into an Underworld where even the rivers burn.

Jung did not live long enough to hear about spiritual ecology, but he would have recognized its lineage because he knew that all our ancestors revered spirits of nature and place. The usual canard that this sensibility was killed off by science fails to note that people who cherish a relationship to the natural world actively oppose the industrialization of entire regions of our planet. Their stories guide them.

Spiritual ecology goes by many names—ecospirituality, nature spirituality, religious ecology, and my own terragnostic version— but remains steadfast in its commitment to a conscious relationship with a reenchanted world alive in ways we might never have suspected. Going well beyond Gaia Theory's mechanistic blueprint of a self-regulating planet making itself optimal for life, spiritual ecology calls for the towering artificial wall between self and world, culture and nature, inner and outer, and material and spiritual to be torn down. With it could fall many us-vs-them dualisms that keep things globally greedy, violent, overspent, and overheating.

This does not mean idolizing Nature, but revering its animated soulfulness, which includes respecting the needs of its breathing, blooming, and crawling emissaries in the web of interspecies kin-ship in which we too are embedded. "Emissaries" because we hear more and more accounts of animals in trouble calling out to us: whales entangled in nets, elephants escaped from the circus, the decomposing manatee that came to me in a dream.

From deep within the existential void growing around the oppressive Roman Empire, the Gnostics creatively reimagined the myths handed down to them, and by doing so revealed the divine powers of the cosmos as accessible from within. At the outbreak of World War I, Jung reimagined them again as psychic forces for which he borrowed the Gnostic term "archetypes." Here on the brink of ecological extermination, our own species ripe for the endangered list, can we welcome the divine in the world while recognizing its presence sparkling within us?

Reweaving the Net: Enchantivism and Archetypal Activism

As leadership consultant Margaret Wheatley explains in the revised edition of *Leadership and the New Science*, a spider when facing a torn web does not slice out segments to repair, but reweaves the net.

The archetype of the Net shows up in every mythology, often accompanied by goddesses who weave (the Fates, the Norns, Frigg, Arachne, Athena). Indra's net of jewels is an example, as is, perhaps, the Internet. What has gone by names like Systems Theory, Complexity Theory, and Nonlinear Dynamics gathers images of where Net meets other archetypes, including Chaos.

> As long as a disequilibrium condition is maintained or increases, and as long as amplifications of departures from equilibrium become rife in the system, and as long as the system is constrained to hold all of this energy, more and more experiments will be tried until a threshold is reached—an unpredictable moment when the entire system may shift.
> —Jeffrey Goldstein, James Hazy, and Benyamin Lichtenstein

How might myth help us reweave the torn nets of psyche, culture, and ecology? Perhaps through an activism of reenchantment?

Activism uninformed by sustained deep reflection easily slips into unhelpful aggression and moralizing. "Quit shaming and depressing people," for example, is advice I often give activists who do not think about the emotional impact of their words on their audiences. Unending gloom and dismal numbers, melting icecaps and body counts, guilt trips: is it any wonder people with no way to deal with all this apocalyptic news retreat and numb out? The unreflective activist shines a spotlight into the eyes of people asleep and expects them to wake up. Instead, eyelids close tighter.

Activists must also deal with burnout, lack of funding, lack of support, rage from opponents, misunderstanding from allies, and, very often, state violence and the lingering emotional and physical costs of it.

Activism is responsible for protecting most of the rights we still enjoy, but when split from self-care skills and knowledge of human nature, it can also reinforce and energize what it wants to curtail.

On the other side flies the lofty idealist who believes that meditation, chanting, or inner work will cure the world of its ills—which they have never done in any of the societies that practiced them. In the United States, where millions flock to yoga studios and therapy jargon permeates politics, unlimited campaign contributions go on flowing into elections as ecosystems die off, state violence looms, and millions do without three meals a day.

When permeated by energy talk of "vibes" and "manifestation," appeals to prismatic cosmic principles look foolish to those still on the ground. As clouds of incense rise, the ruthless seize high office, the super-rich get richer, and the tractors crush entire forests.

Inner work kept separate from the messy business of outer life also tends to collapse when confronted with serious opposition, leaving the world stage to the shallow, the greedy, and the ambitious.

What is available for people either disenchanted with ordinary activism or not called to it to begin with? For followers of synchronicity, oracle, and dream who see their intuitions pointing out into the world? What is a third alternative to unreflective activism and insulated subjectivism?

Enchantivism describes the many ways we make lasting change by reenchanting our relations with ourselves, each other, and our ailing but still-beautiful planet. Being an enchantivist requires no shouting or preaching, although at need it can supplement more conventional and confrontational forms of activism and reform. The quiet can use it so long as they possess a lively imagination, a deep care for life on Earth, and a willingness to plant stories in the space of fertile soil between real and ideal. An enchantivist by vocation is a *transrevolutionary*.

Because "enchantivism" is a relatively new coinage, many have done and are doing it without being aware of the term. A few examples:

> Nichelle Nichols was praised for playing Star Trek's Uhura by Martin Luther King Jr. Black watchers wept with joy to see themselves represented in the future community of courageous explorers.
>
> Jacqueline Suskin saved a stand of redwoods by writing poems for the CEO of the logging company preparing to cut them down. Later, she helped design for him a permaculture dwelling.
>
> Thyonne Gordon uses nature walks to recharge her storytelling, consulting, and community advocacy work: "What if we paralleled nature and focused on purposed giving for the time we have instead of wallowing in what was?"
>
> Devdutt Pattanaik retells Hindu myths as part of increasing diversity awareness in educational and business settings worldwide.
>
> Generations of women have been inspired by the feminist science fiction and fantasy works of Ursula K. Le Guin.
>
> Environmental activists have taken heart from J. R. R. Tolkien's *The Lord of the Rings*.

Although enchantivism does not require a public audience, these examples share a bridging of reflection and action that begins in fantasy and moves into personal and cultural transmutation through a change of story. We speak of "transmutation" because transformation, a popular but vague word, can refer to superficial change, as when you put on a hat to transform your appearance. Transmutation refers to deep, alchemical, lasting change of the type Jung referred to when he wrote that the big problems in life are not worked through, but outgrown.

An inspiration-based storytelling approach also triggers less push-back. With the elevation of Trump into the White House we see just how strong reactionary forces can be. It is never enough merely to oppose racism or sexism: the racist and the sexist need reeducating. The same applies to the violent.

Powerful, the focus on how things *could* be. Although quite clear on injustices, MLK did not say, "We're a bunch of victims." He said he had been to the mountaintop and *seen*, and by saying this, he moved mountains. He denounced racism, violence, poverty, and warfare—and while doing so gave us a visionary glimpse of the Beloved Community. Never one to stay only with what went wrong, he dared to imagine how things could go right.

In its own quiet way, enchantivism draws on the power of imaginative vision through telling and retelling of old myths, fairy tales, reborn legends, surfacing fantasies, and personal accounts. Unlike lecturing or debating, storytelling invites us into a shared imaginal landscape, leaving its interpretation, if any, to the listener. It seeks common ground by collecting visions of times and places that can delight us. In story, the activist and corporatist, rebel and cop, artist and financier come together in a commons of image and language as fellow humans dwelling in more-than-human terrain.

In April 2002, Pacifica Graduate Institute hosted a conference called *The World Behind the World*. With 9/11 only a year in the past, the conference featured many political perspectives. One of these was Aizenstat's call for an "archetypal activism" capable of listening into and responding to collective catastrophes like terrorism and global warming.

Aizenstat outlined four moves of archetypal activism:

1   *Moving into the event by translating it into metaphor.* One of my students did this by amplifying the image of the falling World Trade Center towers with meanings gathered from the Falling Tower card of Tarot. This move creates new questions: What else is collapsing, around us and within us? Who is falling? What hurls the lightning at the tower?

2 *Maintaining compassion by withholding judgment while understanding events from within multiple viewpoints.* Moralizing gives way to resonance, reflection, and self-questioning. When Donald Trump was elected president of the US, his followers were condemned as racists and bigots. Can I try to imagine their point of view, however uncomfortable the effort, without taking refuge either in reflexive condemnation or in blithe denial of what has happened? Can I do the same with those who condemn? With those on the sidelines?

3 *Getting curious instead of reactive, especially about the particularities of the event.* This requires setting aside habits of thought and perception so we can look for the novel and the unexpected. Instead of railing against too much digitization and mass media, what if we noticed the presence of Indra's Net shimmering behind the Internet? What does the collective psyche intend with all these nodal cross-connections?

4 *Hold the tension of the opposites so what is new can emerge from turbulence and rupture.* Recall former Irish president Mary Robinson's invocation of the mythical Fifth Province in the center of Ireland as an ideal for hubs of reflection, storytelling, and reconciliation. Imagine a restoration project dually devised by industrialists and environmental poets. All this relies on an ability to acknowledge and endure polarized oppositions in ourselves as well.

When teaching archetypal activism, I have included a few of my own additions. Dreams make good starting points, but we can also tend our strong, heart-based emotional reactions and persistent fantasies and even symptoms as they respond to outer events. While tending as many conflicting viewpoints as possible, we maintain the awareness that some of these viewpoints have been oppressed or otherwise marginalized by powers that be. We also use imagination to explore the positions of beings who are not human (e.g., factory-farmed animals, ecosystems under siege). We must remember to receive adequate support and to assess the results of our actions. And we must continue absorbing myths.

Putting all this together, we arrive at the following overlapping activities involved in doing archetypal activism:

- Witnessing or dreaming something (a "pressing concern") in and from the world that needs tending,
- Heeding its images as potent metaphors in motion,
- Resolving to reflect on and respond with soul to the concern,
- Creating a support network for the effort,
- Viewing the concern empathically and non-judgmentally from different points of view, especially those pushed to the margins,
- Maintaining openness and curiosity about the particularities and details of the concern,
- Amplifying them (Jung) by doing cultural and historical homework on them,
- Staying in a space of uncertainty, exploration, and tension until new understandings emerge,
- Allowing these understandings to shape action on behalf of what is witnessed or dreamed,
- Taking three concrete steps on its behalf, including storytelling and work with myth
- Assessing the effects of these steps, and
- Either ritualizing a closure for the project or deciding on further efforts on its behalf.

These could be thought of as modes of a two-phase operation: *Listen to the guidance of imagery in an event, and act on behalf of that imagery.* In systems theory terms, the moves above provide a potentially continuous feedback loop for encouraging a complex social system to evolve. Telling and retelling myths applies particularly impactful feedback.

The following projects were created by participants in Stephen

Aizenstat's DreamTending™ workshops and in my Deep Storytelling and Archetypal Activism classes. All began as responses to a pressing concern that arrived through a dream or other signal event reaching across the inner-outer split to touch the heart directly:

- After recurring nightmares about an old woman weeping near a cathedral in a deserted village, an attorney remembers this to be a place he knew in childhood. Visiting the village, he learns that an old section of it is to be bulldozed to make way for a resort. As a result of his actions and some effective community networking, the cathedral is saved and renovated.
- A management-level engineer initiates a series of informal in-house conversation circles on the topic of leadership that can inspire and mentor potential leaders. These circles in turn inspire others and give rise to presentations that contain figures from mythology to teach organizational lessons.
- A middle school teacher draws on mythology to give students living in ecologically damaged areas important lessons in emotional resiliency. The students also make use of this safe, non-judgmental space to creatively tend the images and feelings that arise through art, video, and photography.
- A hospice volunteer adds storytelling and listening to end-of-life stories to the usual activities offered to the elderly, who receive deep attention and witnessing. On another level, these practices modify public attitudes with new and positive narratives about how life can end with warmth and grace.
- A psychotherapist and educator creates a series of life story writing courses followed by an open community event in which participants share one of their stories. Although the stories focus on struggles with mental health, addictions, and other kinds of trauma, the tellers

are not diagnosed or required to visit a clinic. The events are open to the public and include music and food. Tellers and listeners tend the myths arising from the tales.

- A museum curator combines stories about Artemis and Diana with designs of myth-rich graphics, logos, and social media campaigns to organize action on behalf of abandoned pets, dogs in particular. She also trains animal rights activists in these techniques.
- A rainforest aid worker solicits funds, donations, and volunteers by changing from fact- and number-based reports to presentations of the stories of the local community interacting with staff.
- A writer plans an Earth-honoring holistic health center at the edge of a forest. The center includes courses on herbalism, growing food, ceremony, myth-telling, and "practical dreaming" focused on the question: *How do we come home to an ensouled world?*

A beauty of enchantivism, whether performed as spontaneous storytelling, community myth work, conscious ceremony, or archetypal activism, is what it offers to those of us who avoid protests and crowds and public activist endeavors. It works for introverts and extraverts alike. And it enlists those who would normally not consider themselves activists.

It also comes with a myth:

According to Taoist monk Lieh Tzu, the Yellow Emperor of China searched everywhere for enlightenment so his people and their lands would be happier. After going on long journeys and consulting with hermits, he came home, frustrated, only to wake one morning in joy.

Calling his ministers, he said, "I spent three months in seeking and seclusion trying to learn how to govern the country and cultivate myself, but thinking this out did not help. This morning I woke up enlightened, at last, from a dream."

Everyone in the kingdom got to work to make it resemble the mythical land in the dream. After twenty years they came very close indeed. When the Yellow Emperor finally died, the people mourned the passing of a visionary leader.

As Eva Wong writes in her "hermetic opening" of Lieh Tzu,

> On the islands in the eastern seas are immortal beings who live on dewdrops and pinecones. They do not eat grain, they feed on the wind and vapor, and their minds are as clear and still as the mountain lake.... They are open, friendly, and have no inhibitions.... There is no fear, no anger, no tension, and no dissatisfaction. No one is superior or inferior to anyone else. Everything is bountiful and everyone enjoys the providence of heaven and earth.... The deities bless the land, and the monsters never go near it. This is the land the Yellow Emperor visited in his dream.

But archetypal activism doesn't take an emperor.

In his letters, JRR Tolkien coins the word *sarumanism* to denote the customary belief that only money, power, and publicity create change in the world. He firmly disagrees with this. It is (he points out to one fan) not the great generals, armies, or wizards who transform Middle-earth, but the determined actions of little hobbits. And so it is in life.

Change on a large scale does not depend on huge, spectacular programs so much as on more modest actions performed soulfully and with devotion. Telling one relevant myth at an appropriate time, for example. The impact of such actions increases when they are linked.

The enchantivist approach recognizes the importance of stating facts but sees clearly that this will not suffice to change actions or worldviews, especially when the facts bounce off an entrenched story tenaciously held. Only a better story movingly told can overcome that. Not louder words or cleverer arguments. As Le Guin expresses it:

> It is by such statements as, 'Once upon a time there was a dragon,' or 'In a hole in the ground there lived a hob-

bit' — it is by such beautiful non-facts that we fantastic human beings may arrive, in our peculiar fashion, at the truth.

Forward Terrania

I am English by origin but I am early World-Man, and I live in exile from the world community of my desires. I salute that finer larger world from across the genera-tions, and maybe someone down the vista may look back and appreciate an ancestral salutation.
— H.G. Wells

In this chapter we have considered several fanciful applications of myth dreamed onward: as an archetypal study of historical forces; as a reenchantment of worldviews, including the scientific; as an updated, Earth-honoring tradition of spiritual immanence; as ter-rapsychology; as the means to carry reflective action into the world.

It seems appropriate to end with a final fancy: of updating the Golden Age archetype through retellings of how we might live in an Earthrise era of justice, happiness, generosity, and peace on our ail-ing world.

As a boy, I loved reading fantasy and science fiction stories about advanced societies of people who lived in verdant, spacious homes, led healthy lives, cared for each other, and felt at home. As I got older, images of these inviting societies pursued me, each describing one little corner of possibility—Modern Utopia, 24th Century Earth, Pala, Ecotopia, Terra, Beloved Community, Magic Theater—while stimulating a question I could not escape: *Why don't we live like this already?*

We can make stupendous, terrifying, marvelous things, we humans: cities dwarfing their inhabitants, worldwide libraries, ocean-crossing ships, sky-crossing aircraft. We have landed on the Moon and can contemplate the possibility of standing on other worlds as well. Our telescopes reveal the very edges of the universe. The best of humanity's music, art, literature, science, philosophy, mythology, and wisdom await as close at hand as an Internet connection.

Clearly, building safe, beautiful, and just places to live isn't a question of technological capability. Nor is it a question of mere finance: people made miracles long before money existed. Yet today, most of humanity goes hungry, thirsty, and homeless, undeclared wars rage continually, entire countries are ruled by delusional zealots, foreign policy descends into thuggery, and unregulated heavy industry carves the planet into mass extinction, intercontinental pollution, ocean acidification, and global warming.

In spite of all this, and much to my surprise, fantasies, hopes for, and even dreams persist about Terrania, to give a fanciful name to the just, peaceful, planet-honoring world civilization whose fantasy presence has tracked me across the years. Terrania: the protomythos of Earth lovingly and responsibly inhabited by a species of psychological adults.

In one dream, which visited many years ago at a time of despair,

> *I walk in the wind up a grassy hill. I'm with other people. We all sit down in the grass and look out over the vista.*
>
> *Before me rolls the most beautiful valley I have ever seen. Beyond low pink bungalows perfectly placed into the slopes on which we sit stand coppices of trees—waving leaves as green as perfect emeralds—above grottos and clearings in which large brown and tan animals pass through patches of sunlight and cool shade. Herds of distant horses graze the plains, and at the valley's bottom winds a blue creek flowing with such crystal clarity that the schools of fish within it seem to glow.*
>
> *Above and behind the valley, storm clouds puffy with moisture bring rain to green lands lit by flashes of lightning. The storm moves on to reveal an impossibly blue sky above a sea so rich in royal blues and purples that it could have been painted by Van Gogh.*
>
> *As my eyes rove this scene of indescribable loveliness, my despair slips away, replaced by a growing feeling of*

elation. When the other viewers and even the hillside and valley "tell" me subvocally that I am part of what-ever work makes this fresh, clean place possible, the ela-tion heightens into joy.

How long I sit here I cannot tell, but after some time-less time, I nod to one of my companions— "I'm ready to go back now" —and...

...I awaken in bed on Christmas Day with the joy still cresting through me.

Since that dream—a gift followed by other hopeful dream-gifts through the years—I have never doubted that we could find on Earth a paradise of our desire. In fact, it often feels to me as though future Earth—not Utopia, but Heretopia—shimmers just up ahead, sum-moning us to bring it forth, like a baby appearing in the dreams of a woman about to become pregnant. Warfare, collapse, and terror, then, not as hopeless regressions, but as the birth pangs of a fresh new world.

Parts of it live today, in a million local explorations and experi-ments going by names like ecovillage, storytelling circle, civil rights, women's rights, environmental justice, sharing economy, restorative justice council, permaculture, biomimicry, fair trade, urban farming, reskilling, Cradle-to-Cradle industries, micro-lend-ing, mycoremediation, rewilding, Great Turning. Earthrise. The tools lay all about us. What do we need to scale up what they can fashion?

Good stories, perhaps. Good dreams. *Good myths.* Not from any individual, but from many. What we can speak and imagine, we can do.

My own path forward toward such possibilities has taken a turn that continues to amaze me. After years of writing and speaking, reflecting and teaching, I have finally realized that all of my work fits together into a single complex story, composed in the form of a planetary mythology: Terraniana. Not a mythology for everyone, or a big narrative to squeeze everything into, but, arising spontaneously down the years of studying and listening, my own way of storying together who I am, where I belong, why I am here, and how the stories I love so much hold hands across time and place around the world.

> With our view of Earthrise, we could see that the earth and the heavens were no longer divided but that the earth is in the heavens.
> —Joseph Campbell, late interview

I invite you to explore the archetypal Golden Age on Earth yourself and see what arises. Perhaps the gleam of worldwide renewal reaches from behind us in the dawn of myth, with all our stories together weaving our true planetary mythology, to storied possibilities beckoning from just up ahead.

Let us go on our way now with a thought from Sallustius (*On the Gods and the World*) as we continue our mythic meanderings:

> *Tousauta peri mython eipousin hemin autoi te hoi theoi kai tôn grapsantôn tous mythous hai psychai hileoi genôito.*

> To those of us who have spoken in these ways about the myths, may the gods themselves, and also the souls of those who wrote the myths, be kind.

Appendix 1: Theories of Myth: The Longer Version

> And isn't it odd that none of the mythologists, neither the prigs nor the lunatics, has seen the need for an interpretation on different levels?
> —Sigmund Freud, letter to C. G. Jung

> Myth is the garment of mystery.
> —Thomas Mann

What is myth?

Evidently, something so obscure that centuries of theorizing from a multitude of standpoints (theological, political, linguistic, biological, psychological, sociological, anthropological, philosophical, ecological, etc.) have not given us a solid definition. It was for this that psychologist Henry Murray referred to myth as a "notorious semantic hobo of our time." Myth, Jean-Pierre Vernant observed, is often defined not by what it is, but what it is not.

Could it be, though, that the search for a solid definition is part of why we so often fail to appreciate the living reality of myth? "Those who attempt theories of myth," wrote Voltaire, "are blockheads and pedants."

Nevertheless, let us survey this intellectual ancestry and see what we are left with.

* * * *

Preliterate societies tend to just tell mythic stories without ana-

558

lyzing them to pieces. Myths are not considered problematic enough to warrant study until someone tries to separate the historical from the fabled and the rational from the nonrational. Myth becomes available for classification as institutionalized science and abstract philosophy rise, and as writing allows story collection. As Levi-Strauss would announce one day at the Sorbonne, they (oral cultures) listen, and we (after printing) read.

In ancient Greece, *mythos* (formerly transliterated as *muthos*) originally meant an utterance performed in public or a narrative plot, as Harrison, Sienkewicz, Stambovsky, Doty, and a host of other scholars have observed. But then divisions set in, as happens when a rationalism uncritical of itself seeps into a society. In Euripedes' *Electra* mythos is a story that both reveals and conceals, and by the time of the *Iliad* mythos is distinguished from *ergon* ("deed"). Herodotus the historian uses "mythos" to mean a false story in opposition to "logos," a true story.

It has often been suggested that skeptical stances toward a mythology set in when that mythology is already in decline. Xenophanes of Colophon is an early Western example. Around 530 BCE, he attacked sacred stories of the gods, polytheism, and the state religion as human projections. According to Clement of Alexandria, the Ionian argued that

> ...If cattle and horses and lions had hands or could paint with their hands and create works such as men do, horses like horses and cattle like cattle also would depict the gods' shapes and make their bodies of such a sort as the form they themselves have.

In his monotheistic crusade to amputate blasphemous (to him) tales, it didn't occur to Xenophanes that whatever transhuman forces animate myth would best serve their self-expression by taking on human appearance. Phillip Stambovsky credits him and not Plato with launching the Western project of rationalism.

In Greece, myth studies begin with suspicion (via Pindar the pious moralizer, Theagenes, Thucydides, Plato) and the equation of myth with falsehood, although Empedocles promoted myth as higher truth.

The Orphics, Stoics like Chrysippus (3rd century BCE), and Heraclitus tried to rescue it by making *allegory* (Porphyrus) of it as the first myth *naturalists*: Hera standing for air, Hades vapor, Hephaestus fire, and Demeter earth. "Allegory" comes from *allos*, "other," an Other it tries to domesticate. Theagenes was the first in the West (followed by Fontanelle, Tylor, Lang, and too many others to mention) to reduce myth to *pre-scientific explanation*: mythos as inferior logos. Stoics like Zeno also argued for a moralizing allegorizing of myth: Kronos, whom they confused with Chronos, as a lesson in how Time devours. All this shrinks the mysteries of myth into something knowable, cognitive, and readily exploitable by conscious agenda. Plato, who refers to allegorizing as insinuation (*huponoia*), called for its use by *mythoplasts*: state-sponsored storytelling-propagandists seeking to control the public.

Of course, Plato indulged in his own mythopoetics, those of lost Atlantis, the rebirth tale of Er, and the mythic Demirge creating the world between raw matter and the realm of pure Ideas. Stanley Roberts nominates Plato for popularizing the supposed dependence of logos on mythos. In the *Phaedrus*, the character of that name asks Socrates if he believes that the north wind abducted the daughter of a mythic Athenian king. Socrates plays with this a bit, offering a rationalistic explanation for the story, but then says he finds such explanations "too ingenious and belabored." He does not envy the interpreter, who after finishing with the daughter "must go on to put the Hippocentaurs into proper shape and after them the Chimera..." Socrates would prefer to inquire into "whether I am a more complicated and puffed-up sort of animal than Typho or whether I am a gentler and simpler creature, endowed by heaven with a nature altogether less typhonic." This is using myth for self-study. For Lawrence Hatab, however, Plato consistently uses mythos to serve logos.

Xenophanes' rationalistic take on myth, Heraclitus's emphasis on logos over mythos (an early version of logic over myth), Parmenides's on being over becoming and on judging by reason,

Anaximander's on the changeless ground of being, and Plato's favoring of Forms over forms (including mythic stories he denigrated as copies of copies) joined with early Hebrew historicizing under the jealous eye of an absolutely transcendent God to reduce myth, an expression of sacred and embodied storytelling, to pale moralizing, fake history, pseudoscience, propaganda, inferior philosophizing, or anthropomorphism: in any case, to something less than itself.

Furthermore, the collection of myths in books (starting around the fourth century BCE) read by individuals instead of recited in groups conditioned later theorizings and interpretations to regard myth as literary and visual rather than collectively heard and witnessed. This was a foundational cultural shift.

The fictional *Sacred Record* of Euhemer the Messenian claimed to find an old inscription on an island called Panchaea off the Arabian coast in the Indian Ocean, an inscription written by Zeus declaring that stories of gods are based on a king from early Crete. Plutarch said he was lying. Before either of them, Prodicus of Ceos suggested that discoverers of useful arts had been raised to divinity: Demeter a founder of agriculture, Dionysus the first viniculturalist. The long line of **euhemerists** tying deities to dead humans of long ago would come to include Hecateus, Herodotus, Ennius, Joannes Malalas, Saxo Grammaticus, Léon de Pella, Diodorus, Cicero, Persaios, Polybius, Strabo, Lactantius, Dādū of the Dadupanthis, Snorri Sturluson (for whom the Norse Aesir were Asians and Thor a grandson of Priam named Tror), Sir Isaac Newton, Samuel Shuckford, Jacob Bryant, Antoine Banier (who makes room for esthetic and philosophical explanations by myth), David Hume, Herbert Spencer (myth as ancestor worship), Robert Wood, and William Ridgeway, among many others.

In Japan, kami were sometimes seen as elevated nobles; in Paraguay, shamans could be deified; in the Pacific Islands, chiefs could be. In Confucian hands, Chinese myths would undergo reverse euhemerism by reinterpreting deities as culture heroes like Houyi and the Yellow Emperor. Christian monks did likewise when gathering old tales in Ireland. (Euhemerism, a reductive intellectualization, should not be confused with *apotheosis*, the attainment of godhood by a mortal: the deification of the Japanese Emperor Ojin, for example, or the Tangiia belief in Raratonga as a former chief.)

Herodotus also argued for **diffusion**: a common origin of Greek and Egyptian myths spreading outward. Perhaps myth proceeding from Ionia, named after Ion the orphan, was in search of a home elsewhere. The **autochthonous** explanation would send myth home by claiming that it arose spontaneously in many different places: hence the cross-cultural similarities of motif and plot. As Franz Boas would complain one day against Jung, these similarities were often, and wrongly, taken to indicate causal similarities as well, whereas symbols resembling each other often sprang from quite different cultural sources.

In India, the Charvaka materialist philosophers had argued since 600 BCE for critical doubt as a basic research attitude and empirical sense perception as final arbiter of reality. In China, the *Heavenly Questions* (*Tian Wen*: 300 BCE) skeptically queried various myths through verse. In making fun of myth, they perpetuated it.

* * * *

Myth fell into disrepute for centuries in Europe, where materialism and abstract reason had weakened indigenous resistance to Christianity. Missionaries were eager to disprove every myth but their own as "pagan."

According to the doctrine of **condescension** favored by Irenaeus, Augustine, and Eusebius, God allowed myths prefiguring the life of Jesus to play out in non-Christian nations in order to make way for conversion. Natale Conti's *Mythologia* (1616) would interpret the return of Odysseus to Ithaca as a model for Christian endurance. On the other hand, Christians like Justin Martyr, Tertullian, and Cyprian argued that Satan was responsible for deceiving potential believers with such myths. John Toland would denounce myth as corrupted monotheism; to Fourmont, Warburton, Pluche, and Shuckford, all Christians, Egyptian gods were false ones, period. Although applying myth-interpreting methods to Christian story and doctrine was forbidden, Thomas Aquinas had distinguished four levels of biblical understanding: the literal, allegorical, moral, and anagogical (or spiritual). Dante was aware of these levels when he published the *Divine Comedy* in 1320. In still-pagan rural regions and even within the heart of Christian art, allegory, and imagery, myth lived on, disparaged but persistent.

The artists and poets of the Renaissance brought myths recovered from ancient texts newly translated back into the forefront of European taste. Boccaccio allegorized myths as hidden natural truths artfully hidden (1375). In a Christian context, allegory led the way, as in Giovanni Boccaccio's "On the Genealogies of the Gentile Gods," which translated the victories of Perseus into those of virtue over vice. The emergence of Tacitus's *Germania* in 1457 celebrated what would later be reconfigured as Germanic heroic ideals. Natale Conti saw Greek myths as philosophical allegories.

Francis Bacon's continuation of myth held as allegory (e.g., Pan as Mechanic, for some reason; the Sphinx's claws as scientific grasp), Galileo's exaltation of primary over secondary qualities, and Descartes' splitting of inner and outer highlighted a new reduction of myth to matter intellectualized. For the most part, Christian officials tolerated myth in painting and sculpture: witness the popularity of Lorenzo Cartari's *Imagini degli dei degli antichi* (1556). In 1685, however, Van Dale published an attack on pagan magics and miracles — and wound up including those of Judaism and Christianity.

In 1697, philosopher Pierre Bayle published his *Historical and Critical Dictionary* to destroy (destory) myth by use of reason and argument. Instead, he brought the ancient tales renewed attention and interest. His criticism of philosophical extremism might have been applied to his own take on myth: "Philosophy at first refutes errors. But if it is not stopped at this point, it goes on to attack truths. And when it is left on its own, it goes so far that it no longer knows where it is and can find no stopping place." It would have infuriated him to know how much he had done to bring myth back into the limelight.

* * * *

The year 1724 saw publication of Joseph-François Lafitau's *Customs of American Savages Compared to the Customs of the Beginnings of Time* as well as Bernard Fontenelle's *On the Origin of Fables*. Father Lafitau (and, later, Charles de Brosses) drew **comparativist** parallels between the legends and myths of the ancient Greeks and those of Natives of the New World. This launched the idea of the psychic unity of humanity as well as the confusion of indigenous with early and primitive.

Influenced by Van Dale, Fontanelle, whose last name is now a medical term for a gap between cranial bones in an infant's skull, maintained in the brief "Of the Origin of Fables" (1724) that myths were pre-rational speculations from the infancy of human consciousness. Such arguments fed the colonial project of invading and exploiting non-European lands Fontanelle had never visited. Previously, the invaded lacked Jesus; now they lacked scientific reason. One day Robert Jewett, Shelton Lawrence, and M.W. Sexson would refer to this idea of progressing beyond myth into reason as "the myth of mythlessness" (1977).

Giambattista Vico, philosopher, historiographer, and professor of rhetoric, published his ambitious book *The New Science* (*Scienza Nuova*) in 1725. In it he argued that knowledge is constructed, not snatched objectively from the gap of a Cartesian split, as well as rooted, like language, in myth's power of "true narration" (*vera narratio*). Taking an evolutionary and what would now be called a Systems Theory view of society, he posited three phases of its evolution: the divine, the heroic, and the human, each stamped by its own language and characteristic tales. Working allegorically with a soft euhemerism (e.g., heroes as the emotional states of a nation) applied to folktales, myths, and fantastical tellings silenced by the Enlightenment, Vico called for a New Science of comparativism of myths and traditions across cultures to study their evolutionary activity through what served for early concepts: *imaginative universals* dreamed forth through "poetic logic." Whereas empirical science hunts for regular laws, the New Science seeks basic patterns of action throughout human history as revealed in myths, "a mental language common to the nations." His observation that myth, a natural creative product of the poets of every human culture, must change with the times remains important. He also considered metaphor the foundation of culture. Imagination, not reason, is the key to fathoming the "poetic truth" of myth. He anticipated Jung: "Whatever appertains to men but is doubtful or obscure, they naturally interpret according to their own natures and the passions and customs springing from them. This axiom is a great canon of our mythology."

Andrew Ramsay, another early comparativist (and *structuralist*: interested more in the form of myth than its content), wrote the historical romance *The Travels of Cyrus* (1728). In it he distinguished between myth and theology and asserted that the myths of China, Egypt, Greece, India, Israel, and Persia describe an initial state of goodness followed by a fall and a restoration by a presiding deity. Although he made no overt claims for this, the Christian parallel was clear. For a time, comparativism would fall under the spell of the archetype of the Golden Age.

As international trade and warfare intensified, what people had noticed since the time of Alexander the Great increasingly piqued scholarly attention: similarities and variances across the myths, legends, and religious stories held by different cultural groups. Throughout the 1750s, myths that would feed later comparativist analysis came forth and were popularized by trend-setting Nordic Renaissance figures like Paul Henri Mallet, Hugh Blair, and James Macpherson, although the latter's stories of Ossian were weakened by inadequate sources. Even so, people in England, France, and Germany rushed to claim Ossian as their national bard.

During this period George Stanley Faber pioneered the *typological* approach to myth—looking only for similarities in Egyptian, Greek, Persian, Indian, Chinese, Scandinavian, British, American, and South Sea stories made this easier—and repeated Christian allegorizing by classifying all goddesses as aspects of the Ark of Noah. But he left out the Gnostic goddess Norea, who burned down the Ark when Noah refused to allow her aboard. (By the time he built the second Ark he had learned his lesson.) Antoine Pernety believed myth to be an arcane code by Egyptian alchemists for hiding their secrets of longevity from peasants and, worse, women. The Abbé Bergier suggested a less paranoid idea: that myths present a symbolic natural history of the Universe, making them compatible after all with Christian truth.

Comparativism grew with a flurry of Indic translations and studies by Anquetil-Duperron (who had published the Zoroastrian *Zend-Avesta* in 1771) and William Jones ("On the Gods of Greece, Italy, and India," presented to the Asiatic Society in 1785, and with rather accurate archetypal parallels: Jupiter and Indra, for instance). Jones had uncovered linguistic similarities between Sanskrit, Latin, and Greek, sparking interest in Indo-European cultural origins. Myths for him were historical, poetical, metaphysical, and especially astronomical: specifically, solar, anticipating the sunstruck Max Müller. For Jacob Bryant (*Analysis of Ancient Mythology*, 1774), myths were euhemeristic anticipations of the Bible lacked by sun-worshipping pagans looking forward to monotheism. Bryant anticipated linguistic theories of myth by delving into etymologies to bolster his efforts at prehistorical reconstruction.

The *Bibliotheca Classica* published by John Lempriére in 1788 was not a theoretical work, but its catalogue of classical and mythological entries included deity names and anecdotal details that would delight generations of readers. One such reader was Lord Sandwich, who named vessel after vessel of the British Royal Navy after Greek and Roman deities. This Olympian fleet would sally forth as the last defense of England against titanic Napoleon's invading armies.

Many societies have viewed planets and stars as deities and even done design in their image, as with the Han dynasty of China's construction of the capital to parallel Ursa Major and Minor; likewise for Ninevah with Ursa Major, Babylon with Aries and Cetus, Assur with Arcturus, and Sippara with Cancer. Mary Barnard suggests that a comparative study of stellar myths be accompanied by a study of calendars such as those used for planting. Allegorist Charles-François Dupuis introduced ***astrological*** explanations for myths in 1795 in Paris. He also believed Jesus to be a mythical solar deity. Later schools of mythic astrology attributed constellations to human projection, but eerie similarities of astronomical and astrological meaning often reach right across cultures, times, and earthly places.

* * * *

In Europe, a cultural counter-reaction to industrialization and Enlightenment prompted an entire **Romantic** movement not only in literature, philosophy, and the arts, but in myth studies too. English poet Joseph Warton had foreshadowed this by emphasizing imagination as the poet's key power. Walpole, Poe, Hawthorne, Melville (standing in as Jonah), Lord Byron, Keats (i.e., Adonis), Coleridge, Wordsworth, Yeats, and Percy and Mary Shelley (Prometheus and Pandora) relied on this power to bring forth the Gothic, fantastic, macabre, and mythic, as in Tennyson's great Arthurian poem *The Idylls of the King*. Echoing Emerson, Carlyle called for "a new Mythus," Novalis for welcoming the returning gods via myth-replacing poetry, and Hölderlin for lamenting that our forgetting of the gods prompts their withdrawal. Mark Akenside ("Hymn to the Naiads") found value in drawing on "mythological passion" to rewrite myths to express poetic truths. Myth, he wrote, is "the mutual agreement or opposition of the corporeal and moral powers of the world."

In Romanticism it's difficult to say where philosophy stops and poetry starts. Wordsworth revivified myth even while suggesting a new kind of humble, everyday mythmaking. Keats made his gods sensuous and beautiful. No friend of either Romantic Platonism or Victorian materialism, Yeats said the mythic symbol is "a transparent lamp about a spiritual flame" and "an endlessly inter-marrying family," connecting an infinity of truths. Scientific forms are themselves mythic. Coleridge contrasted the metaphorical and the allegorical, the first an expression of "fancy," the second rooted in imagination, "that reconciling and mediatory power, which incorporating the Reason in Images of the Sense, and organizing (as it were) the flux of the Senses by the permanence and self-circling energies of the Reason, gives birth to a system of symbols, harmonious in themselves, and consubstantial with the truths, of which they are the *conductors*." Where allegory remains a pale abstraction, metaphor, basic to thought and expression, forms the symbol, "characterized by a translucence of the Special in the Individual or of the General in the Especial or of the Universal in the General. Above all by the translucence of the Eternal through and in the Temporal." No thought, let alone story or myth, does without symbol and imagination.

Although cast out of the factories and lecture halls, the animate marble statue, the Sandman, the cornucopia, the vampire, the Ancient Mariner, Proteus, Klingsohr, Faust, the Raven, Prometheus and his monstrous shadow, Child Roland, and other mythic figures reappeared in art and literature. This mythologizing directly countered the Enlightenment tendency toward abstraction (as Gockel, Frank, and Fried point out). In Germany, a renewed focus on myth and legend came forth from Herder, Hölderlin, Schelling, Schlegel, the degenerationist Creuzer (who focused on mythic symbols as ultimately Indian esoterica only priests could reveal), Görres the German nationalist and racist, and the Brothers Grimm. In 1805, Achim von Arnim and Clemens Brentano published *The Boy's Magic Horn* (*Des Knabens Wunderhorn*), an influential collection of German folksongs. In France would emerge Hugo, Baron Eckstein, Quinet, Michelet, Dumas, Nerval, Gautier, and Chateaubriand. In 1925, Yeats published his own try at myth as *A Vision*.

Johann Gottfried von Herder believed myth to be communal poetic philosophy as an embodiment of nature's expressive powers of vegetative growth: "All things are full of organically operating omnipotence." Naturally: he was a poet, but also a philosopher, literary scholar and theorist, and student of philology and natural science. His connection of myth with features of the land (the country, not Nation or *Boden*) shaping the psyche of its dwellers impressed the Grimms, although for Herder myths come later than legends or folktales.

> A depressing, cold, cloudy atmosphere, gives rise to images and feelings of the same character; where the sky is serene, open and expanded, the soul also expands itself, and soars without restraint... The mythology of every people is an expression of the particular mode, in

which they viewed nature; particularly whether from their climate and genius they found good or evil to prevail, and how perhaps they endeavoured to account for the one by means of the other. Thus even in the wildest lines, and worst-conceived features, it is a philosophical attempt of the human mind, which dreams ere it awakes, and willingly retains its infant state.

As "a personification of effective powers," coming upon its teller like a visiting animal rather than merely decorous or invented (a point taken up later by poet Robert Duncan), myth is one example of the natural self-expressive tendency of all living beings, a tendency most perfectly realized in language and its symbols. Like early religion, myth begins in awe, not fear. Through imagination, myth allows us to empathize with, if not understand completely, what its original tellers felt, saw, and heard. Myth evolves and adapts but never (as in Voltaire) goes extinct: it gains new life from poeticizing. Nor can it simply be converted into allegory, taken over from another culture, or imitated from the lost past of one's own, as Lessing and Winckelmann had recommended. "Heavens! I have all this in my own land, in my own history; around me lies the material for this poetical achievement." Herder's work led to the Romantic and, later, psychological revitalization of myth as an autonomous mode of symbolically interpretable knowing.

Even before Coleridge, who said of imagination, "It dissolves, diffuses, dissipates, in order to recreate," Goethe counterposed allegorical and symbolic art. Although pleasing, allegory was conceptual rather than imagistic and tended to "destroy the interest in the representation itself and drive the spirit back into itself, so to speak, and remove from its eyes what is actually represented." He also opposed, in himself and others, what he called "stiff-necked realism." Beginning in 1770, inspired by Herder, Goethe began the European trend of deploying and updating myth in poetry, lyric, drama, narrative, and epic. "Archetype" for him is not an abstract otherworldly noun, as he confirms in a letter to Schilling; rather, its dynamic unfolding joins nature and image, ideal and organic, on the level of exact sensorial imagination. Karl Philipp Mortiz developed Goethe's observations, claiming that through the gods of art and myth, and mythic poetry in particular, nature reveals itself: "Thus, each of these beings born from imagination in some way represent Nature complete with all its luxurious, wanton growths and its whole brimming overflow...."

The Four Zoas, *Milton*, and *Jerusalem*. The man who wrote these, William Blake, and who left a cast of mythic characters occupying a brilliantly imagined cosmogony, was surely gifted with the mythopoetic "vision" (his word) which he opposed to "allegory"; yet he had little to say in favor of myth in the abstract, which he opposed to his own esoteric brand of Christianity. Preceding Yeats and Tolkien, Blake wove his mythical worlds and their casts of characters without identifying them as mythical. He also moved across traditions, including voices from Plato, Orphism, Norse myth, the Emerald Tablet, Greek myth, and the Bible. "...If we fear to do the dictates of our Angels & tremble at the Tasks set before us, if we refuse to do Spiritual Act...Who can describe the dismal torments of such a state!" –so he writes in a letter dated Jan. 10th, 1802. Two years later he added,

> Vision or Imagination is a Representation of what Eternally Exists, Really and Unchangeably. Fable or Allegory is formed by the daughters of Memory. Imagination is surrounded by the daughters of Inspiration... The Oak dies as well as the Lettuce but its Eternal Image & Individuality never dies, but renews by its seed. Just so the Imaginative Image returns by the seed of Contemplative thought..."

–in direct anticipation of Goethe's use of "archetype." How different the mentality of dry analysis locked outside the experience:

> ...But many stood silent and busied with their families
> And many said We see no Visions in the darksome air
> Measure the course of that Sulphur orb that lights the darksome day
> Set stations on this breeding Earth & let us by & sell

Others arose & schools Erected forming Instruments
To measure out the course of heaven.
–from *The Four Zoas*

Since 1802, Achim von Arnim and Clemens Brentano had been gathering German folksongs for their three-volume *Des Knabens Wunderhorn*. With Bettine von Arnim, Friedrich Creuzer, Karoline von Günderrode, Joseph von Eichendorff, and Sophie Mereau they formed the Heidelberg Romantics interested as poets in collecting German songs, myths, and fairytales. This interest would catch the attention of the Grimms. As the group worked in a cultural atmosphere of growing nationalistic fervor spurred by the Napoleonic wars, Joseph Görres joined their circle. For purposes of patriotic propaganda, Görres distorted Herder's non-nationalist and non-elitist admiration for the *volk* into pro-German rhetoric about a religious-cultural lineage of purity originating in India. This ran counter to Goethe's emphasis on individuation and to Herder's message that each *volk* should express its own unique version of its *Humanität*.

To the study of myth Friedrich Schelling brought idealist Romantic philosophy. For him, Nature remained unconscious until awakened by human art, with its symbols a "genial imitation." In art, which includes story and myth, abides the possibility of unifying subject and object, culture and nature, in moments of experiential obliteration. Myth is not allegorical or euhemerist, but "tautegorical," speaking not beyond itself but in its own trans-rational voice to seize and awaken the mind to self-consciousness and revelation of the Absolute God beyond polytheism. Even there, though, the gods symbolize the Infinite, with myth reconciling pagan immersion in nature with Christian transcendence. Eventually succumbing to what might be called a Galahad Complex, the later Schelling regarded all this as preliminary to dissolving in the Idea of an absolute God beyond all form or representation: what Martin Buber would refer to one day as a doctrine of absorption. Through myth as Schelling spun it, the ideal consumes the real.

In contrast to this, Friedrich Schlegel (who coined the Romantic movement's name) placed myth-making in the hands of the individual poet. This pre-Wagnerian creator of a "progressive, universal poetry" would mix philosophy with poetry to overcome all genres, polarities, and limitations to unify thought, culture, and art. His "Discourse" (1800) called for a new mythology. By 1828, however, his Catholicism got the upper hand over "old heathenism," mythoclasm had replaced poeticism, Romantic poetry was the only valid kind, and he had stopped proclaiming the rejuvenation of humanity just around the corner. Friedrich's brother August saw myth as a progressive, explicitly aesthetic product of imagination: nature in poetic costume. His chief god was Prometheus, presumably pre-Caucasus.

* * * *

As India displaced Greece, Rome, and Palestine as primordial homeland of human culture, the brothers Grimm felt free to concentrate on what made their own nation unique. In 1812 they started publishing the folktales they had collected. (They were also fond of **degeneration theory:** the idea that folktales are remnants of once-mighty myths. E.S. Hartland and Andrew Lang thought the reverse.) Thomas Keightley did likewise for England with *The Fairy Mythology* (1828). Keightley eschewed the popular notion of myth as universal and kept instead to Karl Otfried Müller's linkage of myth with local *history*, an emphasis foreshadowing the work of Otto Gruppe, Jean Bérard, Carl Robert, Martin Nilsson, Edouard Willthis, Robert Graves, and Peter Munz. Müller, by the way, was an early advocate of the quest for original versions of myths purified of later influences, a quest now known to be fruitless. The example set by the Grimms and by Keightley would influence Elias Lönnrot's quest for Finnish epic as well as Tolkien's *Lord of the Rings*.

Gradually, the influence of German mythography, especially Indic, passed into France: to Michelet via Herder, to Quinet via Creuzer, to Eckstein and Hugo via Friedrich Schlegel. By 1820, French novelists, philosophers, and poets made free use of myth. Most used it well, but some used it badly. In 1853, for example, the French aristocrat and novelist Arthur de Gobineau published his *Essay on the Inequality of Human Races* on the relationship between myth and race. Placing the origin of the white "race" in Siberia, he divided it into two branches, Aryan and non-Aryan, and humanity into whites, yellows, and blacks. In Gobineau's hands, myth hardened into ideology, impressing Richard Wagner, for whom myth was a dramatic propaganda of racial "purity"; Southern slavery defenders in the States, two of whom gave the *Essay* its first English translation; and, later, Hitler, whose first name recalls the Fenrir Wolf from Ragnarok. Gobineau's political take on myth points back to Voltaire, Plato, and Anacreon of Samos, who noted *mythietai* (rebel narrators of myth) in revolt against the tyrant Polycrates.

Adalbert Kuhn, a comparativist contemporary of Gobineau, used philology to trace an original Indo-European source of "Aryan" myth based on a heroic Promethean model. George Dasent too was an Aryanist. Later myth theorists linking myth to politics would criticize such reactionary use: Roland Barthes, for example, whose "Myth Today" interprets myth as a "depoliticized speech" of rightwing ideology; Marxists such as Louis Althusser, who thinks of ideology as itself a kind of myth; and Frederic Jameson, who by contrast sees in myth a deeper and potentially salvific stratum of human experience than that of material artifacts of history. Later political theorists of myth include Murray Edelman, who believes that simplifications offered by myths soothe anxiety in complicated social situations; Raoul Girardet, who holds myths as dream-like fantasies projected during alienating times of crisis; and John Girling, who maintains that myths can be agents of change by representing political transformations symbolically and by helping us understand why certain ideological positions hold such an intense charge for us.

Back in 1830, F. W. Bateson remarked on the initial reluctance of the English language to adopt the word *myth* at all. By the early 15th century, Lydgate was using *mythologies*, and in the 1600s, *mythic*, *mythical*, *mythographer*, *mythologer*, *mythologian*, *mythologic*, *mythological*, *mythologically*, *mythologist*, *mythologize*, and *mythologizer* came into use. But not until 1830 did *myth* itself follow suit. Did the motion of myth resist hardening into a noun?

Charles Darwin published *The Descent of Man* in 1871. That

year, and in admiring response, E. B. Tylor published *Primitive Culture*, a book that impressed Darwin. Its inflated subtitle was, "Researches into the Development of Mythology, Philosophy, Religion, Language, Art, and Custom." Tylor, the son of Quakers, was on a mission: "Ethnography . . . has solemn duties, sometimes even painful ones; it behooves him to shed light on what the course civilization of Antiquity has handed down to our posterity in the form of lamentable superstitions, and to relegate those superstitions to sure destruction. This job, though disagreeable, is nevertheless indispensable to the welfare of mankind." To support his missionizing, Tylor coined the word "animism" to label one of these "superstitions" of the "lower races"; in this he was influenced by Charles de Brosses, who in 1760 had called for wider studies of tribal religions and their fetishes, both of which expressed the same religiosity whether in Egypt or West Africa.

Tylor's myth is pre-linguistic and comes in two flavors: philosophical and nature-explaining. Like Fontanelle, Tylor considers myth to be primitive science as expressed in literalized animism; but unlike him, Tylor does not call for a reversal of Homer, who put human qualities into gods instead of finding the godlike in humanity. To interpret myth is to fail to take it as seriously as its believers do. Later Tyloreans include Robert Marett (who posited "pre-animism": before the tree spirits, the tree is itself a spirit: myth is "animatism grown picturesque"), Henry Balfour, Robin Horton, Samuel Noah Kramer, Paul Radin (for whom myths are primitive speculations), and David Bidney (*Theoretical Anthropology*). Comparitivists in his footsteps are Bastian, Spencer, Andree, and Post; those touting geographical influence include Ratzel, McGee, Guyot, and Ritter.

Starting in 1860 and expanding on the premise of Lafitau and Fontanelle that the human mind was the same wherever found, Adolf Bastian argued for **polygenesis**, a variant of the autochthonous origin idea that similar motifs and "elementary ideas" in myth sprout from the human psyche's similarity everywhere. This is contrary to the diffusionist view of Herodotus, Theodor Benfrey (Pan-Indian), William Perry and G. Elliot Schmidt (Pan-Egyptian), and so many to come. Bastian came out of the naturalist tradition that included

Johann Herder and Alexander von Humboldt, and his own ideas influenced C. G. Jung's later linkage of myth with archetype and collective unconscious.

* * * *

Waves of translations of myths from many lands fed the rise of *comparative religion*. It crested with Max Müller, who joined the likes of comparativists Bastian, Andree, Spencer, Post, Kuhn, Burnouf, Bréal. Gubematis, Goldzieher, Cox, Brown, Brinton, Fiske, Preller, Krappe, Decharme, Jung, and, still later, Doniger. Well-known for his translation of the *Rig Veda* into English, which he paid someone else to do while taking full credit for it, Müller was also guilty of the kinds of flimsy linguistic parallels criticized later by J.Z. Smith ("In Comparison a Magic Dwells," 1982). Linguistic studies enjoyed a lineage back to the 1600s via Kircher, Fourmont, Bochart, Jones, Lowth, and Heyne.

Nevertheless, when Müller, a degenerationist who had studied with Schelling and worked with Indo-European expert Franz Bopp, published *Comparative Mythology* in 1856 (*Contributions to the Science of Mythology* would follow in 1897), he opened a new roadway into myth studies, one whose signposts were linguistic and naturalistic. When the "Aryan" people historians now regard as Indo-Europeans moved into Greece (he argued), they remembered their metaphors but forgot what they meant: that sleepy Endymion, for instance, is a metaphor of the sunset. Myth is therefore a "disease of language," an allegoristic leftover in need of clarification through etymological research invariably solar and celestial, as it had been for sun-loving Sir William Jones, Charles Dupuis, Leo Frobenius, Émile Senart, and James C. Moloney. "Mythology, in the highest sense, is the power exercised by language on thought in every possible sphere of mental activity; and I do not hesitate to call the whole history of Philosophy, from Thales down to Hegel, an uninterrupted battle against mythology, a constant protest of thought against language." Logos had resurfaced, this time without sunglasses.

Although Müller had allies like Tylor, Daniel Brinton, John

Fiske, Robert Brown (who looked at Semitic rather than Aryan origins), Angelo de Buernatis, Ignaz Goldzieher, A. Smythe Palmer, and George Cox, his linguistic, monomythic arguments were so unconvincing that in "The Oxford Solar Myth," R. F. Littledale pointed out that Max Müller's name meant "Chief Grinder": "The more scientific aspect of the question recognizes here the Sun-God, armed with his hammer or battle-axe of light, pounding and crushing frost and clouds alike into impalpability." In *Middlemarch*, George Eliot pilloried Müller as the dry pedant Casaubon. However outdated his philology and the logocentric ideology behind it, Müller was genuinely appalled by the nationalist spin on Aryanism, and he praised Jewish tradition as an oasis in a cultural desert.

As comparativism spread, so did ***naturalism***, regrown from the cognitive speculations of Epicharmus, Theagenes, and Pythagoras. Müller was a naturalist. Samuel Noah Kramer thought of myth as allegorical observations about nature compiled by intelligent scribes; Thorkild Jacobsen accepted this in part but insisted that myths possess an emotional factor beyond rational allegory. Alfred Jeremias too was spellbound by the solar zodiac. On the other hand, the Society for the Comparative Study of Myth, founded in Berlin in 1900, shaded itself from solarism long enough to seek the lunar origins of myth. Also moonstruck was John Tu Er-Wei, who wrote decades later that all of Buddhism and Taoism came from stories about the moon. Adalbert Kuhn favored lightning and thunder, Hermann Usener a plurality of natural forces. Philosopher David Hume believed myth to derive from the need to master the frightening forces of nature: better the god you know than the storm, fire, or earthquake you don't. Hume was also a euhemerist. More recently, Mary Barnard traces some of the gods of hunters and gatherers to encounters with narcotic plants; however, "There are also deities of time and space, earth and sky; there are shaman gods: deities of healing, death and destiny. The deified hero and the deified ancestor."

Without direct experience in how story mediates relations with the natural world, Müller-type linguistic naturalism stood little chance. Ridiculed in academia, especially by Andrew Lang, linguistic comparativism died down for a while, although not before

Johannes Goropius Becanus of Holland claimed the ancestral language of humanity to be Dutch, a patriotic fallacy now known as *goropianism*.

* * * *

The comparativist approach gave way before sociological and anthropological field data entering Europe and lost status as a basic approach, although it remained an adjunct to others.

Theorists of myth began to emphasize ***ritual***. With accounts of indigenous cultural life pouring into Europe as it continued its colonization and missionary campaigns, myth came to be considered by Tylor, Andrew Lang, Sir James Frazer, Jane Harrison (rituals are initiatory), Francis Comford, Arthur Cook, and Gilbert Murray, all members of the English anthropology school, as an oral adjunct to religious ceremonialism. Other ritualists included Sylvain Lévi, Marcel Mauss (for whom myth equated to unconscious ideas and codified verbal behavior emitted by ritual), Marcel Granet, Louis Gernet (Gernet, Granet, and Mauss were French linguistic sociologists), Abel Bergaigne, Arthur van Gennep (a totemist like Durkheim, Lang, and Freud), Lord Raglan (myth accompanies ritual: simple as that), H. S. Hooke (ritual is to secure food), J. A. K. Thompson, Margaret Murray, W. .J. Gruffydd (for whom myth starts as ritual and becomes history, folklore, and then literary tales), Clifford Geertz (myth as model of *and* model for reality), Theodor Gaster, John Robertson, William Simpson, Gertrude Kurath, the euhemerist Robert Graves, Monica Wilson (who distinguishes between religious ritual and conventional ceremony), H. S. Versnel, Herbert Weisinger, who called himself "a simple follower of Frazer," and Lauri Honko, who builds her definition of myth on its form, content, function, and context:

> Myth, a story of the gods, a religious account of the beginning of the world, the creation, fundamental events, the exemplary deeds of the gods as a result of which the world, nature and culture were created together with all the parts thereof and given their order, which

still obtains. A myth expresses and confirms society's religious values and norms, it provides patterns of behavior to be imitated, testifies to the efficacy of ritual with its practical ends and establishes the sanctity of cult. The true milieu of myth is to be found in religious rites and ceremonial....The events recounted in myths have true validity for a religious person. For this reason the use of the term myth in everyday language is from the scholarly point of view inexact (in ordinary language myth is often used expressly for something untrue, utopian, misguided, etc.).

An early exponent of ritualism, if only in "primitive" religions less advanced than Calvinism, William Robertson Smith had attached Darwin's evolutionary framework to the comparative method to define mythology as archaic explanation of religious ritual: "In all the antique religions, mythology takes the place of dogma" (*Lectures on the Religions of the Semites*). Thanks in part to the Cambridge Ritualists (Harrison, Cornford, Cook, Murray), who blended French sociology with anthropological fieldwork and James Frazer (below), ritual theory was applied by Cornford, Murray, and Cook to Greek tragedy and comedy; by Ivan Engnell, Aubrey Johnson, and Sigmund Mowinckel to biblical studies; by Jessie Weston to Grail stories; by Herbert Weisinger and C. L. Barber to Shakespeare; by C. M. Bowra to folksongs; by Francis Fergusson, Rene Girard, and Stanley Hyman to tragic and other literature; by Lord Raglan to hero myths; and by E. M. Butler to the legend of Faust. Lang distinguishes unconvincingly between the explanatory "primitive science" and "practically useful ghosts" of myth and the rational ritual of religion ("moral theism"). T. Gaster treats of myth as a ritual presentation of an eternal, idealized now. Other ritualists include Hocart, Widengren, Engnell, Preuss, de Vries, and many extraverts to come.

To some extent, though, hard distinctions between myth and ritual blur in actual practice. Is not telling a myth a ritual? For Mary Barnard, myth spontaneously emerges from ritual: "Was the arche-

typal dragon first conceived in the imagination and later imperson-
ated by dancers, or was he not, rather, invented by the serpentine
dancers themselves when one of them suddenly cried: 'Look, we're
making a big snake!'" And what about myths unconnected to any
detectable rituals, and vice versa? Few verbally recount myths while
putting up a Christmas tree, even after plenty of eggnog.

The ritualist comparativist Sir James Frazer deserves highlight-
ing because of the impact made by *The Golden Bough* (1890),
where, combining Tylor's evolutionism with Smith's comparativism
into a "law of similarity" gotten from Wilhelm Mannhardt, Frazer
wrote that as society evolves from magic to religion to science, myth
bridges magic and religion, preceding rituals and sometimes left
behind by them. Although he too thought of myth as early scientific
explanation, he changed his mind about exactly what a myth could
be: pre-philosophy, euhemeristic tales, explanations for abandoned
rituals... From his central mythologem, however, he did not deviate.
In all societies (Frazer tells us), a ruler who stands in for the god of
vegetation is eventually killed by his successor. The name of his big
book commemorates the branch plucked from a sacred tree at Nemi
near Rome by the newly named King of the Wood. (Speaking of
names, "James" means "he who supplants"; his middle name,
"George," means "farmer," and his wife's name was Lily. One can
understand his preoccupation with vegetative Attis going to meet
Persephone, goddess of spring and death.)

In any case, Frazer shared the comparativist blind spot: failing
to see that, like psychological symptoms, myths and rituals that
resemble each other across societies might spring from entirely different sources, values, and goals. Also, as R. de Langhe remarks,
"While the study of the myths and ritual practices of so-called primitive peoples has in some cases revealed a close relationship between
myths and the rituals, it is equally true that it has also shown the
existence of myths which are unaccompanied by any ritual performance. Between these two extremes many intermediate types can be
attested." Mary Barnard, for whom the sense of a god emerges from
ritual and revel, writes, "One of my many quarrels with Sir James
Frazer hinges on his seeming inability to imagine that any act asso-

ciated with religion could have been performed in the first place simply because it was fun." Samuel Noah Kramer argues that Sumerian myths had little to do with rite or ritual. Frazer, a would-be younger king killing off the old king of pre-scientific myth, instead revived interest in it.

What William Doty refers to as the anthropological ***sociofunctional*** approach started with Ibn Khaldû (1332-1406) of Tunis: in *The Mugaddimah* he wrote that religion and myth symbolize and express the structures of their society of origin. Centuries later, Émile Durkheim (uncle of Marcel Mauss) equated "god" with what a society values (1912); religion, ritual and myth guard institutions, relationships, and mores and change with them.

But the time of speculating about "primitives" was ending, except in Jungian circles, as scholars like Bronislaw Malinowski did actual fieldwork in places like the Trobriand Islands. Of course, this did not always repair prejudice, as when Malinkowski wrote in his journal, "I see the life of natives as...remote from me as the life of a dog." His mood was probably not improved by the fact of being marooned with them. "Myth, as it exists in a savage community, that is, in its living primitive form, is not merely a story told, but a reality lived"—myth is social glue. All myths are *charter myths* that sanction norms, rituals, traditions, institutions. They are not symbolic (agreeing with Franz Boas), they always contain gods, and they must be studied in their cultural context. Malinowski was influenced by how Frazer and Nietzsche took myth seriously as a societal force.

Sociofunctionalists include Boas, A. R. Radcliffe-Brown (in his emphasis on myth as culturally pragmatic), Clyde Kluckhorn (who worked among the Navajo), Julius Krohn, R. M. and C. H. Berndt, Elizabeth Vandiver, Bruce Lincoln (emphasizing how myths affirm ideologies), Ake Hultkrantz, P. Van Baaren, Dorothy Eggan, Barre Toelken, Francisca Cho Bantly, and Georges Dumézil, who relied on the etymological and sociological work of Mauss, Granet, Meillet, and Benveniste to sort gods into an ideological trinity of Indo-European social castes: priestly Sovereignty / Wisdom / Sorcery, kingly Force / Honor / Bravery, and the artisanal-agricultural-herder Wellbeing / Productivity / Fertility. However, in *Myth and Epic* he admitted that he had never understood the difference between a story and a myth. Hierarchically inclined, he had been influenced by Dutch linguist and Nazi propagandist Jan de Vries. Dumézil wrote under a pen name in praise of Mussolini.

Adorno, Althusser, Bakhtin, Barthes, Baudrillard, Benjamin, Chomsky, Deleuze and Guattari, Derrida, Eco, Foucault, Gramsci, Habermas, Hall, Jameson, Lacan, Lyotard, Nietzsche, Said, Sartre, and others would agree that mythological (or any other) "texts" are situated within a complex interaction of economic, ideological, semiotic, and hermeneutical components of social meanings. Barthes would even brand myth a "depoliticized speech" striving to make its message sound natural and inevitable. However, as J. C. Crocker notes, sociofunctionalists have trouble explaining the persistence of myths whose original cultural purposes have been lost.

To the ritualists' collective emphasis Clyde Kluckhohn added the thought that myths linked to rituals—for him they can exist separately—also provide personal satisfaction to the conscious or unconscious needs of individuals, as when a medicine ceremony restores a patient's psychological health. He holds myths and rituals as "cultural forms defining individual behaviors which are adaptive or adjustive responses." As a storehouse of such responses, myths offer cultural solutions to problems we all face. In his thought about ritual being obsessive and repetitive we see the hand of Freud. However, reversing Kluckhohn's argument that evocative individual fantasies become myth, Dorothy Eggan, who worked among the Hopi, argues that individuals make use of congenial myths for personal fantasy, identification, secondary elaboration, and healing. Hultkrantz shuffled Shoshoni myths into the cosmological, institutional, ritual, and literary. They have no cultic significance. "Their aim is, and has been, to supply prototypes or original descriptions of cosmos, the kingdom of Nature, or cultural and religious institutions....They give sanction to the prevailing conditions." Fixed ties between myth and rite seem most common in highly stratified cultures containing the role of sacred kingship.

Robert Graves is often considered a myth critic (see below), and he is one on the level of a myth's poetic content, but its functions include answering the sorts of questions that children (and not adults?) would ask about who made the world, who was the first human, where do we go after death, etc.; and justifying an existing social system while accounting for its traditional rites and customs. "Mythology is the study of whatever religious or heroic legends are so foreign to a student's experience that he cannot believe them to be true." Graves also argued that myths found near the Mediterranean and in Northern Europe reflect the replacement of matrilineal with patriarchal societies. The prepatriarchal have to do with religious rituals celebrating the Great Goddess. In Graves, a devotee of Frazer, ritual meets euhemerism and historicism as every story he touches turns into a struggle between the old and new sacred king, an animal cult, a lesser goddess standing in for a greater, a numerical calendar symbol, and a triple goddess, each phase of whom is a moon goddess celebrated by orgies, all of this made up by ancient people looking at even more ancient icons. *The Greek Myths* gathers into two volumes a well-written summary of the ancient stories whatever one makes of the accompanying explanations for them.

The sociofunctional Austrian Culture Circle School (*Kulturkrieslehre*) of Fritz Graebner, Wilhelm Schmidt, Kaarle Krohn, C. W. von Sydow, and Axel Obrik sought to trace the diffusion of myths to their sources. To do this they examined *cultural complexes:* related groups of traits emanating from their places of origin. In this view, similarities and parallels found in myth could be explained better anthropologically by widening circles of influence than by a supposedly timeless human nature. The Finnish School carries on this work. Unfortunately, it also tends to be reductive. In the exclusive and narrow sociofunctional equation of myth with societal cement lurks an underestimation of human imagination and of the liberatory potential of myth and story.

The Grimms had thought that folklore contained **historical** facts. So did Karl Otfried Müller, Victor Bérard (for Greek myth anyway) and W. R. Rivers. These theorists and others of like mind—Otto Gruppe, Martin Nilsson, Carl Robert, Edouard Willthis, Graves—looked for the history in myth, a project akin to euhemerism. Nilsson saw Greek myth as a reworking of primitive folk-tale material with a basis in past events.

Karl Müller published his *Introduction to a Scientific System of Mythology* in 1844 to argue quite dogmatically that all myths except the cosmogonic reflect real historical events. Myths are "narrations in which the deeds and destinies of individual personages are recorded and which all relate, by the way they are connected and interwoven, to a period antecedent to the historical era of Greece and separated from it by a tolerably distinct boundary." He believed they combine the real and the ideal: the myth of Demeter combines the fact of her worship at Eleusis with a fanciful idea of how she arrived there. In general, however, historical reads of myth do not ask whether historicism itself betrays a mythic position toward its materials. ("The characteristics of old vanished gods," wrote Heinrich Zimmer, "overgrow the historical memory, and figures which in the baldness of the chronicles appear as little more than mute names begin to speak with the timeless language of dream.") Eric Dardel's position is that history is exactly what myth does *not* contain: as a tale of events perennialized, myth is how we read the world, make sense of it, and how we live in it, concretely and esthetically. Myth is a source of all culture until the stories dry up into secularized speculation and formalistic allegorizing. Still, Müller also suggested a useful precedent: that we exclude no idea from "primitive" mentality without proof that it does not belong there.

* * * *

Most myth theorists have at least acknowledged the role of consciousness in mythmaking. Mythology for John Dewey "is much more an affair of the psychology that generates art than an effort at scientific explanation."

Sigmund Freud popularized *psychological* approaches to myth by theorizing about the Oedipus complex and the "primal horde" vying for overlordship (like his competitive Psychological Wednesday Society?) and by speculating that Moses had been a rebellious Egyptian. Like a dream, a myth was a kind of symptom, an expression of unconscious desire. The father god of religion, for example, represents a projection of one's father complex. Yet Freud draws freely on myth (as Plato had) to underline his points and even calls psychoanalysis "our mythology." Analyst Bruno Bettelheim considers myths regressive, but Otto Rank writes enthusiastically about the birth of the Hero, and, following Freud, Karl Abraham compares dreams and myths. Leo Schneiderman writes that "myths communicate unconscious wishes or fears expressed as miraculous stories," differing from folktales in receiving community sanction as unassailable. Like a dream, a myth comes replete with symbolic disguises and totems to defuse the impact of the underlying wish or fear. When these myths lose vitality, mystic seekers go looking for new ones. Schneiderman does not address the fact that many mystics remain embedded in traditional religions. The strict distinction between folktale and myth is also problematic, as Franz Boas remarks: when we study a single cultural area like the American Northwest Coast, we see how folktales and myths blend into each other.

C. G. Jung left the Freudian circle in part because of Freud's reduction of myth to instinct and regression. At first Jung tended to see in myth the quest of the Hero to break away from the Monster (mother); but as his ideas matured, he came to see myths as expressions of psychological *archetypes*: universal patterns of potentiality. "...The whole of mythology could be taken as a sort of projection of the collective unconscious." Mythic language, he writes, is truer to life than scientific concepts. "Myths are original revelations of the preconscious psyche, involuntary statements about unconscious psychic happenings, and anything but allegories of physical processes." And: "...The whole of mythology can be taken as a sort of projection of the collective unconscious." As productions of the ever-active psyche, myths do not die so much as re-constellate: "Mythological motifs frequently appear, but clothed in modern dress; for instance, instead of the eagle of Zeus, or the great roc, there is an airplane; the fight with the dragon is a railway smash; the dragon-slaying hero is an operatic tenor; the Earth Mother is a stout lady selling vegetables; the Pluto who abducts Persephone is a reckless chauffeur..." Severance from our archetypal psychic foundations saddles us with neurosis; the task for individuation is "to dream the myth onward by giving it a modern dress."

Karl Kérényi was interested in ritual, but he also worked with Jung to develop the beginnings of an archetypally based "science of myth." Myth is "an immemorial and traditional body of material contained in tales about gods and god-like beings, heroic battles and journeys to the Underworld... Myth is the movement of this material....In a true mythologem this meaning is not something that could be expressed just as well and just as fully in a non-mythological way." Also: "Myth gives a ground, lays a foundation. It does not answer the question 'why?' but 'whence?'" To Thomas Mann he wrote that hermeneutic self-reflexivity must prevail to correct both positivism and biological determinism. He preferred "primordial image" to "archetype" and held it descriptively rather than as an entity.

Starting out in the field of literature, Joseph Campbell saw myth as a metaphoric expression of Jungian archetypes rooted in the body and expressive of the monomythic Hero's Journey. "A mythology," he told Bill Moyers, "is a system of images that incorporates a concept of the universe as a divinely energized and energizing ambience within which we live.... And a myth, then, is a single story or a single element of the whole mythology, and the various stories of the mythology interlock—they interlock to be consistent within this great world image." Campbell also described four functions of myth: mystical/metaphysical (awe), cosmological (worldview), sociological (laws, norms), pedagogical (developmental, guiding us through life stages). Religion distorts and literalizes tales whose ultimate purpose is to guide *individual* consciousness into the ultimate silence or void beyond all forms.

For modern people this spiritual quest replaces premodern reliance on mythic systems no longer intact. Like Eliade, Campbell values myth as a doorway to sacred experience. He died while working on a multi-volume comparative "natural history" of world myths, tracing what he saw as their evolution from animistic hunter-gatherer cultures to matriarchal planting societies to industrial civilization, where fragments of myths lay in ruins.

> Obviously, an outward-directed intellect, recognizing only such historical ends and claims, would be very much in danger of losing touch with its natural base, becoming involved wholly in the realization of "meanings" parochial to its local time and place. But, on the other hand, anyone hearkening only inward to the dispositions of feeling, would be in equal danger of losing touch with the only world in which he would ever have the possibility of living as a human being.
> —"Mythological Themes in Creative Literature and Art"

Comparativism of the variety revived by Freud, Jung, and Campbell received vociferous criticism, starting with Boas in "The Limitations of the Comparative Method in Anthropology," 1896: "We cannot say that the occurrence of the same phenomenon is always due to the same causes, and that thus it is proved that the human mind obeys the same laws everywhere." Lévi-Strauss thought the theoretical signification of the archetype to be as arbitrary as the pairing of words with what they stood for. The symbols must be investigated in their relation to the total culture of origin first before comparisons are made. For Marina Warner and Naomi Goldenberg, archetypal theory threatens social justice by imprisoning women in stock gender definitions framed as eternal and immutable. Anthony John Harding, for whom the very idea of "myth" is a label for something lost, agrees: "...The very process of imagining or constructing an archetype obscures *both* the historically determined nature of the sources from which that archetype is constructed *and* the historical situation of the critic who is doing the constructing." Including the apologetic uses to which archetypalizing is put.

Marc Maganaro accuses Campbell of psychologism, Western ethnocentricity, and "piecework universalism" even though Campbell emphasizes that "universals are never experienced in a pure state, abstracted from their locally conditioned ethnic application." Karen King faults Campbell for using Gnostic myths he does not examine in detail as support for his own views; his equation of femininity with body, earth, and reproduction is also problematic. Dundes used his last lecture to denounce Campbell as amateurishly sloppy for ignoring differences between myths and folktales. A myth is a sacred narrative explaining how the world and its peoples came to be in their present form; William Bascom's definitions of myth, folktale, and legend are sacrosanct. Campbell's teacher Heinrich Zimmer refers to this kind of criticism as "morbid dread before the virtual infinity that is continually opening out from the cryptic traits of the expressive picture-writing which it is their profession to regard."

The emphasis on the Hero has also elicited criticism. Campbell's friend Jonathan Z. Smith asked, "If that's all it is, if all myths tell the story of a hero who at a certain stage in his life blah blah blah blah, why read more than one?" In Japan, observes Hayao Kawai, myths don't always carry a heroic motif, and sometimes the "message" of a myth is aesthetic rather than individuative. What counts is the mood they leave in us, not where we or the "hero" have to go. Jerome Bruner's view of myth is more dramatic than heroic:

> The myth as a work of art has as its principal form the shape of drama. So too the human personality: its patternings of impulse express themselves as identities in an internal drama. The myths that are the treasure of an instructed community provide the models and the programs in terms of which the growth of the internal cast of identities is molded and enspirited.

Jungian approaches also gave birth to the field of *myth criticism* (Myth Crit): the study of literature as it embodies myths, archetypes, and universal narratives. Scholars associated with this are Maud Bodkin, Kenneth Burke, Francis Fergusson, Northrop Frye, Leslie Fiedler, Robert Graves, John Livingston Lowes, G. Wilson Knight, Caroline Spurgeon, Philip Wheelwright, and Philip Withim. This transdisciplinary inquiry explores the commonality of our experience, including the passages we all face, and of the lasting concerns of humanity. "In the beginning was mythos," says Fiedler, who subordinates logos to myth, "and each new beginning must draw again from that inexhaustible source."

Northrop Frye developed myth crit as a kind of literary social science, with literature as displaced myth. In the endless culture-building artistry of myth he saw the archetypal Quest as well as the four seasons of nature translated into *mythoi*: spring for romance, summer for comedy, autumn for tragedy, and winter for irony and satire. Each of these breaks down into phases sprinkled with *signs* subordinated to motifs. Signs are a surface *descriptive* aspect of the symbol, which also possesses *formal* (imagistic, allegorical), *mythical* (archetypal), and *anagogic* (transcendent) aspects. In all this, much of it laid out in his *Anatomy of Criticism,* Frye sketches a grand conceptual organization of archetypal images in (Western) literature, for which myth serves as its deep grammar; in religion; in philosophy; and in most other spheres of culture, with mythic motifs forever recurring to enrich other fields and endeavors. To many scholars his schema seems more imposed on literature than detected at work in it. Others object to his restriction of myths to tales containing gods. Notice, however, that, like Hazard Adams, he puts the allegorical on a continuum with the symbolic instead of setting them in relentless opposition.

As one of the few to consider myth developmentally, myth critic Philip Wheelwright sorts myth into three types. *Primary myth* originates in primal storytelling and serves as a basis for language; *romantic myth* treats myth as a contrived literature; and *consummatory myth* is "a post-romantic attempt to recapture the lost innocence of the primitive mythopoeic attitude....Admittedly the line between the romantic and the consummatory is wavering and obscure..." He also distinguishes between the *steno-language* of literal meaning and the earlier, trans-logical *expressive language* of poetry, some prose, and myth. "Later myths, and later retellings of the earlier myths, betray their essentially romantic character by the degree to which such semantic fluidity and plentitude have been exchanged for tidier narratives relying on firmer grammatical, logical, and causal relationships." Other theorists emphasize the difference between oral and written myth, although Levi-Strauss considers the written to be a legitimate variant of a myth. Expressive language (says Wheelwright) is apt to contain concretely imagined archetypes, but more like Goethean metaphors than Jungian abstractions.

Laurence Coupe defines myth as a traditional sacred story of anonymous poetic authorship and archetypal or universal significance, recounted in a community, linked often with ritual, involved with the deeds of anthropomorphic superhuman beings, and rooted in primal or supernatural time. We make sense of our lives by seeing them in a larger mythic context; as Ricoeur states, myth is "an opening on to other possible worlds which transcend the established limits of our actual world." Contrary to what allegorical typologies of myth maintain, mythos *produces* logos, pulls us toward the future in hope, and is not true or false so much as viable or not. Coupe calls his approach to myth as openness and possibility *radical typology*. According to Marjorie W. McCune, Tucker Orbison, and Philip M. Withim (*The Binding of Proteus*), myth "has never been merely a matter of using logic but of engaging all our powers of intuition and synthesis, of employing our whole mind until we break into truth. Any approach to myth and poetry that limits itself only to analysis...is bound to fail simply by missing the central point."

As might be expected, not everyone was happy with myth crit. Philip Rahv referred to its exponents as "mythomanics" blind to history (Rahv was a Marxist). Charles Moorman disliked its universalizing, its reliance on myth as a tool of literary evaluation, its implied reduction of literature to myth, and its distortion of the authenticity of the myths selected for such uses. A myth can be summarized because its essence is in the story, whereas one word removed from a Yeats poem or James novel alters what they say: the Christ in Malory is not the same Christ in Melville. "...In the end myth is as useless in dealing with *McTeague* as is Marxism in coming to grips with *The Bear*, as is either in explicating Wodehouse." Nor was it legitimate to dig up supposedly unconscious motifs or drives in works of literature not deliberately put there by the author. Additionally,

...just as myths are often falsely applied to works that do not reflect them, so pseudo-myths are sometimes created by authors and critics in order to provide mythic depth to an otherwise shallow work. One recalls the "Marilyn myth" and the "JFK myth" as attempts to create symbols, or rather to distill into symbolic personages...The definition and application of such pseudo-mythic patterns is at best a circular and hence question-begging strategy, rather like the historians' use of *Piers Plowman* to construct a picture of fourteenth-century life with which to praise the realism of *Piers Plowman*. By such reasoning *Main Street* becomes a great novel because it so beautifully reflects the "myth" of small-town America, for which it is the chief source.

Richard Chase holds myth *as* literature, an expressive and aesthetic act of imagination dreamed up by individual poets (or, today, novelists). Myth is a narrative uniting real and ideal (Otfried Müller's definition), but not all literature is myth. Chase also vouches for a kind of euhemerism: "The magical or terrible beasts, the witches and sorcerers, the tricksy or noble heroes of mythology should not be described as 'faded gods,' as they have sometimes been called; rather are the gods faded beasts, magicians, and heroes. Stated thus negatively, euhemerism is profoundly true." On the other hand, Robert Duncan:

> In the orders of the poem the poet is commanded by necessities of a form that will not be turned to exemplify moral or aesthetic preconceptions. Writing, one follows through a series of events having their own imperative. So myths—the story of Enkidu and Gilgamesh, the story of Adam and Eve and the Garden of Eden, the story of Ouranous, Kronos and Zeus—resist our interpretations and understandings and confound our philosophies.

Harvey Birenbaum presents a literary model of myth that dips into multidisciplinary waters: as a condition of consciousness and a valid way of registering recurrent human experience, myth (which can be looked at phenomenologically, psychologically, anthropologically, etc.) can be approached through a "define-it-yourself kit" with the following parts, to use in accord with one's needs or taste:

> 1. impossible or unrealistic stories, probably with 2. miraculous or supernatural elements, possibly through 3. the presence of deities, suggesting 4. a religious framework, implying 5. the probability of belief or ritual adherence, sharing therefore 6. communal acceptance, derived in part from 7. the justification of cultural standards, based upon 8. purported explanation of natural phenomena, derived from 9. primeval, impersonal origin, followed by 10. traditional evolution within the society, perhaps upon the basis of 11. archetypal, or at least typal form, conveying 12. representative power, a capacity to capture and magnify typical situations, that may have 13. transcultural applicability, conveyed through 14. subjective expressiveness, establishing 15. a special imaginative reality.

"By omitting most terms between three and nine, we can include fairy tales. By speaking only of the last five, we can further extend the word to include literary mythmaking" (*Myth and Mind*). "In myth, then, the inspired self, the community, and the world of nature, coalesce. We should add a fourth element to the list, however. It is a world that is sensed through the self but beyond it. We can call it, loosely, the supernatural, including within its reach all aspects of experience that do not correspond to objective data."

$$* \quad * \quad * \quad *$$

When the 20th century opened, philology in myth studies had craned its head back at Vico's "poetic metaphysics," nodded to Romantics like Schlegel and Schelling, and resurrected itself around the belief that myth was a function of *language*.

Christian Gottlob Heyne had tried to uncover "raw" myth—he agreed with Hume that some sort of terror of the world had inspired it—by examining mythic poetry. In myth he saw primitive philosophizing built on *philosophemes*: thought units such as ethics, cosmogonies, and etiological explanations. By 1926, the Prague School of Linguistics under Nicholas Troubetzkoy also worked with stories' structural units. Vladimir Propp (along with Dmitry Segal and E. M. Meletinskij) worked the formalist premise that all Russian folktales were reducible to a Quest of thirty-one motif-functions, not all of which appeared in every story. These included being driven from home, marrying the princess, and exposure and return. Propp seems to have thought of tales as filled with "narratemes," elements— Greimas' "actants" leading back to "recalcitrant facts"—like those of chemistry. The emphasis of form over content in this kind of **structuralism** impressed Roland Barthes (for whom myths were a form of repressive ideological speech), A. J. Greimas, Johan Georg von Hahn, and Claude Lévi-Strauss, who favorably compared the approach to the analysis of chemical elements. Revised by Heda Jason, Alan Dundes, and Erhardt Guttgemanns, this approach also shaped all later folklore studies whose objects of inquiry are classified by the Aarne–Thompson Indices.

Lévi-Strauss thought content could be included in myth analysis, but mainly as a subset of structure. He looked at how *mythemes*, the storied counterpart to morphemes, organize tales in series of binary oppositions like nature and culture (preeminent for every society), life and death, female and male, self and other, time and eternity. Myth, he stated in 1958 after studying Native American tales from the Pacific Northwest, was an attempt to reconcile these conflicting opposites by arriving at their solution: "The purpose of myth is to provide a logical model capable of overcoming a contradiction," at bottom that between culture and nature. For example, the Oedipus myth's oppositions—over- and underrating of blood relations, difficulties vs ease of walking, and denial of the earthly origin of humanity—give us the meaning of the story: the inability of a culture believing itself autochthonous to realize that its members are born of unions of women and men. (One wonders what the Sphinx would have made of this.) Lévi-Strauss thought it necessary to analyze all available myths together with their interpretations to arrive at a comprehensive meaning; to compile this data he recommended large boards with pigeon holes for data-bearing punch cards. Objections soon mounted: theorizing myth as prelogical problem-solving fails to address myth's numinosity or embodied telling or hearing; a lame foot in one tale can signify something vastly different from a lame foot in another tale; what a tale means to a particular audience depends on many factors besides an underlying linguistic code; a tale is a whole that means more than its parts; meaning is not reducible to structure in either myth or language (G.S. Kirk); reduction of myth to culture-vs-nature amounts to saying that myths contain conflict, which is obvious; and what of myth-telling societies in which culture and nature are not held as separate?

Later structuralists and semioticians include Althusser, Bourdieu, Detienne (before turning to allegory and history), Dumézil, Genette, Liszka, Loraux, Hartog, Svenbro, Schnapp, Frontisi-Ducroux, Sourvinou-Inwood, Metz, Mosko, Serres, Calame, and Todorov. Heirs to Propp are Alan Dundes, Heda Jason, and Erhardt Güttgemanns, A.J. Greimas, and Roland Barthes, all coders, some French cultural historians looking for communal frames of context for myths. René Girard presents as scientific hypothesis the idea that myths and great literature reveal both mimetic desire (all desire is copied from the desires of other people, which seems circular) and, at the root of spreading mimetic rivalry, historical acts of scapegoat sacrifice, with post-violent intervals of peace, ritual, and taboo the foundations upon which all later civilization and guiding (allegorical) myth are built. Myth, in order words, authorizes and decorates ritual.

A later approach known as *biogenetic structuralism* (Eugene d'Aquili, Charles Laughlin) draws on biology, sociology, cognitive psychology, ethology, and neurology to study myth and ritual as evolutionary survival responses. Borrowing from Information Theory, Edmund Leach identifies characteristics like redundancy and binary opposition: "An object is alive or not alive and one could not formulate the concept 'alive' except as the converse of its partner 'dead.' So also human beings are male or not male..." The aliveness or lack of it in these formulations is perhaps debatable. In general, structuralism has ignored aspects of myth, queer and otherwise, that do not conform to such tidy distinctions, and many "oppositions" (male versus female) seem culture-bound.

Meanwhile, the ***post-structuralists*** got busy emphasizing the semiotics of story. The French were particularly keen on this: Jean-Pierre Vernant, Pierre Vidal-Naquet, Marcel Detienne, Nicole Loraux, Christianne Sourvinou-Inwood, Françoise Lissarrague, Françoise Hartog, Jasper Svenbro, Claude Bérard, Françoise Frontisi-Ducroux, and Alain Schnapp. Some who called themselves "cultural historians" favored an approach less mechanical and reductionistic than traditional structuralism and more attuned to cultural and communal nuance within societies instead of between them. Detienne included aspects of myth overlooked by sociofunctionalists: "To discover the complete horizon of a society's symbolic values, it is also necessary to map out its transgressions, interrogate its deviants, discern phenomena of rejection and refusal, and circumscribe the silent mouths that unlock upon underlying knowledge and the implicit." But his allegorical filter has Greek myths teaching lessons, and he regards "myth" as an invented Enlightenment category.

Eric Gould's "Myth is *a metaphysics of absence implicit in every sign*" echoes Derrida, for whom myth is a play of language whose signifiers point just at each other, signifying nothing. Without true myth, which does not exist in modern times anyway, we are left with the semiotic fact of *mythicity* (Wilhelm Dupré), a verbal conjuring for understanding the world and recovering the sense of the sacred, whether or not we succeed. Myth "reminds us strongly today that without a sense of Nothing, there is no selfhood or freedom." As in Heidegger, myth records our inability to authenticate our knowledge of Being. Archetypes share in these negations as signs of where language cannot be spoken ultimately, mere metaphors shared by speaker and listener (William Doty agrees): "The mythic, I believe, emerges from that very existential awareness [of Nothingness] and not from some primitive wonder-world." Also, "Quite literally, all myth reveals that man cannot get out of this paradox of language or history; even his yearning for the supernatural has this existential basis."

Frank Kermode underscores the dangerous side of myth in short-circuiting intellect and linguistically rearranging the world, as the Third Reich attempted—unlike fictions, which find things out and make sense of the present, and which simply fade when no longer useful. This is the reverse of Diderot's and D'Alembert's claim in their *Encyclopedia* that fables are accompaniments of the arts: they "embellish nature and please the imagination." Kermode's mythicity is a tool for making meaning. "Myth is both hypothesis and compromise. Its meaning is perpetually open and universal only because once the absence of a final meaning is recognized, the gap itself demands interpretation which, in turn, must go on and on, for language is nothing if it is not a system of open meaning" (*The Sense of an Ending*). No trans-linguistic archetypes need apply. Because we use fictions to make sense of the world, myth is in no danger of going away forever.

Kermode was one of a group of British myth theorists who looked critically upon Myth Crit itself, as did A. S. Byatt, David Daiches, John Holloway, Graham Hough, Raymond Williams, and Paul West. They sought to provide a more nuanced protest against both the positivistic leveling down of story and meaning and modernity's other dehumanizing impacts. Daiches argues that imaginative literature carried its own epistemic value (just as Stambovsky argues for myth).

Beyond structuralism and post-structural critiques, language-based approaches to myth proliferated. "Myths to us, then, are not just ancient and thus untrue fables," claims Langdon Gilkey in *Religion and the Scientific Future*; "rather, they signify a certain perennial mode of language, whose elements are multivalent symbols, whose referent is in some strange way the transcendent or sacred, and whose meanings concern the ultimate existential issues of actual life and the questions of human and historical destiny." Out of myths come philosophy, theology, history—and science, with the lab-coated scientist a symbol out of modern myth.

*   *   *   *

Going back to the ancient Greeks, Paul Veyne presents their mythology as a popular oral (pre)literature that did not distinguish between what we now think of as fiction and reality. The element of legend was simply accepted, although not in terms of hard belief. Edith Hamilton agrees that the truth of these myths cannot be read as a kind of Greek Bible. They are entertaining stories with bits of religion mixed in on occasion. According to the literary perspective of Scott Leonard and Michael McClure (see *Myth and Knowing*), myths are ancient narratives attempting to answer the enduring and fundamental human questions, such as: *How did existence come into being? Who are we, and what is our role here? What are our values? How should we act? How should we not act?*

The poets have had much to say about working with mythic material. T. S. Eliot hoped the use of myth could redeem the "futility and anarchy" of the modern world; in *The Waste Land* the reader detects the rebirth theme described by Frazer. Robert Calasso recognized no fixed plan in myth; rather, myth's meanings arise from its contradictions and literary turbulence. "Myths are made up of actions that include their opposites within themselves. The hero kills the monster, but even as he does so we perceive that the opposite is also true: the monster kills the hero. The hero carries off the princess, yet even as he does we perceive that the opposite is also true: the hero deserts the princess. How can we be sure? The variants tell us. They keep the mythical blood in circulation" (*The Marriage of Cadmus and Harmony*).

C. S. Lewis thought of myth as bunk until his friend J. R. R. Tolkien woke him to its poetic potential. Lewis, who dismissed the "chronological snobbery" of relegating myth to a past age, came to see myth as an awe-inspiring conveyor of Truth mediating between the sensual and the abstract, the thought and the lived:

> What flows into you from myth is not truth but reality (truth is always about something, but reality is that about which truth is)....Myth is the mountain whence all the different streams arise which become truths down here

> in the valley....Or, if you prefer, myth is the isthmus
> which connects the peninsular world of thought with the
> vast continent we really belong to. It is not, like truth,
> abstract; nor is it, like direct experience, bound to the
> particular.

...but his own mythic writing remained allegorical, privileging Christianity as the best of all possible myths.

Like Lewis, Tolkien was a Christian, but, despising the heavy-handedness of preachy allegory, he represented Middle-earth as pre-Christian. He also opposed placing analysis above content. Myth was best presented by poetic implication, not overt explication. To feel the "elvish craft" of its enchantment required willing entry into the story while holding daytime considerations — including those of using the stories to prove a theory — firmly at bay. "Faërie cannot be caught in a net of words; for it is one of its qualities to be indescribable, though not imperceptible. It has many ingredients, but analysis will not necessarily discover the secret of the whole." Imaginative *sub-creation* by visionary poets brings forth a Secondary World of myth from language; and interest in the story itself, not only its social function, allegorical archetype, or speculative historical origin, is what keeps a myth alive.

As for fairy stories, their faces are "the Mystical towards the Supernatural; the Magical towards Nature; and the Mirror of pity and scorn towards Man." The difference between fairy tale and myth is of degree, not of kind. Both can evolve, but only insofar as they remain grounded in a tradition. Taking a cue from the folktales in the *Kalevala*, Tolkien wrote *The Lord of the Rings* to provide an updated myth for England. The continuity with past tales, and the inward "elvish" source, lifted the work above the level of simple fiction.

In *On Fairy Stories*, Tolkien explains that

> ....When we cross the border of Faërie we believe (or, if
> our interest is only literary, we put ourselves in the men-
> tal posture of believing) that the scientific, measurable,
> facts and "laws" of the relationship of things and events
> are only one aspect of the world....In Faërie one can con-

ceive of a demon or ogre that possesses a castle of
hideous nightmare shape (for that is his will or nature);
but one cannot conceive of a house built with a "good"
purpose—a hospital, an inn or refuge for travelers—
being ugly or squalid.

"Just as speech is invention about objects and ideas, so myth is
invention about truth." The distinction between higher mythologies
of the gods and lower fairy tales of little powers is one of degree
rather than kind. In the end, all distinctions must bow to the effect
the stories produce on us now, today. Tolkien seems to imply that
secondary belief (similar to what Coleridge calls "poetic faith") matters more in the end, at least in some cases, than literal belief.
"Horses have been ennobled by Pegasus: and still may be. For all we
know, indeed we may fairly guess, in Fantasy we may actually be
assisting in the evolution of Creation." The mythology we require
must be anchored in traditions and tales "which we can bring up to
our own grade of assessment," modernized to fit our time.

Kiowa novelist N. Scott Momaday's deft retellings of Native
American myth carries it forward as a weave of meaning joining
people to a place, self, cosmos, and spirit in a poignant seamless
whole. No wonder the alienated and the rootless so often denigrate
indigenous stories: we have largely lost this sense of wholeness, of
belonging to a world that makes sense. Listening to his grandmother
tell stories of their tribal heritage, Momaday felt as though he also
listened to the speech of the land itself.

Outside the West, the study of myth as story and language tends
to avoid dichotomous categories. Lu Wei agrees that myths are
sacred stories told as narrative, legitimizing social institutions,
employing symbols like god images, and seeking cosmological
understanding through origin stories; but Lithui Yang points out that
myths aren't always sacred, and to endure they must entertain or be
sung as songs. For Yuan Ke, myth can include folklore and even
ancient mythic novels. Isidore Okpewho of Nigeria likes Richard
Chase's definition of myth as art but emphasizes the aesthetic
dimension of the telling: myth is "a tale of the oral tradition which

lays stress on fanciful play." Myth knows no rigid distinctions between itself, epic, legend, folklore. Past and present interfuse, as when a train appears in an ancient story. Myth informs all varieties of human culture and can best be understood qualitatively. Also, the audience co-creates the story with the mythteller, who relies heavily on the entertaining, engaging, and performative dimensions of myth.

In theories of myth that emphasize language, can there be a post-postmodernism? In *Myth, Truth and Literature*, Colin Falck combines a modernist complaint about multicultural bullying ("this revenge of the uncreative sensibility upon the creative") with an argument for restoring the aesthetic and spiritual dimensions to myth studies. Myth remains necessary because mythic apprehension is a stage on the way to developing linguistic consciousness, as is the gestural use of the body. A fairy tale is accessible before a theory of science or economics. "Myth is a form of integrated perceptual awareness which unites 'fact' and 'explanation,' because it is a form of awareness in which fact and explanation have not yet become *dis*-united. It is a mode of perception or of vision, rather than a mode of explanation..." —and in fact objective explanation is preceded by a gut sense of, "How does this story apply to my situation?" Knowing this, it is possible now "to re-familiarize ourselves with those mythic agencies which have for so long been operative in the depths of our imagination, along with such newer spirts or presences as recent centuries may have added to their pantheon." Poetry and the arts, and realistic fiction in particular, can help in this endeavor of re-mythologization even if they can't give us the full sense of pre-Christian immersion in myth. Literature can sustain us spiritually where religion no longer can.

* * * *

Inevitably, in the West at least, a biological approach to myth surfaces now and then. Richard Payne Knight had seen fertility cults and sexual symbolism in myth even before Freud came along. According to Walter Burkert, myths are biological events, with narrative elements constituting certain basic types of tale. For example, in a tale about a girl forced to leave home, after which she suffers a violent encounter with a god, pregnancy, tribulation, rescue, and reintegration into society, the tale suggests to Burkert the stages of a girl's puberty and what follows it: deflowering by a male, childbirth, marriage. Myth sanctifies ritual and vice versa; at the heart of religion is ritual killing and its resulting society-building reparations. Burkert seems not to have gotten out much this century, but he was nice to his students.

Hans Blumenberg's *Work on Myth* traces storytelling to the need to overcome our biological helplessness as mortal creatures struggling in a changing world. The "work" is reinterpreting the old stories to allay existential anxiety, not to provide proto-scientific explanations. Myths selected for the significance they bestow on "the absolutism of reality" survive (his phrase is "Darwinism of words," anticipating what Richard Dawkins would argue about memes). Biological approaches to myth are *functionalist* because they describe what myth does, at least from a despiritualized, depsychologized, abstract somatic standpoint.

For some—Mircea Eliade, for instance—much of myth theory feels like arid intellectualism. (Doty: "Determination of a rationalistic, non-mythic 'interpretation' signifies at the most elemental level the *elimination* of the mythic.") Eliade had been brought to the École pratique des hautes étude (EPHE) in Paris by Dumézil, who had also brought Lévi-Strauss as post-WWII interest in myth swung from Germany to France. Eliade's *spiritual/esoteric* view placed the sense of the sacred (the *numinous* in Rudolf Otto's terminology) in the center of mythic meaning. Myths are: 1. the actions of the Supernaturals outside of time in primordial history, 2. true and sacred because about spiritual realities, 3. related to a creation or origin and providing models to be imitated and recovered by remembrance, 4. control over something by knowing its origins, and 5. a transcendence of profane time: myth is regenerative because we dip back into sacred time and undergo a symbolic rebirth.

Eliade tended to see all myths as creation myths and "folklorization" as their decay into fairytales as they fell into historical time. Like W. K. C. Guthrie and Lewis Spence, he paired myth with religion; and like Rudolf Otto, Joachim Wach, and Gerardus Vander Leeuw, he defended religious experience as irreducible. He wanted his archetypes in front of him, phenomenologically, rather than as Jungian formal-structural patternings. In much of his life and work he possessed the political reactionary's obsession with regaining a golden past, with universalizing, and with being serious and not playful with myth. To Christianity he gives the credit of preserving (!) "pagan" myths by lending them a wider spiritual and cultural context. However, "When, in one or two generations, perhaps even earlier, we have historians of religions who are descended from Australian, African, or Melanesian tribal societies, I do not doubt that, among other things, they will reproach Western scholars for their indifference to the scale of values *indigenous* to these societies." He was right about that.

The *philosophical* approach to myth evident in ancient Greece and India and, later, in Vico and Schelling and David Hume (who distinguished between the moral, theistic level of myth and a lower, amoral, animal level) resurfaced in Hans Jonas, who reinterprets Gnosticism along existential lines, and in Heidegger fan Rudolf Bultmann, who calls for a demythologizing of the Bible to get at its existential truth. Myth is not an explanation of the world, but a story of human choices, fears, and actions about birth, life, and death. What counts is faith, not a futile search through myth for facts. Henri Bergson considers myth a product of smart instinct wielded to counter the divisiveness of intellect. This is why intelligent people also tend to be superstitious. Susanne Langer compares the images of myth to the elements of dream, "all manner of shifting, fantastic images which speak of Good and Evil, of Life and Death," all carrying a quality of holiness as a primitive phase of metaphysical thought. She regards myth as a primary type of philosophical human expression along with language and art.

Ernst Cassirer agrees with Marett, Preuss, Vierkandt, and others that religion begins with intuition of the sacred power in things: "Myth is from its very beginning potential religion." Myth supplies subjective, emotional, passionate truth to be felt more than thought. "When external reality is not merely viewed and contemplated, but overcomes a man in sheer immediacy, with emotions of fear or hope, terror or wish fulfillment: then the spark jumps somehow across, the tension finds release, as the subjective excitement becomes objectified, and confronts the mind as a god or a daemon." Myth is "objective insofar as it is recognized as one of the determining factors by which consciousness frees itself from passive captivity in sensory impression and creates a world of its own in accordance with a spiritual principle."

Arising from ritual (because we act first and rationalize why later: Durkheim, Mauss) and its evocation of participation mystique (Lévi-Bruhl), myth serves as "emotion turned into image," an artful exteriorization of our felt sense of cosmic solidarity. Mythic symbols spring forth because the experience they express crashes into us. "Language and myth stand in an original and indissoluble correlation with one another, from which they both emerge but gradually as independent elements. They are two diverse shoots from the same parent stem, the same impulse of symbolic formulation, springing from the same basic mental activity, a concentration and heightening of simple sensory experience." This is why nearly all forms of culture arise from a mythic matrix, and why story precedes any attempts to explain it. Cassirer also calls for "transposing the Kantian principle" of mental synthesis "into the key of myth" as creative mythopoesis through art, and, writing in the 1940s, for careful analysis of how politics abuses myth. Susanne Langer and W. M. Urban expanded on Cassirer's views throughout the 1950s and 1960s.

Sanford Krolick roots myth in the phenomenological lifeworld expressed in language, with myth a legitimate mode of being in the world, at least in "preobjectivized" and "prepersonal" oral cultures where "the intentional relations uniting body-subject and the world-as-lived by the body are not yet lost in abstract categorizations and thematizations." "I want to argue that we find the source of mythic anonymity, the powerful ground of the myth-making experience, precisely in this pre-personal, anonymous subjectivity" similar to that described by Merleau-Ponty in reference to the body. Myth "'gathers together' into a symbolic whole the entire spectrum of human experience, disclosing the relations between the life-world of concrete existence and the essential ground of being as Power or the Sacred." Rafaele Pettazzoni shares Krolick's phenomenological bent; additionally, the truth of myth is not historical, but religious and magical, for myth serves the ends of cult through the power of words.

For Milton Scarborough, a critic of how Modernist approaches (unlike myth itself) split inner and outer, subject and object, "Only when we can acknowledge that myth is good enough to keep company with us in our most advanced thinking, indeed, only when we can acknowledge our indispensable dependence upon it, are we likely to take myth seriously enough truly to understand and appreciate it" (*Myth and Modernity*). A myth is a form of intentionality, an orientation for existence in the lifeworld, that works on us tacitly even if we've never heard the original tale. "We think with myths, even when myths themselves are what we think about." The crisis of modernity is not an absence of myths, but a profusion, with none dominant. Mythic language cannot be pinned down by a literal-vs-metaphoric binary absent from pre-reflective tellings of the story. Myth serves as an embodied backdrop, a tacit, comprehensive and primordial grasp of the lifeworld and of our values, symbols, facts, etc., with the smaller just-so tales serving as "mythlettes."

> Rather than theories or criteria judging myth, myths help generate and lend credibility to theories and criteria. If myth is not a theory but a form of language, apprehension, and intention linking background and foreground, the tacit and explicit, and orienting people for all activities, including the activity of reflection, even the activity of creating and applying theories of truth, then to mistake myth for theory and to test it by techniques or criteria designed for testing theories can only ensure that myth will be discredited.

Alan Watts saw myth as a complex of stories, their roots largely unconscious, demonstrating the inner meaning of the universe and of human life by way of the perennial philosophy as described by

Coomaraswamy. Paul Ricoeur positions myth as a "social imaginary" between imagination as ideology and as utopia, with the latter humanizing the former unless literalism makes of utopic imagining a totalitarianism. Ricoeur notes that belief in myths has given way to their interpretation: "[Modern man] alone can recognize the myth as myth, because he alone has reached the point where history and myth become separate." Lucky us. "A genuine myth cannot be conscious of itself as a myth, or even of the phenomenon of myth; once myth, or the people conceiving it, attains that consciousness, it ipso facto becomes something else: what Tillich called a 'broken myth.'" He also presents the image of chains of dead metaphors, killed off once they've been absorbed by the community, and adds that the claim of logos to rule mythos is itself a mythical claim. But so perhaps is the claim that people in pre- or non-industrial cultures cannot recognize their stories as stories.

The philosopher R. G. Collingwood, who in childhood enjoyed inventing imaginary worlds, wrote a series of essays on folktales, published posthumously as *The Philosophy of Enchantment*. There he argues that the commingling of reason and imagination was common to both "civilized" and "primitive" cultures. It is dangerous to disaggregate reason and the imagination, for modern progress actually depends on animistic reason: "It is only in a society whose artistic life is healthy and vigorous that a healthy and vigorous scientific life can emerge." He observes that "the mind here discovers its true nature as the creator not only of imaginary worlds but of the real world." Phillip Stambovsky makes a related point: "Leave open the possibility that certain forms of myth and mythopoetic thinking may actually forward the Enlightenment project of critiquing rational understanding."

Kevin Schilbrack considers myths as religious models and as holders of insight into the general character of reality. They also contain metaphysical claims (Frankforts, Eliade, Geertz) and raise important philosophical questions such as:

> What are the differences between the understandings of reality as such in one culture and those in another? Attention to the metaphysics in myths also points to (and

certainly does not hinder one from asking) important sociological questions, such as: are the metaphysical myths used to justify particular social arrangements? And, does the interest in certain metaphysical myths correspond to different sections of society, or to different types of society?

Schilbrack agrees with Michèle Le Doeuff's observation of myth, especially in its images, as an imaginary accompaniment of reason. Myth brings reason and passion together in narrative.

Lawrence Hatab maintains that myth (particularly Greek) creates the existential world of meaning from which reason and abstraction gradually emerge over historical time. "A myth is a narrative which discloses a sacred world." This sense of the sacred is found coming from the lived world, not projected into it; world and self form a circle prior to (mythic!) delineations of subject and object. Drawing upon Cassirer, Heidegger, and phenomenology, Hatab presents myth as an opening, an event that happens existentially and is *lived*, from the inside, not an explanation from a self not yet formulated:

> Myths established social and educational values; prescribed daily tasks and ceremonial responses; inspired painting, sculpture, music, dance, poetry, and architecture; gave meaning to birth, maturation, marriage, and death—in other words, myths shaped the cultural life of a society.

Following Cassirer:

> The sacred does not mean exclusively the supernatural or otherworldly, but simply the *extraordinary*, the uncommon, both wondrous and terrifying. The profane, therefore, does not mean something sacrilegious but simply the *ordinary*, the common. This distinction does not speak of two worlds but rather a single, two-dimensional world.

This is why explanation via symbol is suspect: it implies a duality not present in the myth. "A god was not identical with a natural element but was rather the sacred dimension of that element. Consider Poseidon and the sea. When Homer tells us of Poseidon riding over the waves (*Iliad,* XIII. 21ff.) we witness an example of the sacred-profane distinction." Likewise, Kerényi writes that Hades for the ancient Greeks was presence of the nonexistence in the world, not a separate underworld.

By and large, *feminist* perspectives on myth criticize the mythic valorization of the heroically masculine (Charlene Spretnak), reclaim myths on behalf of women's interpretations of them (starting with Marija Gimbutas), and highlight less-known mythic figures as exemplars of feminine power and wisdom. Merlin Stone's *When God Was a Woman* (1976) brought a resurgence of interest in the figure of the Goddess.

Gimbutas's archaomythology describes a Goddess-honoring Old Europe of six thousand years ago overrun by patriarchal Kurgan nomads hauling their sky gods with them. Her interpretations of goddess images found at archeological digs have been criticized by many, including Bernard Wailes, Ruth Ringham, Linda Ellis, and David Anthony, who denounce her reliance on folklore, but defended by Gerda Lerner, Spretnak, et al. As Spretnak reminds, Gimbutas did not make a case for matriarchy, but for egalitarian forms of community; too, scholarship on religion and folklore has often been unwelcome in archeology.

Feminist approaches have also set plurality against mono-mythologizing. In *The Lost Beliefs of Northern Europe* (1993), the year Judy Gran traced the rise of ritual and myth to menstruation rites, Hilda Ellis Davidson deconstructed the dual notions of a golden age of ritual and of a single conceptual key for unlocking myth, ritual, or religion. To feminists eager to dump all myth as patriarchal Luce Irigaray suggests the alternative of a reconfigurative "miming" to disrupt the very idea of a universal identity, feminine or otherwise, to achieve new possibilities of social life. (Toni Morrison's rewriting of the Medea myth in *Beloved* might be an example of this.) In 1979, Angela Carter offered feminist reinterpretation in *The Bloody Chamber*, as did Anne Baring and Jules Cashford in *The Myth of the Goddess* (1991), Carolyne Larrington with *The Feminist Companion to Mythology* (1992), and works by Sandra Billington, Miranda Green, Iris Furlong, M. W. Seton-Williams, Tao Tao Liu, Isobel White, Helen Payne, Margaret Orbell, Athalya Brenner, Julia Vytrovskaya, Birgitte Sonne, Marta Weigle, Penelope Harvey, Jane Caputi, Diane Purkiss, and Susan Seller.

Spretnak, Adriana Cavarero, and many others have shown that cultural sanctioning of only masculine deities pushes all other figures—feminine, androgynous, asexual, transsexual—out of public discourse. Marina Warner traces current images of the Monster in film and video games to male violence. Popular authors retelling myths to empower women include Clarissa Pinkola Estes, Jean Shimoda Bolen, and Gertrude Mueller Nelson. In *La Frontera*, Gloria Anzaldua uses myth as an access to liminal thresholds of culture such as *nepantla*, the bridge world of the in-between, where deep transformations simmer and hybrid consciousness grows.

*   *   *   *

Recent mythography resurrects old arguments like fragments of myth returning in altered form. Myth makes truth claims, is held as credible, and possesses authority, notes Bruce Lincoln; but myth is full of distortions: culture passed off as nature, projection of the narrator's values and categories into fictive prehistory, reconciliation of unresolvable opposites, groups represented with only one member or character. Texts, contexts, subtexts, consequences, advantages, and variants must all be taken into account to see who benefits by which tellings when and how. Meanwhile, myth no longer believed degenerates into fable and legend. Eric Csapo thinks myths survive because they help combine societal oppositions into unifying ideologies; where Nicole Loraux declares the Heracles myth too widely popular to be political, Csapo sees in it the glorification of heroic deeds from which even a slave can supposedly benefit. Klaus Antoni makes a similar ideological argument for how the Japanese government of WWII exploited the Momotary myth to promote wartime nationalism. Jean-Pierre Vernant sees in Greek myths the celebration of warlike patriarchy.

Barre Toelken considers myths to be culturally constructed narrative fictions whose plots mirror human potentialities, as when a hero demonstrates an admirable quality. Classicist Elizabeth Vandiver deciphers traditional stories a society tells itself as encodings representing the worldview, beliefs, principles, and often fears of that society. In her view, legends are rooted in historical fact, describing adventures of people who actually lived; folktales center on entertaining and often involve animals or clever human beings; and kinds of traditional tales can overlap. There are no mythless societies, but myth is especially important in preliterate societies, where traditional stories have to do the work of theology, history, psychology, science, etc. She believes the idea of a collective psyche that dreams up myths to be undemonstrated.

Max Müller's take on myth as a "disease of language" has been resurrected by Elizabeth and Paul Barber, who attempt to link myth to worldly events important to remember, e.g. earthquakes, volcanoes, tsunamis, and celestial movements of planets and stars through condensed metaphors hardened into tales. What began as a tomb filled with the explosive gas of decomposing bodies mutated over time into a fire-breathing dragon guarding the Underworld. Those who do not write or compute, mythologize. The list of Mytho-Linguistic Principles offered by the Barbers goes without reference to their antecedents (Levy-Bruhl's *participation mystique*, for instance, unmentioned behind the new-minted Principle of Metaphoric Reality: an example of the Silence Principle at work?). If nothing else, the ingenious if reductive parallels (can the spirit world really be shrunk down to reflections in mirrors and lakes?) reveal the forgotten importance of the natural world in how the stories are woven and rewoven.

Although the sociofunctional slant on myth has never gone away, it has gained interesting complexities, especially when linked to other perspectives. In myth Francisca Cho Bantly sees an articulation and perpetuation of "archetypes": not the Jungian variety, but cultural templates used to make the world recognizable and meaningful. In Chinese myth these archetypes contradict the Western split between myth and history by operating within historical time and not outside of it. The supposed reverse euhemerism of Confucius actually blends the mythic and the historic by holding up gods as examples for moral behavior. Nor is there a hard progression from the mythical to the rational or historical, a progression that implies a non-Asian rupture between present and past.

Once largely replaced by sociofunctionalism, comparativism is making a return, especially through Borofsky, Doniger, Eilberg-Schwartzwich, Grottaneli, Nader, and Jake Sherman, who, acknowledging the difficult colonial past of comparative religion, points out that appreciation of real similarities can include valuing difference. "We reclaim the term 'magic,'"—this from Kimberly Patton and Benjamin Ray in their collection *A Magic Still Dwells*—"to endorse and to extend [Smith's] claim that comparison is an indeterminate scholarly procedure that is best undertaken as an intellectually creative enterprise, not as a science but as an art—an imaginative and critical act of mediation and redescription in the service of knowledge." Diana Eck: "This very multiplicity is one meaning of 'comparative' study, for no tradition or community speaks with a single voice, but contains its own inner disputations and multiple perspectives."

Where Lincoln and Barthes equate myth with naturalized ideology, scholars like Wendy Doniger offer examples of how tending myths—including myths compared—can increase cross-cultural appreciation and bring forth cultural and political diversity. To dwell only on difference brings just what is not wanted: absolute Othering that kills conversation, as when Christian fundamentalists insist that Allah is not their God. "....We find ourselves trapped in the self-reflexive garden of a deconstructed Wonderland, forever meeting ourselves walking back through the cultural door we were trying to escape from." And what about how myths detail the human experiences we all share? The big questions we all ask about why we are here? The meanings and values that are shared? What about myths or fairytales like Cinderella that begin in one culture (China) and take root elsewhere? Or are told by people of other nations who now live within our own borders, on soil that gives new growth to transplanted tales? What about when the study of other people's myths opens insight into our own, and when their study of ours sheds light on theirs?

> Picasso called art a lie that tells the truth, and the same might be said of myths. A myth is a story that is sacred to and shared by a group of people who find their most important meanings in it; it is a story believed to have been composed in the past about an event in the past, or, more rarely, in the future, an event that continues to have meaning in the present because it is remembered; it is a story that is part of a larger group of stories.

Doniger agrees with Mary Barnard that only later, when remembered, does a story take on the sheen of true myth by linking us to its past.

Ritualism too has returned, revivied in part through the work of Victor Turner, who defined ritual as quintessential custom condensed through enacted symbols dense with a significance that resists linear analysis. Karen Armstrong calls myth "the discourse we need in extremity": to be deeply transformed by the stories and their enactments, with myth a resacrilizing therapeutic fable carrying mysteries and timeless energies supporting human existence.

> For my money, too much of our mythographic history has been marked by the assumption that *only a single approach* will predominate, so that myths or rituals are considered to have *only one function*, to be of only *one type*, and so forth—we can refer in these cases to *monomythic* mythographies and *reductionist* ritologies.
> —William Doty

A handful of scholars have worked to supply **multidisciplinary** or **pluralist** views of myth. G. S. Kirk argues against the idea that all myths have the same kind of origin or function, although they do exhibit some common attributes: their life in fantasy, their freedom to develop, their complex structure. Nor do all display a clear social application, a ritual connection (a point also made by R. de Langhe et al), or a sharp distinction from fairy tales. Defining myth as "traditional tale," he notes that not all myth is either sacred or about gods. However, unlike the Romantics, Boas, Jung, and Campbell, Kirk bypasses the idea of myth-making in the present. Furthermore, myths are best interpreted with multi-functional and open-ended approaches as symbolized by the multi-patterned weaving cloth of Penelope. Although E. W. Count's argument that the folktale concept is a modern invention, much as Jack Zipes argues for fairy tales, myths act differently by using identifiable characters and family relationships anchored in specific regions. They also carry a more serious tone. Etiologies seem tacked onto myths rather than an integral part of them. "The following might be suggested as a simplified working typology of mythical function. The first type is primarily narrative and entertaining; the second operative, iterative, and validatory; and the third speculative and explanatory."

Vedic expert and historian of language E. J. Michael Witzel defines myth as

> a narrative that is told or recited at certain special occasions; that is standardized (to some extent); that is collectively owned and managed (often by specialists); that is considered by its owners to be of great and enduring significance; that (whether or not these owners are consciously aware of this point) contains and brings out such images of the world (a cosmology), of past and present society (a history and sociology), and of the human condition (an anthropology) as are eminently constitutive of the life society in which that narrative circulates, or at least where it circulated originally; that, if this constitutive aspect is consciously realized by its owners, may be invoked (etiologically) to explain and justify present-day conditions; and that is therefore a

powerful device to create collectively underpinned meaning and collectively recognized truth (regardless of whether such truth would be recognized outside the community whose myth it is).

In his compendious *The Origins of the World's Mythologies* Witzel draws on linguistics, molecular genetics, anthropology, and archeology to lay out a diffusionist comparativist schema wherein myth comes down to us from two great prehistoric branches: the Laurasian from North Africa, Eurasia, and the Americas, and the much older Gondwanan from sub-Saharan Africa, the Andamans, Papua, Australia, South India, and Malaya. An exodus from Africa 40,000 years ago gave rise to the younger Laurasian myths, which tend to be longer and, thematically, concerned with primal Creation and Destruction, Father Heaven and Mother Earth, families of gods, killing the dragon, the Flood, and Trickster deities. By contract, Gondwana mythology takes the world's existence as given instead of created and tells mainly of human emergence from it. Anthropologist Tok Thompson has denounced this theory for having the racist overtones of South/Gondwana = static and incomplete, North/Laurasia = more differentiated. According to Witzel, both branches reach back to a lost primal Pangaean source.

In *Mythography*, William Doty describes myth as tacit-intuitive rather than rational, stocked with cultural wisdom, poly- rather than mono-functional, and functioning differently in different social settings. (Richard Comstock: "Myth, properly understood, is not an early attempt to do what modern science can now do better, any more than a poem is an early attempt to express what a geometrical theorem and proof can state more clearly and convincingly.") Myth is a form of poetry which transcends poetry in that it proclaims a truth; a form of reasoning which transcends reasoning in that it wants to bring about the truth it proclaims; and a form of action, of ritual behavior, which does not find its fulfilment in the act but must proclaim and elaborate a poetic form of truth. Doty writes,

> I see myths as a *particular kind of fiction*, and I see myths and other literary fictions as having an important

function in our society—that of modeling possible personal roles and concepts of the self. But *ultimately mythic narratives themselves are "special."* They are not little but big stories, touching not just the everyday, but sacred or specially marked topics that concern much more than any immediate situation. And myths generally concern repeated (archetypal) themes that humans face over and over again, rather than problems that are relevant only to one person or one group or at one particular period of life.

A mythological corpus consists of: 1. a usually complex network of myths that are 2. culturally important 3. imaginal 4. stories, conveying by means of 5. metaphoric and symbolic diction, 6. graphic imagery, and 7. emotional conviction and participation, 8. the primal, foundational accounts 9. of aspects of the real, experienced world and 10. humankind's roles and relative statuses in it. Myths may 11. convey the political and moral values of a culture and 12. provide systems of interpreting 13. individual experiences within a universal perspective, which may include 14. the intervention of suprahuman entities as well as 15. aspects of the natural and cultural orders. Myths may be enacted or reflected in 16. rituals, ceremonies, and dramas, and 17. may provide materials for secondary elaboration, the constituent mythemes having become merely images or reference points for a subsequent story like a folktale, legend, novella, or prophecy.

Selected by Doty from Morris Freilich's structural strategy of myth analysis:

> Myths attempt to resolve the fundamental human dilemma: to be smart and stay (physically) alive, or to be proper and stay sane
>
> Myths attempt to resolve contradictions, among them contradictory smart and proper norms
>
> Myths attempt to explain paradoxes, including why

properness sometimes leads to tragedy and why smartness sometimes leads to losses

Myths resolve dilemmas, paradoxes, and puzzles by identifying mediators

The key subsystems that together constitute a myth are (a) content—"history," a story that amuses; (b) structure—technology, paired opposites that carry messages: and (c) hidden messages—instructions as to what is proper and what is smart.

Doty also provides a developmental schema of three phases of myth's vitality: *primary myth* newly conceived and linked directly to the needs of a culture; *implicit myth* in which the central story is accepted, elaborated, and made orthodox; and *rationalized myth* once the myth, no longer so vital or whole, is rewritten and explained to strengthen it against competing myths and to align it with contemporary knowledge and discovery. These phases are not necessarily progressive. Doty's schema has the virtue of scope but the disadvantage of being somewhat ponderous. It would be interesting to know what indigenous storytellers from myth-honoring cultures would make of it.

* * * *

Mythoclasm, the disparagement of myth (and its study) as archaic, primitive, or simply useless to modern concerns, is at least as old as iconoclasm. At its best it shatters frail idols to make way for new imaginings; applied recklessly, it undermines imagination itself as well as its best productions, including myth. Rather than ignore myth altogether, it attacks it, unable to dispense with it. David Miller thinks we always harbor both sides, mythoclasm and mythophilia, as we explore myth.

In any case, we have already seen examples of mythoclasm: myth Procrusteanized down to primitive science, superstition, deliberate ideology, essentializing and universalizing social constructions; stereotypical rather than archetypal, irrelevant to or even evasive of contemporary concerns, etc., with much of this unable to distinguish between myth and *how myth is used*. Overt mythoclasts include Roland Barthes (who somehow misses the fabulous side of myth and considers it "poverty-stricken"), Donald Stauffer, Robert Eichner, Naomi Goldenberg, Gabriel Vahanian, Wolfgang Giegerich, Carlo Ginzburg, Sophia Heller, Thomas Altizer, Marc Manganaro, Phillip Rahv, and Daniel Dubuisson.

Echoing a point made by Dubuisson, Robert Eisner positions "myth" as we mistakenly understand it as historically late. Tellings surviving in texts do not give much of a sense of what the tales meant: "A myth, uprooted from its native context, washed clean of jungle dirt, and brought back barely alive to civilization in a Victorian vasculum, has little content and no context left except that which the collector imposes on it." So psychoanalysts appropriated the remains. "The corpus of Greek myth has seemed a fair-game preserve of documentation to many other theoreticians on safari from the consulting rooms, but the rare beasts at large in that ancient paradise do not breed in captivity and can be tracked to their lairs only with proper knowledge of their habitats, habits, and life cycles." Furthermore, "The contrary versions of a given myth are conflated, even bits of unrelated material are collated and juxtaposed, and then all are thrown together into some alchemical retort—with no respect for the variety of incident and detail wrought by generations of poets and artists—to create any Ur-myth the writer fancies." Details and context are lost in the rush to archetypalize and to extract psychological truths from what for pre-individualistic ancient peoples were mostly tales of plain deeds.

Analyst Wolfgang Giegerich holds the search for a higher meaning in life responsible for the modern mood of meaninglessness. We don't ask about meaning when we feel embedded in life and contained in the world. Myths celebrated this instead of providing frameworks for seekers. We seek today because we who embrace rationalism and individuality long for that lost "is-ness." When we find it, it often looks like totalitarian states and fundamentalist sects. The myths and religions that did so much to give birth to individual consciousness are dead; their current use is for the self-numbing turning away from embracing our individuality. "The gods have not become diseases, as Jung and Hillman wanted us to believe, they have become memories, memories of former modes of man's being-in-the-world." Myths are like sugar dissolved in the coffee of modern consciousness. Giegerich prefers his coffee black.

In *The Many Meanings of Myth,* Martin S. Day distinguishes between four forms of myth arising from cultural levels not often accounted for in our theories: Myth I (archaic) from non-literate food-gathering societies, Myth II (intermediate) committed to writing, Myth III (derivative) popularized and released to the public, and Myth IV (ideological), as when Hitler misused Teutonic motifs. Although Day also discriminates between an emblem (what Jung called a sign), which points to the known, and a symbol, which points beyond the concrete to mystery, he locates myth in the past and the archaic.

Some mythoclastic attacks focus on theorists as much as theories. Robert Ellwood knew and worked with Eliade long enough to criticize his early fascistic politics, as do Strenski, Lincoln, and other critics, but says little about his later turn away from them. "Fascists favored a 'spiritual' view of nationhood based on common myths, archetypes, and *Geist,*" he reports; but so do non-authoritarian indigenous priests and elders. Campbell too he treats to *ad hominem* attacks, although he also discusses methods: "Campbell uses the traditional equipment and methods of the literary critic, for whom comparison and analogy are tantamount to proof and fact." Anti-religious Campbell uses King Arthur as a pagan hero "despite the fact that we know King Arthur only as a Christian hero," although Arthur actually begins as a pre-Christian Welsh hero. "Whether there was ever such a thing as living primordial myth in the sense the mythologists envisioned it may be questioned. Myth as we know it is always received from an already distant past, literary (even if only oral literature), hence a step away from primal simplicity." It is reconstructed, whereas the original is fragmentary, more image than word; but was it not first *told*?

Marc Manganaro fires at an entire group of theorists, including Campbell, Eliot, Frazer, and Frye, for modernist reductionism, arbitrary interpretations of motifs cut from contexts and cultures, and ethnocentric evolutionism.

Many of the mythoclastically inclined glimpse myth through a Modernist glass darkly, seeing in myth a spent remnant of another time. Batto, Heller, Miller, Mauss, Dumézil, Malinowski, Voss, and quite a few others think we moderns have no myth anymore, just concepts and imaginings about what we've fallen out of and can no longer take as literally real. In this they receive some support from Campbell and Eliade, who both wrote about gathering up the glittering shards that remain. In a moment both mythoclastic and humanistic, Campbell writes that sea, sky, and animals no longer hold the sacred power: now it is within us, because "there are no more intact monadic horizons: all are dissolving..."

Why then doesn't this failure of myth eradicate religion, which goes on and on? How do we know that the question of meaning never arises for the myth-immersed indigenous? And if they live it instead of wielding it as a method, where do vision quests and sacred ceremonies come from, and why do these so often bring transformation to the non-indigenous as well? What about indigenous Modern people who keep their stories and traditions going, like Navajo storytellers reenacting Nayenezgani (Monster-Slayer) to fight mining conglomerates defiling Dinetah? The mythoclastic equation of myth with pre-subjectivity leans on the old "primitive = preindividual" trope. As for the New Guinea tribe that supposedly disintegrated when shown mirrors and cameras, they're around: they fled into the forest when photographers invaded their homes. No doubt they still have some stories to tell.

According to David Miller, it's not the purpose of myth to settle on any meaning or to fill any gaps. "Serious dogmatism in religion, the ideology in culture, and the literalism in historiography are smashed by myth, which, through dealing with powerful ideas and meanings, is after all merely myth. It is fiction, story, and hypothesis misread as biography, science, and history." The point is to evoke a state of being and a reality beyond meaning. "What is the meaning of a flower?" Campbell asks. "And having no meaning, should the flower, then, not be?" Yet these arguments, Miller points out, are still

concerned with meaning. What if we embraced absence and meaninglessness? "It is an irony of history, I suppose, that the study of
myth began to be a strong presence in the mid-seventeenth century,
just at the time when a mythological worldview was dissolving and
collapsing. Perhaps it is often the case that an academic interest
begins in things that are in the process of dying." In the end, Miller
is a mythoclast. But he leaves out the rest of Campbell's argument,
and Thomas Berry's too: that the absence reflects the sunrise glow
of new myths on the horizon.

* * * *

In contrast to mythoclasm, the psychological approach to myth
as popularized by Freud and Jung has been reinvigorated by a number of theorist-practitioner-mythographers interested in how myth
shows up today.

Rollo May believed that most of his therapy patients were concerned, at bottom, with a search for myths; loss of myth in the West
gave rise to psychotherapy. Unlike fairy tales, which lack an existential dimension, myths can make sense of the world and of ourselves:
"Myths are like the beams in a house: not exposed to outside view,
they are the structure which holds the house together so people can
live in it." When myths are not enough to heal us, the result is
mythoclastic disappointment and retaliatory attacks on the inward
approach to myth. But as a totality and not a solution, "myth unites
the antinomies of life: conscious and unconscious, historical and
present, individual and social... Myth refers to the quintessence of
human experience." Myth augments identity ("Who am I?"), brings
up what is repressed from awareness (the regressive function),
reveals new goals, insights, and possibilities (the progressive function), offers a feeling of community, undergirds our moral values,
presents life's great existential dramas, and makes sense of the cosmos. Myth is therefore permanent and in need of reinterpretation by
each generation. In the end, it is not history that determines myth,
but myth that determines history, as when the need for a change of
perspectives resulted in the Apollo missions that gave us the mythic

image of Earthrise.

James Hillman would not psychologize myth so much as mythologize psychology by revealing its mythic structures and archetypal motifs: myths as adverbs that personify. He begins *A Terrible Love of War* by stating that he stands at the altar of, and thus in the discourse of, Mars. The pathologies of the gods are the pathologies of the psyche. For James Hollis, myth precedes, follows, and occasionally dominates consciousness as the deepest possible level of knowing, "the symbolic expression of the soul." Even in their absence "the gods do not die—they depart the image and go into the underworld for a while and reinvest elsewhere," personifying not only in idea but in affect, body, value, history, and ailment. Myth is expressed through dramatized tribal value systems, through personal histories, and in symptoms and complexes: "Just as Jung called complexes splinter personalities, so one may call symptoms and complexes splinter, or fractile, mythologies."

Psychotherapist Thomas Moore:

> Myth is not merely a kind of intellectual interpretation of events, it guides us out of the modernist template that lives by natural law, by perception of the sense, and by physical technologies toward a sacred world in which meaning is not limited to human categories and where the laws of imagination have dominance....Therefore, the restoration of a mythic sensibility calls for nothing less than a radically post-modern way of living. It allows a vision, not of Greek mythology once more incarnated, but of the goddess of the sensual body and the sea breaking through in an ordinary passage of time.

Moving beyond folklore indexing, Stith Thompson writes that "the actual reason for the existence of stories about the gods, and perhaps about the heroes, is the fact that there are certain psychological compulsions which impel people to tell tales of particular kinds. Dreams, fears, and stresses—it is from these that come the gods, the heroes, and the tales about them." Also, "...Myth has to do with the gods and their actions, with creation, and with the general nature of the universe and of the earth." Studying Jung's views on myth, Robert Segal adds: "Today, it is suggested that myths can be reintroduced into the world of physical phenomena by interpreting them on the level of playful interaction. Play is something in between truth and falsehood." Christine Downing reminds us that myth is first of all a *story*, and stories need retelling. Mythology is logos thinking about mythos even as the myths address us. Nor will myths stay in the myth books: they come back to life and seek us out.

Bringing a psychohistorical perspective, Lloyd De Mause highlights the religious state: "Here glows the very essence of myth and its sacral nature. Most of the rational theorists of myth from Thales onwards have totally missed the point in interpreting myth as allegory, theology, nonsense, or whatever. The fundamental purpose of all true archaic myth is the communication of that heightened state of awareness. A myth can never hold to the mundane world of everyday fact for it must soar, it must evoke the marvelous, the fantastic, the uncanny." In *Meaning and Being in Myth*, Norman Austin writes that the gods provide an Other in whose presence we come to know ourselves. "As long as we continue to be sentient beings we shall continue to need myth, since myth is the primary ground on which we articulate our experience of ourselves in our social and natural environment."

Even in the midst of myth's resurgence, critics like those casting myth studies out of the academy attack the very word "mythologist" for its colonial connotations. Devdutt Pattanaik pushes back:

> To me, mythology is the study of a subjective truth of people that is communicated through stories, symbols and rituals. Unlike fantasy that is nobody's truth, and history that seeks to be everybody's truth, mythology is somebody's truth....This definition of mythology is broad enough to include religious as well as non-religious beliefs. It is respectful of all truths, those of a tribe as well as those of a nation-state or a political party.... This definition allows for discussions (*samvaad*) rather than arguments (*vivaad*) as multiple truths are acknowledged and accommodated. No single idea dominates.

Ecological approaches to myth move beyond naturalism's merely cognitive allegorizing to enjoy closeness to the natural world through the medium of story. Marcus Jacobsen touches on parallels between Enki's tricky deviousness and the coaxing of water through Sumerian irrigation channels: "The key to understanding the forces which one meets in nature is felt to lie in the understanding of their characters, exactly as the clue to understanding men lies in understanding their characters." Think of all the sacred mountains and springs and sites in the world's mythologies, each associated with a god, *kami*, or spirit.

Although the relationship of deities to landscapes, animals, and elements was obvious to preliterate storytellers, only a few myth theorists have taken that connection as more than fanciful or projective. Jakob Grimm and J. G. Herder held up myth as a bridge between the lands shaping it and the people telling and retelling it. Grimm considered Christianity a disruption of this bond between places, stories, and dwellers and collected folktales to give voice to what missionaries had tried to erase. Rodney Needham observes how the perceived split between nature and culture prevents us from appreciating nature as symbolic, as he notes in "Blood, Thunder, and Mockery of Animals":

> Certain things in nature seem to exert an effect on the human mind, conducing to symbolic forms of the most general, and even universal, kind. They seem, namely, to make a primordial impress on the unconscious mind of man as a natural species, producing an affective response which is as natural to the organism (to its distinctive brain) as the motor language of bees or the phototropism of marigolds is natural in other realms of life. This response, when translated (however variously) into language or ritual, constitutes a universal symbolism.

"Wisdom about nature, that wisdom heard and told in animated pattern, that pattern rendered in such a way as to preserve a place whole and sacred, safe from human meddling: these are the concepts with which to begin an exploration of myth," suggests Sean Keen in *Wisdom of the Mythtellers*. "Of these, the notion of the sanctity of place is vital. It anchors the other concepts. ...Once the power of the place is lost to memory, myth is uprooted; knowledge of the earth's processes becomes a different kind of knowledge, manipulated and applied by man." When our theories of myth are mainly urban, then *fabula*, the Latin counterpart to "myth," comes to mean a lie. "Once this anthropocentrism settles in the outlook of a people who have learned to domesticate animals, the animals stop talking in myth." R. S. McCoppin: "It has been scientifically confirmed that life emerged from water eons ago, and numerous creation myths from around the globe capture this accurately with their representations of life emerging from a primordial sea....The underworld, though it is depicted as a place of death, is not in many myths portrayed as an evil place. The mythic underworld most often serves as a representation of the womb of the earth." Jake Berry speaks of "mythopoetic site origin," the location of the mythic impulse prior to its establishment in a finite structure.

> No people, regardless of the simplicity of their culture, ever took a stone carving to be divine. Modern anthropological scholarship now tells us as much. We have lost some quality of experience that would allow us to see the world as they did—or rather to see through it as they did. I take the animist worldview to be just that: things were once transparent to the human eye; greater realities moved behind and within them, were seen in this and that, here and there as if through a lens. This is where the concept of "spirit" comes from, this once-homely, utterly normal sense that something other than matter moves behind matter, animates it, sustains it.
> —Theodore Roszak, *Voice of the Earth*

* * * *

Down the centuries, the majority of Western myth theorists have worked from the outside in, from a stance of depletion trying to glimpse the elusive mythic abundance of other times and peoples. As Ursula K. Le Guin summarizes in *The Language of the Night*,

> Myth is an expression of one of the several ways the human being, body/psyche, perceives, understands and relates to the world. Like science, it is a product of a basic human mode of apprehension. To pretend that it can be replaced by abstract or quantitative cognition is to assert that the human being is, potentially or ideally, a creature of pure reason, a disembodied Mind.

It won't do, then, to see myths just from the outside, like Apollo surveying an archery target. Birenbaum: "As we may say more obviously about dreams, I must *have* them in order to know them, not merely observing them as though they were concrete objects and analyzing them 'objectively' but entering into them subjectively." Theorists have oversimplified—much like the fabled Nasreddin, who did not search for his keys where he had dropped them, but under a lamp, "because the light is better here."

The logos of theory and explanation is ultimately parasitic upon myth. Understanding their relationship frees those of us who care about myth to reenchant our theoretical musings while we encourage a more beneficial symbiosis between them and what animates them.

What we hold most dear as we work is the ecology of Faerie, however conceived—Pleroma, Harqalada, *mundus imaginalis*, Xanadu, Meru, collective unconscious—as it aligns with that of our precious homeworld. May our tellings and retellings honor the iridescence as bright rays of Otherworld shine into this one.

Appendix 2: Glossary of Mythological Terms

Aarne–Thompson Index: a system for classifying myths and folk-tales by motif. Some examples: AT 945 - Luck and Intelligence; A110 - Origin of gods; A301 - Mother Earth conceived as mother of all things.

Aetiological Myth: a myth that explains how something came to be (e.g., how Raven's feathers came to be black).

Allegory: a story or account told to convey a specific, known, and often moralistic lesson. Some myth theorists take myth for allegory. See *Literalism*.

Animism: E.B. Tylor's term for the belief that non-living objects are ensouled.

Archetype: originally a Gnostic term, C. G. Jung used it to refer to what he believed were universal motifs in mythology and folklore. Descent to the Underworld, Goddess, God, Divine Child, Death, Rebirth, and many other archetypes express themselves in specific cultural images (Freya the erotic love goddess in one culture, Bastet, Oshun, and Aphrodite in others). Archetypes are deep structures of experience, not just repeating plot lines.

Blason Populaire: the use of stereotypes to make one nation or cultural group look good at the expense of another.

Charter Myth: Bronislau Malinowski's term for a myth that supports an institution, sanctioned belief, or custom.

Comparative Method: the comparison of folkloric motifs or plots across cultures or cultural groups. Early uses of the comparative method triggered controversy by ranking mythologies such that the European were made out as more advanced than anybody else's.

Cultural Appropriation: exploitation by members of a dominant cultural group of the stories and traditional practices, rites and imagery of a less privileged cultural group. Taking intellectual property, traditional knowledge, cultural expressions, or artifacts from someone else's culture without permission (Susan Scarfidi). An example would be stamping a definitive Western psychological interpretation on a story originating in, and held very differently by, another culture. By contract, *cultural appreciation* finds value and meaning in other people's stories without making dogmatic interpretations of them or advancing overconfident outsider arguments about what the stories "really" mean.

Culture Hero: a celebrated entity, often a deity or hero, who represents the ideals of a culture or cultural group and who usually achieves something great to create, benefit, or protect that culture. Nuwa, Ditolane, Mopo, Thor, and Princess Bari are examples.

Diffusion: the spread of folkloric stories, motifs, images, etc. from one culture into others.

Epic: a long and usually oral narrative poem centered on the struggles of a great hero. The *Ramayana*, *Beowulf*, the *Odyssey*, and *Shahnama* are examples.

Euhemerism: the interpretation of myths as time-exaggerated stories about actual historical persons later believed in as deities (e.g., interpreting Zeus as an actual king nobody remembers anymore except as a god).

Eye Dialect: simulation in writing of the syntax, pronunciation, and pacing of spoken speech.

Fable: a story in which an animal's behavior makes a moral point. See *Allegory*.

Fairy Tale: folklore in which magical beings are predominant and events happened long ago or in some unspecified time. If a dilemma to solve is present, it is usually solved with magic.

Fakelore: Richard Dorson's term for giving a folkloric appearance to material that is not folklore. For example, a marketing campaign by Montgomery Ward created Rudolph the Red-Nosed Reindeer in 1939.

Fennmärchen: fairy tale.

Fertility Goddess: a hugely overused category. Relatively few goddesses are actually experts on fertility, and even those possess many other attributes beyond the ability to procreate. This category tends to say more about its user than about the material being discussed.

Folklore: a general term that includes myth, folktale, fairy tale, and legend. Alan Dundes calls this *prose narrative.*

folktale: a folklore narrative understood to be fictional, often introduced by a traditional formula ("Once upon a time..."), and populated by generic characters (the princess, the woodcutter, the genie, etc.) who use cleverness to get out of a dilemma.

Formalism: a brand of *Structuralism* that keeps to the text of a story while ignoring outside influences.

Frame Story: a story that includes other stories, usually arranged such that one transitions into another, as in the *1001 Nights.*

Imramm (plural Imramma): an Irish folkloric term for a voyage to the Otherworld.

In Illo Tempore: Mircea Eliade's Latin term ("in that time") for the timelessness in which mythic events take place.

Kunstmärchen: fairy tales created by known storytellers.

Legend: set after the creation of the world, a tale taken to be true for a time but eventually treated as fictional. Also, usually local. Example: The Loch Ness Monster.

Literalism: treating a story as a factual account, whether or not one believes it. For the literalist, a myth of a god eating his children means exactly that, with no symbolic or metaphoric overtone. In religion this is known as *fundamentalism.* Literalism is usually tactically applied in support of an ideological agenda.

Märchen: folktale.

Metamyth: a myth with a myth in it (Wendy Doniger); a mythic tale that reflects on another tale. For example, in one myth of Dionysus, Pentheus refuses to grant credence to the mythic rites of that god.

Modern Myth: a myth arising in contemporary or recent times. Some definitions of *myth* hold it to be an ancient and traditional oral story, but the story had to have started sometime. See *protomyth*.

Monomyth: Joseph Campbell borrowed this word from James Joyce to describe the Hero's Journey, a basic adventure cycle based on Arnold van Gennep's three phases of rites of passage (Separation, Liminality, Incorporation). It has come to mean a grand myth to which others can be reduced or referred.

Myth: a collective oral mystery story that is traditional, fantastic, highly personified, archetypally rich, once believed in, and often sacred. Part of a mythology, a set of such stories.

Mytheme: Claude Levi-Strauss's term for the smallest analyzable unit or basic element of a myth. An example would be the leitmotif of atomization occurring throughout a particular tale.

Mythicity: mythic consciousness (Wilhelm Dupré); the use of myth for making meaning.

Mythification: the application of *pseudo-myths* (see below) created by authors and critics to provide mythic depth to otherwise shallow work (Charles Moorman).

Mythoclast: a debunker and disparager of myths. Rollo May: "In mythoclasm people attack and mock the thing they used to venerate," especially by those let down by their former literal belief in it (*Freedom and Destiny*).

Mythography: the study of written myth (similar to what historiography is to history); the study of theories of myth and ritual. For a comprehensive treatment, see William Doty's *Mythography*.

Mythologem: a recurrent image or motif, whether in a single myth or across myths: for example, Trickster bringing fire to humans, or the journey to the Underworld.

Mythopoesis: the creative making and remaking of mythically themed material. Examples include Gnostic reimaginings of the Garden of Eden story, much of William Blake's *Four Zoas,* Tolkien's *The Lord of the Rings,* and the Finnish *Kalevala.*

Mythos: the Greek word for "myth." Also, a cultural set of basic beliefs. Often contrasted with Logos, the principle of reason, opinion, and logic. Mythography and theories of myth could be considered examples of Logos investigating Mythos.

Myth-Ritualism: an approach that subordinates myth to ritual.

Mythuse: degrading myth into ideology or propaganda.

Naturalism: the perspective that myths are personifications of natural forces (e.g., Zeus is the sun).

Numinous: Rudolf Otto's coinage for a sense of "fearful and fascinating mystery": a felt spiritual charge in what gives rise to overpowering awe.

Paramyth: Richard Chase's term for the reductionistic treatment of myth; specifically, the use of one aspect of a myth to explain the whole. In *Quest for Myth* he explains, "The danger is to seize upon one facet of the myth, one ghost precipitated from the artistic whole, and suppose that this is the myth or the explanation of the myth. A philosophical concept, a moral allegory, a symbol seized upon, cut off from the living whole—this is what I should call a paramyth.... To see one form in the whole to the exclusion of others is to see a paramyth."

Participation Mystique: Lucien Lévy-Bruhl's retracted idea that "primitive" people do not differentiate between the natural and the supernatural and are therefore incapable of logic and abstract thought. The term has evolved to mean the opposite: an experience of shared consciousness, not shared unconsciousness.

Personal Myth: the English translation of Jung's German phrase "Mythus meines Lebens" ("myth of my life"), meaning: the specific myth we are living. In a letter Jung described being personally confronted by the story of Faust the alchemist. See *Storied Lives: Discovering and Deepening Your Personal Myth* for accounts of coming upon and working with such myths.

Post-structuralism: the criticism of universal structures or units supposedly uncovered in folklore. We find in stories what the ideologies and power relations in our cultures condition us to find. At best, post-structuralist approaches sharpen awareness of how societal forces condition consciousness; taken too far, they promote cynicism and intellectual nihilism.

Pseudo-myth: an example of *Fakelore* (see above). A story promoted as a myth with no tradition attached to it from which it grew. Charles Moorman: "...Pseudo-myths are sometimes created by authors and critics in order to provide mythic depth to an otherwise shallow work....One recalls the 'Marilyn myth' and the 'JFK myth' as attempts to create symbols....By such reasoning *Main Street* becomes a great novel because it so beautifully reflects the 'myth' of small-town America, for which it is the chief source." See *Submyth*.

Psyche: conscious and unconscious as operative together. (Similar to *mind*, which has a more cognitive connotation.)

Riteme: the smallest analyzable unit of a ritual.

Secondary Belief: the reader's or listener's willing entrance into the world of the storyteller (J. R. R. Tolkien). Not just suspension of disbelief, but active imaginative participation.

Secondary Revision: Sigmund Freud's term for how remembering and working on dream material changes it; this applies also to work with folklore. Even retelling a story reflects a certain approach or interpretation, contradicting the notion of some pure original version.

Sociofunctional: the perspective that myths provide storied glue for holding societies together. See *Charter Myth*.

Structuralism: the reduction of folklore to linguistic units.

Submyth: Ursula K. LeGuin's term for fabled or mythic-feeling images, figures, and motifs with no religious resonance or profound intellectual or aesthetic value but alive and powerful nevertheless, like Superman and Wonder Woman. Science fiction and fantasy in general are submythic, whereas genuine myth accumulates meanings and traditions over many generations.

Superstition: a word used to denigrate beliefs, practices, and rites that do not fit the worldview of Modernism.

Symbol: an image or theme that points to a deeper meaning or experience not immediately evident. Different from the *sign*, which points to a fixed meaning (e.g., a green light for "Go"). To be symbolic is to carry many meanings highly concentrated and metaphorically evoked.

Urban Legend: a legend told in an industrialized society in contemporary times. Chain letters, the Slender Man, chemtrails, and hungry alligators in the sewers are examples.

Unconscious, the: the realm or layer of mind in which past and future mingle. Some of the unconscious is emotional material repressed out of awareness, but much is potential awaiting entry into and realization through conscious living.

Variant: a retelling of a narrative. folktales, fairy tales, and myths commonly have many variants.

Xenia: a Greek term for showing hospitality to strangers. A useful attitude for welcoming the presence of folkloric figures who address us in tellings, texts, films, works of art, and even dreams.

Selected Bibliography and Online Resources

Books:

Adams, H. (1983). *Philosophy of the literary symbolic*. Gainsville: University Press of Florida.

Aisenberg, N. (1994). *Ordinary heroines: Transforming the male myth*. New York: The Continuum Publishing Company.

Altizer, T., Beardslee, W. A. & Harvey Young, J. (1962). *Truth, myth, and symbol*. Englewood Cliffs: Prentice-Hall, Inc.

Andrews, T. (1998). *A dictionary of nature myths*. Oxford: Oxford University Press.

Anzaldua, G. (2012). *Borderlands / La Frontera: The new mestiza*. San Francisco: Aunt Lute Books.

Armstrong, K. (2012). *A short history of myth*. Edinburgh: Canongate.

Ashkenazi, M. (2003). *Handbook of Japanese mythology*. Oxford: Oxford University Press.

Austin, N. (2008). *Meaning and being in myth*. University Park: Penn State University Press.

632

Baeton, E. (1996). *The magic mirror: Myth's abiding power*. New York: State University of New York Press.

Barber, E., & Barber, P. (2006). *When they separated earth from sky: How the human mind shapes myth*. Princeton: Princeton University Press.

Barnard, F. (2003). *Herder on nationality, humanity and history*. Montreal: McGill-Queen's University Press.

Barnard, M. (1979). *The mythmakers*. Athens, Ohio: Ohio University Press.

Beckwith, M. (1976). *Hawaiian mythology*. Honolulu: University of Hawaii Press.

Bierhorst, J. (2002). *The mythology of South America*. Oxford: Oxford University Press.

Bierlein, J. (1994). *Parallel myths*. New York: Random House.

Birenbaum, Harvey. (1988). *Myth and mind*. Lanham, MD: University Press of America, Inc.

Birrel, A. (1993). *Chinese mythology: An introduction*. Baltimore: John Hopkins University Press.

Blumenberg, H. (1988). *Work on myth*. Massachusetts: The MIT Press.

Borges, J. (1964). *Labyrinths: Selected stories and other writings*. New York: New Directions.

Burrows, D., Lapides, F., & Shawcross, J. (1973). *Myths & motifs in literature*. New York: The Free Press.

Calasso, R. (2001). *Literature and the gods*. New York: Vintage.

Campbell, J. (2009). *The flight of the wild gander: Explorations in the mythological dimension.* New York: HarperPerennial.

Campbell, J. (1972). *The hero with a thousand faces.* Princeton: Bollingen.

Campbell, J. (1986). *The inner reaches of outer space: Metaphor as myth and as religion.* Novato: New World Library.

Campbell, J. (1974). *The mythic image.* Princeton: Princeton University Press.

Cassirer, E. (2012). *Language and myth.* Mineola: Dover Publications.

Chalquist, C. (2009). *The tears of Llorona: A Californian odyssey of place, myth, and homecoming.* Walnut Creek: World Soul Books.

Chance, J. (Ed.)(2008). *Tolkien and the invention of myth: A reader.* Lexington: University Press of Kentucky.

Chang, D. (1970). *The folk treasury of Korea.* Seoul: Society of Korean Oral Literature.

Chase, R. (1949). *The quest for myth.* Baton Rouge: Louisiana State University Press.

Chevalier, J., & Gheerbrant, A. (1994). *The Penguine dictionary of symbols.* New York: Penguin Books.

Collingwood, R., & Boucher, D., James, W., & Smallwood, P. (Eds.) (2007). *The philosophy of enchantment: Studies in folklore, cultural criticism, and anthropology.* Oxford: Oxford University Press.

Connor, R., Sparks, M., & Sparks, D. (Eds.)(1997). *Cassell's encyclopedia of queer myth, symbol, and spirit: Gay, lesbian, bisexual and transgendered lore.* London and New York: Cassell.

Couple, L. (2009). *Myth (The New Critical Idiom)*. New York: Routledge.

Curtin, J. (1999). *Myths and folktales of the Russians, Western Slavs, and Magyars*. Mineola: Dover Publications.

Curtis, V. (1993). *Persian myths*. London: British Museum Press.

Davidson, H. (1990). *Gods and myths of Northern Europe*. New York: Penguin Books.

Day, M. (1984). *The many meanings of myth*. Lanham: University Press of America.

DeConick, A. (2016). *The Gnostic new age: How a countercultural spirituality revolutionized religion from antiquity to today*. New York: Columbia University Press.

Delcourt, M. (1961). *Hermaphrodite: Myths and rites of the bisexual figure in classical antiquity*. New York: Studio Books.

Dell, C. (2012). *Mythology: The complete guide to our imagined worlds*. New York: Thames & Hudson.

Detienne, M. (1986). *The creation of mythology*. Chicago: University of Chicago Press.

Dimmitt, C., & Buitenen, J. (Eds.)(1978). *Classical Hindu mythology*. Philadelphia: Temple University Press.

Dorson, M., & Wilmot, J. (1997). *Tales from the rain forest*. Hopewell: The Ecco Press.

Doty, W. (2000). *Mythography: The study of myths and rituals*. Tuscaloosa: University of Alabama Press.

Downing, C. (1996). *The goddess: Mythological images of the feminine*. London, New York: Continuum.

Downing, C. (2006). *Myths and mysteries of same-sex love*. Lincoln: iUniverse.

Duncan, R. (1985). *Fictive certainties*. New York: New Directions.

Eliade, M. (1991). *Images and symbols*. Princeton, NJ: Princeton University Press.

Ellwood, R. (1999). *The politics of myth: A study of C. G. Jung, Mircea Eliade, and Joseph Campbell*. New York: State University of New York Press.

Dundes, A. (1980). *Interpreting folklore*. Bloomington: Indiana University Press.

Dundes, A. (Ed.)(1984). *Sacred narrative: Readings in the theory of myth*. Berkeley: University of California Press.

Eisner, R. (1987). *The road to Daulis: Psychoanalysis, psychology, and classical mythology*. Syracuse: Syracuse University Press.

Eliade, M. (1998). *Myth and reality*. Long Grove, Il: Waveland Press.

Ellis-Davidson, H. (1993). *The lost beliefs of Northern Europe*. New York: Routledge.

Endo, S. (1980). *Silence*. New York: Taplinger Publishing Company.

Erdos, R., & Ortiz, A. (1984). *American Indian myths and legends*. New York: Pantheon.

Estes, C. (1996). *Women who run with the wolves: Myths and stories of the wild woman archetype*. New York: Ballantine Books.

Eugenio, D. (1993) *Philippine folk literature: The myths*. Quezon City: University of the Philippines Press.

Falck, C. (1994). *Myth, truth, and literature: Towards a true postmodernism*. Cambridge: Cambridge University Press.

Field, S. (Trans)(1984). *Tian wen: A Chinese book of origins*. New York: New Directions.

Feldman, B., & Richardson, R. (2000). *The rise of modern mythology, 1680-1860*. Indianapolis: Indiana University Press.

Feldman, S. (Ed.)(1963). *African myths & tales*. New York: Dell Publishing.

Flieger, V. (2005). *Interrupted music: The making of Tolkien's mythology*. Kent: Kent State University Press.

Foss, F. (1993). *World myths and legends II: The Caribbean*. New York: Simon & Schuster.

Foster, B. (1995). *From distant days: Myths, tales, and poetry of ancient Mesopotamia*. Bethesda: CDL Press.

Frazer, J. (2009). *The golden bough: A study in magic and religion*. Oxford: Oxford Classics.

Freud, S. (1992). *Totem and taboo*. New York: W. W. Norton & Company.

Frobenius, L., & Fox, D. (1999). *African genesis: folktales and myths of Africa*. Mineola: Dover.

Frye, N. (2000). *Anatomy of criticism: Four essays*. Princeton: Princeton University Press.

Gantz, T. (1996) *Early Greek myth: A guide to literary and artistic sources*. Baltimore: Johns Hopkins University Press.

Goss, L., & Barnes, M.(Eds.)(1989). *Talk that talk: An anthology of*

African-American storytelling. New York: Touchstone.

Gould, E. (1987). *Mythical intentions in modern literature*. Princeton: Princeton University Press.

Harding, A. (1995). *The reception of myth in English Romanticism*. Columbia, MO: University of Missouri.

Hatab, L. (1992). *Myth and philosophy: A contest of truths*. Chicago: Open Court.

Hazen-Hammond, S. (1999). *Spider woman's web: Traditional Native American tales about women's power*. New York: Penguin Books.

Hesse, H. (1999). *Demian*. New York: Perennial.

Hillman, J. (1997). *The soul's code: In search of character and calling*. New York: Random House.

Hillman, J. (2005). *A terrible love of war*. New York: Penguin Books.

Honko, L. (Ed.)(2011). *Religion, myth and folklore in the world's epics*. Berlin: De Gruyter.

Hurston, Z. (2002) *Every tongue got to confess: Negro folk-tales from the Gulf States*. New York: Harper Perennial.

Jung, C. (1973). *Answer to Job*. Princeton: Princeton University Press.

Jung, C., & Kerenyi, C. (1969). *Essays on a science of mythology*. Princeton: Princeton University Press.

Jung, C. (1989). *Memories, dreams, reflections*. New York: Vintage.

Jung, C. (1953). *Psychology and alchemy*. Princeton: Princeton University Press.

Jung, C., & Shamdasani, S. (Ed.)(2009). *The red book*. New York: W. W. Norton & Company.

Kalsched, D. (1996). *The inner world of trauma: Archetypal defenses of the personal spirit*. New York: Routledge.

Kane, S. (1889). *Wisdom of the mythtellers*. Ontario: Broadview Press.

Kawai, H. (1995). *Dreams, myths & fairy tales in Japan*. Einsiedeln: Daimon.

Kerenyi, C. (1995). *The gods of the Greeks*. New York: Thames & Hudston Inc.

Kirk, G. (1970). *Myth: Its meaning & function in ancient & other cultures*. Cambridge: Cambridge University Press.

Knapp, B. (1997). *Women in myth*. New York: State University of New York Press.

Knipe, R. (1989). *The water of life: A Jungian journey through Hawaiian myth*. Honolulu: University of Hawaii.

Kroeber, T. (1963). *The inland whale*. Berkeley: University of California Press.

Krolick, S. (1987). *Recollective resolve: A phenomenological understanding of time and myth*. Macon: Mercer University Press.

Larrington, C. (Ed.)(1992). *The feminist companion to mythology*. New York: HarperCollins.

Leonard, S., and McClure, M. (2004). *Myth and knowing: An introduction to world mythology*. New York: McGraw-Hill.

Le Guin, U., & Wood, S. (Ed.)(1979). *The language of the night: Essays on fantasy and science fiction*. New York: Putnam.

Levi-Strauss, C. (1995). *Myth and meaning: Cracking the code of culture*. New York: Schocken Books.

Lincoln, B. (2000). *Theorizing myth: Narrative, ideology, and scholarship*. Chicago: University of Chicago Press.

Lonnrot, E. (2008). *The kalevala*. Oxford: Oxford World Classics.

Lupack, A. (2005). *Oxford guide to Arthurian literature and legend*. Oxford: Oxford University Press.

MacCulloch, J. (2004). *Celtic mythology*. Mineola: Dover.

Mahaffey, P. (Ed.)(2014). *Evolving god-images: Essays on religion, individuation, and postmodern spirituality*. Lincoln: iUniverse.

Malinowski, B. (1992). *Magic, science and religion and other essays*. Long Grove, Il: Waveland Press Inc.

Matthews, J., & Matthews, C. (Eds.)(2004). *The encyclopaedia of Celtic myth and legend*. Guilford: The Lyons Press.

May, R. (1991). *The cry for myth*. New York: W. W. Norton.

McCoppin, R. (2015). *The lessons of nature in mythology*. Jefferson: McFarland & Company.

McCune, M., & Orbison, T. (Eds.)(1978). *The binding of Proteus: Perspectives on myth and the literary process*. Plainsboro: Associated University Press.

Meade, M. (1993). *Men and the water of life: Initiation and the tempering of men*. New York: HarperCollins.

Metraux, A. (1972). *Voodoo in Haiti*. New York: Schocken Books.

Momaday, N. (1976). *The way to rainy mountain*. Albuquerque: University of New Mexico Press.

Monaghan, P. (2000). *The new book of goddesses & heroines*. St. Paul: Lewellyn Publications.

Müller, M., & Stone, J. (2002). *The essential Max Müller: On language, mythology, and religion*. New York: Palgrave Macmillan.

Murdock, M. (1990). *The heroine's journey: Woman's quest for wholeness*. Boston: Shambhala.

Murray, H. (Ed.)(1968). *Myth and mythmaking*. Boston: Beacon Press.

Noel, D. (1990). *Paths to the power of myth: Joseph Campbell and the study of religion*. New York: Crossroad.

O'Flaherty, W. (1988). *Other peoples' myths: The cave of echoes*. Chicago: University of Chicago Press.

Okpewho, I. (1983). *Myth in Africa*. Cambridge: Cambridge University Press.

Olson, A. (1980). *Myth, symbol and reality*. Notre Dame, IN: University of Notre Dame Press.

Pagels, E. (2013). *The Gnostic gospels*. New York: Random House.

Paris, G. (1998). *Pagan meditations: The worlds of Aphrodite, Artemis, and Hestia*. Dallas: Spring Publications.

Pattanaik, D. (2003). *Indian mythology: Tales, symbols, and rituals from the heart of the subcontinent*. Rochester: Inner Traditions.

Patton, K., & Ray, B. (Eds.)(2000). *A magic still dwells: Comparative religion in the postmodern age*. Berkeley: University of California Press.

Patton, L., & Doniger, W. (Eds.)(1996). *Myth & method*. Charlottesville: University Press of Virginia.

Puhvel, J. (1987). *Comparative mythology*. Baltimore: John Hopkins University Press.

Reed, A. (1999). *Maori myths & legendary tales*. Auckland: New Holland Publishers.

Robinson, R. (1968). *Aboriginal myths and legends*. Melbourne: Sun Books.

Roszak, T. (1992). *The voice of the earth*. New York: Simon & Schuster.

Rue, L. (2004). *Amythia: Crisis in the natural history of western culture*. Tuscaloosa: University of Alabama Press.

Schilbrack, K. (2003). *Thinking Through Myths: Philosophical Perspectives*. New York: Routledge.

Sebeok, T. (1968). *Myth: A symposium*. Indianapolis: Indiana University Press.

Seznec, J. (1972). *The survival of the pagan gods*. Princeton: Princeton University Press.

Sienkewicz, T. (1997). *Theories of myth: An annotated bibliography*. Lanham: The Scarecrow Press.

Simpson, W. (2003). *The literature of ancient Egypt: An anthology of stories, instructions, stelae, autobiographies, and poetry*. New Haven: Yale University Press.

Slattery, D. (2012). *Riting myth, mythic writing: Plotting your personal story*. Carmel, CA: Fisher King Press.

Slattery, D., & Slater, G. (Eds.)(2008). *Varieties of mythic experience: Essays on religion, psyche and culture*. Einsiedeln: Daimon Verlag.

Soyinka, W. (1992). *Myth, literature, and the African world*. Cambridge: Cambridge University Press.

Spretnak, C. (1984). *Lost goddesses of early Greece: A collection of pre-Hellenic myths*. Boston: Beacon Press.

Stambovsky, P. (1996). *Myths and the limits of reason*. Atlanta, GA: Rodopi.

Stebling-Kamenskij, M. (1982). *Myth: The Icelandic sagas and eddas*. Ann Arbor, MI: Karoma Publishers, Inc.

Sterenberg, M. (2013). *Mythic thinking in twentieth-century Britain: Meaning for modernity*. New York: Palgrave Macmillon.

Stone, M. (1990). *Ancient mirrors of womanhood: A treasury of goddess and heroine lore from around the world*. Boston: Beacon Press.

Tolkien, J., & Tolkien, C. (Ed.)(2000). *The letters of J. R. R. Tolkien*. New York: Mariner Books.

Tolkien, J., Flieger, V. (Ed.), & Anderson, D. (Ed.)(2014). *Tolkien on fairy-stories*. New York: HarperCollins.

Trzaskoma, S., Smith, R., & Brunet, S. (Eds.)(2004). *Anthology of classical myth: Primary sources in translation*. Indianapolis: Hackett Publishing Company.

Van Cleef, J. (2008). *God wears many skins: Myth and folklore of the Sami people*. Madison: Spirit Song Text Publications.

Vernant, J. (1990). *Myth and society in ancient Greece*. New York: Harvester Press.

Veyne, P. (1988). *Did the Greeks believe their myths? An essay on the constitutive imagination*. Chicago: University of Chicago Press.

Vico, G. (1992). *New science*. New York: Penguin Books.

Von Eschenbach, W. (1961). *Parzival*. New York: Vintage.

Von Franz, M. (1995). *Creation myths*. Boston: Shambhala.

Walker, S. (2002). *Jung and the Jungians on myth*. New York: Routledge.

Witzel, E. (2013). *The origin of the world's mythologies*. Oxford: Oxford University Press.

Wong, E. (1995). *Lieh-tzu: A Taoist guide to practical living*. Boston: Shambhala.

Yang, L., & An, D. (2005). *Handbook of Chinese mythology*. Oxford: Oxford University Press.

Young, J. (1996). *Saga: Best new writings on mythology*. Ashland, OR: White Cloud Press.

Zimmer, H., & Campbell, J. (Ed.)(1989). *The king & the corpse: Tales of the soul's conquest of evil*. Princeton: Princeton University Press.

Online Resources:

http://www.immanencejournal.com - Immanence: The Journal of Applied Mythology, Legend, and Folktale

http://home.comcast.net/~chris.s/myth.html - myths and legends from around the world

http://www.pantheon.org/ - Encyclopedia Mythica

http://www.mythencyclopedia.com/ - Myth Encyclopedia

http://www.aboriginalaustralianart.com/dreamtime_art.php - Australian Aboriginal art

http://www.egyptianmyths.net/ - Egyptian mythology

http://traditions.cultural-china.com/13two.html - Chinese myths and legends

http://chinavine.org/ - Chinese folklore

http://www.japanesemythology.jp/ - Japanese mythology

http://devdutt.com/ - website of Indian mythologist Devdutt Pattanaik

http://www.mythome.org/asiang.html - Asian gods

http://www.gateway-africa.com/stories/ - African fables and stories

http://www.ancient.eu.com/Mesopotamian_Religion/ - Mesopotamian religion

http://www.pantheon.org/areas/mythology/middle_east/persian/articles.html - Persian myth

http://dastaneshab.com/ - Persian Storyteller Radio

http://public.sd38.bc.ca/~mcmathlib/First_Nations_Myths - First Nations myths and stories

http://www.native-languages.org/legends.htm - Native American languages and myths

http://www.theoi.com/ - Greek mythology

http://www.sacred-texts.com/neu/sfs/ - sixty-four Slavic folktales

http://www.native-languages.org/carib-legends.htm - Carib myths and legends

http://www.janeresture.com/oceania_myths/ - Oceania mythology

http://www.seasite.niu.edu/Tagalog/folktales/mythsintroduction.htm - Philippine myths and legends

http://www.mythome.org/SouthAm.html - South American mythology

http://www.americanfolklore.net/index.html - American folklore and myth, including Native

http://www.sacred-texts.com/neu/celt/ - Celtic folklore and myth sources

http://norse-mythology.org/ - Norse myth and religion

CPSIA information can be obtained
at www.ICGtesting.com
Printed in the USA
BVHW041255301221
625049BV00023B/1349

9 780982 627969